REQUIEM

The Quiet Bloom

Harrison C Songolo

Xkaii Verse Publishing

CONTENTS

Prologue   V

1. A Life in Monotone   1

2. Greetings   24

3. The Missing Puzzle Pieces   46

4. Shadows in the Daylight   70

5. A Restless Storm   99

6. The Labyrinth of the Mind   126

7. A World of New Sensations   157

8. Fractured Reflections   177

9. The Hunt for Answers   199

10. The Rush   221

11. Into the Wild   242

12. World Reset   275

13. Master of the Wild   300

14. In Search of Marcus   333

15. Shadows in the Dark   356

16.	Into the Lion's Den	376
17.	Dance of Shadows	399
18.	The Awakening	438
19.	The Plan	468
20.	No Way Out	488
21.	Benji's House	516
22.	Palantir Technologies	543
23.	Kirkwood	574
24.	Into the Abyss	601
25.	Tickets Please	627
26.	Run & Hide	657
Afterword		677

PROLOGUE
THE QUIET BLOOM

The city buzzes with its usual chaos, but I feel the weight of silence pressing down on me.

I stand at the corner of 34th and 8th, watching the throngs of people rush by. Their laughter blends into a murmur, an indistinct hum against the roar of traffic. No one glances at the bulletin board plastered with flyers.

"Another one gone," a woman mutters to her friend as they pass, pointing at a poster. A young girl's face stares back at me, wide eyes frozen in fear, beneath the words "MISSING."

"Who even cares anymore?" her friend shrugs. "It's New York. People disappear all the time." They walk on, leaving that little girl behind.

I tear my gaze from the flyer and pull my collar up against the chill creeping in. The news had covered it—brief snippets of reports about people vanishing without a trace—but nobody seems to pay attention. It's like they've learned to ignore what doesn't directly touch them.

Inside a nearby café, I sit alone at a small table by the window, sipping lukewarm coffee. A TV hangs in the corner, broadcasting another missing person report.

"Police say she was last seen near Central Park," a reporter states, her voice smooth but lacking urgency. "If you have any information..."

I glance around; everyone remains absorbed in their phones or conversations, blissfully ignorant of the world beyond their screens.

"Hey," a barista leans over the counter, tapping my cup lightly. "You alright? You look kinda out of it."

"Yeah," I reply too quickly, forcing a smile that feels more like a grimace. "Just thinking."

She nods and moves on to another customer as I sink deeper into thought. The missing faces linger in my mind—their absence echoes louder than sirens in this bustling city.

As night falls and shadows stretch across the pavement, I step outside again. The air carries an electric chill that raises goosebumps along my skin.

The city lights flicker on one by one like stars struggling to pierce through heavy clouds. But it's not enough to banish this gnawing unease gripping my gut.

"Something isn't right," I whisper under my breath as I walk toward home, knowing full well no one else sees what I see—the stories behind those empty smiles on those flyers or the chilling silence that accompanies their disappearance.

CHAPTER ONE

A LIFE IN MONOTONE

The fluorescent lights overhead buzz with the insistent drone of trapped insects, a sound that burrows its way into the marrow of my bones. They cast a cold, unforgiving glow over the rows of cubicles, each one a miniature cell in this meticulously organized prison. It isn't the kind of light that inspires creativity or energy; it is functional, clinical—the kind of light designed to keep people awake but not alive, merely... present.

My screen stares back at me, a sterile, emotionless mirror reflecting my own apathy. A grid of numbers, neatly aligned into rows and columns, a testament to order and precision, waits patiently for me to care about them. They wait in vain.

The report is finished early—like always. Efficiency is my brand. Dependability, my carefully constructed facade. I am the kind of employee every boss wants on paper: compliant, productive, a cog that never jams the machine. But sitting there, staring at that screen, I can't help but wonder why it matters.

What is the point of all this meticulous data entry, this relentless pursuit of optimization? Who am I helping by finishing this report? Whose day improves, even marginally, because I hit send? The truth, stark and un-yielding, is that it is just another task in a never-ending stream of tasks, each one as meaningless as the last, each one a step further into the quicksand of routine.

I lean back in my chair, a cheap, ergonomic monstrosity that promises comfort but delivers only mild relief from the perpetual ache in my lower back. The faint hum of the air conditioning fills the silence, a constant white noise that serves as both a blanket and a suffocating weight. The ceiling tiles above me are speckled with stains—small, irregular patches that hint at past leaks, of forgotten struggles, of institutional neglect.

They've been there since I started this job, a quiet, persistent reminder that nothing ever really changes here—just the slow, steady decay of the infrastructure around us, mirroring the slow, steady decay of our souls.

Around me, the office hums with its usual, predictable rhythm. Key-boards click softly, a digital rain falling on a barren landscape, punctu-ated by the occasional cough or rustle of papers, the shifting of bodies in uncomfortable chairs. It is a symphony of monotony, a soundtrack I come to know by heart, a tune I can hum in my sleep, a melody of muted desperation. I know every note, every beat, every subtle variation in the tempo of despair.

Ash's voice rises above the hum, cutting through the quiet like a poorly tuned radio.

"Crushed it this morning," she announces to no one in particular, her voice dripping with saccharine enthusiasm that feels utterly artificial. "Al-most hit a PR."

Her Peloton escapades have become a daily ritual, a performance piece designed to elicit envy and admiration, and so has her need to broadcast them to the entire office. I don't need to look to know she is near the coffee machine, holding court as she recounts every detail of her workout, every drop of sweat, every calorie burned, every personal record nearly shattered. Ash is the kind of person who thrives on being heard, even if no one is really listening. She is a black hole of attention, sucking in the meager energy of th e office and converting it into a self-serving narrative.

I glance across the aisle at Tom from marketing. He hunches over his desk, his shoulders slumped, his eyes glued to his monitor, his face illuminated by the cold, blue light. He mutters under his breath, his words barely audible above the hum of the air conditioning—a litany of anxieties and frustrations.

"If I lose this week… my fantasy league's done. Done," he says, his voice laced with desperate urgency, his fingers tapping anxiously on the edge of his keyboard—a nervous tic that betrays the depth of his investment.

Tom's fantasy football obsession is well-known around the office. It is his escape, his passion, his reason for being—at least from Monday to Sunday. He talks about it constantly, analyzing stats, strategizing trades, agonizing over injuries as if the outcome of his league is a matter of life and death. For him, it probably is. It is a world where he has control, where his decisions matter, where he can experience the thrill of victory and the agony of defeat without any real-world consequences.

Farther down the row, Lisa stands by the thermostat, her arms crossed tightly over her chest, her brow furrowed in a perpetual frown. She wages a silent war against the office temperature for weeks, a clandestine battle fought with subtle adjustments and passive-aggressive sighs. She adjusts it up and down several times a day, a futile attempt to impose her will on the unyielding climate control system. It doesn't matter that most people don't notice the change—Lisa does, and that is enough. It is a small act of rebellion against the oppressive conformity of the office, a tiny spark of individuality in a sea of sameness.

I glance at the clock. 4:30 PM. That strange, liminal space—that twilight zone where the office seems to pause, caught between productivity and escape. A few people start packing up, slipping laptops into bags and gathering their coats, their movements furtive and hurried, like thieves in the night. Others stay glued to their screens, pretending to work, scrolling aimlessly through social media, composing emails that will never be sent, as they count down the minutes until they can leave without looking like they are leaving too early. It is a delicate dance, a carefully choreographed performance of feigned diligence.

I look back at my screen. The report is finished. My inbox is empty. My tasks are all wrapped up. There's nothing left for me to tackle, no looming deadlines, no immediate demands, no justification for remaining. Yet, I linger at my desk, frozen by inertia, ensnared by the heaviness of my own habits. Departing early feels like conceding defeat, like recognizing the void in my life, like admitting that I have nothing more worthwhile to occupy my time.

The truth is, I don't.

My phone buzzes against the desk, a small, insistent vibration that pulls me out of my thoughts—a jarring intrusion into the quiet contemplation of my own insignificance. I hesitate for a moment, reluctant to break the spell of monotony, before reaching for it.

Benji: "Don't bail on me. 8 PM at The Garret. Vibes are immaculate. No excuses, Tris."

I stare at the message for a moment, the stark white letters on my phone screen seeming to mock the grayness of my surroundings. Benji has a way of cutting through the monotony of my life with his relentless enthusiasm, like a vibrant splash of color on a grayscale canvas. He is the kind of person who can turn a trip to the grocery store into a grand adventure, finding magic in the mundane, seeing potential stories in every stranger he passes.

Most of the time, I admire that about him—envy it even; his unwavering optimism feels like a superpower in a world that often feels determined to grind you down. Tonight, however, I am not so sure. Tonight, the thought of mustering the energy to be social feels like climbing a mountain in lead boots.

I type out a response, my fingers moving slowly, deliberately delaying the inevitable.

Me: "What's The Garret?"

The reply comes almost instantly, buzzing against my palm with the urgency that is so characteristic of Benji. I half expect him to teleport into the office and drag me out himself.

Benji: "Bar. Cozy. Cool. Chill. You'll love it. Seriously. Don't ghost me."

I smirk despite myself, a small, involuntary twitch of my lips. The man is persistent; I'd give him that. He is like a particularly enthusiastic golden retriever, perpetually eager to please and utterly incapable of taking no for an answer. Before I can think of another excuse, before I can craft a sufficiently convincing story about a sudden illness or a family emergency, his voice cuts through the low hum of the office, startling me slightly.

"Going out tonight?"

I look up to see him leaning over the edge of my cubicle, his signature grin firmly in place, radiating an energy that seems almost unfairly bright compared to my own subdued mood. His tie is loosened, the knot pulled down slightly as if it is already chafing against the confines of the workday, and his dark curls have that artful messiness that makes him look like he belongs anywhere but here—anywhere but trapped within these sterile, soul-crushing walls. He has the effortless charm of someone who is genuinely comfortable in their own skin, a quality I have always found both admirable and slightly intimidating.

"Maybe," I say, deliberately keeping my tone vague, trying to project an air of nonchalance that I certainly don't feel. I am hoping to buy myself some time, to delay the decision, to perhaps even magically disappear before I have to commit one way or the other.

Benji rolls his eyes dramatically, leaning further into my space, invading my personal bubble with his infectious enthusiasm. "Tris, come on. Don't be a hermit. Eight o'clock. Bring that brooding energy of yours. It'll be good for the atmosphere. Jess will be there too."

I sigh, running a hand through my hair as I consider Benji's invitation. Jess is like a sister to me, someone who has been there through the best and worst of times. We've weathered so many storms together, our bond forged in the crucible of shared experiences. But that very familiarity can be a double-edged sword, a connection that cuts both ways.

"Jess, huh?" I murmur, my voice tinged with a hint of uncertainty. "I don't know, Benji. It's been a long day, and the thought of being around people right now..." I trail off, unable to articulate the heavy weight that seems to settle on my shoulders whenever I contemplate social interaction.

"Yeah, she says she'll come," he replies casually, too casually perhaps, but there is a flicker of something unspoken in his expression—a hint of mischievousness that suggests he is enjoying this a little too much. "You two are practically siblings anyway. It'll be fun."

I hesitate, glancing back at my monitor, pretending to be absorbed in the rows of data that swim before my eyes. My report is finished, painstakingly completed hours ago, every cell checked and double-checked for errors. My inbox is clear—a rare and almost unsettling state of emptiness. There is no logical reason to stay late, no pressing deadline looming, but I linger out of habit, clinging to the familiar routine as a shield against the uncertainty of the evening ahead.

Leaving early would force me to confront the emptiness—the vast expanse of hours stretching before me like a desolate landscape—a quiet apartment, a frozen dinner consumed in solitude, maybe a show I'd half-watch while mindlessly scrolling on my phone, seeking a fleeting connection in the digital void.

Benji grins wider, tilting his head in mock impatience, his eyes sparkling with an almost predatory gleam. He can always sense when I am wavering, when my resolve is beginning to crumble. He is like a heat-seeking missile, locked onto my indecision and determined to break through my defenses.

"Fine," I sigh, the word escaping my lips with a puff of resignation. I feel a reluctant smile tug at the corner of my mouth—a small flicker of amusement in the face of my impending social obligation. "I'll go."

Benji clasps a hand on my shoulder triumphantly, the force of his enthusiasm nearly knocking me off balance. "That's the spirit! You won't regret it, I promise. Tonight will be legendary!"

I doubt that, but I don't say anything. Benji has a way of making you believe that every plan is the best plan, that every outing will be an unforgettable adventure, even when deep down you know it is likely to be just another evening, punctuated by awkward conversations and overpriced drinks. His unwavering optimism is both his greatest strength and his most infuriating quality.

As he walks back to his desk, his buoyant energy leaving a slight vacuum in its wake, I glance at the clock again. 6:03 PM. Most of the office has started trickling out—a quiet exodus of weary souls seeking refuge from the fluorescent lights and the endless drone of corporate life. Sarah is still by the coffee machine, chatting animatedly with someone who looks half asleep, her voice carrying snippets of office gossip and weekend plans.

Tom gathers his things, his phone pressed to his ear as he rattles off some last-minute instructions about his fantasy league, his brow furrowed in concentration. Lisa finally steps away from the thermostat, her long-fought battle to control the office temperature temporarily suspended, but I notice her glancing at it one last time before she leaves—a silent promise of renewed conflict tomorrow.

I stand up slowly, shrugging on my jacket and grabbing my bag, the weight of its contents feeling heavier than usual. The office feels quieter now, the absence of bodies amplifying the hum of the air conditioning and the distant clatter of keyboards. Sarah is still at the coffee machine, chatting animatedly with someone who looks half-asleep—her voice carrying snippets of office gossip and weekend plans.

As the last few stragglers begin to filter out, I allow the familiar heaviness to settle on my shoulders again. The mundane ritual of exiting the office becomes an ordeal, the movements calculated as if I am walking through a minefield of expectations and unspoken judgments.

I step outside, and the cool night air hits me like a splash of icy water to the face, instantly snapping me out of the stagnant fog that has been clinging to me all day. The city is alive in the way it always is after dark—chaotic, restless, and electric. A million stories unfold simultaneously on every block, none of which have anything to do with me.

Streetlights cast pools of jaundiced yellow onto the damp pavement, their artificial glow reflected in the shimmering surfaces of puddles left behind by an earlier drizzle—transforming the mundane concrete into an abstract art installation, if you look at it just right. Somewhere nearby, the faint screech of brakes echoes off the towering buildings like a mechanical scream, followed by the sharp, indignant bark of a cab driver shouting at a pedestrian who wanders a little too carelessly into the street—a typical symphony of urban discourtesy.

I instinctively pull my worn leather jacket tighter around me, adjusting the strap of my messenger bag on my shoulder. For a moment, I hesitate—my feet hovering between heading toward the grimy entrance of the subway station and turning back to the familiar, predictable solitude of my cramped apartment. Home is only a few blocks away—a siren song of quiet desperation. The idea of sinking into the worn cushions of my couch, lost in a book, or even daring to start a new video game I have been putting off is incredibly tempting. The siren calls my name.

But Benji's voice echoes in my head—a persistent, unwelcome intrusion: Don't ghost me. The guilt, a familiar companion, stirs within me.

I sigh, the sound lost in the ambient noise of the city, and start walking. Each step feels heavy—leaden with the weight of obligation and a vague, undefined sense of disappointment.

The streets are crowded, even for a Thursday night. It seems like everyone else in the city has a purpose, a destination, a connection. Couples stroll arm in arm—faces illuminated by the glow of their phones or the shared anticipation of an evening together, laughing softly as they duck into dimly lit restaurants, escaping into the warm, inviting glow of shared meals and intimate conversations.

Groups of friends gather outside bars, their voices overlapping in excited chatter—fueled by cheap drinks and the intoxicating energy of collective camaraderie. The energy of the city is palpable—a tangible force buzzing beneath the surface like a high-voltage current I can't quite tap into. I am an observer—a ghost drifting through their vibrant world.

I descend into the subway, the reek of metal and damp concrete hitting me like a physical blow. The air is thick with the smell of stale urine, and the distant rumble of approaching trains vibrates through the soles of my shoes. The platform is busy but not completely packed—a churning mass of faces, each lost in its own private world. I find a relatively clean spot near the edge—leaning against a cold, graffitied column as I wait for the train to arrive, trying to make myself as invisible as possible.

A busker plays an old, mournful blues tune on a battered acoustic guitar farther down the platform—his voice raw and soulful, filled with a kind of weary resignation that resonates deep within me. The music is melancholic—a stark contrast to the clamor of the city. I catch snippets of the lyrics as they float through the air—carried on the drafts of the underground wind—something about love lost and found again— a familiar theme of heartache and hope that feels both universal and deeply personal. I wonder if he has ever been as alone as I feel now.

The train roars into the station, a mechanical beast of steel and electricity. The gust of wind it carries tugs at my jacket and whips my hair across my face as it screeches to a jarring stop—momentarily drowning out all other sounds. The doors hiss open, and I step inside, joining the throng of commuters pushing their way into the crowded car. I manage to find a seat near the door, settling in as the car jerks forward and begins to move—plunging back into the darkness of the tunnels.

The ride is profoundly uneventful. Each stop is a reminder of a destination for someone else. People around me stare blankly at their phones, scrolling through endless feeds of meaningless information, or at the grimy floor—faces expressionless—masks of fatigue, indifference, and the accumulated weight of the day's struggles. The air is thick with a mixture of stale perfume, sweat, and the faint, lingering aroma of fast food.

I catch fleeting glimpses of my reflection in the darkened windows—a pale, almost spectral face framed by rumpled hair, eyes shadowed from too many late nights spent staring at a screen and too little purpose guiding my days. I look tired, worn down by the invisible pressures of a life lived on the periphery.

As the train rattles and sways through the dark tunnels, I find myself thinking about The Garret. Benji's description has been typically vague, bordering on cryptic, as usual, but I can picture it in my mind's eye—dimly lit, cozy, probably with overpriced drinks and a carefully curated crowd that leans more hipster than corporate—a haven for those seeking an alternative escape from the mainstream.

It isn't the kind of place I usually go to—my usual haunts being more dive bar than dimly lit lounge—but maybe that is precisely the point. Maybe a change of scenery—even one orchestrated by Benji—is exactly what I need to break free from my self-imposed monotony.

When I finally surface onto the streets of the West Village, the energy of the city feels palpably different—more refined, more electric in a subtle, understated way. The cacophonous noise of Midtown—the relentless pressure of its towering skyscrapers and bustling crowds—feels distant and almost unreal, replaced by the gentle hum of conversations spilling out of cozy wine bars and the occasional, delicate clink of glasses raised in celebratory toasts.

The buildings are shorter, their facades older and more charming, and the soft, ambient glow of string lights hanging above restaurant patios gives the narrow streets an almost romantic quality—a sense of intimacy and warmth that is decidedly absent from the rest of the city.

I navigate the route Benji sent me earlier—twisting through a maze of narrow, cobblestone lanes, each flanked by brownstones and concealed courtyards—until I arrive at a Five Guys burger place, the aroma of oily fries thick in the atmosphere.

"This can't be right," I mutter to myself, pulling out my phone and double-checking the address against the glowing screen. But there it is—clear as day—listed as the location: 123 Bleecker Street. Tucked discreetly to the side of the bustling burger joint, almost hidden in plain sight, is a narrow, unassuming staircase that looks like it leads nowhere—a secret entrance to a world unknown.

I hesitate for a long moment, the aroma of burgers warring with my curiosity, before taking a deep breath and starting to climb the steps—the aged wood creaking softly and protesting under my weight. As I ascend, the familiar noise of the city—the blare of horns and the murmur of voices—fades behind me, gradually replaced by the low thrum of music and the muffled hum of conversation—hinting at the clandestine gathering that awaits me above.

When I reach the top of the staircase and tentatively push open the heavy, unmarked door, the atmosphere shifts completely—as if I have stepped through a portal into another world.

Warm light spills from vintage sconces, casting flickering shadows on exposed brick walls. The mismatched furniture gives the space a curated charm—plush armchairs paired with rustic wooden tables, a scattering of barstools that look like they've been salvaged from a 1920s speakeasy. Candles burn on every table, their flames dancing softly and filling the room with a faint, spicy aroma that I can't quite place. It is a comforting scent—like cinnamon and cloves steeped in warm wine, with a hint of something woodsy underneath—as if the very walls exhale the scent of aged timber.

The Garret is busy but not crowded. Groups of people cluster around the tables, their conversations blending into a low hum that fills the air. It is a pleasant cacophony, a symphony of laughter and shared secrets—of whispered hopes and boisterous pronouncements. The clinking of glasses and the shuffling of feet form a rhythmic backdrop to the evening's unfolding drama.

"Over here!"

Benji's voice cuts through the noise, and I spot him near the back, waving me over to a table surrounded by familiar faces. His smile is a beacon—a promise of easy camaraderie and lighthearted banter. He always manages to command attention without demanding it—his genuine warmth drawing people to him like moths to a flame.

Jessica is the first to greet me—her smile warm and familiar as always. She has a way of making you feel instantly at ease—her genuine concern radiating from her like a soft light. "You made it," she says, scooting her chair to make room. Her touch is light and fleeting, but it grounds me momentarily, reminding me of the simple pleasure of connection.

"Didn't think you'd show," Ash adds—her tone casual but laced with the kind of sharpness that makes it hard to tell if she is teasing or serious. It is her trademark—a carefully constructed ambiguity that keeps everyone on their toes. Her eyes, sharp and intelligent, seem to dissect you with a single glance, leaving you feeling both intrigued and slightly exposed.

"Tristan," I reply softly, taking a sip of the whiskey Benji has ordered for me. The liquid burns a warm path down my throat, momentarily distracting me from the undercurrent of tension.

Benji laughs, clinking his glass against mine. "Humble, too. Truly the whole package."

"Yeah, yeah," Ash says, rolling her eyes. Her movements are precise and deliberate—as if every gesture is carefully calculated. "He's perfect. We get it."

Jessica nudges me with her elbow, her tone playful. "Seriously, though. You've got to teach me how you pulled off that report. It's like magic." Her eyes are filled with genuine curiosity—a refreshing contrast to the veiled barbs thrown about.

"Hardly magic," I say. "Just... focus." It is the truth, but it feels like a hollow explanation—a superficial answer to a question that goes much deeper. The focus comes at the expense of everything else—a trade-off I have long since accepted.

The conversation around the table flows easily—the way it always seems to when Benji is involved. He has this magnetic energy that pulls everyone into his orbit—his quick wit and infectious laugh smoothing over any awkward silences before they have a chance to settle. He is the social glue that holds the group together—the catalyst that transforms individual personalities into a cohesive whole.

"So then," Benji is saying, gesturing animatedly, "the guy actually says, 'You should try turning it off and back on again,' like I haven't already done that three times. And of course, the second I walk away, it works perfectly. He just gives me this smug little nod—like he's the IT whisperer or something."

Jessica laughs—her eyes crinkling at the corners. "People always think they're tech geniuses as soon as something starts working. It's like they've unlocked the secrets of the universe."

"Yeah, well, I've unlocked the secret to never asking Tom for help," Benji quips—a mischievous glint in his eyes as he glances at Tom, who is scanning the room while sipping his drink.

Tom raises his glass in mock offense. "Hey, I'm not that bad. Just because I can't fix your janky laptop doesn't mean I'm useless."

"Janky?" Benji gasps, clutching his chest dramatically. His performance is exaggerated, but it serves to diffuse the underlying tension. "I'll have you know my laptop is a masterpiece of modern engineering. It's a miracle of functionality and beauty."

"Sure it is," Ash says dryly, swirling her drink. The ice clinks softly against the glass—a delicate sound that punctuates her dismissive tone. Her tone is casual, but there is an edge to it—like she isn't fully in on the joke.

I stay quiet, letting the banter wash over me as I sip my drink. This is the dynamic I come to expect from this group: Benji playing the lovable instigator, Jessica smoothing over any rough edges, Tom laughing along while trying not to take the bait, and Ash hovering on the outskirts—her sharp remarks landing like well-aimed darts. It is a delicate ecosystem—a carefully balanced web of personalities and unspoken alliances.

And then there is Ethan.

He sits across from me, nursing his drink with the kind of tight-lipped focus that makes it hard to tell if he is enjoying himself or just tolerating the company. His gaze is intense. Every now and then, he throws in a comment—a dry observation or a sarcastic quip—but he rarely lets the conversation linger on him. He is an enigma—a puzzle wrapped in layers of stoicism and guardedness.

"Tristan," Jessica says, pulling me out of my thoughts. Her voice is gentle but insistent—drawing me back into the present moment. "What about you? Any ridiculous work stories to share?"

I hesitate, glancing around the table. All eyes are on me now, waiting. The weight of their attention feels heavy—a spotlight illuminating my discomfort.

"Nothing exciting," I say, trying to deflect. "Just the usual reports and emails."

"Come on," Benji says, leaning forward with a grin. "There's gotta be something. A Sarah in the making? Someone who microwaved fish in the break room?"

"Microwaved fish?" Jessica wrinkles her nose. "Who does that?"

"Monsters," Benji replies solemnly.

I can't help but smile at that, but I shake my head. "No fish-microwaving incidents. Sorry to disappoint."

"Typical Tris," Ash says—smirking. "Mysterious as ever." The smirk hardly reaches her eyes.

There it is again—that edge, sharp and precise. It isn't hostile, exactly, but it always leaves me feeling like I am under a microscope—as if she is searching for something I don't even know I am hiding. There is an intensity in it—a feeling of being scrutinized that makes my skin crawl.

"Leave the poor guy alone," Jessica says—nudging Ash with her elbow. "Not everyone has a treasure trove of office drama to share."

"Thank you," I say—raising my glass to Jessica. Her support is a welcome shield—a buffer against Ash's persistent probing.

The conversation shifts after that—sliding into easier topics: movies we've been meaning to watch, restaurants Benji insists we have to try, the latest ridiculous office rumors. I find myself relaxing a little, the warmth of the whiskey and the flicker of candlelight softening the edges of the evening. The tension in my shoulders eases, and the constant hum of anxiety that usually plagues me quiets to a murmur. For a brief moment, I almost feel like I belong.

The night goes on with more laughs and drinks. Jessica has me laughing so hard whiskey comes out of my nose. Benji gets a little tipsy and is now dancing by himself in the corner. I catch Ethan smirking at me—I smirk back at him and continue the conversation. More drinks are poured, and more jokes are told. The night is a success.

One by one, the group begins to peel away—each with their own excuses— their own lives pulling them back into the mundane rhythms of existence.

Tom is the first to leave, draining the last dregs of his ale with a noisy gulp. He pushes himself up from the worn wooden chair, stretching his arms above his head with a groan that suggests his muscles are protesting the sudden movement. "Alright," he announces—the word slightly blurred at the edges—betraying a level of intoxication he is trying to downplay. "I've got an early meeting tomorrow," he says—though the faint slur in his words suggests he might be regretting that commitment already. He ruffles his hair—a nervous habit I've seen him do a thousand times before.

"Don't let the fantasy league stress you out too much," Benji teases—a mischievous glint in his eyes, knowing how seriously Tom takes his team—dissecting player stats and agonizing over trades with the intensity of a seasoned general planning a campaign.

Tom rolls his eyes—a familiar gesture of exasperation. "You're just jealous I'm still in the running," he retorts—his voice laced with mock superiority. He knows Benji has been knocked out of the playoffs weeks ago—a fact that still stings his friend's pride. He clasps Benji on the shoulder—a gesture of camaraderie before turning to leave. He weaves slightly as he makes his way through the crowded tables—a testament to the potency of the bar's signature brew.

As he disappears into the crowd, I rise and pull on my weathered leather coat, its soft creaks barely heard over the noise. A fleeting smile crosses my lips—a practiced mask hiding deeper emotions. "I'm out too," I say softly, nodding to the group before merging into the throng with unsettling ease. I glide like a shadow, weaving through bodies and conversations—vanishing as quickly as I arrived. There's always something distant about me—an aloofness that keeps me out of reach.

"Lightweights," Ash mutters, but her contemptuous tone seems to lack its usual bite. She glances at her phone, her brow furrowing slightly as she scans the screen. Then, with a sigh that suggests she is fighting a losing battle against responsibility, she finishes her drink with a single, decisive gulp—the ice clinking against her teeth. Her tone makes it clear she doesn't care if anyone believes her.

She has a deadline, yes, but it isn't quite as pressing as she makes it out to be. Procrastination is her specialty—a skill she has honed to an art form. "See you guys around," she adds, grabbing her bag and striding toward the door with purpose. As she leaves, I notice a small notepad sticking out of her satchel, filled with sketches of fantastical creatures.

Jessica lingers a little longer—the warmth of her presence a comforting contrast to the growing emptiness around the table. She leans back in her chair with an easy smile—her gaze gentle and assessing. "You good, Tris?" she asks softly—her eyes scanning my face as if she can read something in it that I am not saying. She has a knack for seeing through my carefully constructed facades—a talent that both comforts and unnerves me. I know she is worried about me—about the quiet desperation that has been gnawing at me for weeks.

I nod, offering a weak smile in return. "Yeah. I'll hang out a little longer." The lie tastes like ash in my mouth. I am not good. I am far from good. But I can't burden her with the weight of my discontent. She has enough on her plate as it is.

She reaches over and squeezes my hand briefly—a touch that is a silent reassurance. "Don't stay out too late, okay? Someone's got to keep you in line." Her words are lighthearted, but there is a thread of genuine concern woven beneath the surface. She has always been the responsible one—the caretaker of our little group, the one who makes sure we don't stray too far from the path.

"Thanks, Mom," I say with a faint smirk—earning a laugh from her before she stands and leaves. She knows I appreciate her—even if I don't always show it. She gives me a final wave as she disappears into the departing crowd.

That leaves just me and Benji.

"Well," he says, leaning back in his chair and crossing his arms behind his head—his expression smugly satisfied—"I'd call this a solid success. You actually show up, no one fights, and I don't even have to bribe you with free drinks." He is referring to my recent tendency to isolate myself—to avoid social gatherings and retreat into the solitude of my own thoughts. Getting me to leave the house has become a Herculean task.

"High bar," I say dryly—a faint smile tugging at the corner of my lips. Benji's standards are notoriously low.

Benji grins, unperturbed by my sarcasm. "What can I say? I'm a man of simple pleasures." He is anything but simple. Beneath the jovial facade, he is a complex and layered individual, brimming with untapped potential. But he prefers to play the role of the carefree jester—deflecting any attempts to delve deeper.

We sit in companionable silence for a while—the hum of the bar filling the space between us—a comforting backdrop to our unspoken thoughts. The crowd has thinned slightly—leaving pockets of empty space between the remaining patrons. The air is thick with the scent of stale beer and lingering perfume. The bartender—a burly man with a salt-and-pepper beard and a perpetually weary expression—moves with practiced ease, pouring drinks and chatting with patrons as if he has been doing it for decades. He is a fixture of the bar—a silent observer of countless dramas and fleeting moments of joy.

Eventually, Benji checks his watch—the luminescent dial glowing faintly in the dim light. He sighs—a sound that holds a hint of regret. "Alright, I'm calling it. Don't forget to text me when you get home, yeah?" He stands, stretching languidly, his joints popping audibly.

I nod—watching as he grabs his coat from the back of his chair and disappears into the crowd. He pauses for a moment, turning back to give me a final, knowing look before vanishing completely.

And then, I find myself by myself. The burden of my loneliness drapes over me like a thick shroud—oppressive and unavoidable.

I move to the bar, taking my half-finished drink with me. The polished surface is cool beneath my fingertips. I perch on a stool—watching the bartender as he expertly mixes cocktails—the clinking of glasses a rhythmic counterpoint to the low murmur of conversation that fills the room. The flicker of candlelight casts dancing shadows on the walls, creating a warm cocoon that feels at odds with the restless energy thrumming beneath my skin. The music playing is some generic pop song, but even that seems to give a hint of a deeper emotion within me.

I am not ready to go home yet. The thought of returning to the empty silence of my apartment fills me with a sense of dread. I need something—anything—to distract me from the growing emptiness inside. I swirl the remaining liquid in my glass—the ice clinking softly against the side. I debate whether I should just walk out and find something else to do. Maybe I could go for a walk in the city, but that also sounds so emotionally draining.

I end up giving the bartender a slight shake of my head and a small smile. I don't want to get too drunk tonight if I can help it. I don't want to risk the chance of doing something dumb. I end up just pulling out my phone and scrolling through it. Hours pass by and I realize the bar is almost empty. I debate if I should just give up for the night and head home. Maybe it would be nice to sleep. But I can't help but feel like I am missing something, like there is something important that is within my reach.

CHAPTER TWO

GREETINGS

I swirled the whiskey in my glass, the amber liquid catching the flickering candlelight, creating miniature, dancing suns within the cut crystal. The scent, a heady mix of oak and caramel, wafted up, momentarily distracting me from the restless unease that had settled over me. The bartender moved with the kind of practiced efficiency that suggested he could craft a perfect martini blindfolded—a silent ballet of shakers and strainers.

Yet, despite the inherent mundanity of his task, his movements were almost hypnotic to watch, the rhythmic clinking of glass a soothing counterpoint to the inner turmoil that threatened to overwhelm me. Around me, conversations rose and fell, a cacophony of laughter, murmured secrets, and drunken boasts, all blending into a steady hum that filled the smoky space of the bar. It was a familiar sound, a comforting blanket of anonymity, yet tonight it felt grating, a constant reminder of my own isolation within the bustling crowd.

I glanced down at my phone; its blank screen reflected my weary expression. I debated whether to succumb to the digital abyss, to scroll aimlessly through the endless stream of curated realities, or to simply tuck the device away and attempt to find some solace in the present moment. My thumb hovered over the power button, caught in the eternal struggle between connection and detachment, when I felt it—an odd shift in the air, subtle but undeniable.

It was less a physical sensation and more a prickling awareness, a sudden heightening of my senses as if the very atmosphere around me had thickened, become charged with an unseen energy. The hum of conversation seemed to momentarily fade, replaced by a low, almost imperceptible thrum that resonated deep within my bones.

He was sitting at the far end of the bar, alone, shrouded in the dim light like a creature of the shadows.

At first, I thought I'd imagined him, a fleeting apparition conjured from the depths of my own loneliness. He seemed almost too still, his pale skin catching the light in a way that made him look almost ethereal, as if he were sculpted from moonlight and mist. The other patrons of the bar flowed around him, oblivious to his presence, as if he occupied a space slightly out of sync with their own reality.

He wasn't looking at me—not directly, anyway—but there was something about his posture, the way he seemed so effortlessly anchored in the chaotic energy of the room, that made it impossible to look away.

He possessed a stillness that bordered on unnatural, a quiet intensity that radiated outward like an invisible force field.

He was dressed simply—dark, well-worn jeans that spoke of countless journeys, and a fitted jacket of midnight blue that seemed designed to blend in rather than stand out, conforming to the bar's dress code without drawing unnecessary attention—but there was a weight to his presence that made him feel larger than life, an aura of quiet power that belied his unassuming attire. It was in the set of his shoulders, the unwavering gaze that seemed to penetrate the superficial layers of the world, and the subtle tension in his hands resting on the bar.

His dark eyes flickered toward mine for the briefest moment, a fleeting connection that felt both accidental and profoundly significant. I felt a strange jolt, like I'd been caught staring at something I wasn't meant to see, glimpsing a secret truth hidden beneath the surface of ordinary reality. It was a look that held both curiosity and a hint of warning, a silent invitation to a path I wasn't sure I was ready to tread.

I turned back to my drink, the amber liquid now seeming to mock me with its placid stillness. My pulse quickened for reasons I couldn't explain, a primal response to something unknown and potentially danger-ous. I took a large gulp of the whiskey, the burning sensation momentarily grounding me in the present, anchoring me to the familiar weight of the glass in my hand. I tried to rationalize my reaction, to dismiss it as the product of an overactive imagination and too much time spent alone with my thoughts, but the feeling of unease persisted, a persistent whisper at the edge of my consciousness.

By the time I glanced back, he was gone, vanished into the smoky haze as if he were nothing more than a figment of my imagination.

I frowned, a knot of confusion tightening in my stomach. I scanned the room as discreetly as I could, my eyes darting from face to face, searching for any sign of the enigmatic stranger. He wasn't at the bar, his absence leaving a palpable void in the space he had occupied, nor was he mingling with the dwindling crowd, lost in the sea of faces that were now beginning to thin as the night drew on.

For a moment, I wondered if I'd imagined the whole thing—a figment of my restless mind conjured up by too many late nights fueled by cheap whiskey and not enough excitement. Perhaps I was simply projecting my own desires and anxieties onto a random stranger, seeking meaning where there was none to be found.

And then he was beside me, his presence materializing seemingly out of thin air, a silent ghost taking form.

"Mind if I join you?"

His voice was smooth, low, and deliberate, each word carefully chosen and precisely articulated. It cut through the ambient noise of the bar like a knife through butter, slicing through the layers of chatter and clinking glasses, settling into my ears as if it had been meant just for me—a private message delivered in the midst of a crowded room. It was a voice that resonated with authority and a hint of something else, something indefinable that sent a shiver down my spine.

"Sure," I said cautiously, gesturing to the empty seat beside me with a hesitant wave of my hand. My mind raced, trying to anticipate his intentions, to decipher the meaning behind his sudden appearance and his unnervingly direct manner.

He sat with practiced grace, every movement calculated, making the transition from standing to seated seem effortless and unsettling. Up close, his sharp features—high cheekbones casting dramatic shadows, a strong jawline radiating determination, and dark eyes that absorbed the bar's light—revealed a depth of experience and secrets I couldn't fathom.

"I'm Marcus," he said, offering a faint smile that didn't quite reach his eyes, a fleeting expression that revealed nothing of the man beneath.

"Tristan."

"Pleasure," he said softly, the word laced with something I couldn't quite place—a hint of amusement, perhaps, or maybe something darker, something predatory. His gaze lingered on me for a moment too long, as if he were studying me, analyzing my every feature, peeling back layers I didn't even know I had, searching for something hidden beneath the surface. It was an unnerving sensation, like being dissected by an invisible scalpel, my vulnerabilities laid bare to his cold, calculating gaze.

"You've had an interesting night," he said, his tone casual but weighted with unspoken meaning—as if he were privy to thoughts and feelings I hadn't even acknowledged myself.

"What do you mean by that?" I asked, my voice betraying a nervousness I couldn't quite suppress.

Marcus tilted his head slightly, a small knowing smile playing on his lips, as if he were enjoying my discomfort. "You're different," he said, almost to himself, his voice barely a whisper, as if he were speaking a secret truth that only he could hear.

Marcus sat beside me, his posture relaxed yet deliberate. He didn't seem hurried or restless like so many others in the bar, and yet his presence felt oddly commanding. The dim light of the tavern seemed to pool around him, highlighting the sharp angles of his face and the dark intensity of his eyes. He carried himself with an air of quiet confidence—a stark contrast to the boisterous energy that filled the room. It was as if he were observing the chaos around him from a detached, almost scholarly distance. I found myself subtly adjusting my own posture—a subconscious attempt to match his composed demeanor.

"So," I said, glancing at him. "What brings you here?" The question felt clumsy, almost intrusive, but I couldn't shake the feeling that I needed to know more about this enigmatic stranger. The air crackled with unspoken tension, a silent challenge hanging between us.

Marcus's dark eyes shifted toward me, his expression calm and unreadable. They were deep and fathomless, like pools of still water reflecting the starless night. It was impossible to discern his true thoughts behind that impenetrable gaze. "I was curious," he said simply, his voice low but clear—a sound barely audible above the din of the bar, yet resonating with undeniable authority.

"Curious about what?" I asked, trying to keep my tone light—to mask the flicker of unease that his presence sparked within me. The question hung in the air, suspended between the clinking of glasses and the raucous laughter of the other patrons.

He shrugged faintly—a subtle movement that barely disturbed the stillness of his frame. His gaze drifted toward the row of bottles behind the bar. Amber liquids glowed invitingly beneath the flickering lamplight, their labels obscured by layers of dust and grime. "About the kind of people who find their way to places like this." His eyes lingered on a bottle of dark, viscous liquid before returning to me.

It was a vague answer, and yet it carried a weight that I couldn't quite explain. It was as if he were hinting at something deeper, something hidden beneath the surface of the mundane. A shiver ran down my spine, a primal instinct warning me to be cautious. I took another sip of my drink, the lukewarm ale doing little to soothe my nerves, using the motion to steady myself.

"What about you?" Marcus asked, turning his attention back to me. The intensity of his gaze made me feel like I was under a microscope, every flaw and insecurity magnified for his inspection.

"What about me?" I repeated, stalling for time, trying to formulate a response that wouldn't reveal too much.

"Why are you here?" he pressed, his voice unwavering. There was no judgment in his tone, only genuine curiosity.

I hesitated, caught off guard by the directness of the question. It felt like a probe delving into the hidden recesses of my soul. "A friend dragged me out," I said finally, offering a partial truth. "He thought I could use some socializing." It was a weak excuse, I knew, but it was the best I could come up with on the spot.

Marcus tilted his head slightly, a small smile tugging at the corner of his mouth. It was a fleeting expression, gone as quickly as it appeared, but it hinted at a hidden amusement. "And what do you think?" he challenged, his eyes twinkling with an unspoken invitation to be honest.

I paused, unsure how to answer. The truth was, I hadn't wanted to come. The city—its relentless noise, its crowded streets, its constant de-mands—had become overwhelming. I preferred the solitude of my work-shop, the quiet hum of my tools, the predictable rhythm of creation. But my friend, bless his well-meaning heart, had insisted. There was something disarming about the way he spoke, the way he managed to ask questions that felt more personal than they should have. It was as if he possessed some innate ability to bypass my defenses. "I think he's probably right," I said carefully, choosing my words with deliberate precision.

Marcus nodded, as if my answer had confirmed something for him. A strange satisfaction settled over his features. He reached for his drink—a dark, swirling concoction that smelled faintly of spice and something else I couldn't quite identify—and took a small sip. "This city has a way of swallowing people," he said quietly. "It's easy to lose track of yourself here." His words echoed the very sentiments I had been trying to suppress.

I frowned slightly, unsure of where he was going with that. The city was a melting pot of dreams and desperation, a place where fortunes could be made and lives could be broken. It had a seductive allure, but also a sinister undercurrent that I couldn't ignore. "You're not from around here, are you?" I asked, stating the obvious.

He gave a faint smile, a fleeting expression that hinted at a deeper, more complex humor. "Is it that obvious?"

"A little," I admitted, returning his smile with a hesitant one of my own. There was something undeniably foreign about him, something that set him apart from the other inhabitants of the city. Perhaps it was the way he carried himself or the way he spoke, or simply the air of quiet mystery that clung to him like a cloak.

Marcus chuckled softly, the sound low and almost melodic. It was a warm, comforting sound that momentarily eased the tension between us. "No, I'm not from here. But I've spent enough time in places like this to recognize the patterns."

"Patterns?" I prompted, intrigued by his cryptic statement.

He nodded, his gaze drifting briefly to the crowd around us. He observed them with a keen, almost predatory intensity, as if he were studying a particularly fascinating species of animal. "The way people move, the way they talk. Everyone's searching for something, even if they don't know what it is." His observation felt insightful, almost profound.

I wasn't sure why, but his words struck a chord. Maybe it was the way he said them, with a quiet certainty that made them feel like a truth I hadn't wanted to confront. I had always considered myself to be a pragmatic, logical person, but lately, I had begun to feel a nagging sense of dissatisfaction, a vague yearning for something more.

"What about you?" I asked, turning the question back on him. "What are you searching for?" I wanted to know what drove him, what secrets he held, and what lay beneath that calm, unreadable exterior.

For the first time, Marcus hesitated. His dark eyes flickered briefly, revealing a glimpse of vulnerability that he quickly masked. A shadow of something unspoken passed over his face—a fleeting expression of pain or regret. "That's a good question," he said finally, his tone lighter but no less deliberate.

It felt like a deflection, a carefully constructed wall designed to keep me at bay. But I didn't press him. Instead, I studied him for a moment, trying to make sense of the strange pull I felt toward him. There was something about Marcus that didn't fit—something that made him feel both out of place and completely at ease at the same time. He was an enigma, a puzzle I couldn't resist trying to solve.

"You're a quiet one," Marcus said, his tone almost amused, breaking the silence that had descended between us. "Not many people would let a stranger sit down without asking a dozen questions." He tilted his head, studying me with a curious intensity.

"I guess I'm not like most people," I said lightly, trying to deflect his scrutiny with a casual remark.

His smile widened just slightly, but there was something behind it that I couldn't quite read. It was a knowing smile, a smile that suggested he knew more about me than I knew about myself. "No," he said softly. "You're not." The way he said it sent a shiver down my spine—as if he was implying I was different from everyone else in ways I couldn't comprehend yet.

He took a small, silver object from his pocket. It looked like a dragon scale with strange runes on it. He flipped it in his fingers and placed it back in his pocket.

Marcus's gaze lingered on me for a moment longer, a beat suspended in time, before he finally turned back to his drink. I felt the weight of that look—a question unspoken, a hint of something else I couldn't quite decipher. He finished his drink in a slow, deliberate sip, as if savoring the last drop of a rare vintage. The dark liquid disappeared, and the silence stretched on, punctuated only by the low hum of the bar.

He placed the empty glass on the polished bar top with a soft clink—a sound barely audible above the din, yet it echoed in my ears like a small, significant announcement. The motion was as unhurried as everything else he did, each movement precise and measured, giving the impression of someone who had all the time in the world—or perhaps someone who controlled time itself. It was unnerving.

"Well, Tristan," he said quietly, his voice low and smooth, like aged velvet. The sound seemed to brush against my skin, sending a shiver down my spine. It was a voice that could command a room or whisper secrets in the dark—a voice that could charm or intimidate with equal ease. "Enjoy the rest of your evening."

Before I could even formulate a response—before I could attempt to latch onto the thread of our conversation and pull it back from the precipice of ending—he stood. His movements were fluid and purposeful, a stark contrast to the languid pace with which he had consumed his drink. He rose like a predator, uncoiling with silent grace, ready to move on to his next pursuit.

He began weaving his way through the crowd—a human river parting before him as if drawn by an unseen current. He navigated the maze of bodies with an almost supernatural awareness—never bumping into anyone, never hesitating. He was a phantom, a ghost moving through the living, and all I could do was watch him go.

I observed him leave, an odd blend of intrigue and discomfort swirling inside me. It felt like gazing into an abyss—enticed by its enigma yet apprehensive of its depths. What had that expression signified? What was he on the verge of saying? My thoughts raced, attempting to keep pace with the delicate subtleties of the exchange, reaching for ephemeral impressions as if trying to capture smoke.

Marcus didn't look back as he moved toward the exit, his tall frame disappearing into the throng of patrons. He was swallowed by the crowd, absorbed into the collective energy of the bar. He didn't offer a final glance, a parting word—nothing to anchor the moment in reality. It was as if he had never been there at all, his presence evaporating into the air like smoke.

I turned back to my drink, the amber liquid now seeming dull and lifeless. I gripped the glass tighter than I realized, my knuckles turning white. The cold glass was a stark reminder of the chill that had settled over me. The conversation replayed in my mind—fragments of his words echoing louder than they had when he'd said them. You're not like most people. The phrase hung in the air, heavy with unspoken meaning.

It wasn't necessarily what he'd said that unsettled me—it was the way he'd said it, the knowing glint in his eyes, as if he possessed some secret knowledge about me—as if he knew me better than I knew myself. It was an unsettling feeling, like having someone see through a carefully constructed façade, exposing the raw, vulnerable core beneath. Was that a good thing or a bad thing? And more importantly, what did Marcus intend to do with that knowledge?

The space surrounding me felt more vibrant, the soothing hum of chatter and the well-known clinking of glasses transforming into a jarring symphony of sound that grated on my eardrums. The Garret, which had always been a haven—a place of refuge—now felt claustrophobic, oppressive. I glanced at my phone, considering texting Benji or Jessica, seeking the familiar comfort of their presence, but the idea of explaining what had just happened felt impossible. How could I even begin to put it into words? How could I convey the subtle shift in atmosphere, the weight of his gaze, the feeling of being...seen?

I drained the last of my whiskey, the burning liquid doing little to thaw the chill that had settled in my bones. I stood, shrugging on my jacket. The worn leather felt rough against my skin—a small comfort in the face of the growing unease. The air in The Garret suddenly felt stifling—the once-inviting glow of candlelight now too dim, too close, like a spotlight highlighting my own discomfort. I needed to escape, to breathe, to find some semblance of normalcy.

The staircase creaked beneath my weight as I descended back into the city—each step echoing in the sudden silence. The worn wood groaned under my boots, as if mirroring my internal struggle. The noise of the street hit me like a wave the moment I pushed open the heavy oak door—honking taxis, distant sirens, the murmur of pedestrians passing by. It was grounding in a way, a chaotic symphony of urban life that pulled me back from the brink of introspection. It was a stark reminder that the world continued, regardless of the unsettling encounters within the dimly lit confines of The Garret.

But even as I walked, the feeling lingered—that strange pull Marcus had left behind, like an invisible tether connecting us, like a shadow that wouldn't let go. It was a persistent feeling, a nagging sense that something was not quite right—that the world had shifted on its axis ever so slightly. I tried to shake it off, to dismiss it as mere paranoia, but the unease remained—a constant companion in the bustling city streets.

As I turned onto Bleecker Street, the familiar landscape felt foreign, tainted by the encounter. I thought I saw something move out of the corner of my eye—a flicker of motion just at the edge of my vision, a fleeting impression of darkness. I stopped, my heart skipping a beat, my breath catching in my throat. I spun around, my eyes scanning the surrounding area, searching for any sign of movement, any indication of what I had seen. But when I turned to look, there was nothing there.

Just the faint scent of rain on the pavement, a damp, earthy aroma that clung to the air. The streetlights cast long, distorted shadows—playing tricks on my eyes. I could hear the distant rumble of a subway train, the pulse of the city throbbing beneath my feet. Everything seemed normal, mundane, yet the feeling of being watched persisted.

I shook my head, convincing myself it was just my imagination—spurred by too much whiskey and an unsettling conversation. I walked on, trying to regain my composure and banish the lingering fear gnawing at my mind. Yet, as I headed home, unease settled in my chest like an inaudible whisper—a secret I couldn't decipher. It felt as if something had shifted, that I had crossed a threshold with no return. The city lights dimmed, street sounds faded into a dull murmur as I walked into the darkness—the shadow of Marcus's gaze still upon me.

The walk home was uneventful, the city's usual chaos humming around me like a distant melody. The relentless horns of impatient taxis, the ragged strumming of a street musician's guitar, the snippets of heated arguments and boisterous laughter spilling from the dimly lit doorways of nearby bars—all blended into a familiar soundtrack, a constant thrum that vibrated through the very pavement beneath my feet. Years of living in the city had dulled the edge of the noise, transforming it into white noise that I barely noticed anymore. It was the background to my life—the constant hum of the machine that never slept.

I stopped at the bodega near my apartment, the fluorescent lights inside buzzing with a similar frenetic energy to the city outside. I grabbed a cold bottle of water from the refrigerated case—the condensation slick and cool against my skin—and a bag of pretzels, their salty aroma a comforting promise of late-night snacking.

The cashier, a young man with tired eyes and a perpetually bored expression, barely looked up as he rang me out. His earbuds were firmly in place, blasting some unheard rhythm directly into his skull as he bobbed his head almost imperceptibly to a beat only he could hear and feel. He mumbled a perfunctory "Next," already lost in his personal soundscape. The interaction was transactional, devoid of any genuine human connection—a common occurrence in the city's daily grind.

Inside my apartment, the sudden quiet was almost jarring—a heavy blanket of silence that descended the moment the door clicked shut behind me. The outside world—with its clamor of noises and visuals—felt like it was light-years away. The hum of the refrigerator—a low and constant thrumming—and the occasional creak of the old pipes, a chorus of groans and sighs—were the only sounds, a stark contrast to the relentless noise outside. My apartment, small and slightly cramped, was my sanctuary—a refuge from the constant stimulation of the city.

I tossed my heavy messenger bag onto the worn fabric of the couch, the contents shifting with a soft thud, and kicked off my shoes—the sudden freedom a small but welcome relief. My feet ached after a long day spent navigating the crowded streets. I headed straight for the kitchen, the linoleum cool beneath my bare feet. The bottle of water went into the fridge, joining a motley collection of leftovers and condiments, and the bag of pretzels landed unceremoniously onto the speckled countertop.

It was the kind of mindless routine I could do without thinking—a series of familiar actions etched into my muscle memory. My body moved on autopilot, efficiently performing the mundane tasks while my mind wandered, drifting like a cloud through the vast expanse of my thoughts.

I thought about texting Benji, my closest friend and confidant—maybe telling him about the strange encounter at the bar. I replayed the conversation in my mind, searching for the exact words that would capture the peculiarity of the situation. But what was there to say, really? Met someone interesting. Kinda weird, but not in a bad way. Seemed like he knew me—or at least that he knew something about me. But maybe that's just me overthinking the whole thing, reading too much into a simple conversation fueled by alcohol and late-night anxieties. Benji would probably just tell me I was being paranoid—that I needed to relax and stop seeing mysteries where there were none.

I shook my head—the fleeting thought evaporating as quickly as it had come. The urge to share the experience with Benji faded, replaced by a desire for solitude and quiet contemplation. Instead, I grabbed a tall glass of water from the tap—the cool liquid a welcome contrast to the dry heat of the apartment—and sank onto the couch, its familiar contours molding to my body. I flipped on the TV—not really intending to watch anything in particular, but more for the comforting presence of background noise—a buffer against the oppressive silence.

The news anchor's voice droned on about some city council meeting—a tedious discussion about zoning regulations and budget allocations—the kind of thing I usually tuned out completely. It was the same old political rhetoric, the same endless cycle of promises and disappointments. My eyes drifted to the window, drawn by the flickering lights of the city outside. The glow of streetlights cast long, distorted shadows across the room, transforming familiar objects into strange and unsettling shapes. The city, even in its slumber, was a canvas of light and shadow—a constantly evolving work of art.

It had been a good night, I realized with a sudden surge of clarity. Different, certainly, but undeniably good. There was a strange undercurrent of excitement that had taken hold and lingered with me. The meeting with that man was odd, but not threatening. His eyes, although piercing, were also warm and welcoming. He offered something to my life that had been missing for quite some time.

Marcus crossed my mind briefly—his sharp features and calm demeanor flashing like a vivid snapshot before fading quickly into the hazy background of my thoughts. The memory of his intense gaze, the lingering pressure of his hand on my arm, stirred a strange mix of curiosity and unease within me. He was just another stranger in a city full of them—another face in the endless crowd, someone I'd probably never see again. A casual meeting in a bar—no real harm.

Probably. The word echoed in my mind, tinged with a faint sense of doubt. There was something about the encounter that lingered—a subtle feeling that the universe had altered, that a thread had been pulled from the tapestry of my existence. I couldn't shake the feeling that our meeting was not as random as it seemed.

I shook off the nagging thought and leaned back further into the soft cushions of the couch, letting the bland, repetitive sound of the TV fill the quiet spaces in my mind. Tomorrow would be another day, another relentless stream of reports and emails, another seemingly endless stretch of monotony to push through. The cycle would continue: get up, go to work, come home, sleep, repeat. But for tonight, I was content to simply let the city settle around me, its rhythm as steady and familiar as ever—a comforting lullaby that promised a few hours of oblivion before the dawn arrived. And then everything would start again. One more day, one more step forward, one more attempt to fulfill my daily work.

The city never sleeps, and neither does my mind. It is a constant barrage of thoughts, ideas, worries, and dreams.

I close my eyes and let the city wash over me.

After a while, the soft murmur of the TV became little more than background noise—the anchor's voice a disembodied drone blending seamlessly with the steady hum of the city outside; a low, constant thrum that vibrated through the very foundations of the building. The blue light flickered across the opposite wall, casting elongated, shifting shadows that danced with the dust motes suspended in the air.

I finished my water—the last few drops clinging to the bottom of the glass—and set the empty vessel on the worn surface of the coffee table. The wood, scarred with rings from countless forgotten drinks, felt cool beneath my fingertips. My body, heavy and leaden, seemed to sink even deeper into the overstuffed cushions of the couch, as if the furniture itself were trying to swallow me whole.

The weight of the day—a relentless tide of responsibilities and anxieties—was finally catching up to me, pulling insistently at my eyelids. Each blink felt heavier than the last, threatening to plunge me into the oblivion of sleep. A glance at the digital clock on the microwave told me it was just past midnight—the early hours of tomorrow already creeping in like a thief in the night. Another day over, and I was no closer to figuring anything out.

I stretched—my muscles protesting with a symphony of pops and cracks. My limbs felt heavy, weighted down with a mix of bone-deep exhaustion and the pleasant, slightly fuzzy haze from the whiskey I'd had earlier. It had been a single, medicinal shot meant to dull the sharp edges of the day, but it lingered still—a warm ember in my chest.

In the small, cramped bathroom, the fluorescent light above the mirror buzzed softly—a high-pitched whine that grated on my nerves. The cheap fixture flickered erratically—threatening to plunge the room into darkness at any moment. I leaned over the sink and splashed cold water on my face. The shock of the icy liquid bit sharply against my skin—a welcome jolt that grounded me in the present, forcing me to focus on the immediate sensation. The evening's peculiar events replayed themselves in my mind in fragmented, disjointed images: the crowded bar, the clinking of glasses, the murmur of conversations, and, most prominently, Marcus.

Marcus's voice lingered at the edge of my thoughts—quiet but persistent, like a recurring melody you can't quite place. You're not like most people. The words echoed in the silence of the bathroom, amplified by the stillness. I hadn't asked what he meant by that—caught off guard by the unexpected statement. Now, standing here alone in the dead of night, I wished I had. What had he seen? What had prompted him to say such a thing? Was it a compliment? An accusation? A warning? The uncertainty gnawed at me.

I turned off the faucet, letting the last few droplets trail down my face like errant tears before patting my skin dry with a rough, threadbare towel. The faded floral pattern was barely visible—worn away by years of use. When

I looked up, my reflection stared back at me from the mirror—tired eyes clouded with confusion, rumpled hair that stuck out at odd angles, a face that seemed older than it should've been—etched with the subtle lines of worry and weariness.

The fluorescent light cast harsh shadows—exaggerating every flaw, every imperfection. For a moment—a fleeting, unsettling moment—I thought I saw something shift in the glass—a flicker of movement just behind me, at the very periphery of my vision. A dark shape, indistinct and ephemeral—like a shadow trying to take form.

I spun around quickly, my breath catching in my throat—a sudden surge of adrenaline coursing through my veins. My heart hammered against my ribs—a frantic drumbeat in the silence.

The bathroom was empty. Utterly, completely empty. The shower curtain hung motionless, the toilet stood silent, the chipped porcelain sink gleamed faintly under the buzzing light. There was nothing there. Just the small, familiar space I had occupied countless times before.

I stood there for a few moments—my pulse pounding in my ears, the blood rushing in my head. The logical, rational part of my brain desperately tried to assert itself, offering explanations, dismissing the unsettling feeling as nothing more than a trick of the light—the hallucination conjured by my tired mind playing games. It was late, I was exhausted, and I'd had a drink. It was perfectly reasonable to be experiencing minor sensory distortions. But despite the logical explanations, the feeling stayed with me—a cold knot of unease tightening in my stomach. It lingered like a phantom limb—a persistent reminder that something was not quite right.

I forced myself to take a deep breath, trying to regain my composure. I left the bathroom, switching off the light and stepping into the shadowed hallway. The darkness felt thicker here, pressing in around me, amplifying the silence.

I made my way to the bedroom—the soft creak of the floor-boards following my steps like a ghostly accompaniment. Each footstep echoed in the stillness, sounding far louder than it should have. The apartment was old—the building settling with age—but tonight, the familiar sounds felt different—imbued with a sense of foreboding. The streetlight outside cast a faint, ethereal glow through the window, cutting across the room in long, slanting bars of pale orange. The light illuminated the dust motes dancing in the air, turning them into fleeting, ephemeral shapes.

Sliding into bed, I pulled the blanket up to my chest, seeking comfort in its familiar weight. The cotton felt soft against my skin, but it did little to dispel the lingering sense of unease. I stared up at the ceiling—the plaster slightly cracked and stained with old watermarks—as my mind churned, replaying the events of the evening, searching for some logical explanation for the unsettling feeling that clung to me.

I thought about Marcus again—his calm demeanor, the quiet confidence that radiated from him. He had seemed so...ordinary. Just another face in the crowd. And yet, there had been something else there—something beneath the surface that had unsettled me. The way he had looked at me, the intensity in his eyes, the weight of his presence. It was as if he knew something I didn't.

If anything, he'd seemed completely ordinary. That was part of what bothered me. He was unremarkable in almost every way, and yet he had managed to completely unnerve me with a few simple words. How could someone so seemingly normal have such a profound effect?

And yet he wasn't—not entirely. There was something hidden—something lurking beneath the surface. I could feel it—a subtle vibration in the air around him—a sense of restrained power.

I turned onto my side, pulling the pillow closer and closing my eyes, willing sleep to come. I tried to empty my mind, to focus on my breathing, to shut out the relentless thoughts that threatened to overwhelm me. But it was no use. The questions kept swirling, the doubts kept nagging.

As the city settled into its familiar nighttime rhythm outside my window—the distant sirens and the muffled rumble of traffic fading into a low, constant hum—I felt the strange sensation of being watched—a faint prickling at the back of my neck that wouldn't go away. It was a subtle sensation—almost imperceptible, but it was there nonetheless—a persistent reminder that I was not alone. I told myself it was nothing—just the remnants of an unusual night clinging to me like a shadow—a lingering echo of the unsettling encounter with Marcus. It was probably just my imagination—amplified by exhaustion and a touch of paranoia.

But even as I drifted toward sleep—succumbing to the heavy pull of exhaustion—I couldn't shake the feeling that Marcus's words hadn't been idle. That maybe—just maybe—he'd meant them as something more than a casual observation. That they were a clue, a hint, a veiled warning about something I didn't yet understand.

Somewhere outside, a dog barked—its sharp, piercing cry cutting through the quiet of the night. The sound reverberated through the empty streets, echoing off the brick walls of the surrounding buildings. It was a lonely, desolate sound—full of a primal energy that sent a shiver down my spine.

And then—silence.

Chapter Three

THE MISSING PUZZLE PIECES

The morning unfolded with the predictable monotony of a recurring dream. The digital shriek of my alarm clock, a sound I had grown to both despise and rely upon, tore me from the depths of sleep. My hand, still heavy with slumber, fumbled across the nightstand until my fingers found the snooze button. Silence descended, a brief respite before the inevitable.

I lay there, suspended between wakefulness and the lingering tendrils of the dream world. The ceiling above was a blank canvas, gradually illuminated by the faint, ethereal glow of dawn seeping through the slats of the blinds. My body felt strangely rested, devoid of the usual aches and stiffness, but my mind was a churning sea of half-formed thoughts and shadowy impressions.

Fragments of dreams, elusive and intangible, danced just beyond the grasp of my conscious memory. Images flickered: a towering cityscape bathed in an unnatural light, a faceless figure whispering cryptic words, a labyrinthine corridor that seemed to stretch into infinity. They were gone as quickly as they appeared, leaving behind only a vague sense of unease and a persistent feeling that something important was just out of reach.

I shook off the lingering effects of sleep, forcing myself to confront the reality of the day ahead. The world wouldn't pause to accommodate my mental wanderings. It marched forward, relentless and unforgiving.

With a sigh, I swung my legs over the side of the bed and stood up, the cold floor sending a shiver through my bare feet. The motions of my morning routine were as ingrained and mechanical as the inner workings of a clock. A quick shower, the invigorating rush of hot water washing away the last vestiges of sleep; a strong cup of coffee, the rich aroma filling the air and promising a jolt of much-needed energy; a piece of toast, consumed quickly and efficiently.

Everything had its rhythm, its prescribed sequence, a pattern so familiar that I could navigate it blindfolded. There was a strange comfort in this predictability, a sense of order in the chaos. It was like muscle memory taking over, carrying me forward even when my thoughts lagged behind, lost in the labyrinth of my own mind.

At Palantir Technologies, the office greeted me with its usual, soul-crushing gray monotony. The walls, painted in a shade that could best be described as "corporate beige," seemed to absorb all light and color. Rows upon rows of identical desks stretched out before me, each one occupied by a faceless drone diligently contributing to the corporate machine. The air hung heavy with the faint, stale scent of day-old coffee and the sterile, metallic odor of electronic equipment. The muted chatter of coworkers, a low, constant buzz of voices discussing spreadsheets and deadlines, blended into an ambient hum that was both ever-present and easily ignored.

Sliding into my assigned chair, I powered on my computer, the familiar click of the power button a small act of rebellion against the prevailing silence. The screen flickered to life, displaying the Palantir logo before resolving into the stark, demanding interface of the day's work. A fresh spreadsheet stared back at me, a vast grid of numbers and formulas promising hours of tedious analysis. It demanded my full attention, but my focus remained stubbornly elsewhere, still clinging to the fragments of forgotten dreams and the nagging feeling that something was amiss.

"Tris!"

Benji's voice, loud and cheerfully intrusive, rang out from the neighboring cubicle, instantly shattering the illusion of quiet concentration. A moment later, his head popped up over the fabric-covered divider, his unruly brown hair sticking up at improbable angles. His grin was wide and irrepressible, a beacon of genuine enthusiasm in the sterile corporate environment.

"Morning," I said, already reaching for my mug and heading toward the coffee machine. The promise of caffeine was the only thing keeping me afloat at this point.

"You good?" he asked, tilting his head slightly, his brow furrowed in concern. "You've got that 'I was up too late wrestling with existential dread' look. It's not a good look on you, by the way."

"I'm fine," I replied, hoping to shut down the conversation before it went any further.

"Come on, spill. Did you stay at the bar longer than I thought? Did you finally meet the girl of your dreams Or maybe you were busy saving the world again, after work hours? Mysterious late-night adventures?" He wiggled his eyebrows in mock intrigue, his eyes sparkling with playful curiosity.

"No adventures," I said, striving to keep my tone neutral and unrevealing. "Just... ended up thinking about stuff."

Benji nodded sagely, as if he understood completely the complexities of my inner life. "Ah, one of those nights. The dreaded overthinking spiral. You overthinkers always have it rough. Well, if you need a distraction from the voices inside your head, I've got a story about the absolute disaster that was my last date. It involves a karaoke machine, three shots of tequila, and a near miss with a rogue chihuahua."

I managed a faint smile, appreciating his attempt to lighten the mood, but before I could formulate a response, Ash strode past our cubicles, a stack of meticulously organized folders clutched tightly in her arms. Her movements were sharp and precise, radiating an aura of controlled efficiency.

"Morning, Ash," I said casually, hoping to avoid any unnecessary confrontation.

"Tristan," she replied, her voice clipped and professional, devoid of any warmth.

Her gaze lingered for a moment, her eyes sharp and assessing, before she continued down the aisle, her heels clicking sharply on the linoleum floor. Benji watched her retreating figure, then turned back to me with a low whistle, his expression a mixture of amusement and concern.

"She's still pissed about the Kintech proposal, huh?"

"Probably," I said, keeping my tone even and noncommittal.

"That's putting it mildly." Benji leaned in conspiratorially, lowering his voice as if fearing that Ash might overhear us. "Word is she's been fuming ever since you swooped in to save the presentation. Which, by the way, was badass. If it weren't for you, the client would've walked, and we'd all be screwed. You saved the day, Tris. You're basically a corporate superhero."

The Kintech project had been Ash's responsibility, a massive account she'd been diligently handling for weeks. It was a high-profile client, a major player in the tech industry, and securing their business was considered a significant win for Palantir Technologies. But when the client unexpectedly requested last-minute revisions just hours before the final presentation, Ash had faltered, clearly overwhelmed by the sheer scope of the changes.

She had frozen, unable to cope with the pressure. I'd stepped in, working through the night to reorganize the data, refine the presentation, and deliver the pitch myself. The client had been undeniably impressed, showering praise on the revamped proposal and formally accepting Palantir's bid. But Ash... not so much.

"She had it under control," I said, though the words felt hollow and unconvincing, even to my own ears.

Benji snorted, rolling his eyes. "Not from where I was sitting. She looked like she was about to have a panic attack. Look, you didn't do anything wrong, Tris. You just... well, you were better. And Ash is one of those people who hates feeling outshined. Especially by you. Just let her stew for a while. She'll come around eventually. Or at least, she'll find someone else to blame for the project's success."

I wasn't so sure about that. Ash was nothing if not persistent, and her ambition burned with a fierce intensity. I had a feeling this wasn't over.

By lunchtime, the monotony was settling over me like a heavy fog. The morning had crawled by, each tick of the clock a tiny hammer blow against my patience. Each task blurred into the next with an almost maddening sameness. Spreadsheets, emails, and meetings – it was a cycle that seemed designed to drain the very life out of me, leaving behind a hollow shell. I longed for something, anything, to break the spell, a crack in the routine to let some light shine through. But the office remained stubbornly ordinary, a landscape of beige cubicles and fluorescent lighting, a testament to the crushing weight of corporate existence.

The cafeteria was already filling up with people, the noise level rising like the tide. Groups formed at tables, islands of chatter amidst the sea of lunchtime diners, exchanging office gossip or dissecting last night's game with the fervor of seasoned analysts. The air was thick with the smells of lukewarm coffee, perpetually brewing since dawn, and microwaved lunches, a comforting yet somehow depressing aroma that spoke to the daily grind, to the compromises made for convenience and the sacrifices of culinary ambition. I grabbed a prepackaged sandwich, the same turkey and Swiss on stale rye I'd had every day for the past two weeks, and scanned the room, a familiar exercise in social cartography.

The usual suspects were present: the marketing team animatedly discussing the latest ad campaign, their laughter and debates punctuating the air; the grim legal department, faces etched with the weight of contracts; and scattered individuals lost in their own worlds, staring blankly at screens

or flipping through magazines, eyes glazed with boredom. A pang of loneliness hit me, a sense of drifting among strangers, each navigating their
own struggles. This feeling often washed over me, a wave of isolation in
a crowded room.

"Tristan!" Jessica's voice cut through the hum of conversation, a welcome
beacon in the cafeteria din. She waved me over to a table near the back,
where she sat with Dan from IT and Emily from data analytics. Their table
was relatively secluded, tucked away in a quieter corner of the cafeteria,
near a window that offered a view of the parking lot and the distant
cityscape. They seemed to be enjoying a relaxed, informal conversation,
their body language suggesting a level of comfort and camaraderie that I
envied.

I hesitated for a moment before heading over, a flicker of self-consciousness washing over me. I wasn't particularly close to Dan or Emily. We were
more acquaintances than friends, bound together by the shared experience
of working in the same soul-crushing environment. But I also didn't have
any other compelling lunch options. And, truth be told, the prospect
of sitting alone with my stale sandwich, lost in my own thoughts, was
becoming increasingly unappealing.

I took a deep breath, trying to project an air of casual confidence, a façade
of effortless sociability. I straightened my shoulders, adjusted my tie, and
started toward them, hoping I didn't look too desperate or pathetic. I slid
into a seat across from her, forcing a small smile.

"You looked lost," she said with a grin, her tone teasing but light, devoid of any genuine malice. "Thought I'd rescue you." Her smile was warm and genuine, a flash of brightness that momentarily lifted the gray cloud hanging over my head, and I felt a little of my anxiety dissipate. Jessica had a knack for making people feel at ease, for disarming even the most guarded individuals. It was probably why she was so popular around the office, a natural social lubricant in the often awkward ecosystem of corporate relationships.

"Thanks," I said, unwrapping my sandwich. The rye bread was even drier than I remembered, bordering on fossilized, and the turkey looked suspiciously pale, as if it had been bleached of all color and flavor. I took a tentative bite, trying to ignore the blandness of it all, the complete lack of any discernible taste. It was a culinary void, a testament to the triumph o f efficiency over quality. "Appreciate the save."

The table's conversation was easy and meandering, a mix of work complaints—the universal language of office workers—and weekend plans, those fleeting glimpses of freedom that sustained us through the drudgery of the week. Dan, as usual, was glued to his phone, his thumbs flying across the screen at lightning speed, occasionally interjecting with a sarcastic comment or a tech-related observation, his attention divided between the digital world and the physical one. Emily was recounting some recent incident involving a malfunctioning spreadsheet and a near-catastrophic data breach, her voice animated with a mixture of frustration and amusement.

"Ugh, look at this," Dan muttered, holding up his phone to Emily, his face illuminated by the harsh glow of the screen. His eyes were fixed on the display, and his brow was furrowed in a mixture of annoyance and morbid curiosity. He seemed both fascinated and repulsed by whatever he was seeing.

"What now?" Emily asked, rolling her eyes playfully. "Another cat video gone viral? Or did someone finally figure out how to hack the coffee machine?"

"Worse, kinda. Something about the police dragging the river downtown. They found a backpack or something." He shrugged, already scrolling past it, his attention span seemingly measured in milliseconds. The brief interruption seemed to have barely registered with him, and he was already moving on to the next piece of digital detritus, the endless stream of information and distraction that consumed his waking hours.

Jessica frowned slightly. "What's that about?" Her tone was curious, but also laced with a hint of concern. She had a soft spot for the city and its people, a deep-seated empathy that extended to the anonymous masses who shared its streets and struggles. She always worried about the undercurrent of darkness that seemed to lurk beneath the surface, the hidden currents of violence and despair that flowed beneath the glittering façade of urban prosperity.

"No idea," Dan replied, his attention already drifting back to his phone. "Some random thing. Probably nothing. You know how it is." He dismissed it with a wave of his hand, a casual disregard for the potential significance of the event.

"City drama," Emily added dismissively, taking a sip of her coffee. She clearly wasn't interested in dwelling on the matter, and her tone suggested that she considered it to be nothing more than a trivial distraction, a fleeting moment of morbid curiosity that had no bearing on her own life. "Happens all the time."

The topic fizzled out almost as quickly as it had come up, dissolving into the background noise of the cafeteria. The conversation shifted back to lighter chatter about an upcoming office happy hour, a scheduled dose of forced camaraderie and watered-down cocktails. The conversation flowed around me, a gentle stream of words and laughter that I found strangely comforting, a temporary escape from the relentless pressure of my own thoughts. I focused on my sandwich, dissecting it bite by bite, tuning out most of the conversation, letting the familiar voices wash over me like a soothing balm.

It wasn't unusual to hear odd stories like that in a city this size. They were part of the fabric of urban life, woven into the tapestry of everyday existence. There were always rumors, always strange headlines that felt disconnected from the lives we led, whispers of tragedies and mysteries that played out on the fringes of our awareness.

The city was a melting pot of dreams and despair, of triumphs and tragedies, and it was inevitable that some of that chaos would spill over into our everyday lives, like oil slicks spreading across a placid lake. Still, a faint thread of unease tugged at the back of my mind, a subtle discord in the otherwise harmonious symphony of lunchtime chatter, though I pushed it aside as quickly as it came, dismissing it as mere anxiety.

The image of the river, dark and murky, flashed through my mind, unbidden and unwelcome. I'd always felt a strange fascination with the river, a sense that it held secrets beneath its surface, that its depths concealed stories that the city had long forgotten. The thought of a backpack being dragged from its depths sent a shiver down my spine, a feeling that something wasn't quite right, a premonition that something significant had been unearthed. The river, that silent witness to all the city's sins and sorrows.

I tried to dismiss the feeling as mere coincidence, as a product of my overactive imagination, fueled by too much coffee and too little sleep. But the unease lingered, a persistent little voice whispering in the back of my mind, a nagging intuition that refused to be silenced. It was a feeling that I knew all too well, a sense of foreboding that had often proven to be justified in the past. I tried to ignore it, to focus on the mundane reality of my surroundings, but the image of the river remained, a dark and unsettling premonition.

By the time lunch was over, the mention of the river and the backpack had faded into the white noise of the day, becoming just another fleeting moment in the relentless flow of information. I returned to my desk, the monotony of the morning quickly reasserting itself, like a tide pulling me back into its relentless rhythm. Spreadsheets and emails filled my screen, demanding my attention, vying for my focus with their urgent requests and endless data points. I tried to focus, to immerse myself in the world of numbers and data, to lose myself in the intricate patterns and complex algorithms.

The afternoon passed in a haze of repetition. Each minute seemed an echo of the last, stretching into an indistinguishable blur. The fluorescent lights hummed their monotonous tune, a soundtrack to the soul-crushing symphony of corporate life.

Emails, spreadsheets, meetings—everything blended together into a dull, endless rhythm. The kind of work that made time both crawl and disappear all at once. One moment, the morning coffee was still warm in my hand; the next, the shadows outside were lengthening, painting the neighboring buildings in hues of fading gold. By the time I glanced at the clock, its digital face glared back at me, the numbers creeping toward three with agonizing slowness, though it felt like no progress had been made.

I leaned back in my chair, the faux leather groaning in protest. Rubbing my eyes, I pressed my fingertips against the throbbing pressure points at my temples. The familiar ache of staring at a screen too long was starting to set in, a dull throb that resonated deep within my skull. The air in the cubicle felt stale, recycled, devoid of any real oxygen. I longed for the crisp, clean air of the outdoors, the feeling of the sun on my skin.

"Tristan," a voice called from across the cubicle wall, momentarily piercing the veil of monotony.

It was Sarah, my manager. The sound of her voice, though not unpleasant, was enough to trigger a surge of mild anxiety. I sat up straighter, adjusting my posture and attempting to appear more engaged than I actually felt. I watched as she rounded the corner, her heels clicking softly against the linoleum floor. She carried a stack of papers in her hand, their edges slightly frayed from constant handling.

"Do you have a minute?" she asked, her tone polite but brisk, the practiced cadence of a seasoned professional. Her eyes, though kind, held a hint of the weariness that seemed to permeate every corner of this building.

"Sure," I said, gesturing to the empty chair beside me, a silent invitation. I tried to imbue my voice with a semblance of enthusiasm, hoping to mask the quiet desperation simmering beneath the surface.

She didn't sit, instead remaining standing and flipping through the papers with deft fingers, her focus intense. The rustling sound filled the small space, momentarily drowning out the hum of the computers and the distant murmur of conversations. Finally, she pulled out one with a highlighted section, the vibrant yellow ink stark against the pale paper. "This is the report for Kintech," she said, handing it over. The paper felt cool and smooth against my palm. "I just need you to double-check these numbers before we send it out. Shouldn't take long."

"No problem," I replied, taking the report and scanning the document quickly. My eyes darted across the columns of figures, searching for any glaring errors or inconsistencies. The numbers seemed to dance before me, blurring together in a dizzying array.

"Thanks," Sarah said, her professional demeanor softening slightly, a hint of genuine gratitude flickering in her eyes. "You've been a lifesaver with this account. I don't know what we would have done without you."

I nodded, offering her a small smile, a gesture that felt both automatic and strangely hollow. "Just doing my job."

As she walked away, her heels clicking softly against the floor once more, I turned my attention back to the report. The numbers blurred together at first, my mind wandering as I tried to focus. The report was for Kintech, a company we had just signed a deal with that would drastically change the company; these numbers had to be perfect.

Random fragments of the day drifted through my thoughts—the clatter of trays in the cafeteria, the lingering smell of stale coffee, the brief mention of the river during a water cooler conversation, the quiet hum of the office around me, a constant, almost imperceptible drone. It was all so routine, so predictable, a carefully orchestrated symphony of the mundane. And yet, there was something beneath it all that felt... off. A discordant note, a subtle vibration that resonated just outside the realm of conscious awareness.

I shook my head, forcing my focus back to the spreadsheet in front of me. Whatever it was, it wasn't worth dwelling on. It was probably just the stress, the lack of sleep, the cumulative effect of weeks spent buried in spreadsheets and reports. I needed to focus, to get this report done, and to escape the soul-crushing gravity of the office.

I took a slow, deliberate breath, trying to center myself. It wasn't easy. The office felt like a cage, its invisible bars closing in around me. The air was thick with the weight of unspoken anxieties and unfulfilled dreams. I wanted to be anywhere but here.

My eyes drifted back to the report, and I began to meticulously check each number, each calculation, each decimal point. The work was tedious, but it required focus, and that was exactly what I needed. To lose myself in something tangible, something concrete, something that could distract me from the unsettling feeling that gnawed at the edge of my consciousness.

The minutes ticked by slowly, each one a small victory against the encroaching tide of despair. I checked and double-checked the figures, ensuring that everything was accurate and consistent. The numbers swam before my eyes, threatening to blur together once more, but I persevered, determined to complete the task at hand and escape the confines of th e office, and maybe then I could try to understand why I was feeling so off.

I scanned the report again, desperately hoping to find an error, a reason to prolong the task and delay the moment when I would be forced to confront the unsettling feeling that continued to linger.

But there it was.

A number was off by a significant margin. I highlighted the error, a surge of adrenaline coursing through my veins. This was it, the distraction I needed. I corrected the number, recalculated the totals, and double-checked everything one last time.

The report was finally complete.

By the time I stepped outside, the sun had dipped lower in the sky, painting the city in hues of orange and gold. The usual chaos of Midtown Manhattan swirled around me—a symphony of car horns blaring in gridlocked traffic, a relentless chorus of pedestrians weaving through each other on the sidewalks, the distant, almost hypnotic rhythm of a street performer's drum echoing off the sheer glass and steel of the surrounding buildings. The sounds were familiar, a constant backdrop to my life in the city, but tonight they seemed amplified, a little sharper, a little more insistent.

I adjusted the strap of my worn leather messenger bag on my shoulder, its weight a comforting presence, and allowed myself to be carried along by the seemingly chaotic but ultimately ordered flow of people. My footsteps, almost unconsciously, began to sync with the unspoken rhythm of the city—a steady pulse that resonated through the concrete and steel, a beat that thrummed in the chests of millions. Each footfall was a tiny note in the grand urban composition.

The crisp air was a welcome and refreshing change after spending hours trapped under the stale, recycled atmosphere of the office. Fluorescent lights and the hum of computers had been replaced by the fading warmth of the sun and the murmur of the city. For a moment, I allowed myself to simply enjoy it—the cool breeze that kissed my face, carrying with it the faint, tantalizing scent of roasted nuts from a nearby vendor's cart, the way the fading sunlight caught on the myriad windows of the towering buildings around me, transforming them into shimmering beacons against the darkening sky. It was a momentary escape, a chance to breathe and simply be.

I hadn't decided where I was going yet, and truthfully, that indecision was part of the appeal. Walking without a fixed destination, allowing the city to guide my steps, felt like the closest thing to genuine freedom I could find within the confines of my daily routine. It was a rebellion in miniature, a small act of defiance against the rigid structure of my life. Each unscripted turn was a victory.

Eventually, my aimless wanderings led me to Bryant Park. The open space, a vibrant oasis amidst the concrete jungle, was dotted with small clusters of people—friends animatedly chatting on the sprawling lawn, their laughter punctuating the air; couples strolling hand in hand, lost in their own private worlds; a lone man sitting under the soft glow of a lamppost, his nose buried deep within the pages of a well-worn book.

The collective hum of life here was noticeably different from the frenetic chaos of the surrounding streets, quieter and more subdued, but no less vibrant or full of energy. It was a pocket of tranquility, a space for reflection and connection within the bustling city.

I scanned the park for an empty spot, my eyes finally settling on a vacant bench near the edge of the park, close enough to observe the activity but far enough to maintain a sense of solitude. I sat down, gently placing my bag at my feet on the cool paving stones. The accumulated tension in my shoulders, a physical manifestation of the day's stresses, began to ease incrementally as I leaned back against the worn wooden slats of the bench.

I closed my eyes for a moment, taking a deep breath and letting it out slowly, willing the residual anxieties to dissipate with each exhale. Then, I opened my eyes again, allowing my gaze to drift slowly over the serene scene unfolding in front of me.

The day had been ordinary, unremarkable, really—a predictable sequence of meetings, emails, and deadlines. But something about the hushed quiet of the park, juxtaposed against the relentless energy of the city, made it feel like a much-needed reprieve, a moment of sanctuary carved out from the everyday. The trees formed a natural barrier, muffling the sounds of traffic.

For a while, I just sat there in contemplative silence, allowing the insistent noise of the city to gradually recede into the background, fading into a low, almost imperceptible hum. My thoughts, initially tangled and chaotic, began to wander aimlessly, drifting from the lingering frustrations of work to tentative plans for the weekend ahead, and then to nothing in particular.

It was a form of mental decluttering, a way to clear the mental space and allow myself to simply exist in the present moment.

And then I felt it—that faint, almost imperceptible, prickling sensation at the back of my neck. It was a familiar feeling, one I hadn't experienced in a long time, but one that I recognized instantly. It was the distinct sensation of being watched.

I straightened up slightly on the bench, my eyes involuntarily scanning the surrounding crowd without really knowing what I was looking for or even expecting to find anything at all. The park looked exactly the same as it had a moment ago—just ordinary people going about their ordinary lives, engaged in ordinary activities. It was the kind of scene I'd witnessed countless times before, a typical tableau of urban life. There were no obvious threats, no suspicious characters lurking in the shadows, nothing to justify the unsettling feeling that had suddenly washed over me.

But despite the apparent normalcy of the scene, the feeling of being watched didn't go away. If anything, it intensified, growing stronger with each passing second. It was a subtle but persistent sensation, like a tiny alarm bell ringing in the back of my mind.

Shaking my head slightly, I tried to brush it off, dismissing it as nothing more than a figment of my imagination—the exaggerated product of a long and stressful day finally catching up with me. Maybe I was just tired, or maybe it was just a random, inexplicable feeling with no real basis in reality. I told myself that I needed a break, that I was being paranoid.

The wind picked up suddenly, rustling the leaves in the branches of the trees above me with a soft, whispering sound. The sky was undergoing a transformation now, the vibrant deep orange of the sunset slowly but surely giving way to the soft, muted gray of twilight. The change in light altered the atmosphere of the park, casting long, elongated shadows across the lawn and imbuing the scene with a sense of quiet mystery.

I stood up from the bench, slinging my bag back over my shoulder. The strap felt heavier now, the weight of the bag amplified by the growing sense of unease that had settled over me. It was time to head home, to retreat back to the safety and familiarity of my apartment. The feeling of freedom I had experienced earlier in the evening had vanished, replaced by a growing sense of apprehension.

As I turned to leave, I couldn't shake the feeling that I was being watched. I glanced back one last time, my eyes sweeping across the park, but I saw nothing out of the ordinary—just people, trees, and the fading light of day. But the prickling sensation at the back of my neck remained, a silent warning that I couldn't ignore. I quickened my pace, eager to escape the park and its unsettling atmosphere.

The streets were alive with their usual evening energy as I made my way back toward the subway. A symphony of urban sounds swelled around me—car horns blared in a discordant harmony, the rhythmic rumble of distant buses echoed through the canyons of buildings, and the chatter of a thousand conversations mingled into an almost indistinguishable murmur.

The air had grown cooler, the faint bite of autumn brushing against my face like a playful spirit. It was a welcome change from the humid stuffiness of the afternoon, a promise of crisper days to come. Pedestrians moved with purpose now, their steps quick and efficient, heads down, shoulders hunched against the deepening chill, eager to get to their destinations before the night fully settled in and chased away the last vestiges of daylight.

I blended into the crowd, becoming just another face in the sea of humanity that flowed along the sidewalks. I let the rhythm of the city carry me, a current of motion that required no conscious effort. My thoughts drifted, a restless flock of birds flitting between the mundane and the nagging. I mentally reviewed the spreadsheets I hadn't quite finished at work, the seemingly endless columns of numbers blurring together in my mind.

Then my thoughts jumped to the weekend plans I hadn't made, the empty expanse of Saturday and Sunday looming before me like a blank canvas. And underlying it all, like a low, persistent hum, was the faint unease I couldn't seem to shake—the residue of the strange encounter from the night before. It was a prickling feeling at the back of my neck, a whisper in the silence between thoughts.

The buzz of conversation, the hum of engines, the occasional bark of a street vendor calling out his wares—pretzels, hot dogs, roasted nuts—each distinct call a small piece of the city's vibrant tapestry; all of it blended together into the kind of background noise I barely noticed anymore. It was the soundtrack of my life, a constant, familiar drone that both soothed and numbed. Years of living in the city had trained me to filter it out, to focus on the immediate and necessary.

And then I saw him.

Across the street, standing just beyond the glow of a flickering street-lamp, was Marcus. The light cast long, dancing shadows around him, distorting his features in a way that made him seem both familiar and otherworldly. The streetlamp itself seemed to struggle against the encroaching darkness, its bulb wavering and sputtering as if reluctant to illuminate him.

My breath caught in my throat, a sudden, painful constriction that stole the air from my lungs. I froze mid-step, my body rigid and unresponsive. It was as if someone had pressed pause on the remote control of my life. He was perfectly still, an island of calm in the bustling sea of pedestrians. His dark eyes, even from that distance, seemed to pierce through the noise and confusion, fixed on me in a way that made it feel like the chaos of the city had evaporated, leaving only the two of us suspended in a bubble of silent awareness. The honking cars faded, the chattering voices softened, and the city itself seemed to hold its breath.

My rational mind screamed at me, trying to assert control. It couldn't be him. What were the odds, the astronomically small probabilities, of running into the same stranger twice in a city of millions? It was absurd, illogical, statistically impossible. And yet, there he was—his sharp features unmistakable, the distinctive curve of his jaw, the way his dark hair fell across his forehead. His presence was as magnetic as it had been the night before, drawing me in despite my better judgment. It was an undeniable pull, a force that seemed to bypass my conscious thought and speak directly to something deeper within me.

For a moment, neither of us moved. We were locked in a silent tableau, two figures caught in the amber of a shared moment. The world around us continued its relentless motion, but we remained frozen, suspended in time. His gaze held mine, an unspoken question hanging in the air between us. I felt a strange mixture of fear and fascination, a dangerous curiosity that urged me to step forward, to break the spell.

And then a bus rumbled into view, its hulking frame a monstrous interruption. It was one of those articulated buses, the kind that snaked through the city streets like a metallic serpent, its windows filled with the blurred faces of weary commuters. The bus roared into the intersection, its bright headlights momentarily blinding, blocking him from sight.

I stood there, rooted to the spot, my muscles tense and unyielding as the bus roared past, its engine drowning out the noise of the city around me. The sheer size of the vehicle felt oppressive, a symbol of the city's impersonal force, its ability to swallow individuals whole. The air vibrated with the bus's passage, the force of its displacement buffeting me like a physical blow. I squeezed my eyes shut for a moment, willing the bus to disappear, to reveal him still standing there.

When it finally cleared, he was gone.

I stared at the empty space where he had been, my heart pounding in my chest like a trapped bird. The streetlamp flickered erratically, casting dancing shadows that seemed to mock my confusion. People continued to stream past me, their faces indifferent, their eyes focused on their own destinations, oblivious to the drama that had just unfolded. They navigated the crowded sidewalks with practiced ease, their movements fluid and efficient. The spot beneath the streetlamp was empty now, devoid of any trace of his presence, as if he'd never been there at all. The city had swallowed him whole, erasing him as quickly as he had appeared.

It had to be a coincidence—a trick of the light, a misinterpretation of shadows, or simply someone who just looked like him. The city was full of faces, a constantly shifting mosaic of features. But the rational explanation didn't settle the unease creeping through me. It felt like a flimsy excuse, a desperate attempt to cling to logic in the face of something inexplicable. The memory of his gaze, the intensity of his presence, lingered in my mind, defying any easy dismissal.

I took a deep breath, forcing my feet to move again. The city didn't stop for anyone, and neither could I. I had to keep moving, to keep functioning, to pretend that everything was normal. But the normalcy felt like a fragile mask, threatening to slip at any moment.

As I walked, my pulse remained unsteady, a frantic drumbeat against my ribs. My mind replayed the moment over and over again, dissecting every detail, searching for some clue, some explanation. The way he had looked at me—calm, deliberate, almost expectant—like he'd been waiting for me to see him, like our meeting was preordained. It was that sense of purpose in his gaze that unsettled me the most.

When I reached the subway station, the entrance yawning before me like a maw into the earth, I hesitated for a moment before descending into its depths. The stairs seemed steeper than usual, the journey downward suddenly fraught with uncertainty. The lights overhead buzzed faintly, their cold glow flickering in time with the distant rumble of approaching trains, a mechanical heartbeat echoing from the depths. The air that drifted up from the tunnel was stale and heavy, carrying the scent of dust and metal, a stark contrast to the crisp autumn air above.

When I stepped onto the platform, I was surrounded by the jostling bodies of my fellow commuters, the encounter with Marcus felt like a strange, fleeting dream. The harsh reality of the subway, the grimy walls, the screeching trains, seemed to push the memory further into the realm of the unreal. But the unease remained, a persistent shadow clinging to the edges of my consciousness.

The subway ride home had been a blur. The rhythmic clatter of the train and the faint hum of fluorescent lights had done little to settle the unease gnawing at me. I'd tried to push it all aside—Marcus's fleeting presence, the strange weight of his gaze—but it clung to me, lingering at the edges of my thoughts like a shadow I couldn't escape.

By the time I got home, the routine of dinner and a show I barely paid attention to did little to ground me. Sleep came in fits, fragmented and restless.

CHAPTER FOUR

SHADOWS IN THE DAYLIGHT

Morning arrived with unwelcome haste, its intrusion particularly jarring. Sleep had offered no respite, only a tumultuous arena where unnamed anxieties clashed and lingered. It always seemed this way, as if the universe conspired to rob me of true rest.

The feeble barrier of cheap plastic blinds was no match for the sun's determined rays. They pierced through the gaps, painting harsh lines across the room, feeling like a violation, a forceful expulsion from the murky depths of unconsciousness. My dreams had been a vibrant, chaotic spectacle—a fleeting exhibition of colors and emotions, ultimately unresolved and frustratingly elusive.

I was left with only fragmented images that slipped through my mental grasp like grains of sand in a torrential river. Yet, amidst the swirling chaos, Marcus's face surfaced and strangely remained. It wasn't a clear, detailed picture, but rather a persistent emotion, a subtle shadow lingering at the periphery of my awareness. His presence was both ephemeral and indelible, a glitch in the otherwise well-oiled machine of my mind.

A sigh, barely audible, escaped my lips—a silent acknowledgment of the daunting day ahead. With deliberate effort, I banished the unwelcome thought, attempting to disperse the lingering unease that clung to me like a stubborn mist. I forced myself to rise from the depths of the bed, my feet touching the cold floor. The old, worn floorboards emitted a mournful creak beneath my weight as I traversed the small room, dragging myself through my established morning ritual like a weary soldier trudging through thick mud.

Brushing my teeth, the sharp, invigorating taste of minty paste offered a momentary reprieve from the persistent taste of anxiety coating my tongue. Combing my hair, I attempted to smooth not only the physical tangles but the mental knots that had formed during the night. Brewing coffee, the rich, comforting aroma provided a temporary sanctuary.

It was all autopilot now, a sequence of small, almost insignificant victories—mundane rituals I clung to as I desperately tried to shake off the oppressive fog clouding my thoughts. These familiar anchors prevented me from being swept away by the sea of anxious thoughts.

The apartment was unusually quiet, the silence only broken by the monotonous hum of the refrigerator and the muffled murmur of the news playing softly in the background as I dutifully packed my lunch. Peanut butter and jelly, a simple, nostalgic comfort from childhood, was today's choice. The news droned on with the usual predictable narrative: political squabbles that seemed to lead nowhere, weather patterns that defied all prediction, and the obligatory feel-good story about a rescued kitten or a local hero—inevitably sandwiched between reports of minor chaos and petty crime.

My attention drifted, lost in the mindless routine of spreading peanut butter, when a few carefully chosen words, delivered with practiced gravity and intended to grab attention, snagged my wandering mind and held it captive.

"Police are still investigating a series of incidents downtown. Details remain scarce, but witnesses have described... unusual circumstances. While authorities have not confirmed any connection between the cases, citing the ongoing nature of the investigation, residents are advised to remain vigilant and report any suspicious activity..."

The rest of the segment faded into indistinguishable background noise, nothing more than a dull drone, as my mind became fixated on those phrases, replaying them like a broken record. It wasn't unusual to hear about such occurrences in the city—incidents, disappearances, petty crimes escalating into something far more ominous.

The kind of stories that rarely impacted my day, unless, of course, I found myself in the wrong place at the wrong time, a statistic waiting to materialize. This was simply an unwelcome reality of city life, in all its gritty and relentless glory.

Still, the unease stirred within me once more, a cold knot tightening in the pit of my stomach. It was faint, almost imperceptible, but undeniably persistent, like a low hum in the distance you couldn't quite pinpoint. Was it merely residual anxiety from the unsettling dream, a lingering echo of the night's turmoil? Or was it something more tangible, something more substantial? The feeling was oddly familiar, reminiscent of the sensation of being watched, of knowing that unseen eyes were upon you even though you couldn't discern their source.

I glanced at the digital clock on the microwave. The red numbers blinked back at me, mocking my tardiness. Time was slipping away faster than I realized, each passing second a precious grain of sand filtering relentlessly through the narrow neck of an hourglass. Grabbing my worn canvas bag, the strap digging uncomfortably into my shoulder, I silenced the news abruptly, cutting off the anchor mid-sentence, and headed out the door into the unknown of the day.

The stale, recycled air of the hallway assaulted my senses first, followed immediately by the biting, unforgiving cold of the early morning. It was a brutal slap to the face, an awakening far more effective than lukewarm coffee could ever hope to achieve. I shivered involuntarily, my body reacting to the sudden temperature change. The sky was a bruised, ominous purple, an ill omen promising a day of unrelenting gray skies and fierce, biting wind. It looked like the world was joining me in my dread of the day.

The walk to the subway station was, for the most part, uneventful. The usual cast of characters populated the pre-dawn streets: hurried commuters with their faces buried in the glowing screens of their phones, their minds already lost in the digital world; dog walkers bundled in layers of scarves, hats, and gloves, braving the cold for their furry companions; and the homeless man who always occupied the same corner, his hand perpetually outstretched, his eyes vacant and devoid of hope.

I, like most others, avoided eye contact, a practiced maneuver honed over years of navigating the complex social landscape of the city. To acknowledge them was to acknowledge the despair and poverty the city tried to hide.

Deep in the subway station, the air hung thick and heavy with the unmistakable stench of stale urine, a pungent aroma that permeated everything it touched. The echoing rumble of distant trains reverberated through the dark tunnels, a constant reminder of the mechanical beast lurking beneath the city's surface.

A smattering of other early-morning travelers waited on the platform, their faces etched with the same weariness and quiet resignation that I felt mirrored on my own. The train finally arrived with a screech of metal against metal, a jarring sound that momentarily pierced the silence. We all shuffled inside, like cattle being herded into a pen, finding our places among the already crowded carriages. Each of us, stuck in our own heads.

As the train rattled and lurched its way through the labyrinthine tunnels, I found myself staring blankly out the window, watching the blurred lights of the tunnels streak past in a dizzying array of colors. My mind, despite my best efforts, drifted back to the unsettling news report, the phrase "unusual circumstances" echoing in my thoughts. What did that even mean, in practical terms? And more importantly, why did it evoke such a profound sense of unease within me, planting seeds of anxiety that threatened to take root and flourish?

I tried to shake it off, to dismiss it as nothing more than a fleeting distraction. I sternly reminded myself that I had far more pressing matters to concern myself with: work, the ever-present stack of bills threatening to bury me, and the endless, monotonous cycle of daily life stretching out before me like an unyielding desert.

But the feeling persisted, a nagging doubt lingering at the periphery of my thoughts, refusing to be ignored. It was as if a tiny, persistent voice was whispering warnings in my ear, a voice I couldn't quite decipher but couldn't quite dismiss.

When I finally arrived at my designated stop, I pushed my way through the throng of commuters, a sea of faces all focused on one thing: their destination, and stepped out onto the platform. The morning air was even colder here, the wind whipping around me with a vengeance, stinging my face and making my eyes water as I walked toward the towering office building, a monolith of glass and steel that housed my place of employment.

The office was already humming with activity by the time I arrived. The usual gray monotony greeted me—rows of identical desks, the faint hum of computers, and the lingering smell of stale coffee. It was a landscape I knew intimately, each chipped corner of a desk, each stain on the worn carpet, a familiar and comforting, if uninspiring, presence. But today, something felt different in the air. It clung to the edges of the fluorescent lighting, a subtle distortion in the familiar drone of the workplace.

It wasn't just the noise of keyboards clacking and the muted drone of conversations; it was sharper, more urgent. The collective murmur of the office was punctuated by staccato bursts of hushed voices, quick, nervous laughter, and the unmistakable undercurrent of anxiety. People huddled in small groups, their heads bent close, speaking in low voices, their expressions tense and guarded.

Eyes darted nervously toward the entrances, as if expecting some unseen authority to descend and quell the unrest. The usual morning camaraderie was absent, replaced by a pervasive sense of unease that settled in the pit of my stomach like a stone.

Sliding into my chair, I powered on my computer, the screen flickering to life with its usual grid of emails and spreadsheets. The familiar icons and folders swam into focus, offering a momentary distraction from the unsettling atmosphere. I logged in, and the system's cheerful chime felt jarringly out of place.

I'd barely settled in, my fingers hovering over the keyboard, when Emily leaned over the divider from her cubicle, her eyes wide and frantic. Her normally bright and cheerful face was pale, and her usual bouncy ponytail seemed to have lost its spring.

"Tristan," she whispered, her voice barely above the hum of the office. She glanced around furtively, as if afraid of being overheard. "Did you hear what happened yesterday?"

I looked up, frowning slightly. The question hung in the air, laden with unspoken implications. "Not really. Something about a client losing it?" I vaguely recalled snippets of conversation earlier but had dismissed them as office gossip.

Emily nodded quickly, glancing around again to ensure no one was listening. She pressed a finger to her lips, urging me to keep my voice down. "Yeah, it was bad. It was Kirkwood—one of the Gordon & Blake guys. He completely freaked out during a demo."

I set my coffee down, the ceramic mug clinking softly against the desk, giving her my full attention. The name Gordon & Blake was enough to pique my interest. They were one of our biggest clients, and any issues with them were serious business. "What happened?"

Emily leaned closer, her voice dropping even lower, barely audible above the whirring of the computer fans. "Apparently, he saw the predictions from the model we built, and they were way off. Like, catastrophic-level wrong. He started yelling about how it was going to ruin their entire business. He demanded to see everything—the raw data, the algorithms, all of it."

"That doesn't make sense," I said, shaking my head in disbelief. The models we delivered were solid. They had been rigorously tested and peer-reviewed. We prided ourselves on our accuracy and reliability. "We double-checked everything before the handover."

"I know," Emily said, her eyes pleading. "But he wasn't hearing it. He stormed out of the conference room and went straight to the developers' area. That's when things got... physical." She winced, as if reliving the scene.

My stomach tightened, a knot of apprehension forming in my gut. The air in the office seemed to grow colder, shadows lengthening around us. "What do you mean, 'physical'?" I asked, my voice barely a whisper.

"Sarah said he attacked Laura," Emily said, her voice trembling slightly. Her gaze flickered toward the developers' area, a cluster of desks situated near the back of the office. "He threw her laptop across the room and shoved her into a desk. She hit her head—there was blood everywhere. Security showed up, but Kirkwood was gone by the time they got there."

The words hung heavy in the air between us, thick and suffocating. The hum of the office faded into the background, replaced by a ringing silence in my ears. Assaulting a coworker was beyond the pale. It was incomprehensible.

"Why would he snap like that?" I asked, my voice quieter now, barely audible. "Even if the model was wrong – and I still don't believe it was – that kind of reaction..." I trailed off, unable to articulate the sheer irrationality of it all.

Emily shrugged helplessly, her shoulders slumping. "I don't know. But Sarah thinks there might've been tampering. Someone messing with the data or algorithms to sabotage the predictions."

"Tampering?" I repeated, my frown deepening. The thought was disturbing. It suggested a deliberate act of malice, a betrayal from within.

She nodded. "It's just a rumor, but it makes sense. Kirkwood must've seen something that made him think we were trying to tank his company." She paused, chewing on her lip nervously. "It's crazy, I know. But what else could explain it?"

Before I could respond, before I could even fully process the implications of her words, Sarah appeared at the edge of my cubicle, her face pale and drawn. The color had drained from her cheeks, leaving her looking gaunt and haunted.

"Tristan," she said, her tone clipped and urgent. Her eyes darted between Emily and me, conveying a silent message that this conversation was not to be overheard. "Can I talk to you for a second?"

I nodded, pushing back my chair and standing up. The motion felt strangely mechanical, as if I were moving through treacle. I followed her to the conference room, the tension in my chest tightening with every step. The fluorescent lights flickered ominously overhead, casting long, distorted shadows on the walls.

A sense of foreboding washed over me, a premonition that whatever Sarah had to say would only deepen the mystery and unravel the fragile sense of order that remained. The air crackled with unspoken anxieties, and I felt like I was walking into an ambush. The familiar path to the conference room now felt like a gauntlet, each step heavy with the weight of uncertainty.

As I followed Sarah, I couldn't shake the feeling that there was more to this incident than met the eye. Kirkwood's violent outburst, the rumors of tampering, and the palpable tension in the office all pointed to a deeper conspiracy, a shadow lurking beneath the surface of our daily routines.

Sarah closed the door behind us, her movements sharp and deliberate, each click of the latch echoing in the tense silence of the room. She didn't sit, instead standing near the end of the long conference table, her arms crossed tightly over her chest. The fluorescent lights overhead, cold and unforgiving, cast harsh shadows on her face, etching the lines of worry and frustration deeper into her features. It was a mask of controlled anxiety, barely concealing the storm brewing beneath.

"This thing with Kirkwood," she began, her tone brisk and devoid of its usual warmth, "is worse than I thought." Each word was precise, measured, as if she were trying to contain the enormity of the situation within the confines of the sterile room.

I sank into one of the uncomfortable chairs, its faux leather groaning slightly under my weight, a small sound in the weighty atmosphere. I tried to match her seriousness, to mirror the urgency that radiated from her like heat from a forge. "Emily told me some of it. What's going on, Sarah? Lay it all out."

Sarah exhaled, the sound heavy with frustration, like a gust of wind sighing through a narrow passage. It was the sound of someone carrying an immense burden, a burden that threatened to crush her. "Kirkwood's meltdown yesterday wasn't just about the model predictions being wrong. That was just the surface. He's claiming that we—or someone on our team—deliberately sabotaged him."

"What?" I said, leaning forward, the chair protesting again with a sharper squeak. The accusation hung in the air, thick and suffocating. "That doesn't make any sense. Why would we do that? We've poured months into this project."

"It doesn't have to make sense to him," Sarah replied, her voice laced with weary exasperation. "He's not thinking rationally, Tristan. He's looking for someone to blame, a convenient target for his own failings, and right now, that's us. He's throwing around words like 'fraud' and 'litigation.' He's threatening to drag us all through the mud."

I frowned, the implications of her words sinking in like stones tossed into a still pond. "Does he have any proof, Sarah? Or is he just making noise, trying to intimidate us?"

Sarah shook her head, the gesture sharp and decisive. "He doesn't have proof. Not yet, anyway. But he's threatening to bring in a third-party auditor to comb through everything—the raw data, the algorithms, even our internal communications. He wants to dissect every line of code, every email, every whispered conversation."

That was a problem. A significant, potentially devastating problem. Not because we had anything to hide—our work had been meticulous, our integrity unwavering—but because an audit would stall the Gordon & Blake project indefinitely. It could cripple us, damage our reputation beyond repair, even if the findings ultimately cleared us of any wrongdoing. The mere suggestion of impropriety could poison the well, leaving a lingering stench of suspicion.

"Why would he go nuclear like this?" I asked, my voice tinged with disbelief. "It seems like a massive overreaction, even for Kirkwood."

Sarah hesitated, her eyes narrowing slightly, as if weighing her words carefully. "That's what I've been trying to figure out. From what I've heard, Kirkwood's been under a lot of pressure lately. A failed acquisition, a disastrous quarterly report—things aren't going well for him, Tristan. The cracks are starting to show."

"So he's using us as a scapegoat," I said, my voice flat, devoid of emotion. The idea was repugnant, but it fit the facts. "Deflecting the blame to protect himself."

"It looks that way," Sarah replied, her gaze unwavering. "But there's something else. Something deeper, more insidious. One of our engineers, Sam, thinks Kirkwood was trying to game the model—feeding it specific inputs, cherry-picking data to get the predictions he wanted. When the final demo didn't align with his carefully crafted narrative, he lost it. Sam says he's never seen Kirkwood so unhinged."

The pieces began to click together in my mind, forming a disturbing picture. Kirkwood, the master manipulator, had been seeking an edge, trying to bend the system to serve his own agenda and bolster his own position. But when it backfired and the truth was revealed, he needed someone to blame—someone to take the fall for his own hubris.

"That's why he's pushing this fraud angle," I said slowly, the realization dawning on me. "He's trying to cover his tracks, burying his mistakes under a mountain of accusations."

Sarah nodded grimly. "That's my guess. But whatever his reasons, whatever twisted logic is driving him, we need to get ahead of this, Tristan. We must be proactive, not reactive. I need you to go through the project files—every single one. Triple-check everything: data sets, test cases, every piece of code. If there's even a single inconsistency, a minor anomaly, I want to know about it. No stone can be left unturned."

I nodded, mentally preparing for the long hours and painstaking work ahead. It would be like searching for a grain of sand on a vast beach, but the stakes were too high to take any shortcuts.

"And Tristan," Sarah added, her voice softening slightly, a flicker of genuine concern in her eyes. "Be careful. Kirkwood's erratic right now—unpredictable. If he really believes we're trying to sabotage him, if he feels cornered and desperate, there's no telling what he might do next. He could lash out in any direction."

The weight of her words settled heavily on my shoulders, a tangible burden. It wasn't just about protecting the project or the company's reputation; it was about protecting ourselves from a man clearly capable of anything. The shadows in the daylight had suddenly become much darker and more menacing. The air in the room felt colder. I thought to myself, "Time to get to work."

I sat back in my chair, organizing the files and beginning the review as quickly as I could. I grabbed a red pen and started to highlight anything that seemed out of place. I knew I would have to do it all again, and again, and again. I asked Sarah for an extra monitor, and she got one for me ASAP. I was focused and determined to find something—and hopefully it wasn't us!

Back at my desk, I stared at the blinking cursor on my computer screen, the Gordon & Blake project files open and waiting for me to dive in. The task felt monumental, even though it shouldn't have. Data was data—neutral, unchanging, just numbers waiting to be interpreted. But today, it felt different.

A weight pressed down on me, a feeling of unease unrelated to debugging or algorithms. It was the human element: Kirkwood's unsettling actions, Sarah's suspicions, and the nagging sense that something far more significant lurked beneath the surface of this failed demo.

I started with the raw inputs, cross-checking them against the original data sets we'd received from Gordon & Blake. Every number matched, every variable was accounted for. I double-checked, then triple-checked, my eyes scanning the columns for even the tiniest discrepancy. Negative. It was all there. All... perfect. That was exactly the problem. How could something so flawlessly constructed lead to such a catastrophic failure? Doubts began to creep into my mind, whispering possibilities of unseen forces and hidden agendas beyond corporate finagling.

Next came the algorithms—a complex web of equations, loops, and subroutines designed to predict market trends. I took a deep breath and plunged in.

As I scanned through the lines of code, a familiar rhythm returned—the methodical process of troubleshooting, the satisfying click of logic falling into place. It was like slipping into an old, comfortable pair of gloves. The world outside—Kirkwood's outburst, the accusations—faded away as I immersed myself in the intricacies of the code. Yet, the farther I delved, the more an unsettling feeling crept in. It was subtle, like a draft on the back of my neck, but relentless, growing stronger with each passing line.

Nothing was wrong. That was the terrifying part.

No errors, no tampering, no anomalies. The predictive model was exactly as it should have been: elegant, efficient, and inexplicably, devastatingly wrong. Every function performed as intended, every calculation was accurate, but the final result was a complete mess. I felt like an explorer charting a perfect map of a land that didn't exist. The more I confirmed the model's integrity, the deeper the puzzle became. A shiver ran down my spine; it was as if a ghost haunted the machine, its presence felt but never seen.

So why had it failed so catastrophically during the demo? The question echoed in my mind, a persistent drumbeat drowning out the hum of the office. The demo was a make-or-break moment for the company. What was at stake that could drive someone to that kind of behavior?

"Find anything?" Emily's voice startled me, pulling me out of my focus. The sudden intrusion was jarring, like waking from a deep sleep. I blinked, trying to reorient myself to the real world.

I looked up to see her standing at the edge of my cubicle, a coffee mug in hand. The aroma of dark roast wafted toward me, a small comfort amid the frustrating task. Her face was etched with worry, the lines around her eyes more pronounced than usual.

"No," I said, leaning back in my chair, the springs groaning in protest. "Everything looks clean so far." The words tasted like ash in my mouth. Clean. Too clean. I had a sinking feeling we were all missing something—something crucial.

She nodded, though her expression was far from relaxed. "I didn't think we'd find anything, but... I don't know. Something about this whole situation feels off." She glanced around the office, as if expecting someone to be listening.

"Tell me about it," I muttered, glancing back at the screen. The lines of code seemed to mock me, their flawless execution a testament to the mystery. "Kirkwood's accusing us of sabotage, but from where I'm sitting, it looks like he's the one who's been playing games." I resisted the urge to slam my fist on the desk.

Emily tilted her head, her brow furrowing slightly. "What do you mean?" Her eyes were sharp and intelligent, always able to cut through the noise and get to the heart of the matter.

I hesitated, my fingers hovering over the keyboard. I debated whether or not to share Sarah's theory. It was still just speculation, after all. But Emily deserved to know what we were thinking. "Sarah thinks Kirkwood was trying to finesse the model—feeding it specific inputs to make the predictions work in his favor. But when it didn't go the way he planned, he panicked."

"Typical corporate drama," Emily said with a faint smirk, though her eyes remained serious. "A tale as old as time: inflated egos, backstabbing, and desperate attempts to climb the corporate ladder." She took a sip of her coffee, her gaze distant.

"Maybe," I said, my voice trailing off. "But it still doesn't explain why he snapped. I mean, even if the demo went sideways, there's no reason to..." The image of Kirkwood's face, contorted with rage, flashed through my min d.

"Throw a laptop? Attack someone?" Jessica finished for me, appearing seemingly out of nowhere. She leaned against the adjacent cubicle, her expression a mask of weary resignation.

"Exactly," I replied, shifting my gaze between the two.

She let out a sigh, leaning against the cubicle wall. "Well, let me know if you need help combing through the files. Sarah asked me to pull some test cases from the sandbox environment, so I'll be buried in those for the next few hours." She pushed herself off the cubicle wall. "I'm diving in; wish me luck."

"Thanks," I said, my attention already drifting back to the screen. The weight of the task settled back on my shoulders, heavier than before. The pressure to find something—anything—was immense.

As Emily and Jess walked away, I scrolled to the next section of the project files, searching for anything—no matter how small—that might explain the mess Kirkwood had created. I felt like I was sifting through sand, looking for a single grain of gold. Hours passed. The light outside shifted, painting the office in hues of late afternoon.

And then I saw it. A subtle tick in the matrix, a tiny imperfection that broke the illusion of perfection.

It wasn't an error, exactly. More like... an outlier. A single data point buried deep in the test results, flagged but unexamined. It had been dismissed as insignificant—a rounding error, a minor deviation.

I clicked on it, the file opening in a new window. It was just a string of numbers and variables, meaningless without context. A jumble of digits and symbols that looked like random noise. But something about it felt... wrong. Like it didn't belong there. Like a foreign object lodged in a well-oiled machine.

I jotted down the details and closed the file, my mind racing. The office had grown unnaturally quiet, the distant sounds muffled by the hum of the computers. Only my heart beat loudly in my ears.

It was probably nothing—a hiccup, an oversight, the kind of thing that happened in complex systems like this all the time. A random fluctuation, a statistical anomaly—nothing to worry about.

But I couldn't shake the feeling that I'd just stumbled onto something bigger than a bad prediction model. The nagging feeling at the back of my mind refused to be silenced. I continued staring at the screen.

I couldn't stop fixating on the flagged data point. It was like a splinter in my mind, a persistent itch I couldn't scratch.

On the surface, it appeared to be a simple anomaly—an outlier in a sea of perfectly normal variables. A blip on the radar, easily dismissed. But the longer I studied it, the more it nagged at me. This wasn't the kind of mistake you'd expect to find in a predictive model this polished. It felt deliberate, hidden in plain sight.

I traced its origin through the logs, pulling up the test cases to see where the anomaly had first appeared. It was like following a breadcrumb trail through a forest, each crumb leading me deeper into the unknown. Each line of data told a story, a series of inputs and outputs meant to simulate real-world scenarios. The patterns should have been predictable, consistent, reliable.

But they weren't. A ripple effect, a subtle distortion that changed everything it touched.

The flagged point rippled through the system, subtle but undeniable. It skewed the predictions just enough to destabilize the entire model. It was like finding a needle hidden in a haystack—but the needle had been placed there intentionally. The realization hit me like a cold wave, a sudden understanding of the true nature of the problem.

What are you hiding, Kirkwood? What were you trying to accomplish? The questions swirled in my head, each one more disturbing than the last.

I leaned back in my chair, the glow of the monitor casting faint shadows on the desk. My eyes burned, and my muscles ached from hours of concentration. The office around me had grown quieter, the end-of-day lull setting in. The faint hum of the HVAC filled the space, punctuated only by the occasional clatter of a keyboard. I felt as if I were alone in the world.

The office felt colder now, the shadows deeper, the silence more profound. The outlier in the model gnawed at me, its implications growing with each passing moment. It wasn't just a data point; it was a key. I looked at the screen, and the numbers blurred slightly as I understood what I needed to do.

The demo hadn't just failed; it had been sabotaged, and I wanted answers.

The anomaly wouldn't leave my mind. It felt too precise to be an accident, too targeted to be random. Someone had tampered with the data—of that I was certain. But why? What could drive someone to such lengths to distort the results? Did they stand to gain something from the chaos that would ensue? My thoughts spun in an endless loop, fragments of possibilities swirling around my consciousness like fallen leaves caught in a restless wind.

"Still here?" Her voice pulled me from my reverie. I looked up to see Sarah standing at the edge of my cubicle, her arms crossed tightly over her chest. She wore that expression again, the one that always indicated both concern and determination.

"Yeah," I said, motioning toward the screen. "You might want to see this."

Her curiosity piqued, she stepped closer, pulling a chair over to sit beside me. "What have you found?"

I gestured at the monitor, my heart racing in sync with my thoughts. "There's a flagged data point buried in the test results. At first, I thought it was just an outlier, but it's not random. Look—here's where it originated." I clicked through the logs, highlighting the corresponding entries with a trembling hand.

Sarah leaned in, her brow furrowing as she studied the screen. "This is... deliberate," she said slowly, the realization dawning on her. "It's small, but it's enough to throw off the predictions in just the right way. If someone fed this into the model, it could easily destabilize the whole system."

"Exactly," I said, a tingle of urgency sparking within me. "It's almost too precise, like whoever planted it knew exactly what they were doing. It's as if they orchestrated a symphony of errors just for a moment like this."

Sarah sat back, crossing her arms protectively. "Are you saying someone tampered with the model?"

"I'm saying it's possible," I replied, the weight of the implications settling heavily on my shoulders. "The flagged point isn't random. It was placed here for a reason."

Her jaw tightened, and I could almost hear the gears turning in her mind. "That explains why Kirkwood lost it during the demo. If he was feeding the model specific inputs and this anomaly disrupted his results, he'd think we sabotaged him."

I nodded, our eyes locked in an unspoken agreement, each of us recognizing the stakes involved. "But why would someone plant something like this? And who?"

"Good questions," Sarah said, her voice quiet but laced with tension. She glanced around the office—an instinctual check for eavesdroppers, perhaps—and then leaned closer, her voice dropping to a whisper. "This could get messy, Tristan. If Kirkwood finds out about this before we do, he'll use it as ammo to blow up our entire team. He won't hesitate to pin the blame on us."

"I know," I said, resolve hardening in my chest. "I'll dig deeper and see if I can trace it back to whoever planted it."

Sarah hesitated, her eyes narrowing slightly, and I could sense a warning hanging in the air. "Be careful with this. If someone's gone to the trouble of tampering with the data, they won't want us uncovering it. They're likely more dangerous than we anticipate."

She stood, giving me a final nod before walking away. The sound of her footsteps faded into a soft echo, leaving me alone once more with the glowing screen. I turned back, the flagged point shining faintly in its highlighted box—a tiny spark in the darkness, illuminating questions I wasn't sure I wanted answers to.

The office was nearly empty now, the silence amplifying the faint hum of my computer. I should have gone home hours ago, but I couldn't shake the feeling that I was on the verge of something important—something bigger than just Kirkwood's impending meltdown. My intuition screamed at me that a storm was gathering on the horizon, and I needed to prepare for it.

With a deep, grounding breath, I pulled up another log file, my fingers flying across the keyboard. The numbers danced before my eyes, strings of data weaving together like a complex tapestry, each thread hinting at more than mere metrics. I scrolled deeper, letting the information wash over me, each entry a potential key to understanding the underlying malice that had just thrust itself into our world.

Every artifact I examined felt like a piece of a puzzle—a puzzle missing its central image, one I was desperate to complete. The more I probed, unraveling layers of information, the tighter the feeling in my gut grew. Whatever this was, I needed to know. It was not just about answering the why but also about protecting everything and everyone I held dear in this office.

As the minutes slipped by, I sank further into the rabbit hole. My computer screen flickered with endless columns and rows of data, numbers that once seemed innocuous now morphed into a sinister smokescreen. I knew I was playing a dangerous game, diving headfirst into an abyss that could consume me, but the risk felt justified.

I typed a search command for every instance correlating with the flagged point. Each moment I spent sifting through the data felt like peeling back layers of skin, exposing raw nerve endings. How had I missed this before? The enormity of the oversight weighed on me, but I pushed through it, fueled by determination and a flicker of fear.

A notification popped up—another anomaly noted in a different section of the model. My pulse quickened. I opened it and began dissecting this new data point. With each occurrence I uncovered, a chilling realization settled over me: this wasn't just one isolated incident. This was part of a larger scheme, an orchestrated series of manipulations designed to mislead us.

I could almost envision the shadowy figure behind the curtain, pulling the strings and orchestrating the chaos in the office, night after night. A ghost in the machinery—an unsettling concept, a whisper that sent a shiver down my spine.

As I returned to my data search, the office around me faded into the background, the fluorescent lights buzzing softly overhead like distant whispers from an unseen counsel. I scrolled through entries, my eyes scanning for patterns, connections that would illuminate the darkness sprawled across my screen.

Hours seemed to slip away, the steady rhythm of my typing a strange comfort amidst the chaos brewing in my mind. I absorbed every scrap of information, piecing elements together like shards of glass waiting to form a cohesive picture, though I could feel the pressure mounting around me.

It was well past midnight when I stumbled upon something—a thread that pulled at my awareness. A scatter of instances appeared, connected by a singular attribute that felt too coherent to be mere coincidence. The whispers of the past converged with the present, and for a brief moment, clarity washed over me like a cleansing tide.

I leaned closer to my screen, heart hammering in my chest. This wasn't just an anomaly; it was a breadcrumb leading toward a far darker reality than I had anticipated. As the realization struck me, I could hardly breathe. Whatever path lay ahead was fraught with uncertainty, a descent into shadows where secrets and motives lurked, waiting to be unveiled.

Drawing in a shaky breath, I felt an unfamiliar sense of resolve take hold—this chaos couldn't simply be allowed to unfold unchecked. Not while I had the chance to uncover it, to piece it together before it all spiraled into a nightmare for us, for the entire team.

Determined, I noted every detail and relevant data point swirling through my mind as I began to forge a plan. This was my fight now, and retreat was no longer an option. I would delve deeper, expose the truth behind the shadows, and if I had to confront whoever was behind this, I would do so with clarity and conviction.

The night enveloped the office like a heavy cloak as I continued scouring the depths of data, each keystroke echoing in the silence—a heartbeat in the impending storm. Whatever this was, I would unravel it, and the lurking darkness would soon learn that I was not just another cog in the machine.

The office lay wrapped in a suffocating silence that felt almost tangible, each sound of my keystrokes echoing against the walls like distant gunshots in the night. The fluorescent lights buzzed overhead, flickering intermittently and casting ghostly shadows across the empty desks. Most of my coworkers had long since departed, their chairs neatly pushed in, their monitors dark and abandoned as the echoes of their chatter faded with their footsteps. But for me, leaving wasn't an option—not just yet.

Not while the anomaly hung over my head like a storm cloud, its weight pressing down on my mind. It was like a nagging itch I couldn't scratch, a piece of a puzzle that refused to fit neatly into any corner of the larger picture I was trying to assemble. I had poured over everything—scanning logs like a detective sifting for evidence, retracing the complex data pipelines like an explorer navigating a labyrinth, and cross-checking test results like a scientist in a frenzy—but no matter how many angles I examined, something still felt fundamentally wrong.

With determination, I leaned forward, my chair creaking softly as I opened yet another log file, my eyes racing across the endless stream of entries flickering in the dim light of my screen. Most of what I encountered was routine—standard data pulled from various sources, algorithms humming away as they executed their preprogrammed functions. Yet, amid this sea of mundanity, something lurked beneath the surface: an irregularity, an anomaly that was entirely out of place.

Then I spotted it: a command, subtle and insidious, cleverly nestled within what appeared to be unremarkable automated scripts. The flagged anomaly hadn't emerged from the chaos of random errors; it had been carefully injected into the system. An unauthorized manual override had shifted crucial data at its source, just enough to unleash chaos upon our carefully calibrated model.

Staring at the screen, my thoughts rushed in a tumultuous wave. Someone had deliberately chosen to sabotage our system, just as Sarah and I had feared. But who was the culprit lurking behind this act of deceit? Fueled by rising agitation, I followed the breadcrumb trail left in the logs, meticulously tracing the override back to its origin. The logs were precise, every action timestamped down to the millisecond. Amid this sea of digital fingerprints, one name began to emerge—like a shadow creeping across the screen.

Kirkwood.

Shock rippled through me as I froze, staring unblinkingly at the screen. The override had come from his credentials. He had infiltrated the system days before the critical demo, stealthily planting the anomaly within the unassuming data pipeline. The logs told no lies; they revealed his betrayal, confirming he had orchestrated this sabotage with cold precision.

"Why would you do that?" I whispered, my voice barely cutting through the oppressive quiet of the office, the echo lingering hauntingly in the air. The pieces began to snap together in a disjointed rhythm; Kirkwood's earlier accusations against us fell into chilling clarity. It wasn't anger over the model's failure that had driven his paranoia—no, he was terrified of being exposed. His plot to manipulate the model had backfired spectacularly, leaving a gaping hole instead of the shield he had hoped for, and now he was scrambling to cover his tracks.

How brazen. To think he believed he could maneuver every piece on the board to suit his needs without the risk of being caught.

But now the very gamble he had employed had spiraled beyond his control, the anomaly rendering predictions so volatile that even he could not grasp the narrative anymore. He had unwittingly unleashed a Pandora's box, threatening to explode into chaos.

Leaning back in my chair, I took a slow, deep breath, allowing the realization to wash over me. Kirkwood had orchestrated this sabotage, albeit clumsily, with his ambitions clouding his judgment. However, when everything had spiraled out of hand, panic set in. Now, he was clawing to pin the blame on Sarah and me, seeking to divert attention away from his catastrophic missteps.

This was bigger than I had initially assumed. The implications of what I had uncovered were staggering. If news of this revelation slipped out, it would not only jeopardize Kirkwood's career; it could plunge Gordon & Blake into a scandal so profound it could irrevocably tarnish our reputations and connections as well. If anyone got wind of what Kirkwood had done, it would be a tidal wave crashing upon us all, and I could already feel the swell rising.

The sudden buzz of my phone jolted me from my spiraling thoughts, its sound cutting through the quiet like a siren. I glanced down—Sarah's name flashed on the screen, and adrenaline surged as I swiftly answered.

"Hey," I croaked, urgency tightening my words.

"Any progress?" she asked, skipping the customary niceties with a brusqueness that was unnerving.

"I found it," I replied, a taut thread of tension woven through my voice. "The anomaly—it wasn't random. Kirkwood planted it himself."

A heavy silence stretched across the line, the realization pressing between us like the weight of reality.

"You're sure?" she finally asked, her tone sharp and cautionary, the tension palpable even through the speakers.

"Absolutely," I affirmed. "I traced the logs back to his credentials. He accessed the system intentionally and injected that anomaly days before the demo. He's the one we need to watch out for."

"Jesus," she muttered, the gravity of the news hanging like a cloud above us. "That explains why he was so paranoid. He wasn't worried about us screwing up—he was worried about us finding out."

"Exactly," I confirmed, the fight igniting in my veins. "But there's more. I believe he was attempting to manipulate the model to fit his own agenda. When things went disastrous, he panicked."

Sarah inhaled sharply, the sound echoing on the other end of the line. "This changes everything. If we can prove this, it completely clears us. But if the higher-ups at Gordon & Blake find out about what Kirkwood did…"

She didn't need to finish her thought, because the menace of that unstated consequence hung heavily in the air like a sword poised to drop. The reputation of a firm thrived on trust and integrity; a scandal like this could deeply compromise everything we had built.

"What do we do now?" I asked, my mind racing with possibilities while my heart thudded unevenly in my chest.

"For now, we keep this between us," Sarah instructed, her voice low and calculated. "I'll loop in legal and start plotting our next steps. But Tristan, be extra cautious. If Kirkwood's willing to sabotage the model, we have to consider the depth of his capabilities. We know he's desperate."

Her words lingered, heavy with an unsaid warning, as the call came to an abrupt end. I stared at the glowing screen in front of me, the evidence of Kirkwood's treachery glaring back like a titan ready to crush us. The puzzle pieces had finally begun to coalesce, but the picture they formed was darker than I had anticipated.

Something felt off, though. Kirkwood's actions, desperate as they were, reeked of calculated deliberation beneath the surface. It was as if a cornered animal was lashing out, trapped and grasping for the smallest semblance of control among the growing chaos of his own making.

With focused resolve, I saved every log, making extra copies to ensure nothing could be lost in a catastrophic failure. The silence that enveloped the office felt oppressive now, the faint hum of the lights hovering like specters, watching my every move.

I gathered my belongings, the weight of the situation settling heavily on my shoulders, and as I stepped toward the elevator, a single burning question warred in my mind:

What had Kirkwood gotten himself into? And how far was he willing to go to maintain the façade he had created for himself?

CHAPTER FIVE

A RESTLESS STORM

The tension in the office was suffocating, a thick, invisible fog that clung to every surface and permeated every conversation. The air crackled with unspoken anxieties, fueled by the unsettling events of yesterday. As I walked toward the lunchroom, the fluorescent lights reflected harshly off the polished floor, and I could feel the undercurrent of unease threading through the air—sharp and inescapable, like the biting wind that sometimes swept through the city streets. It was more than just office gossip; it was a collective holding of breath, a shared anticipation of something else, something worse, to come.

Near the elevator, Benji and Ash were deep in conversation, their heads close together, their bodies angled away from prying eyes. Their voices were too low for anyone else to hear, a conspiratorial murmur that vibrated with urgency, but just loud enough for me to catch snippets as I passed. I pretended not to notice, my gaze fixed on the scuff marks on the elevator doors, but my ears strained to decipher their hushed exchange.

"...Heard they're still looking for Kirkwood," Benji muttered, his eyes darting around nervously as if he expected Kirkwood himself to materialize from behind a potted plant. He shifted his weight from one foot to the other, a subtle indication of his unease, and ran a hand through his already disheveled hair.

"They'd better find him," Ash replied, her tone edged with frustration and something akin to anger. Her voice had a sharp, brittle quality, like thin ice threatening to crack. "Laura didn't deserve that. I mean, who throws a laptop at someone over data? It's insane."

"Apparently Kirkwood," Benji said grimly, a flicker of fear crossing his face. "You should've seen her face when they wheeled her out—there was blood everywhere. It was... it was awful." He shivered, a physical manifestation of the horror he had witnessed.

The words hit me harder than I expected, a punch to the gut that stole my breath. The casual brutality of their description, the image of Laura's injury, was jarring—a stark reminder of the fragility of order and safety. I quickened my pace, desperate to escape the conversation, to distance myself from the grim details and the unsettling atmosphere they created.

But the lunchroom was no better. The space, usually a haven of lunchtime camaraderie, buzzed with overlapping voices—a cacophony of speculation and conjecture. Every table was filled with coworkers dissecting the same story in increasingly dramatic detail, adding their own embellishments and interpretations to the already sensational account. The air was thick with anxiety, a palpable tension that made it hard to breathe.

"Do you think Laura's okay?" someone at the next table asked, her voice tinged with worry and a hint of morbid curiosity. She nervously chewed on her lip, her eyes wide with concern.

"I heard she has a concussion," another replied, her voice lowered as if sharing a dangerous secret. "Maybe worse. HR isn't saying much, though. Typical. They're probably trying to cover their asses."

"Well, they'd better figure out what to tell us soon," a third voice cut in, sharp and demanding. "Kirkwood's clearly unhinged. What if he comes back? What if he decides to finish what he started?"

"That's not going to happen," someone else scoffed, their voice dismissive and laced with bravado. "Security's on high alert now. They've got guards posted at every entrance. Besides, he's probably halfway out of the state by now, trying to cover his tracks and avoid the cops."

I grabbed a pre-made sandwich from the cooler, the cold plastic a stark contrast to the heat of my anxiety. The sandwich felt heavy and unappetizing in my hand, but I forced myself to take it anyway, needing something to occupy my hands and distract my mind. I found a seat near the window, hoping to drown out the incessant chatter and the unsettling atmosphere. But their words lingered, echoing in my mind, blending with my own thoughts until it was impossible to ignore the weight of the situation.

Laura's injury wasn't just a story to pass the time; it was a stark reminder of how quickly everything could spiral out of control, how easily the veneer of civility could shatter. Kirkwood's desperation, his anger—whatever had driven him to violence—had crossed a line, and we were all caught in the fallout, forced to confront the unsettling reality that lurked beneath the surface of our mundane lives.

I stared out at the skyline, the familiar shapes of buildings distorted by the midday sun. The glass facades shimmered and wavered, reflecting a distorted image of the city back at me. The world outside seemed almost mockingly normal, a sharp contrast to the unease simmering inside the office—the palpable fear that hung in the air like a storm cloud.

After lunch, I stepped outside, needing air, needing to escape the claustrophobic atmosphere of the office. The tension felt heavier now, pressing down on me as if the walls were closing in. The air outside was thick with humidity, but it was a welcome relief from the stale, recycled air of the office. The nearby park offered a fleeting sense of space, a pocket of green in the concrete jungle, a place where I could let the noise of the city drown out the noise in my head.

I wandered along the winding paths, letting the hum of passing conversations and the rustling of leaves blur together, trying to find some semblance of peace amidst the chaos. But even as I focused on the mundane—the sound of footsteps crunching on the gravel path, the faint scent of street food wafting from a nearby vendor, the cheerful chatter of children playing in the distance—I couldn't shake the feeling that something wasn't right. It was a prickling sensation on the back of my neck, an instinctive awareness that I was being watched.

And then I saw him.

Across the street, through the ebb and flow of cars and pedestrians, Marcus stood beneath the shadow of a sprawling oak tree. He was still—almost unnaturally so—his figure a sharp contrast to the chaotic energy of the city around him. He stood like a statue, radiating an aura of calm amidst the frantic pace of urban life.

My breath caught in my throat, my heart skipped a beat, and my hands became clammy.

It was the same as before—the magnetic pull, the calm intensity that radiated from him even at a distance. His eyes seemed to pierce through the crowd, focusing solely on me.

I froze, rooted to the spot, my heart pounding in my chest like a trapped bird. The logical part of me insisted it couldn't be him, not here, not now. It had to be a trick of the light, a figment of my imagination fueled by stress and anxiety. But the way his gaze locked onto mine, the unmistakable spark of recognition in his eyes, left no doubt in my mind.

Then, as though a switch had been flipped, Marcus moved.

Without breaking eye contact, his gaze unwavering, he stepped into the crowd. He navigated the throng of people with effortless grace, his movements fluid and purposeful. His figure dissolved into the sea of pedestrians, swallowed up so seamlessly it felt almost deliberate, as if he possessed the uncanny ability to blend into his surroundings.

I stood there, my pulse racing, scanning the sidewalk for any sign of him. I craned my neck, desperately trying to catch another glimpse of his face, but he was gone. Vanished.

The crowd surged onward, oblivious to the man who had just disappeared among them, their faces blank and unseeing. The city continued its relentless march, uncaring and unaware of the strange encounter that had just taken place.

Was it really him? Or was my mind playing tricks on me, warping my unease into something tangible, conjuring up a ghost from my past? The question echoed in my mind, a persistent whisper I couldn't ignore.

Back at the office, the tension hadn't eased. If anything, it had intensified, fueled by rumors and speculation about Kirkwood's whereabouts and Laura's condition. Benji caught me on the way to my desk, his face unusually serious, his brow furrowed with concern.

"Hey," he said, keeping his voice low and glancing around to ensure no one was eavesdropping. "You okay? You've been... off today. You seem distracted and... I don't know... kind of pale."

"Yeah," I lied, brushing past him and trying to avoid his probing gaze. "Just distracted. Lots on my mind."

He didn't look convinced; his eyes narrowed with suspicion, but he didn't press further. He knew me well enough to recognize when I was trying to avoid a conversation, and he respected my boundaries, even if he didn't understand what was going on.

The rest of the afternoon was a blur of half-hearted attempts at work, punctuated by the steady buzz of whispered conversations about Laura and Kirkwood. Every email, every phone call, every meeting was overshadowed by the unsettling events of the past day. By the time I shut my computer down, the screen reflecting a tired and anxious face back at me, and packed my things, I was no closer to making sense of anything. The image of Marcus's face, the memory of his intense gaze, haunted me, adding another layer of confusion and unease to the already chaotic mix.

As I stepped outside, the city lights beginning to twinkle against the darkening sky, my phone buzzed. I was surprised to see Rebecca's name light up the screen.

The screen of my phone glowed faintly in the dimming evening light, an insistent beacon in the encroaching twilight. Rebecca's name stared back at me, stark and unwavering, her message short and to the point, devoid of any unnecessary embellishment.

Rebecca: "Party tonight. Penthouse downtown. 8 PM. You should come."

I stared at the text, the words hanging in the air like a silent challenge. My thumb hovered over the reply button, paralyzed by indecision. Each tap felt like a commitment, a step closer to a world I was trying desperately to avoid.

Rebecca.

The name echoed in the chambers of my mind, a familiar melody laced with a bitter undertone. It had been months since we'd spoken—months of carefully constructed distance and deliberate avoidance. But her presence still lingered in the corners of my memory, a persistent ghost I couldn't seem to shake. She had this uncanny ability to always pull me back in, like a moth drawn to a dangerous flame, even when I knew better, even when every instinct screamed at me to run in the opposite direction. It was a siren song, a tempting lure promising excitement and drama, but ultimately leading to inevitable disappointment.

I sighed, the sound heavy with resignation, and slipped the phone into my pocket without responding. The digital message burned against my thigh, a constant reminder of the decision I was trying to postpone. The last thing I needed tonight was to be dragged back into her meticulously crafted orbit, forced to endure an evening of forced smiles and thinly veiled passive-aggressive conversations about how much better her life was now, how much further she had climbed the ladder of success, leaving me in her wake. I knew the script—the carefully rehearsed lines, the subtle jabs designed to make me feel inadequate.

But as I walked toward the subway, the rumble of the approaching train a dull counterpoint to the swirling thoughts in my head, her message played on a loop, a broken record spinning relentlessly. Rebecca didn't do anything without a reason. Every action was calculated, every word carefully chosen. She had always been deliberate, as if every move was part of some larger, intricate game only she could see—a game with rules I didn't understand and stakes I couldn't afford. I was a pawn in her world, a player to be manipulated and discarded at her whim.

What was she after this time? What benefit did she hope to gain from my presence at her party? Was it simply a desire to flaunt her success, to bask in the envy of those she had left behind? Or was there something more, a deeper motive hidden beneath the surface of her carefully constructed facade? The questions gnawed at me, relentless and insistent.

When I finally made it home, the apartment felt smaller than usual, the familiar comfort replaced by a sense of claustrophobia. The quiet pressed in on me, suffocating and heavy, amplifying the anxieties that buzzed beneath my skin. I tried to settle into my usual routine—a quick dinner of reheated leftovers, a lukewarm beer, some mindless scrolling on my laptop, hoping to lose myself in the endless stream of online distractions—but Rebecca's message wouldn't leave me alone. It was like a persistent itch, a nagging reminder of the decision I was trying to avoid.

It wasn't just her, I realized, as I stared blankly at the flickering screen. It was everything—the mounting tension at work, the unsettling chaos surrounding Kirkwood, and the strange encounters I'd had with Marcus, the fleeting glimpses of him that I couldn't explain, the unsettling feeling that I was being watched. It all felt connected somehow, threads of a vast and intricate web tightening around me, slowly constricting my movements and limiting my choices. Each event, each encounter, seemed to be part of a larger pattern, a puzzle I couldn't quite solve.

And maybe, just maybe, Rebecca's party was another piece of the puzzle—a crucial clue that could unlock the secrets of my existence. Perhaps it was a dangerous gamble, a step into the unknown that could unravel everything I held dear. But the alternative—remaining in the dark, allowing the shadows to consume me—was even less appealing.

By 7:30, I found myself standing in front of the mirror, staring at my reflection with a mixture of apprehension and defiance. I was running my hands along the collar of a shirt I hadn't worn in months, a relic from a past life, a symbol of the person I used to be. The fabric felt stiff and unfamiliar against my skin, a reminder of the changes I had undergone in recent months. My reflection looked as uncertain as I felt—a ghost of my former self staring back at me with haunted eyes.

Why are you doing this? The question echoed in my mind, a silent accusation.

I didn't have an answer—not a good one anyway. I couldn't articulate the reasons behind my decision, the complex web of emotions and anxieties that had led me to this point. Was it curiosity? A desperate need for answers? Or simply a masochistic desire to inflict pain upon myself? Whatever the reason, I knew I couldn't stay away; I had to see what Rebecca had planned, even if it meant walking into a trap.

The penthouse was downtown, perched atop one of the tallest buildings in the city—a glittering beacon in the night. The building's entrance was a sleek facade of glass and steel, an imposing structure that seemed to pierce the sky. It was the kind of place Rebecca had always dreamed of, a symbol of the wealth and success she so desperately craved. The air thrummed with an unspoken energy, a sense of exclusivity and privilege that made me feel like an outsider looking in.

I stepped into the elevator, the faint hum of classical music filling the space as it carried me upward, ascending through the layers of the city. The music was sterile and impersonal, a soundtrack to the artificial world I was about to enter. With each floor, the anticipation grew, the knot in my stomach tightening with each passing second.

When the doors opened, I was greeted by a view that could have been ripped from the pages of a glossy magazine. The penthouse was immaculate—polished marble floors that reflected the city lights, crystal chandeliers casting a dazzling glow, and floor-to-ceiling windows showcasing the sprawling cityscape below. The air was thick with the scent of expensive perfume and the murmur of polite conversation. It was a world of artifice and illusion, a carefully constructed stage set designed to impress and intimidate.

Rebecca spotted me almost immediately, her eyes lighting up with a predatory gleam. She excused herself from a group of impeccably dressed guests and made her way over, her smile as polished and perfect as her surroundings. It never reached her eyes; it always felt like a performance, a carefully rehearsed routine.

"Tristan," she said, drawing out my name like it was a punchline to some private joke, a subtle reminder of her power over me. "You made it."

"Yeah," I said, forcing a small smile that felt brittle and insincere. "Nice place."

She waved a manicured hand dismissively, her diamond ring glinting in the light. "Oh, it's not mine. Just a friend's. But it's fabulous, isn't it? You should see the view from the balcony."

Before I could reply, she slipped an arm through mine, her touch sending an uncomfortable shiver down my spine, and steered me toward the center of the room, her grip surprisingly firm. "Come on, I want to introduce you to someone."

I should have known better. I should have anticipated this. Rebecca never did anything without an ulterior motive.

Standing in the center of a small crowd of admirers was a man who looked like he belonged in a catalog for designer suits. His perfectly styled hair, dazzlingly white teeth, and expensive watch screamed success. He radiated an aura of wealth and confidence that was both impressive and unsettling.

"This is James," Rebecca said, her voice dripping with pride, her eyes sparkling with triumph. "My fiancé."

The word hit me like a punch to the gut, stealing the air from my lungs. It was unexpected, a cruel twist in a game I didn't even know I was playing.

I managed a polite nod, extending my hand to shake James's. "Congratulations."

Rebecca's smile widened, a look of pure satisfaction on her face. "Thanks. I knew you'd be happy for me."

Happy? That wasn't the word I'd use. Stunned, perhaps. Betrayed, maybe. But happy? No. I swallowed my feelings, forcing a smile that felt like a mask, and stepped back, letting her bask in her moment, allowing her to revel in her carefully constructed happiness.

Ash appeared out of nowhere, a drink in hand and her usual sharp gaze fixed on me, her presence a welcome distraction from the awkwardness of the situation.

"Didn't think I'd see you here," she said, her tone flat, betraying nothing.

"Yeah, well, Rebecca has a way of pulling people in," I replied, trying to sound nonchalant, but my voice betrayed my unease.

Ash snorted, taking a sip of her drink, her eyes narrowed in observation. "Don't let her get to you. She thrives on this kind of thing."

"I know," I said, glancing toward the balcony, hoping to escape the suffocating atmosphere of the party. "I just need a minute."

The balcony offered a sanctuary, a detached observatory far removed from the cacophony that reigned within the penthouse. The sprawling metropolis unfolded beneath a velvet sky—a tapestry woven with shimmering lights that pulsed with life. The city's constant thrum, a low and persistent drone, was muted by the towering glass walls, serving as a transparent barrier between the vibrant party inside and the tranquil night beyond.

My fingers tightened around the cool, smooth railing, my gaze lost in the breathtaking panorama of the skyline. The crisp night air was a balm against the suffocating heat that had been building within me—a pressure cooker ignited by Rebecca's startling announcement. Each breath I took felt shallow, insufficient to quell the turmoil churning in my gut.

Fiancé.

The word reverberated within the chambers of my mind, a shard of ice piercing through the carefully constructed walls of my composure. A single word, yet laden with implications, a declaration that shattered the fragile equilibrium of my world. Rebecca hadn't merely invited me to this extravagant gathering; she'd orchestrated it, meticulously planning every detail to maximize its impact. Every fleeting glance, every calculated gesture, every carefully chosen word had been a subtle twist of the knife, a deliberate attempt to inflict pain.

"I want you to be happy for me," she had said, her voice dripping with a saccharine sweetness that grated against my nerves. As if I were some distant acquaintance, an ex-lover she barely remembered, not the man who had dedicated years to making her happiness a priority. The galling indifference in her tone starkly contrasted the years of shared dreams and whispered promises.

Behind me, the muffled sounds of forced laughter and the delicate clinking of crystal glasses drifted through the partially open sliding door. Within that glittering throng, Rebecca was undoubtedly reveling in her perceived victory, regaling anyone who would listen with the charming tale of her whirlwind romance, glossing over the inconvenient truth of our shared history. The thought sent a fresh wave of anger surging through me, threatening to shatter the fragile control I was desperately clinging to.

I exhaled slowly, a conscious effort to release the pent-up tension that had coiled itself around my chest. I focused on the distant pinpricks of light that dotted the horizon, trying to find solace in their unwavering glow. Each light represented a life, a story, a world unto itself. My own felt suddenly small, insignificant in the face of such vastness.

That's when I felt it.

A presence.

It wasn't a boisterous intrusion or an overt display of power; it was something far more subtle, more unsettling. Just the faintest tremor in the air behind me, like the imperceptible shifting of a shadow in the periphery of my vision. A prickling sensation danced across my skin, raising goosebumps in its wake.

Before I could react, before I could even turn to confront the source of this strange disturbance, a voice sliced through the stillness of the night.

"Beautiful view, isn't it?"

The voice was a low, resonant rumble, a smooth caress that seemed to vibrate through the very air around me. Instantly recognizable, it sent a shiver down my spine.

I turned sharply, my heart pounding against my ribs like a trapped bird, to find Marcus standing a few feet away. His posture was relaxed, almost nonchalant, his hands casually tucked into the pockets of his impeccably tailored trousers. His dark eyes, pools of fathomless depth, were fixed on the sprawling skyline, as if he were merely admiring the scenery.

"How did you—" I started, the words catching in my throat, strangled by a mixture of surprise and apprehension. His presence here was unexpected, unwelcome, and deeply unsettling. I had hoped to escape the suffocating atmosphere of the party, to find a moment of solitude to compose myself, but it seemed that solitude was a luxury I could no longer afford.

Marcus smiled faintly, a subtle curve of his lips that didn't quite reach his eyes. He took a purposeful step closer, closing the distance between us. "I've always preferred moments like these. Quiet. Unassuming. Don't you?"

My pulse quickened, a frantic drumbeat echoing in my ears. There was something about his presence, an aura of controlled power, calm but deliberate, that set every nerve ending in my body on edge. It was like standing on the precipice of a storm, the air thick with anticipation, the sky pregnant with unspoken menace.

"What do you want?" I asked, my voice surprisingly steady despite the growing unease curling in my chest. I refused to show him my fear, to give him the satisfaction of knowing how deeply he unsettled me.

Marcus tilted his head slightly, as if genuinely considering the question. The gesture was practiced, refined, a subtle performance designed to maintain the upper hand. "The same thing you do. A moment of clarity in all this chaos."

His words hung in the air, laden with implications that I couldn't quite decipher. Was he referring to the chaos of the party, the orchestrated drama of Rebecca's engagement, or something far more profound? I sensed that his motives were far from simple, that he was playing a game with rules I didn't understand.

Before I could formulate a response, before I could even attempt to unravel the enigma of his intentions, he moved.

It was so fast, so seamless, that I didn't fully comprehend what had occurred until it was over. One moment he was standing there, a figure of enigmatic calm, and the next, his hand brushed against mine, a fleeting contact that left me reeling.

A sharp warmth blossomed on the back of my hand, a sudden surge of energy that spread through my veins like sunlight breaking through a storm. The sensation was intoxicating—euphoric, even—a rush of pure, untainted power that left me breathless. But it vanished just as quickly as it came, leaving behind only a lingering echo of its intensity.

I stumbled back, clutching my hand to my chest, my mind struggling to process the inexplicable event. My skin tingled where he'd touched me, a faint heat lingering like the afterglow of a summer day. It was a subtle sensation, almost imperceptible, but it resonated with an undeniable power.

"What the hell—" I started, my voice a strangled whisper, but Marcus was already gone.

The sliding door to the balcony stood ajar, the noise of the party filtering back into the quiet night, a stark reminder of the world I had momentarily escaped. I glanced around wildly, searching for any sign of his presence, but there was no trace of him—just the empty space where he'd been standing moments ago. He had vanished into thin air, leaving me to grapple with the unsettling reality of what had just transpired.

My heart raced as I stared down at my hand, searching for some visible evidence of the encounter. The skin was unbroken, unmarked, offering no tangible explanation for the intense sensation that still lingered. But the warmth persisted, a subtle hum that felt too deliberate to ignore. It was as if he had imprinted something on me, a hidden message etched into my very being.

I leaned against the railing, trying to steady my breathing, to regain some semblance of composure in the face of this bewildering experience. What had he done? What was the meaning behind his cryptic words, his fleeting touch? The questions swirled through my mind, a maelstrom of confusion and apprehension.

The noise of the party beckoned me back inside its gilded cage, its constant hum grounding me in the present, reminding me of the charade I was expected to play. But as I reluctantly stepped through the sliding door, the memory of Marcus's presence clung to me like a shadow, a constant reminder that I was no longer entirely alone in this game. The storm within me remained, now fueled by a new and unknown element, a sense of impending change that both terrified and intrigued me.

The clamor of the celebration grew louder. As I crossed the threshold, the din of chatter and unrestrained laughter washing over me with the force of a rogue wave. The air, thick with perfume and the cloying sweetness of cheap wine, felt suddenly oppressive. My muscles tensed instinctively, a primal urge to retreat battling with the thin veneer of composure I struggled to maintain.

I burrowed deeper into myself, keeping my gaze fixed on the worn Persian rug beneath my feet. A labyrinth of intertwined patterns blurred before my eyes as I navigated the throng, a silent plea echoing in my mind: Don't let her see me. The last thing I needed, the absolute last thing, was to become the unwilling subject of Rebecca's triumphant gaze or, worse, the target of one of her fiancé's carefully crafted barbs.

I remembered, with a jolt of renewed resentment, the preening smile plastered on his face as he'd shaken my hand earlier, the subtle pressure of his grip a clear indication of his dominance. He was everything I wasn't: successful, confident, and undeniably suitable. A perfect match for Rebecca's ambition, a shining trophy to display to her circle of equally polished friends.

My internal monologue was abruptly cut short as Ash's sharp eyes, honed by years of cynical observation, locked onto me from across the room. It was as if she possessed some kind of radar for my discomfort, an uncanny ability to zero in on my vulnerabilities with unnerving precision. Her brow furrowed slightly, a silent question forming in the space between u s.

With a sigh that barely registered above the party noise, she began to weave her way through the crowd, her progress swift and purposeful. There was a certain elegance to her movements, a quiet confidence that set her apart from the giddy revelers around her. Despite my irritation, a small part of me was relieved by her approach. Ash, for all her sharp edges, was the closest thing I had to a friend in this suffocating charade.

"Tristan," she said, her voice a familiar blend of exasperation and morbid curiosity. The sound, though laced with her characteristic cynicism, was a welcome anchor in the swirling chaos of the party. "What's with you? You look like you've seen a ghost... or perhaps remembered one."

I flinched as the truth of her words hit a raw nerve. Marcus's face flashed unbidden in my mind, his eyes burning with unsettling intensity. "I'm fine," I muttered, attempting to brush past her. My shoulder bumped awkwardly against hers, a clumsy maneuver that only highlighted my disquiet.

"Sure you are," she retorted, effortlessly falling into step beside me. I felt her gaze boring into me, dissecting my carefully constructed facade. "You've been off all night, ever since we got here. Let me guess—Rebecca dragged you here to show off her new life, her new ring, and now you're sulking because she's marrying Mr. Perfect and living some kind of domestic dream that will probably bore her to tears within a year."

Her words, delivered with her usual brand of acerbic wit, struck a little too close to home. The truth, as always, was a bitter pill. "Not now, Ash," I snapped, my voice sharper than intended. The last thing I wanted was to dissect my complicated feelings for Rebecca under the harsh glare of the ballroom lights.

She raised a perfectly sculpted eyebrow, her expression unreadable. It was a skill she had mastered over the years: the ability to mask her true emotions behind a wall of sardonic detachment. "Whatever you say," she replied, her voice flat. But I saw it—a flicker of something in her eyes, maybe concern, maybe just plain curiosity, but the understanding was there.

I left her standing there, a solitary figure amidst the swirling mass of bodies, and made my way toward the bar. The thought of alcohol, of dulling the sharp edges of my anxiety, suddenly felt incredibly appealing. A strong drink seemed like the only plausible solution to the whirlwind churning in my chest.

I flagged down the bartender, ordered a double whiskey neat, and downed half of it in one go. The burning liquid slid down my throat, offering a momentary respite from the turmoil within. But even as I nursed the remaining alcohol, it failed to soothe the restless energy coursing through my veins.

My left hand, the one Marcus had touched, still tingled with an unsettling heat. The warmth that had started as a faint, almost imperceptible sensation was growing exponentially, spreading like wildfire up my arm and into the very core of my being.

I set the glass down with a clatter, my breathing becoming shallow and erratic. The sound of glass on marble felt discordant, like nails scratching on a chalkboard.

The room felt brighter, sharper, as though some unseen hand had cranked up the volume on every sensory input. The laughter, which had previously been a mere annoyance, now felt like a relentless assault on my eardrums. The clinking of glasses, the rustling of dresses, the murmur of conversations—all of it coalesced into a deafening roar.

A wave of dizziness washed over me, threatening to pull me under. I gripped the edge of the bar, my knuckles turning white as I fought to maintain my balance. The polished marble felt cold and smooth beneath my trembling fingers, a temporary anchor in the face of the rising tide.

"You okay?" the bartender asked, his voice cutting through the haze like a shard of ice. He was a young man, barely out of his teens, with kind eyes and a perpetual air of weary resignation.

I nodded quickly, mumbling something incoherent about needing some air. I fumbled in my pocket for cash, tossed it onto the bar, and then stumbled away, desperate to escape the oppressive atmosphere.

My steps felt uneven and unsteady as I made my way toward a quieter corner of the room, a small alcove shrouded in shadow. Each breath came faster and shallower than the last, my chest tightening as if an invisible vise was constricting my lungs. The air, once thick with perfume, now felt thin and inadequate, offering no relief from the suffocating pressure.

Then, just as I thought I might faint, the warmth in my chest erupted.

It wasn't painful—not at first. It was more like being submerged in pure sunlight, a radiant heat flooding my veins in a way that felt almost alive. It was an alien sensation, both terrifying and strangely exhilarating. But the feeling didn't stop or plateau. It continued to intensify, spreading relentlessly to my head, my legs, my fingertips, until every inch of my being buzzed with an intensity that bordered on unbearable.

The first spasm hit me out of nowhere, a sudden and violent contraction that ripped through my muscles like a lightning bolt.

My hands clenched involuntarily, twisting and turning. My vision went white for a split second, the world dissolving into a blinding void. I stumbled, my legs giving way beneath me. I instinctively reached out, my fingers grasping desperately for something, anything, to hold onto. My hand landed on the back of a nearby chair, the rough texture of the fabric a small comfort as the room tilted violently.

"Tristan?"

Ash's voice cut through the fog, distant but insistent. The sound, though muffled by the cacophony of the party, was laced with genuine concern that surprised me.

I tried to respond, to reassure her that I was alright, that I was just feeling a little unwell. But the words caught in my throat, choked by rising panic. Another spasm hit, even stronger than the first, convulsing my body with an almost unbearable force. My knees buckled, and I sank into the chair, trembling uncontrollably as I fought to stay upright.

"Hey!" Ash was in front of me now, her sharp features softened by something that looked suspiciously like genuine concern. "What's going on? You look like you're about to pass out... or spontaneously combust."

"I'm fine," I managed, though my voice was barely a whisper, a rasping croak lost in the general din.

"No, you're not," she said, her tone uncharacteristically firm. She glanced around, her eyes darting nervously, before lowering her voice. "What the hell is going on with you? You look like you're burning up. Are you sick? Did Rebecca poison you?"

I didn't have an answer. I didn't know the answer. All I knew was that something was happening to me—something strange and terrifying—and I had no idea how to stop it.

The warmth in my body surged again, this time accompanied by a jolt of pain that made me clench my teeth. It wasn't a sharp, stabbing pain, but something deeper, something more fundamental. It felt like something inside me was shifting, breaking apart, and rearranging itself in some bizarre and incomprehensible pattern.

I gripped the edge of the chair, my knuckles white, focusing all my attention on the feeling of the worn wood beneath my fingers. It was a desperate attempt to ground myself, to anchor to reality in the face of the overwhelming sensations that threatened to consume me.

"I just need... air," I said, forcing the words out, each syllable a monumental effort. My lungs burned, and my head swam.

Ash hesitated, her eyes scanning my face with an intensity that made me uncomfortable. "I'll come with you," she said.

"No," I said quickly, shaking my head. The thought of Ash witnessing whatever was happening to me, of seeing me in such a vulnerable state, was unbearable. "I'll be fine. Just give me a minute."

She didn't look convinced, but after a moment of tense silence, she nodded reluctantly. "Fine. But if you keel over, don't say I didn't warn you."

I waited until she retreated back into the crowd, her shoulders stiff with unspoken concern, before attempting to stand. My legs were shaky and unsteady, but at least functional. The tingling in my hand had spread to my fingertips now, the warmth pulsing in time with my erratic heartbeat. It felt like I was holding some kind of dangerous power, raw and untamed.

Each step felt heavier than the last as I made my way toward the balcony again, the cool night air calling to me like a lifeline. The promise of escape, of solitude, was almost enough to keep me moving, to propel me forward despite the overwhelming urge to collapse. The night was the only thing keeping me sane.

The cool air on the balcony was a palpable relief, the crisp breeze a welcome contrast to the stuffy, overheated ballroom. It sliced through the lingering warmth pulsing beneath my skin, a persistent reminder of the unnerving events that had unfolded inside. For a moment, I simply stood there, ignoring the glittering panorama of the city stretching before me. The endless rows of lights blurred together, becoming an indistinct canvas of shimmering gold against the dark backdrop of the night. I closed my eyes, focusing solely on the rhythm of my breathing.

In and out.

Each inhale was a conscious act, a deliberate attempt to anchor myself to the present. The dizziness that had threatened to overwhelm me just moments ago had eased to a manageable level. My thoughts, which had been a tangled mess of fragmented images and disjointed ideas, were slowly beginning to coalesce, forming coherent patterns. My body felt lighter somehow, as if an invisible weight I hadn't even realized I was carrying had been lifted from my shoulders. The sensation was subtle but undeniable, a freeing lightness that allowed me to stand a little straighter, breathe a little d eeper.

I flexed my fingers, my gaze drawn to my hand. The tingling sensation, which had been so intense earlier, was still there, but it had dulled to a faint hum, like static electricity clinging to my skin. It was a subtle, almost imperceptible vibration that ran up my arm, a lingering echo of the violation I had experienced.

Maybe it's over, I thought, hope echoing softly in my mind. Perhaps whatever this is—this strange affliction, this unwelcome intrusion into my life—has passed. The thought was fragile and easily shattered, but I clung to it nonetheless, desperate for a return to normalcy.

The door behind me slid open with a soft whoosh, and Ash stepped onto the balcony, her arms crossed tightly over her chest. Her expression was unreadable, a carefully constructed mask that revealed nothing of her inner thoughts. The music from the party spilled into the night air, a muffled thump of bass and high-pitched chatter.

"You look better," she said, her tone skeptical, laced with a hint of cautious optimism. It was clear she was still unsure of my stability, wary of a sudden relapse.

"Yeah," I replied, my voice steadier than it had been all night. The words felt genuine, a reflection of the tentative improvement I felt within myself. "I think I just needed some air."

Ash raised a perfectly sculpted eyebrow, leaning against the railing with effortless grace. The city lights glinted in her dark eyes, reflecting the vibrant energy of the metropolis. "You're not going to pass out on me, are you?"

I shook my head, managing a small laugh, the sound surprisingly light and genuine. "No. I'm good. Really." I met her gaze, trying to convey the sincerity of my words. "I promise."

For the first time all night, it wasn't a lie. My body felt steady again, the earlier heat replaced by a strange sense of clarity and newfound awareness of my surroundings. Even the sounds of the party behind us felt less overwhelming, as if the volume had been turned down, allowing me to focus on the present moment.

Ash studied me for a moment, her sharp gaze softening slightly, the lines of concern around her eyes relaxing. "Well, that's a relief. I don't want to explain to HR why one of my coworkers collapsed at a party." She pushed a stray strand of hair behind her ear, a gesture that revealed a hint of nervousness.

"Don't worry," I said, leaning against the railing beside her, mimicking her relaxed posture. The cool metal felt grounding beneath my fingertips. "I'll spare you the trouble."

Ash smirked, shaking her head with wry amusement. "You really are a magnet for chaos, aren't you?"

"Maybe," I said, glancing at the glittering skyline. The city stretched out before us, a vast and complex tapestry of light and shadow. "But chaos makes life interesting, doesn't it?"

Ash snorted, the sound laced with playful disbelief. "You've got a funny definition of interesting."

We fell into an easy silence after that, the hum of the city filling the space between us, a constant, low-frequency drone vibrating through the air. The distant sirens, the rumble of traffic, the faint strains of mu-sic—all blended into a symphony of urban sound. For the first time all night, I felt normal again—grounded, present, even... content. The feeling was subtle, a quiet sense of peace settling over me like a warm blanket.

And then it hit me.

It started as a faint tremor, a barely perceptible flicker of warmth in my chest that I almost dismissed as a trick of the imagination. But within seconds, it surged, spreading through my body like wildfire, consuming me from the inside out. It was a heat unlike anything I had ever experienced, an intense, burning sensation that made my skin prickle and my muscles tense. My vision blurred at the edges, the city lights dissolving into hazy streaks of color. My knees buckled, threatening to give way beneath me as a wave of dizziness washed over me, disorienting and overwhelming.

"Tristan?" Ash's voice was sharp now, edged with genuine concern that cut through the fog in my mind. The lighthearted banter was gone, replaced by urgency and alarm.

"I'm fine," I tried to say, but the words came out slurred, tangled in the sudden rush of heat and pressure building within me. My tongue felt thick and clumsy, my mouth dry. The lie tasted bitter on my lips.

The world tilted violently, the horizon spinning as my legs gave out beneath me. I stumbled, grabbing the railing for support, my fingers scrabbling against the smooth, cold metal. But my grip slipped, weakened by the overwhelming sensations coursing through my body, and I sank to the ground, the hard concrete jarring against my knees.

"Hey! Tristan!" Ash dropped to her knees beside me, her hands on my shoulders, her grip firm and reassuring. "What's happening? Talk to me!" Her voice was close to my ear, a beacon of clarity in the swirling vortex of sensations threatening to engulf me.

I opened my mouth to answer, to reassure her that I was okay, that this was just a momentary lapse, but the words wouldn't come. My body felt like it was shutting down, every muscle going slack, every thought dissolving into static. I was losing control, becoming a passenger in my own body, watching helplessly as the darkness closed in.

Ash's voice grew faint, her features blurring as darkness crept in at the edges of my vision, like ink spreading through water. The city lights flickered and dimmed, the music faded into a distant murmur.

"Tristan!"

And then everything went black.

Chapter Six

THE LABYRINTH OF THE MIND

Darkness enveloped me, thick and endless, a suffocating blanket woven from the absence of light. I had no sense of time, no anchor to tether me to a specific place. My body felt as if it had dissolved, its familiar boundaries erased. Yet, I could feel the weight of the void pressing down, an immeasurable force crushing me from all sides. It wasn't pain, exactly—more a profound disorientation, a terrifying sense of being untethered from everything I knew, adrift in an infinite ocean of nothingness. The very foundations of my existence crumbled, leaving behind only a raw, exposed core.

For what felt like an eternity, there was nothing. No sound pierced the silence, no glimmer of light disturbed the darkness, and no thought stirred within the vacant expanse of my mind. I was a blank canvas, a vessel emptied of its contents, waiting for something—anything—to fill the void. The nothingness threatened to consume me entirely, to erase my identity and leave behind only an echo of what once was. Then, faintly, a whisper against the silence reached my ears: a rhythm.

A heartbeat.

Not the steady, comforting thrum I was accustomed to, the dependable metronome that marked the passage of my days. This was different—faster, more urgent, echoing in the blackness like a distant drum, its frantic pulse reverberating through the void. It was a primal sound, a desperate plea in the face of oblivion, a fragile spark of life refusing to be extinguished. Each beat resonated deep within me, stirring something dormant and awakening a long-forgotten sense of hope.

Then came the warmth. It started faint and gentle, like sunlight breaking through a cold, impenetrable fog, a tentative promise of relief from the oppressive darkness. It was a subtle shift at first, a barely perceptible change in the atmosphere around me. But slowly, gradually, it bloomed into something more substantial, a comforting presence that filled the void with its radiant energy. It wrapped around me, safe and protective, soothing my frayed nerves and calming my racing heart. A strange peace settled over me, a tranquility I hadn't known was possible, as the rhythm grew louder, steadier, more reassuring—a beacon in the darkness guiding me home.

I wasn't floating anymore, lost in the infinite expanse of the void. I was... somewhere. A place both familiar and alien, a realm suspended between reality and dream. The sense of disorientation began to fade, replaced by a growing awareness of my surroundings, though they remained shrouded in a veil of mystery. I was no longer alone; I was surrounded by an unseen presence, a comforting energy that filled the void with anticipation.

Images began to form, blurry at first—indistinct shapes swirling in the darkness. But with every passing moment, they grew clearer, sharper, resolving into recognizable forms and colors. I saw light filtering through a veil of red, a soft, diffused glow that hinted at a hidden world. The muffled sound of voices came from outside, their tones soothing and familiar, like a lullaby whispered from a distant shore. There was a sense of safety and comfort in their voices, a promise of protection and love.

This is impossible, I thought, a flicker of disbelief in the face of the surreal. But even as the words came unbidden to my mind, I realized where I was. The truth dawned on me with the force of a revelation, shattering the illusion of the void and revealing the reality beneath.

The womb.

I was reliving my very beginning, the genesis of my existence, the earliest moments of my being. The memories were too primal to have words or context—raw emotions unfiltered by the lens of language. I could feel the heartbeat that wasn't mine but was still a part of me, the steady, rhythmic pulse that sustained my life, the unwavering presence of my mother. Her voice reached me—distorted but filled with love—a lullaby hummed just beyond my comprehension, a symphony of affection echoing in the confined space. It was a symphony of love and hope, a promise of a future filled with joy and happiness.

The peace shattered as the memory shifted, twisting violently, the serenity replaced by a sudden surge of panic and fear. I was no longer safe, no longer warm; the comforting embrace was replaced by a sense of impending doom. A blinding white light pierced through me, searing my senses, and I was pulled into the world, screaming—the transition brutal and unforgiving.

My birth.

The violent expulsion from the only world I had ever known, the sudden assault of light and sound, the shock of cold air on my skin. It was a traumatic experience, a painful awakening to the realities of existence. The transition from the serene world of the womb to the harsh world of reality was a rude awakening, a painful reminder of the challenges that lay ahead.

The memories came faster after that—a torrent of images and emotions washing over me, each one more vivid and intense than the last. My life flashed before my eyes, a whirlwind of experiences condensed into a fleeting moment.

I saw myself as a toddler, wobbling on unsteady legs, my arms outstretched, my face alight with determination. My mother's hands reached out to catch me before I fell, her eyes filled with love and encouragement. The sound of my father's laughter filled the room—deep and rich, a comforting rumble that resonated within my soul. It was a scene of pure joy and innocence, a moment of carefree happiness untouched by the worries of the world.

The scene shifted again; the idyllic memory was replaced by one tinged with sadness. I was older, standing on the sidewalk outside my school, waiting for my parents, my small frame shivering in the cold. Rain poured down, soaking my shoes, and I felt the chill seep into my bones. But the feeling that lingered most was loneliness, a gnawing ache I couldn't explain, a sense of isolation that cut me off from the world. It was a feeling of being lost and abandoned, a sense of not belonging.

The flood of memories didn't stop; each one was a fleeting glimpse into the past, a fragment of my life replayed before my eyes. Birthdays, arguments, triumphs, failures. My first kiss—an exploration of emotion and intimacy—my first heartbreak, a devastating loss that left me shattered and broken. The nights spent staring at the ceiling, wondering if this was all there was to life, questioning my purpose and searching for meaning.

And then Rebecca.

Her laughter was like music to my ears; her touch was a spark that ignited my soul, the way she made me feel like I was finally enough—accepted and loved for who I was. She was the light in my darkness, the missing piece that completed my puzzle. And then came the betrayal, the shattering of trust, the devastating realization that everything I thought I knew was a lie. The look in her eyes when she told me it was over, the cold indifference that pierced my heart like a shard of ice.

The memories sped up, hurtling toward the moment that cofused me most, the event that irrevocably changed my life—the turning point from which there was no return.

I was at the party, standing on the balcony, the city stretched out before me—a tapestry of lights twinkling in the darkness. I felt the cold air on my skin, the weight of Rebecca's announcement still pressing on my chest, a leaden burden that threatened to crush me. The city seemed indifferent to my pain, its glittering lights a cruel reminder of the joy I could no longer share.

Marcus's voice came from behind me—a low murmur that sent a chill down my spine. I turned, startled, and there he was—calm and deliberate, his presence like a shadow that had finally stepped into the light. He was a figure of darkness, his eyes devoid of emotion, his face a mask of indifference.

I felt the bite before I saw it, a warmth spread through my hand—a disconcerting heat that raced up my arm, stealing my strength and paralyzing my senses. And then, just as quickly as it had happened, he was gone, vanished into the night, leaving me standing alone.

The memory of collapsing into darkness replayed—the familiar sensation of my consciousness fading away, the feeling of my body succumbing to the inevitable. But this time, it didn't end; the comforting oblivion was replaced by something else, something unexpected and unknown.

I wasn't falling anymore, drifting into the abyss. I was standing in a field, the grass beneath my feet damp with morning dew, the soft blades tickling my toes. The air smelled different—not like the city, polluted and stale—but earthy and wild, filled with the scent of trees and unspoiled nature. It was a sensory overload, a symphony of scents and sensations that awakened my senses and filled me with a sense of peace

.

This wasn't my memory.

The realization hit me like a jolt, a surge of adrenaline coursing through my veins and sharpening my senses. I turned, scanning the horizon, searching for an explanation, for a clue to unravel the mystery of my surroundings.

The field stretched endlessly—a sea of green dotted with simple thatched huts, their rustic charm a stark contrast to the sterile cityscape I was accustomed to. Smoke curled from the tops of some, a sign of life and activity, and the faint sound of voices carried on the wind—whispers in a language I didn't understand. It was a scene of tranquil beauty, a pastoral idyll that seemed to exist outside of time.

Before I could take another step to explore this strange new reality, the world shifted again. The peaceful field dissolved into a sprawling forest, its depths shrouded in shadow and mystery. Shadows danced between the trees, playing tricks on my eyes, and I felt the weight of a bow in my hands, its smooth wood familiar against my skin. My heart raced—not with fear, but with anticipation, a thrill of excitement coursing through my veins. I wasn't me anymore; I was no longer the person I had always known myself to be.

I was Marcus.

The world around me began to dissolve, the familiar bite of the forest air replaced by an encroaching warmth, a comforting embrace of imagined firelight. The dense trees, the damp earth, the rustling leaves—all receded like a half-remembered dream, giving way to a scene both achingly familiar and impossibly distant.

Marcus stood firm and imposing, the focal point of a scene filled with domestic serenity in the center of his village. His strong arms, typically marked with dirt and sweat from tending to the fields, enveloped his wife and their infant. The baby, a delicate bundle of vitality, cooed gently, its tiny hands instinctively grasping at the woven threads of Marcus's tunic.

The soft sounds were music to Marcus as he gazed down at his new-found purpose—his very essence. Elara, his wife, nestled against him, her face glowing in the flickering light of the central fire blazing in the square, her smile as wide as the flames that reached high into the night sky.

The village throbbed with the comforting rhythms of evening. Laughter, like distant bells, drifted from groups sharing the day's end. Whispers exchanged secrets and stories, mingling with the clatter of pots as families cooked. Occasionally, a dog's bark reminded them of safety. Children, carefree, darted between mud-brick huts, their bare feet stirring dust motes that danced in the firelight, creating an ethereal haze that softened reality.

It was peaceful—a scene of idyllic serenity, a moment stolen from the relentless march of time. A memory encased in amber, perfect and whole.

And then it wasn't.

A scream, sharp and piercing, tore through the carefully woven tapestry of sound, shattering the fragile calm like glass. It was a sound of pure, unadulterated terror, a primal cry that resonated deep within the bones, raising the hairs on the back of the neck and chilling the blood in the veins.

Marcus's grip tightened instinctively around his wife and child, his protective instincts flaring to life. He snapped his head toward the periphery of the village, his eyes scanning the darkness beyond the comforting circle of firelight. Shadows flickered and danced at the edge of his vision, moving with a speed and fluidity that defied human capabilities. They twisted and elongated, reforming into different shapes. The speed at which they moved could only mean one thing.

The villagers froze, their laughter abruptly silenced, their conversations dying in their throats. The air grew heavy with anticipation, every breath held, every muscle tense. A deep, guttural sound—like a predator's growl mixed with a mournful wail—echoed through the darkness, slithering into the hearts of everyone present, feeding on their fear. It was the sound of something ancient and malevolent, a sound that spoke of pain, hunger, and an insatiable darkness.

Then it emerged.

The creature stepped into the firelight, and Marcus felt his blood turn to ice. His heart hammered against his ribs, a frantic drumbeat against the sudden silence. He felt the primal instinct to run, to hide, to protect his family at all costs flood through his veins.

It was humanoid, bearing a crude resemblance to a man, but only just. Its skin was as pale as bone, stretched taut over a frame that was too thin, too angular, as if the flesh had been forcibly molded over a skeleton far too large for it. The bones in its face were sharp and prominent. Long, claw-like fingers, tipped with points sharper than any knife, twitched at its sides, scraping against the rough material of its tattered garments. Its eyes—dark and endless—seemed to pierce through everything they touched. They were black holes in its face, swallowing light and hope, reflecting back only the fear and despair of those who dared to meet their gaze.

It moved with a strange, unsettling grace, each step silent despite the loose dirt and scattered stones beneath its feet. It was as if it floated across the ground, disconnected from the earth, a phantom given form. The creature was death.

The villagers stood frozen, paralyzed by fear, their eyes wide with disbelief and horror. The air crackled with palpable tension, thick and suffocating. Then the creature lunged, breaking the spell of paralysis with a burst of terrifying speed.

Its attack was wild and chaotic, a whirlwind of teeth and claws unleashed upon the unsuspecting villagers. It moved from one person to the next with terrifying speed, a blur of pale limbs and snapping jaws. Fangs flashed in the firelight as it bit into necks, shoulders, arms—anything it could reach. The creature's hunger was insatiable. The only thing that mattered was to eat.

Marcus watched in horror as his neighbors fell, one after another, their lives extinguished in a brutal, senseless wave of violence. Some collapsed instantly, their bodies convulsing in their death throes before going still. Others screamed, their voices rising in agony as they clawed at their throats, desperately trying to staunch the flow of blood gushing from their wounds.

"Inside!" Marcus shouted, his voice raw with panic, shoving his wife and child toward their small mud-brick hut. "Go, now! Get to safety! I will catch up." He prayed that he could. He needed to protect them at all costs.

He grabbed his hunting bow from the wall of his home, notching an arrow as he backed away from the escalating chaos. His heart pounded in his chest, the weight of his family's safety driving every movement, fueling his adrenaline. It was the only thing that mattered. If he was going to die, he was going to go down fighting.

The creature's head snapped toward him, its dark eyes locking onto his with unnerving intensity. It paused its bloody rampage, its attention now solely focused on Marcus.

Marcus froze, his fingers tightening around the bowstring, his knuckles white. He knew, with chilling certainty, that he was the creature's next target.

The creature tilted its head, studying him with an intensity that made his skin crawl. It seemed to be assessing him, measuring his strength, anticipating his next move. It took a step forward, its movements now deliberate and measured, each footfall a silent threat.

Marcus released the arrow.

The projectile flew straight and true, aimed directly at the creature's heart. But the creature moved faster than anything he had ever witnessed. It twisted its body with impossible precision, the arrow whistling past harmlessly, missing its mark by a hair's breadth.

And then it was upon him.

Marcus barely had time to raise his arms in defense before the creature struck, knocking the bow from his hands with a force that sent it clattering across the ground. Its claws, sharp as razors, wrapped around his throat, lifting him off the ground with terrifying ease. He struggled to breathe, his lungs burning, his vision blurring.

The creature's face was close now, its breath cold and rancid against Marcus's skin, the stench of death and decay filling his nostrils. Its eyes bored into his, and for a fleeting moment, he thought he saw something there—something more than rage, more than hunger. There was something deeper.

It was searching for something. Something within him. Something important.

The baby cried.

The sound cut through the chaos like a blade, piercing the veil of terror that had enveloped the village. The creature's head snapped toward the source of the sound. Marcus's wife was crouched near the entrance to their hut, clutching the child tightly to her chest, her eyes wide with fear.

The creature's grip on Marcus loosened slightly, its attention momentarily diverted.

He fell to the ground, gasping for air, his throat burning, his body trembling. He scrambled to his feet, his eyes fixed on the creature as it turned toward his family.

"No!" Marcus shouted, his voice hoarse and desperate, scrambling to his feet.

He moved between the creature and his wife, spreading his arms wide, his body a shield against the impending danger.

The creature stopped, its dark eyes flicking between Marcus and his family, its expression unreadable.

For a moment, the air was still, the only sound the soft whimpering of the baby.

The creature's gaze settled on Marcus, and something shifted within its eyes. Its body, previously tense and coiled, relaxed slightly, its head tilting as if it were trying to understand the emotions radiating from Marcus.

The raw, unfiltered love radiating from Marcus and his family seemed to catch the creature off guard, momentarily disrupting its predatory focus. It reached out, its clawed hand trembling slightly, and touched Marcus's face with hesitant curiosity.

The touch was cold, like death itself, but also strangely gentle, almost reverent. It was as if the creature was trying to connect, to understand the essence of humanity.

Then its fangs sank into Marcus's neck.

The pain was immediate and blinding, a searing fire spreading through Marcus's veins, consuming him from the inside out. He tried to cry out, but his voice failed him, choked off by the creature's relentless attack.

As the creature fed, its movements slowed, the initial frenzy subsiding. The chaotic energy that had defined its attack faded, replaced by something unexpected.

It wasn't rage; it wasn't hunger—it was sorrow. A deep, profound sadness seemed to emanate from the creature as it drank his blood, as if it were consuming not just his life force, but also his pain, fears, and regrets.

The creature pulled back, blood dripping from its mouth, its eyes reflecting the firelight in a way that made it seem as though it were crying. It stared at Marcus for a long moment, its expression unreadable, its eyes filled with a complex mixture of emotions.

Then it turned and disappeared into the shadows, vanishing as quickly and silently as it had appeared, leaving Marcus kneeling in the dirt, trembling, his lifeblood seeping into the earth.

He turned to look at his wife, to reassure her, to tell her everything would be alright. But she was slumped against the hut, her eyes wide and unseeing, her body limp and lifeless. The baby was silent in her arms, its cries extinguished forever.

Marcus's vision blurred, his heart pounding weakly in his chest as the fire in his veins grew stronger, consuming his remaining strength. His body convulsed, his legs giving way beneath him as he collapsed onto the ground, darkness overtaking him, silencing his thoughts and stealing his life.

The first thing Marcus felt was the cold.

It seeped into his skin, deeper than the air or the ground beneath him—it was a chill that came from within, as if his own body had turned against him.

His eyes opened slowly, and the world around him sharpened in ways he couldn't understand. The grass beneath him wasn't just green—it was alive with detail, every blade distinct. The cracks in the dirt were miniature canyons, intricate and deep.

He blinked, but the darkness didn't leave. His reflection in the nearby stream caught his attention: his eyes were black voids, swallowing the light around them. It was terrifying and unnatural, and he couldn't look away.

Instinctively, his hand shot to his neck, searching for the bite marks he remembered. But there was nothing—no wounds, no scars. His skin was smooth and unbroken, as if he'd never been bitten at all.

He pushed himself up, his limbs trembling. The village was silent, unnaturally so. Smoke still rose from the dying embers of the central fire, but there were no voices, no laughter.

Bodies littered the ground.

The faces of his neighbors stared back at him, their expressions frozen in fear and pain. Just a few feet away, his wife and child lay crumpled together. Amara's arms were wrapped protectively around Sion, her face turned toward Marcus as if she'd been looking for him with her last breath.

Marcus's chest tightened as he staggered forward, his legs unsteady.

"Amara?" he called, his voice hoarse. "Sion?"

He dropped to his knees beside them, his hands shaking as he reached for their lifeless forms. His fingers brushed Amara's cheek, and the coldness of her skin sent a jolt through him.

"No."

His voice cracked as he pulled them into his arms. They were so still, so quiet. The warmth that had always radiated from them, the love that had filled his world, was gone.

"I'm sorry," he whispered, his voice breaking. "I couldn't... I couldn't stop him."

A low sound came from behind him.

Marcus spun, his body reacting on instinct. His vision blurred for a moment, then sharpened, locking onto the source of the noise.

The creature.

It stood at the edge of the clearing, its pale form stark against the dark forest. Its movements were slow, almost hesitant, as it approached.

Marcus's fists clenched, anger and fear warring within him. "What are you?" he demanded, his voice raw.

The creature didn't answer. It tilted its head, its dark eyes scanning Marcus as if trying to decipher something.

"Why me?" Marcus continued, his voice rising. "Why did you spare me?"

The creature stepped closer, and Marcus scrambled back, his hands searching for anything he could use as a weapon. But the creature didn't attack.

It knelt in front of him, its movements unnaturally smooth, and pointed to Marcus's chest.

Marcus looked down, confused, and realized his heart was still beating—faster than it should have been, like a drum pounding in his ears.

The creature touched its own chest, then pointed to Marcus again.

It was trying to tell him something, but the meaning was lost in the weight of the moment.

"What do you want from me?" Marcus asked, his voice barely above a whisper.

The creature rose to its feet, its towering form casting a shadow over Marcus. It turned and began walking toward the forest, stopping once to glance back, as if beckoning him to follow.

Marcus hesitated. Every instinct screamed at him to run, to get as far away from this thing as possible. But there was nowhere to go.

The village was gone. His family was gone.

And something inside him had changed.

With a heavy heart, he pushed himself to his feet and followed the creature into the trees.

The forest was alive with sound.

Every rustle of leaves, every chirp of insects, every distant crack of a branch was deafening. Marcus stumbled after the creature, his senses overwhelmed.

The chill in his veins hadn't subsided, but it was joined by something else now—a hunger that gnawed at him, growing stronger with every step.

He tried to ignore it, to focus on the creature ahead of him. It moved effortlessly through the underbrush, its pale form a ghost among the shadows.

They reached a stream, its surface shimmering in the moonlight. The creature stopped, motioning for Marcus to kneel.

Marcus hesitated, but the hunger in his chest was becoming unbearable. He dropped to his knees beside the water, his reflection staring back at him.

The void-like blackness of his eyes startled him, drawing a gasp from his throat. His face was still his own, but it was wrong—inhuman.

The creature crouched beside him, cupping its hands in the water and bringing it to its lips. Then it pointed downstream.

Marcus followed its gaze and froze.

A deer stood at the edge of the water, its head bent as it drank. The creature gestured for Marcus to approach, then mimed biting into the animal's neck.

"You... want me to..." Marcus trailed off, horrified.

The creature nodded.

The hunger clawed at him, sharper now, almost painful. He staggered to his feet, his body moving without his permission. His heart raced, his breath quickening as he approached the deer.

The animal didn't notice him at first. It raised its head as he drew closer, its ears twitching.

Marcus's hands trembled as he reached for it.

His mind screamed in protest, but his body was no longer his own. He lunged, his teeth sinking into the deer's neck.

The taste of blood filled his mouth, warm and rich. The hunger ebbed, replaced by a rush of energy that coursed through him like wildfire.

When he pulled back, the deer collapsed, its body limp. Marcus stared at his bloodstained hands, his chest heaving.

His reflection in the stream caught his eye again.

The black void was gone, replaced by his own eyes—but brighter, clearer, almost unnaturally vivid. His heart beat so fast now that he couldn't feel or hear it, but the energy coursing through him was undeniable.

His complexion was no longer pale. His skin looked radiant and flawless, as if the imperfections of humanity had been stripped away.

He stared at himself, breath catching. "What am I?"

The creature stood, its dark eyes meeting his.

It didn't speak, but in that moment, Marcus understood.

He was no longer human.

The memory shifted, pulling me deeper into the fragmented tapestry of Marcus's life. It was as if I were a leaf caught in a relentless current, swept away from familiar shores and into the unknown depths of his past. The sensations were vivid, almost overwhelming, a cacophony of sights, sounds, and emotions that threatened to consume my own identity.

The forest was gone, replaced by a sprawling village nestled in a valley, cradled by rolling hills like a precious jewel. The sight was unlike anything I had ever seen, a tableau of impossible harmony woven into the fabric of reality. Humans and vampires moved together as if they shared one world, their interactions devoid of the animosity and fear I had come to expect. Farmers tilled fields under the watchful eyes of vampires, their presence not a threat, but a reassurance. They worked alongside them, their hands stained with the same earth, or stood guard at the edges of the village, protecting their shared haven from external da ngers.

This was harmony, a delicate balance struck between two species historically defined by conflict. It was a testament to the power of change, the possibility of coexistence in a world saturated with prejudice. I could almost taste the air, thick with the scent of freshly turned soil and the faint metallic tang of blood—a unique blend that spoke of compromise and shared sustenance.

I could feel Marcus's amazement, his awe at how far they'd come since his transformation. He radiated a sense of wonder, a palpable joy at witnessing the fruits of their collective labor. The Fallen, though still a mystery to Marcus, a cryptic figure shrouded in enigma, had shown them how to live with humans, how to sustain themselves on animal blood. Slowly, painstakingly, the surviving vampires built something more than mere survival—they built a community, a sanctuary where they could find solace and purpose.

The Fallen didn't speak much; his communication relied on gestures and demonstrations—a language that transcended words. His guidance had been pivotal, his presence a steady beacon in their uncertain journey. Marcus watched, with a mixture of fascination and trepidation, as the creature bit others one by one, sometimes succeeding and sometimes failing. Not all survived the transformation; their bodies rejected the poison of his chaotic emotions, and their systems were unable to adapt to the volatile influx of power.

But those who lived, like Marcus, thrived. They emerged from the ordeal stronger and more resilient, their senses heightened and minds sharpened. They carried the mark of the transformation, a visible reminder of their unique heritage, but they also bore the promise of a new beginning. They were reborn, forged in the crucible of pain and sacrifice, ready to embrace a future free from the shackles of their past.

The memory blurred, leaping forward through the corridors of time. The seasons changed in a heartbeat, and years collapsed into fleeting moments as Marcus's life unfolded before my eyes. I felt like a ghost, a silent observer adrift in the currents of his existence, unable to intervene or alter the course of events.

Marcus stood in the village square, surrounded by others like him—Moon Blooded, though they had yet to call themselves that. The name hung unspoken in the air, a future designation waiting to be claimed. Their clear, vivid eyes reflected the vibrant colors of the world around them, burning with an inner light that dispelled the shadows of their vampiric nature. Their skin, no longer pale and ashen, glowed with a healthy radiance, infused with the lifeblood they now shared with the animal kingdom. They were strong, capable, and yet indistinguishable from humans in appearance, blending seamlessly into the tapestry of the village.

The Fallen stood at the center of the group, a solitary figure amidst the burgeoning community, gesturing with his long, clawed hands. He was teaching again, imparting his wisdom through action rather than words, demonstrating the principles of survival and coexistence. His movements were fluid and graceful, a silent ballet of predator and prey.

Marcus watched, captivated, as the Fallen stalked a deer, his movements precise and deliberate, each step calculated to minimize detection. He caught the animal with ease, his speed and strength a testament to his enhanced abilities, feeding quickly before retreating into the shadows. The message was clear: vampires were predators, but their prey needn't be human. It was a lesson in restraint, a reminder of the responsibility that came with their power.

The memory shifted again, whisking me away to another point in Marcus's life. The village had grown, expanding beyond its original boundaries to accommodate the increasing population. New homes had been built, fields expanded, and the sense of community had deepened, solidifying into an unbreakable bond.

More villages had risen, each a testament to the delicate balance between vampires and humans. Marcus became a trusted figure among the growing vampire community, his wisdom and compassion earning him the respect of his peers. He helped maintain order, ensuring that the harmony the Fallen had instilled was not broken, mediating disputes and resolving conflicts with fairness and impartiality.

For decades, it worked. The villages flourished, becoming beacons of hope in a world still plagued by prejudice and fear. The Moon Blooded proved that coexistence was possible, that vampires and humans could live together in peace and harmony. They were living proof that the past didn't have to dictate the future.

But peace is fragile, a delicate ecosystem susceptible to disruption. It requires constant vigilance, unwavering commitment, and a willingness to compromise. And in a world as complex and volatile as theirs, such ideals were often challenged by the harsh realities of power and ambition.

The next memory hit me like a hammer, shattering the idyllic image of harmony and plunging me into the depths of despair. The sudden shift was jarring, the transition from serenity to carnage almost unbearable.

Marcus stood in the aftermath of a slaughter, the harmony shattered beyond repair. The bodies of vampires and humans alike littered the ground, their blood mingling in the dirt, creating a macabre tapestry of death. The air was thick with the stench of death and copper, a suffocating miasma that choked the senses and filled the lungs with dread.

I felt Marcus's horror and fury as he turned to face the attackers—a group of vampires with eyes like deep, dark rubies, burning with malevolent intensity. Their presence radiated an aura of power and cruelty, a chilling contrast to the peaceful existence of the Moon Blooded.

The Blooded.

The name echoed in my mind, a chilling premonition of the darkness that lay ahead. They were the antithesis of everything the Moon Blooded stood for—a force of destruction and corruption that threatened to consume the world.

"Why would you do this?" Marcus demanded, his voice raw with grief and disbelief. The words were barely audible above the moans of the wounded and the crackling flames of the burning buildings.

A tall figure stepped forward from the Blooded ranks, his expression cold and unfeeling, devoid of empathy or remorse. He wore the look of someone who had seen too much and cared too little, a jaded cynicism that permeated his entire being. I felt Marcus's rage spike at the sight of him, a surge of pure, unadulterated hatred.

The Overlord.

His title resonated with an ominous weight, a symbol of absolute power and ruthless ambition. He was the architect of this carnage, the mastermind behind the assault, and the embodiment of everything Marcus despised.

"You waste yourselves," the Overlord said, his voice smooth but laced with disdain, dripping with arrogance and superiority. "Drinking from animals when the humans you protect offer so much more. You could be powerful, unstoppable. And yet you choose weakness."

"This isn't weakness," Marcus spat, his voice filled with defiance despite the overwhelming odds. "It's balance. It's survival without destruction. You don't see that?"

The Overlord smirked, a cruel twist of his lips that revealed a hint of his predatory nature. "I see what I need to see. I see strength, and I see those unwilling to take it."

The Blooded stepped forward as one, their movements synchronized with unnatural precision, their shadows shifting unnaturally at their feet.

Marcus's eyes widened as the shadows took form, transforming into jagged spears that hovered in the air, crackling with dark energy.

The first attack came without warning, a blitzkrieg of violence and devastation. The Blooded moved with terrifying speed, their blood-enhanced strength and shadow-crafted weapons overwhelming the Moon Blooded defenders. I felt the weight of Marcus's fear and frustration, the crushing realization that they were outmatched and outgunned. The Moon Blooded were strong, but they lacked the Blooded's supernatural abilities and sheer destructive force.

It was a massacre, a brutal and merciless slaughter that left no one untouched. The village, once a symbol of hope and harmony, was reduced to a smoldering ruin, a testament to the destructive power of hatred and greed.

Marcus fought with everything he had, his body moving with the precision of years of training, his senses honed to a razor's edge. But for every Blooded he felled, three more took their place, their numbers seemingly endless.

In the chaos, Marcus caught sight of the Overlord. The Blooded leader stood at the center of the carnage, untouched, watching with a cruel smile. It was as if he reveled in the destruction, drawing strength from the suffering of others.

The memory fractured again, pulling me forward through the tumultuous currents of Marcus's life. The war between the two factions escalated, consuming everything in its path.

I felt the weight of his emotions more intensely—rage, fear, and something deeper, an ache that sat heavy in his chest like a stone. I could feel it all as though it were my own, yet I couldn't shake the sense that I didn't belong here.

Marcus knelt in the dirt, his arms bound behind him, and the Overlord loomed over him like a shadow.

"You disappoint me, Marcus," the Overlord said, his voice a cruel sneer. "All that strength, all that potential, and yet you cling to your so-called balance."

Marcus strained against his bindings, his breath ragged. "I'll never be like you."

The Overlord's laughter cut through the air, sharp and mocking. "You already are, whether you admit it or not. The difference is that I've embraced what I am. You, Marcus, are still pretending to be human."

I could feel Marcus's frustration and desperation bubbling beneath the surface.

Behind the Overlord, two Blooded vampires dragged a young man forward. The human's face was pale, his wide eyes brimming with terror. Blood trickled from a shallow cut on his neck, the scent so vivid in Marcus's senses that it made my own stomach twist with hunger I didn't understand.

"No," Marcus growled, his voice trembling. "I won't."

The Overlord crouched beside Marcus, his tone dropping to something low and menacing. "You don't have a choice."

I could feel the Overlord's grip on Marcus's head, forcing him closer to the terrified human. Marcus fought it, his resolve barely holding, but I could sense his control slipping. The smell of blood—sharp, metal-lic—was overwhelming.

"You'll thank me for this," the Overlord hissed, shoving Marcus forward.

Marcus's teeth sank into the human's neck.

The memory twisted sharply, sensations blurring into a tidal wave of emotions. I could feel the rush coursing through Marcus—the taste of blood, rich and intoxicating, igniting something primal and unstop-pable.

The human's cries grew faint, fading into silence as his body went limp. Marcus stumbled back, horror and power warring within him.

"No..."

His hands shook as he stared at the lifeless figure on the ground. I could sense his disgust at himself, his revulsion at what he'd done, but also the undeniable surge of strength that accompanied it.

"There it is," the Overlord said, clapping his hands in mock triumph. "That's the power you've been denying yourself."

Marcus looked down at his hands, his vision blurring. Shadows began to pool around him, coiling and twisting as if they were alive.

"What's happening to me?"

"The Blood Shadow," the Overlord replied, his tone dripping with satisfaction. "A gift for those who truly embrace their nature. You've unlocked it, Marcus. You're finally one of us."

The shadows solidified into a jagged spear in Marcus's hand. He stared at it, horrified, before letting it dissolve.

"This isn't me," he whispered. "This isn't who I am."

The Overlord stepped closer, his crimson eyes glinting with malice. "Oh, but it is. The sooner you accept it, the stronger you'll become. There's no turning back now."

The conflict between the Blooded and the Moon Blooded had escalated into full-scale war. Villages burned, their once-thriving communities reduced to ashes. The Blooded hunted humans and Moon Blooded vampires with ruthless efficiency, draining them dry and turning those they deemed worthy, swelling their ranks with new recruits.

Marcus had witnessed it all. He had watched the world the Fallen had helped them build crumble under the weight of greed and bloodlust. The dream of harmony lay shattered, replaced by the grim reality of endless war.

I could feel Marcus's guilt, his shame. He had survived where so many others hadn't. He had fought, but it hadn't been enough. The Moon Blooded were scattered, forced into hiding, while the Blooded grew stronger with every Moon Blooded they turned.

As the memories blurred and shifted, I felt my own sense of self slipping away, dissolving into the torrent of Marcus's experiences. The weight of his past was crushing, threatening to drown me in sorrow and regret, blurring the lines between his identity and my own.

This isn't my life. This isn't my pain.

But the memories wouldn't let go. They dragged me deeper, showing me more of Marcus's struggles, his defeats, his fleeting victories, binding me to his past with an unbreakable chain. His regrets became my regrets, his sorrows my sorrows.

My heart pounded in my chest. I could feel the pull of the memories, the way they tried to anchor me to Marcus's world, erasing my own identity and replacing it with his.

No. I can't stay here. I have to wake up.

I focused on the faint thread of light in the distance, the tether that connected me to my own life, to my own reality. It was dim, fragile, but it was there, a beacon of hope in the encroaching darkness.

I'm Tristan. I'm Tristan.

With every ounce of willpower, I pushed back against the tide of memories, fighting to reclaim my own identity. I could feel them trying to pull me under, to consume me entirely, but I refused to let them win.

The light grew brighter, closer, as I fought to break free.

The memory shifted, dragging me to a different moment in Marcus's life.

Marcus stood at the edge of a burning village, his shadow spear shimmering faintly in the firelight. The cries of the dying echoed around him, but his gaze was fixed on a single building—a crude wooden structure at the edge of the settlement.

The Blooded were slaughtering everyone they could find, offering survivors only two options: death or the chance to be turned. It was a grim, calculated effort to wipe out the Moon Blooded and any humans who aligned with them. But Marcus had his own rules.

He moved through the chaos with practiced precision, avoiding the homes and shelters where families huddled in fear. Instead, he slipped into the village's crude prison, a grim place of stone and iron, meant for those society had deemed unworthy of freedom.

The cells were filled with terrified humans, their faces pale as they realized what was happening outside. Some begged for their lives. Others simply stared, their eyes empty. Marcus ignored them all, his focus sharp and unyielding.

He stopped at the last cell, where a young woman sat in the shadows. Her hands were bound, her clothes torn, and her hair matted with dirt. She looked up as he approached, her eyes burning with defiance.

"Who are you?" she demanded, her voice hoarse.

Marcus didn't answer immediately. Instead, he unlocked the cell door, stepping inside with careful movements.

"They said I was a witch," she continued, watching him warily. "But I'm not. I didn't do anything wrong."

Marcus crouched beside her, his expression unreadable. "They don't care. Innocent or guilty doesn't matter to them."

She blinked, surprised by his response. "Then why are you here?"

"To give you a choice," Marcus said simply. "Stay here and die with the others, or come with me."

She hesitated, her gaze flicking to the chaos outside the prison. "Why would you help me?"

Marcus didn't answer. He extended a hand, waiting.

After a moment, she took it.

The memory blurred, skipping forward.

Marcus stood before the Overlord, his face an emotionless mask. The girl stood behind him, her hood pulled low over her face.

"You broke the law," the Overlord said, his tone cold. "No human is allowed to know about us. You know the punishment for this."

"I do," Marcus replied, his tone steady.

The Overlord's crimson eyes gleamed with something dark and calculating. "You've gone too far this time, Marcus. You've tested my patience for the last time. But I won't kill her. No, that would be too easy."

The Overlord stepped closer, a cruel smile on his lips. "I'll turn her myself. She'll be mine, as will every thought, every memory, every part of her."

Marcus's jaw tightened, but he said nothing.

The Overlord chuckled. "I'll make a grand occasion of it. The turning will be my gift to you—a reminder of where your loyalty should lie."

The memory fractured, leaping to the night of the turning.

The Blooded gathered in a clearing, the Overlord standing at the center with the girl kneeling before him. Marcus stood among the others, his expression unreadable.

The Overlord gestured for Marcus to step forward, a mocking smile on his lips. "Come, Marcus. Witness her rebirth."

But Marcus didn't move toward the Overlord. Instead, he advanced toward the girl. In one fluid motion, he grabbed her arm and pulled her to her feet.

The Overlord's smile vanished, replaced by a snarl. "What are you doing?"

Marcus didn't answer. He turned and ran, his shadow spear forming in his hand as he cut through the Blooded who tried to stop him.

The girl clung to him, her fear evident, but she didn't slow him down. Together, they disappeared into the forest, the sounds of pursuit fading behind them.

The memory shifted one last time, and I found myself in a small cabin deep in the woods. Moonlight filtered through the cracks in the walls, casting eerie shadows around us.

"They'll come for us," the girl whispered, her voice trembling with fear.

"Let them try," Marcus replied his tone firm, a calm protector amidst uncertainty. "I'll protect you. No matter what."

The scene began to blur around me, and I heard Marcus's voice echo faintly as the memory dissolved, pulling me under once again.

Suddenly, I was on the balcony.

I felt Marcus's presence before I saw him—a cold, unnerving stillness washed over me, setting my nerves on edge. Marcus stood there, calm and composed, as if he belonged here more than I did. The world around us faded, sharpened to a fine point. The sounds of the party inside felt muted, almost irrelevant. All I could focus on was Marcus, his piercing gaze locked onto me, my heartbeat thundering in my ears like a drum.

He moved with deliberate precision, each step silent and calculated. Before I could react, Marcus grabbed my hand, and in one swift motion, he sank his teeth into it.

A quick surge of pain ran through me from the bite, but it felt different—more intense as if a rush of warmth and power flowed into my veins.

Then, just as quickly, Marcus pulled back, slipping away into the shadows without a word.

The memory ended abruptly, and darkness enveloped me. I felt myself falling, the light around me dimming as I was pulled back into my own body.

My last thought before everything went black was simple but chilling.

Hold on, he actually bit me!

Chapter Seven

A World of New Sensations

Darkness faded, and my eyes fluttered open, reluctantly greeting the sterile white of the hospital lights. They were too bright, too sharp—an affront to my newly awakened senses. It felt like staring directly into the sun, an unbearable glare that forced a wince from me. I turned my head away, overwhelmed and struggling to process the unnerving clarity and precision that had taken hold.

The bed beneath me was unyielding and stiff, and the sheets, normally unnoticed, felt rough against my skin. Every fiber of the fabric was distinct, magnified as if under a powerful microscope. I could hear the soft hum of fluorescent lights overhead, a constant, unwavering drone. The faint clicking of heels echoed down the hallway, each step precise and measured. The rhythmic beeping of machines in nearby rooms created a symphony of sterile sounds, each pulse a reminder of this strange, clinical environment.

I sat up slowly and cautiously; my movements felt too smooth, too fluid—almost unnatural. There was a grace, a precision to my actions that felt foreign and unsettling. My hands trembled, but it wasn't from weakness. It was from the raw, untamed energy coursing through me, a potent force that made my body feel like a coiled spring, ready to run, leap, or fight at the slightest provocation.

Where am I? The question echoed in my mind, a desperate plea for context and understanding.

The last coherent memory was the balcony, the cold air brushing against my exposed skin, the city lights twinkling below. And then Marcus... Marcus biting me. He bit me?! A flood of warmth, an unexpected invasion. A rush of something I couldn't name—something potent and transformative. And then... darkness, a merciful oblivion that had stolen me away until this very moment.

My heart raced, pounding against my ribs, but the beat was strange—too fast, almost mechanical, like the hum of a finely tuned engine operating at peak performance. It lacked the organic rhythm I was accustomed to, replaced by something precise and almost artificial. I pressed a hand to my chest, trying to ground myself, to find some semblance of familiarity in this alien landscape, but it only heightened the surreal quality of my situation.

Swinging my legs over the side of the bed, I glanced around the room, taking in the details with unnerving clarity. It was a standard hospital setup—machines with blinking lights and cryptic readouts, monitors displaying vital signs in green and red, and the ever-present scent of antiseptic lingering in the air, a sterile perfume meant to mask the unpleasant realities of illness and injury. But something was off, a subtle dissonance that set my teeth on edge. There were no nurses bustling about, no doctors making their rounds, no concerned faces peering in to check on my well-being. No sign of anyone checking on me.

How long have I been here? The thought wormed its way into my consciousness, feeding my growing unease. Had it been hours? Days? The passage of time felt distorted, irrelevant in this strange, isolated bubble.

I caught a glimpse of myself in the reflective surface of the window, the glass offering a distorted image of the world outside. For a moment, I didn't recognize the person staring back at me. The face was familiar yet alien, subtly altered in a way I couldn't quite articulate. My skin was pale, almost luminous, radiating a faint glow that seemed to defy the dim lighting of the room. It had an ethereal quality that made it look both flawless and utterly alien, as though sculpted from porcelain. My eyes... they were black voids, bottomless pits that seemed to absorb all light. They were endless and unnatural, devoid of the warmth and humanity I was accustomed to seeing reflected there, yet somehow mesmerizing, drawing my gaze into their dark depths.

A surge of panic hit me, a cold wave that threatened to drown me in fear. I stumbled back, clutching the edge of the bed for support, my knuckles white against the metal frame. What is happening? What's wrong with me?

The hospital room suddenly felt too small, too suffocating. The walls seemed to be closing in, pressing against me in a silent, invisible threat. I had to get out. I didn't know where I was going; I didn't have a destination in mind, but staying here, confined within these sterile walls, wasn't an option. It felt like a prison, a confinement that loomed over me, ready to ensnare me in this unwelcome change.

Moving to the door, I hesitated, my hand hovering over the cold metal handle. I peered into the hallway, scanning the empty space for any sign of life. It was quiet—unnervingly so. The silence was thick and heavy, broken only by the faint hum of the fluorescent lights, their glow casting stark, unnatural shadows along the white walls. I took a cautious step forward, my bare feet silent against the cold tile.

With each step, my senses sharpened further, growing more acute and discerning. I was picking up every detail with unnerving clarity: the faint scent of cleaning chemicals clinging to the air, the hum of machinery hidden behind closed doors, the distant murmur of voices from another wing, carried on the ventilation system like ghostly whispers. It was disorienting, like someone had turned up the volume on the world and removed all the filters, rendering me vulnerable to a clamor of sensations.

I turned a corner and spotted a nurse at the far end of the hall, her back to me as she busied herself at a medication cart. My first instinct was to call out, to seek help and answers from a familiar face, but something stopped me—an inexplicable hesitation that held me back. I couldn't explain it, but I didn't want to be seen—not like this, not in this altered state.

Keeping to the shadows, I moved past her, my footsteps so silent it was as if I wasn't even touching the floor. There was a lightness to my movements, a grace that defied gravity. My body felt weightless, each movement effortless and precise, as though I were floating rather than walking. It should have been reassuring—this newfound agility and strength—but it wasn't. It only made me feel less... human, more like a phantom gliding through the halls.

The moment I stepped outside, the world hit me like a freight train, a sudden and overwhelming assault on my heightened senses.

The air was crisp and biting, carrying the sharp tang of exhaust fumes and the subtle sweetness of blooming flowers. The sounds of the city, normally filtered into a dull background hum, were overwhelming—a symphony of blaring horns, sirens, and shouting voices that threatened to shatter my eardrums. Every honk of a car horn, every snippet of conversation, every rustle of leaves in the nearby trees was amplified to an almost unbearable degree. My vision zoomed in and out, as though my eyes were a malfunctioning camera, struggling to find focus. I could see every crack in the pavement, every imperfection on the faces of the people passing by, every minute detail magnified to an absurd degree.

I stumbled down the sidewalk, my head spinning from the sensory overload. People were staring at me—some with concern etched on their faces, others with suspicion lurking in their eyes. I must have looked like a lunatic, wandering barefoot in ill-fitting hospital clothes, my movements erratic as I tried to navigate the chaotic landscape and block out the overwhelming sensations.

"Are you okay?" someone asked, their voice too loud, too sharp, cutting through the noise like a knife.

I flinched, my head snapping toward them, my body recoiling instinctively. It was a woman, her expression a mix of concern and wariness, her eyes narrowed as she assessed me. Her perfume hit me like a wave—floral and overpowering, a cloying scent that threatened to suffocate me.

"I'm fine," I muttered, my voice strained and raspy, barely audible above the din of the city. "Just... need to get home." The words felt hollow, inadequate to explain the turmoil raging within me.

She hesitated, her gaze lingering on me for a moment longer before she nodded, stepping aside to allow me passage. I didn't wait for a response. Relief washed over me as the moment passed; it was time to move on. I kept going, my focus narrowed to a single, desperate goal: putting one foot in front of the other, blocking out the chaos around me, and surviving this sensory onslaught.

By the time I reached my apartment building, I was trembling uncontrollably. My skin felt like it was on fire, every nerve ending alive and raw, screaming in protest against the constant barrage of stimuli. My hands shook as I fumbled with the key, struggling to insert it into the lock. Finally, after what felt like an eternity, I managed to unlock the door and stumble inside.

The relative silence of my apartment was a momentary relief, a brief respite from the chaos outside, but it didn't last long. The hum of the refrigerator, the creak of the floorboards beneath my weight, the distant sounds of the city filtering through the closed windows—it was all still there, amplified and inescapable, a constant reminder that I couldn't escape my own heightened senses.

I collapsed onto the couch, my breath coming in ragged gasps. My mind raced, a whirlwind of thoughts and emotions, trying to make sense of what was happening to me and the transformation I was undergoing.

My reflection in the window caught my eye again, and I turned to face it, drawn to the image like a moth to a flame. A morbid curiosity compelled me to confront the changes in my appearance. The black voids of my eyes stared back at me, unblinking, their depths concealing secrets I couldn't comprehend. My complexion, remaining pale and unblemished, appeared nearly otherworldly in the soft glow, emanating an unsettling allure.

"What am I?" I whispered, my voice barely audible, a fragile question carried on the silent air.

The hunger gnawed at me, a deep, insistent ache that I couldn't ignore. It wasn't just physical hunger, the familiar pangs of an empty stomach. It was something deeper, primal, and all-consuming. It was a hunger for something I couldn't name, something that resonated within the very core of my being. I clenched my fists, trying to push it down, to suppress the rising tide of need, but it felt like trying to hold back a tidal wave with bare hands.

My mind drifted to Marcus, to the moment he bit me—the searing pain and the strange, exhilarating pleasure that had accompanied it. The warmth, the rush of power—it all came flooding back, bringing with it a thousand unanswered questions. Why had he done this to me? What did he want? What was his purpose?

I didn't have any answers, only the faint, sinking realization that my life would never be the same. The bite had changed me, altered me in ways I couldn't yet fully understand.

The first few hours in my apartment passed in a haze of confusion and burgeoning dread. I sat on the edge of the couch, the worn fabric digging slightly into the back of my legs, staring at my hands as if they belonged to someone else entirely. I rotated them, flexing my fingers, watching the tendons move beneath the newly pale skin. Every minute detail was now sharply in focus. I tried to understand what had happened, what unholy transformation had been forced upon me.

My skin was pale and flawless, as if every imperfection, blemish, and scar that told a story had been erased, leaving behind a blank canvas devoid of history. But it wasn't human anymore. It didn't feel like my own, a foreign substance grafted onto my bones.

The sounds of the city, once a familiar and comforting background hum, now clawed at my sanity. Horns blared with aggressive insistence, people shouted snippets of conversations that felt impossibly loud and clear, and a distant siren wailed its mournful song—each note a fresh wave of panic. Every noise was sharp and intrusive, like shards of glass slicing through my thoughts, shattering any semblance of calm.

I pressed my hands over my ears, digging my fingers into the cartilage, but it barely dulled the noise. The sounds seemed to penetrate my skull, vibrating within my very being. It was as if my ears had become ultra-sensitive, amplified to an unbearable degree.

I stood, pacing the cramped room, the limited space exacerbating my growing agitation as the sensory overload threatened to crush me, to suffocate me beneath the weight of amplified reality.

Every detail of my surroundings seemed magnified beyond recognition: the uneven texture of the walls, the subtle imperfections in the plaster that I had never noticed before, the faint smell of detergent from my freshly laundered clothes—an aroma that now assaulted my nostrils with an almost chemical intensity. The incessant hum of electricity running through the appliances resonated deep within my bones,

a low-frequency drone that felt overwhelming.

The world had gone from muted to deafening, from blurry to hyper-defined, and I was powerless to turn it down, trapped in a nightmare of heightened awareness.

Then there was the hunger, the insidious emptiness gnawing at my insides. It had started as a dull ache in the pit of my stomach, a subtle discomfort I initially dismissed, but it was growing with alarming speed. It wasn't the kind of hunger I'd felt before—no familiar pang for a burger or a slice of pizza. It wasn't for food or drink, for anything tangible or recognizable. It was something deeper, more primal, a need resonating within my very core. It felt ancient, instinctive, something I couldn't name yet knew I had to satiate.

I ran my tongue over my teeth, a nervous habit from my former life, and froze, my blood turning to ice in my veins. They felt... different. Sharper. More defined. Less human. I hurried to the bathroom, flipping on the light and leaning over the sink to get a closer look in the cracked and smudged mirror.

My black void-like eyes stared back at me, alien and unsettling in their unnatural darkness, and my heart lurched at the sight, a wave of nausea rising in my throat. I looked like a stranger, a grotesque parody of the man I once was.

This isn't me. This can't be me. This has to be a dream, a nightmare from which I will soon awaken. The world can't be this twisted.

My hands gripped the cold porcelain edges of the sink as I leaned in closer, my breath fogging the glass as I opened my mouth slightly. My canines were longer, faintly pointed, almost unnoticeable unless you looked carefully, unless you knew what to look for. But I felt them—sharp and alien against my tongue, a constant reminder of the monstrous transformation I was undergoing. They were subtle, yes, but undeniably present. They were the teeth of a predator—a being I never dreamed I might become.

I stumbled back, shaking my head, desperate to deny the evidence of my own eyes, to cling to the fading memory of my former self. This couldn't be real.

"Marcus, what the hell did you do to me?" I whispered, my voice trembling, a raw and broken sound echoing in the small, tiled room, foreign to my own ears. The words hung in the air, heavy with fear and anger.

I tried to push him from my mind, to block out the memories threatening to overwhelm me, to focus on something—anything—else, a distraction, a lifeline in this sea of madness. But it was impossible. Memories of the balcony flooded back, unbidden and unwelcome.

His cold presence, the unnatural stillness of his movements, the way he appeared out of nowhere—a phantom emerging from the shadows. The warmth that spread through me when he bit my hand felt like a violation. It had felt like sunlight, something pure and comforting, a strange and inexplicable sense of euphoria. But now it felt like a curse, a dark and insidious poison that had corrupted my very being.

I sank onto the worn couch again, burying my face in my hands, trying to shut out the world, to escape the horrifying reality of my situation. The hunger gnawed at me with increasing intensity, a relentless and unforgiving tormentor. I clenched my jaw, trying to ignore it, to suppress the growing urge that threatened to consume me. But the more I fought it, the stronger it became, until it was all I could think about. My throat was dry, burning like I hadn't had a drop of water in days.

I stagger to the kitchen, the hunger clawing at me like a wild animal trapped inside my ribcage. The refrigerator door opens with a soft vacuum sound, the light inside blinding my sensitive eyes. The contents look like they always have—leftover Chinese takeout, half a rotisserie chicken, some wilting vegetables, and various condiments—but something feels profoundly wrong.

My hands shake as I grab the chicken container, not bothering with a plate. I tear into the meat with my fingers, stuffing it into my mouth with desperate, animalistic movements. The flavor explodes across my tongue with an intensity I've never experienced—every subtle note of herbs and spices magnified tenfold, the texture of the meat impossibly detailed against my palate.

"Jesus," I whisper, momentarily stunned by the sensory overload.

But even as I swallow, the gnawing emptiness persists. I reach for the Chinese food next, shoveling cold lo mein into my mouth. Again, the flavors are overwhelming, almost psychedelic in their intensity, but the hunger remains untouched, unaffected by what should be satisfying it.

I grab a carton of orange juice, tearing it open and drinking directly from the container, juice dribbling down my chin. The sweetness is almost painful, like liquid sunshine burning my throat, but it does nothing to quench my thirst.

Frantically, I pull out more food—cheese, deli meat, a container of hummus, an apple—consuming each with increasing desperation. Each bite is a symphony of flavor, yet each swallow is followed by the same hollow emptiness. It's like pouring water into a bottomless pit.

"What the hell is happening to me?" I slam the refrigerator door shut, sliding down against it until I'm sitting on the kitchen floor, surrounded by empty containers and discarded food.

The hunger remains, persistent and growing. My stomach feels physically full, stretched and uncomfortable from the amount I've consumed, but the deeper hunger—the one that seems to emanate from every cell in my body—remains unsatisfied, untouched by ordinary sustenance.

I run my tongue over my sharpened teeth, a terrible realization beginning to form in the back of my mind.

A knock at the door jolted me from my thoughts, sending a jolt of adrenaline through my veins.

My head snapped toward the sound, my senses suddenly hyper-focused, amplified to an almost unbearable degree. I could hear the faint shuffle of feet outside, the subtle creaks of the floorboards as someone shifted their weight, and the steady rhythm of a heartbeat—a palpable pulse of life that both fascinated and terrified me. The scent of something faintly metallic drifted under the door, a subtle aroma that sent a wave of nausea washing over me, and I realized with horror what it was.

Blood.

I stood frozen, my body tense, every muscle coiled tight like a spring ready to unleash, my mind racing to anticipate any potential threat. Another knock echoed through the apartment, louder this time, more insistent, demanding attention.

"Tristan? It's Jess."

Her voice, familiar and comforting, cut through the haze in my mind, a beacon of normalcy in this sea of madness. Jessica. My friend, my confidante, my anchor in the chaos of work and life. I took a shaky step toward the door, my hands trembling, unsure of what to do or say.

"Tris, are you okay?" Jess asked, her tone laced with concern, genuine worry tugging at my heart.

I hesitated, my mind racing as I weighed the options and calculated the risks. She couldn't see me like this—not with my black eyes, my pale skin, and my unsteady movements. Not with the monster lurking just beneath the surface. But I couldn't ignore her either; I had to protect her from this, from the darkness that now clung to me.

"I'm fine," I called out, my voice raspier than I intended. It was a strained sound that betrayed my inner turmoil.

"You don't sound fine," she replied sharply, suspicion lacing her tone. "I was really worried when I came to check on you, and the hospital had no clue where you were. Benji and I were panicking! You haven't been to work since you passed out at your ex's party. Ash said you collapsed because of the news that she was getting married, but dude, that doesn't add up. It's been seven days!"

Panic rose within me, and I snapped. "No!" The word came out harsher than I intended, a sharp bark that echoed in the small apartment. I winced at my own forcefulness, the animalistic quality of my voice startling me. I forced myself to take a deep breath, trying to steady my voice, regain control of my emotions. "I'm just... not feeling well. I needed a break."

"Tris, this doesn't sound like just needing a break! What happened? Did something go wrong when you were in the hospital?" Her worry was palpable, spilling through her words.

I racked my brains for something to say. "It wasn't a big deal. I just got overwhelmed after everything that happened at the party. The doctors said I needed some time to recuperate, and I thought it would be best to do that in peace, you know?"

"So you just... went home?" she pressed, still not fully convinced. "Tris, you could have at least texted me!"

"I didn't think it was necessary," I lied, forcing a laugh that fell flat. "I just wanted some time to be alone and clear my head. You know how I get."

"I know you!" she said, her tone softening as if she was trying to reassure me. "You don't just disappear into thin air for days. If I didn't care, I wouldn't be here knocking on your door. I was worried you'd gotten lost or worse!"

"I'm fine, really." I tried to sound convincing, hoping she'd buy it. "Being alone helps me think, Jessica. Believe me, it's what I need right now. Just... trust me."

Her silence lingered in the air again, and I could hear her heartbeat quicken, the faint shuffle of her feet as she shifted uncomfortably. After what felt like an eternity, I heard her exhale slowly, trying to process my words.

"Okay," she said finally, though her voice was still tinged with disappointment. "But if you need anything at all, call me. Please. You know I'm here for you, right?"

"Yeah, I know," I assured, my heart aching at the thought of disappointing her. "I appreciate it, really. I promise I'll reach out once I'm feeling a bit more... myself. I just need some time, alright?"

"Alright," she said, her tone softening again, almost resigned. "I just want to make sure you're safe. That's all."

"I'll be fine, Jess. You don't have to worry about me," I said, my conviction wavering.

"Okay. I really hope so." There was a pause, her uncertainty hanging in the air. "Just... take care of yourself, alright? I'm counting on you to check in."

"I will," I promised, swallowing hard. "Thanks for checking on me. It means a lot, really."

After a moment, I heard her footsteps retreating down the hall. I waited until the sound faded into the background noise of the city before I exhaled, the tension leaving my body in a rush. But I couldn't shake the heaviness in my chest. My hands were shaking, and my jaw was clenched tightly, a physical manifestation of the internal struggle raging within me.

The hunger was unbearable now, a searing pain consuming my every thought. I could feel it clawing at my insides, a primal urge that refused to be ignored, a ravenous beast demanding to be fed. My body trembled uncontrollably, my vision swimming and threatening to black out at any moment. I pressed my palms to my temples, trying to keep myself together, to maintain some semblance of control, but it was no use. The darkness was closing in.

The faint scent of blood lingered in the air, a cruel reminder of what I had become, of the monster I was now destined to be. I didn't understand it and didn't want to accept it, but the truth was undeniable, staring me in the face, mocking my denial. I was... different. Changed. Transformed into something I didn't understand—something I feared.

I curled up on the couch, my knees drawn to my chest in a fetal position, and closed my eyes, trying to shut out the horrifying reality of my existence. I didn't want to think about Marcus or the hunger or the terrifying clarity of my senses. I just wanted to disappear, to cease to exist, to go back to the way things were before—a life that now seemed like a distant and unattainable dream.

But there was no going back. The door had been slammed shut. The past was over, and my new and terrifying existence had begun.

The hours dragged on with excruciating slowness, each minute an eternity of torment as the hunger gnawed at me until I thought I would lose my mind. My body felt like it was on fire, every nerve ending alive and raw, screaming out in protest. I couldn't sit still, couldn't think straight, couldn't find any respite from the relentless assault on my senses.

I paced the apartment, my movements restless and erratic, like a caged animal desperate to escape its confinement. The walls felt like they were closing in, the ceiling pressing down on me, the limited space exacerbating my growing panic. The sounds of the city outside were too loud, too invasive, too overwhelming. I pressed my hands over my ears, digging my fingers into the cartilage until it hurt, but it didn't help. The noise was inside me now, a constant and inescapable torment.

And then, something inside me snapped. The last vestiges of my self-control crumbled, leaving me vulnerable to the darkness that now consumed me.

I stumbled to the window, my legs weak and unsteady, throwing it open and leaning out into the cool night air, gasping for breath as if I had been drowning. The city stretched out before me, vibrant and alive, a glittering tapestry of light and sound, but it was too much. The lights, the sounds, the smells—it was all too much, an overwhelming sensory assault threatening to shatter my sanity.

I gripped the windowsill, my knuckles white, my fingers digging into the wood, and closed my eyes, trying to block out the chaos, to find some semblance of peace. I needed to focus, to ground myself, to regain control, but it felt impossible. My mind was racing, my thoughts tumbling over each other in a chaotic spiral—a maelstrom of fear and confusion.

As the night wore on, exhaustion began to creep in, my body rebelling against the unnatural demands placed upon it. My body was strong, unyielding, imbued with a newfound power, but my mind was fraying at the edges, unraveling under the strain. I sank onto the floor, my back against the cold, hard wall, and buried my face in my hands, giving in to the despair that threatened to consume me.

"What am I?" I whispered, the question a desperate plea lost in the vastness of the night.

The hunger answered me—a relentless force that refused to be silenced. It was all-consuming, overwhelming, and terrifying.

And yet, deep down, I knew that this was only the beginning.

The next morning, I woke to the relentless blaring of my alarm. The sound pierced through my skull, amplified to an unbearable level. It wasn't just the volume; it was the quality of the sound—a grating, digital shriek that vibrated deep within my bones. I slapped the off button and sat up, clutching my head as a dull ache throbbed in my chest. My body felt like a stranger's, every movement too smooth, too controlled. It was as if I were a puppet and some unseen force was guiding my limbs with unnerving precision.

Just get through the day, I told myself, but even as I thought it, I wasn't sure how I would. The words felt hollow—a desperate mantra whispered into the void. Getting through the day now felt like scaling a sheer cliff face, each moment a precarious handhold threatening to crumble beneath my weight.

I stumbled to the bathroom, avoiding the mirror until I couldn't anymore. When I finally looked up, the face staring back wasn't mine. Not entirely. The structure was familiar—same jawline, same nose—but the eyes... those weren't mine. Where warm hazel had once been, now black voids stared back, like windows into an endless abyss. No whites, no iris, just pure darkness that seemed to swallow light.

"Shit," I whispered, leaning closer to examine them. "How am I supposed to explain this?"

I couldn't stay locked in my apartment forever. Eventually, I'd need supplies, food—though what kind, I wasn't sure anymore. But I couldn't walk around with these eyes. People would stare, ask questions, maybe even call authorities. I needed a disguise.

Contacts. The solution hit me suddenly. There was a pharmacy three blocks from my apartment that sold colored contacts. If I could get there without drawing attention, I might find something close to my original hazel color.

I pulled a hoodie over my head, tugging it low to shadow my face, and grabbed sunglasses from my nightstand. The thought of stepping outside terrified me—too many people, too many heartbeats, too much temptation—but I had no choice.

"Just walk in, grab the contacts, pay, and leave," I muttered, rehearsing the simple steps as if they were a complex mission. "Don't look at anyone. Don't talk to anyone. Just get what you need and get out."

My hand trembled on the doorknob. Beyond this door was a world I no longer belonged to, filled with people who would fear me if they knew what I had become. A world where I was now the monster lurking in the shadows.

I took a deep breath—a useless human habit that provided no comfort to my still lungs—and opened the door.

I stepped outside, the brightness of the day assaulting my senses. Every sound amplified—cars honking three blocks away, conversations from apartment windows, even the rustle of leaves in the breeze. The scent of humanity hung thick in the air, a mixture of perfumes, sweat, and beneath it all, the tantalizing iron-rich smell of blood pumping through veins.

My legs moved mechanically, carrying me forward while my mind screamed to retreat back into isolation. The pharmacy was just around the corner, barely a minute's walk, but it felt like crossing a desert. I kept my head down, sunglasses firmly in place, hood pulled low.

The electronic bell chimed as I entered the store, the sound piercing through my skull. I flinched visibly, drawing the attention of the cashier—a middle-aged man with thinning hair and suspicious eyes.

I wandered the aisles aimlessly, pretending to browse while feeling his gaze follow me. My movements were too stiff, too calculated. I could hear his heartbeat quicken, smell the subtle change in his chemistry as adrenaline entered his bloodstream. He thought I was going to steal something.

The cashier's footsteps approached, heavy and deliberate. "Can I help you find something?" His tone was clipped, professional but wary.

"Contacts," I managed to say, my voice rougher than I intended. "Colored contacts. Where do you keep them?"

His suspicion didn't fully dissipate, but he gestured toward the back corner. "Cosmetics section, bottom shelf."

I nodded my thanks and moved quickly to the indicated area, feeling his eyes on my back. The selection was limited, but I found a package labeled

"Hazel Dream" that looked close enough to my original eye color. The irony of the name wasn't lost on me.

At the counter, I kept my gaze down while he rang up my purchase. His pulse was right there, throbbing visibly in his neck. I swallowed hard and focused on counting out the exact change.

"Have a good day," he said as I grabbed the small bag, clearly relieved to see me leaving.

Outside, I ducked into an alley, tore open the package with trembling fingers, and carefully inserted the contacts. They felt foreign, uncomfortable against my new eyes, but when I checked my reflection in a store window, a semblance of my old self stared back.

The station wasn't far. I moved toward it, joining the stream of commuters, a wolf in sheep's clothing.

CHAPTER EIGHT

FRACTURED REFLECTIONS

The ride to work was a haze of overwhelming sensations. The screech of the subway train against the tracks drilled into my skull, and the jumble of voices around me felt directed straight into my ears. It wasn't merely noise; it was a symphony of separate sounds, each one unique and clamoring for recognition. The rhythmic thump of a bass in someone's headphones, the sharp ping of a text message, the murmur of a conversation about last night's game—all of it slammed into me with brutal intensity.

Every smell—the faint perfume of the woman to my left, a floral scent layered with a synthetic undertone; the tang of sweat from the man clutching the pole, a musky, almost animalistic odor; the metallic scent of the train itself, a cold, sterile aroma overlaid with the faint, greasy smell of machinery—swirled together, making my stomach churn. It was a sensory overload, a tidal wave of stimuli threatening to drown me.

I kept my head down, gripping the metal pole until my knuckles turned white. The cold steel was the only anchor in a sea of chaos, a tangible reminder of reality. No one paid me any mind—just another face in the sea of commuters. Eyes glazed over, lost in their own worlds, oblivious to the internal turmoil raging within me. But the anonymity didn't comfort me; instead, it amplified my isolation. I felt like an alien observer, trapped within a human guise, forever separated from the ordinary lives unfolding around me.

The office was another story. The anonymity I clung to on the subway evaporated the moment I stepped inside.

As soon as I walked through the glass doors, a ripple of tension spread through the room. It was subtle, almost imperceptible, but I felt it like a physical blow. Heads turned, conversations faltered, and whispers began to fill the space. The air crackled with unspoken curiosity and cautious apprehension. It was as if I had walked into a room filled with fragile glass, each step threatening to shatter the delicate peace.

"Tristan!" Benji's voice rang out, breaking the awkward silence. He was the first to approach, weaving through the rows of desks with a wide grin. His energy was like a burst of sunlight, a welcome distraction from the oppressive atmosphere. "Man, it's good to see you back! Thought you were out for the count."

I forced a smile, grateful for his familiar energy. It was a weak smile, a pale imitation of my usual jovial expression, but I hoped it was enough to mask the turmoil within. "Yeah. Just needed some rest."

Benji's grin faltered for a moment as he studied me. His eyes, usually filled with playful mischief, were now narrowed with concern. "You, uh... you look good. Like, really good. Like you've been photoshopped or something. Did you finally take my skincare advice?"

I chuckled weakly. The sound felt foreign, forced. "Something like that."

Before I could say more, Jessica appeared, her arms crossed and her expression filled with concern. Her presence was a balm to my frayed nerves, a reminder of genuine care in a world that suddenly felt alien. "Tristan, what are you doing here? You should be resting."

"I'm fine," I said quickly, brushing off her worry. My voice sounded too sharp, too insistent. "Really. I needed to get back to work."

She didn't look convinced, her eyes narrowing as she studied my face. She was searching for something, some sign of weakness or vulnerability that I was desperately trying to conceal. "If you say so. But seriously, take it easy. We were all worried about you."

Not everyone shared their concern. Some were driven by curiosity, others by something darker.

"Well, well," Ash said as she sauntered by, her tone dripping with sarcasm. Her presence was a jarring note in the already discordant symphony of the office, a reminder of the petty rivalries and unspoken resentments that simmered beneath the surface. "Look who decided to grace us with his presence. Didn't think we'd see you upright again."

"Good to see you too, Ash," I replied, keeping my tone neutral. I carefully controlled every syllable, ensuring that no hint of my inner turmoil betrayed my composure.

She stopped, giving me a once-over with a smirk. Her eyes lingered on me, dissecting my appearance with predatory interest. "You do look... different. New haircut? Or is it that whole 'near-death experience' glow?"

Benji scoffed. "Don't you ever get tired of being a pain, Ash?"

Ash shrugged, her smirk widening. Her eyes glittered with amusement, clearly reveling in the discomfort she caused. "Just calling it like I see it." She shot me one last glance before walking off, her high heels clicking a sharp, staccato rhythm against the polished floor.

Benji shook his head, muttering under his breath, "She's impossible."

Jessica sighed. "Don't let her get to you, Tristan. She's probably just mad because you didn't take her advice on the Kintech project."

I nodded, though my focus was already slipping. The sounds of the office surrounded me—keyboards clicking, papers shuffling, hushed voices murmuring—but I couldn't tune them out. It was a relentless barrage of noise, each sound amplified to an unbearable degree. Everything felt too loud, too sharp. The fluorescent lights hummed with an irritating buzz, the air conditioning unit rattled and wheezed, and the distant drone of traffic filtered through the closed windows.

At my desk, I tried to lose myself in the routine of work. The spreadsheets on my screen should have been mind-numbing, a comforting shield against the overwhelming stimuli, but the words and numbers seemed to leap out at me, too clear, too vivid. Each line of text was etched in sharp detail, each number pulsated with an almost tangible energy. My senses were in overdrive, picking up every detail, every sound, every scent. It was like staring into the sun, the intensity almost blinding.

And then it hit me—the smell.

Sharp and metallic, like copper. It was faint at first, a subtle undertone to the usual office smells, but it grew quickly, overwhelming everything else. My head snapped up, my eyes scanning the room until they locked on Daniel by the coffee machine. He was holding his hand, a small bandage covering his palm. A tiny, almost invisible speck of red stained the white gauze.

The scent of blood filled my nostrils, intoxicating and overwhelming. It was a primal, almost irresistible aroma, like the finest perfume and the most addictive drug combined. My throat burned, my muscles tensed, and I gripped the edge of my desk until my knuckles turned white. The desire to taste it, to experience its essence, was a visceral, overwhelming urge. It was a hunger unlike anything I had ever known, a hunger that threatened to consume me.

"Tristan?" Jessica's voice snapped me back to reality. The sound was like a splash of cold water, momentarily shocking me out of my trance. She stood a few feet away, her brow furrowed in concern. Her eyes were filled with a mixture of worry and apprehension. "Are you okay?"

"I... I need some air," I muttered, standing abruptly. My voice sounded too smooth, too controlled, like it didn't belong to me. It was the voice of a predator, calm and calculating, masking the inner beast that clawed at its cage.

I didn't wait for a response. Grabbing my phone and bag, I headed for the exit, ignoring the worried glances that followed me. I could feel their eyes on my back, analyzing my every move, searching for an explanation for my sudden departure.

The cold air outside hit me like a wave, but it did little to calm the storm inside me. It was a temporary reprieve, a brief moment of clarity before the hunger reasserted itself. I leaned against the building, pressing my palms into the rough brick as I tried to steady my breathing. The texture of the brick was abrasive against my skin, a grounding sensation that helped me cling to reality.

"What is happening to me?" I whispered, my voice trembling. It was a plea for answers, a desperate cry for help in the face of an unknown force.

The hunger gnawed at me, relentless and primal. It wasn't just physical—it was a pull, an instinct I didn't understand but couldn't ignore. It was a siren song, luring me toward the edge of a precipice.

I closed my eyes, trying to shove it down, to bury it deep where it couldn't consume me. But it was no use. The hunger was part of me now, woven into the very fabric of my being, and no matter how much I fought it, it wasn't going away. It was a parasite, feeding on my willpower, slowly eroding my humanity.

I didn't know how long I stood outside the office, trying to regain some semblance of control. The sounds of the city buzzed around me—honking horns, chattering pedestrians, the rumble of a distant construction site—but it all merged into a chaotic symphony of sound that caused my head to ache. The usual symphony of urban life, once a comforting backdrop, now crashed against my newly heightened senses like a rogue wave against a fragile shore.

Each individual sound, amplified and distorted, fought for dominance, creating a disorienting and overwhelming wave of sensory input. The rhythmic pulse of a distant jackhammer was now a brutal, insistent hammering in my skull, and the cheerful banter of passersby became a jarring, intrusive symphony. It was as if the volume of the world had been cranked up to an unbearable level, pushing me to the brink of sensory overload.

You can do this, I told myself, gripping the edge of the building for support. But my hands trembled, and the cool brick beneath my fingers felt like sandpaper, every grain and groove scraping against my skin. The tactile world, once a source of comfort and familiarity, had become abrasive and unsettling.

The smooth, weathered surface of the brick, ordinarily unremarkable, now assaulted my fingertips with a thousand tiny, irritating sensations. Each minute imperfection, each subtle variation in texture, screamed for attention, creating a relentless barrage of tactile information that my overwhelmed mind struggled to process. The very act of holding onto the building, of seeking stability and grounding, became an exercise in discomfort and heightened awareness.

I couldn't go back inside. Not like this. The concerned glances, the well-meaning questions, the suffocating atmosphere of normality—I couldn't face any of it. The risk of exposing what I had become, of losing control and giving in to the gnawing hunger, was too great.

The office, once a sanctuary of routine and purpose, now felt like a potential trap, a place where my carefully constructed facade could crumble at any moment. The thought of interacting with my colleagues, of forcing a smile and engaging in meaningless small talk, filled me with a profound sense of dread. It was as if an invisible barrier had sprung up between me and the rest of humanity, separating me from the familiar comfort of ordinary life.

Without a clear plan, I started walking, driven by an instinctive need to escape, to outrun the physical and emotional turmoil roiling within me. The act of walking, of putting one foot in front of the other, offered a small measure of control in a world that had suddenly spun out of control. Each step was a deliberate act of defiance, a refusal to succumb to the overwhelming forces that threatened to consume me. I was adrift in a sea of uncertainty, but the simple act of forward motion provided a temporary sense of direction, of purpose, however illusory it might be.

The streets were crowded, the air thick with the mingling scents of exhaust fumes, hot pretzels, and perfume. My heightened senses latched onto everything, my brain struggling to process the overload of information. Colors seemed brighter, sounds sharper, and the faintest scents teased my nose like an invasive whisper. The visual landscape of the city had transformed into a hyper-realistic tapestry of vibrant hues and stark contrasts.

Neon signs blazed with an almost painful intensity, the metallic sheen of passing cars shimmered with an unnatural brilliance, and even the drab facades of the buildings seemed to pulse with a hidden energy. My ears, attuned to the subtlest of vibrations, picked up the faintest sounds—the rustle of leaves in distant trees, the distant wail of a siren, the hushed conversations of strangers blocks away. And the smells!

The fragrant scent of roasted nuts from a street vendor, the sharp tang of industrial cleaner wafting from a nearby alley, the cloying sweetness of cheap perfume clinging to passersby—all these blended into a heady, intoxicating cocktail that threatened to overwhelm my senses.

I didn't have a destination in mind. I just needed to move, to escape the oppressive walls of the office and the concerned eyes of my coworkers. Escape was key, a desperate need to put distance between myself and the life I'd once known. Perhaps time alone would give me some clarity.

But the hunger followed me. An ever-present, nagging reminder of my new reality, a constant companion that gnawed at my insides and clouded my thoughts. It was a primal urge, a desperate craving that transcended mere physical need. It was a dark, insistent voice that whispered promises of power and pleasure while simultaneously threatening to strip me of my humanity.

Every step felt heavier, my muscles tense and coiled like a spring. My throat burned, dry and raw, as if I hadn't had a sip of water in days. But it wasn't water I needed. The physical discomfort was merely a symptom of a deeper, more profound deprivation. My body was a prison, its needs a constant reminder of my altered state. The tension in my muscles, the dryness of my throat, the ache in my bones—all were manifestations of the insatiable hunger that consumed me.

I passed a coffee shop, and the smell of freshly baked pastries mixed with the bitter tang of espresso hit me like a punch. My stomach twisted, but the hunger gnawing at me wasn't for food. The aroma, once a comforting trigger of happy memories, now felt like a cruel taunt, a reminder of the simple pleasures I could no longer fully enjoy. The rich, sugary scent of the pastries and the robust bitterness of the espresso were mere window dressing, pale imitations of the true sustenance I craved.

When I stopped at a crosswalk, I noticed a man standing beside me, typing on his phone, oblivious to the world around him. A faint red line ran across his knuckle—a paper cut, perhaps—and a single drop of blood welled up at its edge. The man's focus was solely on the screen, a tiny world displayed in his hands, while he stood unaware on the cusp of something darker.

The scent was faint, almost imperceptible, but it might as well have been a shout in my ears. My vision tunneled, narrowing on the tiny bead of crimson, and my breathing hitched. The world around me faded into a muted blur, all sound and color dissolving into a gray fog. My focus became absolute, my attention consumed by the single drop of blood that pulsed with an irresistible allure. It was as if my entire being had been compressed into a single point, a laser beam of pure, unadulterated hunger.

Walk away. Just walk away. The mantra repeated in my head, a desperate attempt to regain control. It was a battle against instinct, a war waged within the confines of my own mind. Sanity versus desire, light against dark. The line was thin.

The light changed, and the man stepped into the street, disappearing into the crowd. I stumbled forward, my head swimming as I fought to keep myself in check. His departure was a momentary reprieve from the overwhelming temptation, but the hunger lingered, a coiled serpent waiting to strike. The effort to control it left me drained and disoriented, my body trembling with suppressed desire.

Somehow, I ended up at Bryant Park. The small patch of green amidst the concrete jungle should have been calming, but even here, the world felt overwhelming. A supposed sanctuary of peace had become a reminder of what I had lost.

I found a bench near the edge of the park and collapsed onto it, my head in my hands. The cool metal offered a stark contrast to the burning in my blood. The world spun.

"What's happening to me?" I whispered, the question echoing in my mind. A desperate plea for understanding, a hope that there was some explanation for the transformation that had befallen me. The words hung in the air, unanswered, a testament to the isolation and confusion consuming me.

I didn't recognize myself anymore. My pale skin, my black void-like eyes, the hunger that clawed at me every waking moment—it was as if I had been replaced by someone, something else. The reflection I saw in the darkened windows was not of myself.

The park was bustling with life. Children laughed as they chased each other across the grass, couples strolled hand in hand, and joggers weaved through the pathways. I watched them, feeling a strange mix of longing and detachment. They were part of a world I no longer belonged to, a world I couldn't fully return to. They had not had their humanity taken from them.

A dog barked nearby, and I flinched at the sharp sound, my head snapping in the direction of the noise. A golden retriever was tugging at its leash, its owner struggling to hold it back. The dog's gaze locked onto me, its lips curling back in a low growl.

I froze, a cold dread settling over me. Animals had always liked me—at least, they used to. But now, the dog looked at me like I was something to be feared, something unnatural. Animals could sense things that people couldn't, the purity in the world. That was now gone.

The owner dragged the dog away, casting me an apologetic glance, but I couldn't shake the unease that lingered. The other patrons of the park stared with contempt.

Even they can tell something is off.

I stayed in the park longer than I should have, trying to steady myself. The hunger didn't subside, but I learned to ignore it, to push it to the back of my mind. For now, at least. The park was now empty, and I was alone.

As the sun dipped lower in the sky, casting long shadows across the grass, I knew I couldn't avoid going home forever. Nightfall was approaching, and with it, the hunger would grow.

The walk back to my apartment was a blur. The sights and sounds of the city passed me by, muted and distant, like I was walking through a dream. The moon began to peek through. By the time I reached my building, exhaustion had settled deep in my bones. My muscles ached, my eyes burned, and my mind was numb, but I had to continue.

I climbed the stairs slowly, each step feeling heavier than the last. The familiar scent of old wood and dust seemed foreign, almost sinister. When I finally reached my door, I hesitated, my hand hovering over the handle. The door felt cold and unwelcoming.

The thought of being alone with my thoughts, of facing the reality of what I had become, was almost too much to bear. But there was nowhere else to go. The hunger grew worse, and I was trapped.

I unlocked the door and stepped inside, the familiar space feeling foreign and cold. The place I once called home now felt like a prison, its walls closing in on me. The darkness of my transition had followed me.

The first thing I noticed was the silence. The hum of the refrigerator, the faint creak of the floorboards—all the little noises I had taken for granted before—now felt deafening. The lack of sound was anything but peaceful.

I dropped my bag by the door and collapsed onto the couch, burying my face in my hands. The once-soft and comforting cushions now felt stiff and unyielding. What little comfort I had was now gone.

What do I do now?

By the time I reached my apartment, it was just after three in the afternoon. The sunlight poured in through the windows, bathing everything in a warm glow. It should have felt comforting, but instead, it felt oppressive. Too bright. Too sharp.

The first thing I did was lock the door behind me, the simple motion giving me a small, fleeting sense of control. I kicked off my shoes and collapsed onto the couch, staring at the ceiling as the events of the day churned in my mind.

My skin still felt too tight, my senses buzzing with an intensity I couldn't shut off. Every sound in the apartment—from the hum of the refrigerator to the faint tick of a clock I'd never noticed before—pressed down on me like a weight.

What is happening to me?

My thoughts kept circling back to the same point: Marcus. His face loomed large in my mind, his calm, composed presence a stark contrast to the chaos he had left me with. I didn't know what he had done to me, but I knew it was his fault.

I replayed the moment on the balcony in my head. The way he had appeared out of nowhere, silent and swift, and then disappeared just as quickly. I could still feel the ghost of his touch, the strange warmth on my hand before everything went dark.

I sat up, running a hand through my hair as the hunger hit me again. It was sharper now, gnawing at my insides like a live wire.

I stumbled into the kitchen, throwing open the fridge in the desperate hope that something—anything—would make this stop.

Leftover pasta. Half an apple. A carton of milk.

Nothing seemed appetizing. Nothing seemed *right*.

I grab the apple from the fridge, examining its red skin. My stomach growls, a painful reminder of the hollow feeling that's been growing inside me. Maybe this will help. Maybe this is all I need.

I take a large bite, and flavor explodes across my tongue. The apple tastes incredible—sweeter, more complex than any apple I've ever eaten. I can taste every nuance: the subtle tartness beneath the sweetness, the crispness of its flesh, even hints of the soil it grew from.

"Wow," I whisper, staring at the fruit in amazement.

I devour the rest in seconds, each bite a symphony of flavor. But as the last piece disappears, I realize something terrible. The hunger hasn't subsided at all. If anything, it feels worse.

The apple was delicious—perfect, even—but it did nothing for the gnawing emptiness inside me. It's like throwing a single drop of water on a raging fire.

I slam my fist against the counter, the impact sending vibrations through my arm. The hunger remains, persistent and demanding. My body knows what it wants, and it isn't food—at least, not the kind I've always eaten.

"This isn't right," I mutter, pacing across the kitchen floor. "This isn't happening."

The hunger wasn't going away. If anything, it was getting worse.

I wandered back into the living room, glancing at the clock. 3:45 PM. The minutes dragged, each one stretching into an eternity.

I couldn't just sit here. I had to do something—anything.

My gaze fell on my laptop sitting on the coffee table. It was a lifeline to the outside world, a way to find answers—or at least, a distraction.

But what would I even look up?

I hesitated, my fingers hovering over the keyboard. Typing out "changes to the body after a bite" or "what happens when you black out for five days" felt ridiculous. And yet, it was all I could think about.

I sighed, shutting the laptop before I even started. Maybe later, when I wasn't so wound up.

I glanced at my phone on the table beside me. There were a few missed calls and texts from Benji and Jessica, their concern clear from the messages they'd left. I knew I should call them back, but I couldn't bring myself to do it—not yet.

The idea of facing anyone right now, even the people closest to me, was too much.

My stomach twisted, and I let out a slow, shaky breath. I wasn't going to figure this out tonight. Hell, I wasn't sure I could figure it out tomorrow, either.

That's when it hit me.

I can't go back to work—not like this.

The thought was both a relief and a source of anxiety. Taking time off would give me space to figure out what was happening to me, but it also meant stepping away from the safety net of routine.

Still, I knew it was the right call.

I grabbed my phone and set a reminder to call out in the morning. My fingers hovered over Jessica's name in my contacts list, but I didn't press it. Tomorrow. I'd deal with it tomorrow.

For now, I just needed to rest—and maybe start figuring out what to look up on my laptop.

As I lay back on the couch, staring at the ceiling, one thing became painfully clear: my life wasn't normal anymore. It was up to me to figure out what to do next.

I sat on the edge of my bed, staring at my phone, my fingers hovering over the screen, trembling. The past few days felt like a fever dream, each moment dragging me further from reality. Calling out of work felt like the final thread snapping, but I had no choice. My body didn't belong to me anymore; it felt like a stranger's, a machine governed by new rules I didn't understand.

With a deep breath, I pressed the call button.

"Palantir Technologies, this is Jean," a cheerful voice answered.

"Hi, this is Tristan Blake," I said, my words dry and brittle. "I'm not feeling well... I need to take a few sick days."

There was a brief pause. "Of course, Mr. Blake. I hope you feel better soon. Is there anything else I can assist you with?"

"No, that's all. Thanks."

I hung up before she could reply, the call cutting off with a finality that left the air heavy. For a moment, I just sat there, staring at the darkened screen, as if it held some hidden answer I hadn't found yet.

But there were no answers. Not in my phone. Not in my reflection. Not anywhere.

The faint hum of my laptop broke the silence, the screen casting a cold light across the room. I hadn't closed it from earlier when I'd scrolled through endless pages of nonsense. Reluctantly, I turned back to it and typed the same questions I'd already asked a hundred times.

Sudden change in eye color. Extreme sensory perception. Heightened senses.

The results were as useless as before—medical forums with vague theories, articles about rare conditions, and threads filled with people speculating on ailments that didn't match my symptoms.

Nothing fit.

My hands shook as I rephrased the question, desperation driving my fingers across the keyboard. My mind wandered to Marcus. *Who is he? What did he do to me?*

I typed his name, adding every modifier I could think of: *Marcus New York, mysterious man Marcus, Marcus vampire.*

The results were absurd—pages of irrelevant social media profiles and conspiracy theories. I scrolled aimlessly, the tension in my chest growing tighter with each failed search. Then, buried in the noise, a grainy photo caught my attention.

A man stood in the shadows of an alley, his face partially obscured, with the caption reading: *Are vampires real? NYC's urban legends explored.*

The figure bore a passing resemblance to Marcus, but the image was too blurry to be sure. I clicked on the link, skimming through the article. It was nothing but tabloid fodder, full of wild claims about "blood cults" and "eternal beings" lurking beneath the city.

Still, something about it gnawed at me. Stories of disappearances, whispers of pale figures haunting the edges of the urban sprawl. They sounded like campfire tales spun from fear and imagination, yet the uneasy part of me wondered if there was a sliver of truth buried beneath the exaggerations.

The thought sent a shiver down my spine.

I opened another tab, diving deeper into the rabbit hole of vampire lore. The pages were a chaotic mess of gothic tropes and supernatural clichés. Wooden stakes, garlic, crosses—all of it felt like fiction. Yet certain details stuck out, pulling at the edges of my mind.

Vampires were described as predatory, their senses sharper than any human's. They could smell blood from miles away, hear whispers through walls, and see with perfect clarity in complete darkness.

That's me.

I shook my head, instinctively denying it. It wasn't possible. This wasn't possible.

Another site detailed the transformation process—how the body changed, adapted, and heightened itself to become a predator. It described the hunger, an unrelenting need for blood that would consume everything else if left unchecked.

My chest tightened as I read the words. The description fit me too perfectly.

Then, the page veered off: "Vampires must avoid sunlight, as it burns their flesh within seconds. They are repelled by holy objects and cannot enter a home without permission."

I slammed the laptop shut, frustration boiling over. The initial spark of recognition was crushed under a mountain of absurdity. None of it matched my reality. I wasn't burning in the sunlight or recoiling at crosses. I wasn't sleeping in coffins or turning into a bat.

It was all just a bad joke.

"This is insane," I muttered, running my hands through my hair.

But the words didn't stop the unease twisting in my gut.

I paced the room, my body vibrating with restless energy. Every sound, every movement seemed amplified. The distant hum of traffic outside, the faint creak of my apartment settling—all of it rang in my ears like a symphony of chaos.

My thoughts spiraled back to Marcus. His calm demeanor, the weight in his voice, the way he'd seemed so sure of himself, so sure of *me.*

Who was he? What had he done to me?

The memory of his face lingered, unshakable. He wasn't just a man. That much was clear. But the details slipped through my fingers like water. Everything I knew about him came from fragmented memories and gut instincts. There was no trail to follow, no clues to chase—just questions and silence.

The hunger surged again, sharp and relentless. I gripped the edge of the desk, my knuckles white. It wasn't like normal hunger—it didn't gnaw at my stomach or make me crave food. It was deeper, more primal, like a fire burning beneath my skin.

I couldn't escape it.

The thought of blood flashed through my mind, unbidden. The memory of Daniel's cut at work, the scent that had nearly driven me mad, sent a jolt through my chest. My pulse quickened, but not with fear.

I shook the thought away, horrified at the darkness creeping into my mind.

"This is insane," I muttered again, gripping the desk tighter.

The laptop's faint glow caught my eye, pulling me back toward it. My fingers itched to type, to keep searching, to find *something*. But what could I possibly uncover that would make sense of this?

I turned away, crossing to the window and pulling the curtain back. The city stretched out before me, alive and chaotic, as if mocking the stillness inside me.

Somewhere out there, Marcus had answers.

And somewhere within me, the monster he'd awakened waited, patient and hungry.

"This is insane," I said again, the words hollow and desperate. "I'm not a vampire."

But a small, nagging voice whispered otherwise.

I stood and paced the room, trying to calm myself. My thoughts were a storm, chaotic and unrelenting. What if this was real? What if Marcus had turned me into...?

I halted before the mirror, examining my reflection. The dark emptiness of my eyes gazed back, unwavering. My ashen complexion appeared perfect, nearly glowing, yet somehow foreign. It felt like I was looking at someone else entirely.

The thought hit me like a punch to the gut: what if I'm not me anymore?

I clenched my fists, trying to suppress the rising panic. "There has to be another way," I whispered.

An idea formed in my mind, desperate and flimsy but better than nothing. If this hunger was real—if—then maybe there was a way to satisfy it without becoming a monster.

Animal blood.

The thought was absurd, but it gave me something to hold onto. If vampires were real, then maybe not all of them fed on humans. Perhaps there was another way.

I reopened the laptop, searching for any mention of vampires surviving on animal blood. The results were scarce—most sources dismissed the idea as a myth or a sign of "weakened" vampires. But a few accounts claimed it was possible, though difficult. Animal blood was said to be less potent, less satisfying, but it could sustain a vampire without the need to harm humans.

I clung to the idea like a lifeline. It was my only hope of holding onto the person I used to be.

The hunger surged again, stronger this time, clawing at my insides. I doubled over, clutching my stomach, as a wave of nausea washed over me. My mouth felt dry, my throat raw.

I can't do this.

I grabbed a bottle of water from the desk and drank it in one long gulp, but it didn't help. The hunger wasn't for food or water—it was for something darker, something I didn't want to name.

I collapsed onto the bed, staring at the ceiling as the hunger gnawed at me. My mind raced, searching for answers, for solutions, for anything that could explain what was happening to me.

But one thought kept rising to the surface, no matter how much I tried to push it away.

Marcus.

He had done this to me. He had turned me into... this. Whatever I was now, it was because of him.

I needed answers. And I had a feeling Marcus was the only one who could give them to me.

CHAPTER NINE

THE HUNT FOR ANSWERS

I couldn't stop pacing. My body buzzed with restless energy, hunger clawing at the edges of my thoughts like a starving animal. Every second that passed felt heavier, like a weight pressing down on my chest. I kept glancing at my laptop, the ghost of those ridiculous forum threads lingering in my mind.

Some of the things I read lined up too well with what I was feeling. But the rest? Unicorns and aging backward? It had to be a joke. Yet, the more I paced, the more I felt the unsettling truth gnawing at me. I couldn't deny the changes in my body—heightened senses, insatiable thirst.

Here I was, pacing like a madman, trying to figure out how not to lose my mind—or hurt anyone. My mind flicked back to the moment in the alley, the scent of blood filling my nostrils, the hunger taking control. I shuddered at the memory, realizing what I could become if I didn't find a way to manage this.

My stomach twisted again, sharp and insistent, as if to remind me what was at stake. I stopped in my tracks, leaning against the wall and pressing my fists into my temples. The coolness of the wall did nothing to soothe the burning inside me.

"What do I do?" I muttered, my voice shaking. "What the hell do I do?"

The memory of Daniel's blood hit me like a freight train—the scent, the way it had filled my nostrils and consumed my every thought. The hunger wanted more than to be fed; it wanted to devour. I couldn't let that happen again. I couldn't risk hurting those I cared about, not like that.

There had to be another way. Animal blood. The thought circled back again, persistent and hopeful, like a lifeline in a sea of chaos. If this was real—if I truly was becoming... something—then maybe there was a way to face it without losing myself entirely. Perhaps I could find a balance, a way to feed the hunger without succumbing to it.

But how could I trust that? Nothing about this felt trustworthy. My senses were sharper than ever, every detail in the room screaming for attention. The ticking of the clock, the hum of the refrigerator, the distant murmur of voices outside—all of it was amplified and overwhelming. Yet my instincts felt unreliable, pulling me in too many directions—one toward survival and the other toward something I couldn't even define.

I collapsed into the chair by my desk, the wood groaning beneath me, its sound too sharp in the stillness. My eyes fell on the darkened laptop screen. Its reflection stared back at me—my pale skin, my disheveled hair, and those haunting hazel eyes with faint swirls of silver and gold that seemed to mock me.

"Try again," I muttered, forcing myself to open the laptop. I had to find answers, no matter how ridiculous or far-fetched they seemed. I couldn't keep living like this, torn between the human I once was and the vampire I was becoming.

Its glow stabbed at my retinas, making me wince. The contrast between the brightness and the dim light of the room felt like a physical blow, but I pushed through it, blinking furiously until the screen came into focus. My fingers hovered above the keyboard, hesitant and unsure of what to type. I felt a strange mix of desperation and absurdity, as if I were grasping at straws in the dark.

Heightened senses.

The words looked ridiculous on the screen, as if they would unlock some secret truth. I hit enter and scrolled through the results. Articles about rare conditions, sensory processing disorders, and meditation techniques filled the screen with information, none of which came close to what I was experiencing. Each click led to another dead end, the frustration building like a pressure cooker inside me.

Frustrated, I erased the query and tried again. Pale skin. Black eyes. Craving blood.

This time, the results were worse. Stories about vampires popped up, filled with gothic tropes and movie clichés. One article even had a title so ridiculous it made me groan: "10 Signs You Might Be a Real-Life Vampire!" The sheer absurdity of it all made me want to scream. How could something so outlandish be the closest thing to an explanation for what was happening to me?

I scrolled past the ridiculous articles, my frustration growing with each click. Then something caught my eye—a link to a website that looked like a kid's cartoon show, complete with bright colors and playful fonts. The name "Vampire Fun Zone" seemed like a joke, but something about it tugged at my curiosity. I clicked on it, expecting more nonsense.

The site loaded with a cheerful jingle, a cartoon vampire dancing across the screen. It was absurd, but I couldn't look away. The homepage was filled with links to videos and stories, all presented in a way that made it seem like a fun game rather than a source of actual information. I clicked on a video titled "How to Survive Your First Week as a Vampire!" expecting more silliness.

But as the video played, my amusement faded. The cartoon vampire spoke with a mix of humor and seriousness, detailing experiences eerily similar to mine. The heightened senses, the insatiable hunger, the changes in appearance—it was all there, wrapped in a colorful, kid-friendly package. I watched another video, this one about the dangers of being a new vampire. It discussed the importance of staying hidden, avoiding sunlight, and the risks of being discovered by other vampires.

I scrolled through the site, my disbelief growing with each click. There were stories about missing people, about blood farms where humans were kept captive to feed vampires. It was horrifying, but the site presented it all with a mix of truth and wonder, as if it were a grand adventure rather than a nightmare.

The more I read, the more confused I became. This couldn't be real, could it? It was too absurd, too over-the-top. And yet, there was a kernel of truth in every story, every video. It felt like the site was designed to be both a guide and a warning, wrapped in whimsy to make it all seem less terrifying.

I clicked on the "About" section, curious about who was behind this strange site. The profile name was "Captain Kirk," the handle "@USS_Enterprise." The bio was short and vague, filled with references to Star Trek and a love for all things vampire. It was impossible to tell if the person behind the site was serious or just having a laugh at the expense of people like me.

I leaned back in my chair, my mind racing. This site was a mix of truth and confusion, a strange blend of the ridiculous and the real. I couldn't take it seriously, not entirely. But I couldn't dismiss it either. There was too much that lined up with my own experiences, too much that felt like a warning.

"Helpful," I muttered bitterly, slamming the laptop shut. The sound echoed through the room, making me jump. The silence that followed was deafening, a stark reminder of how alone I felt in this ordeal.

This wasn't working. I wasn't finding answers—I was just running in circles, each dead end making the reality of my situation feel heavier. The weight of it all pressed down on me, suffocating.

My fingers itched to throw something, to lash out and break the growing tension in the air. But what good would that do? I needed a plan. Something tangible. Something to pull me out of this spiral.

I got up and started pacing, my steps quick and uneven. Every creak of the floorboards sounded like a gunshot, every shadow in the room seemed darker than before. The frustration built inside me, an ever-tightening coil, threatening to snap at any moment.

"Think, Tristan," I muttered, my voice cracking with desperation. "There has to be a way to fix this. There has to be."

But the hunger surged again, sharp and relentless. It clawed at my insides, dragging my thoughts back to the office, to Daniel's blood, to the terrifying pull I felt in that moment. The memory made my mouth water, even as I tried to push the thought away.

I pressed a hand to my stomach as if I could physically suppress the hunger, but it didn't help. It was like trying to hold back a tidal wave with a paper dam. The craving was all-consuming, a force that seemed to defy all logic and reason.

I drifted to the window, pulling back the curtain to stare out at the city below. The view was as familiar as ever—the flickering streetlights, the occasional honk of a car horn, the people rushing past one another on the sidewalks. But everything felt different now. The world outside seemed both more vivid and more dangerous, filled with potential threats and temptations.

The glow of the lights burned brighter than they should, casting shadows that stretched and twisted unnaturally. My ears caught snippets of conversations I shouldn't have heard—someone arguing with their partner two stories down, a jogger talking to their dog across the street, a mother scolding her child for not holding her hand. Each sound was crisp and clear, as if I were standing right next to them.

And then there was the smell.

It was faint, almost imperceptible, but it hit me like a punch to the gut. Blood. Somewhere out there, someone had cut themselves—maybe just a tiny nick—but the scent carried to me on the breeze, sharp and metallic.

It was a siren call, a temptation that tugged at the very core of my being. I clenched my fists, my nails digging into my palms, as I fought to resist the urge to follow the scent, to give in to the hunger that threatened to consume me.

I staggered back from the window, my breath coming in short, shallow bursts. The hunger surged again, fiercer than before, gripping me like a vice. I clenched my fists, fighting to keep it at bay, my nails digging into my palms. The scent of blood from outside still lingered in my nose, taunting me, pushing me to the edge.

"I can't... I can't live like this," I whispered, my voice barely audible, choked with desperation.

My mind circled back to the only viable option left: animal blood. It was a grim thought, but it was better than the alternative. If I needed blood to survive, maybe I could get it without hurting anyone—without becoming the monster I was starting to fear I already was. I couldn't let the vampire within control me, not like this.

I let the curtain fall back into place, blocking out the fading light, and began pacing again. The rhythm of my steps was uneven and frantic, echoing the chaos inside me. My body felt like it was running on overdrive, every muscle coiled and ready to snap. The hunger burned through me, insistent and unrelenting, clouding my thoughts like a storm. I couldn't think straight—couldn't focus on anything but the gnawing need.

I had to act. I had to do something before I lost control completely.

* * *

A plan began to form in my mind, shaky and uncertain but enough to hold onto. I'd go to the woods, find an animal—anything—and test if it worked. It sounded insane, even to me, but what choice did I have? If I didn't feed soon, I didn't know what I'd do. The risk of hurting someone, of exposing what I was, was too great.

I crossed to the closet, yanking it open with more force than necessary. I pulled out dark clothing—something that wouldn't stand out in the shadows. My hands shook as I grabbed a jacket and stuffed a flashlight into a backpack, along with a few other essentials. I was a mess, but I had to push through. This was about survival now.

The sun was sinking lower, the last golden rays of daylight fading into deep oranges and purples. The room darkened with each passing second, the shadows lengthening and creeping up the walls, mirroring the darkness inside me. I slung the backpack over my shoulder and took a deep breath, trying to calm my nerves. But the hunger was a relentless beast, clawing at my insides, demanding to be fed.

This was survival. I didn't have the luxury of second-guessing myself anymore. I had to act, had to find a way to satiate this hunger without becoming a monster.

But as I stood there, staring at the horizon and the darkening sky, one thought refused to leave me: what if it's not enough? The thought of feeding on a person crossed my mind more times than I wanted to admit. Each time, it filled me with disgust.

I couldn't hurt someone, let alone take their life, to satisfy this monstrous hunger. But if I didn't do something soon, I wasn't sure how long I could hold on. The line between human and monster was blurring, and I was terrified of what I might become.

My phone buzzed on the nightstand, jolting me from my spiraling thoughts. I hesitated before answering, my thumb hovering over the screen as if it could somehow sense the weight of the conversation to come. The name *Sarah* blinked back at me, a stark reminder of the life I used to have, the normalcy that now felt so distant.

"Hey, Sarah," I said, trying to keep my voice steady, pushing down the turmoil that churned inside me.

"Tristan! How are you feeling? Everyone's worried," she said, her voice filled with genuine concern, a warmth that seemed to belong to a different world.

"I'm... managing," I replied, unsure how else to put it. How could I explain the storm raging within me, the hunger that gnawed at my very being? "Just trying to figure some things out."

A brief pause followed, the kind that usually signaled someone choosing their words carefully, treading lightly around a sensitive topic. "I get it. But seriously, you should take care of yourself. You don't sound like yourself."

"I know, I know," I said, rubbing my temple. "Just... dealing with some stuff."

"Anything you want to talk about?" she asked gently, her voice a lifeline to the humanity I desperately clung to.

For a moment, I considered telling her everything—about the transformation, the hunger, the nightmares that haunted me even when I was awake. But the idea was absurd. Who would believe me? I barely believed it myself.

"Nah," I said instead, the lie tasting bitter on my tongue. "I'm good. Just need a bit more time."

"Alright," she said, though her voice carried a note of hesitation, a sign that she wasn't entirely convinced. "But don't hesitate to reach out if you need anything, okay? We're all here for you."

"Thanks, Sarah. I appreciate it," I said, the words heartfelt even as I knew I couldn't take her up on the offer. Not with this. Not with the monster I had become.

We exchanged a few more pleasantries before hanging up. I stared at the phone for a moment, the weight of her concern settling heavily on me. Everyone was worried about me, and here I was, planning how to sneak into a forest to drink blood from a wild animal. The hidden nature of it all ate away at me, a persistent reminder of the gulf between my former existence and the unfamiliar realm I now found myself in.

I shoved the phone into my pocket and grabbed my keys from the counter. The jangle echoed through the apartment, a stark reminder of the silence that now defined my life. The isolation was palpable, a void that seemed to grow with each passing day. I headed out, locking the door behind me with a finality that made my stomach churn. The click of the latch felt like a seal on a fate I never asked for.

The city streets were a blur of noise and lights as I walked to my car. Each step felt like a march toward the inevitable, a point of no return. The cool night air did little to calm the storm raging inside me. I could feel the hunger gnawing at my insides. The neon signs and bustling crowds seemed distant, a world I was no longer truly a part of.

My car sat in the parking garage, a silent witness to my descent into this new world. I slid into the driver's seat, the leather creaking beneath me. The engine roared to life, the sound echoing off the concrete walls, amplifying the sense of isolation. I pulled out, the city lights reflecting off the windshield as I navigated the familiar streets. Each turn felt like a step deeper into the shadows, a journey into a life I could barely recognize as my own.

The drive to the woods was a slow burn, each mile marker a ticking clock counting down to the moment I'd have to face the reality of my situation. The cityscape gradually gave way to suburbs, then to open fields and dense forests. The road stretched out before me, a dark ribbon under the moonlight, as if leading me into an inevitable confrontation with my new nature.

I gripped the steering wheel tighter, my knuckles turning white as the hunger within me intensified. It was a constant companion now, a nagging voice in the back of my mind that grew louder with each passing mile, demanding to be acknowledged.

I tried to focus on the road, on the steady hum of the engine, on anything but the gnawing need inside me. The scent of pine and earth wafted through the open window, a stark reminder of the wilderness I was entering, both physically and metaphorically.

The woods loomed ahead, a dark mass against the night sky, seemingly impenetrable and full of secrets. I turned off the main road, the car bouncing along the uneven dirt path, each jolt sending a shiver up my spine. The trees closed in around me, their branches reaching out like skeletal fingers, beckoning me deeper into the shadows. I parked the car at the edge of the forest, the headlights casting eerie shadows on the trunks of the trees, as if the very woods were alive with whispers of the unknown.

I sat there for a moment, the engine idling, the headlights cutting through the darkness like a knife. The woods were silent, the only sound the distant hoot of an owl and the quiet ticking of the car engine as it cooled. I took a deep breath, the scent of pine and earth filling my lungs, a stark contrast to the stale air of the office I'd left behind. This was it. There was no turning back now.

I turned off the engine, the sudden silence deafening. I stepped out of the car, the crunch of gravel under my feet echoing through the stillness, each step a reminder of the path I'd chosen. The forest loomed before me, a dark and unknown world waiting to be explored, a stark contrast to the bright, sterile environment of the office. I shouldered my backpack, the weight of it grounding me, reminding me of the stakes and the reasons behind my journey.

Night had fully settled by the time I reached the edge of the forest. It loomed before me, dark and endless, like the mouth of some ancient beast waiting to swallow me whole. I adjusted the straps on my backpack, the faint city lights behind me flickering like dying stars, their glow too distant to offer any comfort.

Out here, the world felt quieter, but not in a comforting way. It was a stillness heavy with expectation, a silence that wrapped itself around my senses and refused to let go, a stark reminder of the solitude that now defined my existence.

I took a step forward, then another, as the forest swallowed me whole. The city, the office, the worries of my old life—they all faded away, leaving only the woods and the hunger. I was a predator now, a creature of the night, driven by instincts that were both exhilarating and terrifying. I was hunting, not just for sustenance, but for answers, seeking a way to reconcile the person I was with the creature I'd become.

My breaths came shallow, and my pulse drummed steadily—just a touch faster than normal, though even that felt off, a constant reminder of the change coursing through my veins. Something primal stirred within me, a mix of anticipation and dread that made my hands tremble, starkly contrasting with the steady control I had once prided myself on. The deeper I ventured into the woods, the more I felt the pull of my new nature, the allure of the unknown, and the constant, gnawing hunger demanding to be satisfied.

The woods felt alive in a way I hadn't noticed before. My heightened senses picked up every detail—the breeze brushing through the treetops, the rich, damp soil beneath me, the faint rustle of animals moving in the shadows. Even the distant hoot of an owl echoed in my mind with startling clarity.

I swallowed hard as I took my first step into the forest. The crunch of leaves underfoot sounded like thunder to my sensitive ears.

The air grew colder as the trees enveloped me, their towering forms blotting out the faint glow of the moon. I moved cautiously, my feet landing almost soundlessly on the forest floor. It felt strange to move this way—graceful, deliberate, yet uncoordinated all at once. My body had changed so much, but I hadn't yet learned how to wield this newfound strength. Each step was a dance between control and instinct, a constant reminder of the transformation coursing through my veins.

The hunger inside me stirred, sharper now, more demanding. It clawed at my stomach, winding its way up my throat until I could barely breathe past it. I clenched my jaw, forcing myself to stay calm, to maintain some semblance of the person I used to be. But the primal urge was relentless, gnawing at the edges of my restraint.

And then it came.

A scent unlike anything I'd ever encountered before. Sweet, metallic, sharp—it cut through the earthy smells of the forest like lightning through a stormy sky. My mouth watered, my fangs ached, and my body surged forward before I even realized I was moving. It was as if every cell in my body was drawn to this scent, pulled by an invisible force.

The scent led me deeper into the woods, my legs carrying me faster than I thought possible. The world around me blurred, trees whipping past as I honed in on the invisible trail. Every step felt effortless; my movements were almost too quick, too light. The forest floor seemed to disappear beneath me, and the wind rushed past my ears in a constant whisper.

Then, through the dense trees, I saw it.

A clearing bathed in silver moonlight. Standing at its center, grazing peacefully, was a large elk. Its sleek coat glistened under the soft glow of the moon, and its antlers stretched skyward, casting jagged shadows across the clearing. The sight brought me to a halt, instincts warring within me.

The hunger screamed at me to lunge, to take, to drink. But the human part of me—the part that still clung to reason and morality—hesitated. My hands clenched into fists at my sides, and I crouched low, watching the animal from the shadows. Every sense was on fire. I could hear its steady breaths, the subtle crackle of its hooves on the dry leaves, the rhythmic pounding of its heartbeat.

The scent of its blood filled my nostrils, and my vision sharpened until I could see the smallest movements of its muscles beneath its skin. The elk's every twitch and flicker of its ears was amplified, drawing me in, urging me closer. The tension between my primal desires and my human conscience was a tightrope, and I teetered on the edge, unsure which side would win.

I crouched low, the world around me fading into a muted backdrop as I fixated on the elk. The rush of adrenaline mingled with a gnawing realization: I was lost. The dense canopy above blocked out most of the sunlight, casting dappled shadows that danced on the forest floor, disorienting me further.

With trembling fingers, I fished my phone from my pocket and pressed the button to wake it up. The screen lit up in the dim light, a harsh contrast to the natural surroundings. I quickly pulled up the GPS, my hands shaking slightly as I waited for the signal to lock on. It took a moment for the little dot representing me to materialize on the map, a small blue beacon in a sea of green.

The forest stretched endlessly in every direction, an overwhelming sea of trees and shadows. A sense of dread washed over me as I recognized just how far I had wandered from my car. The thought of retracing my steps felt daunting, like trying to find a single needle in a haystack, but the GPS offered a glimmer of hope—a winding path back through this tangled maze.

I found a patch of dry ground beneath an old oak, its gnarled roots snaking across the earth, and set down my backpack. Letting out a breath I didn't realize I'd been holding, I tried to steady myself. However, as I glanced at the map, that sense of relief was short-lived. The reality of my situation began to sink in, along with a growing unease.

The hunger surged again—sharp and insistent—clawing at my insides like an animal desperate for escape. My stomach tightened as the sweet scent of the elk overwhelmed my senses, drowning out everything else. It was a primal, all-consuming need that threatened to override all reason.

I forced myself to look away from the glowing screen and back at my surroundings. The elk remained oblivious, still grazing peacefully, its powerful form a stark contrast to my inner turmoil. Yet something deep inside urged me to stay alert. I couldn't afford to let my guard down, not here, not now.

My instincts screamed at me to be cautious; if there were people nearby, they could ruin everything. Slowly scanning the clearing, I peered into the shadows between the trees. Nothing moved—just silence filled with whispers of leaves rustling in the breeze. Yet the forest felt alive, watching, waiting. I knew I had to tread carefully, one wrong move could spell disaster.

Panic bubbled under my skin as another wave of hunger washed over me, sharper than before, clawing at my insides with an intensity that was almost painful. This time it wasn't just about survival; it was about control—a desperate fight against the monster lurking within me, threatening to consume my humanity.

I inhaled deeply again, the rich, sweet aroma of the elk enveloping me, drowning out everything else. I looked back at the creature, its soft, graceful movements making it seem so inviting, so utterly unaware of the impending doom that hung in the air. The sight of it, so peaceful and vulnerable, sent a shiver down my spine.

I couldn't let myself lose control—not now, not ever. But every instinct within me urged me closer to that animal; each beat of its heart resonated with a silent, primal rhythm that seemed to summon me forward, like a drumbeat calling me to action. The temptation was overwhelming, a siren song of hunger and desire threatening to overpower my senses.

But what if there were hunters nearby? What if someone had followed me here, tracking my every move? The thought sent a cold chill through my veins, a stark reminder of the danger that lurked in the shadows. For now, I forced myself to stay still, torn between two primal urges: one that sought sustenance, that craved the warmth and life of the elk, and another that warned me not to lose myself completely in this darkened wilderness, to remain vigilant and alert.

I took a cautious step forward, my muscles tensing with anticipation. The elk's head shot up, its ears twitching as it sensed the danger lurking in the shadows. Its wide, dark eyes scanned the darkness, searching for the source of the threat that had disturbed its peaceful grazing.

Then, with a sudden burst of motion, it bolted.

"Shit!" I hissed, springing after it, my instincts taking over as I gave chase, the hunger within me driving me forward with a force that was almost uncontrollable.

The chase was chaotic from the start. My legs moved with incredible speed, but my body felt unbalanced, my strides too long and my movements too powerful. I stumbled over roots, crashed through low-hanging branches, and nearly collided with a tree. The sheer force in my muscles was intoxicating, but it was wild, untamed, and nearly impossible to control. Each misstep sent jolts of sensation through me, a mix of exhilaration and frustration.

The elk zigzagged through the trees with a precision I couldn't match, its body sleek and fluid as it darted between obstacles. My own movements were clumsy in comparison, sending leaves and debris flying in my wake, the forest floor churning beneath my feet. The elk seemed to know the terrain intimately, while I was a stranger, my newfound strength more of a hindrance than a help.

"Focus," I muttered, gritting my teeth, trying to rein in the chaotic energy coursing through my veins.

I leaped over a fallen log, my trajectory too high, my body too light. I landed hard on the other side, rolling to a stop as the elk disappeared into the shadows. The impact barely hurt, but the frustration burned deep, a hot coal in the pit of my stomach. I was a predator unlike any other, yet I couldn't even catch a simple elk.

The hunger roared louder, a primal force demanding to be fed. It spurred me back to my feet, my breathing steady, my body surging with adrenaline—or something far more potent. The scent of blood filled my nostrils, sweet and metallic, guiding me like a beacon through the darkened forest. The elk's heartbeat thudded in my ears, a steady drumbeat growing louder with every step, a promise of the satiation I so desperately craved.

My strides began to steady, my body adjusting to the power coursing through it like a wild river finding its course. Each movement became more deliberate, more controlled, as if my muscles were finally understanding the language of this new, raw energy.

I ducked under low-hanging branches, leaped over gnarled roots and fallen leaves, and pushed off the damp earth with just the right amount of force, propelling myself forward with an agility that felt both exhilarating and unsettling.

The elk was within sight now, its sleek, tawny form darting through the moonlit trees like a fleeting ghost. It veered sharply to the left, perhaps hoping to throw me off, but I anticipated the move. I cut through the forest with a precision that surprised even me, my senses heightened to a point where the world around me seemed to slow down.

"Not this time," I growled, the hunger overtaking everything else, reducing my world to a single, all-consuming need.

The forest around me blurred into a wash of greens and grays as I pushed myself harder, faster. The elk's frantic breathing filled my ears, its fear palpable in the air, a tangy, metallic scent that fueled my pursuit. I was so close now, close enough to see the glistening sheen of sweat on its coat, to feel the heat radiating from its body like a beacon guiding me in.

With a final burst of speed, I lunged forward. My hands, fingers splayed wide, reached out and grabbed the elk's flank. The force of my momentum sent us both tumbling to the ground, a tangle of limbs and desperation. Its cries echoed through the forest, sharp and panicked, as it thrashed beneath me, fighting for its life with a ferocity that mirrored my own inner struggle.

For a moment, I froze. Time seemed to stand still as the elk's wide, terrified eyes locked onto mine. Its body trembled under my grip, each shiver resonating through me like an accusation. The human part of me—the part that still clung to reason, to the echoes of who I used to be—screamed to let it go. This wasn't who I was. This wasn't what I wanted to become. I was a man, not a monster.

But the hunger... the hunger didn't care. It roared within me, a relentless, primal force that demanded to be fed.

The elk's heartbeat pounded in my ears, a steady, thrumming rhythm that drowned out everything else—the rustle of leaves, the distant hoot of an owl, the whispered pleas of my own conscience. My fangs throbbed, the primal urge to feed overwhelming every thought, every emotion, every last shred of my humanity.

Tears blurred my vision as I whispered, "I'm sorry." The words tasted like ashes in my mouth, a bitter acknowledgment of the line I was about to cross. A line that, once breached, would forever change who I was, who I am.

The elk beneath me was a magnificent creature, its body a landscape of tawny fur stretched taut over powerful muscles. It was warm, so warm, like a furnace against the chill of the night, its heat radiating into me, a stark contrast to the cold emptiness I felt inside.

Its breaths came in short, sharp bursts, each exhale a cloud of mist in the cool air, the scent of its fear a tangy, metallic taste on my tongue. Every inhale the creature took seemed to echo in the silence, a countdown to an inevitable end.

I could see the pulse of its life force, the great veins in its neck throbbing with each terrified heartbeat. They were like ropes beneath its skin, thick and corded, a testament to the power and vitality coursing through this creature. Its eyes, wide and dark, reflected the moonlight, a sheen of terror glazing them as it stared up at me, frozen in that primal dance of predator and prey. In those eyes, I saw a reflection of myself, a monster looming over an innocent creature, and I shuddered.

My hands, trembling with a mix of hunger and revulsion, hovered over its neck. The elk's coat was coarse yet soft, the hairs tickling my palms, a sensation so real and vivid it anchored me to the moment. I could feel the creature's life, the thrum of its heart, the rush of its blood—all of it a symphony of existence that called to the void within me. Each beat of its heart was a reminder of the life I no longer possessed, the warmth I could no longer generate on my own.

I leaned down, the world narrowing to the space between us. My lips brushed against its neck, the contact sending a jolt through me. The elk's pulse was a drumbeat against my mouth, a rhythm that echoed through me, resonating with the hunger clawing at my insides. The scent of its blood was overpowering, a sweet, metallic aroma that filled my nostrils, drowning out everything else. It was a scent that promised sustenance, power, and a fleeting sense of fulfillment.

For a split second, I hesitated, teetering on the edge of a chasm from which there would be no return. The warmth of the elk's body, the throb of its life beneath my touch, the sheer vitality of it—all of it starkly contrasted the cold, empty hunger gnawing at me. This was the line, the point of no return, and I wavered, caught between the monster I was becoming and the man I used to be.

The man who loved his family, who cherished life, who would never have dreamed of taking another's blood to sustain his own existence. But that man was fading, replaced by a creature driven by primal instincts, a creature of the night, a vampire.

Then, with a deep, shuddering breath, I sank my fangs into its flesh.

Chapter Ten

THE RUSH

The moment the blood hit my tongue, the world tilted on its axis, the familiar ground beneath my feet becoming uncertain and dream-like. It wasn't an unpleasant sensation, not exactly, but disorienting—like being spun too quickly on a playground merry-go-round. The forest floor seemed to rise to meet me, then recede, the trees swaying in a silent, dizzying dance. Their leaves blurred into a kaleidoscope of green and silver under the moonlight, and the usual sounds of the night echoed from a great distance, as if heard through a thick fog.

Warmth surged through me, not the comforting warmth of a hearth fire, but something electric and alive, like liquid fire coursing through my veins. It spread rapidly, igniting every nerve ending, making my skin prickle and my muscles twitch. The feeling was all-consuming, obliterating the chill of the night air and replacing it with a furnace-like intensity that seemed to burn from within, awakening parts of me I never knew existed.

The elk's heartbeat, which had been a faint, rapid thrum against my chest, now pulsed with an unnatural force driven by fear. Each beat intensified, echoing in my ears like a frantic drumbeat. It was as if I could feel the life force ebbing and flowing within the creature, its strength becoming my strength, its vitality fueling my own.

My own heart, the one I thought long dead or at least dormant, raced faster until it was impossible to hear or feel—a hum of pure energy resonating deep within my chest, replacing the familiar, steady rhythm I vaguely remembered from my human life. It was a frantic vibration, a chaotic symphony of blood and power threatening to overwhelm my senses, drowning out everything but the primal urge to feed.

As I drank, the elk's struggles weakened, its life force ebbing like a tide receding from the shore. The once vibrant energy I felt emanating from the creature began to dim, its pulse growing fainter and more erratic. The taste was overwhelming, intoxicating—a primal satisfaction unlike anything I'd ever known.

It was more than quenching a thirst; it was a deep, instinctive need fulfilled, a hunger that had gnawed at me for an eternity finally being appeased. The blood was rich and earthy, tinged with the scent of the forest, the taste of life itself—a potent reminder of the power now coursing through my veins, both exhilarating and terrifying in its intensity.

Stop.

The thought—a tiny, fragile seed of reason—broke through the intoxicating haze enveloping my mind. It was a struggle to grasp it, to hold onto the thread of my former self, but the urgency in the command was undeniable. With a monumental effort of will, I wrenched myself away, stumbling back, my body protesting the abrupt interruption.

Blood dripped from my lips, warm and metallic, a stark reminder of what I had done and what I had become. The crimson droplets stained the ground, each one a testament to my new life. I wiped them away with a trembling hand, the movement clumsy and uncoordinated, my body buzzing with the alien energy coursing through me.

The elk collapsed onto its side, its breathing ragged and shallow, panting but alive. Its wide, glassy eyes met mine, and a wave of guilt, sharp and unexpected, twisted in my stomach. It was a foreign emotion, one I hadn't felt in what seemed like an age, yet its sting was undeniable.

With a shuddering breath, I stepped back, creating distance between us. Slowly, with visible effort, the elk rose to its feet, its legs shaking and body trembling. It stared at me for a moment longer, its gaze filled with a mixture of fear and confusion, before bolting into the trees, disappearing into the darkness.

I sank to my knees, the damp earth cold against my skin, my hands digging into the soil as I tried to steady myself, anchoring myself to reality. The world still swam before my eyes, the residual effects of the blood still coursing through my veins. The hunger, which had been unbearable moments ago, a gnawing emptiness consuming my every thought, was gone, replaced by a strange sense of fullness, of satiation.

I felt whole, complete, as though every cell in my body vibrated with newfound vitality. It was an exhilarating sensation, a rush of pure, unadulterated power surging through me like a relentless tide. But beneath the surface, a disquieting unease lingered—a nagging feeling that this newfound strength came at a terrible price, a debt that would one day need to be repaid.

What am I?

The question hung heavy in the cool night air, a silent plea for understanding, for recognition of the creature I had become. But my body wouldn't let me linger on it, wouldn't allow me to dwell on the implications of my actions. A restless energy surged through me, demanding an outlet, a release, as if every moment of stillness was a moment wasted.

I stood, my muscles coiled like springs, ready to launch. It was as if I were a predator poised to strike, every fiber of my being attuned to the hunt, to the primal instincts now coursing through me. The energy within me threatened to burst, to overwhelm me if I didn't find a way to channel it. I could feel it pulsating, resonating with the very essence of the forest around me, as if the wilderness recognized one of its own.

I took a hesitant step forward, then another. My movements felt light, fluid, effortless, as if I were floating on air. The limitations of my former human body seemed to have vanished, replaced by something faster, stronger, more powerful. The world around me shifted, colors becoming more vibrant, scents sharper, and sounds crystal clear, as if the very atmosphere was alive and whispering secrets to me. Testing the limits of my newfound strength, I crouched low and sprang upward, clearing the trees with ease, soaring through the air like a creature of myth, the wind whipping around me in a symphony of sensation.

I landed awkwardly, my feet skidding on the damp earth, nearly sending me sprawling. My breath hitched, but a surprised, involuntary laugh escaped my lips—a laugh born of exhilaration and disbelief. It was a sound I hadn't heard in years, a sound that felt both foreign and familiar, a reminder of a time before the Blood, before the transformation that had irrevocably changed me.

Do it again.

The thought—a command this time—echoed in my mind. The urge to test my limits, to explore the boundaries of my newfound abilities, was irresistible. I pushed off again, this time with more focus, more control. My body soared through the air, higher and farther than before, the trees below becoming a blur of green and brown.

When I landed, I stayed upright, the impact barely registering, my body absorbing the shock with an ease that felt almost magical. A wide, uninhibited grin spread across my face as I began to run, testing my speed, pushing myself to the edge of my capabilities. The forest around me became a living entity, challenging me, urging me on, as if it too wanted to see just how far I could go.

The forest blurred around me as I picked up the pace, the wind whipping past me in a rush of sensation. My legs moved with a speed and precision that felt almost alien, but there was a raw power in it, a primal thrill that made my heart sing, or rather, made the energy within me resonate with joyful intensity.

I darted between trees, dodging branches with instinctive ease, leapt over fallen logs without breaking stride, and climbed rocks with the agility of a mountain cat. But for all my newfound abilities, I wasn't graceful—not yet. I stumbled over roots hidden beneath the leaves, misjudged distances, and tripped more than once, each misstep a reminder of my inexperience.

Each fall was a reminder: this body, this strength—it wasn't mine. Not really. It was a new experience, something I hadn't fully grasped yet, something I had gained through Marcus's mysterious action or perhaps an instinctual urge. But it was a borrowed power, a gift and a curse all in one.

But with every step, every leap, I felt more in tune with myself, more connected to this new reality. The awkwardness began to fade, replaced by a growing confidence, a sense of mastery over my movements. I was learning to inhabit this new body, to understand its strengths and weaknesses.

The wind carried a thousand scents to me: the earth's damp richness, the musk of animals hiding in the shadows, the faint metallic tang of blood lingering in the air. I could hear every rustle of leaves, every distant call of nocturnal birds, the faint scurrying of rodents beneath the forest floor. The world felt alive in a way I'd never experienced before, my senses heightened to a degree that was both exhilarating and overwhelming.

I stopped in a clearing, breathing heavily but not out of breath. My lungs didn't burn, my muscles didn't ache. The moon hung low in the sky, casting silver light on the forest floor, illuminating the trees in an ethereal glow. My skin tingled with the energy coursing through me, my heart humming in my chest like a finely tuned engine, ready to unleash its pow er.

The rush of adrenaline began to fade, replaced by a quieter, deeper hunger. The elk's blood had satiated me, but only partially. It had quenched the immediate thirst, but it hadn't filled the void within me. Something inside me stirred, insistent and primal, a constant, gnawing need that threatened to consume me once more. I could feel it clawing at my insides, a reminder of the power now coursing through my veins and the price that came with it.

And then I heard it.

A low growl rumbled through the night, a guttural sound that resonated deep within my bones and sent a shiver down my spine. It was a sound that spoke of power, aggression, and territoriality. I turned toward the source, my heightened senses locking onto it with an uncanny precision that was still new to me. The scent hit me next—musky, earthy, and laced with the sharp tang of iron, a scent that spoke of raw, untamed power. It was a stark contrast to the pleasant earthy aroma I had grown accustomed to since my transformation.

The bear emerged from the shadows, its massive form illuminated by the moonlight. It was a creature of immense size and strength, an apex predator in its natural habitat. Its dark eyes glinted as they locked onto me, unwavering, while its lips pulled back in a snarl, revealing rows of sharp, formidable teeth. It was a chilling reminder that I wasn't the only dangerous creature lurking in the night.

Instinct kicked in, and I tensed, my muscles coiling like springs, ready to react. The bear growled again, a deep, resonant sound that vibrated through my chest—a clear warning that I was encroaching on its territory. I felt the energy within me pulsating, ready to unleash, but I hesitated, caught between the urge to fight and the instinct to flee.

Do I run? Fight?

The choice was made for me as the bear charged, its heavy paws thundering against the earth, shaking the ground with its approach. I leapt to the side, my movements clumsy yet quick, narrowly avoiding the brunt of its attack. The bear's claws swiped through the space I had just occupied, tearing through the air with terrifying force that sent a jolt of fear and exhilaration through me.

I stumbled, nearly losing my footing, but managed to regain my balance, adrenaline coursing through my veins. The bear turned, growling menacingly as it prepared for another attack, its eyes fixed on me with predatory intensity. I could see the hunger in its gaze, a reflection of the hunger I felt within, a hunger that demanded to be fed.

Adrenaline surged through me, and I pushed off the ground, launching myself over the bear's head in a desperate attempt to escape. I landed behind it, my feet skidding uncontrollably on the damp earth. The bear wheeled around, its massive form blocking out the moonlight as it reared up on its hind legs, a towering display of power and aggression. It was a chilling sight, but I could feel my own power rising to meet the challenge, the vampire blood within me igniting a fierce determination to survive.

I darted forward, faster this time, driven by a primal need to survive that burned through me like wildfire. I sank my fangs into the bear's thick fur, tearing through the matted layers with newfound ferocity. The taste of blood flooded my mouth, warm and metallic, silencing the hunger that had clawed at me, satisfying the primal urge that had taken control.

The bear roared in pain and rage, thrashing wildly, its massive body shaking with desperate struggles. But I held on, my grip tightening as I drank, refusing to release my hold. Its struggles weakened with every passing second, its massive body growing still beneath me, its life force slowly ebbing away, absorbed into my being.

I forced myself to stop before it was too late, before I consumed every last drop of its vitality. Pulling away just as the bear collapsed onto the ground, its breathing shallow and ragged. Blood dripped from my lips as I staggered back, my body thrumming with energy, my senses heightened to an almost unbearable degree. The forest around me seemed to come alive, every whisper of wind and rustle of leaves amplified a hundredfold.

The bear lay still for a moment, its massive form unmoving, before letting out a low groan—a sound of defeat and exhaustion. Slowly, with visible effort, it rolled onto its stomach and lumbered to its feet, its movements sluggish but deliberate. It turned to look at me, its dark eyes wary but calm, filled with a strange mix of fear and respect, acknowledging the power it had encountered.

And then, with a huff, it disappeared into the trees, melting back into the darkness and leaving me alone in the clearing. The taste of blood still lingered on my tongue, a constant reminder of what I had done, the hunger finally, blessedly gone, replaced by a sense of satiation and lingering unease. My body felt alive, electric, as though I could take on the entire world and win—invulnerable, yet deeply aware of the line I had crossed.

I wiped my mouth, trying to erase the evidence of my actions, to cleanse myself of the blood that stained my lips, but I knew deep down that the stain would never truly disappear. The tang of it, that metallic hint of power and life, lingered on my tongue, a constant reminder of what I had become.

The first rays of dawn lit the city streets as I stumbled back into my apartment, my body vibrating with energy but my mind heavy with exhaustion. Every part of me felt different—sharper, stronger, more alive—but the rush of power was tangled with confusion and lingering unease from the forest.

I closed the door behind me and leaned against it, letting out a long, shuddering breath. The city sounds that usually faded into the background of my daily life now felt like a symphony I couldn't escape. Each honk, every fragment of dialogue, and the gentle rustling of leaves beyond my window were painfully clear, each noise a piercing note in the discord of the stirring city.

I clenched my jaw and took a shaky step forward, focusing on grounding myself. My shoes scuffed lightly against the floorboards, and even that tiny noise seemed to echo in my ears. *Just move. Just keep moving.* I needed to process what had happened, to make sense of the change coursing through my veins.

The bathroom mirror was calling to me, and I dreaded what I might see. The memories of the night—of the elk, the bear, the blood—were too fresh, too vivid. But I needed answers, even if they were written across my own face. I needed to see if the transformation was as evident on the outside as it felt on the inside.

When I flipped on the light and looked into the mirror, I froze.

My eyes, once black voids after Marcus turned me, now held something new. Faint streaks of color swirled beneath the surface, like molten silver trying to break free. They weren't just different; they felt alive, shifting subtly as though responding to my emotions. The hazel that had once been there was now intertwined with gleaming threads of silver and gold, a dance of light and dark that seemed to reflect the turmoil within me.

I leaned closer, studying the subtle changes in the dark pools. The silver shimmered just beneath the surface, twisting and swirling like smoke trapped in glass. It was hypnotic, a strange and beautiful reminder of the power that now coursed through me—a power that both thrilled and terrified me. A power that tied me irrevocably to this new world and all its dangers.

But it wasn't just my eyes. My skin was flawless, almost unnaturally smooth, with a faint glow that seemed to catch the light in all the right ways. The pale, sickly tone that had haunted me for days was gone, replaced by a healthy vibrancy that bordered on unreal. I ran my fingers over my forearm, marveling at the texture. No scars, no imperfections—just perfect, unblemished skin.

I flexed my hand, noting how my tendons moved beneath the surface like taut cables. My fingers looked the same but felt different—stronger, more precise. I raised my other hand to my jaw, tracing the sharp lines of my face. My cheekbones were higher, more defined, and my jawline...it looked like it belonged on a magazine cover, not my own body.

I took a step back, struggling to process the changes. My reflection was beautiful, almost painfully so, but it was wrong. It wasn't me. The eyes staring back at me were mine. I leaned closer, inspecting the flawless skin, the high cheekbones, the sharp jawline. It was all so perfect, so unreal.

This isn't me.

My gaze dropped to my teeth, and I caught sight of my canines. They were sharper, slightly longer than I remembered. A chill ran down my spine as I tentatively pressed a finger to one, only to jerk my hand back when it pricked me. A tiny bead of blood welled up—crimson and glistening under the harsh bathroom light.

The scent hit me like a freight train. Sweet, metallic, and impossibly enticing. My stomach twisted, and a low growl escaped my lips before I could stop it. I stared at the tiny drop of blood, feeling an ache deep in my chest. It wasn't hunger—not exactly—but something more primal, more consuming. An urge that seemed to claw at the very core of my being.

I turned on the faucet and washed the blood away, my hands trembling. The cold water rushed over my fingers, grounding me for a moment. I gripped the edge of the sink, leaning forward as I tried to steady my breathing. My heart was racing—or at least, I thought it was. I pressed a hand to my chest, searching for the familiar thud. But it wasn't there. Not like before. Instead, my heart beat so fast it was almost imperceptible, a silent hum that resonated through my body.

"So fast I can't hear it. So fast I can't feel it," I murmured.

"What did you do to me, Marcus?" I whispered, the question hanging in the air like a challenge.

I forced myself to step back from the sink, pulling my eyes away from the stranger in the mirror. The blood had dulled the gnawing hunger, but it had left behind something else—restlessness, an unease I couldn't shake. I felt like a caged animal, pacing the confines of my own skin.

Memories of the hunt flooded back: the thrill of the chase, the rush of power, the taste of life coursing through my veins. I could still feel the strength of the bear surging through me, amplifying every part of my being. But the elation I'd felt in the woods was gone, replaced by a cold, creeping dread. The forest that had once been a sanctuary now felt wild and untamed, a reflection of the primal instincts awakening within me.

I wasn't human anymore. I was something else, something more. And it terrified me.

I paced the bathroom, my thoughts racing faster than I could keep up with. The blood had changed me, and I didn't know if I could ever go back.

My body felt alien, my senses overwhelming, my reflection unrecognizable. Every sound echoed too loudly, every scent was too intense, and the very air seemed to hum with an energy I couldn't ignore.

I returned to the mirror, staring at the stranger before me. The flawless skin that shimmered under the harsh bathroom light; the sharper angles of my face—they all belonged to someone else. Someone stronger, faster, more powerful. But someone who wasn't me. My eyes, still black but now there is an unusual faint shimmer of silver and gold patterns, served as a vivid reminder of the change I am experiencing.

This wasn't the Tristan Blake I knew. This wasn't the face I saw every morning, the body I'd grown used to inhabiting. The person staring back at me was a stranger, a creature of the night, not the human I had been just days before.

My phone buzzed from the bedroom, breaking the silence. I hesitated before checking it, grabbing it off the nightstand. A text from Jessica lit up the screen.

Jessica: "Hey, heard you're still out sick. Let me know if you need anything, okay?"

The message made my chest ache. Jess had always been there for me, always looked out for me. But how could I tell her what was happening? How could I explain any of this? The weight of the secret pressed down on me, making it hard to breathe.

I put the phone down without replying and collapsed onto the bed, staring up at the ceiling. The events of the night replayed in my mind: the elk, the chase, the bear, the blood. The hunger. The taste of life coursing through my veins, the surge of power that had filled me. It was all too vivid, too raw.

I closed my eyes, trying to shut it all out, but sleep wouldn't come. Every sound, every scent, every flicker of movement outside my window kept me on edge. My senses were too sharp, my mind too restless. The forest seemed to call out to me, a primal force I couldn't ignore.

What am I supposed to do now?

The hunger might have been satisfied for now, but I knew it wouldn't last. And when it came back, when it clawed its way to the surface again, what then? The thought sent a shiver down my spine, a cold dread settling in the pit of my stomach.

I turned onto my side, clutching the pillow as though it could anchor me. My body felt like it was humming, every nerve alive with energy, but my mind spiraled into a pit of questions I couldn't answer. Would I ever feel normal again? Could I even *be* normal again?

The face in the mirror flashed in my mind, and a wave of fear washed over me. I didn't know who that person was or what I was becoming. The absence of a heartbeat, the eerie stillness in my chest, was a constant reminder of the change.

But one thing was certain.

This was only the beginning.

Dawn seeped into the cracks of the blinds, painting faint golden streaks across the walls. The city outside began to stir, the hum of life growing louder as morning inched forward. I stepped inside my apartment, closing the door behind me with a soft click. The warmth of the hunt still thrummed in my veins, a lingering buzz of adrenaline and raw power, but it was starting to fade.

The elation I'd felt while running through the forest, testing the limits of this new body, was slowly being replaced by something else—an unease that crept over me like a shadow. The power, the speed, the clarity—they had been intoxicating, overwhelming even. But now, with the rush behind me, they felt alien, as though I'd stepped into a stranger's skin and hadn't yet learned how to wear it.

Leaning against the door, I let out a shaky breath, listening to the faint sounds of the building around me. My breaths came evenly, but my chest didn't rise and fall the way it used to. It was subtle, the way my body no longer mimicked human rhythms, but I noticed it now, and the realization sent a shiver down my spine.

Then there was my pulse—if it could still be called that. I was sure it was there, but it didn't beat like it used to. It was too fast, a humming vibration buried somewhere deep inside me, so rapid it seemed to exist beyond sound or touch. I pressed a hand to my chest, searching for the comforting thud of my heartbeat, but all I felt was a faint flutter, like the wings of a moth trapped behind a glass pane.

The apartment was quiet, but my senses picked up every sound beyond its walls—the creak of wood as the building settled, the muffled drone of a television from the apartment below, the faint rustle of a newspaper being unfolded somewhere down the hall. Even further still, I could hear the distant, rhythmic steps of someone walking their dog, the scrape of a leash dragging against concrete. It wasn't just sound. I could almost feel it, as if the vibrations were traveling through the air and into my skin.

I pushed off the door, my movements slower, more deliberate than they needed to be. Each step across the hardwood floor felt magnified, the faint scrape of my shoes reverberating in my ears like a drumbeat. The apartment felt smaller somehow, its walls closer, the space more suffocating than it had ever been.

My feet carried me to the kitchen, where I opened the fridge out of habit, the motion as automatic as it was futile. The faint hum of the motor filled the silence, but the cold air that wafted out was unappealing, carrying no temptation. My eyes scanned the shelves—eggs nestled in their carton, a few slices of leftover pizza, a half-eaten sandwich, a carton of milk—but none of it stirred even the faintest pang of hunger. It all looked... artificial. Props on a stage, food meant for someone else, someone whose body still functioned with a human's rhythm and needs.

I closed the fridge without taking anything, the hollow thud of the door echoing behind me like a dismissive farewell. The sound resonated within me, another reminder of the chasm that now existed between who I was and who I used to be.

The couch in the living room caught my eye, its familiar contours o-ffering a promise of comfort, a sanctuary from the strange new world I inhabited. I crossed the room, my steps measured, and sank into it, letting the cushions absorb the tension that had settled deep within my body.

My limbs coiled and relaxed in a way that felt strange, as if they were adjusting to a new set of rules I didn't fully understand. The sensation was unsettling, a stark reminder of the transformation that had taken place within me.

I leaned my head back against the cushions and closed my eyes, trying to quiet the thoughts racing through my mind. The stillness of the apartment pressed down on me, amplifying the questions I couldn't seem to escape. Each tick of the clock on the wall felt like a drumbeat, counting out the seconds of my new existence.

The night replayed in my head—the chase, the feeding, the primal satisfaction that came with it. I'd felt alive out there, powerful, as though the world had finally revealed its hidden layers to me. The wind in my hair, the scent of the night, the rush of blood—it had all been intoxicating. But now, in the harsh light of morning, that power felt like a chain, tethering me to something I didn't ask for and didn't want.

The reality of my situation settled over me like a shroud, heavy and inescapable. I was no longer just Tristan; I was something more, something dangerous, something forever tied to this strange world and its relentless demands.

My eyes drifted to the ceiling, where the faint patterns of sunlight filtering through the blinds danced like ghosts. Everything had changed so quickly, so completely, that it was hard to believe any of it was real. The black voids of my eyes had once been the most alarming thing about my transformation, but now they were something else entirely.

They weren't just voids anymore. The streaks of color I'd glimpsed in my reflection earlier weren't an illusion—they were real, swirling beneath the surface like molten silver struggling to break free. My eyes had been windows into nothingness, but now they were something in-between—something I didn't understand.

I opened my hand, turning it palm-up and studying the lines and creases etched into my skin. My body had changed, every muscle and sinew honed and sharpened like a blade. My skin was flawless, my movements fluid, my senses sharper than I'd ever thought possible. But it didn't feel like my body anymore.

This isn't me.

The thought came unbidden, cutting through the haze of my mind like a blade. I was no longer Tristan Blake—not entirely, anyway. The reflection in the mirror wasn't the man I'd been yesterday or the week before. It was someone new, someone I didn't recognize.

I leaned forward, resting my elbows on my knees as the weight of it all pressed down on me. The hunger had been sated, at least for now, but the questions it left behind gnawed at me just as fiercely.

What was I now?

The question lingered, heavy and unanswered. My reflection in the mirror revealed more than I wanted to know. The black voids in my eyes were fading, replaced by streaks of color so vivid they seemed almost alive. But that didn't mean I was returning to who I was. If anything, the changes served as a reminder that I had crossed a line, that the Tristan Blake I once knew was gone.

My thoughts drifted to the hunt, to the moment I sank my fangs into the elk's neck and felt its life force surge into me. The rush had been unlike anything I'd ever experienced—pure, unfiltered vitality coursing through my veins, sharpening every sense, every thought. It wasn't just physical sustenance; it was something deeper, more primal. Then there was the second feeding, the bear. That had been different, sloppier, but no less intense. It had filled me, satisfying a hunger I hadn't fully understood. But it hadn't extinguished the questions.

Marcus's face came unbidden to my mind, his cold, unrelenting gaze, the words he'd spoken to me on the balcony. He had turned me into this... this *monster*, and then vanished without giving me any answers. I clenched my fists, my nails biting into the flesh of my palms—not enough to hurt, but enough to ground me. The memory of his voice echoed through my thoughts, each syllable a taunting reminder of the transformation he'd forced upon me.

"What do you want from me, Marcus?" I whispered into the empty apartment, my voice barely audible even to my heightened senses.

The silence that followed was deafening. I leaned my head back against the couch, staring at the ceiling as the weight of it all pressed down on me. Marcus had changed me, but why? What did he see in me that made him choose this path for my life? And more importantly, what did he expect me to become in this new, dark world he'd thrust me into?

My gaze drifted to the stack of unopened mail on the coffee table, buried beneath a layer of dust. Somewhere in there was a photo—a snapshot of my old life, a reminder of who I used to be. I didn't want to look at it, didn't want to see the face of the man I was losing. But my hand reached for it anyway, compelled by a mix of nostalgia and a desperate need for clarity.

The photo was from last year, a work event that now felt like a lifetime ago. Benji, Jessica, and I were front and center, grinning like idiots with beers in hand. Even Ash, who hated being in photos, had been caught mid-eye-roll in the background. We were carefree, ordinary, human. The contrast between that moment and the present was stark, a chasm that seemed impossible to bridge. The old Tristan in the photo was a stranger now, replaced by the creature I had become.

I stared at my own face in the photo, tracing the lines with my thumb. That version of Tristan Blake didn't exist anymore. The man in the picture had flaws, doubts, fears—but he also had a sense of himself, a connection to the world around him. He was part of something, even if he didn't always appreciate it.

I placed the photo back on the table, my chest tightening, the edges of the print leaving a faint impression on my fingertips. I didn't feel connected to anything anymore. The mirror had shown me someone else—someone sharper, stronger, more dangerous. My reflection was a stranger, his vivid hazel eyes gleaming with an otherworldly glow of silver and gold swirls. I couldn't reconcile that image with the memories of who I used to be, the person staring back at me from the photograph.

The city outside was waking up, the hum of life growing louder with each passing minute, a stark contrast to the silent, still world I now inhabited. I stood and walked to the window, staring down at the street below. People hurried by, caught up in their routines, their hearts beating in a rhythm I could no longer share. They were oblivious to the existence of someone like me, a creature lurking in the shadows of their ordinary lives. Their world hadn't changed, but mine had been turned inside out, shaken by the profound transformation that now defined me.

You don't belong here anymore.

The thought came unbidden, whispering through my mind like a cold wind. I pushed it aside, refusing to accept it, yet deep down, I knew it was true. This apartment, this life, this version of me—it was all slipping away, replaced by something darker, something I didn't fully understand. The echoes of my past seemed to fade with each moment, drowned out by the relentless beat of a new existence.

As the sun climbed higher, its light cutting through the blinds and casting sharp angles across the room, I returned to the couch. My mind was a tangled mess of thoughts and fears, each vying for dominance. The hunger had been sated, but it hadn't disappeared. It was still there, lurking beneath the surface like a predator waiting to strike. And I knew it would resurface, demanding to be fed, reminding me of the insatiable thirst that now defined my existence.

This wasn't just a change. It was a transformation, one I couldn't outrun or undo. And as much as I wanted to cling to who I used to be, I couldn't ignore the truth any longer. The old Tristan Blake was fading away, replaced by a creature of the night, a vampire with a thirst for blood. This was my reality now, and I had to find a way to navigate it, no matter how dark and uncertain the path ahead might be.

I wasn't Tristan Blake anymore. Not entirely.

And whoever I was becoming, I wasn't sure I wanted to know.

INTO THE WILD

I couldn't stay here. The thought clung to me like a shadow, impossible to ignore, its claws deep in my bones. My apartment felt alien, each familiar corner now suffocating. The walls contracted with every breath, exhaling stale air from a life I no longer recognized. The city's hum grated on my nerves; every car horn, hurried footstep, and arrhythmic heartbeat pulsed through concrete veins, taunting me. Each sound carried a primal scent of humanity, echoing within me like war drums, even the neighbor's faucet drip vibrating against my eardrums.

The hunger was quieter now, tamed for the moment by last night's feeding. The animals I'd managed to catch had taken the edge off, but it hadn't silenced the ache completely. It lingered at the edges of my thoughts, a dull sawing at the base of my skull, reminding me how fragile my control was.

I caught my reflection in the microwave door as I leaned against the counter. My eyes—once hazel—had become something else entirely. They were still, the pupils almost swallowing the irises, but faint swirls of color danced within the voids, like oil spreading across black water, iridescent and treacherous. They shifted and changed in the dim light, catching fractured glints from the dying bulb above, becoming kaleidoscopes of absence. They were hypnotic in a way that unsettled me, beautiful yet alien, windows to a storm brewing behind my sternum.

"What am I becoming?" I whispered, my voice barely audible. The reflection didn't answer, though its lips moved a fraction slower than mine, as if the glass held truths my throat couldn't shape.

The thought of staying here, surrounded by people, was unbearable. Every moment felt like a risk, every stray sound or scent a trigger waiting to push me over the edge. The perfume of the florist's shop below had become a funeral bouquet, and the chatter of children at the bus stop was a siren's song. I couldn't trust myself, not yet. Maybe not ever. The city wasn't a home anymore—it was a minefield, every smiling stranger a potential casualty.

"I need to leave," I said aloud, as if saying it would make it real. My hand gripped the counter, the cool metal grounding me for just a moment, leaving crescent moon indents in the steel. "I need to figure this out before it's too late." The words tasted like a lie. Wasn't it already too late the moment Marcus' teeth found me? The moment my own heart began its silent sprint?

The decision to leave wasn't easy, but it was necessary. Necessary like cauterizing a wound, like swallowing broken glass to quiet a scream. By the time the sun dipped below the horizon, I had packed a bag with whatever I thought I'd need: some clothes, stiff with disuse and smelling of mothballs; my phone, a dead weight of dead connections; a charger, its cord coiled like a noose; and a knife I'd picked up years ago for a camping trip that never happened. The blade glinted when I tested its edge, singing a silver note that harmonized with the itch beneath my skin. It wasn't much, but it would have to do. Survival, I was learning, required not preparation but surrender.

I drove out of the city in silence, the skyline shrinking in my rearview mirror like a receding tide of steel and glass. The forest loomed ahead, its pine-crowned heights breathing shadows across the windshield. The roads grew narrower, the trees pressing closer in leafy exhalations until I finally reached a dirt path and pulled over. The air here was different—cleaner, sharper, piercing my nostrils like icicle daggers—and filled with the scents of earth and leaves, a symphony of decay and growth that made my jaw ache

.

I stepped out of the car, slinging my bag over my shoulder as I faced the forest. The engine ticked its disapproval behind me. The towering trees seemed to watch me, their branches swaying gently in the breeze, needles hissing secrets in a language older than blood. A shiver ran through me, not from cold, but from the terrible understanding that I was the intruder here, but I pushed it aside.

This was where I needed to be. Where the monsters lived. Where I belonged.

The forest felt alive in ways that defied language. Every step I took was met with the crunch of leaves screaming their final protest or the snap of a twig sharp as a bone fracture, the sounds stark against the backdrop of rustling branches and distant birdcalls. My senses were dialed up to eleven, needles jammed into their redlined gauges, every detail magnified to the point of overwhelm. The damp earth beneath my boots smelled rich and loamy, layered with hints of pine and moss and the iron tang of a thousand decomposed lives. I could taste the age of the oaks, their sap running bitter and slow like congealed time.

I moved cautiously at first, testing my footing on the uneven ground. My shadow stretched long between the trunks, mimicking my hesitations. Surprisingly, I wasn't clumsy; the forest seemed etched into my muscle memory. My strides became longer and smoother, and when I ran, the trees blurred into a green-grey watercolor.

It wasn't perfect—I stumbled over roots like spiteful serpents and snagged my jacket on branches with splintered claws—but it felt natural, as if I was meant to be here, a phantom threading through the woods.

Leaning against a tree, bark biting into my shoulder blade, I stared up at the canopy. The sunlight filtering through the leaves felt warm and golden, though I could still see faint halos of violets and crimsons bleeding around each beam like prismatic bruises.

The tree shuddered under my touch. Or maybe I did.

The first night was a challenge. Here, night was a presence—thick and velveteen, pressing against my pupils until they swallowed the world. I found a small clearing, dropped my bag, and sat cross-legged on the hard ground, which felt as unyielding as a church pew. The air was cool, sharp like freshly whetted knives, and the forest sounds were louder than expected.

Every creak, scuttle, and rustle made my muscles tense, my spine crackling with static anticipation. My heightened senses were both a gift and a curse, spinning me in every direction like a mad compass.

I closed my eyes, trying to block it out, but my eyelids offered little protection against the sensory flood. Sleep wouldn't come. Instead, fragments of memories slipped through my mind—vivid yet disjointed. They weren't mine; I knew that much.

I saw Marcus, younger and less hardened, running through a forest much like this one. His laughter was a foreign country, bright and jagged. His movements were fluid, almost hypnotic, as he weaved between trees with a predator's grace. Moonlight stippled his skin like war paint. There was a thrill in the chase, the electric joy of the hunt, a hunger that mirrored my own.

The memory shifted, slipping through my fingers like black sand, showing me glimpses of battles—clawed hands slick with gore, blood arcing in slow-motion crescents—and faces I didn't recognize. A woman screamed soundlessly. A man's eyes widened as his throat became a fountain. Each image carried a weight that pressed down on me, a lodestone of guilt, filling my chest with an ache I couldn't explain. Were these his sins or just dreams?

When dawn broke, staining the eastern sky the color of a healing wound, I was still sitting in the clearing, the faint light painting the forest in shades of green and gold. My muscles were stiff, petrified wood beneath flesh, but I felt sharper, more awake than I had in days. The woods had etched their teachings into my soul throughout the night—survival meant transforming into rock, transforming into tempest.

The following days tested my will and instincts, a brutal lesson in monstrous survival. I devoted myself to adapting, eager to explore my body's limits. Initially, I stumbled, tripping over roots that seemed to twist beneath me and slipping on treacherous wet rocks. My movements lacked the precision I had witnessed in Marcus's memories. Each failure left me snarling at the indifferent trees, my new fangs biting into my lower lip.

But with each stumble, I learned. The forest was a harsh tutor, its curriculum written in scars and adrenaline.

Running became easier. My strides grew longer, my footing more sure. Wind became an accomplice, howling encouragement through the pines. I started timing myself, weaving between trees so closely their bark grazed my ribs and vaulting over fallen logs in arcs that defied gravity's pull. The forest became a playground, each obstacle a challenge to overcome, each successful maneuver a temporary salve for the rot in my soul.

Hunting, though, was another matter entirely.

The first time I caught the scent of blood, I froze. It was faint but unmistakable, cutting through the other scents of the forest like a blade. My pulse quickened as the hunger flared to life, sharp and insistent. I followed the trail instinctively, moving through the woods with a silence that surprised even me.

When I found the source—a wounded deer caught in a hunter's trap—I hesitated. Its wide, terrified eyes locked onto mine, and for a moment, I felt a pang of guilt. But the hunger wouldn't let me walk away.

The deer's wide eyes stared into mine, glimmering with fear and pain. Its leg was twisted awkwardly in the steel jaws of a hunter's trap, the skin torn and bloodied. The scent of its blood filled my senses, sharp and electric, and I could feel the hunger roaring back to life. My chest tightened as I fought to suppress it, but the animal's pain made it difficult. The smell of fresh blood felt like tendrils wrapping around my body, tempting and taunting me.

For a moment, I stood frozen, torn between the urge to feed and the guilt gnawing at me for even considering it. The deer's body trembled with every shallow breath, its chest rising and falling like a dying heartbeat. With each whimper, my resolve weakened, the vampire side of me screaming to take over. It was a battle I was beginning to realize I might not win. My hands twitched, my nails elongating slightly as the hunger threatened to consume me.

"I'm sorry," I whispered, though I wasn't sure what I was apologizing for—being here, being this, or being tempted by its suffering. The words felt hollow, insufficient against the primal urge coursing through my veins. My throat burned, my fangs aching to be released.

I crouched slowly, trying not to startle the animal further. My mind raced, flicking through half-formed plans, but none felt right. The memory of Marcus's hunts flitted across my mind, vivid and visceral, and I could almost hear his voice in the back of my head: Survival comes first. The clarity in his voice was shocking but cruel.

"No," I muttered, shaking the thought away. "That's not who I am." But was it? Was I fooling myself? Every fiber of my being yearned for the release that feeding would bring, the satisfaction of quenching the burning thirst that never truly went away. The idea of giving in, of succumbing to my nature, was terrifying.

My gaze drifted to the blood pooling around the deer's leg, and an idea sparked. It was ridiculous, but it was all I had. A desperate act of selflessness to combat the selfishness growing inside me. If I could save this creature, perhaps I could save a little bit of myself.

What if it works? The question echoed in my mind, a fragile hope flickering amidst the darkness. It was a long shot, a gamble based on nothing more than a far-fetched idea and a desperate desire to do something good, and I really wanted this to work.

My favorite scenes from *Underworld* flashed in my head, moments where vampires used their blood to heal. I had always thought it was just cinematic flair, but now... now I wasn't so sure. Could there be some truth to it? Some ancient knowledge lost to time? Or was I just grasping at straws, seeking any justification to avoid the inevitable? Still, I was hopeful because I knew it was better than nothing.

I hesitated, then sank my teeth into my wrist. The skin yielded easily, and crimson blood welled up. It didn't hurt as much as I expected, but the sight churned my stomach. It felt wrong to use my own life force like this, a violation of my being.

"This is so stupid," I muttered, pressing the bleeding wound against the deer's leg. My words were self-deprecating, laced with fear—fear of failure, disappointment, and what I was becoming. Despite the impossible odds, a sliver of hope remained.

For a moment, nothing happened. The deer struggled weakly, but I held firm, whispering soothingly to keep it still. I knew it would be fine soon. Then, I saw it—tiny tendrils of my blood seeping into its flesh, knitting the torn skin together. The transformation was subtle yet undeniable; the gash began to close, fur regrowing in patches. It was fascinating, horrifying, and strangely beautiful.

The deer flinched, its large eyes darting between its leg and me. I stepped back as it scrambled to its feet. We locked eyes, a strange understanding passing between us—a silent acknowledgment of the impossible act I had just performed. The deer sensed my help, and I caught a flicker of gratitude in its gaze.

"Go," I said softly.

The deer bolted, disappearing into the trees with a grace I envied. I stood there, watching the shadows swallow it whole, a strange mix of relief and hunger twisting in my gut. Relief that I had been able to help, but also a gnawing emptiness where the hunger used to be. The act of giving had only intensified the need to take. This wasn't going to be easy.

My stomach growled, low and insistent, and I pressed a hand to it as if that would help. Saving the deer had felt right, but it hadn't solved my problem. The hunger was still there, sharper now that I had tasted my own blood. It was a reminder of what I was, what I needed, and what I was trying so desperately to deny.

I wiped my wrist against my shirt, noting how quickly the bite mark had vanished. My body was a puzzle I didn't understand, and every new discovery brought more questions than answers. But one thing was clear: I couldn't ignore the hunger any longer. It was a constant companion, a shadow lurking just beneath the surface, threatening to consume me entirely. I hated knowing there was nothing I could do about it.

The plan came together as I moved through the forest, my senses tuned to the sounds and scents around me. I needed to hunt—needed to feed. I had to do it soon, before the hunger overwhelmed me completely. But this time, I was determined to do it differently. I couldn't let myself become a monster.

The scent of the mountain lion hit me before I saw it. It was faint at first, a musky, earthy smell that grew stronger as I followed it. A predator, like me, but one that didn't have the luxury of choice. It killed to survive, without remorse or guilt. I wondered if that was what awaited me if I couldn't find a way to control my hunger.

I moved silently through the underbrush with natural precision. My footsteps were light, my body instinctively dodging branches and leaves that could betray me. The trees blurred as I pushed forward, moving faster than any human could. It was exhilarating and terrifying, this newfound strength and speed, a sign of the power dormant within me, ready to be unleashed.

When I spotted the mountain lion, my breath caught. It was perched on a low rock, its sleek body coiled with muscle, golden fur glinting in the sunlight. It was beautiful, powerful, and completely unaware of my presence. A perfect specimen, perfectly adapted to its environment. And I was about to violate the natural order by preying on it.

I hesitated, crouching low behind a fallen log. The predator in me screamed to strike, to take what I needed, but a small voice in the back of my mind whispered doubts. The lion meant no harm, yet, in order for me to live and continue to survive, the lion had to be the sacrifice.

Is this who I am now? The question haunted me, a constant reminder of the person I used to be. Was I still that person? Or had the transformation changed me so fundamentally that I was no longer recognizable, even to myself? I hated not knowing the answer.

The mountain lion's ears twitched, its head turning slightly as if it had sensed me. I tensed, every muscle in my body ready to spring into action. The moment of truth had arrived. There was no turning back now. I had to do this.

Yes, I thought, silencing the doubts. This is survival. It was a justification, a rationalization, but it was enough to propel me forward. I was doing what I had to do to survive.

I lunged, my body moving faster than I had expected. The mountain lion barely had time to react before I was on it, my hands gripping its shoulders as we tumbled to the ground. It snarled, claws raking at my arms, but I didn't feel the pain. My instincts took over, guiding me with a precision that was equal parts terrifying and exhilarating. It was as though some part of me had been waiting for this moment, eager to embrace my true nature.

As I pinned the animal beneath me, I pressed my face close to its neck, the scent of its blood overwhelming. My teeth sank in, and the taste was unlike anything I had ever experienced—rich, wild, and electric. A symphony of flavors ignited my senses. It was intoxicating.

But as I fed, I felt its heart slowing beneath my fingers, the steady rhythm weakening with each passing moment. The realization of what I was doing hit me like a physical blow.

"That's enough," I gasped, pulling back. The horror of my actions washed over me, a wave of nausea and self-loathing. I had almost crossed the line. Almost became the monster I feared.

The mountain lion's eyes fluttered open, its breath shallow but steady. I staggered away, wiping my mouth with the back of my hand. The hunger had eased, but the guilt remained, heavy and unshakable. The taste of blood lingered on my tongue as I watched the lion with concern and worry.

The mountain lion rose slowly, glaring at me before slinking off into the trees. I watched it disappear, a strange mix of relief and unease coursing through me. I had spared its life, but at what cost? The guilt was building up inside me even more than before.

I stare at the spot where the mountain lion disappeared, my breathing ragged not from exertion but from the emotional turmoil raging inside me. The taste of its blood still coats my tongue, rich and satisfying, yet tainted by my own disgust at what I've become. I make a silent vow then, standing alone in the forest with blood on my lips: I will never kill for survival. Never. This hunger that claws at me, this monstrous need that threatens to consume my humanity—I refuse to let it dictate who I am.

If I must feed to survive in this new existence, I'll ensure that whatever animal provides that sustenance walks away afterward. Their survival matters as much as mine. I'll take only what I need, leaving them weakened perhaps, but alive to continue their own journey through this world.

The mountain lion's retreating form becomes a symbol of this promise—proof that I can maintain some semblance of humanity despite the changes Marcus forced upon me. My fangs retract as I wipe my mouth clean. I had fed, but I hadn't killed. It was a small victory, but one that left me questioning whether I could keep this up.

The forest had become my training ground. The towering trees, sprawling roots, and scattered boulders presented challenges I never could have imagined back in the city. At first, I stumbled—misjudging distances and tripping over uneven terrain—but now, after weeks of practice, I moved with a confidence that felt almost instinctual.

I wasn't just surviving anymore; I was thriving.

Mornings were my favorite. The cool air was crisp against my skin, carrying the faint scent of dew and pine. My body hummed with energy, the hunger a distant murmur instead of a roar. I began each day with a run, weaving through the trees at a speed that made the world blur around me.

The first time I leapt over a fallen log, something inside me clicked. My body seemed to know what to do before my brain caught up, muscles coiling and releasing with perfect timing. I landed lightly on the other side, barely making a sound beneath my boots.

I wanted more.

That's when I started experimenting.

The fallen logs became hurdles, and low-hanging branches turned into obstacles to vault over. I tested myself, running harder, leaping higher, pushing my body to its limits. When I wasn't running, I was climbing. The trees here were ancient, their trunks thick and gnarled, their branches high and sturdy. At first, scaling them felt impossible, my hands slipping on the bark and my footing unsure.

But I kept trying.

Every failure taught me something new. I adjusted my grip, shifted my weight, and soon I was climbing faster than I thought possible. I scrambled to the highest branches, balancing on limbs that should have snapped beneath me, and looked out over the endless expanse of forest.

From up there, the world felt different—smaller, perhaps. More manageable.

The idea to practice flips came from a memory of watching parkour videos online back in the city. I had always been fascinated by how those athletes seemed to defy gravity, their movements fluid and deliberate. If they could do it, why couldn't I?

My first attempts were... ugly.

I tried a simple backflip off a low rock, and instead of landing on my feet, I sprawled onto my back with a loud oof. The impact didn't hurt—not the way it would have before—but it bruised my pride enough to keep me going.

By the end of the week, I was landing cleanly. By the end of the month, I was adding twists and spins, my movements smooth and controlled. I felt like a different person—like I was finally embracing the potential of what I had become.

There was something freeing about it. The flips, the leaps, the speed—it all felt like a celebration of this new version of myself. For the first time, I stopped questioning and started asking what I could do.

The realization about my feeding came almost by accident.

It had been a month since I left the city, and I had fallen into a routine of hunting every few days. I didn't track how much blood I consumed at first; I was too focused on easing the hunger and staying in control. But as the days turned into weeks, I started to notice a pattern.

Three gallons. That was the magic number.

Whenever I drank more than that, the hunger vanished entirely, replaced by a calm, almost euphoric clarity. It was as if my body was telling me, That's enough. What surprised me even more was how long it lasted—nine days, give or take, before the hunger started creeping back in.

The discovery felt monumental, like I had unlocked a secret to my survival.

One afternoon, I sat by the edge of a small stream, staring at my reflection in the rippling water. My eyes, still dark but flecked with swirling colors, stared back at me with a calm I hadn't seen before. The face looking back wasn't the same as the one I remembered, but for the first time, that didn't scare me.

"I'm a vampire," I said aloud, the words strange on my tongue.

It was the first time I'd admitted it to myself, and saying it felt like a weight lifting off my shoulders. I wasn't human anymore—that much was clear. But I wasn't a monster either.

I traced my fingers over the surface of the water, watching the ripples distort my reflection. I had spent weeks running from what I was, fighting it, resenting it. But out here, in the quiet embrace of the forest, I found something I hadn't expected: acceptance.

I was still me. Still Tristan Blake.

And for the first time since this began, I felt... okay.

The next morning, I climbed to the top of a tree as the sun rose, bathing the forest in hues of gold and green. The wind tugged at my hair, carrying with it the faint scent of rain. I closed my eyes, letting the breeze wash over me, and smiled.

The hunger would return eventually. Challenges would come. But for now, I was ready.

The forest held more secrets than I realized. Beyond physical challenges, I was undergoing a different kind of training, sharpening my senses. The world transformed from a blur into a symphony of details. I could hear leaves rustling before the wind arrived, smell damp earth beneath the trees, and sense creatures moving through the undergrowth.

My enhanced hearing surprised me. Initially overwhelming, it threatened to drive me mad. But as I learned to filter the noise, it became invaluable. I could distinguish a squirrel scampering from a deer cautiously stepping through leaves, even hear the distant murmur of a stream, hidden from view.

And then there was my heart; I imagined it beating like a humming-bird's wings, so fast it was almost a blur. So silent that it echoed in the chasm where normal hearts could be heard. It fueled my speed and strength, but it also kept me on edge. I could feel the pulse of energy coursing through my veins, a constant surge that made me feel both powerful and vulnerable.

I learned to use this hyper-awareness. It aided my balance, agility, and reflexes. I was a predator now, and the forest was my hunting ground.

Hunting wasn't just about survival; it was a test of skill, a way to hone my abilities. I tracked deer, followed their trails through the dense undergrowth, learning their habits and movements. I studied the way the wind shifted, carrying scents that could betray my presence. I practiced moving silently, my feet barely touching the ground, my body a shadow among the trees.

When the time came, I struck with precision and speed. No pro-longed chase, no unnecessary suffering. A swift, clean hunt, and then the replenishing drink. I was careful not to take more than I needed, respectful of the forest's balance. I was part of this ecosystem now, and I had a responsibility to maintain its harmony.

The nights were different. The forest transformed into a realm of shadows and whispers. The trees loomed like silent sentinels, their branches clawing at the inky sky. The sounds of the day faded, replaced by the nocturnal chorus of owls and crickets.

At first, the darkness unnerved me. I missed the artificial lights of the city and the feeling of safety they provided. But as the weeks passed, I grew accustomed to the night, learning to see in the shadows and navigate by the faint light of the moon and stars.

My vision had adapted, becoming sharper and more sensitive to light. I could see details that would have been invisible to human eyes—the faint shimmer of moonlight on a spider's web, the subtle glow of phosphorescent fungi, the glint of eyes in the darkness.

The night became my ally, a time when my senses were at their peak. I would run for hours, pushing myself harder than ever before, reveling in the freedom of movement. The forest was my playground, and the darkness was my cloak.

One night, while perched high in a tree, I witnessed a meteor shower. Streaks of light blazed across the sky, igniting the darkness with fleeting brilliance. I felt a sense of awe, a connection to something larger than myself. It was a reminder that I was just a small part of a vast and wondrous universe.

In that moment, I felt a surge of gratitude. Gratitude for the challenges that had brought me here, for the strength I had discovered within myself, and for the beauty that surrounded me.

I closed my eyes, taking a deep breath of the cool night air, and made a promise to myself. I would not squander this gift. I would not succumb to despair. I would embrace this new life, learn from it, and use my abilities to protect the innocent.

The forest had become my sanctuary, my teacher, my home. And I was ready to face whatever challenges lay ahead.

However, solitude began to breed a different kind of challenge: loneliness. It crept in subtly, a quiet whisper in the back of my mind. At first,

I barely noticed it, too preoccupied with survival and training. But as the days turned into weeks, it grew louder, more insistent.

I missed the companionship of others, the simple act of conversation. I missed the laughter, the debates, the shared experiences that had once filled my life. I missed the connection to humanity, the sense of belonging.

I tried to ignore it, burying myself in my training, but the loneliness persisted. It was like a phantom limb, an ache for something that was no longer there.

One day, I found myself talking to the trees. Silly, I know. But I could almost feel them listening. I'd tell them about my old life, my family, my friends, my dreams. I'd share the challenges I was facing, the doubts that plagued me, the fears that haunted my nights.

It helped a little. It was a way to vent my emotions, to release the pent-up energy building inside me. But it wasn't the same as talking to a real person, someone who could offer advice, support, and understanding.

I considered returning to the city, just for a visit, but I knew it was a dangerous idea. I wasn't ready to face the world yet, not while I was still struggling to control my hunger and impulses. Besides, what would I say to my friends and family? How could I explain what I had become?

No, the city was out of the question. For now, I had to stay here in the forest and face my demons alone.

I decided to focus on my strengths, on the things I could control. I redoubled my efforts to master my abilities and refine my skills. I spent hours meditating, trying to calm the storm within me and find a sense of inner peace.

I also began to explore the woods more thoroughly, venturing into areas I had previously avoided. I discovered hidden glades, cascading waterfalls, and ancient ruins that spoke of a forgotten past.

The forest was full of surprises, beauty, and wonder. As I explored, I began to feel a sense of connection to this place, a sense of belonging.

Maybe this was my home now. Perhaps I was meant to be here, in the wilderness, far from the distractions and temptations of the city. Maybe this was where I would find my purpose and destiny.

The sun began its fiery descent, painting the sky in hues of orange, purple, and red. I watched in silence, feeling a sense of peace wash over me.

The hunger would return eventually, and the challenges would come. But for now, I was ready.

The forest had become more than just a refuge—it was a part of me now. Every tree, every rock, every stream felt like an extension of my senses. I moved through it with ease, my steps light and deliberate, my presence blending seamlessly with the world around me.

I wasn't just surviving anymore; I was living.

For weeks, I roamed aimlessly, setting up makeshift camps wherever I felt like it—one night beneath a fallen tree, the next among boulders. But as time passed, I craved something permanent, a place to call my own. It was about more than practicality; it was about belonging. This forest was my home, and it was time to treat it as such.

I found the perfect spot by accident while chasing a buck through the dense underbrush. The creature had been too fast and clever, and I lost it near a rocky outcrop hidden deep within the woods.

Frustrated, I stopped to catch my breath and looked around. The outcrop rose like a natural fortress, its craggy surface dotted with moss and lichen. The ground below was sheltered, surrounded by thick bushes and uneven terrain that made it nearly impossible for anyone—or anything—to approach unnoticed.

A stream ran nearby, its water glistening like liquid glass in the dappled sunlight. The canopy above provided ample cover, the interwoven branches forming a natural roof that kept the area shaded and cool.

"This is it," I murmured, running my fingers over the rough bark of a nearby tree.

The thought of having a place to call my own filled me with a strange sense of hope. For the first time in weeks, I felt a spark of excitement—not the frantic rush of a hunt or the fleeting thrill of a successful leap, but something quieter and steadier.

I got to work.

The first few days were a blur of trial and error. I scavenged fallen branches, sturdy and thick, and wove them together with vines to create a framework for the shelter. My strength made it easier to carry the heavier pieces, and my heightened senses helped me find the sturdiest materials, but building something that wouldn't collapse under its own weight was a challenge.

Branches snapped, vines slipped from my grip, and more than once, an entire section of the frame came crashing down just as I thought I had it secured. Each failure was frustrating, but it also taught me something. I learned to test the tension of the vines, to layer the branches in a way that distributed weight more evenly, and to take my time instead of rushing to finish.

By the end of the week, the shelter began to take shape.

The walls were made of interwoven branches, layered with moss and leaves to camouflage them against the forest floor. For the roof, I used bark and larger leaves, securing them tightly to keep out the rain. The entrance was small, just big enough for me to squeeze through, and I reinforced it with a makeshift door fashioned from a slab of bark tied together with vines.

It wasn't much to look at, but it was mine.

The first night in the shelter felt different. The forest was still alive with its usual sounds—the rustle of leaves, the chirping of crickets—but there was a sense of peace I hadn't felt before. I sat inside, the earthy scent of moss and bark filling the air, and ran my fingers over the rough walls.

It felt good to have a place to return to, a place where I could rest without constantly looking over my shoulder. The shelter wasn't just a refuge; it was a symbol of how far I'd come since leaving the city.

Over the next few days, I made small improvements. I lined the floor with layers of soft moss and leaves, creating a cushion that made it easier to rest. I added a hidden corner for my few belongings, weaving a small compartment into the wall where I could store my knife and spare clothes.

I even worked on a system to block the entrance from the inside—a tangle of vines that I could pull across to keep out curious animals or any uninvited guests.

Bit by bit, the shelter became more than just a place to sleep; it became a home.

As I settled into my new routine, I felt a deeper connection to the trees. I knew its rhythms now—the way the shadows shifted with the sun, the paths the animals took, the subtle changes in the air before a storm. I had become a part of its ecosystem, moving through it like any other creature.

There were moments when I felt almost human again. I'd sit by the stream, letting the cool water run over my hands, or lie on the forest floor, staring up at the stars. But those moments were fleeting, tempered by the constant reminder of what I had become.

This was my life now. And for the first time, I was okay with that.

Building the shelter had taught me something I hadn't expected: patience. The same patience I had used to piece together the frame and secure the vines now extended to every aspect of my life. Whether I was hunting, running, or simply exploring, I moved with a deliberate calm that felt natural, even comforting.

The forest was my world now, and every day, it felt a little more like home.

The idea of truly settling down, of building something lasting, was a novel sensation. Before, my existence had been a frantic dance of survival, a constant flight from the past. Now, I was building toward a future, however uncertain it might be. The shelter was a testament to that. Each carefully placed branch and tightly woven vine was a declaration of my intent to stay, to make this forest my own.

The forest, in turn, seemed to respond to my efforts. The animals, initially wary, grew accustomed to my presence. Squirrels chattered at me from the branches, their fear replaced by cautious curiosity. Deer grazed nearby, their eyes still watchful, but their bodies relaxed. Even the birds seemed to sing a little louder when I was around.

I learned to read the signs of the woods with uncanny accuracy. I could tell the direction of the wind by the way the leaves rustled, predict the coming rain by the thickness of the clouds, and identify the tracks of every creature that crossed my path. The forest wasn't just a place to live; it was a book to be read, a language to be learned.

As I learned, I grew stronger—not just physically, but mentally and emotionally. The solitude, once a burden, became a source of clarity. The challenges, once overwhelming, became opportunities for growth. I was honing my senses in ways I never thought possible. My hearing was so acute that I could hear the faintest rustle of a mouse in the undergrowth. My eyesight was so sharp that I could spot a hawk circling miles away. And my sense of smell was so refined that I could distinguish between different types of trees simply by inhaling the air.

I practiced moving silently, gliding through the woods without disturbing a single leaf. It was a skill honed by necessity, but it also became a form of meditation. Each step was deliberate, each movement fluid, each breath controlled. I became one with the shadows, a whisper in the wind.

My reflexes, already heightened, became lightning fast. I could react to danger in an instant, dodging falling branches, leaping over hidden roots, and avoiding the snapping jaws of predators. It was as if my body anticipated every threat before it even materialized.

The enhanced senses of a vampire were, in some ways, a burden. The world became an overwhelming symphony of sights, sounds, and smells. But in the forest, those senses were a gift. They allowed me to navigate the wilderness with unparalleled skill, to survive in a world that would have devoured a human in an instant.

The hunt became a ritual. I didn't kill indiscriminately; I only took what I needed to survive, honoring the balance of the forest. I tracked my prey with patience and skill, learning their habits, anticipating their movements, and respecting their lives. It was a dance of predator and prey, a dance that had played out in these woods for centuries.

I began to experiment with new techniques, improving my hunting skills with each passing day. I learned to use the wind to my advantage, masking my scent from my prey. I learned to mimic the calls of other animals, luring unsuspecting creatures into my path. And I learned to blend in with the environment, becoming a part of the landscape, an invisible hunter.

The blood sustained me, of course, but it was more than mere sustenance. It connected me to the life force of the forest, reminding me of the cycle of life and death. It was like dark magic, a forbidden power, but it also came with responsibility. I knew I had to use my abilities wisely, to respect the balance of nature, and to avoid drawing unwanted attention to myself.

The forest had become my teacher, protector, and home. In turn, I had become a part of it—a silent guardian, a creature of the wild.

I launched myself off a low rock, twisting in the air before landing lightly on my feet. The movement was effortless now, my body coiling and releasing with a precision I couldn't have dreamed of before.

It was no longer just about speed; it was about style.

The flips had started as a challenge to push my limits, but now they felt like second nature. Every leap, every vault, every mid-air twist was a celebration of the control I had finally gained over this new body. I was a predator, reborn in the heart of the wild, and my movements reflected that.

I raced through the forest, weaving between trees and vaulting over fallen logs, adding spins and flips. The world blurred into a streak of green and brown, and for the first time in ages, I wasn't thinking—I was just moving. It was pure freedom. Each step whispered against the earth, the forest floor yielding to my strength and speed. The world was a canvas, and my movements painted a picture of exhilaration and liberation.

When I finally stopped, I found myself at the edge of a cliff. The forest stretched out below, an endless sea of green under a sky painted in the soft hues of twilight. The air was crisp and clean, carrying the scent of pine and damp earth. It was a breathtaking view, a panorama of nature's grandeur that filled me with awe.

This was my world now—a realm of endless green, where shadows danced like secrets, and the air hummed with the unseen energy of life.

Yet, the thought of leaving it began to creep in, uninvited and persistent. It was a nagging whisper in the back of my mind, a seed of doubt threatening to sprout and take root. The forest was my sanctuary, my haven, but the echoes of my past grew louder.

I didn't want to leave. The forest had given me everything I needed—a place to grow, to learn, to become. But the part of me that still clung to my old life, that remembered city lights and familiar faces, wouldn't let me rest. It was a constant tug-of-war, a battle between the new me and the ghost of who I once was.

I crouched at the edge of the cliff, staring out over the treetops. The wind rustled through the leaves, creating a symphony of whispers that echoed my internal turmoil. The world was beautiful but also a constant reminder of my sacrifices to become part of it. My reflection in a nearby pool of water caught my eye, and I turned to look. The water was still and dark, reflecting the twilight sky like a mirror.

Dark eyes with swirling colors stared back at me, framed by a face that was both familiar and strange. My jaw was sharper, my cheekbones more defined. The transformation had been subtle but undeniable. I was still Tristan Blake, but I wasn't the same.

"I can't avoid it forever," I muttered, running a hand through my hair. The strands were longer now, tangled with leaves and dirt—another small sign of how much I had changed, how far I had drifted from the life I once knew. The air was cool against my skin, and I could feel the subtle hum of energy coursing through my veins.

The thought of returning to the city filled me with equal parts anticipation and dread. It was a siren's call, a tantalizing whisper of familiarity promising comfort and connection. But it also represented danger, temptation, and the potential for everything I had worked so hard to build to come crashing down.

I'd spent weeks here, away from people, away from temptation. The hunger was under control now—manageable—but I wondered what would happen when I was surrounded by humans again. Would their scent drive me over the edge? Would I lose the control I had fought so hard to gain? The scent of life, the intoxicating aroma of warm blood, would be a constant assault on my senses. It was a test I wasn't sure I was ready to face.

And then there was the other side of it—the life I had left behind. My apartment, my job, the people who might still wonder where I had gone. It felt distant now, like a faded photograph or a half-remembered dream.

The thought of saying goodbye to it all felt heavy—a weight on my chest, a dull ache in my soul. I had built a life, however imperfect, and severing those ties was daunting. The silence of the forest starkly contrasted the noise and chaos of the city, but it had become comforting, a refuge from the constant stimulation of human interaction.

I stood and stretched, my muscles warm and loose from the run. The sun was setting, casting long shadows across the forest floor. The trees loomed like silent sentinels, their branches reaching toward the sky like skeletal fingers. The air grew cooler, and the shadows deepened, painting the forest in shades of gray and black.

I didn't want to leave this place—this sanctuary of solace and solitude.

The shelter I had built, the trails I had carved through the trees, the way the forest seemed to welcome me—it was all a part of me now. I had found something here I hadn't known I was looking for: peace. A quiet understanding with nature. A refuge from the fast-paced world.

But the longer I stayed, the more it felt like I was hiding—a coward running from the echoes of my past.

I turned back toward the forest, breaking into a run. The trees blurred around me as I pushed myself harder, faster, the air rushing past like a whisper of freedom. I leapt over a fallen log, twisting mid-air into a backflip before landing in a crouch. The ground barely felt the impact of my landing.

The movement felt as natural as breathing, as essential as the air in my lungs.

By the time I reached my shelter, the sun had dipped below the horizon, leaving the forest bathed in twilight. I ducked inside, the familiar scent of moss and bark filling my senses, and dropped onto the soft floor of leaves and moss. The shelter was simple but comforting, a small haven in the heart of the wild.

I lay there, staring up at the ceiling of my shelter, my thoughts racing—a mental whirlwind, a chaotic storm of questions and doubts. The image of the city played out in my mind.

Going back wasn't just about saying goodbye; it was about closure. About facing the life I had left behind and making peace with it. But it was also dangerous. It was like stepping back into a cage, knowing that the bars were always there, waiting to trap me.

The hunger was quiet now, but it wasn't gone. It never truly went away. The thought of being surrounded by humans, their scents overwhelming, their heartbeats like drums in my ears... it scared me. The sensory overload would be immense, a constant assault on my heightened senses. The risk of losing control was ever-present, a shadow lurking just beneath the surface.

But I couldn't ignore the pull any longer. The need for closure, the desire to see the faces of those I had left behind, was too strong to resist.

I would go back—not to stay, but to tie up loose ends. To see the life I had left behind one last time. To satisfy my curiosity and my desires.

"I'll come back," I murmured to myself, my voice barely audible in the stillness of the shelter. "This is my home now." The walls of the shelter were comforting, the ground soft and cool against my skin.

The words felt like a promise—a vow to nature.

The morning air was sharp and clean, carrying the faint scent of pine and damp earth. The forest was alive with its usual symphony—the trill of birds, the rustle of leaves stirred by a gentle breeze—but to me, it felt quieter, more intimate.

I crouched by the stream, watching the water flow over smooth stones, my reflection rippling on the surface. The faint swirls of color in my dark eyes shimmered in the sunlight, catching the light like threads of silver and gold.

This forest was my sanctuary, my home. Every tree and trail had shaped my journey, teaching me survival and how to tame my inner chaos. Each sunrise through the canopy felt personal, a reminder of my resilience. The forest bore witness to my struggles and my gradual return to peace, holding my secrets, the weight of my past, and a fragile hope for the future.

I had found balance here, existing in harmony with the world around me. My senses, once overwhelming, now felt like an extension of myself, blending seamlessly into my awareness. The cacophony of the human world had been tormenting; here, the quiet was a balm, the darkness a comfort. I could hear the silent pulse of a hummingbird's wings, the trees' secret language sharing nutrients through their roots, and the subtle tremor of the earth beneath my feet.

This was my world now. But I couldn't avoid the city forever. The thought hung in the air, a discordant note in the otherwise harmonious symphony of the forest. The city represented everything I had tried to escape: the noise, the crowds, the constant temptation, and the ever-present risk of discovery. It was a place where my true nature would be a secret, a burden I would have to carry alone.

"This isn't goodbye," I said softly, my voice carried away by the breeze. The words were meant for the forest, for the trees that had sheltered me, for the creatures that had shared their space with me. But they were also a promise to myself, a reaffirmation that I would return, that this place would always be a part of me.

The shelter felt different as I stepped inside, its walls of woven branches and moss holding a stillness that mirrored my own. The air was thick with the scent of dried leaves and woodsmoke, a familiar and comforting aroma. Sunlight filtered through the gaps in the woven walls, casting dancing shadows on the dirt floor and creating an ephemeral tapestry of light and dark.

I ran my hand along the doorframe, my fingers tracing the grooves I had worn into the bark over weeks of coming and going. Each indentation was a map of my time here, a record of the countless times I had sought refuge within these walls.

This place had been my sanctuary. It had given me the time and space I needed to find myself again and to understand what I had become. The transformation had been brutal, a violent upheaval of everything I had once known. The shelter had been my anchor, a safe harbor in the storm. Here, I had wrestled with my demons, confronted my fears, and slowly, painstakingly, rebuilt myself.

I gathered my belongings with ritual-like care: a worn shirt, my knife, my journal of scattered thoughts, and treasures like a stream-smoothed stone and a cliff-side feather. Each object carried its history—the shirt bearing witness to nights under the stars, the keen-edged knife proving my survival, the notebook documenting my journey to comprehend what I had become.

When my bag was packed, I stood at the doorway, letting my gaze sweep over the shelter one last time. The humble structure seemed to absorb my gaze, holding onto the energy I had poured into it.

"Thank you," I murmured, the words heavy with gratitude. The forest had given me so much, and though I was leaving now, I knew I would return. This was my home—nothing could change that.

The path through the trees was familiar, my feet finding the trails without hesitation. The air was cool and crisp, carrying the scent of moss and pine. I moved with ease, my steps light and deliberate, every motion precise. Each footfall was silent, a testament to my heightened senses and my innate understanding of the forest floor. I could navigate this terrain blindfolded, my body attuned to every subtle shift in elevation, every fallen branch, and every hidden root.

The trees felt like old friends as I passed, their branches swaying gently in the breeze. I brushed my fingers over their rough bark, letting the texture ground me. Each step was a goodbye, but not a final one. I memorized the patterns of the bark, the unique shapes of the leaves, the way sunlight filtered through the canopy. These images would be etched into my memory, a constant reminder of the peace I had found here.

Before I left, I needed one last hunt. The need was a dull ache, a gnawing emptiness that threatened to consume me if left unchecked. The city would be a constant test of my control, a minefield of temptations. I needed to be fortified, both physically and mentally.

The hunger was quiet, a faint whisper in the back of my mind, but I didn't want to take chances. The city would test me in ways the forest hadn't, and I needed to be prepared. My heightened senses would be both a blessing and a curse in the urban landscape, amplifying the allure of blood and the danger of exposure.

The wind shifted, carrying with it the scent of a stag. My senses sharpened, locking onto the musky, earthy smell. It was faint but distinct, and I followed it instinctively. The scent grew stronger with each step, pulling me deeper into the heart of the forest.

The stag appeared in a clearing, its antlers gleaming in the sunlight, its coat sleek and shining. It moved with deliberate grace, each step a testament to its power. It was a magnificent creature, a symbol of the wildness and freedom I had come to embrace.

I crouched low, blending into the shadows, my body sinking into the familiar rhythm of a hunt. The forest seemed to hold its breath as I moved, the world narrowing to the steady beat of the stag's heart.

When I lunged, the movement was swift and practiced. My hands gripped the stag's powerful frame as we tumbled to the ground, my teeth sinking into its neck. The blood flooded my senses, rich and electric, silencing the hunger as it coursed through me. It was a primal experience, a moment of pure instinct and raw power. The world dissolved into a vortex of sensation: the taste of blood, the feel of fur, the scent of the earth.

But I pulled back before its heart could falter. Control was paramount. The goal wasn't to kill, but to sustain. The beast's quickening pulse vibrated against my lips, each pump sending a wave of warmth through me, a reminder of the fragile life I held in my hands. The forest demanded respect, and needless destruction was a violation of its delicate balance.

The stag staggered to its feet, its wide eyes locking onto mine for a moment before it bolted into the trees. I stayed where I was, watching it disappear, the taste of its blood still lingering on my tongue. The creature's frantic heartbeat now echoed in the trees.

This was control. This was balance. This was the life I had chosen, a life lived on the edge, defined by both power and restraint.

The place where I had left my car was almost unrecognizable, buried beneath layers of dirt and leaves. It was a stark reminder of the passage of time, of the days I had spent immersed in the wild.

I brushed the debris away, running my hand over the cool metal. The sight of it brought back memories of the life I had left behind—the city streets, the late-night drives, the person I used to be. It felt like a lifetime ago, a distant echo of a past that no longer defined me.

Climbing inside, I took a moment to adjust to the confined space. The air was stale, carrying the faint scent of leather and time. My fingers rested on the steering wheel, tracing its smooth surface as I let the moment sink in. It was a strange feeling, returning to this machine after so long in nature. The car represented a different kind of freedom, one of movement and connection to the human world.

I turned the key, and the engine sputtered before roaring to life. The sound shattered the quiet, sending birds scattering into the sky. The mechanical roar seemed jarring after the subtle symphony of the forest, a harsh reminder of the artificiality of the urban landscape.

I stared into the rearview mirror, the forest behind me blurred into a sea of green. It was a comforting image, a reminder of the sanctuary I was leaving behind, but also a symbol of hope.

"This isn't goodbye," I said firmly, my voice steady. It wasn't just wishful thinking; it was a vow. A commitment to return, to reconnect, to find solace in this wild place whenever the city threatened to overwhelm me.

It wasn't a farewell. I would come back—not just because I wanted to, but because I belonged here. The forest was a part of me now, just as much as the blood in my veins. I would never be truly free of it, and I wouldn't want to be.

But for now, I needed to go. The city was waiting, and I had unfinished business.

Shifting the car into gear, I pressed down on the gas. The tires crunched over dirt and leaves as I pulled away, leaving the forest behind—but only for a little while.

Chapter Twelve

WORLD RESET

It had been weeks since I last stepped foot in my apartment, but the moment I walked through the door, it hit me like a wave. The stale air hung heavy, carrying the faint scent of dust and forgotten time. Everything was just as I'd left it—the cluttered desk, the couch with its uneven cushions, the jacket I'd tossed on the floor the day I walked away.

But now, it all felt foreign. Smaller. Duller.

The walls felt closer than I remembered, the space stifling. Out there, in the forest, I had felt alive—connected to something vast and untamed. Here, surrounded by these four walls, I felt... wrong. Out of place.

I ran a hand over the stack of unopened mail on the kitchen counter, the paper damp with neglect. My phone sat nearby, blinking with unread messages and missed calls. I had avoided it for so long, but now, with nowhere left to run, I grabbed it and sat down.

The first voicemail was from my sister.

"Tristan, where are you? Mom and Dad are freaking out. You missed the wedding. Call me, please."

Her voice cracked slightly at the end, and I clenched the phone tighter. Guilt twisted in my chest. How could I have forgotten something so important?

I scrolled back to her number, my finger hovering over the call button. She deserved answers. They all did. But how could I explain why I had disappeared? How could I make her understand without telling her the truth?

Finally, I pressed the button, holding my breath as the line rang.

"Tristan?" Her voice came through sharp and frantic. "Oh my God, is that you?"

"Yeah, it's me," I said softly.

"Where the hell have you been? We've all been worried sick! You missed the wedding! Do you have any idea what that did to Mom and Dad?"

"I know," I said, my voice tight. "I'm sorry, Kat. I... I needed time."

"Time?" she repeated, her voice tinged with disbelief. "You disappeared for weeks, Tristan! No calls, no texts—nothing. Do you have any idea what it's been like for us?"

"I didn't mean to worry you," I said. "I just... needed to figure some things out."

There was a pause on the other end of the line. I could picture her pacing, her free hand gesturing wildly as she tried to make sense of what I was saying.

"Are you okay?" she asked finally, her voice quieter now.

"I am," I said. "Better than I've been in a long time."

She didn't answer right away. "You don't sound like yourself."

"I'm still me, Kat. Just... different."

"Different how?"

"I can't explain right now," I said, my voice tight. "But I promise, I'm okay. And I need you to know that, no matter what happens, I'm figuring things out."

"'No matter what happens'?" she repeated, her voice rising slightly. "What the hell does that mean?"

"It means... I might not be around much," I said carefully. "I don't know what's next for me, but I need you to trust me on this."

Another pause, this one longer.

"Tristan," she said finally, her voice trembling, "are you dying? Is that what this is? Are you sick, or on drugs, or—"

"No," I said quickly. "It's nothing like that. I'm healthy. I'm fine."

"Then what is it?"

"I can't tell you yet."

Her frustration boiled over, her voice sharp. "That's not good enough, Tristan! You don't get to disappear for weeks, miss my wedding, and then call out of nowhere and expect me to just—"

"I'm sorry," I said, cutting her off. "I really am. But I can't explain it right now. I just... needed to hear your voice. To tell you I'm okay. And to apologize for everything."

She sighed heavily, the sound filled with a mix of anger and worry. "You're not making any sense, Tristan. But... I'll try to trust you. Call Mom and Dad, okay? They need to hear from you."

"I will," I lied, knowing I couldn't face them yet.

"Don't disappear again," she said softly, her voice breaking slightly. "Promise me."

"I'll try," I said, my throat tight.

We said goodbye, and when the call ended, I stared at the phone in my hand. The weight of everything I hadn't said pressed down on me, heavy and suffocating.

After talking to my sister, I forced myself to dial my boss's number, Sarah. The line rang a few times before a familiar, slightly exasperated voice picked up.

"Tristan? Is that really you?"

"Yeah, it's me."

There was a long pause. "Do you have any idea the position you've put us in? No calls, no emails, nothing? People have been covering your shifts for weeks!"

"I know," I said, my voice tight. "I screwed up. I'm sorry."

"Sorry doesn't cut it, Tristan. We had to let you go. You didn't leave us a choice."

"I get it," I said, the words heavy. "I just... needed time."

"Well, if you ever figure out what's going on, give me a call," he said with a sigh. "You're a good guy, Tristan. I hope you find whatever it is you're looking for."

Jessica picked up after only two rings.

"Tristan? Is this a prank?"

"It's me," I said, forcing a smile into my voice.

"Oh my God, where have you been? Do you know how worried we've been? Benji and I even went to your apartment—"

"I'm fine," I said, cutting her off. "I just... needed some time to figure things out."

"That's not an answer," she snapped. "We thought something happened to you. You don't just disappear for weeks without telling anyone."

"I know," I said softly. "I'm sorry."

There was a pause. "You don't sound like yourself," she said cautiously.

"I'm still me," I said, though the words felt hollow.

"Where are you now? Can we meet?"

"I can't," I said quickly. "I'm not staying long."

"Not staying long?" she repeated, her voice tinged with suspicion. "What does that mean? Tristan, you're scaring me."

"Jess, listen to me," I said, my voice steady. "I'm okay. I just needed to hear your voice. To tell you that I'm fine and that... I'm sorry."

"Sorry for what?" she asked, her voice rising.

"For everything," I said quietly.

"Tristan, what's going on? Are you sick? On drugs? What's happening?"

"I'll explain when I can," I said, knowing it was a lie. "Tell Benji I'm sorry, too. And... thank you for always being there."

"Tristan—"

I hung up before she could say anything else.

As I stood by the window that night, looking out at the city below, I felt the growing pull of the forest. The lights, the sounds, the hum of humanity all felt so distant, so disconnected from the life I had come to know.

But I wasn't ready to leave just yet.

The city felt heavier at night, like it carried the weight of everything I was leaving behind. The muffled roar of distant traffic hummed through the walls of my apartment, blending with the occasional wail of a siren. It all seemed so far away now, like a song I had forgotten the words to.

I sat by the window, staring out at the sea of lights stretching into the horizon. They blurred together, shimmering in shades of orange and white, their glow muted compared to the brilliance of the stars I had grown used to in the forest.

The forest.

Even now, I could feel its pull, like a thread wrapped around my chest, tugging gently but insistently. Out there, I was free—alive in ways I couldn't explain. My senses were sharper, my movements faster, my body a vessel of strength and precision I hadn't known I was capable of.

Here, in this apartment, in this city filled with noise and chaos, I felt like I was suffocating.

I leaned my forehead against the cool glass, closing my eyes. When I opened them again, my reflection stared back at me—familiar but not. My eyes, once ordinary and easy to overlook, were brighter now, almost unnervingly vibrant. Swirls of silver and gold danced through the irises, catching the dim light and making them appear as if they were glowing faintly.

The changes had been gradual, subtle at first, but now they were undeniable. I touched the glass, tracing the outline of my face. I was still me, wasn't I?

My bag was already packed, sitting by the door like a silent reminder of the choice I had made. I had spent the evening tying up loose ends, reaching out to the people I cared about, trying to offer closure without saying too much.

But what I hadn't said lingered in the back of my mind, clawing at me.

I hadn't told my sister that I might never come back. I hadn't told Jessica or Benji the truth about why I had disappeared. I hadn't told my parents anything at all.

And now, it was too late.

The fridge hummed faintly as I opened it, the dim light flickering on to reveal an assortment of forgotten leftovers and expired cartons. The stillness of it all was oppressive, the silence broken only by the soft thud of the fridge door as I closed it again.

I rummaged through the kitchen drawers, pulling out a pen and a scrap of paper. Sitting at the table, I stared at the blank page, the words refusing to come.

Dear Mom and Dad, I began. I'm sorry for leaving without an explanation. I'm sorry for missing Kat's wedding. I'm sorry for being a disappointment.

No. That wasn't right.

I crumpled the paper and tossed it aside, grabbing another sheet.

I'm okay. Please don't worry about me. I just need more time.

The words stared back at me, stark and insufficient. I set the pen down, leaning back in the chair. It wasn't enough. It didn't feel like enough.

But what else could I say?

The clock on the wall ticked steadily, each second marking the time slipping away. I glanced at my phone, the screen dark and silent. No new messages. No calls.

I should have felt relief, but instead, I felt hollow.

I walked to the bathroom, flipped on the light, and leaned against the sink. My reflection stared back at me, unfamiliar and strange. My eyes, once a shade too muted to stand out, were now impossible to ignore. The vibrant swirls of silver and gold caught the fluorescent light, shifting and shimmering with every movement.

I touched my face, tracing the sharp angles of my jawline and the curve of my cheekbones. It was still me. But it wasn't.

Out in the forest, I hadn't needed to face this. The wild didn't care what I looked like or what I was becoming. But here, under the harsh glow of city lights, the changes felt stark and undeniable.

"I'm still me," I said aloud, as if saying it would make it true.

The words hung in the air, unanswered.

The decision to leave had been easy; the execution was harder.

As much as I hated this place—the noise, the confinement, the weight of my old life pressing down on me—it was familiar. Comfortable, in its own way.

Leaving it behind meant letting go of my job, my friends, my family, of everything that had once defined me.

I returned to the table, my movements slow and deliberate, and picked up the note I had written. It wasn't perfect, but it would have to do.

I folded it carefully, tucked it into an envelope, and left it on the counter where I knew my sister would find it. She'd be the one to come here first, to check on me when I didn't respond.

She'd understand eventually. I had to believe that.

I paused, staring at the note one last time. It felt final in a way I hadn't expected—a quiet goodbye to the life I was walking away from.

The weight of the moment pressed down on me as I grabbed my bag and slung it over my shoulder. I hesitated at the door, my hand resting on the cool metal of the doorknob.

The forest was waiting.

And this time, I wasn't coming back the same.

The quiet of the apartment felt oddly inviting, almost like it was holding its breath, waiting for a decision I'd already made. Everything remained exactly as I had left it—dishes still in the sink, books scattered on the coffee table, that old sweater draped over the back of my chair. For a moment, I could almost pretend this was just another day, that I wasn't about to vanish from my own life. But the stillness seemed to know better, embracing me one last time before I stepped away forever.

I thought of my sister, Kat. Her wedding. Her bright, infectious laugh. Guilt twisted in my stomach. I should have been there, helping her plan and supporting her through the pre-wedding jitters. But I couldn't. Not like this. Not when I was becoming something... else.

Jessica and Benji—my best friends since childhood. We had shared everything: secrets whispered in the dark and dreams painted on late-night canvases. How could I explain my sudden departure, the abrupt severing of our bond? What could I possibly say that wouldn't sound like a lie, a flimsy excuse masking a truth too terrifying to speak? The thought of their confusion and hurt gnawed at me.

And my parents. The disappointment in their eyes, the unspoken questions that hung in the air whenever I failed to meet their expectations. I had always strived to make them proud, to be the daughter they had envisioned. But somewhere along the way, I had lost myself, trapped in a life that felt increasingly suffocating. Now, I was about to shatter their expectations completely, to vanish without a trace, leaving them with nothing but unanswered questions and a lingering sense of unease.

The forest offered an escape—a sanctuary from the suffocating expectations of my old life. Out there, I was free to be myself, to embrace the changes coursing through me. But that freedom came at a cost: abandoning the people I loved, severing ties that had bound me for so long.

I closed my eyes again, picturing the forest. The towering trees, their branches intertwined like grasping fingers, filtering sunlight into dappled patterns on the forest floor. The earthy scent of damp soil and decaying leaves, the symphony of birdsong that filled the air. The feeling of raw power surged through me as I moved through the undergrowth, my senses heightened, my body responding with newfound agility and strength.

It was a dangerous place, filled with creatures I didn't fully understand. But it was also a place of profound beauty and untamed freedom—a place where I could finally come to terms with what I was becoming.

I opened my eyes, my gaze fixed on the bag by the door. It was a symbol of my decision, a tangible representation of the path I was choosing. I had packed only the essentials: a few changes of clothes, a knife, a flashlight, and a map of the surrounding area. I had left behind everything that reminded me of my old life, the possessions that had once defined me.

The apartment felt smaller now, the walls closing in around me. The city outside pressed in, a constant reminder of the life I was leaving behind. I took a deep breath, trying to calm my frantic nerves. It was time to go.

I walked to the door, my hand trembling slightly as I reached for the doorknob. The metal was cold against my skin, a stark contrast to the warmth of my own hand. I hesitated for a moment, my mind swirling with doubts and regrets. Was I making the right decision? Was I strong enough to face the challenges ahead?

I pushed the door open and stepped into the hallway. The dim light illuminated the worn carpet and faded wallpaper. It was a familiar sight, a comforting reminder of the place I had called home for so long. But it was also a reminder of the life I was leaving behind.

I closed the door behind me, the click echoing in the silent hallway. It was a final goodbye, a severing of ties. I turned and walked away, my footsteps muffled by the carpet.

The forest was waiting.

I descended the stairs, each step taking me further from my old life. The air grew cooler as I reached the ground floor, the scent of the city filling my nostrils—car exhaust, stale food, and the faint aroma of salt from the nearby ocean. It was a familiar smell, once comforting, but now felt oppressive—a suffocating reminder of the chaos and pollution that permeated the city.

I stepped onto the street, the sounds of the city washing over me. The din of vehicles, the honking of horns, the murmur of passersby—a symphony of sound, an unending barrage on my perception.. I closed my eyes for a moment, trying to block it all out.

I started walking, my footsteps quick and purposeful. I didn't know where I was going, but I knew I had to get away from the city. I had to reach the forest to find the sanctuary I so desperately craved.

As I walked, I thought of the changes happening to me: the increased strength, the heightened senses, the subtle but undeniable alterations to my appearance. I was becoming something different, something more than human.

I didn't know what the future held, but I knew I couldn't stay in the city. I had to embrace the changes, to find my place in the world. The forest was calling to me, beckoning me to discover my true potential.

The night air was cool against my skin as I stood by the car, my bag slung over one shoulder. The keys were heavy in my hand, the metal biting into my palm. I clenched them tighter, feeling the ridges press into my skin, as if the physical sensation could ground me in the moment. The weight of the keys symbolized more than just their physical mass—it represented a decision, a choice that would change everything.

I glanced at the car—a relic of my old life, but not forgotten. It sat there, clean and functional, a testament to the effort I'd put into maintaining it after driving it back home. The metallic sheen of its surface caught the faint glow of the streetlight, and for a moment, it looked almost alive, as if waiting for me to climb in and return to the life I'd left behind.

I could have driven; the road would have been faster, easier. But the thought of sitting in the driver's seat, surrounded by the hum of the engine and the empty sound of the highway, made my chest tighten. The monotony of the road, the endless stretch of asphalt, the isolation—it all felt suffocating. This wasn't about speed. It wasn't about convenience.

It was about the journey.

I tucked the keys into my bag and started walking.

The city stretched out before me, its streets alive with a hum I had never noticed before. The soft murmur of conversation drifted from open windows, mingling with the distant blare of a car horn. Neon signs flickered above shuttered storefronts, their colors bright and unnatural against the dark sky. It was as if the city had taken on a new life and energy in the hours since I had last walked these streets.

Everything felt sharper now, more vivid. I could hear the faint scuff of shoes on pavement half a block away, the rhythmic drip of water from a leaky pipe in an alley. Scents swirled around me—oil and asphalt, cigarette smoke, the faint sweetness of flowers in a window box. It was overwhelming but not unpleasant. It felt as if my senses had heightened, as if I were seeing, hearing, and feeling the world for the first time.

I turned down streets I had never walked before, letting my feet guide me. This was the same city I had lived in for years, but tonight, it felt like a different world. The familiarity of the grid-like streets and towering buildings was still there, but there was something new, something almost magical in the air. It was as if the city had been reset, its edges softened, its colors brighter.

I passed a group of street performers on a corner, their music blending with the laughter of a small crowd gathered around them. A man played the guitar, his fingers dancing over the strings with practiced ease, while a woman beside him sang softly, her voice clear and sweet. The haunting melody seemed to echo through the streets and linger in the air long after I had passed.

I paused for a moment, listening. The notes curled around me, warm and alive, and I felt an ache in my chest—a longing for something I couldn't quite name. It wasn't just the music; it was the sense of connection, the way the crowd swayed and smiled, the way the performers poured their hearts into every note. For a moment, I wanted to stay, to lose myself in the music and laughter, to forget about the journey ahead.

But I couldn't.

I continued walking, the streets growing quieter as I moved farther from the heart of the city. The buildings around me changed, their facades older and their windows dark. I passed an old bookstore, its sign faded and its shelves visible through the glass, crammed with titles I couldn't make out. The store looked as though it had been frozen in time, a relic of a bygone era. I wondered how long it had been since anyone had stepped inside and how long it had been since the bell above the door had rung.

A stray cat darted across my path, its movements quick and silent. It paused to look at me, its green eyes catching the light before disappearing into the shadows. I watched it go, feeling a strange sense of kinship with the creature. It, too, was navigating this world alone, finding its way through the darkness.

The farther I walked, the more the city seemed to fade. The roads grew narrower, the streetlights fewer and farther between. The hum of traffic was replaced by the rustle of leaves and the chirp of crickets. The air smelled different here—cleaner, fresher, with a hint of earth and moss.

The forest wasn't far now.

I reached the edge of the city just as the first light of dawn began to creep over the horizon. The sky shifted from deep indigo to soft shades of pink and gold, the stars fading one by one. The trees loomed ahead, their silhouettes dark against the growing light. They stood like sentinels, guarding the boundary between the world I had known and the world I was about to enter.

I stopped for a moment, turning back to look at the city behind me. The buildings rose like shadows, their outlines blurred by the haze of morning. For a brief moment, I felt the weight of everything I was leaving behind:

my family, my friends, the life I had built here, the memories—both good and bad—that had shaped me into the person I was.

But then I turned back to the forest, the pull of it steady and unrelenting.

This was where I belonged now.

The forest was alive in a way the city could never be. The trees whispered to each other in the breeze, their leaves rustling like a secret language. The ground beneath my feet was soft, cushioned by layers of fallen leaves and moss. The air was thick with the scent of pine and damp earth, and the sound of birdsong filled the air.

As I stepped into the forest, I felt a sense of peace wash over me. The chaos of the city, the noise, the constant motion—it all fell away, replaced by the quiet rhythm of nature. This was a world that moved at its own pace, a world that didn't care about deadlines or schedules or the endless rush of modern life.

I walked deeper into the forest, the trees closing in around me. Sunlight filtered through the canopy above, casting dappled shadows on the ground. I could hear the distant sound of a stream, its water bubbling over rocks, and I followed the sound, drawn by its gentle melody.

The stream was small, its waters clear and cool. I knelt beside it, dipping my hand into the water and feeling the chill against my skin. I cupped the water in my hands and brought it to my lips, drinking deeply. It tasted pure, untouched, as if it had come straight from the heart of the earth.

I sat by the stream for a while, listening to the sounds of the forest. The birdsong, the rustle of leaves, the gentle flow of the water—it was a symphony, a reminder that there was still beauty in the world, even after everything that had happened.

As I sat there, I thought about the journey ahead. I didn't know what I would find in the forest, what challenges or wonders awaited me. But I knew that this was where I needed to be. This was my reset, my chance to start over, to find a new path.

The city was behind me now, its noise and chaos fading into the distance. The forest stretched out before me, vast and unknown.

I took a deep breath, feeling the cool air fill my lungs, and stepped forward into the trees.

This was my new beginning.

The forest welcomed me like an old friend, its arms wide and familiar. The air was different here—crisper, cleaner, carrying the faint scent of pine and earth. It wrapped around me, grounding me in a way the city never could. The city was a cacophony of noise and motion, a place where the air felt heavy with the weight of countless lives intersecting in chaos. But here, in the embrace of the wild, the world felt lighter, simpler, and infinitely more alive.

The light was softer, filtered through the thick canopy above, casting the forest floor in a patchwork of gold and green. Every sound felt alive, from the rustle of leaves in the breeze to the distant call of a bird hidden among the branches. The forest was a symphony, each note perfectly in tune, each instrument playing its part in harmony. I stood still for a moment, letting the music of the wild wash over me, filling the spaces in my soul that had been hollowed out by the relentless grind of urban life.

This was home.

I dropped my bag at the base of a large oak, its trunk gnarled and ancient, its roots sprawling like the fingers of a giant buried beneath the earth. Stretching my arms over my head, I let out a slow breath, feeling the tension I hadn't realized I was carrying begin to melt away. It was as if the forest itself reached out to me, its calm seeping into my bones, replacing the unease that had clung to me like a second skin.

Crouching down, I ran my fingers over the moss that clung to the tree's roots. The texture was soft and damp, a reminder of the life teeming beneath the surface. The forest was alive in ways that were invisible to the eye but palpable to the senses. The earth beneath my feet pulsed with energy, a steady, rhythmic heartbeat that seemed to sync with my own.

For weeks, this place had been my sanctuary, the only place where I could truly be myself. Out here, there were no expectations, no judgment—only the quiet rhythm of the wild, steady and unchanging. The forest didn't care about my past or my mistakes. It didn't demand anything from me. It simply existed, and in its existence, it offered me a kind of peace I had never found elsewhere.

I closed my eyes, letting my senses expand.

The hum of the forest surrounded me, filling the space between each breath. I could hear the soft buzz of insects, the gentle rustle of small creatures moving through the underbrush, the faint trickle of a nearby stream. The air was thick with the scent of pine and damp earth, and I breathed it in deeply, letting it fill my lungs.

It was all so familiar. So right.

I grabbed my bag and started walking, weaving through the trees with ease. My feet moved instinctively, finding the paths I had carved out over weekss of exploration. The forest had changed in subtle ways—the underbrush thicker in some places, the scent of fresh blooms lingering in the air—but it was still the same place that had shaped me.

As I moved deeper into the woods, I began testing myself again, pushing my body to its limits. I leapt over fallen logs, scaled low-hanging branches, and vaulted from rock to rock, my movements fluid and controlled. The confidence I had gained in my time here came rushing back, my body remembering the lessons the forest had taught me.

The forest was a teacher, harsh but fair. It demanded respect and rewarded perseverance. It had taught me how to listen, how to move, how to survive. It had shown me that strength wasn't just about physical power but about adaptability, about finding balance in the face of chaos.

I climbed to the top of a rocky outcrop, the stone cool beneath my palms, and looked out over the endless expanse of trees. The sight was breathtaking, the forest stretching as far as the eye could see, bathed in the warm light of morning. The canopy rippled like a green ocean, the leaves catching the sunlight and shimmering like waves.

"This," I murmured to myself, my voice barely louder than the wind, "this is where I'm supposed to be."

The words felt true in a way that nothing else had in a long time. The city had always felt like a borrowed space, a place where I was constantly out of sync with the world around me. But here, in the forest, I felt like I belonged.

I made my way toward the stream I had discovered early on, the sound of rushing water guiding me. When I reached it, I knelt by the edge, cupping my hands and letting the cold water run over my skin. The stream was clear and bright, its surface dappled with sunlight. I could see small fish darting beneath the surface, their silver bodies flashing like blades.

The forest had a way of stripping everything down to its essence. Out here, there was no noise, no chaos—only the clarity that came with being connected to something greater than yourself. The stream was a reminder of that, its waters flowing endlessly, carving their path through the earth with quiet determination.

I leaned down, splashing the cool water onto my face. As it dripped down, I caught my reflection in the surface.

My eyes stared back at me, brighter than they had ever been, swirls of silver and gold shimmering in the dappled light. They looked almost otherworldly, glowing faintly in the rippling water. For a moment, I simply stared.

This was who I was now.

The person I had been in the city felt like a stranger, a shadow of who I was meant to be. Out here in the forest, I felt like I was finally coming into myself, as if the wild had stripped away the layers of pretense and revealed the core of who I was.

Hours slipped away as I explored, reacquainting myself with the forest. I found the shelter I had built months ago, hidden beneath the thick canopy of trees. It was still standing, its walls of woven branches and moss blending seamlessly with the surrounding landscape.

I stepped inside, running my fingers over the rough texture of the walls. The air was cool, carrying the faint scent of earth and leaves. It was comforting, like returning to a favorite childhood haunt. The shelter was small, barely large enough to lie down in, but it had been my refuge, my safe haven.

This place had been my refuge, my home, my anchor.

And now, it was mine again.

That evening, I sat by the stream, watching the sun dip below the horizon. The sky turned shades of pink and orange, casting long shadows across the forest floor. The air grew cooler, and the scent of pine and earth deepened as day gave way to night.

The forest came alive around me, the sounds of nocturnal creatures stirring in the cool air. Fireflies blinked like tiny stars among the trees, their glow soft and fleeting. The world felt quieter now, the sounds of the day replaced by the gentle hum of the night.

For the first time in weeks, I felt... at peace.

The city lay in my past now, its clamor and turmoil retreating into recollection. Out here, amidst the tranquility of the forest, I felt complete. The woods had a unique ability to clarify my thoughts, reminding me of what truly held significance. It wasn't about the things I had abandoned or the life I had turned my back on. It was all about this moment, this place, this sensation of being exactly where I was destined to be.

This was my world. And I was ready to embrace it.

As the stars began to appear in the darkening sky, I lay back on the soft earth, letting the forest envelop me. The fireflies danced above, their light mingling with the stars, and I felt a sense of contentment settle over me.

The forest had always been my sanctuary, my place of healing and renewal. And now, as I lay beneath the canopy of trees, I knew it would always be a part of me. No matter where life took me, no matter what challenges lay ahead, I would carry this place with me, a quiet reminder of who I was and who I could be.

Back in the woods, it felt like slipping into my true skin.

The trees stretched high above me, their branches swaying gently in the breeze, their leaves whispering secrets to one another in a language only the forest could understand. The scent of pine and wet earth filled the air, crisp and clean, grounding me in a way the city never could. The city was a labyrinth of steel and concrete, a place where the air tasted stale and the sky was a distant memory. But here, in the heart of the wild, the world felt alive, vibrant, and unbroken.

The soft hum of a nearby stream reached my ears, its rhythm blending seamlessly with the rustling of small critters moving through the underbrush. The forest was a symphony, each sound a note in a melody that had been playing long before I arrived and would continue long after I was gone. I stood still for a moment, letting the music of the wild wash over me, filling the spaces in my soul that had been hollowed out by the relentless grind of urban life.

Everything felt sharper here, clearer. The forest wasn't just a place—it was a part of me now. It had seeped into my bones, into my blood, into the very core of who I was. Out here, I wasn't just surviving. I was thriving.

I began testing my strength again, picking up where I had left off months ago. The familiarity of it was exhilarating, each motion reminding me of the progress I had made. The forest had been my training ground, my teacher, and my sanctuary. It had shaped me, honed me, and now it was time to see just how far I had come.

I approached a massive rock, its surface rough and cool under my hands. The stone was jagged and uneven, its weight formidable, but I had faced it before. My muscles flexed as I pushed, the stone resisting for a moment before giving way. I lifted it off the ground as if it weighed nothing, my arms steady and sure. The power coursing through me was intoxicating, a reminder of the strength I had gained through months of relentless effort.

With a grin, I hurled the boulder forward, watching as it smashed into a nearby tree. The impact sent a tremor through the forest, shaking loose a cascade of leaves and startling a flock of birds from the canopy above. The sound of their wings beating against the air was like applause, a fleeting acknowledgment of the raw power I now wielded.

But it wasn't enough.

I needed to test my speed and agility—the skills I had honed through months of practice. The forest was my playground, and I was determined to master every inch of it.

I took off running, the ground blurring beneath me as I weaved between trees and vaulted over fallen logs. My feet moved faster than I could process, each step precise, every motion fluid. The wind whipped past my face, carrying with it the scent of pine and earth, and I felt alive in a way I never had before.

A low-hanging branch loomed ahead, but I didn't slow. Instead, I launched myself upward, gripping the branch and using it to swing forward before landing gracefully on the other side. The thrill of the movement sent a surge of adrenaline through me; if I could feel my heart, I imagined it pounding in time with the rhythm of the forest.

I felt unstoppable.

The first time I had tried this, I had stumbled, crashed, and slid across the dirt more times than I cared to admit. But now, my form was nearly perfect, my movements effortless. Confidence surged through me, my body alive with the thrill of the run.

One morning, as I practiced flips and tricks I'd seen in parkour videos, something changed.

I smelled it before I saw it—blood.

Not animal blood. Human blood.

The scent hit me like a wave, sharp and intoxicating, igniting my senses. My body moved on instinct, drawn to the source before I could think to stop myself. The hunger that had been lying dormant within me roared to life, a primal force that threatened to consume me.

I found them a few minutes later: a group of hikers—three of them—gathered around one of their own.

The injured hiker sat on a rock, his leg propped up as blood oozed from a fresh gash. The scent filled the air, thick and overwhelming, making my throat burn with hunger. I stopped a safe distance away, forcing my feet to stay planted as I fought against the primal urge to get closer.

"Hey!" I called, my voice steady despite the fire in my veins. "Are you guys okay?"

The injured hiker looked up, his face pale with pain. "Yeah, just an accident. A rock tore me up a bit."

I approached slowly, keeping my movements deliberate and unthreatening. "Let me help," I said, pulling a small first-aid kit from my bag.

The woman crouched next to him straightened, her eyes narrowing as she looked me over. "What are you doing out here alone?"

"Photographer," I lied smoothly, kneeling next to the injured man. "Looking for rare bugs. Nature shots. You know, that sort of thing."

Her suspicion didn't fade, but she didn't argue. "Well, we're lucky you showed up, I guess."

"Let's see the cut," I said, keeping my voice calm.

The scent of his blood was almost unbearable as I unwrapped the torn fabric of his pants. The gash was deep, jagged, and still bleeding heavily. My fingers trembled slightly as I cleaned the wound, the hunger clawing at me with every breath.

"You're good at this," the third hiker said—a younger man with a nervous energy about him. "You a medic or something?"

"Just prepared," I said, securing the bandage tightly around the wound. "These trails can be rough."

The woman crossed her arms, watching me closely. "Strange place to be on your own."

I shrugged, standing up and stepping back. "I like the quiet. Less distraction out here."

I pointed them toward the nearest road, giving clear directions to safety. "You should be able to get help from there."

The injured man nodded, wincing as he tried to stand with their help. "Thanks, man. Seriously."

"Take care," I said, my voice even.

I waited until they disappeared into the trees before I let out a shaky breath, my body sagging with relief.

That had been too close.

I walked deeper into the woods, the weight of the encounter pressing down on me. Their scent lingered in my mind, the memory of their blood a sharp reminder of what I had become. But I had resisted.

It hadn't been easy, but I had done it.

As the forest swallowed me whole, I felt the tension begin to ease. The city was behind me now, its noise and chaos nothing but a faint echo. This was my life now, and I was determined to master it.

Chapter Thirteen

MASTER OF THE WILD

The forest had become my world. Every waking moment was dedicated to refining my abilities, pushing my limits, and discovering just how far I could go. The trees weren't merely part of the scenery—they were my allies, my mentors, the backdrop against which I was learning to thrive. Each root, each branch, and each patch of moss seemed to whisper its secrets to me, teaching lessons I could never have learned within the confines of the city.

Each morning began the same way. I woke before the sun, the cold air nipping at my skin as I stepped out of the small shelter I had built. It was hidden among the trees, its walls made of woven branches and moss that blended seamlessly into the forest. The smell of damp earth and pine filled my lungs, grounding me in this place that now felt more like home than anywhere I had ever known.

The shelter was simple but sturdy, a testament to the skills I had developed over time. It wasn't just a place to sleep; it was a sanctuary, a reminder of how far I had come. The first time I tried to build it, the structure collapsed within hours. But now, it stood firm against the wind and rain, a symbol of my growing mastery over this wild, untamed world.

With my phone propped against a tree, I played parkour tutorials, martial arts demonstrations, and climbing techniques on repeat. The shaky, amateur videos from suburban backyards and gyms felt absurdly out of place here, but I absorbed the movements with ease. My eyes followed the flips, strikes, and combinations, breaking them down into sequences I could replicate. The forest was my gym, my dojo, my proving ground.

By mid-morning, I was moving.

The forest became my training ground, each obstacle an opportunity to test myself. Fallen trees served as balance beams, and low-hanging branches became bars to swing from. The uneven terrain forced me to adapt to each twist and dip with precision and confidence. Every step was a lesson; every leap was a challenge.

As part of my training, I started incorporating strikes—punches, kicks, knees, and elbows—into my routines.

One morning, I stood before a towering oak, its bark gnarled and thick. My knuckles cracked as I clenched my fists, my feet shifting into a steady stance. With a sharp breath, I threw a punch.

The impact reverberated up my arm, the bark splintering slightly where my fist connected. I grinned, the sting in my knuckles quickly fading as my body adjusted.

I followed with a combination: jab, cross, hook, elbow. Each strike landed with precision, the tree shaking with every blow. My muscles coiled and uncoiled like springs, my movements fluid and deliberate.

After a few rounds, I switched to kicks. My leg swung in a sharp arc, my shin slamming into the trunk with a dull thud. The sound echoed through the forest, accompanied by the satisfying crack of bark splitting under the force.

Rocks became targets, too. I practiced front kicks and sidekicks, the power behind them strong enough to send smaller boulders tumbling across the forest floor. The larger ones were used to test my elbows and knees, driving them into the stone with calculated force.

This wasn't just about strength—it was about control. Every strike was measured; every movement was precise. The forest wasn't just my playground; it was my sparring partner.

By the second month, my movements became almost instinctive. My leaps were longer, my landings softer. I could vault over fallen logs without breaking stride, scale tree trunks with the ease of a predator, and flip mid-air to avoid snagging branches.

One morning, I crouched in front of a massive fallen tree, its roots jutting into the air like skeletal fingers. Wrapping my hands around its thick trunk, I took a deep breath, feeling the ground beneath my feet. With a grunt, I lifted.

The tree groaned as it shifted, dirt raining down in clumps. My muscles burned, the strain exhilarating. With one final push, I lifted it fully off the ground, holding it there for a moment before letting it fall with a thunderous crash.

I grinned, the sound echoing through the forest. Each day, I felt myself growing stronger, more capable.

Even my senses had sharpened.

I could hear the faintest rustle of a squirrel on a branch, the distant splash of a fish in the stream, the heartbeat of an elk yards away. My vision, too, had changed. Colors were brighter, edges sharper. I could pick out details I would have missed before—a bird's nest hidden among the leaves, the subtle shift of shadows as the sun moved through the sky.

The forest revealed itself to me in ways I had never noticed before. The way the trees swayed together in the wind, their branches brushing like old friends. The patterns of animal tracks in the dirt, each one telling a story of where they had been and where they were going.

At night, the forest transformed into a different world.

The sounds shifted—the hoot of an owl replaced the chatter of birds, and the rustling of nocturnal creatures echoed in the darkness. Moonlight filtered through the canopy, casting the ground in patches of silver.

This was when I practiced my stealth.

I moved through the woods like a shadow, my steps silent as I weaved between the trees. I practiced following animals without them noticing, testing how close I could get before they caught my scent or sensed my presence.

Sometimes, I would sit for hours, watching the world move around me. A family of deer grazing in a clearing. A fox stalking its prey. The gentle sway of the trees in the wind.

I felt as if I was part of it all—woven into the fabric of the forest itself.

The forest wasn't just a place to train; it was a place to reflect.

Each night, as I sat by the stream or under the stars, I found myself thinking about who I had been before. The Tristan who had struggled with a mundane job, who had been consumed by the grind of daily life.

That version of me felt like a stranger now.

Here, in the forest, I was something else. Stronger. Faster. Sharper.

But there was still a part of me that wondered what I had lost in the process.

The forest had given me so much—strength, clarity, purpose. But it had also taken something from me. The person I had been before, the one who had lived in the city, who had worried about bills and deadlines and the opinions of others—that person was gone.

And yet, I couldn't help but feel a pang of nostalgia for that simpler, more predictable life.

I shook my head, pushing the thought aside. This was my life now. The forest had chosen me, and I had chosen it in return.

As I lay back on the soft earth, staring up at the stars, I felt a sense of peace settle over me. The forest was my home, my sanctuary, my teacher. And I was its student, its protector, its master.

The hunger was always there—a low, steady burn in the back of my mind. It wasn't as overwhelming as it had been during the first few weeks, but it was persistent, like a quiet whisper I couldn't ignore. It was a part of me now, as much as the blood in my veins or the air in my lungs—a constant reminder of what I had become.

I had learned to manage it, to keep it at bay until the time came to feed. My hunts were calculated, deliberate. I no longer stumbled through the woods, clumsy and desperate. Now, I moved with the precision of a predator, my senses guiding me toward my prey with unerring accuracy. The forest had taught me patience, discipline, and control. It had turned me into something more than human, something that walked the line between man and beast.

It was late afternoon when I caught the scent.

The wind carried it to me, faint and musky, tinged with the metallic edge of warm blood. My body tensed, every nerve alight as I turned toward the source. The hunger flared, sharp and insistent, but I pushed it down, focusing on the task at hand.

I crouched low, my movements silent as I crept through the underbrush. My ears picked up the soft rustle of leaves ahead, the rhythmic crunch of hooves against the forest floor.

A herd of deer.

They moved in graceful unison, their heads dipping low to graze on patches of grass while their ears twitched, alert to any sound. The sunlight filtering through the canopy caught their coats, casting them in a soft, golden glow. They were beautiful, serene, and completely unaware of the danger lurking in the shadows.

I slowed my breathing, focusing. The world around me seemed to fade, the forest falling silent as my attention honed in on the herd. My senses painted a vivid picture—the steady thrum of their heartbeats, the occasional flick of a tail, the subtle rise and fall of their chests. I could almost feel the warmth of their blood, the pulse of life beneath their skin.

Step by step, I closed the distance, careful to stay downwind. My body moved with a fluidity that still surprised me, every muscle working in perfect harmony. The forest itself seemed to aid me, the leaves rustling just enough to mask my approach, the shadows deepening to hide my form.

When I was close enough, I chose my target—a young buck grazing at the edge of the group. Its muscles rippled as it shifted, completely unaware of my presence.

I lunged.

The herd scattered in an instant, their hooves pounding against the earth as they vanished into the trees. But the buck wasn't fast enough.

I chased it down with ease, my feet silent against the ground as I darted between the trees. The wind rushed past me, the scent of the buck growing stronger with every stride. This was what I had been made for, what I had become.

With one final burst of speed, I leapt forward, tackling it to the ground.

The buck thrashed beneath me, its wide, panicked eyes reflecting the light filtering through the canopy. My teeth ached with anticipation, hunger flaring hot and urgent as I leaned in.

The taste of its blood was electric, a surge of warmth spreading through my veins and quieting the hunger in an instant. It was more than sustenance; it was power, life, and energy all at once. For a moment, I lost myself in it, the world narrowing to the pulse of the buck's heartbeat and the warmth of its blood.

But I didn't take too much.

I forced myself to stop, pulling back as the buck's heartbeat began to slow. Its breath came in short, sharp bursts, its chest heaving against the ground.

I released it, stepping back as the buck scrambled to its feet. It stumbled for a moment, its legs unsteady, before bolting into the trees, disappearing into the shadows.

I sat back, wiping the blood from my lips.

Moments like these were a strange mix of triumph and guilt. The power I felt during the hunt was undeniable, intoxicating even. But there was always a weight that came afterward—a reminder of what I had become.

I didn't need to kill to survive, and I made sure not to. But the act of feeding, of taking, left a mark on me all the same. It reminded me that I was no longer fully human, that I existed in a space between worlds. The forest had become my home, but it had also changed me in ways I was still trying to understand.

The forest around me was alive again, the sounds of birds and insects returning as the tension of the hunt dissipated. I leaned against a tree, letting the cool bark press into my back as I closed my eyes.

And that's when it happened.

A memory.

It came unbidden, sharp and vivid, flashing across my mind like lightning.

Marcus.

I saw him standing over me, his face shrouded in shadow, his voice low and deliberate. The memory was fleeting, just a fragment, but it was enough to send a chill through me. I could almost hear his words, though they were muffled, distorted, as if coming from a great distance.

I opened my eyes, the forest coming back into focus.

Marcus. The man who had started all of this, the one whose memories I had glimpsed during my transformation. The one who had left me to figure this out on my own.

I clenched my fists, my jaw tightening.

I had tried not to think about him, to push him out of my mind. But now, the thought of him lingered, clawing at the edges of my consciousness.

Marcus had answers—answers I needed.

Who was he? Why had he chosen me? What was I supposed to do with this power, this hunger, this new life?

The forest felt quieter now, the weight of the memory settling over me like a shroud. The trees seemed to close in around me, their branches reaching out like silent observers. Even the air felt heavier, the scent of pine and earth now tinged with something darker, more foreboding.

For the first time in months, I found myself wondering if I should leave. Not forever, but long enough to find him. To confront him.

I didn't know what I would say.

But I knew one thing for certain.

I couldn't ignore this any longer.

The forest had given me strength, clarity, and purpose. But it had also given me questions—questions that only Marcus could answer.

As I stood there, the weight of the decision pressing down on me, I felt a strange sense of resolve settle over me. The forest had been my teacher, my sanctuary, my home. But it was also a place of transformation, a place where I had been reborn.

And now, it was time to leave.

Not forever. Just long enough to find the man who had started it all.

I took a deep breath, the scent of the forest filling my lungs.

This was my world.

And I was ready to face it.

The memory of Marcus clung to me like the remnants of a storm, swirling at the edges of my thoughts no matter how hard I tried to push it away. It was a shadow I couldn't shake, a whisper that grew louder the more I tried to ignore it. His presence lingered in the recesses of my mind, a phantom that refused to be exorcised. Every time I thought I had buried him, every time I believed I had moved on, his face would resurface, his voice would echo, and I would be pulled back into the labyrinth of questions I had no answers to.

I sat by the stream, staring at the water as it rushed over smooth stones, its surface catching the pale light of the moon. The sounds of the forest—the chirping of crickets, the rustle of leaves in the wind—seemed muted, distant, as if the world itself had paused to let me think. The forest had always been my refuge, a place where I could escape the noise of my own mind. But tonight, even its familiar embrace felt hollow, as though it too had turned its back on me.

Marcus.

His name was a knot in my chest, tightening with every breath.

For months, I had avoided thinking about him. The man whose blood had transformed me, whose memories I had glimpsed during those five days of agony. He was a ghost, a specter that haunted the edges of my consciousness, always there but never fully seen. I had tried to bury him, to lock him away in the darkest corners of my mind, but he always found a way to claw his way back.

I had seen fragments of his life—flashes of unfamiliar faces, moments of violence and despair, a darkness I couldn't fully understand. But I had also seen strength. Control. A sense of purpose that I hadn't found in myself.

Why had he chosen me?

The question burned in my mind, a wound that refused to heal.

I looked around the forest, taking in the towering trees, the dappled moonlight filtering through the canopy. This place had given me peace. It had become my sanctuary, a world where I could be free from the noise and chaos of humanity. The forest had taught me how to survive, how to harness my strength, how to master my senses. It had become a part of me.

And yet...

It wasn't enough.

I stood, pacing along the edge of the stream, my footsteps silent against the soft earth. The cool night air brushed against my skin, carrying with it the faint scent of pine and damp earth. The forest was alive around me, teeming with life, but I felt disconnected from it, as though I were an outsider looking in.

For all the clarity I had found here, there was still a void inside me—questions that only Marcus could answer.

What had I become?

Why had he left me to figure this out on my own?

And what did he want from me?

The thought of returning to the city was daunting. The idea of walking among people again, of exposing myself to the world I had left behind, filled me with unease. I wasn't the same Tristan who had lived there, who had worked late shifts and texted his sister and friends without a second thought. I had changed in ways I couldn't fully articulate, ways that made me feel like a stranger in my own skin.

I didn't know if I could go back.

But the pull was undeniable.

I closed my eyes, leaning against a tree as I let my thoughts drift. The bark was rough against my back, grounding me in the present even as my mind wandered into the past. Marcus's face came to me again, shadowed and intense. I saw his lips move, his words lost to the haze of memory.

In that moment, I hated him.

I hated the way he had upended my life, the way he had left me to piece myself back together without so much as a hint of what I was becoming. He had taken everything from me—my normalcy, my sense of self, my place in the world—and replaced it with uncertainty and fear.

But I also needed him.

I needed to understand.

The forest had become my world, but it wasn't my entire world. Not anymore.

I thought of the city—the streets I had walked, the people I had left behind. My sister. Jessica and Benji. The guilt I had buried for months began to surface, a weight pressing down on me as I considered what it would mean to face them again.

Would they recognize me?

Would I recognize myself?

The decision felt impossible.

Staying here meant holding on to the life I had built in the woods, the sense of freedom and control I had fought so hard to achieve. It meant continuing to live in the shadows, away from the world that had once been mine.

But leaving meant answers. Closure.

I sat down again, running a hand through my hair as the thoughts churned in my mind. The night stretched on, the stars above winking faintly through the gaps in the trees. I stayed by the stream, my reflection rippling in the water as I wrestled with the choice before me.

The forest was quiet, as if waiting for me to decide.

I thought about the first time I had seen Marcus. It had been in a dream—or what I had thought was a dream. He had been standing in a clearing, his eyes piercing, his presence commanding. He had spoken to me, his voice low and urgent, but the words had been lost in the haze of sleep. When I woke, I had dismissed it as nothing more than a figment of my imagination.

But then the changes had started.

The heightened senses. The strength. The hunger.

It had taken me weeks to realize that the dream hadn't been a dream at all. It had been a memory—a memory that wasn't mine.

I had tried to run from it, to deny it, but the truth had been inescapable. Marcus had changed me, and there was no going back.

Now, as I sat by the stream, I wondered if I had been running from the wrong thing. Maybe the answers I sought weren't in the forest. Maybe they were in the city, in the life I had left behind.

But the thought of returning filled me with dread.

I had spent months learning to control my new abilities, to harness the power coursing through my veins. But I had also spent months hiding, avoiding the world that had once been mine. I didn't know if I was ready to face it again.

And yet...

The pull was undeniable.

I stood, my decision made.

The forest had been my sanctuary, but it was time to leave.

I took one last look at the stream, at the moonlight dancing on its surface, and then I turned and walked away.

The path ahead was uncertain, but I knew one thing for sure: I couldn't keep running.

It was time to face Marcus.

It was time to face myself.

Morning came slowly, the soft glow of dawn creeping through the trees like a hesitant breath. Pale light filtered through the canopy, painting the forest floor in fractured gold, each beam trembling as leaves shivered in the breeze. The air hung heavy with dew, dampening my clothes and hair, the chill seeping into my bones. Around me, the forest stirred—leaves rustled like parchment, branches creaked in conversation, and somewhere far off, a woodpecker drummed a staccato rhythm against bark. Birdsong spilled from the treetops, bright and liquid, but their melodies felt distant, as if muffled by the weight pressing against my chest.

I hadn't slept.

The decision had coiled around me all night, serpent-tight, squeezing the air from my lungs. I'd sat with my back against the broad trunk of an ancient cedar, its roots cradling me like gnarled hands, while the moon traced its slow arc across the sky. Sleep had been impossible. Every time I closed my eyes, memories surged—fragmented and sharp. This place had remade me. But remaking, I realized now, was not the same as healing.

For months, the forest had been my refuge—a womb of shadows and silence where I could shed the skin of the man I'd been. Here, I'd learned to quiet the chaos in my veins, to bend the wildness inside me to my will. The trees had been my teachers. They'd shown me how to listen—not just with ears, but with skin and sinew. To track the shift in wind that warned of storms, to taste the metallic tang of prey in the air, to feel the vibration of a rabbit's heartbeat through the soil. The forest had stripped me of everything soft, everything human, until all that remained was instinct and hunger. The noise of my old life—the clatter of subway cars, the shrill ping of text messages, the hollow laughter of crowded rooms—had dissolved into the rhythm of rainfall and the whisper of roots drinking deep from t he earth.

But now, the forest felt smaller.

It wasn't the trees or the trails—it was me. I'd grown beyond the boundaries of this place, restless and ravenous. If I stayed, I could carve out a life here, simple and safe. I'd hunt at dawn, sleep beneath the stars, let the seasons wear me down to something timeless and uncomplicated. But the questions would rot inside me, festering. What am I? Why did this happen? And beneath it all, relentless as a tide—Marcus.

I stood by the stream, its waters black and glassy in the predawn hush. My reflection wavered as I leaned closer—a stranger's face stared back. My hair hung wild, streaked with dirt and moss, framing features honed by months of solitude. I looked feral. Unrecognizable.

I crouched, plunging my hands into the water. The cold stabbed through me, sharpening the fog in my mind. Droplets clung to my skin as I splashed my face, the shock grounding me. The forest would endure. Its roots would dig deeper, its creatures would thrive. But I could no longer hide among them.

The next hours blurred into ritual.

My shelter—a cocoon of woven branches, moss, and desperation—stood nestled between two boulders, nearly invisible beneath a curtain of ivy. Inside, the remnants of my life here lingered: a bed of flattened ferns, a fire pit choked with ash, a chipped mug I'd stolen from a forgotten campsite. I packed methodically: an old hoodie, its fabric stiff with dried mud, to hide my face; my phone, long dead but kept like a talisman; my knife, which I grabbed from home before I left, its edge gleaming dull. At the last moment, I tucked a sprig of pine into my pocket, its resinous scent a fleeting anchor.

Before leaving, I knelt at the shelter's entrance. My fingers traced the grooves in the wood, the notches I'd carved to count the days. "Thank you," I whispered. The wind answered, scattering leaves across the threshold like a blessing.

The journey to the forest's edge felt like walking through a dream.

Familiar landmarks guided me—the lightning-scarred oak where I'd weathered my first storm, the creek where I'd learned to fish with bare hands, the clearing where I'd faced down a coyote, our snarls echoing like thunder. The trees seemed to lean closer as I passed, their branches brushing my shoulders. Stay, they seemed to murmur. Stay, and stay safe.

I didn't look back.

When the first glint of the city pierced the horizon—a jagged line of steel and glass—I froze. The wind shifted, carrying the stench of exhaust and fried grease. My pulse quickened. Climbing a lichen-crusted boulder, I balanced between worlds: behind me, the endless green; ahead, the gray sprawl.

I thought of Jessica and Benji. Jessica, with her razor wit and reckless loyalty, who'd once driven three hours to bail me out of a bar fight I didn't start. Benji, whose laughter could flood a room, who'd smuggled me coffee during endless night shifts at the garage. They'd tried to find me. Texts lit up my dead phone for weeks—Where the hell are you? and Talk to us, Tris—until the messages stopped. Had they mourned me? Or had they buried the man I'd been, the way you bury something too broken to fix?

I thought of my sister, missing her wedding—the biggest day of her life. The voicemails she'd left, her voice fraying with fear. Please, Tristan. Just tell me you're alive.

I thought of Marcus. Always Marcus.

And I thought of the forest. The way it had held me when I had nothing left. The way it had made me strong.

It wasn't a goodbye.

The forest would wait.

But I had to go.

The tree line thinned, sunlight glaring where shadows once soothed. I hesitated, toes digging into the soil. A jay screeched overhead, indignant. Last chance, it seemed to warn.

I stepped onto asphalt.

The city swallowed me in waves. First the sounds—engines growling, horns blaring, a busker's guitar wailing a distorted tune. Then the smells: gasoline, sweat, greasy street meat, the acrid bite of urine. My hoodie clung to me, damp with nervous sweat, as I tugged the hood lower. Faces blurred—a man shouting into his Bluetooth, a toddler wailing in a stroller, a group of teens vaping under an awning. I moved like a ghost, shoulders hunched, footsteps silent.

Yet the city had its own pulse. Neon signs flickered, bleeding color onto the pavement. Graffiti screamed from alley walls, cryptic and urgent. A subway train rumbled underground, its vibration humming in my teeth. For a heartbeat, I missed the forest's stillness.

But danger hummed here too. A cop car idled at the corner, radio static crackling. A man in a doorway tracked my movement, eyes gleaming with calculation. The prickle on my neck—someone's gaze, lingering too long. I ducked into a bodega, fluorescent lights scalding my eyes. The clerk glanced up, disinterested, then returned to his crossword.

I bought a pair of hazel contacts and a lukewarm bottle of water, the plastic slippery in my grip. At the counter, my reflection glared from a security mirror—hooded, hollow-cheeked, a predator in stolen skin. This is what you are now, this is what he made you.

Night fell as I reached the old neighborhood. Brownstones loomed, windows glowing like watchful eyes. My apartment building hunched at the end of the block, its bricks stained with decades of grime. A curtain twitched in Mrs. Petrovic's window—she'd always watered her geraniums at 7 p.m., rain or shine.

I didn't linger.

The building looked the same as I approached it, yet everything about it felt different. The cracked sidewalk, its fissures spiderwebbing toward the gutter like veins, held memories of sprinting to catch the morning bus, of stumbling home after late shifts at the diner. The peeling paint around the doorframe, once a cheerful robin's egg blue, had dulled to the color of ash. Even the faint hum of the streetlights overhead, their orange glow pooling on the pavement like spilled nectar, felt colder now, harsher. This place had been a sanctuary once—a cramped, leaking, roach-riddled sanctuary, but mine all the same.

But standing there now, staring at the place I had once called home, I felt like a stranger. The weight of the forest clung to me, its whispers tangled in my bones. I wondered if the walls would recoil at the scent of wolf musk and crushed juniper that followed me like a second shadow.

I reached into my bag and pulled out my old key, the metal cold and worn against my palm. The teeth were uneven, filed down by years of impatient jiggling. Funny, I thought. This thing survived bar fights, subway floods, and that time Benji tried to "fix" it with a pocketknife. Sliding it into the lock, I twisted it with a faint hope that maybe, just maybe, some piece of my old life had stayed intact.

The lock didn't budge.

I tried again, my brow furrowing as I jiggled the key in the slot. Still nothing. The mechanism ground stubbornly, as if offended by the intrusion. A bitter smile tugged at the corner of my lips. Of course, they'd have changed the locks by now. It had been months since I'd vanished without a word—no notice, no forwarding address, just a half-finished carton of milk in the fridge and a Netflix subscription quietly hemorrhaging cash from my drained bank account. The landlord, old Mrs. Petrovic, with her cigarette-scorched voice and hawkish eyes, had probably assumed I'd joined the ranks of the city's ghosts. Cleared out my stuff, moved on. Erased me.

Leaning against the door, I closed my eyes. The wood pressed into my shoulder blade, unyielding. The faint sounds of the city buzzed around me—distant conversations in languages I couldn't place, the rumble of a passing car with a misfiring engine, the chirp of a bike bell as a delivery rider wove through pedestrians. Life here pulsed on, indifferent. I wondered if the neighbors still fought on Thursdays, if the bodega downstairs still sold those stale croissants I'd pretended to enjoy.

They've erased me, I thought. Just like that.

But erasure required effort. Had she boxed my things herself? Donated my threadbare flannels to the thrift store? Thrown out the Polaroids tacked to the wall—Benji grinning with a ketchup mustache, Jessica mid-laugh at Coney Island, the blurry shot of Dad teaching me to cast a fishing line? Or had she simply dumped it all into the alley dumpster, where rain and rats would finish the job?

I took a step back, scanning the building's facade. My gaze snagged on a small window near the fire escape, its latch slightly loose. The metal grate sagged, rust eating at its hinges. No one was watching.

In a single fluid motion, I leaped up, gripping the edge of the fire escape. The iron groaned under my weight, flakes of paint crumbling like dried blood. My muscles burned—not with strain, but with the memory of scaling cliffs in the wilderness, of outrunning storms that howled through the pines. I pulled myself onto the metal platform, its gridwork imprinting diamonds onto my palms.

The window slid open with a shriek that set my teeth on edge. I froze, listening for footsteps, for the creak of a neighbor's floorboards. Nothing. Slipping inside, I landed softly on the floor, my boots sinking into carpet that was... different. Thicker. Beige instead of the moth-eaten gray I remembered.

The smell hit me first—stale air and dust, mingled with the sharp tang of fresh paint. The apartment was nearly empty, save for a few boxes stacked near the wall labeled *KITCHEN – FRAGILE* and a single leather suitcase leaning against the couch. A *new* couch, I realized. Sleek, black, nothing like the sagging plaid monstrosity I'd salvaged from a sidewalk.

Someone else was moving in.

I drifted through the rooms, trailing my fingers along the walls. The scuffed hardwood floors were still the same, though someone had tried to buff out the deepest scars. The cracks in the ceiling still branched like lightning, but now they'd been painted over, whitewash failing to conceal the damage beneath. My bookshelves were gone. So was the dented fridge plastered with takeout menus and Jessica's crayon drawings from third grade.

A pang of loss rippled through me, sharp enough to steal my breath. The Tristan who had lived here—who'd burned toast at 3 a.m., who'd pinned maps of hiking trails to the bathroom door, who'd whispered secrets to the mold creeping along the baseboards—that boy was gone. The forest had hollowed him out and stitched something fiercer in his place.

But the shower still worked.

I moved quickly, locking the door behind me and heading to the bathroom. The tiles were cold under my bare feet, the same cracked hexagons, the same grout stained by hard water. The overhead light flickered to life with its familiar epileptic hum.

The mirror above the sink was speckled with grime, but it was enough to catch my reflection.

I paused, staring at the face that looked back at me. My hazel eyes, alive with shimmering silver and gold patterns—a side effect of the wild magic or just sleep deprivation?—seemed to glow in the dingy light. I wiped a streak of condensation from the mirror, leaning in closer as my reflection became clearer.

My cheekbones stood out sharper than I remembered, giving my face an angular, sculpted look that hadn't been there before. My jawline was more defined, my features striking in a way that felt almost intentional—like I had been refined, perfected.

But it was my skin that stopped me cold.

It was no longer pale.

After months in the forest, I had expected my complexion to be dull, maybe a little rough from the dirt and, of course, pale—almost sickly. But instead, my skin looked... flawless.

Too flawless.

The color was warm, rich, and impossibly smooth. No blemishes, no uneven texture, no scars—not even the faint childhood scar I knew had once been at my temple. Every imperfection, every trace of the person I used to be, was gone.

I turned my face side to side, watching the way the dim bathroom light caught the surface of my skin. It didn't shine unnaturally, but it reflected light in a way that made it look soft, like polished marble. My skin wasn't just healthy—it was something more.

Not human, but not monstrous either.

I had expected some change after my transformation. I knew I was faster, stronger, that my senses had sharpened beyond anything I could have imagined. But this? This was different.

I had seen myself before, in glimpses of reflections in water, in brief flashes when passing by glass surfaces. But I had never taken the time to truly *look*.

And now that I was, I wasn't sure how to process it.

I lifted my hand and ran my fingers along my jaw. My skin was impossibly smooth, like the surface of a perfect porcelain doll. It wasn't unnatural in the way a statue looked artificial—it was too natural, *too* ideal, as if my body had been sculpted into the most visually perfect version of itself.

This wasn't just an improvement. This was... deliberate.

I had assumed my body would adapt to my new nature, that I'd be stronger and heal faster. But I hadn't expected *this*.

I looked normal enough to blend in. If anything, I looked better than I ever had before. And yet, the perfection of it unsettled me.

Because nothing was ever perfect.

Nothing human, at least.

My hair was long, a chaotic mess of waves that brushed my collarbone, streaked with hints of sun-bleached bronze. Dirt smudged my jawline, the faint scent of pine and earth clinging to me like a confession.

I barely recognized myself.

The water was freezing when I turned the shower on, but I didn't care. I stripped off my hoodie—threadbare, smelling of wood smoke—and jeans caked with dried mud. Stepping under the spray, I let the cold water cascade over me. It was a shock, the chill biting into my skin, needling my ribs and thigh. But soon the water warmed, steaming as it sluiced away the grime of the forest, the blood, the sweat.

I scrubbed at my arms, my chest, my face, watching as the dirt swirled down the drain. It felt like shedding a layer of my old life, peeling back the months of isolation to reveal the person I'd become. The soap stung, cheap and citrusy, nothing like the herbal poultices I'd made from crushed yarrow and rainwater. But it was a human sting. A familiar one.

For the first time in weeks, I felt clean.

After the shower, I toweled off with a rag I found crumpled behind the door—stiff, sun-bleached, possibly mine. The bathroom cabinet yielded half a bottle of aspirin, a rusty razor, and a pair of scissors buried under expired coupons. My fingers trembled slightly as I held them, the blade catching the light.

I faced the mirror, studying my reflection.

My hair was too long, unruly, a reminder of mornings spent finger-combing tangles, of twigs and leaves caught in the strands after nights spent sleeping under the stars. It was a wild thing, this mane, a testament to the chaos I'd survived. But chaos had no place here. Not anymore.

I combed my fingers through it, lifting a section before snipping it away. The strands fell into the sink, dark and damp, as I worked to tame the mess. Memories flickered—Mom shearing my hair in the kitchen when I was seven, Jessica giggling as she swept up the clumps; Benji daring me to shave a lightning bolt into my temple sophomore year.

When I was done, my hair was shorter, cropped close at the sides with a tousled sweep on top. Neat enough to pass for normal, but still rough-edged, like a cliff face weathered by a storm. It felt like me, but new—a version of myself I could step into.

I ran a hand through it, nodding at my reflection. The eyes that stared back were still feral, still flecked with that unnatural metallic sheen, but the rest? Passable. Human.

I grabbed the small plastic case from the counter, popping it open with a click. Inside, two hazel contacts nestled in solution—$19.99 from a bodega with flickering fluorescents and a cashier who didn't ask questions. Leaning toward the mirror, I carefully placed them over my irises, blinking rapidly as they settled. The hazel color looked almost natural, reminiscent of my human eyes, but couldn't fully mask the silver and gold swirls that shimmered beneath like molten metal. A partial disguise, but better than nothing.

I found my phone in the pocket of my bag, its screen smudged and dark. The case, cracked, a sticker of a howling wolf half-scratched off—was the same. The battery was nearly dead, but it still had enough life to power on.

I plugged it into the charger I'd left behind months ago, watching as the screen flickered to life. Notifications flooded in—missed calls, texts, voicemails, emails. A digital avalanche.

27 Missed Calls: SIS

15 Unread Messages: Benji <3

<3 42 Emails: Overdue Bills, Final Notices, Eviction Warning

I ignored most of them, my thumb hovering over the few that mattered.

KAT: Tristan, please call me. I'm worried about you. (Sent 5 months ago)

KAT: Where are you??? Mrs. Petrovic says you're gone. (Sent 4 months ago)

KAT: I'm coming to the city. If you get this, meet me at Lou's Diner. 8 p.m. Please. (Sent 3 weeks ago)

Benji <3: Dude, did you get eaten by a bear??? (Sent 6 months ago)

Benji <3: Seriously, Trist. Your sister's calling me every night. (Sent 4 months ago)

Benji <3: Alright, fuck this. I'm filing a missing person report. (Sent 47 days ago)

Jessica: Hey Tristan! Kat says you're "off finding yourself" lol. Call me when you're done being a hippie! (Sent 2 months ago)

Kat: ...Tristan? (Sent 17 days ago)

The words hit me harder than I expected. My sister had always been the worrier, the one who bandaged my skinned knees and hidden Dad's whiskey keys. I had let her down, leaving her to spin excuses for my absence and field Mom's brittle questions at Sunday dinners.

But maybe, just maybe, I could fix that.

I leaned back against the couch, the leather creaking beneath me. My phone charged slowly, the red light blinking like a heartbeat. Outside, the city's rhythm continued—taxis honking, a dog barking, the distant wail of a siren. Normal sounds. Human sounds.

The faint smell of paint lingered in the air, a reminder that this place wasn't mine anymore. The thought didn't sting as much as I expected it to. This apartment had been a chapter in my life, filled with burnt coffee, overdue bills, and the kind of loneliness that gnaws at your edges. Now it was closed.

But there were still threads to pick up, fragments to glue back into something resembling a life. Starting with my sister.

The sun was setting by the time I stood, pulling on a clean shirt from my bag—black, nondescript, smelling faintly of cedar. I slipped my phone into my pocket, its weight feeling foreign. The streets outside were bathed in the golden glow of evening, the hum of the city softening as shopkeepers rolled down gates and office crowds thinned.

I grabbed my bag, slinging it over my shoulder. One last look around the apartment: the boxes, the suitcase, the emptiness. A shrine to impermanence.

But as I stepped out into the hallway, locking the door behind me, I felt a spark of determination. The forest had taught me to track, to fight, to listen to the silent language of the earth. It had stripped me raw and rebuilt me with claws and grit.

Now it was time to face the world I'd left behind.

And the first step was seeing my sister.

The city felt different now. Less like a place I had abandoned and more like something foreign—like I was walking through the ghost of a life that no longer belonged to me. The streets hummed with the same restless energy, but the noise grated against my senses now—too sharp, too alive. Neon signs buzzed like angry wasps, car horns blared in staccato bursts, and the thrum of footsteps on pavement vibrated in my bones. I kept my hands buried in my jacket pockets, my nails digging into my palms to ground myself. The hunger was quieter these days, but it still prowled beneath the surface, a wolf on a frayed leash.

Still, I had unfinished business.

The familiar path to Kat's front door felt heavier with every step, the weight of guilt settling in my chest like a stone. Her neighborhood hadn't changed—trim hedges, chalk drawings smudged on the sidewalk, the same crooked oak tree whose branches scraped against her roof in the wind. I paused at the foot of her porch steps, staring at the wreath on her door. Autumn leaves and dried flowers. Seasonal. Normal. Everything I wasn't anymore.

When she opened the door, her face was a whirlwind of emotions—relief, frustration, suspicion. She looked older. Not in her features, which were still sharp and bright, but in the way she held herself, shoulders squared like she'd been bracing for a storm. Her auburn hair was shorter, swept into a messy bun, and her sweatshirt smelled faintly of baby powder. A new detail. A life moving forward without me.

"Where the hell have you been?" she demanded, crossing her arms. No hug. No "it's good to see you." Just raw emotion. I deserved that.

I exhaled slowly, stepping inside without waiting for an invitation. The air was thick with vanilla candles and the yeasty warmth of freshly baked bread. A half-knitted blanket lay abandoned on the armchair, needles still tucked into the yarn. Kat had always fidgeted when she was upset.

"I've been... figuring things out," I said, my voice steady and rehearsed. Too calm. Too composed. It didn't sound like me anymore.

"For months?" She shut the door hard behind me, the sound reverberating in my skull. "Months, Tristan! Almost a year! No calls, no texts—you missed everything! My wedding, holidays, birthdays—Mom and Dad thought you were dead!"

Her voice cracked on the last word, and I flinched. The guilt twisted deeper. I could've told her then—I am dead, in a way—but the lie slipped out smoother.

"I know. And I'm sorry."

We stood in the living room, frozen in the amber of her anger. The mantelpiece behind her was crowded with photos—Kat in her wedding dress, beaming under a summer sun; our parents posing stiffly in matching holiday sweaters; a gap where my graduation photo used to sit. She'd taken it down.

"Sit," she said finally, gesturing to the couch. "You look like you haven't slept in weeks."

I don't sleep at all, I almost said. Instead, I sank into the cushions, the fabric sighing under my weight. Kat perched on the edge of the coffee table, her knees nearly brushing mine. Close enough to reach out. She didn't.

"So?" she pressed. "What happened? Where were you?"

I hesitated, my gaze drifting to the window. Dusk painted the sky in bruised purples, and somewhere beyond the glass, a siren wailed. "I've decided to leave the country," I said. "There are... communities. Remote places that need help—medical care, infrastructure. It's a long-term commitment. I won't be able to communicate much."

Her eyes narrowed. "Since when do you know anything about infrastructure?"

"Since now." I forced a smile, thin and brittle. "I'll send letters when I can."

A beat passed. Then she snorted, shaking her head. "God, you're such a martyr. Always have to be the hero, don't you?"

The old jab should've stung. Instead, it felt like a relic, a script from a play we'd outgrown. "Someone's got to do it," I said lightly.

We lapsed into silence. Kat picked at a loose thread on her sleeve, her jaw working like she was chewing on words she couldn't spit out. Finally, she stood, pacing to the kitchen. "You want coffee? Or—" She glanced at the clock, the unspoken or something stronger hanging between us.

"No. Thanks."

She returned with a mug anyway, steam curling into the air. The smell of it—dark roast, a splash of cinnamon—flooded me with memories: late-night study sessions, her laughing as I burned my tongue gulping it too fast. "Patience, Tristan," she'd say. "It's not going anywhere."

Now, she sipped slowly, studying me over the rim. "This isn't another one of your disappearing acts, is it?" she asked quietly. "Because I don't think Mom and Dad can handle you vanishing again."

The words hung there, fragile. I thought of our mother's hands trembling as she'd dialed my number for the hundredth time, our father staring blankly at the nightly news, as if waiting for my face to flash among the missing persons.

"It's not like that," I said. "I'm doing something good. Something that'll make a difference."

She didn't believe me. I saw it in the way her grip tightened on the mug, in the faint crease between her brows. But she nodded anyway because that's what sisters do. They let you lie when the truth would break them.

When I hugged her goodbye, I held on for a second longer than I should have, memorizing the rhythm of her heartbeat, the warmth of her skin. Human. Fragile. Alive.

"Don't be a stranger," she muttered into my shoulder.

I didn't promise.

My parents' neighborhood was quieter, the houses wider and farther apart. Their porch light flickered as I approached, moths darting in frantic circles around it. The door swung open before I could knock.

"Tristan!" My mother's voice trembled as she pulled me into a hug, her hands clutching the back of my jacket like I might dissolve. She smelled like lavender and the menthol balm she used for her arthritis. "We've been so worried—your father kept saying you'd turn up, but I—"

"I'm here, Mom," I murmured, resting my chin on her head. Over her shoulder, my father stood in the hallway, his eyes glistening.

They ushered me inside, fussing over the paleness of my skin and the sharpness of my bones. "You're too thin," Mom fretted, already heading to the kitchen. "Let me make you a plate."

I let her. I sat at the same oak table where I'd done homework as a kid, its surface scarred with decades of knife scratches and spilled wax. Dad settled across from me, his hands folded tightly.

"Where've you been, son?" he asked, his voice gruff with the effort of staying calm.

I repeated the lie—helping communities, traveling. They accepted it eagerly, their relief palpable. Mom returned with a heaping plate of lasagna, her specialty, and I forced myself to pick at it, the spices clashing violently with my enhanced taste buds.

They filled the silence with stories—Aunt Linda's hip surgery, the Johnsons' new golden retriever, the leak in the church roof that Dad had helped fix. Normalcy. A balm for their fears. I nodded along, smiling at all the right moments, but their voices blurred into static. I was acutely aware of the wrongness of it all—the way my mother's pulse fluttered in her throat, the scent of my father's aftershave mingling with the iron undertone of his blood.

While they talked, I slipped upstairs to my old room, now a guest space stripped of my band posters and track medals. In the closet, however, buried under spare blankets, I found it: a dusty cardboard box labeled "Tristan's Stuff" in Mom's looping cursive.

Inside lay my old kung fu gear—fingerless gloves frayed at the seams, a cracked leather mouthguard, a gi yellowed with age. Beneath it all was a photo from my first tournament at sixteen: me mid-kick, face flushed with effort, Sifu Chen grinning proudly in the background. "Control isn't just in the body," he'd say, tapping my temple. "It's here. Always here."

I packed the gear into my bag, the weight of it comforting.

When I left, my mother pressed a stack of handwritten letters into my hands—updates I'd missed, silly anecdotes, coupons she'd saved. "Write when you can," she said, her smile trembling.

My father squeezed my shoulder. "Make us proud."

I promised I would.

Night had fully settled by the time I returned to the city. I wandered without direction, past dimly lit bars and shuttered storefronts. My senses prickled with every passing crowd—laughter, perfume, the metallic tang of blood. A group of teenagers jostled past me, their voices loud and raw, and I veered into an alley, pressing my back to the cold brick until the roar in my veins subsided.

Discipline, I reminded myself. Control.

In a vacant lot on the outskirts, the gi felt strange against my skin—too stiff, too human. But the movements came back—the snap of a round-house kick, the fluid arc of a backfist. I moved faster now, my body a shadow blurring under the moon. When I struck the makeshift wooden dummy, it splintered with a crack that echoed like gunfire.

Too much. Too strong.

By dawn, the dummy was reduced to kindling, my knuckles raw and healing quickly. But I had lasted the night without slipping. Without feeding, but I can last six more days before I need to go hunting again.

It was a start.

CHAPTER FOURTEEN

IN SEARCH OF MARCUS

I stood on the roof of my apartment building, staring out at the sprawling city that was now my temporary home. The wind carried the stench of humanity up to me—sweat, perfume, rust, and the faint, ever-present rot of garbage fermenting in alleyways. But beneath it all, there was something metallic and electric, like the ozone before a storm. The city's heartbeat.

It pulsed with life, its lights stretching endlessly into the horizon, flickering like artificial stars. Even in the dead of night, the city never truly slept—cars weaved through the streets below, their headlights cutting through the darkness, and distant sirens wailed like restless ghosts. Once, I'd found comfort in the noise. As a human, it had been a lullaby, proof that I wasn't alone. Now, it felt like standing in the center of a collapsing star, every sound and scent a supernova.

I'd lived here before, walked these streets as someone softer, slower, blind to the layers of the world. The memory clung to me like a phantom limb. There—the corner where I'd spilled coffee down my shirt rushing to work. There—the park bench where I'd watched pigeons fight over a half-eaten pretzel.

But the city I'd known was gone, replaced by something sharper, hungrier. The subway's rumble wasn't just vibration now; it was a language, the grind of steel and spark telling stories of decay. The diners I'd loved weren't havens of grease and laughter but symphonies of heartbeats, of blood rushing beneath thin skin.

Everything felt foreign, warped by the unnatural sharpness of my senses.

The sounds were deafening.

I could hear every conversation within a block's radius—a couple arguing about rent, a bartender humming off-key, a child muttering in their sleep. Every inhale and exhale of the people beneath me threaded together into a discordant choir. The faint rustle of fabric as someone shifted in bed behind a closed window might as well have been sandpaper dragged over my skull.

The scents were overwhelming.

The acrid burn of gasoline, the sickly-sweet aroma of street food, the unmistakable metallic tang of blood from the occasional cut or scraped knee. It was all there, pressing against my mind like an invisible weight. Worse were the layers beneath—the salt of fear on a woman walking alone, the sour musk of exhaustion clinging to a night-shift worker, the dizzying rush of dopamine from a laughing group outside a club. My throat burned.

And yet, none of it mattered.

Because no matter how loud the city was, there was only one thing I was listening for.

"Marcus."

He had vanished as suddenly as he had entered my life. No note, no trail, no ripple in the world to suggest he'd ever existed. Not even the faintest imprint of his cologne—bergamot and frost, a smell I'd committed to memory—lingered in the air anymore. I'd checked.

And now, everything about my existence seemed to circle back to him.

Why had he turned me?

What did he see in me?

Why had he left me to figure this out alone?

The questions gnawed at me, refusing to let go. I had combed the city, stalking through alleyways, lingering in forgotten places where I thought he might have been. I'd memorized the graffiti-scarred walls of the industrial district, the damp, echoing silence of empty parking garages, the way moonlight pooled in the cracks of abandoned churches. But Marcus was a ghost, always just beyond my reach. Always in the corner of my vision—a shadow slipping around a corner, a familiar cadence of footsteps that dissolved into chaos when I chased it.

Sometimes, I felt him. A whisper in the back of my mind, a tugging sensation that told me I was close. But close to what? A memory? A hallucination? Or was it something real?

Once, I'd followed that tug for hours, through rain-soaked streets and construction sites clattering with chains. It led me to a crumbling theater, its marquee spelling out "HELLO" in broken bulbs. Inside, I found nothing but dust and the gnawed bones of rodents. No Marcus. Just the hollow ache of hope.

I didn't know.

But I needed to find out.

Without a real home to return to, I had been forced to start over.

The apartment I managed to find was on the outskirts of the city, wedged between forgotten buildings and a strip of abandoned warehouses. The walls were thin, the floors sloped, and the pipes groaned like dying animals. But the windows faced the woods—a jagged line of pines that leaned toward the city as if trying to escape their own shadows. At night, their branches scratched at the glass, a sound that might have unnerved a human. To me, it was a reminder: You don't belong here either.

It wasn't much, but it had one thing I needed—proximity to the woods.

The forest had been my refuge, the only place I could breathe when the city became too much. Once every nine days, I disappeared into the trees, keeping my feeding confined to the animals that roamed the dense wilderness. Deer were easiest—their slow, heavy pulses called to me from miles away. Rabbits were quicker, their hearts frantic drums that left my hands shaking afterward. Once, I'd tried a fox. Its blood was fiercer, wilder, like drinking liquid fire. I'd gagged for hours, my throat raw, as if it had fought me even in death.

Three gallons of blood.

Not a drop more. Not a drop less.

A carefully measured rhythm.

The ritual was clinical now. I'd wake at dusk, count the hours until the woods swallowed the last traces of sunlight, then hunt with the precision of a surgeon. No joy in it. No relief. Just the mechanical act of survival, folding the hunger into a smaller and smaller box inside my ribs.

I had thought feeding would get easier, but the control it required never waned. The hunger was constant—a dull, quiet pull, waiting for a moment of weakness.

So far, I hadn't given it one.

But the city presented new problems.

I couldn't hide in the shadows forever. Not here.

The more time I spent in the open, the more I realized that I was drawing attention. Not because of my strength or speed—those were things I could keep to myself. It was my eyes.

They had returned to a bright, vivid hazel, but they were different now—unnaturally vibrant, flecked with silver and gold swirls that faintly glowed under certain lights. In the dimness of my apartment, they cast faint patterns on the walls, like sunlight through water. I'd caught my reflection in a shattered mirror behind the warehouse last week and froze—not at the sight of myself, but at the way the colors in my eyes seemed to "move," slow and hypnotic, as if alive.

It wasn't something anyone could fully articulate, but I saw it in their expressions—the way their conversations faltered when I passed, the way their gazes lingered a second too long.

At the 24-hour convenience store, the cashier had dropped a jar of pickles when I walked in. "S-sorry," he'd stammered, cheeks flushing as he scrambled to clean the glass. "You just...

startled me." But his pulse had spiked, a frantic thud-thud-thud that echoed in my skull. He hadn't been startled. He'd been afraid.

Whispers followed me.

"Did you see that guy? His eyes are insane. They almost glow."

"He looks... different. Like he's not from here."

A woman in a red coat had followed me for three blocks last Tuesday, her curiosity a thick, syrupy scent in the air. When I finally turned to face her, she'd blinked, disoriented, as if waking from a dream. "I... I thought you were someone else," she'd lied, backing away. Her pupils were dilated, her breath shallow. She hadn't thought anything. She'd felt it—the pull, the magnetism. The predator's charm.

Some were drawn to me, unable to look away. Others avoided me altogether, as if their instincts warned them of something they couldn't explain.

Neither reaction was good.

The contacts were a necessity.

I had scoured the city for the right pair, eventually finding a shade that dulled the unnatural sharpness of my gaze. They were uncomfortable at first—an irritation I hadn't dealt with in months—but they did their job.

Now, at least, I could walk down the street without feeling like prey being watched by a thousand unseen eyes.

And yet, even with the contacts, the feeling never truly faded.

There was something else. Something beyond just my eyes.

It was in the way people felt me before they saw me, as if my presence sent an unspoken ripple through the air. The way birds fell silent when I passed beneath their trees. The way stray dogs tucked their tails and slunk into alleys. The city itself seemed to hold its breath when I moved through it, waiting for me to tip my hand, to stop pretending.

It was the way strangers hesitated before speaking to me, drawn in without understanding why.

I was a magnet.

And the more I tried to disappear, the more the city seemed to notice me.

I exhaled slowly, running a hand through my hair as I stepped away from the edge of the rooftop. The city stretched below, a living, breathing monster. I wondered if it recognized me as one of its own now—something beautiful and terrible, something that didn't quite fit.

I had spent months trying to blend in, forcing myself to exist among humans again. But I couldn't shake the feeling that I was only playing a part.

Because no matter how much I tried to act normal...

I wasn't.

And unless I found Marcus—unless I understood what I had become—I never would be.

It didn't help that my appearance had changed in other ways, too. It was more than just a subtle shift; it was a complete transformation. My body was leaner, sharper, and every muscle was defined in ways that I couldn't hide, no matter how much I tried to blend into the shadows. The very structure of my face seemed altered; my cheekbones were more pronounced, my jawline sharper, as if sculpted by the hands of a master artist.

My skin, once pale and dull, almost fragile in its imperfection, now glowed in the sunlight, radiating an inner light that drew the eye and made it nearly impossible to disappear into a crowd. The paleness remained, but it was now the pallor of alabaster, not the sickly white of illness or fatigue. It was the flawless skin of someone who existed outside the normal confines of mortality.

The faint scar from a childhood accident was gone, vanished without a trace. A foolish tumble from a tree had left its mark just above my left eyebrow—a permanent reminder of youthful recklessness. Now, nothing. It was as if the injury had never happened; the skin was perfectly smooth and unblemished. This erasure of my past was unsettling, a physical rewriting of my very being. It left me feeling disconnected from the person I once was, a stranger in my own skin, no matter how beautiful that skin might be.

The attention made it harder for me to move through the city unnoticed, but I kept searching for Marcus. Casual glances had turned into lingering stares; whispers followed me down the street, and I felt the weight of curious eyes on my back wherever I went. Before, I could fade into the background, just another face in the urban tapestry.

Now, it felt like a spotlight was constantly trained on me, illuminating my every move. This made my search for Marcus infinitely more complicated, forcing me to adopt elaborate disguises and take circuitous routes to avoid drawing unwanted attention.

He was out there somewhere, and I couldn't shake the feeling that our paths would cross again soon. The bond we had shared, however fleeting, was not something that could be easily broken. I felt it like a constant hum beneath my skin, a subtle vibration resonating within me. It was a beacon, faint but persistent, guiding me through the labyrinthine streets of the city.

I knew, with a certainty that defied logic, that he was within my reach, and I refused to give up until I found him.

I spent countless nights roaming the city streets, hoping to find something—anything—that would lead me to him. The darkness had always been my ally, a cloak of invisibility that allowed me to move unseen. But now, even the shadows seemed to betray me, reflecting the unnatural luminescence emanating from my skin.

I'd walk for hours, from dusk until dawn, following any faint trace of him that I thought I could feel. The scent of his presence—a subtle blend of earth and something indefinably metallic—lingered in certain places, a cruel reminder of our shared past. Sometimes, I caught a fleeting glimpse of his shadow in a crowded street or heard a whisper of his name carried on the wind. These were the breadcrumbs I followed, desperate for a sign that I was on the right track.

Every time I thought I was close, he'd slip away, leaving me frustrated and more determined than ever. It felt like chasing a phantom, a mirage shimmering just out of reach. I would find evidence of his presence—a discarded cigarette butt bearing his distinctive mark, a half-finished sketch in a forgotten alleyway, the lingering echo of his laughter in a crowded bar—but when I arrived, he was always gone. It was a game of cat and mouse, and Marcus was proving to be a formidable opponent. The frustration gnawed at me, fueling my desperation and hardening my resolve. I would not be deterred. I would find him, no matter the cost.

But then, one night, something changed. My nightly searches had become almost ritualistic, a predictable pattern of movement through the city's underbelly. On this particular night, however, a sense of unease settled over me, a feeling that something was different, that the familiar rhythm of the city had been disrupted. It was late, and I was walking through a part of town I hadn't explored before, a narrow alleyway tucked between two abandoned warehouses.

The air was damp, and the smell of rain lingered in the cool breeze. The silence was almost oppressive, broken only by the distant wail of a siren and the rhythmic drip of water from a leaky pipe. The darkness here was thicker, more profound, as if the shadows themselves were sentient beings, watching my every move.

As I rounded a corner, I caught sight of something—a flash of movement out of the corner of my eye. It was so quick, so fleeting, that I almost dismissed it as a trick of the light. But there was something about it, a quality of movement that resonated deep within me, triggering a primal instinct I couldn't ignore. It was like a spark igniting a dormant flame, a sudden surge of energy coursing through my veins.

I stopped, adrenaline sharpening my senses and heightening my awareness. The world seemed to slow down, every sound amplified, every detail brought into sharp focus. There it was again, that faint tugging sensation, like someone was calling me from a distance. It was more than just a feeling; it was a tangible connection, a psychic link resonating between us. I turned toward the movement, my eyes scanning the darkness.

Nothing.

But I knew better. Something was there. The air crackled with unseen energy, the silence felt pregnant with anticipation. I could sense a presence lurking just beyond the veil of shadows, watching, waiting. It was close, closer than it had ever been before. This time, I wouldn't let him slip away. I straightened, every muscle tense, every sense alert. The hunt was on.

I stood perfectly still, a statue carved from moonlight and shadow, my enhanced hearing straining to pick up the slightest sound. The familiar clamor of the city—distant traffic, muffled conversations, the rumble of the subway beneath my feet—seemed to fade into a dull background hum, allowing me to focus on the subtle nuances of the alleyway around me.

I could hear the skittering of rats in the darkness, the rustling of leaves caught in the wind, and the faint whisper of the wind through cracks in the dilapidated brick walls. But beneath these ambient sounds, I sensed something else—a subtle shift in the air pressure, a barely perceptible vibration in the ground beneath my feet, the faintest hint of a scent that was both familiar and disturbingly alien.

My transformation had gifted me with senses far beyond those of a normal human, allowing me to perceive the world in ways I never thought possible. I could see in the dark with almost perfect clarity, hear sounds from miles away, and sense the faintest traces of energy fields surrounding all living things. It was both a blessing and a curse, this heightened awareness, amplifying both the beauty and the ugliness of the world around me.

I took a tentative step forward, my senses on full alert, moving with a grace and agility that belied my former clumsiness. The alleyway stretched before me, an endless labyrinth of shadows and secrets. Each step was measured and deliberate as I carefully scanned every nook and cranny, searching for any sign of movement, any clue that would lead me to Marcus. The air grew colder, a chill that had nothing to do with the night and everything to do with the unnatural presence lurking nearby.

I reached the spot where I had seen the flash of movement, a narrow gap between two crumbling brick walls, barely wide enough for a person to squeeze through. I peered into the darkness, my eyes struggling to penetrate the inky blackness. The scent of rain was stronger here, mixed with a faint metallic odor that sent a shiver down my spine.

I stepped forward cautiously, my heightened senses on high alert. The air felt charged, like the moments before a storm, and the hairs on the back of my neck stood up in rigid defiance. It was more than just the prickling awareness of being watched; it was a tangible shift in the very fabric of the atmosphere, a subtle vibration resonating with an unseen presence. The alley, usually a haven of shadows and forgotten refuse, now felt like a stage set for a play with an unknown and potentially deadly outcome.

I listened carefully, trying to pick up any sound that might reveal the presence I was sure was there. My enhanced hearing strained to filter through the city's ambient noise—the distant siren wail, the rumble of a passing truck, the hushed conversations from the street beyond the alley's mouth. I focused, pushing past the cacophony, searching for the subtle telltale sign of another being.

Then, I heard it. A voice. Whispering. It was so faint, so ephemeral, that I almost dismissed it as a trick of the wind, a phantom echo of my own racing thoughts. But no, it was there, a thread of sound woven into the tapestry of the night. It was barely audible, a mere breath against the brick and asphalt, but I caught a single syllable, laden with a weight that belied its delicate form.

I moved toward the sound, my footsteps silent as I approached a crumbling brick wall at the end of the alley. Years of disuse and neglect had taken their toll on the structure, leaving it scarred with cracks and stained with the grime of countless city rains. The bricks themselves seemed to sag under the weight of time, their mortar crumbling to dust.

There, hidden in the shadows cast by an overhanging fire escape, was a small, tattered envelope pinned to the wall by an old rusty nail. The nail, corroded and fragile, looked as if it might crumble at the slightest touch. The envelope was nondescript; its once-white paper was now stained and yellowed, with frayed edges.

I reached out and carefully removed the envelope, feeling a strange sense of foreboding as I turned it over in my hands. The paper felt thin and brittle, threatening to disintegrate at any moment. There was no name, no address, nothing to indicate who had left it there. It was a blank slate, a void filled only with the unspoken weight of its intended message.

But I knew, deep down, that this was meant for me. A certainty settled in my bones, a cold dread spreading through my veins. It was a summons, a warning, a threat—all rolled into one.

I opened the envelope and pulled out a single sheet of paper. The paper was of the same quality as the envelope: thin and aged, as if it had been pulled from a forgotten stack in some dusty attic. The handwriting was elegant, almost old-fashioned, with sweeping loops and delicate flourishes. It resembled the script one might find in a centuries-old letter, a relic of a bygone era.

The ink, once a deep black, had faded to a ghostly grey, but the words were still legible, sending a chill down my spine that had nothing to do with the night air. They seemed to vibrate on the page, pulsing with hidden energy.

"Hide."

No signature. No indication of who had written it. No explanation, no context—just that single, stark word, hanging in the silence like a suspended blade. But I didn't need one. I knew exactly who it was from. The scent, faint but unmistakable, hit me like a wave. It was a complex, layered aroma—a mixture of ancient earth, expensive cologne, and something darker, something inherently predatory. It stirred both fear and a strange, unwelcome fascination within me. It was a scent I had tried to forget, a scent that haunted my dreams.

Marcus.

Visions of him surged in my mind, a fragmented collage of memories: that evening at the bar, the hazy air thick with smoke, the quiet buzz of dialogue, his smile enchanting, predatory, and completely mesmerizing. I recalled how he had moved with a fluidity that masked his power, the way his gaze had felt like it was cutting through me, revealing truths I hadn't even acknowledged.

I remembered his cologne—a sophisticated blend of sandalwood and spices—a scent that had lingered on my skin long after he was gone. But this time, with my vampire senses, I picked up his true scent, the underlying aroma masked by human artifice. It was a scent of power and decay, of immortality and the endless hunger that came with it.

The realization hit me like a punch to the gut, stealing my breath and leaving me reeling. After all these months—months of silence and agonizing uncertainty—he had finally reached out, and it was as cryptic as ever. What did he mean by "Hide"? Hide what? Hide who? Was it a warning, an attempt to protect me? Or was it a game, a twisted invitation to a deadly dance? The questions swirled in my mind, each one more unsettling than the last. I gripped the piece of paper tighter, my knuckles white, as if I could somehow wring the answers from its fragile surface.

Before I could process any more, I felt it—a presence. The feeling intensified, becoming almost unbearable. It was like being submerged in a pool of ice water, the cold seeping into every pore, every nerve ending. Someone, or something, was watching me. I wasn't alone. I knew it with a certainty that transcended logic or reason. It was a primal awareness, a hunter's sixth sense honed by years of survival.

I spun around, my senses on high alert. My enhanced vision pierced through the shadows, revealing every detail of the alley with unnerving clarity. The crumbling bricks, the scattered debris, the flickering neon sign above the street—all rendered in sharp relief. The alley was empty, at least to the casual observer.

But I could feel it, a heaviness in the air, like a suffocating blanket. It was as if a thousand eyes were burning into the back of my skull, scrutinizing my every move. I scanned the rooftops, the shadows, every dark corner but saw nothing. No movement, no flicker of light, no telltale glint of reflection.

Yet, I knew I wasn't alone. The feeling persisted, growing stronger with each passing second. Whatever was out there was close, impossibly close. It was toying with me, letting me know that it was watching, that it was in control. And that filled me with a bone-chilling dread. I was being hunted, and the hunter was playing a game. I had no idea what the rules were.

I clutched the note in my hand, the cheap paper crinkling under my tightening grip. I started backing away, each step slow and deliberate, my senses stretched taut. The air itself seemed to thicken, pressing in on me, heavy with an unseen weight. The alley walls, graffitied and stained with the city's grime, seemed to lean in, threatening to suffocate me.

The presence wasn't Marcus—I could feel that much. Marcus, even in his brooding intensity, possessed a certain familiar energy, a darkness I understood—a shared burden of existence. This... this was alien, cold, and sharp, like a shard of ice against my skin. It lacked the faintest echo of humanity that clung to Marcus. This was something else entirely. And whatever—or whoever—it was, was not friendly. It radiated a predatory hunger, a silent promise of pain that sent shivers down my spine. Not shivers of fear, though that was present too, but something else, a primal recognition of a power far exceeding my own.

As I turned and started walking quickly down the street, I could feel the thing following me, keeping its distance but never letting me out of its sight. It was like an invisible leash, tethering me to its unseen will. The hairs on the back of my neck prickled, an instinctive response to unseen danger. A cold sweat slicked my palms, the unnatural dampness a stark contrast to my otherwise cool skin. Every instinct in my body screamed for me to run, to bolt into the night and lose myself in the labyrinthine city streets. But I forced myself to keep calm, to act like I didn't know it was there. To show fear would invite attack, confirming its power over me. I focused on my breathing, trying to regulate my frantic senses, willing my legs to move with controlled purpose. It was a delicate dance, a battle of wills played out on the crowded streets of the city.

The street was busy, a kaleidoscope of lights and sounds. Cars roared past, their headlights momentarily blinding, painting the buildings in stark contrasts of light and shadow. People jostled on the sidewalks, their faces illuminated by the glow of storefronts and streetlamps. Each face was a fleeting mask, anonymous in the anonymity of the city. A sea of humanity, oblivious to the silent drama unfolding in their midst. I tried to focus on them, to find a sense of normalcy in their mundane existence, but the presence behind me was a constant, oppressive weight—a dark cloud hanging over the bright lights of the city.

I rounded another corner, slipping into the thick crowd of late-night city dwellers, hoping to lose whatever was following me. The sheer volume of humanity pressed in around me, a temporary buffer against the unseen threat. I ducked my head, weaving through groups of laughing teenagers, their youthful exuberance a stark reminder of what I had lost. I passed couples strolling hand-in-hand, their quiet intimacy a poignant counterpoint to my own isolation. I moved around solitary figures lost in their own thoughts, each encased in their own separate world.

The smells of street food—hot dogs, pretzels, and something vaguely spicy—filled the air, a strange and disorienting mix. A sensory overload that did little to mask the persistent dread that clung to me. But even amidst the chaos, I could still feel it, lurking in the distance, watching, waiting. It was like a persistent hum, a low-frequency vibration resonating deep within my bones. A constant reminder that I was being hunted.

I glanced back, a quick, furtive movement, but saw nothing out of the ordinary—just the endless stream of faces, the flickering lights, the urban cacophony. A blur of movement and sound, concealing the threat that stalked me. But I knew it was there. I could feel its gaze, heavy and unwavering, burning into my back. It was playing with me, allowing me a false sense of hope, a brief respite before tightening the noose. A cruel game, designed to break my spirit.

I wasn't sure what kind of danger I was in, but one thing was clear—finding Marcus wasn't going to be easy. This thing, whatever it was, was an obstacle, a barrier placed deliberately between me and my goal. And whatever had left that note was only the beginning of the game he was playing with me. The note, the cryptic warning, the unsettling presence... it all pointed to a carefully orchestrated plan, a twisted game of cat and mouse with me as the prey—a pawn in a larger, more sinister game.

Panic threatened to overwhelm me, but I fought it back. I had to stay focused, to think clearly. Marcus was counting on me. He needed my help, and I couldn't afford to let him down. My friend; my only connection to a life that felt like it was slipping through my fingers. And maybe, just maybe, I could use this situation to my advantage. If I could figure out who or what this thing was and what it wanted, I might be able to turn the tables—to become the hunter rather than the hunted.

The transformation that changed my eyes from a black void to a vividly bright hue, swirling with silver and gold, came with abilities. I could run faster than any human; I was stronger and more perceptive. The enhanced speed and strength of a vampire who fed solely on animal blood was both a blessing and a curse.

For the rest of the night, I didn't dare return to my apartment. The thought of being trapped in that small, confined space with something lurking outside was unbearable. The darkness would only amplify my fear, the walls closing in on me, suffocating me. Instead, I wandered the city, a ghost in the urban landscape, weaving through streets and alleyways, trying to shake the presence that clung to me like a shadow. A creature of the night, lost in the dark. The city, usually a source of comfort and anonymity, now felt like a hostile maze, every corner hiding a potential threat, every shadow a possible enemy.

I found myself drawn to the less populated areas, the forgotten corners of the city where shadows lingered and secrets thrived—places where the veil between worlds seemed thin. I walked along the riverfront, the dark water reflecting the faint glow of city lights. The air was damp and cool, carrying the scent of salt and decay, thick with the smell of rot—the same scent I was emanating as a vampire. I cut through deserted parks, the silence broken only by the rustling of leaves and the distant wail of a siren, the empty swings hanging like headless corpses in the wind.

As dawn approached, painting the sky in hues of pale rose and faint lavender, I felt drawn back to the familiar edge of the woods. The trees seemed to sigh in relief as the first slivers of sunlight pierced the canopy, creating a mosaic of light and shadow on the forest floor. It was a welcome sight, a beacon signaling a temporary reprieve from the relentless pursuit that had shadowed my every move. I ducked into the comforting embrace of the trees, the dense foliage swallowing me whole. The ancient oaks and whispering pines offered a silent sanctuary, a place where I could momentarily shed the weight of my anxieties and gather my thoughts.

As I ventured deeper, weaving through the tangled undergrowth, I felt the unsettling presence that had clung to me finally begin to dissipate. It receded like a tide, leaving behind a chilling emptiness in its wake. The sunlight, growing stronger with each moment, acted as a natural barrier against the unseen forces seeking to control my fate.

I eventually came to a halt in a small clearing, a hidden haven I had discovered during previous periods of refuge. A fallen log lay draped in verdant moss, offering a semblance of comfort amidst the wildness. I settled onto its damp surface, the rough texture grounding me in the present moment. My fingers, still trembling from the night's ordeal, tightened around a crumpled note—a tangible reminder of the chaos unleashed, a physical manifestation of the web Marcus had so carefully constructed.

The words on the note swam before my eyes, each syllable a sharp barb piercing my already frayed nerves. Marcus was out there, a puppet master orchestrating the intricate dance of my existence. He held the strings, pulling me this way and that, forcing me to react to his machinations. Layered upon this already complex game was a new threat, an unseen presence stalking me from the shadows. It was a terrifying revelation, a realization that I was no longer just fighting against Marcus but also against an unknown entity with unknown motives.

The thought sent a shiver down my spine, a cold premonition that this was just the beginning of a much larger and more dangerous game. I closed my eyes, trying to block out the fear threatening to consume me. I needed to focus, to find a logical path through the labyrinth of uncertainty surrounding me.

Taking a deep breath, I unfurled my fist and smoothed the note out on my lap. The paper was worn and creased, bearing the marks of countless readings and nervous crumplings. I traced the familiar words with my fingertip, trying to glean some new insight, some hidden clue I had previously overlooked. But there was nothing—just the cold, hard reality of my situation staring back at me.

I was being hunted, manipulated, and controlled. Yet, despite the overwhelming odds, a flicker of defiance ignited within me. I refused to be a pawn in Marcus's game. I would not allow fear to paralyze me. I was Tristan, and I would fight back.

The memory of my transformation surfaced unbidden—the burning agony, the exquisite ecstasy of the change, the feeling of power surging through my veins. Moments later, my reflection revealed flawless skin, a canvas of unblemished perfection, a testament to my new existence. But it was my eyes that truly captivated me. Once a familiar hazel, they now blazed with vibrant intensity, a kaleidoscope of swirling silver and gold dancing within their depths. It was a beauty born of something ancient and powerful, a beauty that thrilled and frightened me.

The fact that I now subsisted on animal blood, a choice I had made to retain some semblance of humanity, seemed insignificant in the face of everything else. I was still a vampire, still bound to the shadows and the night. But I would not let that define me. I would use my newfound abilities—my enhanced senses and strength—to fight for what I believed in.

And what I believed in was finding Marcus and stopping him.

I knew, with unwavering certainty, that I was closer than ever to uncovering his secrets and bringing him to justice. I had followed the trail for so long, enduring countless hardships and making unimaginable sacrifices. I refused to turn back now.

The sun climbed higher in the sky, bathing the clearing in warm, golden light. The forest around me stirred with life, the chirping of birds and rustling of leaves creating a symphony of nature. It was a stark contrast to the darkness lurking within me, the darkness that threatened to consume me if I allowed myself to be overcome by despair.

I stood up, brushing the dirt and leaves from my clothes. The weight of the log lifted from my shoulders, replaced by a renewed sense of purpose. I would use this time, this brief respite from the hunt, to gather my strength and formulate a plan.

For now, I would lay low, hidden within the shadows, observing and analyzing. I would sharpen my senses, hone my skills, and steel my resolve. I would become a shadow myself, moving unseen and unheard, gathering intelligence and waiting for the opportune moment to strike.

During my time in hiding, I would carefully consider my next steps. The revelation of being followed required adjustments to my strategy. I needed to understand who, or what, was tracking me and their connection, if any, to Marcus. Was this a new player in the game or simply another of Marcus's pawns?

I would also meditate on what I knew about Marcus. I needed to understand his weaknesses and vulnerabilities. What were his motivations beyond merely leaving a letter for me to find? What did he truly desire? These questions swirled in my mind as I attempted to form the first steps of my plan.

This enforced pause was not a setback but an opportunity—a chance to heal, regroup, and emerge stronger and more determined than ever before. I would transform myself into the ultimate weapon, a force to be reckoned with.

Because something told me this was only the beginning. The game was far from over. In fact, it was just beginning to escalate. I had a feeling the stakes were about to get a whole lot higher. The whispers of the wind seemed to carry a warning, a chilling premonition of the darkness that lay ahead.

It was a darkness I knew I had to face, not just for myself, but for the sake of everyone I loved. The time for waiting was over. The time for action was fast approaching. And I would be ready. No, I needed to be ready.

Chapter Fifteen

SHADOWS IN THE DARK

The city had become my new playground, a sprawling canvas of concrete and steel upon which I painted my nocturnal existence. After days of wandering the labyrinthine streets—each alleyway and avenue a new discovery—I finally returned to my apartment: a small, sparsely furnished room tucked away in a relatively quiet district closer to the woods. It wasn't much—a single room without art on the walls and a bed that wasn't as comfortable as I would like—but

it was mine, a small island of solitude in a sea of overwhelming change. I didn't need much. The city was my escape, my real home, where I could roam freely and push the limits of who I was becoming. It called to me every night without fail, and in the dead of night, I would answer, drawn by an irresistible force, a primal urge that resonated deep within my altered being.

During the day, I kept a low profile, a ghost in the machine of human society. I walked among them, unseen and unnoticed; the anonymity of the crowd was a cloak of invisibility. I tried to act like a human when the sun was up, but the pull to the night was always there, calling me back—a constant reminder of my true nature, a siren's song echoing in my soul. The charade was exhausting, a constant effort to suppress the power simmering beneath my skin, the hunger gnawing at my insides.

But the nights were when I came alive, when the transformation was complete, and I embraced the power coursing through my veins. There was something liberating about darting through the streets, a sense of freedom that came with enhanced speed and agility. I felt weightless as I moved with unnatural grace, leaping from one rooftop to another, using the city's structures to hone my newfound abilities. Each jump was a test of my limits, each landing a victory.

I would look down at the humans below, their faces scrunched in concentration or engaged in laughter, never knowing that a vampire lurked above them. Their obliviousness was both amusing and unsettling, a reminder of the vast gulf that now separated us—a chasm of understanding that could never be bridged.

I was no longer one of them, but something else entirely: a creature of the night, a predator in the urban jungle. At least I drank animal blood; I could only imagine how the others felt.

The city's buildings were predictable, rigid in their design, offering me a controlled environment—a stark contrast to the chaos of my existence. Each brick, each window, each steel beam was a constant, a reminder of order in a world that had turned upside down. I practiced parkour in the dead of night, dressed in black, moving like a shadow through the urban maze. The darkness was my ally, concealing me from prying eyes and allowing me to move with a fluidity that defied human limitations.

It was more than just exercise; it was a form of meditation, a way to channel the restless energy surging through me. I became one with the city—a silent guardian, a predator lurking in the shadows. Every night, I returned to the same buildings, climbing them over and over, striving for the perfect balance of strength and grace.

Each movement was deliberate and precise—a dance between power and control. I wanted to be more than just strong; I wanted to be elegant, refined—a creature of both beauty and terror.

Every night, I found myself pushing further, testing how fast I could run and how high I could jump. It was easier than in the woods, where uneven terrain and unpredictable conditions posed challenges. The woods were wild and untamed, a reflection of the beast within me. The city, though, was ordered and structured—a mirror to the control I craved. The woods reminded me of who I could become; the city symbolized who I wanted to be.

Here, I felt like I was flying, moving with a grace and speed I never thought possible. The wind whipped through my hair as I soared through the air, the city lights blurring beneath me—a dazzling display of human ingenuity that both fascinated and repelled me. It wasn't just about getting better; it was about control. I needed to learn how to use my vampire agility without losing myself to its power. I didn't want to become a monster driven by instinct alone.

I wanted to master this new existence, to bend it to my will. The power was addicting, and I knew I had to be careful with it. Each surge of strength, each burst of speed, was a temptation—a whisper urging me to let go and embrace the darkness. But I resisted, clinging to the remnants of my humanity, determined to remain in control.

Yet, no matter how much fun I was having, a single thought nagged at the back of my mind, a persistent unease that refused to be silenced: Marcus. The vampire who left me with this curse hadn't bothered to explain anything. He had disappeared after turning me, leaving me with more questions than answers—a cruel twist of fate, a cosmic joke that irrevocably altered my life's course. Why me? What did he want?

Was I just a pawn in some elaborate game? The last hint of his presence was when I found that note in the alley: Hide. It had been weeks since then, but I still had no idea what he meant. Was I hiding from him or from something more sinister? I didn't even know what he truly looked like—a faceless enemy, a ghost in the shadows, a master manipulator pulling strings from afar.

I tried to find clues, but so far, I had nothing. The whole situation was frustrating and confusing. I was trapped between two lives, neither of which I fully understood. I was a vampire, yes, but what kind? What were the rules? What were the dangers? Was I part of something bigger—a hidden world of ancient rivalries and forgotten secrets? Or was I just a lone anomaly, a mistake that needed correcting? The possibilities were endless, each more terrifying than the last.

I decided to head toward the old part of the city—a labyrinth of narrow streets and crumbling buildings, a place where shadows lingered even during the day. The air hung heavy with the weight of history, the ghosts of forgotten lives whispering on the wind. It was rumored to be a haven for the city's underbelly, a place where secrets were traded and deals made—the perfect place to start my search.

If anyone knew anything about Marcus, it would be here, amidst the shadows and whispers, where the veil between worlds was thin. I felt a strange pull toward this place, a sense of familiarity I couldn't explain. It was as if something was calling me, beckoning me to uncover the truth. I knew I needed to find Marcus and get answers, but I also had to be careful. A place like this could hold danger, and I was walking into the unknown.

As I walked, I focused on my senses, amplifying them, trying to pick up any trace of Marcus. The sounds of the city faded into the background as I honed in on the faintest smells and subtlest vibrations. The air was thick with the stench of garbage and decay, but beneath it, I detected a faint metallic scent—blood.

It was a scent that both disgusted and intrigued me—a reminder of the darkness lurking within, the hunger I constantly had to suppress. I tried to ignore it and focus on my mission, but it was like trying to ignore a roaring fire. It was natural yet something I hated.

It could be nothing—just a stray animal or a discarded piece of meat. But it was worth investigating. I followed the scent, weaving through the crowded streets, my eyes scanning the faces around me. Each face was a mask, hiding secrets and desires, fears and regrets. Nothing—just ordinary people going about their lives, oblivious to the predator in their midst.

Or maybe they were just good at hiding it—a skill honed over years of survival in this unforgiving city. A sudden wave of paranoia washed over me, a sense that I was being watched, that eyes were following me from the shadows. It was probably nothing—just my heightened senses playing tricks. But I couldn't shake the feeling I was walking into a trap.

The scent grew stronger, leading me down a narrow alleyway, the walls closing in around me, the darkness deepening. It was a place where the sun never reached, where the only light came from flickering streetlamps casting long, distorted shadows. I hesitated for a moment, a sense of foreboding washing over me. But I couldn't turn back now; I had come too far. I took a deep breath and stepped into the darkness, ready to face whatever awaited me. I could feel the adrenaline pumping through my veins. The city was alive tonight.

One evening, as I leaped across the rooftops, a thought struck me with the force of a physical blow: the bar. The dimly lit sanctuary where I had first encountered Marcus was etched into my memory with a peculiar blend of hope and nascent dread. Perhaps that was the key—the subtle breadcrumb I had overlooked in my frantic search.

Maybe, just maybe, he would return to the place where it all began, drawn by some unseen force or shared nostalgia mirroring my own desperate longing. It was a long shot, I knew, but in the face of such profound and unsettling silence, even the faintest glimmer of possibility felt like a beacon in the encroaching darkness.

The next night, under a starless sky, I retraced my steps, my movements fluid and almost silent, a phantom navigating the urban landscape. I made my way to the bar, its location etched into my memory. It had been months since I last crossed its threshold, months filled with a gnawing anxiety that threatened to consume me entirely. Stepping inside felt like stepping back in time; the bar hadn't changed at all.

The same low-key, dimly lit atmosphere clung to the air like a second skin, and the familiar scent of stale beer and unspoken stories filled my nostrils. The same faces were scattered throughout the room, some of which I vaguely recognized from that first night—a collection of souls seeking solace or oblivion in the bottom of a glass. But Marcus wasn't among them. His absence hung heavy in the air, a palpable void that transformed the bar's familiar ambiance into a haunting reminder of what I had lost.

For a month straight, driven by a stubborn hope that bordered on delusion, I made the bar my second home, a nocturnal pilgrimage fueled by desperation and the faintest whisper of possibility. I visited every night, taking my usual spot at the far end of the bar, nursing drinks I didn't particularly want, and surreptitiously observing the ebb and flow of the clientele.

I talked to all kinds of people—the weary-eyed bartenders, the grizzled regulars who seemed to have taken permanent residence on their barstools, and the fresh-faced newcomers just beginning to learn the bar's unspoken rules—all the while subtly probing for information, hoping to catch even the faintest scent of Marcus, the smallest crumb of a lead.

I was careful, of course, acutely aware of the delicate balance I had to maintain. I couldn't afford to arouse suspicion or reveal the depths of my desperation. I asked subtle questions, disguised as casual conversation, watching for any signs, any flicker of recognition, any unspoken acknowledgment that someone else knew something about Marcus's whereabouts.

I learned to read the nuances of human interaction, the micro-expressions that betrayed hidden thoughts and emotions.

But night after night, my efforts yielded nothing. No clues, no leads, no whisper of Marcus's name on anyone's lips—just the same old faces, the same tired stories, and the same disappointing emptiness echoing in the hollow chambers of my heart. The weight of my failure grew with each passing day, threatening to suffocate me.

Until one night—a night that began like any other, steeped in routine and punctuated by the dull ache of disappointment.

It was a Thursday, and the bar was quieter than usual, the usual throng of patrons thinned to a sparse scattering of regulars. The air felt heavy, charged with a strange static electricity that prickled beneath my skin. I sat in my usual spot, staring blankly into the murky depths of a drink I didn't care to taste, a concoction of cheap whiskey and even cheaper hope, when I felt it.

That same presence—the unnerving sensation of being watched, the prickling unease that had followed me like a shadow in the weeks after I found that strange letter. It was faint at first, a mere whisper at the edge of my awareness, but it grew steadily stronger, more insistent, until it became an undeniable weight pressing down on me.

My muscles tensed instinctively, coiling like a spring ready to unleash, and I glanced around the room, my senses heightened, my eyes scanning every corner and every face, searching for the source of the unsettling sensation. But everything seemed normal—deceptively so. The bartender polished glasses with practiced hands, the regulars nursed their drinks in comfortable silence, and a lone couple huddled in a corner booth, lost in their own private world.

Yet deep down, I knew it wasn't normal. Something was amiss, something out of place, and the primal part of my brain screamed at me to be cautious. Whoever—or whatever—it was, it was getting closer, its presence intensifying with each passing moment.

I stood up abruptly, making a show of nonchalance, pretending to be uninterested in my surroundings. I tossed a few bills onto the bar, enough to cover the drink I hadn't finished, and made my way toward the exit, my movements deliberate but fluid, my senses on high alert. As soon as I stepped outside into the cool night air, the oppressive weight of the presence intensified, wrapping around me like a suffocating blanket.

I could feel it now, a palpable force lurking just beyond the periphery of my vision—something watching me, studying me, its unseen gaze burning into the back of my skull. The hairs on the back of my neck stood on end, a physical manifestation of the primal fear coursing through my veins. My instincts screamed at me to flee, to put as much distance as possible between myself and whatever was stalking me in the shadows.

I started walking, trying to maintain a veneer of calm, forcing myself to breathe evenly, to control the frantic racing of my thoughts. But the presence persisted, an invisible leash tethering me to the unknown. It followed me relentlessly, trailing me through the labyrinth of narrow streets and dimly lit alleyways crisscrossing the city. It was relentless, implacable, and no matter how many turns I took or shortcuts I tried to navigate, I couldn't shake it.

It was as if it anticipated my every move, knew my intended destination before I did. The realization sent a fresh wave of panic through me, fueling the growing sense of dread threatening to overwhelm me. My breath quickened, hitching in my throat, and I picked up the pace, breaking into a jog, my footsteps echoing in the deserted alleyways, the sound amplified by the oppressive silence of the night. The hunter had become the hunted, and I knew, with chilling certainty, that my life was in danger.

Suddenly, a figure appeared in front of me—a man. He materialized from the inky blackness between buildings, stepping out of the shadows as if conjured from the darkness itself, blocking my path with deliberate menace. The dim streetlights cast long, distorted shadows that danced around him, making him seem even more imposing. His eyes, the color of dried blood—dark red and unnervingly intense—glowed faintly in the meager light, like embers in a dying fire.

He had pale, almost translucent skin that stood out starkly against the darkness, giving him an ethereal, ghostly appearance. His face was gaunt, with sharp angles and prominent cheekbones, adding to his predatory look. He had dark blonde hair, slicked back meticulously, as if he had spent hours perfecting his appearance, and a cold, predatory expression on his face, a look that promised pain and suffering.

But it wasn't just his appearance that unsettled me, though that was certainly enough to send shivers down my spine. It was his smell—an odor that clung to him like a shroud, suffocating and overwhelming. The sharp, metallic scent of blood, raw and visceral, mixed with something else—a cloying sweetness, the unmistakable stench of decaying flesh.

It was revolting, a nauseating cocktail of death and corruption, but familiar in a way that made my stomach churn. It was the smell of human blood.

I took a step back, my mind screaming at me to run, to escape the danger radiating from this creature. Every instinct urged me to flee, to put as much distance as possible between myself and him. My legs trembled slightly, ready to spring into action, but before I could move, before I could even register the motion, he lunged at me with unnatural speed—vampire speed, fast enough to make the eye struggle to follow.

In an instant, I was slammed against the rough, cold wall of a nearby alley, the brick digging into my back. His surprisingly strong hand clamped over my throat, gripping tightly and cutting off my air supply. He held me there effortlessly, as if I were a doll.

His face was inches from mine, his breath hot and fetid against my skin, as he sniffed the air around me like a predator scenting its prey, a wolf trying to determine if its target was worth the effort.

"Why do you smell like Marcus?" he snarled, his voice low and menacing, a guttural growl rumbling in his chest. The words dripped with venom, laced with barely suppressed rage that made my blood run cold. "Is Marcus your master?" The question hung in the air, heavy with threat.

I struggled against his grip, clawing at his hand, trying to pry his fingers from my throat, but it was no use. He was impossibly strong—stronger than I was, stronger than any human could ever be. My struggles were futile, like a fly caught in a spider's web, and he seemed to relish my fear. His red eyes, burning with ancient hunger, bored into mine, searching for answers, trying to penetrate my thoughts, to uncover my secrets.

His nose twitched as he continued to sniff me, like a hound on the trail, examining every inch of my scent, dissecting the complex aroma that clung to my skin.

He suddenly recoiled, a look of disgust crossing his face, his perfect features twisting in revulsion. "You don't have the scent...what are you?" he spat, his voice dripping with disdain, stepping back slightly but still keeping me pinned against the wall. "Human?" The pressure on my throat lessened slightly, allowing me to gasp for a precious breath of air. "No... you smell like... like the woods. Like an animal."

He grimaced, wiping his nose with the back of his hand as if trying to rid himself of the offensive smell. "It's disgusting," he muttered, his eyes narrowed with distaste. "Unnatural."

I could barely breathe, my lungs burning, his hand still pressing against my throat, restricting the flow of air. But I managed to choke out a few fragmented words, my voice raspy and weak. "Who are you?"

The man narrowed his eyes, his grip tightening once more, a silent warning. "That's not important right now. What matters is why you smell like Marcus." He leaned in closer, invading my personal space, his breath hot and foul against my face. He sniffed me again, his expression twisting in confusion, as if he were trying to solve a complex puzzle. "And why you smell like... dirt. Earth. Animal blood?" The words were spoken with a mixture of bewilderment and revulsion.

He released me suddenly, as if burned, letting me drop to the ground in a heap, gasping for air. He took a step back, his expression a mix of confusion and disgust, as if he couldn't comprehend what he was experiencing. "I don't get it," he muttered, more to himself than to me, his voice barely a whisper. "You smell like Marcus, but... you reek of the woods. Like an animal." He shook his head slowly, as if trying to clear his thoughts.

I coughed, trying to catch my breath, my lungs screaming for oxygen. My head spun, and it took a moment to regain my bearings. "What do you want?" I asked, my voice hoarse and shaky.

The man glared at me, his crimson eyes ablaze with fury, as though my mere presence was an insult. "I've been hunting for Marcus for three centuries," he stated, his tone icy and unwavering, stripped of any feeling. "Three centuries, and at last, I've discovered someone who carries his scent." The words flowed from him with an unsettling composure, a threat of suffering and vengeance.

He crouched down in front of me, his face inches from mine once again, invading my personal space, his presence suffocating. "Do you know why I've been looking for him?" he asked, his voice dangerously calm, the calm before a storm. "Because he defied the council. He defied them—for it." The rage he had been holding back was now visible.

My mind raced, a frantic hamster wheel of panicked thoughts. Marcus? The council? It felt like I'd stumbled into a nightmare, a gothic tapestry woven with secrets and ancient vendettas. Just moments ago, I had been worried about the mundane realities of survival—finding a safe place to sleep and scrounging for food.

Now, I was facing something far more terrifying, something that threatened not just my life but the lives of everyone I held dear, even those I barely knew. The weight of it all threatened to crush me, the invisible pressure of a world I never knew existed suddenly bearing down.

The man continued, his voice growing more intense, each word a poisoned dart aimed at my fragile sense of reality. "Marcus has been in hiding for over six hundred years." Six centuries! The sheer timeframe was staggering, a testament to the unnatural lifespan of these creatures. "But that defiance comes with a price." A steep one, no doubt. I thought, trying to guess what it could be. Eternal damnation? Endless torture? Or something far crueler, something designed to break not just the body, but the spirit? The way this vampire spoke suggested the severity of Marcus's crime was beyond my comprehension, a wound that had festered for centuries, demanding retribution.

"Since then, I've been searching for him, resolute in my intent to make him pay for what he's done." His eyes, burning with a cold, unwavering fire, conveyed the depth of his obsession. He'd dedicated centuries to this pursuit, an existence fueled by vengeance. What kind of torment could drive a being to such single-mindedness? What had Marcus truly done?

He stood up abruptly, the movement sharp and predatory, his pale face twisted in a mask of barely contained rage. His features, though undeniably handsome in a chilling, statuesque way, were contorted by an emotion that seemed to consume him from the inside out. Every line, every shadow on his face spoke of an age-old anger.

"I am Lord Constantine Reinhardt, inquisitor of the vampire council," he declared, his voice filled with an authority that seemed to vibrate in the very air around us, demanding obedience, demanding fear. The title itself sent a shiver down my spine. Inquisitor. It conjured images of dark chambers, relentless interrogations, and punishments designed to break the will. He wasn't just a hunter; he was a judge, a jury, and an executioner all rolled into one terrifying package.

"And I've been tasked with bringing Marcus to justice for his crimes." Each word was delivered with the weight of centuries of power, a stark declaration of his purpose. The weight of council approval pressed down on us. I wondered what types of punishments they could impose, being creatures as powerful as they were. What laws did they abide by?

I stared at him, my mind reeling, a chaotic swirl of fear, confusion, and a growing sense of dread. This man—this vampire—had been hunting Marcus for centuries. It was an impossibly long stretch of time, a period that spanned empires and revolutions, wars and plagues. To dedicate such a lifespan to a single pursuit spoke of a depth of commitment, or perhaps obsession, that was both terrifying and strangely sad.

And now, because of me, because I had stumbled into this hidden world, he was closer than ever. My presence here, my connection to Marcus, had inadvertently lit a beacon, guiding this ancient hunter to his prey. The guilt was a bitter pill, a suffocating weight in my chest. I had become a pawn in a game I didn't even understand, a game with stakes far higher than I could have ever imagined.

Constantine leaned down again, the movement fluid and unsettling, his red eyes locking onto mine, piercing through my defenses, seeing into my soul. They were eyes that had witnessed centuries of darkness, eyes that had seen things I couldn't even begin to fathom. "There's something you should know," he said quietly, his voice now a silken whisper, but one that dripped with malice, with the promise of untold suffering.

The change in tone was subtle, but even more chilling than his earlier pronouncements. It was the voice of a predator toying with its prey, savoring the fear before the final strike.

"Any new vampire made outside the council's knowledge must be eliminated. Eradicated." I felt the blood drain from my face. I had no idea that being turned into a vampire meant living in fear of being killed by some vampire council with laws older than any modern laws.

"And that includes you." The words hung in the air, a death sentence delivered with chilling nonchalance. It wasn't just Marcus who was in danger now; it was me. I, a fledgling vampire with no knowledge of their world, no skills to defend myself, was now a target, an anomaly to be erased from existence. It felt like the ground had dropped out from underneath me, leaving me suspended in a void of despair. I hadn't even had time to process my new life, and it was already being threatened.

He straightened up, towering over me, his presence suddenly overwhelming, casting a long, menacing shadow. "Not just you," he continued, his voice cold and final, devoid of any emotion, any hint of remorse. "Your entire bloodline must be wiped out." The finality in his voice crushed me. I stared back into the abyss, the red in his eyes swirling in a vortex of hate and bloodlust. He was an enemy, a being devoid of any compassion, any understanding. My brief taste of this new world was over. I had to leave now and go into hiding.

I had thought I was protecting myself, but it seemed I had doomed my entire family. What do you do when death comes knocking at your door? I wanted to scream, to rage, to lash out against this impossible reality, but I was paralyzed by fear, trapped in the web of this vampire's ancient vendetta. My family? What did they have to do with any of this chaos?

I swallowed hard, trying to find my voice, to muster some semblance of strength in the face of this overwhelming threat. "Why?" I whispered, the word barely audible, a desperate plea for some kind of explanation, some justification for this senseless cruelty. "Why my family?"

Constantine's lips curled into a cruel smile, a chilling display of predatory satisfaction. "To ensure," he purred, "that the seed of this... *abomination* is extinguished forever. To prevent any chance of future defiance, any further contamination of our bloodlines. It's a necessary measure, wouldn't you agree?" His eyes gleamed with dark amusement, as if enjoying my torment, relishing in my helplessness. He took a step closer, the scent of ancient power filling the air, making it hard to breathe.

"No," I choked out, the word a feeble protest against the overwhelming force of his will. "It's not necessary. They're innocent. They don't know anything about this."

He chuckled, a low, guttural sound that sent shivers down my spine. "Innocence is a luxury you can no longer afford. You are tainted, and that taint spreads to all those connected to you by blood. It's a simple equation, really. Eliminate the source, eliminate the spread. Cleanse the bloodline."

My mind raced, desperately searching for a way out, a way to protect my family from this monstrous threat. But I was trapped, cornered, with no resources, no allies, and no hope.

He raised a hand, his long, pale fingers twitching with anticipation. "Don't worry," he whispered, his voice dripping with false sympathy. "It will be quick. Relatively painless. And think of it this way: you'll be sparing them a lifetime of fear, a lifetime of living in the shadows, knowing they are targets, hunted. You'll be setting them free."

But I knew what he was really saying. He was enjoying this. I was his prey.

He savored my torment, reveling in my helplessness.

His words hit me like a punch to the gut, and a cold wave of fear washed over me. My family—my sister, my parents—were all in danger because of me. I, the one who swore to protect them, the one who was supposed to be their shield against the darkness, had become the reason the darkness had found them.

Constantine smiled cruelly, his red eyes gleaming in the darkness. Those eyes, pools of crimson malice, bore into me, stripping me bare. He relished this moment. The power he held, the fear he inspired, fueled his twisted soul. "So, tell me, little vampire," he sneered, his words dripping with venom. "Are you ready to face the consequences of Marcus's actions?"

Marcus. Even his name felt like a stone in my throat. He was a ghost of a memory, a shadow clinging to my past, a constant reminder of the life I had left behind—or perhaps, the life that had left me behind. His choices, his hunger, his reckless disregard for the fragile balance of the world had brought us to this precipice. And now, I, Tristan, was left to clean up his m ess.

I didn't answer. I couldn't. My mind spun in a chaotic vortex of dread and desperation. Each breath felt like a struggle as fear seeped from my pores. What could I do? How could I possibly protect them from someone like Constantine, a vampire who reveled in the consumption of human life, whose very presence exuded the stench of blood and decay?

My family... I pictured my sister, Kat, with her bright smile, the way her laughter could chase away the darkest clouds. I saw my mother's gentle hands, always ready to offer comfort and care. I saw my father, his strong arms radiating unwavering strength. They were innocent. They were good. They deserved to be safe.

The thought ignited a spark within the swirling chaos of my fear. A spark of defiance. A spark of resolve. I would not let Constantine hurt them. I would not allow Marcus's sins to define their fate.

But how? I was still relatively new to this existence, grappling with the limitations and strange freedoms it offered. I knew I possessed a degree of strength and speed, advantages that humans couldn't comprehend. But Constantine... he radiated power, an ancient and terrifying strength that dwarfed my own. He was a predator, honed by centuries of feeding on human blood, fueled by an insatiable hunger.

I had to be smarter. I had to be faster. I had to use every advantage I had, every ounce of my cunning and will, to outmaneuver him.

But first, I needed information. I needed to understand his motives, his plans. Why was he targeting my family? What did he want from me? Was this truly about Marcus, or was there something more?

Before I could react, Constantine turned and disappeared into the shadows, melting into the darkness as if he were a part of it. He left me alone in the alley. The air hung heavy with the scent of decay, a lingering reminder of his presence, a chilling premonition of what was to come.

He was gone. But the threat remained, a palpable darkness clinging to the air, a promise of pain and suffering. I knew, with a certainty that chilled me to the bone, that this was just the beginning.

The hunt was on.

And I was the prey. Or was I?

I closed my eyes, trying to gather my scattered thoughts, seeking a flicker of hope in the encroaching darkness. I had to find my sister, my parents. I had to get them to safety. That was my priority. Everything else could wait.

But where to begin? Constantine could be anywhere, watching, waiting for me to make a mistake. He could be manipulating events from behind the scenes, weaving a web of deceit and danger around my loved ones.

I needed help.

But who could I trust? Who could I turn to without putting them in harm's way?

Perhaps there were others like me, vampires who had chosen a different path, who still clung to their humanity. Maybe they could offer guidance, support, a glimmer of hope in this desperate situation.

But finding them would be a challenge. They would be hidden, wary of outsiders, protective of their own. And Constantine would undoubtedly be watching, waiting for me to expose them, to bring them into his deadly game.

The weight of responsibility settled heavily on my shoulders. I was alone, hunted, and facing an enemy far more powerful than myself. But I couldn't give up. I wouldn't give up. My family's lives depended on it.

Taking a deep breath, I straightened my shoulders and stepped out of the alley, back into the labyrinthine streets of the city. The darkness pressed in on me, whispering threats and casting long, menacing shadows.

But I would not falter. I would not be afraid. I would find Constantine, and I would stop him, no matter the cost.

Chapter Sixteen

Into the Lion's Den

The night air was thick with tension, a suffocating blanket of humidity and a metallic tang that clung to me. I stood alone in the alley, the grimy brick pressing against my back, feeling utterly exposed and vulnerable after Constantine had left me. The flickering gas lamp cast long, dancing shadows, making the familiar urban landscape seem alien and menacing.

My mind was a whirlwind, a chaotic storm of confusion, fear, and anger. He could have killed me right there. He had stared at me, his eyes like chips of ice, the power radiating from him palpable. He had every opportunity, every advantage. One swift move, and I would have been dust—oblivion. But instead, he left me alive, a cruel twist of fate I couldn't comprehend. His cold voice still echoed in my head, each syllable a chilling pronouncement.

Any new vampire made outside the council's knowledge must be eliminated. That meant me. I was an anomaly, a glitch in their meticulously crafted system, and anomalies were to be purged. And it meant my family was in danger. Every breath I took felt like a betrayal, knowing that my existence was a threat to the people I loved most.

The idea of a vampire council... I had always suspected there was more to this world than what Marcus had revealed, more than the shadowed corners and whispered legends. But I never imagined it was this vast, this organized, this... bureaucratic. Rules? Councils? Inquisitors? It sounded like some twisted parody of human governance, a chilling reflection of our own flawed systems. It felt like I had been dropped into the middle of a nightmare, a meticulously constructed stage play where I was a pawn, a nameless extra in a game I didn't even know existed.

Before, I thought I knew what it meant to be a vampire. But now I felt like a naive child who had been lied to his whole life. When I thought about it, no one had ever really explained much to me. I felt even more lost discovering this "council." I had so many questions to ask Marcus. I needed to know what he had been hiding from me. And I needed to know now.

But why didn't Constantine kill me? Why let me live, knowing I posed a threat to their precious order? The answer came to me as soon as I asked the question, a sickening realization settling in my stomach like a stone—he wasn't after me, not primarily. I was merely a means to an end. He was after Marcus. And I was his bait. My existence, my transformation, was a carefully orchestrated trap.

My stomach churned at the thought, the metallic tang in my mouth intensifying. Constantine had been hunting Marcus for centuries, a relentless pursuit fueled by some ancient grudge I couldn't even begin to comprehend. And now I was the perfect lure, the irresistible prize that would draw Marcus out of the shadows. A pawn in a game played by immortals with stakes I couldn't even fathom. It was a terrifying prospect, a suffocating weight of responsibility I wasn't sure I could bear.

But the trap wasn't just for me; he was after my family too. The realization hit me like a physical blow, stealing the air from my lungs. He would use them, manipulate them, exploit their love for me to get to Marcus. My family... Panic rose in my chest, a cold wave of dread washing over me. He knew about them. He knew where they lived, what they did. Constantine would use them to get to Marcus, and if I didn't act swiftly and decisively, they were as good as dead.

I had to warn them. I had to get them out of harm's way. But where could I take them? Where would they be safe from a being as powerful and ruthless as Constantine? The council... Could they offer protection? The thought felt absurd. They wanted me eliminated, likely saw my family as collateral damage in their pursuit of Marcus. Trusting them would be a fool's errand, a suicidal gamble.

No, I was on my own. I had to protect them myself. I had to find Marcus, confront him, demand answers, and formulate a plan. But how? Where do I even begin? Marcus had always been so secretive, so elusive. Tracking him down would be like chasing a ghost through a city of shadows.

Each breath I took felt heavy, laden with the weight of responsibility and the chilling premonition of what was to come. My eyes darted around the alley, searching for... what? Some sign, some direction, anything that could offer a glimmer of hope in this oppressive darkness. But there was nothing, only the city's cold indifference and the street lights' mocking flicker.

I could hear the far-off rumble of a train, the soft notes of music drifting from a nearby bar, the hurried movements of rats lurking in the shadows. And the odors... the sickly sweetness of decaying trash, the acrid bite of urine, the subtle, lingering scent of... blood. It was omnipresent, a relentless reminder of my new, unnatural craving.

I clenched my fists, trying to suppress the rising tide of panic. I had to focus, to think clearly. My family's lives depended on it. What should I do? How should I handle this situation? I tried to channel some composure, to emulate quiet strength. But it was no use. My mind was still racing, my thoughts scattered and fragmented like shards of glass.

I needed information. I needed to understand Constantine—his motivations, his weaknesses. But where could I find such information? The vampire council... they were a possibility, but a dangerous one. They clearly wanted me dead, but perhaps they would be willing to offer some information in exchange for my... cooperation. The thought left a bitter taste in my mouth. The idea of working with them, of betraying Marcus, was repulsive. But what choice did I have?

No. There had to be another way. There had to be someone I could trust, someone who could help me navigate this treacherous landscape. But who? The few people I considered friends before... they were out of the question. They couldn't possibly understand, couldn't comprehend the reality of my new existence. Involving them would only put them in danger.

Marcus... he was the key. He held all the answers, all the secrets. But finding him would be like searching for a needle in a haystack. He had always been careful to conceal his movements, to remain hidden from the prying eyes of the council. How could I possibly track him down when even they couldn't?

I pushed myself off the brick wall, my muscles tense and coiled like a spring. I couldn't stay here, paralyzed by fear and indecision. I had to do something—anything. I had to start moving, to search. But where?

My gaze fell on the city streets that stretched out before me, a labyrinth of shadows and secrets. Somewhere in that vast expanse, Marcus was hiding. And somewhere else, Constantine was waiting, watching, patiently plotting his next move.

I took a deep breath, trying to steady myself. The metallic tang in the air seemed to intensify, filling my lungs with its cold, bitter taste. This was it. This was the beginning of the hunt. And I was the prey.

As I started to walk, a low growl reverberated from the depths of my chest, a sound both animalistic and foreign. I paused, startled by the noise, and then a surge of something primal and powerful coursed through my veins. It was an intoxicating mix of hunger, fear, and determination. I was no longer just Tristan. I was something else, something more. And I was ready to fight for my family, even if it meant facing the most dangerous creatures in the world.

I began walking, pulling my jacket tighter around me. The cold night air bit at my exposed skin, but I barely noticed. My mind was focused, my senses heightened. I was searching.

I walked for hours, scanning every alleyway, every doorway, every shadow. I discreetly inquired about Marcus's whereabouts, but no one seemed to know anything—or if they did, they weren't talking. It was as if he had vanished into thin air.

Frustration gnawed at me, a burning impatience threatening to consume me. I needed to find him, and I needed to find him now. But how?

The frigid night air continued to bite at my exposed skin, but I scarcely noticed. My mind was focused, my senses heightened. I was searching.

I needed to move quickly. My parents, my sister Katherine, Micah, her new husband—none of them had a clue about what was on the horizon. Constantine, that despicable monster, would stop at nothing to reach me, and if I didn't get them out of the city, he would eliminate them one by one, using them as leverage, as pieces in his twisted scheme.

The idea sent a chill through me, not because I feared for my own safety, but from a deep-seated urge to protect my family. They were innocent, unaware of the darkness that lay just beneath the surface of their daily lives. They didn't know about the realm of vampires, they were oblivious to the power, the temptation, and the peril that came with it.

Grabbing my phone, my fingers trembling slightly, I quickly dialed my sister, Katherine. She answered after a few rings, her voice bright and cheerful, completely unaware of the storm closing in on us. The stark contrast between her lightheartedness and the grim reality I was facing was almost unbearable.

"Hey, Tristan! What's up?" she asked, the sound of the TV faintly in the background. Probably some mindless reality show, I thought—a stark reminder of the normal life they still clung to.

"I need to talk to you," I said, trying to keep my voice steady to mask the panic threatening to consume me. I couldn't let her hear the fear or desperation; it would only scare her, and I needed her to listen, to trust me implicitly.

"Okay... what's going on?" she replied, her tone shifting to concern. The cheerfulness was gone, replaced by cautious wariness. "Is everything alright?"

I hesitated for a moment. How could I explain this without sounding completely insane? How could I tell her that vampires were real, that one of the most powerful and ruthless of their kind was hunting me, and that her life—and the lives of everyone she loved—were in imminent danger? There was no elegant way to deliver such a devastating truth.

"I need you, Mom, and Dad to come to the cabin. Now," I blurted out, the words tumbling out in a rush. The cabin, our family's sanctuary nestled deep in the woods, was the only place I could think of where they might be safe, at least for a little while. It was far from any major cities, remote and secluded.

"The cabin? Tristan, it's almost midnight! What's going on?" Her voice was laced with confusion and a hint of annoyance. Midnight was the time for sleep and relaxation, not for unexpected trips to a remote cabin.

"I'll explain everything when you get there. Please, Kat, just trust me," I pleaded, my voice tight with urgency. Trust was all I had to rely on. I couldn't give her the full story over the phone; it was too dangerous.

Constantine could be listening, watching, waiting for any slip-up. My silver and gold swirling eyes darted around the room, paranoia gripping m e.

There was a long pause on the other end. I could almost hear her thoughts racing, trying to make sense of my cryptic words. "Is this about your secret?" she asked, her voice softer now, almost hesitant. "You know, the one you've been avoiding for months?"

My "secret." That's what they called it. The truth about what I was, the life I led, the darkness that had consumed me. It was a secret I had guarded fiercely, afraid of how they would react, of the judgment and fear that would inevitably follow. But now, the secret was no longer mine to keep. It was about to become their reality, whether they wanted it or not.

"Yeah," I lied. It was easier than trying to explain the truth. Easier to frame it as some personal revelation, a dramatic confession, rather than the life-or-death situation it truly was. "It's time I tell you everything."

Another pause. I imagined her weighing her options, torn between curiosity and reservations. Katherine had always been the more adventurous one, the one who embraced the unknown with open arms. But this was different. This wasn't just a new experience; it was a potential disruption to her carefully constructed world.

"Alright. I'll get Micah. We'll meet you there in the morning," she said, finally relenting. Relief washed over me, but it was quickly replaced by a renewed sense of urgency. Morning was too late. Constantine wouldn't wait that long.

"No," I said quickly, my voice sharp with panic. "Not in the morning. You need to leave now."

"What? Tristan, it's the middle of the night—" She protested, her voice rising in frustration. I could hear the wheels turning in her head, trying to understand why I was being so insistent, so irrational.

"Kat, please!" My voice cracked with urgency, and I could tell she sensed how serious I was. The playful banter was gone, replaced by genuine fear. I had finally broken through her skepticism, and now I had her attention.

"Okay... okay. I'll talk to Micah and call Mom and Dad. We'll leave as soon as we can," she agreed, her voice trembling slightly. I knew she was scared, but she was also willing to trust me, to put her faith in me despite her fear.

"Thank you," I breathed, relief flooding through me and momentarily washing away the anxiety. "Just... just be careful."

"Tristan, you're scaring me. What's really going on?" She pressed, her voice laced with genuine concern. The questions were coming, the demands for explanations. I couldn't blame her for wanting answers, but I couldn't give them to her—not yet.

"I'll explain when I see you. Just... be safe." I repeated, my voice firm. It was all I could offer her—a promise of explanation and a plea for safety. It wasn't enough, but it was all I had.

We hung up, and I immediately called my parents. They were more difficult to convince, my father especially. He hated being woken up in the middle of the night for anything, let alone an impromptu trip to the family cabin. He valued routine, order, and predictability. Chaos and spontaneity were anathema to him.

"Tristan, what in God's name is going on?" He grumbled, his voice thick with sleep and annoyance. "Do you have any idea what time it is?"

"Dad, I know this is a lot to ask, but it's important. You need to get Mom and come to the cabin. Now," I said, trying to keep my voice calm and reasonable despite the fear churning inside me.

"The cabin? Now? Tristan, I have a meeting in the morning. I can't just drop everything and drive out to the middle of nowhere," he protested, his voice growing louder.

"Dad, please. This is more important than any meeting. I can't explain it over the phone, but I need you to trust me. This is about our family." I pleaded, my voice cracking with desperation.

My mother came on the line then, her voice softer and more understanding. "Tristan, what's wrong? You sound upset."

"Mom, I'm fine. But I need you and Dad to come to the cabin. Please. It's important." I repeated, hoping she would be able to convince my father.

After a lot of back and forth, a lot of arguing and pleading, they finally agreed to meet us there by morning. I had to hope they would leave in time, that Constantine wouldn't reach them before they could escape the city. The image of their lifeless bodies, their blood drained, flashed through my mind, and I shuddered. I couldn't let that happen. I wouldn't let that happen.

Now that I had a plan—if you could even call it that—I needed to prepare. The word "plan" felt too grandiose for what it really was: a desperate gamble, a flickering candle in the face of encroaching darkness. I made my way to a 24-hour convenience store, the fluorescent lights buzzing overhead as I scanned the aisles, my eyes darting from one item to the next, searching for anything that could serve as a weapon, anything that could give me even the slightest edge.

My mind raced, a chaotic jumble of fear and adrenaline. Constantine. The name was a brand on my soul, a weight in my gut. He was out there somewhere, a predator circling, and I was the prey. Grabbing a handful of hunting knives—their polished blades glinting under the artificial light—felt like a futile gesture, akin to arming myself with twigs against a raging inferno.

I also grabbed duct tape, its industrial-strength promise of holding things together a symbolic counterpoint to the unraveling of my own life. Some rope, a heavy-duty flashlight, and a first-aid kit rounded out my meager arsenal. I had no idea if any of this would actually work against someone like Constantine, a creature steeped in the arcane, someone who had walked the earth for centuries, but I couldn't just sit back and do nothing. Paralysis was not an option. Action, even if misguided, was better than surrender.

After paying for the items and feeling the cashier's curious gaze on me as I hastily shoved everything into a worn backpack, I made my way to the cabin. The air outside was cooler, a welcome relief from the sterile environment of the store. The woods were dense and quiet, the trees looming like silent sentinels, their branches intertwined overhead, creating a cathedral of shadows.

The only sounds were my own footsteps crunching on the fallen leaves and the occasional rustle of leaves in the wind, sounding like whispered secrets. I moved quickly, pushing my way through the undergrowth, my senses on high alert, hyper-aware of every snapping twig, every rustle in the brush.

The cabin had been in our family for generations, passed down through the line—a secluded place deep in the forest, far removed from the noise and chaos of the city. It was a sanctuary, a refuge, a place of fond memories. As a child, it was where I learned to swim in the lake, roast marshmallows by the campfire, and tell ghost stories that scared me half to death. Now, it was a prison, a fortress, a last stand. It wasn't much—just a simple log structure with a stone fireplace and a porch that wrapped around the front—but it was the only place I could think of where we'd be safe, at least for a little while. It was the only place that felt like home.

When I arrived, the place was just as I remembered: rustic, quiet, and far from civilization. The scent of pine needles and damp earth filled the air, a comforting aroma that tugged at my heart. The cabin stood sentinel against the encroaching woods. The windows were dark and vacant. I took a deep breath and pushed open the creaky wooden door.

The interior was musty and cold, the air thick with the scent of disuse. Dust motes danced in the shafts of sunlight that pierced through the gaps in the wooden walls. I spent the next few hours setting up whatever defenses I could—barricading the windows with heavy furniture, wedging chairs under the doorknobs, placing knives within easy reach on every surface. It was a pathetic attempt, a child's game against a master strategist, but I persisted, driven by desperate hope. I also tried to come up with some kind of strategy, pacing back and forth, my mind churning, weighing my options, considering every possible scenario. My efforts were frantic and disorganized.

It wasn't much, but it was all I had. I checked the perimeter, piled wood next to the fireplace, and filled a tub with water. Then I waited.

Constantine... The name echoed in my mind, a dark incantation that conjured images of cruelty and power. This vampire had hunted Marcus for centuries, a relentless predator driven by an insatiable thirst. He was a hunter of the old blood, a creature of the night who reveled in the suffering of others. He would stop at nothing to get what he wanted. I had no illusions about my chances in a fight.

Constantine possessed centuries of experience, knowledge of ancient magic, and a thirst for blood that had been honed over the ages, while I had been a vampire for less than a year, still grappling with the basics of my own transformation. I hadn't even learned to control my heightened senses yet.

While my parkour skills might help me escape, allowing me to navigate the city's treacherous terrain, leaping across rooftops and disappearing into the shadows, I couldn't outrun him forever. He was too strong, too fast, too experienced. Sooner or later, he would catch me. And when he did, the consequences would be dire.

But I wasn't just going to roll over. I wasn't going to sit here and wait for the inevitable. I would fight until my last breath. I would protect my family, even if it meant sacrificing myself. If he wanted my family, he'd have to go through me first. The thought solidified in my mind—a beacon of defiance in the face of despair. I was Tristan, I was a vampire, and I would not be broken. I sat in the darkness, waiting. The cabin was quiet. The forest was watching.

The fear was still there, gnawing at me, but beneath it, a flicker of determination began to grow. I was ready. Or at least, I would be. I had to be. My family's lives depended on it.

By the time my family arrived at the cabin, the sun was beginning to rise, casting a faint golden light over the trees. The crisp, cool air held the scent of pine and damp earth—a scent I usually found comforting, a reminder of simpler times spent hiking and camping with my family. But now, the familiar aroma did little to soothe the knot of anxiety twisting in my gut.

My sister, Kat, was the first to step out of the car, pulling her jacket tighter around herself against the morning chill. Her husband, Micah, followed, stretching his arms above his head in a weary yawn. My parents emerged last, their faces etched with a mixture of concern and confusion. They all looked tired, pulled from their beds in the dead of night and driven to this secluded cabin in the woods.

"Tristan," my mother said, her voice laced with concern, "What's going on? Why did you drag us out here in the middle of the night?" She reached out, her hand hovering over my arm, perhaps to steady herself or me. Her hazel eyes, so similar to my own, searched my face, seeking answers I wasn't yet ready to give.

I took a deep breath, the cool air burning in my lungs. I needed to choose my words carefully, to navigate the treacherous waters of half-truths and carefully constructed lies. The full truth—that vampires existed, that I was entangled in their world, and that their very survival was now intertwined with mine—would shatter their reality and potentially put them in even greater danger. I couldn't risk that. "There's... there's something I need to tell you. Something important."

Kat crossed her arms, giving me a pointed look that spoke volumes. We had always been close, sharing secrets and supporting each other through thick and thin. But lately, I had been distant and withdrawn, and she knew something was amiss. "You said that already. What's going on? You've been acting weird for months." Her voice held a hint of accusation mixed with genuine worry.

I hesitated, my gaze darting around the clearing. The trees seemed to watch me, their branches like skeletal fingers reaching out to grasp the truth. The rising sun, usually a symbol of hope, now felt like a spotlight, exposing my deception. I couldn't tell them the full truth—it was too dangerous, not just for them, but for me too. Revealing their existence to humans was strictly forbidden.

But I had to say something to explain my erratic behavior and justify their sudden relocation to this isolated cabin. "I've been keeping a secret," I began slowly, my voice barely above a whisper. "And... I need you all to be safe while I figure things out. That's why I brought you here. Just... just trust me, okay?" It sounded weak, even to my own ears—a desperate plea masked as reassurance.

My father frowned, his brow furrowed in suspicion. He had always been a man of logic and reason, a scientist who demanded proof and valued tangible evidence. My vague explanations and cryptic warnings were unlikely to satisfy him. "Trust you? Tristan, you're not making any sense. What's really going on?" His voice was stern, laced with a father's expectation of honesty.

Before I could answer, Micah stepped forward, a faint, almost mocking, smile on his face. He was always the outsider, the one who never quite fit into our family dynamic. While he was polite and respectful, there was always a subtle distance, a sense of detachment. "Look, man, I get it. Family's important. But you're acting like we're in some kind of horror movie." There was a dismissive tone in his voice.

His words hit a little too close to home, a stark reminder of the terrifying reality I was desperately trying to conceal. The irony wasn't lost on me. He thought I was being dramatic, exaggerating a situation, and yet, we were undeniably living in a horror movie. But while he perceived it as fiction, for me, it was a chilling reality. "I'm serious, Micah," I said, my voice low and firm, emphasizing the gravity of the situation. "You all need to stay here. Don't leave the cabin for anything. I'll explain more later."

Micah sighed, clearly not convinced, but he didn't push further. Perhaps he sensed the underlying tension in my voice, the desperation in my eyes. Or maybe he simply didn't care enough to challenge me. "Alright. If you say so." He turned and headed toward the cabin, leaving me to grapple with my conscience.

The weight of my secret pressed down on me, heavy and suffocating. I knew I couldn't keep them in the dark forever, but the prospect of revealing the truth terrified me. How could I explain the existence of vampires, the ancient war raging in the shadows, the sacrifices I had made? How could I make them understand the delicate balance I was trying to maintain, the constant threat that hung over our heads?

My gaze drifted toward the woods, where shadows still clung to the undergrowth. I knew they were out there, watching, waiting. The vampires who drank human blood, who reveled in the kill, whose skin was pale, eyes dark red, and whose presence carried a stench of decay, would see right through my lies, through my feeble attempts to protect my family. They would exploit my weakness, using my loved ones as leverage.

The thought sent a shiver down my spine. I had to be stronger, more cunning. I had to find a way to protect them without exposing them to the full horror of my world. My family moved toward the cabin, oblivious to the danger lurking nearby. I watched them, my heart aching with a mixture of love and fear. I was their protector, their shield against the darkness. And I would do whatever it took to keep them safe, even if it meant sacrificing myself.

I took another deep breath, steeling my resolve. It was time to face the lion's den, to confront the forces that threatened to tear my world apart. But first, I needed to buy myself some time. "Mom? Dad?" I called out, my voice echoing in the clearing. "Can I talk to you for a minute? Alone?"

My parents exchanged a knowing look, sensing the urgency in my tone. They nodded, and together we stepped away from the cabin toward the edge of the woods. As we walked, I felt the eyes of the unseen watchers upon us, their presence like a cold, invisible hand on my back. I had to be careful, very careful. The fate of my family, and perhaps something much larger, rested on my shoulders.

As we walked away from the cabin, my mind started to race. I didn't know how much longer they would be safe; I needed to act fast. I had to keep them away from the truth for their own good.

"Mom, Dad," I began, my voice trembling slightly, "I know I haven't been myself lately, and I'm sorry for that. The truth is... I'm working on something, something really big, and it requires a lot of my attention. I can't tell you the specifics right now, but I promise, it's nothing illegal or anything like that. It's just... complicated."

My father raised an eyebrow, his skepticism evident. "Complicated how, Tristan? You're not making any sense. What kind of work requires you to drag us out to a cabin in the middle of nowhere?"

I sighed, trying to maintain eye contact but finding it difficult. "It's hard to explain. It involves... research and a lot of travel. I'm not always able to be in contact, and that's why I wanted you all to be here, safe and sound, while I figure things out."

My mother reached out and took my hand, her touch warm and reassuring. "Tristan, we're your parents. We support you, no matter what. But we also need to know that you're okay. You've been so secretive lately. It's worrying us."

"I know, Mom, and I'm sorry. I promise, I'll tell you everything as soon as I can. Just trust me a little longer, okay? I wouldn't ask if it wasn't important."

My father studied me for a long moment, his gaze intense and unwavering. Finally, he nodded slowly. "Alright, Tristan. We'll trust you... for now. But you need to understand, we expect answers. And we expect them soon."

"I promise," I said, squeezing my mother's hand. "I'll tell you everything as soon as I can. Thank you, Mom, Dad. It means a lot."

As we walked back to the cabin, I couldn't shake the feeling that I was digging myself deeper into a hole. The lies were piling up, and the truth was becoming more elusive. But what choice did I have? I had to protect my family, even if it meant deceiving them.

The day stretched on, long and tense. We spent our time inside the cabin, where I made sure to lock all doors and windows while keeping an eye out for anything suspicious. My family tried their best to make the most of it, but the air was heavy with worry. I attempted to create the illusion of a normal family vacation, but it didn't work; they were still onto me.

As night fell, I knew the real danger would only grow. It was when the predators came out to hunt, and I needed to be ready.

Settling into the cramped confines of the cabin, the air thick with unspoken dread, I fought a losing battle against the rising tide of my anxiety. Each creak of the weathered wood, each rustle of leaves outside the window, sent jolts of adrenaline through me like lightning strikes. The trap was closing; the walls of our sanctuary shrank with every tick of the clock. Constantine was out there, and I had no idea how long we had before he decided to spring his carefully laid plan.

The weight of responsibility pressed down on me. I had brought my family into this, led them to this isolated haven that was proving to be anything but safe. I had hoped the remote location would offer some protection, a buffer against Constantine's relentless pursuit. But now, surrounded by the deepening shadows of the encroaching night, all I felt was exposed and vulnerable.

Every noise outside the cabin made me jump, a reflex honed by years of living on the edge, perpetually anticipating danger. Every shadow seemed to writhe and twist into grotesque shapes, morphing into the looming silhouette of Constantine himself. The forest, which had initially felt like a comforting embrace, now suffocated me, with each tree a silent sentinel guarding our prison.

By evening, an uneasy calm settled over the cabin—a fragile truce in the face of the impending storm. My parents, bless their hearts, attempted to maintain a semblance of normalcy, distracting themselves with the mundane act of preparing dinner. The aroma of simmering vegetables and roasting herbs filled the air, a stark contrast to the metallic tang of fear that clung to the back of my throat. They moved about the small kitchen with forced cheerfulness, their eyes darting nervously towards me every so often. I knew they were worried, terrified even, but they were trying, for my sake, to project an air of composure.

Kat and Micah, usually boisterous and full of life, sat huddled by the fireplace, whispering to each other in hushed tones. The flickering flames cast dancing shadows across their faces, highlighting the worry etched into their expressions. They seemed to have retreated into their own private world, seeking solace in each other's presence. I envied them, their ability to find comfort in shared silence.

I, however, was incapable of stillness. Pacing like a caged animal, I patrolled the perimeter of the cabin, my eyes darting from window to window, scanning the surrounding woods for any sign of movement. The glass felt cold beneath my fingertips, a stark reminder of the flimsy barrier separating us from the darkness outside. I was constantly on edge, every nerve ending screaming, waiting for something to happen. I knew Constantine wouldn't wait forever. He was a predator, patient and cunning, but ultimately driven by a bloodlust that couldn't be contained.

The minutes stretched into an eternity, each laden with the weight of anticipation. The sun dipped below the horizon, painting the sky in shades of orange and purple—a beautiful but fleeting illusion of peace before true darkness descended. The forest grew darker, the shadows deeper, and the silence became almost deafening. It was the kind of silence that precedes a storm, a pregnant pause before the inevitable eruption.

And then it did.

The sound shattered the fragile tranquility of the cabin, a brutal intrusion that sent a shockwave through my entire being. The front door, weakened by years of neglect, burst open with a splintering crash, the wood groaning in protest as it gave way.

Micah stumbled in, swaying precariously, his face ashen. He looked like a ghost, a hollow shell of the vibrant young man he had been just hours before. His breathing was ragged, shallow gasps punctuating the suffocating silence with a desperate plea for air.

Blood dripped from his neck, a crimson river tracing a path down his chest, staining the fabric of his shirt. It was dark and viscous, thick with the unmistakable scent of decay. My stomach churned, a wave of nausea threatening to overwhelm me. The shirt... I recognized it instantly. It was mine, a worn-out sweatshirt I had left here years ago.

He collapsed onto the floor with a sickening thud, his limbs splayed at awkward angles, his eyes wide with a mixture of pain and terror. He clawed at his throat, his fingers smearing the blood across his skin, creating a macabre portrait of suffering.

"Micah!" Kat screamed, her voice raw with fear. She rushed to his side, dropping to her knees beside him, her hands hovering over his wounds, unsure of what to do. "Oh my god, what happened? Who did this to y ou?"

But I already knew. The sight of the wound on his neck, a precise and deliberate puncture, the coppery smell of blood mingling with the faint but unmistakable hint of decay in the air... it all pointed to one inescapable conclusion. Constantine had found us. He had breached our defenses, infiltrated our sanctuary, and left his mark in the most brutal and devastating way imaginable.

And he had used Micah's scent—my scent—on that sweatshirt to track us down. It was a calculated move, a cruel manipulation designed to strike at the heart of our group, sowing chaos and discord. He had turned our own vulnerabilities against us, transforming our trust into a weapon.

Micah's eyes fluttered closed, the light fading from them like a dying ember. His breathing became even more shallow, his chest barely rising and falling. I could feel panic rising in my chest, a cold, suffocating wave that threatened to engulf me.

My family... they were in more danger than ever. Constantine had proven that he could reach us, that he could break through our defenses. He had tasted blood, and now he would be coming for more.

Constantine was closing in. I could feel it in the air, a palpable shift in the atmosphere, a tightening of the noose around our necks. The lion was at the door, ready to pounce. My mind raced, desperately searching for a solution, a way to protect the people I loved from the monster that was hunting us. But all I could feel was fear—a primal, paralyzing fear that threatened to consume me entirely.

I had to act, and I had to act fast. But how could I possibly fight a creature as powerful and ruthless as Constantine, especially when he had already gained the upper hand? The answer eluded me, leaving me trapped in a vortex of despair, watching helplessly as the darkness closed in around us

.

pristine surface. The thick, viscous liquid pulsed with a dark energy, a tangible representation of the life force draining away.

His skin, usually flush with life—a healthy glow that spoke of days spent in the sun and nights filled with laughter—was now pale and clammy, warmth evaporating as rapidly as the lifeblood spilled onto the floor. The vibrant color of life was replaced with the sickly pallor of death.

Kat screamed, a raw, guttural sound that tore through the silence and ripped at my heart. It wasn't a delicate cry of anguish; it was a primal scream, the sound of a wounded animal, a desperate plea against the injustice of the moment. She crumpled to her knees beside him, her lithe frame shaking uncontrollably. Her body, usually so full of graceful movement, was now wracked with tremors of grief and fear.

Tears streamed down her face, blurring her vision and turning the world into a distorted, watery mess. The elegant lines of her face were marred by the tracks of sorrow, each tear a testament to the depth of her pain. Each sob was a shard of glass, piercing the already fragile atmosphere. The air itself seemed to vibrate with her anguish.

My parents stood frozen, statues carved from shock and disbelief. They were pillars of silent horror, their faces masks of utter incomprehension. Their eyes were wide, unable to process the brutal reality unfolding before them. The scene was beyond their comprehension, a horrifying tableau that defied their understanding of the world. They had always lived a life insulated from darkness, shielded from the creatures that lurked in the shadows.

They had carefully cultivated a life of normalcy—dinner parties and Sunday brunches, art galleries and classical concerts—all designed to keep the darkness at bay. Now, that illusion was shattered, the veil torn away to reveal the terrifying truth. The blood, the wound, the sickening stillness of Micah—it was all too much, a nightmare bleeding into their waking world.

CHAPTER SEVENTEEN

DANCE OF SHADOWS

Micah's body lay on the floor, and for a moment, the world seemed to freeze. Not a gentle pause, but a violent, jarring halt, as if the very fabric of reality had snagged on the horror unfolding before me. The vibrant colors of the room—the warm hues of the Persian rug, a masterpiece of intricate knots and faded dyes passed down through generations; the delicate floral patterns on the wallpaper, painstakingly chosen by my mother to bring a touch of the outside world inside—seemed to dull, fading into a monochrome canvas of despair. It was as if some malevolent artist had drained the life from the scene, leaving only a stark, unsettling sketch.

Blood gushed from the wound on his neck, a crimson torrent painting the polished wood a horrifying shade. It wasn't just a stain; it was a macabre masterpiece, a twisting, swirling composition of death etched onto the

Their carefully constructed reality had crumbled, leaving them exposed and vulnerable to the horrors of the night.

I could hear the blood rushing in my ears, a deafening roar that drowned out all other sounds. It was a primal scream within my own body, a frantic pulse of adrenaline urging me to action. My senses were on high alert, amplified to an almost unbearable degree. Every sound was intensified, every scent heightened, creating a discordant symphony of overwhelming sensations.

The air thrummed with a palpable energy, a dark and malevolent presence that sent shivers down my spine. It was like an invisible hand pressing down on us, a weight of dread that suffocated the room.

The scent of death hung thick in the air, a sickeningly sweet combination of decay and fresh blood, a perfume only the creatures of the night could truly appreciate. The metallic tang of blood mixed with the cloying sweetness of decay created an almost intoxicating aroma, a siren's call to the predators lurking in the shadows. It clung to the back of my throat, making me gag. The smell alone seemed to carry a weight, a physical manifestation of the horror unfolding before us.

Constantine had found us. The realization slammed into me with the force of a physical blow, stealing the air from my lungs. It was a cold, hard truth that resonated deep within my bones, a chilling certainty that wiped away any lingering doubt. He had been hunting us, circling us like a predator stalking its prey, and now he had finally struck. We had been living on borrowed time, always looking over our shoulders, knowing that the hunter was out there, somewhere in the darkness.

We were mice in a deadly game of cat and mouse, and the cat had finally cornered us. I knew it wouldn't be long before he finished what he started, before he descended upon us with all the fury and hunger of a centuries-old vampire. The thought of his power and ruthlessness sent a wave of icy fear washing over me. We were trapped, cornered in our own home, exposed and vulnerable. Our sanctuary, the place where we were supposed to feel safe, had been violated, turned into a hunting ground.

Micah's chest rose and fell with shallow, labored breaths, each gasp a painful reminder of the precious life slipping away. His face was contorted in a silent scream, his muscles taut with agony, his features twisted in a mask of unimaginable pain. His eyes were glazed over with a film of approaching oblivion, the light fading from them like the dying embers of a fire. I knew I had to do something—anything—to save him.

The weight of responsibility crashed down on me, a crushing burden that threatened to suffocate me. Time was running out, each second a step closer to the irreversible abyss. The hourglass of his life was emptying rapidly, and I was desperate to find a way to turn it over.

In a panic, my mind raced, desperately searching for a solution, a way to cheat death. It was a chaotic storm of thoughts and possibilities, a frantic attempt to grasp at any straw of hope. I reached for the slimmest thread of hope, any memory, any whisper of a possibility. The first idea that popped into my head was outlandish, almost ludicrous, yet it was all I had.

Could it really work? I had saved that elk, brought it back from the brink with just a taste of my blood. The triumph of that moment danced in the edges of my memory, a faint glimmer of hope in the chaos surrounding Micah's fading life.

If I could heal an animal, surely a human—someone with so much more life and spirit—stood a chance. The logic felt both ridiculous and necessary, as if the universe were aligning to give me this one chance. It was all I had, the only thread of hope left to grasp.

But doubt clawed at me. The mechanics of it all were murky. Would my blood be strong enough? Would it work, or was I grasping at straws? Those questions fizzled away as I looked into Micah's desperate eyes, pleading for salvation. The urgency of the moment overrode my fears.

If it had worked once, what if it could work again? The primal instinct to save those I cared about surged within me. I had to try. I could no longer afford to waver; it was this moment or nothing at all.

I hesitated only for a moment, battling the voice of reason that screamed at me to find a more logical solution. The voice of logic was a stern, unwavering presence, reminding me of the absurdity of the idea, the lack of scientific basis, the sheer improbability of it working. But there was no time for logic, no time for doubt. The luxury of reasoned thought was a distant memory, replaced by the urgent need for immediate action. This was all I had. I bit down hard on my wrist, the sharp, stinging pain a welcome jolt to my senses.

The physical pain was a grounding force, anchoring me to the present and cutting through the fog of fear and panic. The flesh tore easily, and the metallic tang of blood filled my mouth. The taste was both familiar and alien, a potent reminder of my own mortality and the fragile nature of life.

The pain quickly gave way to a strange, almost intoxicating sensation, a feeling of power and vulnerability intertwined. It was a feeling of surrender and control, of offering a piece of myself in the hope of saving another.

This was my life force, my essence, and I was about to offer it to another. It was an act of sacrifice, a desperate attempt to defy the natural order and rewrite the ending of this horrific story.

I knelt beside Micah, my family watching in stunned silence, their faces a mixture of confusion, fear, and disbelief. Their reactions were a kaleidoscope of emotions, reflecting their inability to comprehend the desperate act I was about to commit. They couldn't possibly understand what I was doing, the gamble I was taking.

They saw only madness in my eyes, a descent into the very darkness they feared. To them, it must have seemed like madness, a plunge into the same darkness that had claimed Micah. They saw me offering myself to the monster, sacrificing my own life in a futile attempt to save a dying man.

I gently cradled his head in my hands, tilting it back slightly. His head was heavy and limp, his neck offering no resistance. His skin was cold and clammy, the temperature of death clinging to his flesh. His lips were cold and lifeless, the color leached from them. They were dry and cracked, devoid of the moisture of life. For a terrifying second, I thought it was too late.

The warmth was gone, the spark extinguished. The hope that had flickered so brightly threatened to die with him. Despair threatened to engulf me, to pull me down into the abyss of hopelessness. The darkness beckoned, promising oblivion and an end to the pain.

But then, a flicker. A barely perceptible twitch of his eyelids. It was a tiny, almost imperceptible movement, but it was enough. It was a spark of life in the face of death, a defiant rebellion against the encroaching darkness. Hope surged through me, a blinding light cutting through the darkness. The rush of adrenaline was intoxicating, re-energizing my resolve and banishing the despair that had threatened to consume me.

I pressed my bleeding wrist against his mouth, the warm blood flowing from my wound to his parched lips. The blood was a lifeline, a conduit of energy and hope, flowing from my body into his.

He sputtered, choking on blood, his body convulsing weakly as the substance began to work its way through his system. The violent reaction was both horrifying and encouraging. The sight of his body struggling, gagging and choking, was deeply disturbing, but it also offered a glimmer of hope. It meant he was still alive, still fighting. It meant there was a chance. It was a grotesque display of life clinging to existence, a desperate battle against the inevitable.

The room was dead silent, save for the crackle of the fireplace, the faint, comforting sound suddenly amplified in the oppressive stillness. The fire was a constant, a warm and reassuring presence in the face of the encroaching darkness.

It symbolized life and hope, a flickering flame that refused to be extinguished. Kat's quiet sobs served as a constant reminder of the grief and terror permeating the air. Her sobs were a soundtrack to the horror, a mournful counterpoint to the desperate scene unfolding before us.

My mother took a step forward, her face pale with confusion and fear. The flickering lamplight danced across her features, accentuating the worry lines etched around her eyes. Her hands trembled as she reached out towards me, then quickly retracted them, as if afraid to break the fragile spell that hung in the air.

It was as if she feared that touching me would shatter the illusion of normalcy we had always maintained, an illusion now crumbling before her very eyes. "Tristan, what are you doing?" she whispered, her voice trembling, barely audible above the roaring in my ears.

The roaring wasn't just in my ears; it was the frantic thumping of my own blood, the frantic beat of a pulse that Micah no longer possessed. Her eyes, wide with a mixture of love and concern, pleaded for an explanation, for some reassurance that her son hadn't completely lost his mind. They reflected the terrible truth, the monstrous act in which I was complicit. The air crackled with unspoken questions, fear tasting like ash on the tongue.

The question hung in the air, unanswered, swallowed by the encroaching darkness. What indeed was I doing? Was I saving him, or damning us all? Each course of action felt like a game stacked against us.

The weight of their gazes pressed down on me, heavier than any physical burden. I could see the dread simmering in their eyes, the dawning realization that the son they knew, the boy they had raised, was capable of something... unnatural. The gentle rhythm of their breaths sounded like roaring waves in my ears. I closed my eyes, squeezing them shut, taking a deep breath and holding it for a few seconds. The darkness behind my eyelids was a swirling vortex of doubt and desperation.

I focused on the image of the injured deer, the frail creature whose life I had managed to restore. That had been different, hadn't it? This felt different. I opened my eyes and responded, "I am saving him, Ma." The words felt hollow, inadequate, a flimsy shield against the tsunami of their apprehension. It had worked with the deer when I found one trapped with a broken leg; I hoped this would work too. That had been a desperate act of compassion, a fleeting moment of connection with the wild, unburdened world. This was... a transgression.

The silence in the cabin was thick and suffocating, punctuated only by Micah's shallow, ragged breaths. Every second felt like an eternity, an agonizing wait to see if my desperate gamble would pay off. I didn't have time to explain. Every moment spent explaining was a moment gained for Constantine, a moment closer to whatever cruel plan he had in store. I didn't even know if this would work.

Hope was a dangerous currency in this world, easily spent and rarely replenished. But as the seconds ticked by, Micah's breathing grew steadier, and his complexion less ghastly. The ashen pallor that had clung to his skin began to recede, replaced by a faint flush of color. Slowly, almost imperceptibly, the deep gash on his neck began to close, the flesh knitting itself back together. It was a grotesque miracle, a testament to the dark power coursing through my veins.

My parents stared, wide-eyed and terrified, as the impossible unfolded before them. Horror and disbelief warred in their expressions, a silent struggle to reconcile what they were seeing with everything they thought they knew. The lines on their faces seemed deeper, etched by the shock of witnessing something so far beyond their comprehension.

My father, always the skeptic, the pragmatic man of science and reason, was the first to break the silence. The foundation of his worldview shook as he witnessed a miracle happening before his eyes.

"What the hell...?" he muttered, his voice trailing off. The question hung in the air, unanswered and unanswerable. There were no logical explanations, no scientific principles that could account for what was happening. Only the cold, hard reality of the impossible made manifest. He looked from Micah to me, his eyes searching for some flicker of humanity, some explanation that would ease his troubled mind. He sought reason where only magic could be found.

I pulled my wrist away from Micah's mouth, the wound on my hand already starting to heal. The pain was a distant throb, easily ignored in the face of the larger crisis looming. "I'll explain later," I said, my voice low. The words were a promise, a commitment to unravel the tangled web of secrets and lies that had brought us to this point. But later might never come. "Right now, I have to stop Constantine."

Kat looked up at me, her face streaked with tears. The tracks glistened in the lamplight, reflecting the depths of her fear and confusion. She was just a child, caught in a nightmare she didn't understand. "Who is Constantine?" she asked, her voice shaking. Each word was a fragile plea for understanding, a desperate attempt to find solid ground in the shifting landscape of our lives. "What's going on, Tristan?"

I didn't have time to answer. Every second I spent explaining was a second gained for Constantine. The air outside was heavy, charged with a dark energy that made the hairs on my arms stand on end. I could feel Constantine's presence like a predator stalking its prey. He was close—too close. The scent of blood and malice hung thick in the air, a suffocating reminder of the danger closing in around us.

"I need you to stay here," I said, grabbing the hunting knife I had set on the table earlier. The cold steel felt reassuring in my hand, a tangible weapon against an unseen enemy. He would not win. "Whatever happens, do not leave the cabin."

My mother opened her mouth to protest, to argue, to beg me to stay. But the words died in her throat, choked by the fear that had gripped her. She knew, on some instinctive level, that this was a battle I had to face alone. But I was already moving. Without another word, I darted out the door and into the night.

The cold air hit my face like a slap, jolting me awake and sharpening my senses. The forest was a tapestry of shadows, alive with unseen eyes. The moon, a sliver of silver in the inky sky, offered little guidance.

Constantine was out there, waiting. And I had to find him before he found us. I ran into the night, ready to fight with everything I had to protect my family, whether they understood what I was doing or not. This was the choice I made, and everything that followed was a consequence of it.

The hunt was on. And I had no idea what the outcome would be. Even though the sun did not hurt me, the fact could not change that I was a walking shadow in the night. I was an anomaly. But Constantine would soon find out that I was not one to be trifled with. I was going to bring the fight to him, and he was going to regret ever showing his face around my family.

The forest pulsed with a hidden rhythm, a symphony conducted by unseen creatures. Crickets chirped their incessant melodies, owls hooted mournful ballads to the moon, and the wind whispered secrets through the ancient trees. But within the cacophony of the night, I was deafened by a single, overwhelming sensation: the relentless, inexorable approach of Constantine.

Each rustle of leaves, each snap of a twig under some nocturnal wanderer's foot, amplified the dread coiling in my gut. I moved with frantic grace, a desperate dance through the tangled undergrowth. My feet skimmed the forest floor, barely disturbing the fallen leaves as I vaulted over decaying logs, the wood soft and yielding beneath my weight. Low-hanging branches, gnarled and twisted like skeletal arms, snagged at my clothes, but I slipped beneath them with practiced ease, propelled by a primal fear.

This forest, once a sanctuary, a familiar haven where I could lose myself in the embrace of nature, was now a hostile arena, a battleground lit only by slivers of moonlight filtering through the dense canopy. The air, once fresh and invigorating, now hung heavy with the scent of damp earth and the metallic tang of something far more sinister—the promise of impending danger.

Every shadow seemed to writhe with malevolent intent, morphing into grotesque shapes that threatened to reach out and ensnare me. Each gust of wind carried not the soothing balm of the night, but a chilling premonition, a whisper of Constantine's presence, a ghostly echo of his hunger. The forest, once a place of solace, had betrayed me, transforming into a labyrinth of fear, designed to amplify my terror and lead me directly into his waiting embrace.

And then, through the skeletal branches of the trees, I saw him. A clearing, bathed in the ethereal glow of the moon, offered a stark contrast to the surrounding darkness. There, silhouetted against the silver light, stood Constantine.

He was an apparition, a creature woven from the very fabric of night. His eyes, twin embers of dark red, gleamed with an unholy light, piercing the darkness and locking onto mine with predatory intensity. His pale skin, stretched tight over sharp cheekbones, radiated a ghostly luminescence—a beacon of cold, unnatural beauty. He looked impossibly relaxed, almost languid, his posture exuding an unsettling confidence.

He stood with his weight casually shifted to one leg, arms loosely crossed, as if this were nothing more than a routine exercise, another trivial hunt in a long and blood-soaked existence. There was no tension in his stance, no sign of exertion, only the quiet, chilling certainty of his impending victory.

"You're late," he said, his voice a silken caress that sent shivers down my spine. It was a voice that could charm the stars from the sky, lulling the most wary prey into a false sense of security. But tonight, it carried a faint, almost imperceptible note of amusement, a mocking acknowledgment of my futile attempt to escape. "I was starting to think you weren't going to s how."

The air around me thickened, pressing in from all sides. I tightened my grip on the knife, the cold steel a small, inadequate comfort in my trembling hand. The blade felt insignificant, a child's toy against a force of nature. I knew, with chilling certainty, that it would be utterly useless against him. It was a desperate gesture, a futile attempt to regain some semblance of control in a situation spiraling rapidly beyond my grasp.

Constantine was toying with me, savoring the moment, drawing out my fear like a connoisseur sampling fine wine. He was enjoying the hunt, the anticipation of the kill, the knowledge that my fate was already sealed. We both knew it. He knew that I knew, and that knowledge was yet another weapon in his arsenal, a layer of psychological torment designed to break my spirit before he broke my body.

"You should've stayed inside, little fledgling," Constantine continued, his voice dropping to a low, almost conspiratorial whisper. The scent of him—the cloying sweetness of blood mixed with earthy undertones of decay—filled my nostrils, making my stomach churn. I fought back the urge to gag, to betray my weakness. "You might've lived a little longer."

His words were a cruel taunt, a reminder of my naiveté, my foolish belief that I could stand against him. They were a calculated attempt to undermine my resolve, to break the last vestiges of my hope.

"I'm not afraid of you," I lied, the words catching in my throat, sounding thin and unconvincing even to my own ears. I forced myself to meet his gaze, holding his burning red eyes with every ounce of willpower I possessed. It was a dangerous game, a test of strength and nerve, but I knew I couldn't afford to flinch or show even the slightest hint of fear. To do so would be to surrender completely, to invite him to crush me without mercy.

A slow, deliberate smile spread across his face, transforming his already unsettling features into something truly terrifying. It was not a smile of joy or amusement, but a predatory expression, a glimpse into the dark, empty void residing within his ancient soul. It was the smile of a hunter who had finally cornered his prey, the smile of a predator who knew victory was assured.

"You should be."

He took another step, and the forest held its breath.

The silence became deafening.

The air, thick and heavy, crackled with unseen energy.

I was no longer just afraid.

I was terrified.

But I would not break.

Not yet.

I would fight.

I would survive.

Even if it was the last thing I ever did.

Before I could react, Constantine moved—faster than I could see. One moment, he stood a few feet away, radiating an almost palpable aura of malice, and the next, he was in front of me, his hand wrapping around my throat with a crushing grip. It was a casual, dismissive gesture for him, like swatting a fly, but for me, it was the agonizing prelude to oblivion.

He lifted me off the ground with ease, as though I weighed nothing at all, his red eyes gleaming with amusement, a predatory light dancing within their crimson depths as I struggled to breathe. My hands flew up, clawing at his wrist, but my fingers found no purchase on his smooth, cold skin. It was like trying to grip marble—unyielding and devoid of warmth.

"You're Marcus's little pet, aren't you?" he said, tilting his head as he examined me. His gaze was unnervingly intense, like a scientist dissecting a specimen. He seemed to look right through me, analyzing my very essence. "I can see why he chose you. There's something... different about you." He paused, his eyes narrowing slightly as if trying to decipher a complex puzzle. "Something other than the fear that clings to you so sweetly."

I gasped for air, my lungs burning with a desperate need for oxygen. My vision blurred, the trees swirling into a dizzying kaleidoscope of green and brown as I tried to pry his hand off my throat. But it was no use. Constantine was toying with me, savoring my fear, enjoying the game of cat and mouse, even though the mouse had no chance of escape.

He possessed a terrifying confidence, born from centuries of power and bloodshed. He knew he held all the cards, and he relished the moment. The air crackled with unsettling energy, a silent promise of pain and suffering to come.

"Do you know why I've been hunting Marcus for so long?" he asked, his voice almost conversational, a stark contrast to the agonizing pressure on my windpipe as he tightened his grip. The words were spoken with chilling calmness, like a lecturer explaining a particularly interesting theorem. "It's because he's weak. He thinks he can live outside the council's rules, protect those who don't deserve protection." He spat the last word with contempt, as if the notion of mercy was anathema to him. His gaze flickered with distaste.

My mind raced, scrambling for a way out from beneath the suffocating terror, searching for any weakness, any advantage, no matter how small. But the world was closing in around me, the darkness pressing in from all sides. Panic clawed at the edges of my sanity, threatening to overwhelm me completely. I was losing consciousness, the edges of my vision going black, like ink bleeding into water. My limbs grew heavy and unresponsive, and a strange numbness began to creep through my body.

The forest floor tilted beneath me, the scent of damp earth and decaying leaves filling my nostrils. It was a familiar scent, typically comforting, but now it only served to heighten my sense of helplessness. I thought of Marcus and my family, and a wave of guilt washed over me. I had led Constantine to them, jeopardizing their safety.

Then, with a surge of desperation that blazed through the encroaching darkness, I kicked out, fueled by a primal instinct to survive. Adrenaline coursed through my veins, lending me a fleeting burst of strength. Using my legs to push off from a nearby tree, my foot connected solidly with the rough bark. I propelled myself forward with the last vestiges of my energy.

The force of the movement caught Constantine off guard, momentarily throwing him off balance, and his grip loosened just enough for me to slip free.

I hit the ground hard, the impact sending a jolt of pain through my body, but the agony was a welcome sensation compared to the suffocating darkness that had threatened to consume me. Gasping for breath, my lungs screaming in protest, I didn't stop moving.

I scrambled to my feet, ignoring the throbbing in my head and the burning in my throat, and darted deeper into the woods, weaving between the trees. The sound of Constantine's laughter, cold and mocking, echoed behind me, spurring me onward—a chilling reminder of the danger I f aced.

The forest seemed to close in around me, shadows lengthening and twisting into grotesque shapes. Every rustle of leaves, every snap of a twig, sent a jolt of fear through me. I risked a glance over my shoulder, but the trees obscured my vision, hiding whatever horrors might lurk in the darkness. My breath came in ragged gasps, and my legs burned with exhaustion, but I knew I couldn't stop. Constantine wouldn't give up. He would hunt me down, savoring my fear, prolonging my suffering before finally delivering the killing blow.

I pushed myself harder, driven by a desperate hope that I could escape, that I could somehow find my way back to Marcus, Kat, Mom, and Dad to warn them of the danger coming. My eyes darted around me, searching for any sign of salvation, any glimmer of hope in the suffocating darkness. But all I saw were trees, shadows, and the looming threat of Constantine, the hunter in the night.

My muscles screamed in protest, each stride a monumental effort. My lungs burned, and my head swam, but the image of my family kept me going.

The forest floor became uneven, roots and rocks jutting out like grasping claws. I stumbled, my ankle twisting beneath me, and I cried out in pain. For a moment, I faltered, considering giving up. But then I heard Constantine's voice, closer now, a low, menacing growl that sent shivers down my spine.

"Running won't save you, little pet," he called out, his voice dripping with cruel amusement. "Marcus can't protect you."

His words ignited a fresh surge of defiance within me. He thought I was weak, a helpless pawn in his game. He thought he could break me. But I would prove him wrong. I would survive.

Ignoring the pain in my ankle, I pushed myself to my feet as it began to heal and continued to run, weaving through the trees with renewed determination. I focused on the path ahead, scanning the shadows for any sign of danger or opportunity to escape.

The forest began to thin, the trees becoming sparser and the undergrowth less dense. A sliver of moonlight pierced through the canopy, illuminating a small clearing ahead—a chance, a glimmer of hope in the darkness.

I burst into the clearing, my senses on high alert. It was small and circular, surrounded by a ring of oaks. In the center stood a gnarled, twisted tree, its branches reaching up toward the sky like skeletal fingers.

The forest was silent except for my desperate breaths and the crunch of leaves underfoot, mingled with the distant, mocking laughter. It created a symphony of terror, a dance of shadows, and I was its unwilling participant. I stumbled on, my body aching, my mind reeling, my spirit clinging to a fragile thread of hope. But deep down, a chilling premonition told me this was just the beginning. The game had only just begun.

"You're fast, little fledgling," he called, his voice filled with amusement. "But you can't outrun me forever."

I didn't look back. Every rustle of leaves, every snap of a twig beneath my worn sneakers amplified the sound of his pursuit. It was a twisted symphony of dread, each note a reminder of the peril nipping at my heels. I could feel him gaining on me, his presence like a shadow—elongated and grotesque—creeping closer. The air around me thrummed with dark energy, a palpable sense of dread tightening its grip around my throat, making each breath a ragged, desperate gasp.

My mind raced, a frantic hamster wheel of desperate plans and futile hopes, as I leaped over fallen logs, their decaying surfaces slick with moss, and sprinted through the dense forest. The ancient trees, their gnarled branches reaching out like skeletal arms, seemed to mock my efforts, their silent judgment heavy in the twilight air. They had witnessed countless chases, countless hunts, and I was just another fleeting speck in their timeless existence.

Parkour had always been my escape from the monotony of life, a way to feel alive in a world that felt increasingly dull and predetermined. The adrenaline rush of a perfectly executed jump, the satisfaction of conquering an obstacle with sheer physical skill—it was my solace, my secret rebellion.

A way to prove to myself that I was more than ordinary, that I had the potential to be extraordinary. Now, it was more than just a hobby; it was the only thing keeping me alive. Every vault, every roll, every carefully calculated step was a desperate prayer, a frantic plea to the uncaring gods of fate. It was a language my body spoke fluently, a language of survival I hoped would buy me enough time.

Constantine's laughter rang out again, closer this time, a chilling melody that bounced off the silent trees, distorting into something inhuman and terrifying. It wasn't the joyful sound of mirth, but the cruel amusement of a predator toying with its prey—a sound that promised pain and suffering, echoing through my very bones. "You're making this fun," he said, his voice low and menacing, laced with a dark promise that sent shivers down my spine. "But playtime's over."

Each word was a hammer blow, shattering the last vestiges of hope I stubbornly clung to. I knew what he was—the monster lurking beneath a deceptively human facade. One of the Pale Ones, a vampire who craved not the sustenance of animals, but the lifeblood of humans. His very presence reeked of death and decay, a tangible aura of corruption that poisoned the air around him. The air clung to me like a second skin, suffocating me from all sides. He was everything I had come to fear, everything I had tried to avoid.

I pushed myself harder, summoning reserves of energy I didn't know I possessed. Somewhere deep inside me, a fire still tried to burn, refusing to be extinguished. My lungs burned with each ragged breath, each attempt to suck in air felt like inhaling fire. My muscles screamed in protest, aching with every movement, but I couldn't stop. I wouldn't stop. Not while there was even a sliver of hope left.

The forest floor became a blur beneath my feet, the world reduced to a tunnel vision of survival. Each sense heightened and sharpened by fear and panic. I had to remember everything I learned during my time in the woods and the city—every move, every strategy. Every lesson absorbed through trial and error, every instinct honed by necessity.

I couldn't let him catch me—not yet. I needed to buy time, to find some advantage in this desperate game of cat and mouse. I needed to think, to strategize, to find a way to turn this hunt in my favor, but my mind was a battlefield of fear and adrenaline, a chaotic storm of conflicting impulses. I tried to focus, to clear the fog of terror clouding my judgment, but it was like trying to hold water in my bare hands. There was no clear path—only desperate improvisation.

The forest was a labyrinth of shadows, the moon slicing through the canopy like a silver blade. My breath hitched as I skidded to a halt, leaves crunching underfoot. My grip tightened on the combat knife, its steel edge glinting faintly in the filtered moonlight. The familiar scent of pine and damp earth usually calmed me, but tonight, it was tainted with something else, something ancient and dangerous.

The cold wasn't from the night air. The late spring air was crisp but not biting. This was a deeper chill, one that settled in my bones, heralding something unnatural.

It was primal dread—the deep, instinctual fear of prey sensing a predator. A feeling resonating in the marrow of my bones. I could feel the fine hairs on my arms stand on end, a physical manifestation of the terror gripping my heart. It was the kind of fear that bypassed logic, a biological imperative screaming at me to run, to hide, to survive.

Then... he was there.

Constantine materialized without a sound, as if the air had simply decided to form his body in front of me. He wasn't there one moment, and then he was—impossibly tall and imposing, blocking the path ahead. It wasn't just his sudden appearance that unnerved me; it was the unnatural stillness surrounding him. No rustling leaves, no chirping insects—no sound at all.

The stillness was more terrifying than a roar. His red eyes burned, ancient and endless, locked onto me with a curiosity colder than death itself. They were wells of crimson light, hinting at the power and darkness contained within. His sculpted face, so inhumanly perfect, was unreadable—an executioner deciding whether I was worth his time. Every line, every angle was flawless, a testament to his ageless existence.

The answer came when he moved. It began with a twitch of his lip, a barely perceptible shift in his posture. The air crackled with anticipation, a silent promise of violence.

Constantine struck first—a black blur of speed and ferocity. One moment he was still; the next, he was a whirlwind of deadly motion. My training kicked in, years of discipline and honed reflexes taking over.

I twisted sideways, instincts screaming, barely avoiding the fist that could've shattered a brick wall. Time seemed to slow, stretching each moment into an eternity. I saw the fist coming—a dark shape hurtling toward me—and reacted without thinking. Even grazing my ribs, the force of it nearly caved my side in. Pain roared through me, a blinding flash threatening to overwhelm my senses. I channeled it into motion, pivoting on my heel and slashing upward with my knife. I focused on my training, pushing through the pain, using it as fuel to keep moving.

Steel bit into flesh. The sensation was jarring, the slight resistance followed by the sickening give of the blade.

I saw dark blood spray, sizzling against the cold air as the gash opened across Constantine's forearm. The sight invigorated me, a small spark of hope igniting in the face of overwhelming dread. It was a deep cut—good. Deeper than I expected.

But it healed before I could blink. The edges of the wound pulled together, knitting themselves shut with unnatural speed. The skin shimmered, reforming perfectly, leaving no trace of the injury. My hope flickered, threatened by the impossible reality of his regeneration.

"Cute," Constantine purred, flicking his wrist as if swatting a fly. His voice was deceptively languid, a dangerous contrast to the raw power he exuded.

His backhand caught my jaw, snapping my head back. The force of the blow resonated through my skull, rattling my brain. My skull felt like it cracked against the air itself. I staggered, copper flooding my mouth, the taste of my own blood acrid on my tongue, but I forced myself to stay upright, using the momentum to spin into a low sweep kick. I channeled all my remaining strength into the blow, desperate to throw him off balance.

My shin collided with his ankle—but it was like kicking solid steel. There was no give, no bend—just unyielding resistance. He didn't even budge. It was like kicking a tree trunk.

But I was already moving. I couldn't afford to stay in one place, to give him a stationary target.

I leaped backward, twisting mid-air, landing atop a moss-covered boulder. The moss was slick, threatening to send me tumbling, but I maintained my balance, using the momentum to propel myself forward. Parkour had drilled into me one truth—keep moving or die. Stagnation meant death.

I launched off the boulder, tucking into a roll to evade Constantine's next lunge. I used the environment to my advantage, leveraging every tree, rock, and contour of the landscape to stay one step ahead.

His claws carved through the earth where I had stood just a second ago, dirt and stone exploding into the air. The air smelled of turned earth and ozone, a testament to the raw power he wielded.

I embraced the chaos, ran up the nearest tree trunk, flipped backward, and slashed down mid-air. I moved with practiced grace, my body a weapon honed by years of training.

Blade met flesh. Again.

The steel edge tore through his cheek, splitting skin like parchment. The sound was almost delicate, a horrifying contrast to the violence of the act.

Constantine didn't even flinch. He showed no sign of pain, no reaction whatsoever.

He simply smiled as the wound sealed shut in an instant. The healing was almost casual, a demonstration of his indifference.

"You're fast," he admitted, his voice a low, velvet rumble. The sound sent shivers down my spine, a vibration that resonated in my bones. "But speed without strategy is just... noise." The words dripped with condescension, dismissing my efforts.

He vanished—

Instinct saved me. It was a premonition, a sudden certainty that I needed to move. I ducked just as his elbow obliterated the oak behind me. Wood splintered like a bomb had gone off inside it, a shower of bark and debris raining down around me. The force of the blow was immense, enough to pulverize the tree into dust.

I retaliated with a spinning back kick, putting every ounce of power into it—

And I hit him. The impact was solid, a satisfying crunch of bone and muscle.

My heel crashed against his sternum. I focused all my energy into the blow, hoping to fracture his ribs and slow him down.

Constantine grunted—actually grunted—and slid back half a step. It was the first sign that I had actually hurt him.

A victory. A small one, but a victory. A glimmer of hope in the darkness.

I pressed the attack. I couldn't afford to let him recover or give him time to regroup.

I feinted left, then cartwheeled right, slashing at Constantine's thigh. I aimed for the largest muscle mass, hoping to cripple him and limit his mobility.

The knife sank deep, muscle splitting open. I felt the resistance give way as the blade sliced through flesh. He let out a low snarl, his first real reaction.

For the first time, I felt hope—genuine, unadulterated hope—blooming in my chest. Perhaps I could win. Perhaps I could survive this.

Then his hand clamped around my wrist. The grip was like a vise, constricting my circulation, cutting off the flow of blood.

Bone snapped. The sound was sickeningly loud, a sharp crack that echoed through the silent forest.

Agony shot through my entire arm as my knife clattered to the ground. The pain was blinding, radiating outward from the break, threatening to overwhelm me. I screamed, instinct kicking in—I jabbed my fingers at his eyes, trying to force him to let go. It was a desperate move fueled by pure survival instinct.

He did—but not because he felt pain.

Because he was laughing.

A sound like gravel and broken glass. The laughter was devoid of humor, a chilling expression of amusement at my futile struggles.

"Bravo," Constantine crooned. "You've memorized forms, but you fight like a human—predictable." His words were a slap in the face, a brutal assessment of my weaknesses.

Then the forest itself seemed to bend around him. The air shimmered, distorting the light and creating an illusion of movement.

A root shot from the soil, coiling around my ankle like a vice. It was thicker than my arm, its surface rough and gnarled.

I hacked at it with my healed hand, but Constantine was already upon me. There was no escape.

His fists came down like pistons. Each blow landed with devastating force, shattering bone and crushing muscle.

Ribs cracked. A jaw shattered. I could feel the fragments grinding against each other.

I blocked blow after blow, but it was useless. There was no defense against his relentless assault. Every strike felt like it was tearing me apart, my bones breaking and healing at a sickening pace.

I flipped over him, landing awkwardly but managing to snatch up my knife again. I refused to give up, to surrender.

Blood dripped from my split lip onto the blade. The taste of blood was metallic, a constant reminder of my injuries.

Constantine paused, tilting his head. He seemed genuinely curious. "You remind me of myself. Centuries ago." The words were spoken with a hint of nostalgia, a glimpse into his ancient past.

He lunged—but I was ready. Or at least as ready as I could be, given the circumstances.

I dropped into a sliding split, my knife raking across his abdomen. It was a desperate maneuver, a last-ditch effort to inflict some damage.

The blade gutted him.

For the first time, Constantine staggered. He stumbled backward, his expression a mix of surprise and annoyance.

For a heartbeat, triumph surged in my chest—a fleeting moment of euphoria before the inevitable crash.

Then Constantine straightened. His lips curved into a smile, one of pure evil.

His intestines stitched back into place, sealing like hot wax under a flame. The healing was grotesque, a violation of the natural order.

He exhaled, red eyes gleaming. The crimson light intensified, burning with malevolent energy.

"Almost," he growled. The word was laced with contempt, a dismissal of my efforts.

Then he stopped playing. The casual amusement vanished from his face, replaced by a cold, implacable fury.

Everything became a whirlwind of violence. I could barely track his movements; his speed was blinding.

Constantine's strikes came faster, harder—a punch to the kidney, a knee to the gut, an elbow to the face. Each blow was perfectly placed, designed to inflict maximum damage.

I blocked one claw strike—but my leg was swept out from under me. I was losing, and I knew it.

I hit the ground, the air exploding from my lungs. The impact knocked the wind out of me, leaving me gasping for breath.

His boot crushed my wrist, pinning me down. The force was immense, grinding bone against bone. The knife slipped from my numb fingers. Freedom was no longer an option.

I tried to roll away, to escape his clutches, but his hand closed around my throat, lifting me off the ground like I weighed nothing. His grip was like iron, cutting off my air supply.

"You've entertained me," Constantine murmured, fingers tightening. The words were almost a compliment, but they offered no comfort.

I gagged, clawing at his grip. My vision dimmed, the edges blurring. Desperation fueled my remaining strength.

Desperate, I drove a palm strike upward, aiming for his nose—a blow I had been taught as a last resort. Aim for the soft tissue, for the organs that even a vampire would have trouble healing.

Cartilage crunched. I felt the bone shatter under my palm.

Constantine sighed. The sound was almost bored, as if I had inconvenienced him.

Then—

He slammed me into a tree.

Bark exploded, the impact sending a shockwave of agony through my spine. I felt something crack, something break. My vision went black.

He pinned me against the tree, the rough bark digging into my back, his grip like iron. Inhuman strength radiated from him, a terrifying display of raw power that dwarfed my own feeble resistance. My struggles were futile, the movements of a trapped bird beating against its cage.

He held me effortlessly, as if I were a mere child, his presence suffocating and overwhelming. His shadow loomed over me, casting me in darkness and stealing away the last vestiges of light. I could feel the cold emanating from him, a chilling absence of warmth that seeped into my bones. His gaze was intense, his eyes drilling into my very soul.

"Enough games," he growled, his voice filled with cold malice, devoid of warmth or compassion. His breath was a chilling whisper against my ear, the voice of a predator savoring the moment before the kill—a promise of pain and suffering, a declaration of my imminent demise. He seemed to relish my fear, feeding off the terror that emanated from me.

He was close now, too close. My feeling and vision returned, thanks to my vampire healing ability. I could feel the chilling touch of his skin through my thin shirt, along with the subtle scent of decay that clung to him like a shroud—a musty odor that spoke of ancient secrets and long-dormant desires. I struggled against him, twisting and writhing, kicking my legs in a desperate attempt to gain leverage, but it was no use.

His grip was like iron, unyielding and unbreakable. I could feel life draining from me, a slow, agonizing siphon, as his cold eyes bore into mine, piercing through my fear and stripping away my defenses. It was as if he reached inside me, touching my soul and pulling all the strength from my b ody.

His gaze was hypnotic, drawing me into the abyss, promising oblivion—a dark vortex of despair that threatened to swallow me whole. I felt myself weakening, my muscles losing their strength, my will crumbling under the weight of his power. This was it. This was how it ended. Not with a heroic showdown, not with a valiant sacrifice, but with a whimper in the forest, a forgotten victim of a monster's insatiable hunger—a statistic in the grand scheme of things. I closed my eyes, bracing myself for the inevitable.

The forest held its breath around us, a silent audience to my demise. I knew the animals were there, hidden among the trees, watching with cold, uncaring eyes—witnesses to my last breath. I tried to remember my life. I thought of the smell in my grandmother's kitchen, the way the moonlight looked on the water, and every happy memory I could summon.

But just as Constantine raised his hand, ready to deliver the final blow, something inside me snapped. It wasn't a conscious decision, not a surge of bravery or righteous anger. It was primal—a visceral reaction to impending doom, a desperate clawing at the edge of oblivion. A surge of power, unlike anything I had ever felt before, coursed through my body, igniting nerves I didn't even know existed.

It was as if a dam had broken within me, releasing a torrent of energy that had been building, unknowingly, for years. It felt ancient, raw, un-tamed—a force that threatened to consume me even as it offered salvation. Without thinking, driven by pure instinct, I let out a scream—a primal, desperate scream that seemed to shake the very earth around us.

It wasn't a scream of terror, though fear was certainly a component. It wasn't a scream of pain, though my body ached with every injury. It was something more. It was the scream of someone pushed to the absolute limit, born of desperation and defiance. It echoed with the frustration of being hunted, the injustice of being targeted, the burning desire to survive. It resonated with a power that transcended my physical form, drawing upon something deep within the earth and the very air around us. It was a scream that demanded to be heard, a scream that refused to be silenced.

The force of it sent Constantine flying backward, slamming into a near-by tree with enough impact to splinter the trunk. The sound of cracking wood echoed through the forest like a gunshot. He hit the ground hard, the air leaving his lungs in a whoosh, shock and disbelief etched on his face. The arrogance that had defined him moments before was replaced with utter bewilderment, as if the very laws of physics had been defied. He looked vulnerable. For the first time since this nightmare began, he seemed like he could actually be defeated.

"What... what was that?" he muttered, confusion and anger lacing his voice. The words were ragged and strained, a far cry from the confident pronouncements he'd made only moments before. He pushed himself up, wincing in pain, his eyes darting around as if searching for the source of the attack. He couldn't comprehend what had just happened, couldn't reconcile the image of the cowering victim he expected with the force that had just thrown him across the forest. He was lost, disoriented, unprepared for this sudden shift in power.

I didn't know. I had no idea what had just happened. The power that had surged through me vanished as quickly as it had arrived, leaving me feeling drained and weak. My limbs trembled, my head spun, and I struggled to catch my breath. I was just as confused as Constantine, bewildered by my unexpected strength. But I didn't have time to think about it.

I couldn't afford to dwell on the inexplicable force that had erupted within me, not when survival was still the immediate concern. There would be time for questions later, time for answers, if I lived long enough to find them.

From the corner of my eye, I saw Marcus emerge from the shadows, moving swiftly and silently toward Constantine. He was a predator unleashed, his movements fluid and graceful, radiating an aura of lethal intent. The moonlight glinted off his silver hair, casting long, dramatic shadows that danced around him like restless spirits.

His eyes were cold, devoid of emotion, his face set in grim determination. He moved with a purpose that brooked no argument, no hesitation, no doubt. Focused solely on the task at hand, he was driven by a loyalty that ran deeper than blood.

Without hesitation, Marcus raised a silver blade and drove it into Constantine's chest. The movement was swift, precise, and utterly merciless. There was no flourish, no dramatic pronouncements—just a clean, efficient strike designed to end the threat decisively. The blade plunged deep, piercing flesh and bone, severing the connections that held Constantine's unnatural life together. The silver was pure and radiant.

Constantine let out a scream of pain, a raw, guttural sound that echoed through the forest—a testament to the agonizing power of the silver. His body convulsed violently as the blade pierced his heart, his limbs jerking uncontrollably as his nervous system overloaded. The pain was unbearable—a searing inferno consuming him from the inside out.

He clawed at the blade, desperate to pull it free, but his strength was failing him, his life force ebbing away with each passing second. Flames erupted from the wound, engulfing him in a fiery blaze. The silver ignited his unnatural essence, unleashing a torrent of energy that burned away his corruption, consuming him in a pyre of holy fire. The flames danced and writhed, casting grotesque shadows that flickered across the surrounding trees, painting a macabre scene of destruction and demise.

But even as his body disintegrated into ash, even as the flames consumed him entirely, he managed to speak one final, haunting sentence. "You think this is over, Marcus? You think you've won?" he hissed, his voice echoing through the clearing. "There are others... they'll come for you... for him... for everyone." His voice was weak, raspy, barely audible above the crackling fire, but it carried a weight of malice and a chilling premonition of what was to come.

It was a curse, a warning, a promise of retribution that lingered in the air long after his physical form had vanished. The words were laced with ancient power, forged in centuries of darkness and fueled by an insatiable thirst for vengeance—a seed of evil planted in the heart of the forest, threatening to blossom into something even more terrifying than Constantine himself.

The flames finally subsided, leaving behind only a pile of smoldering ash and the lingering scent of sulfur. Constantine was gone, reduced to nothing but a memory, a fading whisper in the wind. But his final words hung heavy in the air, a dark cloud overshadowing our momentary victory. The battle was won, but the war was far from over.

The silence that followed was deafening, broken only by the rustling of leaves and the distant hoot of an owl. The forest seemed to hold its breath, as if waiting for the next shoe to drop. The tension was palpable, a thick, suffocating blanket pressing down on us from all sides. We had survived, yes, but at what cost? What had that scream been? And what did Constantine's final words mean?

Marcus withdrew the silver blade, wiping it clean on a piece of cloth before sheathing it. His face was grim, his eyes narrowed in thought. He had witnessed the power that surged through me, had felt the earth tremble beneath our feet. He knew that something profound had shifted—something that would change the course of our lives forever. And he had not overlooked Constantine's last words. He understood that this was not the end, but only the beginning of a new, even more dangerous chapter.

The clearing was silent, save for the crackle of dying flames. Embers danced like fleeting spirits, their light painting the surrounding trees in shifting patterns of orange and black. The air hung heavy with the scent of wood smoke and something else—something metallic and sharp that clung to the back of my throat. I collapsed to the ground, my body shaking with exhaustion and shock. Every muscle screamed in protest, a chorus of aches and pains reminding me of the brutal fight and my desperate struggle for survival.

The adrenaline that had coursed through my veins only moments before had finally abandoned me, leaving behind a hollow ache and a bone-deep weariness. I could feel the blood caked on my skin, a grim reminder of the violence I had both witnessed and perpetrated. The image of Constantine's face, contorted in rage and hunger, flashed before my eyes, making me shudder involuntarily.

Marcus stood over me, his tall frame silhouetted against the fading firelight. His dark hair was disheveled, falling across his forehead in a way that might have seemed boyish were it not for the grave expression etched on his face. His expression was unreadable, a mask of stoicism that both comforted and unnerved me. I longed to see some flicker of emotion, some sign of the turmoil I knew he must be feeling, but his face remained an impenetrable fortress.

It was a face that had seen too much, a face that had borne witness to centuries of darkness and despair. I wondered what secrets lay hidden behind those crimson amber eyes, what horrors he had endured in his long and immortal life. Was this how he always dealt with things? An unreadable statue always watching? I yearned to know him more, but something in his demeanor kept me at bay, as if separated by an invisible wall.

"Why didn't you help earlier?" I rasped, my voice hoarse and raw from shouting and the lingering fear that clung to me like a shroud. The words felt like shards of glass in my throat, each syllable a testament to my frustration and resentment. Logically, I knew he must have had his reasons, but the image of him standing by while I fought for my life burned in my memory. It felt like a betrayal, a silent judgment of my abilities.

Was I not worth his intervention? Was I simply a pawn in some larger game that only he understood? The thought stung, adding another layer of bitterness to my wounded pride. I wanted to yell at him, scream at him even, but the words caught in my throat, choked by exhaustion and a lingering sense of dependence. I couldn't deny that I needed him, that my family needed him. And he knew it.

Marcus knelt beside me, his movements fluid and graceful. Even in the dim light, I could see the subtle elegance in his posture, the effortless way he carried himself. It was the grace of a predator, honed over centuries of hunting and survival. He emanated a quiet power that was both alluring and intimidating. His eyes, those mesmerizing pools of red amber, softened slightly, a subtle shift that registered deep within me.

They held a depth of ancient knowledge and a weariness that spoke of centuries lived, centuries of bearing burdens I couldn't begin to comprehend. There was a sadness there, a profound sense of loss that tugged at something deep within my soul. It made me want to reach out to him, to offer some small measure of comfort, but I hesitated, unsure if my touch would be welcome.

"I had to protect your family," he said quietly, his voice a low rumble that resonated within me. "They wouldn't have survived the night without me." Though delivered softly, his words carried the weight of absolute certainty. There was no room for argument, no space for doubt. He had made a choice, a calculated decision based on the needs of many rather than the needs of one. While I understood the logic behind it, it didn't make it feel any better.

His words struck me like a physical blow. Of course. My family. In my frantic fight for survival, I'd almost forgotten about them. The thought of what could have happened to them, of the horrors they might have faced without Marcus's protection, sent a fresh wave of fear washing over me. They were vulnerable, human, utterly defenseless against the monstrous power of Constantine and his followers.

My mother, Dad, and my sister—would they simply become another victim in this reality I had never known? I bit my lip, attempting to hold back the guilt that loomed over me. I ought to have been there for them, safeguarding them as any son ought to. I had let them down.

I swallowed hard, my throat dry and constricted. My mind was still reeling, a chaotic vortex of images and emotions. The fight, the blood, Constantine's twisted face—all swirled together in a nightmarish tapestry. Then there were his words, his cryptic warning that haunted me like a phantom. He had spoken of others, of forces far greater than himself, lurking in the shadows, waiting to strike. His words had been laced with a dark promise of pain and suffering to come, a threat that hung over us like a sword of Damocles, ready to fall at any moment.

"What did he mean?" I asked, my voice barely above a whisper. The question hung in the air between us, heavy with unspoken dread. "About others coming for us?" I searched his face for answers, for some sign of hope, but found only grim resignation. I was beginning to understand that we were not safe, that we would never truly be safe.

We were caught in a war that had been raging for centuries, a conflict between predator and prey, and we were hopelessly outmatched. Was there any chance of peace? Or was our future destined to be one of endless flight and fear?

Marcus's face darkened; the subtle softening vanished as quickly as it had appeared. Gone was the flicker of compassion, replaced by a mask of cold determination. His gaze became distant, focused on something far beyond the confines of the clearing, something that only he could see. It was as if he were peering into the depths of time, searching for answers in the echoes of forgotten ages.

I suddenly felt a chill, a coldness that had nothing to do with the night air. It was the chill of uncertainty, of knowing that we were caught in a web of events far larger and more dangerous than I could possibly imagine. It was like staring into an abyss that stared back, and I felt small and inconsequential.

He remained silent for a long moment, his jaw tight, his brow furrowed in concentration. I could practically see the gears turning in his mind, the calculations he was making as he weighed our options and assessed the risks. The only sound was the crackling fire and the rustling of leaves in the wind, a symphony of nature that seemed oblivious to the darkness surrounding us. The tranquility of the forest felt like a cruel mockery of the chaos unfolding in our lives. Finally, he spoke, his voice low and grave.

"Constantine was not alone," he said, his words measured and deliberate. Each word was enunciated with precision, as if he were choosing them carefully, aware of their weight and significance. "He was part of a larger... organization. A coven, if you will... of vampires." I shivered again. The way he said 'coven' made me believe that this was no mere club of vampires.

"They're already... here." My mind struggled to grasp the enormity of what he was implying.

Marcus sighed, a sound that seemed to carry the weight of centuries. It was a sound of resignation, of weariness, of a soul burdened by too much knowledge and pain. "There are more of Constantine's men. You rest; I'll handle the rest." He kept those red amber eyes locked on mine, ensuring I understood the sheer gravity of the situation.

The words hung in the air, chilling me to the core. The implications were terrifying. Constantine, as monstrous as he was, was just a foot soldier in a much larger, more organized army—an army of bloodthirsty predators who saw humanity as nothing more than food. The idea of living in such a world, of being reduced to nothing more than livestock, was abhorrent. I would rather die than submit to such a fate.

"And they're coming for us?" I asked, my voice trembling despite my best efforts to remain calm. I tried to steel myself, to prepare for the fight to come, but the fear was overwhelming. How could we possibly stand against such a powerful force? We were just ordinary people, thrust into a world of darkness and violence.

Marcus nodded slowly, his eyes filled with grim resolve. "Constantine's failure will not go unnoticed. They will want to know why he failed, and they will want to eliminate any potential threats."

"Threats? But why would they see us as a threat? We're just... trying to survive." I felt a surge of indignation. We hadn't asked for any of this. We were simply trying to protect ourselves, to carve out a safe existence in a world that had suddenly become hostile. Was that so wrong?

"You know about them," Marcus said, his gaze piercing. "You know about the existence of vampires. That alone makes you a liability. If you speak, then others will know. They can't have that."

Chapter Eighteen

THE AWAKENING

The world around me was dark and suffocating, like a thick fog I couldn't escape. It wasn't the comforting darkness of sleep, filled with soft shadows and muted thoughts, but a heavy, oppressive void pressing in on all sides—a crushing weight threatening to extinguish any flicker of consciousness. My limbs felt impossibly heavy, pinned down by an unseen force, as if I were submerged in thick mud or encased in stone.

I tried to move, to twitch a finger or flex a toe, to send even the smallest signal to my dormant muscles, but nothing responded. It was as if my body had become a separate entity, a lifeless shell disconnected from my will.

The forest sounds, usually a symphony of rustling leaves, the gentle caress of the wind through the branches, the incessant chirping of insects heralding each new night, and the distant calls of nocturnal creatures—the hooting of owls and the rustling of small animals in the undergrowth—had dimmed into a distant, echoing hum.

They were there, I knew, flickering at the edge of my awareness, yet muffled, as if heard from the bottom of a well, filtered through layers of cotton and distance. The vibrant tapestry of the night had been reduced to a dull, barely perceptible drone.

I wanted to open my eyes, to see what was happening around me, to penetrate this suffocating darkness and regain my sense of orientation, but I couldn't. The effort felt insurmountable, like trying to lift a mountain, a task so monumental it defied comprehension. My eyelids felt sealed shut, weighted down by exhaustion—not the familiar fatigue of a long day, but a bone-deep weariness seeping from the very marrow of my bones. My body was spent, utterly drained of every ounce of energy after that last surge of power, the final desperate act of defiance.

The fight, the desperate defense, had taken everything, leaving me a hollow shell, a husk devoid of vitality. I remembered the searing heat, the agonizing burn that had licked at my skin, the bone-jarring impacts, the relentless assault that had threatened to overwhelm me, and the raw, desperate need to protect... protect whom? It felt crucial, a connection to something precious and irreplaceable, but the details slipped away like sand through my fingers, dissolving into the oppressive darkness.

Doubt crept into the edges of my awareness, a corrosive whisper threatening to unravel what little remained of my resolve. Was I dying? Was this what it felt like—the slow fade into oblivion, the gradual extinguishing of the self? The thought sparked a flicker of fear, a primal instinct to survive, a desperate clinging to life struggling against the overwhelming inertia, the seductive pull of the void.

I had to fight this, I knew; I had to claw my way back from the brink. But how could you fight a darkness that was both inside and outside you, a force emanating from the very fabric of existence? How could you combat an enemy you couldn't see, touch, or fully comprehend?

I felt Marcus beside me—his presence, his strength—a faint but undeniable anchor in the swirling nothingness, a beacon of stability in the storm. I sensed his steady, controlled energy, the quiet hum of his immortal existence, a stark contrast to my own depleted state and shattered reserves. His very being radiated quiet power, a silent promise of safety, reassuring me that I was not alone in this terrifying darkness.

But even his voice was fading, becoming more distant, beginning to sound like a faint echo, a whisper on the wind, as the darkness pulled me under, deeper into its embrace. Was he trying to reach me, to pull me back from this precipice, to drag me from the clutches of oblivion? I couldn't be sure if I was just imagining the almost-silent murmur—perhaps a plea for me to hold on or a desperate cry for help. The darkness played tricks on the mind, distorting perceptions and blurring the lines between reality and illusion.

I strained, focusing all my will on that single point of contact, that fragile connection to reality, that tenuous link to the world of the living. I clung to it as if it were a lifeline, the only thing preventing me from being swept away completely, desperately trying to draw strength from him, to leech even the smallest amount of his power to fuel my own failing reserves. But the darkness was relentless, a powerful current determined to sweep me away, a force that brooked no resistance.

It felt ancient, patient, and utterly indifferent to my struggles—an entity that had witnessed countless deaths and would witness countless more. It was a force of nature, an inexorable tide that could not be reasoned with, bargained with, or appeased.

Suddenly, I was standing in the cabin, the warm glow of the fire casting long shadows on the wooden floor. The familiar creaks and groans of the old wood, the scent of pine and woodsmoke, painted a canvas of normalcy. Everything seemed calm. My family was sitting at the table, bathed in golden light, laughing and talking as if nothing had happened. Kat's laugh echoed, a bright, melodic sound that usually filled the room with warmth and joy.

My father, his face etched with the stories of a long life, poked at the fire with an iron rod, a contented smile playing on his lips as he recounted some old story, likely one we had heard a hundred times before. My mother, her hands moving with practiced grace, was making her famous tea, the fragrant steam curling upwards in delicate wisps.

And Micah, his presence a comforting anchor, was there too, sitting close to Kat, their fingers intertwined in a silent promise of love and support. A scene of domestic tranquility, a portrait of everything I held dear.

But something was off. A subtle discordance, a hairline fracture in the otherwise perfect picture. The warmth of the fire seemed too bright, almost feverish, radiating an unnatural intensity. The colors, normally comforting and familiar, seemed too sharp, too vivid, assaulting my senses. The cheerful chatter felt forced, the smiles strained, as if everyone were acting a part in a play they didn't quite understand.

A chill, deeper than any winter wind, ran down my spine, prickling my skin and raising goosebumps along my arms. The air, usually crisp and clean, grew heavy, thick with an unseen pressure, pressing down on me like the weight of an impending storm—a suffocating blanket of dread. I felt an overwhelming sense of wrongness, a primal instinct screaming at me to flee, to escape the impending catastrophe.

I opened my mouth to speak, to warn them, to shatter the illusion of peace and tell them something was terribly, irrevocably wrong, but no sound came out. My throat constricted, my vocal cords refusing to obey my desperate commands. I tried to shout, whisper, or even croak out a single word of warning, but my voice was trapped, imprisoned within the confines of my paralyzed body.

Panic began to claw at the edges of my mind, threatening to consume me in a tidal wave of fear. I wanted to reach out, to touch them, to pull them from whatever spell held them captive, but my limbs felt heavy and unresponsive, as if filled with lead.

And then it happened. The world tilted on its axis, the fragile bubble of normalcy shattering into a million pieces.

The door burst open with a violence that stole my breath, the wooden frame splintering and cracking as if struck by a wrecking ball. Shards of wood flew through the air like deadly projectiles, adding to the chaos and destruction. A gust of cold air, sharper than any winter gale, swept into the cabin, carrying with it the stench of death and decay—a palpable wave of malevolence that choked the air from my lungs. And there he was—Constantine.

He stood silhouetted in the doorway, a figure of terrifying grandeur, a predator poised to strike. The flickering firelight danced across his face, highlighting the sharp angles of his cheekbones and the cruel curve of his lips. But it was his eyes that held my attention, that held me captive in their terrifying gaze. They glowed a menacing red, burning with an infernal fire, reflecting the bloodlust simmering just beneath the surface.

Blood, thick and viscous, dripped from his lips, staining his chin and neck—a gruesome testament to his recent depravity. His clothes, once elegant and refined, were now torn and stained with fresh kills, clinging to him like a shroud of death. The scent of blood, mingled with the sickly sweet odor of decay, permeated the air, a nauseating assault on my senses.

His presence was suffocating, overwhelming—a black hole sucking all the light and life from the room. He exuded an aura of power and ancient evil that pressed down on me, crushing my spirit and stealing my will to resist. He was a vortex of darkness, a creature of nightmare, and he had come to claim what was his.

My family froze, their laughter dying in their throats, their faces paling as Constantine stepped inside, crossing the threshold with deliberate, predatory grace. Their eyes widened in horror, reflecting the same fear and helplessness that consumed me. The scene of warmth and happiness evaporated, replaced by a tableau of terror—a chilling reminder of the darkness lurking beyond the edges of our fragile existence. His boots thudded ominously against the wooden floor, each step echoing through the silent cabin like the beat of a death knell, marking the inevitable approach of doom.

I tried to move, to rush forward and stop him, to protect my family from the monster that had invaded our home. But my legs wouldn't obey, refusing to respond to my frantic commands. They felt rooted to the spot, heavy and unresponsive, as if bound by invisible chains. I was trapped, helpless, a spectator to the unfolding tragedy, forced to watch as my world crumbled around me.

Constantine's gaze swept over my family, lingering on each of them as if savoring the moment, relishing their fear. A slow, cruel smile spread across his face, revealing teeth that seemed far too sharp, far too long. "Well, well, well," he said, his voice a low, gravelly rumble that sent shivers down my spine. "What a delightful little gathering we have here. It seems I've arrived just in time for supper." The way he said "supper" made my stomach churn. It wasn't an invitation; it was a threat.

His eyes finally locked onto mine. A spark of recognition flickered within their crimson depths, a cruel amusement dancing there. "Tristan," he purred, my name a venomous caress on his tongue. "How lovely to see you again. I trust you've been... well?" He knew perfectly well I hadn't been. The implication hung heavy in the air: our last encounter had not been pleasant, and this one promised to be far worse.

He took another step forward, and the air crackled with unseen energy. The fire in the hearth flared higher, casting grotesque shadows that danced across the walls, turning the familiar cabin into a chamber of horrors. My father, despite his age, stood up, placing himself between Constantine and my mother. His eyes, though filled with fear, held a spark of defiance, a protective instinct that refused to be extinguished. "Get out of my house," he growled, his voice trembling but firm.

Constantine chuckled, a chilling sound that echoed through the cabin. "Your house? Oh, but, this is where you are wrong. I'm taking what's mine, and he is mine to take." He gestured toward me with a languid hand, his red eyes gleaming with possessiveness. "Tristan and I have... unfinished business."

My mother gasped, her hand flying to her mouth. Kat and Micah clung to each other, their faces pale with terror. I wanted to scream, to tell them to run, to fight, to do anything but stand there like lambs waiting for slaughter. But I was still frozen, paralyzed by fear and the overwhelming power emanating from Constantine.

"You'll need to get past me first," my father declared, stepping forward and raising his hand as if to hit Constantine. Constantine let out another laugh, completely devoid of mirth. In a blur that surpassed human ability, he surged ahead, seizing my father's wrist in a hold that seemed to shatter bone. My father yelled in anguish, his expression twisted in torment. Constantine wrenched his wrist with a grotesque crack, and my father crumpled to the ground, cradling his shattered arm.

My mother screamed, rushing to his side. Constantine ignored her, his attention fixed on me. "Such bravery," he said mockingly, his eyes never leaving mine. "But ultimately, futile."

He turned his gaze to Kat and Micah, who were huddled together, trembling. A predatory gleam entered his eyes. "And who are these... delightful morsels?" he asked, his voice dripping with menace. "Perhaps I'll have a little appetizer before the main course."

Rage, hot and blinding, finally broke through the paralysis that had held me captive. The sight of my family, cowering in fear, my father writhing in pain, was too much to bear. The primal instinct to protect surged through me, overriding the terror that had gripped me. I didn't care that

Constantine was stronger, faster, more powerful than I could ever hope to be. I couldn't stand by and watch him hurt my family.

With a roar that surprised even myself, I lunged at Constantine, my fist clenched, my body fueled by pure, unadulterated rage. He barely reacted, his eyes widening slightly in what might have been surprise. As I neared him, he sidestepped effortlessly, my fist whistling harmlessly through the air. Before I could recover, he grabbed my arm, his grip like a vise, and flung me across the room.

I crashed into the wall, the impact knocking the wind out of me. Pain exploded in my head, blurring my vision. I struggled to get to my feet, but my limbs felt like lead. Constantine advanced on me, his red eyes burning with amusement.

"Such spirit, Tristan," he said, his voice a mocking whisper. "But you are no match for me. You never were." He reached out, his long, pale fingers trailing across my cheek. A shiver of revulsion ran down my spine. "Join me, Tristan," he whispered, his voice hypnotic. "Embrace your true nature. Together, we can rule this world."

I spat in his face.

His smile vanished, replaced by a look of pure, unadulterated fury. He backhanded me across the face, the force of the blow sending me sprawling to the floor. The world swam before my eyes.

"You will learn to obey," he snarled, his voice dripping with venom. He knelt down, his face inches from mine. "You will all learn."

He turned back to my family, his eyes gleaming. "Now, where were we?"

I tried to get up, to stop him, but I was too weak, too injured. All I could do was lie there, helpless, as Constantine prepared to unleash his terror on my family. The cabin, once a sanctuary of warmth and love, had become a stage for a nightmare, and a bloody, terrifying act was just about to begin. I watched the horror unfold through a haze of pain and despair, knowing

I was powerless to stop it. As he moved toward Kat and Micah, a guttural scream ripped through the air, but it wasn't mine; it was Kat's, echoing in my mind even as darkness threatened to claim me completely.

Constantine smiled—an evil, twisted grin that stretched his lips into a grotesque parody of human joy. It was a smile devoid of warmth, a smile that promised pain and suffering, a smile that sent shivers down my spine and turned my blood to ice. It was the smile of a predator, a hunter who had cornered his prey, a monster who reveled in the fear and despair of his victims. It was a smile I would never forget, a smile that would haunt my dreams and fuel my nightmares for the rest of my existence.

The promise of torment lived in that smile, a reflection of the darkness he carried within him, the darkness that threatened to consume us all. His eyes locked with mine, a spark of cruel amusement flickering within their crimson depths, as if he knew the torment I was experiencing, as if he delighted in my helplessness. He knew he had me trapped, knew I couldn't stop him, and the knowledge only amplified his twisted pleasure.

The scene was frozen in time, a tableau of horror that would forever be etched into the deepest recesses of my mind.

"NO!" I screamed, but the sound died in my throat, a pathetic, silent plea in the grand theater of horror unfolding before me. The air, thick with the metallic tang of blood, seemed to swallow any hope of escape, any chance of averting the inevitable.

Blood sprayed across the room, a crimson rain painting the once-pristine walls with the grotesque artwork of death. Constantine, a whirlwind of predatory grace and ravenous hunger, had descended upon Kat with horrifying speed. Her eyes, wide with an understanding of the terror to come, locked with mine for a fleeting, desperate moment—a silent scream of betrayal and disbelief. Then, his fangs, elongated and sharpened to deadly points, plunged into the delicate curve of her neck.

I saw the life drain from her, not in a mystical fading, but in a brutal extinguishing. The vibrant spark that defined Kat, her infectious laughter and unwavering spirit, flickered and died like a candle snuffed out by a storm. Her body went limp in his grasp, the vibrant energy that had animated it moments before now gone. Her head lolled to the side, a grotesque parody of sleep. He tossed her aside like a broken toy, a discarded plaything no longer capable of providing amusement or sustenance. The casual cruelty of the act was almost as sickening as the act itself.

My mother screamed, a raw, primal sound of grief and defiance that echoed the terror seizing my own heart. She rushed to my father's side, desperation fueling her movements, as if she could somehow mend the irreparable, rewind time, or at least offer comfort in his final moments. But it was too late. Hope was a fool's errand in this charade.

The life was already fading from his eyes, leaving behind a hollow emptiness that mirrored the void opening up in my own soul. Constantine's eyes, the color of churning storm clouds, turned to her, cold and merciless. There was no recognition, no flicker of humanity, only the insatiable hunger of a predator that had tasted blood and craved more.

In an instant, he was upon her, a blur of unnatural speed. She hadn't enough time to react. Her scream was cut short as his fangs sank into her flesh, ripping and tearing with savage abandon. The sound of her heartbeat, once a comforting rhythm of life, echoed in my ears, growing fainter with every second, a morbid metronome counting down the moments until her demise. It was a sound I'd never forget. A sound that would forever haunt my nightmares.

I knew, logically, that vampires weren't supposed to have a heart. They didn't need a heartbeat as humans did. But the absence of a heartbeat, coupled with her fading tempo, signified the ending of her life on earth. Just like that, the light left her eyes, replaced by the dull, vacant stare of the dead. Her body crumpled to the floor, joining Kat in the gruesome tableau of death.

Micah stood frozen in shock, his youthful face pale with a fear that far exceeded his years. His body trembled, a visible manifestation of the terror consuming him. He was like a deer caught in the headlights, paralyzed by the overwhelming dread of impending doom.

Constantine turned to him, blood dripping from his mouth like a grotesque parody of a child eating jam. The sight was surreal and horrifying. Micah tried to run, his legs moving with desperate, frantic energy, but it was a futile effort. Constantine caught him easily, his un-natural speed making Micah's desperate flight seem like slow motion.

He slammed Micah against the wall with a sickening thud, the force of the impact cracking the plaster. Micah didn't even have time to scream before Constantine's fangs sank into his throat, severing arteries and silencing him forever. His blood painted the walls, a gruesome mural of despair. The coppery scent filled my nostrils, mingling with the other smells of death.

I watched, helpless, as my family was torn apart, their bodies lifeless on the floor, drenched in blood. Each death was a fresh wound, a new layer of agony added to the unbearable weight crushing my soul. I was a prisoner in my own mind, forced to witness the slaughter without the power to intervene. The world seemed to tilt on its axis, reality blurring into a nightmarish landscape where life was cheap and death was a spectator sport.

Constantine turned to me, his eyes burning with a cold, unholy fire. They were the eyes of a predator who had cornered his prey, savoring the moment before the final kill. There was no triumph, no satisfaction—only a chilling emptiness that spoke of a soul devoid of empathy or remorse.

"They're all dead because of you," he hissed, his voice dripping with venom. Each word was a dagger, twisting in the already gaping wounds in my heart. "You're too weak to protect them. You'll never be strong enough."

His words were like a curse, a self-fulfilling prophecy designed to break me, to shatter my spirit, and leave me vulnerable to his power. He wanted to destroy me, not just physically, but emotionally and spiritually. He aimed to strip me of everything I held dear, leaving me a hollow shell, a broken husk of my former self.

I tried to scream, to deny his accusations, to unleash the rage and grief that threatened to consume me, but no sound came. My vocal cords were frozen, paralyzed by fear. I was trapped in a silent scream, a prisoner of my own terror. I attempted to fight, to summon the strength to defend myself, to avenge my family, but my body wouldn't move. My limbs were heavy and unresponsive, as if weighed down by invisible chains. I was a puppet on strings, forced to watch my own destruction.

I was trapped in my own nightmare, a recurring loop of horror, watching my family die over and over again. Each iteration was more agonizing than the last, each a fresh wave of pain washing over me. The faces of my loved ones, contorted in terror and agony, were etched into my memory, haunting me with their silent pleas for help.

I could feel their pain, their fear, their despair, as if they were somehow still connected to me, their spirits trapped in this horrifying purgatory. I wanted to reach out to them, to comfort them, to tell them that everything would be alright, but I was powerless. I was a ghost in my own life, a silent observer of my own tragedy.

This wasn't just about death; it was about the shattering of everything I believed in. The love, the security, the future—all gone, ripped away in a brutal, senseless act of violence. The world I knew, where good triumphed and families stayed together, was a lie. This... this was the truth. Cold, cruel, and unforgiving. I was alone. Utterly, irrevocably alone.

The weight of that realization crashed down on me, threatening to suffocate me. But beneath the despair, a spark flickered. A tiny ember of defiance, refusing to be extinguished. A whisper of resistance against the overwhelming darkness. I might be weak now, broken and battered, but I was not defeated. Not yet. Something inside me refused to surrender, a primal instinct for survival that clawed its way through the layers of grief and fear.

The nightmare wasn't over. Not by a long shot. But somewhere deep inside, a new awakening had begun. A slow, painful process of rebirth, forged in the fires of tragedy. And I knew, with a certainty that defied logic, that I would emerge from this darkness stronger, more determined, and more dangerous than ever before. Constantine had made a grave mistake. He had underestimated me.

Suddenly, I jolted awake, my body drenched in sweat. The clammy feeling clung to my skin, a testament to the horrors my mind had conjured. But the nightmare clung to me like a heavy fog, suffocating and oppressive, my breath coming in ragged gasps. For a moment, I didn't know where I was—whether the nightmare was real or not, if the monstrous figures I saw in my dreams were here with me or merely figments of my tiring mind. The line between waking and sleeping felt dangerously blurred, and I was frightened.

Then I felt it—someone lifting me. A sense of weightlessness washed over me, a strange sensation that cut through the lingering fear of the nightmare.

"Tristan!" Kat's voice, filled with relief, echoed in my ears. The sound was like a beacon in the darkness, a familiar comfort that helped anchor me back to reality. Her voice trembled slightly, revealing the depth of her worry.

I blinked, my vision blurry and unfocused, as I felt strong arms lift me effortlessly off the ground. Micah. Of course, it was Micah. He was carrying me, his once human strength now amplified by the vampire blood I had given him. He moved with a grace and ease that felt foreign, almost unnatural. His muscles were taut and powerful as he held me like I weighed nothing, a stark contrast to the lanky frame he possessed before. The blood had obviously had an effect on him. The vulnerability I always sensed from him had vanished, replaced by a quiet resolve.

With the way Micah was moving and carrying me with such ease and strength, a terrifying thought crossed my mind: *had* I somehow turned him? Had the act of sharing my blood, even in a desperate attempt to save his life, irrevocably changed him? Was I responsible for turning my friend into one of them? It was a thought that made me want to vomit.

A wave of panic threatened to engulf me, but I forced myself to focus, to observe. I searched for any sign of transformation. He didn't have the elongated, sharper canines, nor did he reek of the coppery, metallic scent or the sickly sweet aroma of decay that defined them. No, he didn't smell like a vampire—he was still human. But my blood had definitely given him a massive boost in strength, and his eyes... they almost had a faint glow to them, a subtle luminescence that hadn't been there before.

It was as if the vampire essence within my blood was resonating within him, changing him on a foundational level without dragging him completely into the life I was trying desperately to escape. His eyes had always been a warm chocolate brown, but now they seemed to flicker with an inner light, like embers glowing in the dark.

As I drifted in and out of consciousness, the truth of my own transformation became undeniable to my parents, Kat, and now Micah. My wounds had healed with unnatural speed, but the greatest change was now visible for all to see. As my body healed, my eyes had reverted to their natural state, the colored contacts that had shielded me from scrutiny now discarded. My family finally saw what I truly was—what I was becoming.

My vivid, bright hazel eyes, now laced with swirling silver and gold, and their faint, inner glow made it clear that I was no longer entirely human.

Even though I looked human, my eyes and fangs gave me away. They were the undeniable marks of my altered state, a constant reminder of the darkness lurking within me. My fangs, usually hidden, were now bared, a clear sign of my defensive mood. They had been triggered throughout the fight with the vampire, ready to defend myself if necessary, and they were still present now, when I felt Micah pick me up. My instincts were on high alert, and my body was ready to protect itself.

"I've got him," Micah said, his voice steady and reassuring, though an underlying edge of concern lingered. "Let's get him inside." He shifted my weight slightly, adjusting his grip to ensure I was secure. His touch was gentle despite his newfound strength.

The cold bite of the night air hit my skin, jolting me further awake as I glanced around. The woods loomed around us, dark and endless, their shadows stretching long and menacing, and the fog rolled in to make things scarier. The trees seemed to press in on us, as if the forest itself was alive and watching. I could feel the weight of its ancient presence, a silent witness to everything that had transpired. My family was gathered close, their faces etched with fear and confusion.

They huddled together for comfort and support, their eyes wide with a mixture of concern for me and apprehension about what they had just witnessed. But they followed Micah without question as he carried me back toward the cabin. The small structure offered a promise of safety, a refuge from the terrors of the night.

The scene felt surreal, like a twisted parody of a family picnic. Instead of laughter and games, there was fear and uncertainty. Instead of a warm blanket and hot food, there was cold air, looming trees, and the undeniable truth of my transformation. I was no longer the same person I had been when we arrived at the cabin. I was something else, something more, and I wasn't sure if that was a good thing.

The cabin itself looked smaller and more vulnerable in the darkness, a tiny speck of light against the vastness of the woods. I knew that inside those walls, we would have to confront the new reality that had befallen us.

We would have to deal with the consequences of my transformation, the secrets I had been keeping, and the uncertain and dangerous future that stretched before us. A wave of guilt washed over me.

My family had been drawn into this world of vampires and violence because of me. I had brought the darkness to their doorstep, and I wasn't sure how to protect them from it. This was not their fight, at least not initially. My mind began to drift again, and as Micah continued toward the cabin, I felt a strange mixture of relief and dread. Relief that I was safe for now, that my family was with me, and that Micah was strong enough to protect us. Dread for what was to come.

"Micah…" I whispered, barely able to form words. "How…?"

His gaze, softly illuminating the deepening shadows under the dense foliage of the forest, locked onto mine. He carried the scents of soil and pine, mixed with the fresh sweat from his efforts—all reassuringly human aromas. Yet beneath those familiar notes was a slight metallic hint, the lingering essence of my own blood. Even though he appeared human, bore the scent of a person, and possessed the fluidity of human movement, my blood had undeniably enhanced him. A wave of relief, intertwined with persistent anxiety and uncertainty, flooded through me.

"You saved me, Tristan. That blood you gave me… I don't know what it did, but I feel better than ever." His voice was stronger, more resonant than I remembered it being just hours before. He stood straighter, his shoulders squared, radiating a subtle energy that was new and foreign. He looked healthier. The blood had changed him somehow, amplifying something within him. Guilt twisted in my stomach. Was this a power I should wield so carelessly? A power I even understood?

I nodded weakly, too exhausted to respond. My limbs felt like lead, each one weighted down by an invisible force. Every muscle in my body ached, screaming in protest from the frantic fight, the adrenaline-fueled sprint through the forest, and the strange new power that had surged through me, leaving me weakened. Every breath felt monumental, my lungs burning with the frigid night air. I needed to rest, to understand what was happening to Micah and to me.

As we neared the dilapidated cabin, our temporary sanctuary, a strange flicker of light in the distance caught my eye. It pulsed from deep within the woods, a distant beacon in the oppressive darkness. A fire, undoubtedly, but this was not like any fire I had seen before. It was not the warm, inviting glow of burning wood, but something far more unnatural.

The flames were an eerie shade of green and blue, colors that should never exist in a natural fire, twisting and writhing like living entities. They crackled with an unnatural energy, an almost visible hunger, as they consumed something hidden in the shadows. The trees around the fire seemed to recoil, their branches contorting as though in pain. A faint, acrid smell, like burning metal and something indefinable, tainted the night air.

"What is that?" my father asked, his voice filled with a mix of fear and curiosity. He stopped dead in his tracks, his hand instinctively reaching for the worn axe strapped to his back. He was a hunter, a survivor, and this unnatural fire had ignited his primal instincts.

Micah paused beside me, his grip tightening on my arm. His previously revitalized face now held a stark look of apprehension. "I don't know, but we need to get inside." His voice was urgent, laced with a fear that resonated deep within my own soul. His gaze darted between the unnatural fire and the relative safety of the cabin, weighing our options with lightning-fast calculation.

I knew what it was. I knew what, or rather who, was responsible for that unholy pyre. It was Marcus. He was disposing of what remained of Constantine's men—silencing the remaining hunter vampires who had foolishly followed the zealot's banner. An image of Constantine's burning body, crumbling into nothingness, consumed by those same unearthly flames, flashed vividly in my mind. It wasn't just a dream—it was a vision, a terrifying glimpse into the brutal reality of the vampire world. It was real.

A cold wave of dread washed over me, chilling me to the bone. Marcus was out there, a predator in the night, and that fire was a testament to his ruthless efficiency. He was cleaning house, eliminating any loose ends. He had been hunted for hundreds of years, so I was sure he knew how to ensure his safety—and mine. In the meantime, we needed to reach the cabin, secure our defenses, and prepare for whatever was to come.

The flickering green and blue flames cast long, dancing shadows that stretched and distorted the familiar landscape, turning the woods into a grotesque caricature of itself. The air thrummed with an almost palpable energy and a sense of wrongness that pressed down on us like a physical weight.

My father, ever vigilant, scanned the surrounding trees, his eyes narrowed, his senses on high alert. He knew, instinctively, that something was amiss. He might not understand the nature of the threat, but he felt it—a primal fear that resonated deep within his soul. He tightened his grip on the axe, ready to defend his family at any cost.

Micah, his face pale in the unnatural light, pulled me forward, urging me toward the cabin with renewed urgency. He kept glancing back at the fire, his eyes wide with a mixture of fascination and fear. He had been thrust into a world he didn't understand, a world of vampires and ancient powers, and he was struggling to comprehend the sheer scope of the danger we faced.

The image of Constantine's immolation burned in my mind and spurred me on. We had to reach the cabin. We had to survive. We had to find a way to escape this nightmare.

As we hurried toward the relative safety of the cabin, I couldn't shake the feeling that we were being watched. The woods felt alive, filled with unseen eyes that followed our every move. The unnatural fire crackled and hissed, a malevolent soundtrack to our desperate flight. It was a reminder of the power lurking in the shadows, the power that threatened to consume us all.

The cabin, with its rough-hewn logs and boarded-up windows, seemed like a fortress compared to the darkness that surrounded us. It was a fragile sanctuary, but it was all we had. We burst through the door, slamming it shut behind us and jamming the crude wooden bolt into place. The darkness inside was almost as oppressive as the darkness outside, but it felt safer, somehow.

We huddled together, catching our breath and listening intently for any sound that might betray the presence of danger. The unnatural fire still flickered in the distance, a distant beacon of dread, but for now, we were safe. For now, we were inside the lion's den. But I knew, with chilling certainty, that the lion was still out there, and it was only a matter of time before it came for us. The distant green and blue flames still burned, a promise of death and destruction. We needed to be ready.

Micah carried me through the cabin door, laying me down on the couch. Every inch of my body ached, a deep, bone-weary exhaustion settling in my marrow. It felt like I had been hit by a truck, pulverized and then reassembled with the wrong parts. But at least I was alive. That was something, wasn't it? Alive, when so many others hadn't been so lucky.

The memory of the fight—the snarling faces, the terrifying speed and strength of my attackers—flashed behind my eyes. I could almost feel the phantom pain of claws tearing at my flesh, the sickening crunch of bone against bone.

My family crowded around me, their faces a tapestry woven with concern, confusion, and a primal, gut-wrenching fear. I could practically taste it in the air, the sharp metallic tang of panic. They didn't understand, and how could they? How could they possibly comprehend the nightmare I had just stumbled out of, the transformation that had ripped through me, leaving me... this. This... thing. I glanced down at my hands, turning them over in the dim light of the cabin. They looked the same, didn't they?

The same calluses from chopping wood, the same faint scars from childhood adventures? But no, everything about me was different. My eyes looked insane to a normal person, my skin flawless like a porcelain doll, and beneath the surface, everything had changed too. The blood that flowed through my veins was different now—colder, quicker, laced with something... other.

"Tristan," my mother whispered, kneeling beside me, her hand hovering just above my arm as if afraid to touch me. Her eyes, usually bright and filled with warmth, were now clouded with a desperate, searching gaze. She was looking for the son she knew, the boy who had left this cabin only hours ago, a boy who no longer existed.

He was gone, lost somewhere in the shadows of the night, replaced by something... else. "What's happening? What's going on?" Her voice was a fragile thread. The realization struck me again with brutal force, a cold, hard truth that settled in my gut: no heartbeat. No warmth. Just... emptiness.

I took a deep breath, the air rasping in my throat. My lungs felt tight and constricted, as if they were struggling to perform a function they no longer needed. I forced myself to focus, to find the words, to somehow articulate the impossible truth that clawed at my insides. My mouth was dry, my throat sore, a burning ache that had nothing to do with a cold.

It felt as if I had swallowed a handful of sand, the grit scraping against my raw flesh. But I had to tell them something. They deserved that much, at least. Their love, their unwavering belief in me, deserved an explanation, however inadequate.

"I... I'm not like I was," I began, my voice hoarse and unfamiliar, a gravelly whisper that barely resembled my own. "I'm different now." I swallowed hard, trying to force the words past the lump in my throat. The lie of omission tasted bitter on my tongue, a betrayal of the trust they had always placed in me. But how could I tell them the truth? How could I explain the impossible, the unbelievable, the terrifying reality of my new existence?

The words felt inadequate, pitifully insufficient to describe the seismic shift that had occurred within me. How could I convey the utter alienness of my new reality in such simple terms? It was like trying to explain the vastness of the ocean with a single drop of water or trying to describe the burning heat of the sun to someone who had only ever known darkness. The chasm between who I was and who I had become was vast and unbridgeable, a gulf that separated me from everything I had ever known.

"Different?" My father stepped forward, his presence suddenly looming, casting a long shadow that seemed to press down on me. His brow was furrowed, a deep crease etched between his eyes, and his jaw was tight, clenched with a mixture of worry and suspicion. He was a practical man, a man of action and logic, and this defied all logic. It was beyond his comprehension. This was something that couldn't be solved with an equation.

"What the hell does that mean?" He was a rock, solid and unyielding, but I could see the tremor of fear in his eyes, the subtle shift in his stance that betrayed his inner turmoil. He was trying to stay strong, to be the man he had always been, but the ground beneath his feet was shifting, crumbling into the unknown.

"It means…" I hesitated, the weight of the truth pressing down on me, a crushing burden that threatened to suffocate me outright. I couldn't tell them everything, not yet. The full horror of what I had witnessed, the depravity and the power, the sheer, terrifying reality of the vampire world—they weren't ready for that.

Images flashed through my mind: sleek, beautiful vampires with glinting eyes full of ancient hunger; pale, gaunt vampires with faces twisted in a mask of eternal suffering and bloodlust; the transformation itself, the searing pain, the agonizing struggle, the complete and utter loss of control.

But they deserved some kind of explanation, a glimmer of understanding in the face of this inexplicable change. They deserved to know why I was different, why I was… broken. "It means I'm not human anymore."

The words hung in the air, heavy and suffocating, like a shroud. They were stark and undeniable, a pronouncement of doom that echoed through the silent cabin.

The silence that followed was deafening, a thick, suffocating blanket that muffled all other sounds. The crackling of the fire in the hearth, the gentle sigh of the wind outside, even the frantic buzzing in my own head—all of it seemed to fade into a distant, muted hum. The air itself crackled with tension, with the unspoken fear and disbelief that hung heavy in the room. I could feel their eyes on me, scrutinizing every inch of my being, searching for some sign, some proof that this wasn't real.

My mother's hand trembled visibly as she finally reached out to touch my arm, her fingers brushing against my skin with a hesitant, almost fearful touch. It was as if she was testing me, trying to determine if I was still flesh and blood or if I had become something... else. Her eyes, swimming with unshed tears, were locked on mine, desperately searching for some indication that I was still the son she knew and loved. But the truth was written on my face, etched into my very being, a stark and undeniable reality she couldn't ignore.

"Tristan," she whispered, her voice breaking, a fragile, wounded sound that tore at my insides. "What... what are you saying?" The question was a plea, a desperate attempt to deny the impossible. She wanted me to take it back, to tell her it was a joke, a misunderstanding—anything but the truth. But I couldn't. I couldn't lie to her, not about this.

I looked away, unable to meet her gaze. The guilt was a sharp, piercing pain, a constant reminder of the burden I had placed upon them. How could I do this to them? How could I inflict this upon the people I loved most in the world? They had always been my anchor, my safe harbor in the storms of life. And now, I was threatening to drag them down into the darkness with me. The weight of my actions was almost unbearable, a crushing burden that threatened to break me completely.

"I don't know how to explain it," I admitted, running a hand through my hair, the strands feeling strangely coarse and unfamiliar against my skin. It was as if my very body was betraying me, transforming into something alien and unknown. "But I've changed. I've been... turned." The word hung in the air, a loaded weapon that threatened to explode at any moment. It was a confession, an admission of guilt, a declaration of war.

I could feel their confusion, their desperation to understand. They were grasping for straws, searching for a rational explanation for something that defied all reason. They wanted to believe this was a nightmare, a terrible misunderstanding—anything but the truth. But the truth was relentless, a cold, hard reality that couldn't be denied.

My father's face twisted in confusion and anger. The anger was a shield, a defense mechanism against the fear that threatened to overwhelm him. He needed to understand, to categorize, to control. And this was beyond his control. It was a force of nature, a cataclysmic event that had shattered his world and left him reeling. "Turned? Into what?" The words were clipped, sharp, demanding an answer he didn't want to hear. He was pushing me, forcing me to confront the truth, even though he knew it would break his heart.

I braced myself, knowing this was the point of no return. Once I spoke the word, there would be no going back. The illusion of normalcy would shatter, and the truth, however terrifying, would be laid bare.

"A vampire," I said quietly, the word hanging heavy in the air. It was a confession, a revelation, a truth I had carried hidden for so long, now finally exposed to the light of day—or rather, the dim light of the cabin. The single word felt like a physical weight, settling upon the already tense atmosphere, thickening the air with disbelief and burgeoning fear. It was out now, though. No taking it back.

For a moment, no one spoke. The silence was thick and suffocating. The crackling fire in the hearth seemed to quiet, as if even the flames were holding their breath, waiting. The disbelief on their faces was palpable, a visible shield against the impossible. Shock and fear coursed through them like a tidal wave, threatening to drown them in its icy grip. They couldn't comprehend it—not yet.

Their minds were struggling to reconcile the Tristan they knew—the son, the brother, the friend—with the monstrous label I had just uttered. The idea was too outlandish, too ingrained in the realm of myth and legend to suddenly become a tangible reality standing before them. But they would. They had to. The truth, however unbelievable, was undeniable.

"You're telling us... you're a vampire?" Kat's voice was barely audible, a fragile thread of sound easily lost in the oppressive silence. Her eyes were wide with disbelief, darting between me and the others, as if seeking confirmation that this was some bizarre dream, a shared hallucination. Her complexion paled, her rosy cheeks losing color, replaced by a sickly pallor. She looked like she might faint. The question hung in the air, desperate for an answer yet dreading the confirmation of her worst fears.

I nodded slowly, deliberately. "Yes." The word was a simple affirmation, yet it carried the weight of centuries, the burden of a hidden existence. It was a declaration of my otherness, a line drawn in the sand separating me from the normalcy I had so desperately clung to.

With that single word, I had shattered the illusion, revealing the creature I truly was. My eyes, usually a source of comfort and familiarity, must have seemed alien now, reflecting the truth of my nature. I wondered what they saw when they looked at me—the brother and son they loved or the monster they feared.

My father shook his head, his face a mask of denial. He took a step back, as if I had just told him the most absurd thing in the world. "No. No, that's impossible. You can't be..." His voice trailed off, choked by disbelief. He couldn't bring himself to complete the sentence, the very idea too repugnant to voice aloud.

The thought of his son, his own flesh and blood, being a creature of the night—a being of darkness and legend—was simply too much to bear. He had raised me, cared for me, and taught me right from wrong. How could he reconcile that with the image of a vampire, a monster that preyed on the living? The foundation of his world, his understanding of reality, was crumbling before his very eyes. He appeared on the verge of collapse, his strong frame suddenly looking frail and vulnerable.

"It's true," Micah interrupted, his voice steady and resolute. He stood beside me, a pillar of unexpected support in the face of my family's shock. "I've seen it. I felt it. He saved my life by giving me his blood. I... I don't know how to explain it, but it's real." Micah was human; I was sure of it. His scent lacked the telltale metallic tang of vampire blood, the intoxicating aroma that both repulsed and fascinated me.

But my blood had healed the bite Constantine gave him, and he seemed better than okay—definitely stronger than before—just by the way he carried me in the cabin like I weighed nothing. The experience had clearly left its mark, imbuing him with newfound strength, both physical and emotional. He was no longer the timid shadow of the man I once knew. He was a warrior, standing tall in the face of the impossible, ready to defend the truth.

My father's gaze shifted to Micah, his disbelief softening slightly, replaced by a flicker of cautious curiosity. "What do you mean, his blood saved you?" The question was laced with desperation, a frantic attempt to find some semblance of logic in this chaotic situation. He needed an explanation—some tangible evidence to support the unbelievable claims being thrown at him. Micah's experience, his firsthand account, offered a glimmer of hope, a potential bridge between the world he knew and the terrifying reality unfolding before him.

Micah stood tall, his newly acquired strength and confidence evident in his posture and the slight glow in his eyes, similar to mine. The subtle luminescence was almost imperceptible, a mere hint of the power that now coursed through his veins. Micah was still human, but undeniably enhanced. My blood had amplified his natural abilities, boosting his strength, speed, and resilience.

It was a temporary gift, I suspected—a fleeting glimpse into the world of the enhanced. Whether it would fade with time or leave a permanent mark remained to be seen. "When I was attacked by that... thing—Constantine—I was dying. My blood was everywhere, and my vision was getting blurry," Micah explained, his voice unwavering. "Tristan gave me his blood, and... it healed me. More than that, it made me stronger." He clenched his fist, demonstrating the newfound power surging within him. "I would not be alive if it weren't for Tristan."

My family exchanged bewildered glances, struggling to piece together the impossible reality they were now facing. They were caught in a whirlwind of disbelief, trying to reconcile the evidence before their eyes with the ingrained beliefs of a lifetime. The idea of a vampire, of blood having healing properties, of a human gaining strength from a vampire's blood, was simply too much to process. Their minds raced, searching for any logical explanation, any way to deny the truth staring them in the face.

I sat up slowly, my muscles aching from the exertion of the fight and the strange power that had overtaken me. The transformation was still new to me, the vampiric instincts raw and unfamiliar. I could feel the heightened senses, the increased strength, the primal hunger gnawing at the back of my mind. It was a constant struggle, a battle between my human sensibilities and the bestial urges threatening to consume me. "I don't know what's happening to me," I admitted, my voice barely above a whisper. "But I'm not the same person I was. I swear I'll protect you. I'll keep you all safe."

The words spilled from my mouth with confidence, a desperate attempt to reassure them—and myself—that I was still in control. But deep inside, I wasn't sure how I would protect my family, not from The Council, not from other vampires, and I wasn't certain how vast this whole situation had become.

The weight of responsibility settled heavily upon my shoulders, suffocating. I knew that the path ahead would be fraught with danger, and protecting the ones I loved would require sacrifices I wasn't sure I was ready to make. But I had to try. For them, I had to try.

CHAPTER NINETEEN

THE PLAN

The cabin was dimly lit, a single lantern casting long, flickering shadows on the walls. My family sat in a tight circle, their faces pale and drawn, still reeling from everything I had just told them. My mother's hands were clasped tightly in her lap, her knuckles white. Kat's eyes darted between me and Micah, unable to fully process what was happening. My father sat with his head in his hands, silent and brooding.

Micah, however, stood tall. He was calm, collected, and had a determined glint in his eyes—almost as if he had already begun planning our next steps. He always had a knack for strategy, a talent for seeing the bigger picture even when chaos reigned. It was one of the many reasons I admired him, even envied him, though I would never admit that aloud.

I cleared my throat, breaking the heavy silence. "There's more," I said, my voice low. "You need to understand why we're in danger. Why I'm in danger."

My father looked up, his eyes dark with confusion and anger. "We already understand enough, Tristan. You've been turned into a... a vampire.

That's more than enough for one night." He spat the word "vampire" like it was a curse, a vile taste in his mouth. I couldn't blame him. It was a curse, just not the kind he imagined. He saw the monsters of folklore, the creatures of the night preying on the innocent. He didn't see the beauty, the enhanced senses, the elongated life. Though, admittedly, that beauty came at a steep price.

"I know it's a lot to take in," I replied, keeping my voice steady. "Believe me, I'm not exactly thrilled about it either. But there are things you don't know. Things that could get all of us killed if we're not careful." I paused, gathering my courage. "I got some information from that psychopath Constantine before he was killed. He found me in the city and told me some of the important rules." The memory of Constantine, a whirlwind of manic energy and cryptic warnings, sent a chill down my spine. He was a creature of pure instinct, a survivor, and yet even he had been consumed by the darkness he lived in.

"They don't like it when humans discover that vampires exist, so they find everyone in our family and kill us all," I said calmly, trying to downplay the horror of the situation. I watched their faces, each one registering the information in their own way. My mother's eyes welled with tears, Kat's face paled further, and my father's jaw clenched tight.

Kat shifted in her seat, crossing her arms tightly across her chest. "What are you talking about? How could things get worse than... this?" She gestured toward me, as if my mere existence as a vampire was the worst possible outcome. I couldn't fault her reaction either. Her life had been turned upside down in a single night. I had become something she feared, something she had only read about in stories.

I took a deep breath, choosing my words carefully. "I was turned illegally," I said, watching their reactions closely. I might as well just rip the band-aid off. My father frowned, his brow furrowed in confusion. My mother's face tensed with worry, a network of fine lines appearing at the corners of her eyes. Kat's eyes narrowed in suspicion, as if she were trying to decipher a complex code. "In the vampire world, there's a council—a governing body that controls who can be turned. They maintain order, enforce the rules, and try, in their own twisted way, to keep the peace between vampires and humans." I sighed. "Any vampire created without their permission is hunted down and killed. And not just the vampire—their entire family, their entire bloodline."

The room fell deathly silent. The only sound was the crackling of the fire in the hearth and my own heartbeat, which, of course, they couldn't hear. Oh, the irony.

My mother's voice wavered as she spoke. "What are you saying, Tristan? Are we... are we in danger because of this?" Her voice was barely a whisper, laced with a fear that resonated deep within me. I never wanted to be the source of her pain, the reason for her tears. I had always strived to protect her, to be the son she deserved. And now, I had become her greatest threat.

I nodded slowly. "Yes. If they find out about me, they'll come for all of us." It was a harsh truth, a brutal reality that I couldn't sugarcoat, but they deserved to know the full extent of the danger. They deserved a chance to fight, even if the odds were stacked against us.

My father slammed his fist on the arm of his chair. The wood groaned under the impact, a testament to his barely restrained rage. "So what do we do?" he demanded, his voice thick with anger and fear. "How do we stop them? How do we protect ourselves?" He was a man of action, a provider, a protector. He wouldn't stand idly by while his family was threatened. He would fight, even if it meant facing an enemy he couldn't comprehend.

"That's the problem," I admitted, running a hand through my hair, a nervous habit, a way of releasing the pent-up tension building inside me. "I don't know how to stop them. But there's someone who does. Marcus."

Marcus... Just the name alone made my blood run cold.

"Marcus?" Micah spoke up, his voice thoughtful. "Isn't he... dangerous?"

I nodded grimly. "He is. But he also knows more about the Council than anyone else. He understands their weaknesses, their secrets. If anyone can help us survive this, it's him."

"Who is this Marcus? How do you even know him?" Kat asked suspiciously.

"The vampire who turned me," I said, the bitterness clear in my voice. It tasted like ash in my mouth, a residue of the horror Constantine had revealed and the desperate need to protect my family. The memory of that night, the violation, the agonizing transformation—it clawed at me constantly, a shadow clinging to my every thought. "He's the one who knows what's coming. He knows the rules, the laws, and the dangers. He understands the intricate workings of their society, the power dynamics, the ancient secrets that are now threatening to unravel everything. I need to find him before it's too late. He's the only one who can help us."

Finding Marcus, however, felt like chasing a phantom. He had vanished after my turning, leaving no trace, no clue as to his whereabouts. A deliberate act, no doubt. He was a creature of secrets, shrouded in mystery, and I was now forced to unravel that mystery to save the very people I loved. The thought of him lurking somewhere, observing, perhaps even manipulating events from the shadows, sent a chill down my spine.

"But how do we even find him?" My mother asked, her voice trembling. It was a fragile sound, laced with fear and desperation. I looked at her, at the worry etched on her face, the lines that had deepened in the past few days, and my heart ached. She had always been the anchor of our family, the one who held us together with her unwavering love and strength. Now, she was crumbling under the weight of this unimaginable threat. "We're just... we're just normal people. We can't fight vampires or outrun them. What can we do?"

Her words were a stark reminder of our vulnerability. We were ordinary, unprepared, thrust into a world we never knew existed. How could we possibly stand against beings of immense power, creatures who possessed superhuman strength, speed, and an insatiable hunger?

"We can't sit around and wait to be slaughtered, that's for sure," Micah said, stepping forward. His voice was firm, resolute, a stark contrast to my mother's trembling tone. He glanced at me, and I could see the fire in his eyes—the same fire that had been burning inside me since this nightmare began. It was fueled by a desperate need to protect, to survive, to fight back against the darkness encroaching upon us. "We need a plan."

Micah, ever the level-headed one, the pragmatist. He always had a knack for cutting through the chaos and finding the most logical course of action. His presence was a comfort, a reassurance that even in the face of overwhelming odds, we wouldn't succumb to despair.

I nodded, grateful that at least Micah was thinking ahead. Panic was a luxury we couldn't afford. We needed clarity, strategy, and a willingness to do whatever was necessary to survive. "We need to move deeper into the forest," I said, my voice gaining strength as I spoke. The words felt foreign, alien, coming from my lips, but I knew they were true. Every instinct screamed at me to get them away from here, away from the immediate danger. "We can't stay here—it's too exposed. We need a place where we can hide, where we can prepare. Somewhere we can survive if... if they come for us."

The forest offered a semblance of protection, a natural barrier against the outside world. It was dense, sprawling, and unforgiving, but it also provided cover, concealment, and a fighting chance. We wouldn't be safe, not truly, but we would be harder to find, harder to reach.

"But we're not vampires," Kat interjected. Her voice was sharp, laced with disbelief and a hint of fear. She was younger than Micah and me, a vibrant spirit who thrived on social interaction and the comforts of civilization. The thought of abandoning everything she knew, of living like a fugitive in the wilderness, was clearly terrifying. "We can't live like that—hiding in the woods like animals."

Kat's words were a valid concern. The forest was not a welcoming place, especially for those accustomed to the conveniences of modern life. It was a harsh environment, filled with dangers both real and imagined. Could they adapt? Could they survive?

"You won't be hiding," I assured her. My voice was calm and reassuring, though I wasn't entirely sure I believed the words myself. I had to project confidence to quell their fears, even if it meant glossing over the harsh realities that lay ahead. "We'll make sure you have everything you need: food, water, shelter. You'll be safe. And I'll make sure you have a way to fight back if it comes to that."

Providing for them, protecting them—it was a heavy burden, one I wasn't sure I was capable of carrying. But I had to try. They were my family, my responsibility, and I would do anything, anything, to keep them safe.

My father looked skeptical. His eyes, normally filled with warmth and affection, were now clouded with suspicion and deep-seated unease. He had always been a man of reason, a man who valued logic and order. This situation defied all reason and logic. "And what do you mean by that? Fight back how?"

His question hung in the air, heavy with unspoken concerns. We were outmatched, outgunned, and outmaneuvered. How could ordinary humans possibly hope to defend themselves against creatures like the ones we were facing?

I hesitated, glancing at Micah before answering. His gaze met mine, and I saw a flicker of understanding in his eyes. He knew what I was about to say, knew the weight of the decision I was contemplating. "I've been thinking," I said slowly, "about turning you. All of you."

The silence that followed was deafening. The shock on their faces was immediate and palpable. Their expressions ranged from disbelief to horror, a mixture of emotions swirling in their eyes. I had just shattered their world, presenting them with a choice that was both terrifying and unthinkable.

My mother gasped, her hand flying to her mouth. My father's face paled, his eyes widening in disbelief. Kat stared at me, her mouth agape, as if I had just sprouted fangs and claws. Micah, however, remained stoic, his expression unreadable.

Turning them. It was a desperate measure, a last resort, but it was also the only way I could see to truly protect them. As a vampire, I possessed abilities they could only dream of. I could shield them, defend them, and give them the strength to fight back against the creatures that sought to destroy us.

But the price... the price was immense. It meant condemning them to a life of darkness, a life of constant hunger, a life forever bound to the shadows. It meant transforming them into creatures they could never have imagined, beings who were both powerful and cursed.

The animal blood that sustains me keeps my appearance of flawless skin and swirling silver and gold eyes intact; the hazel in my eyes wouldn't change. It wasn't really drinking blood that made you look like a monster; it was the human blood, the craving for it that changed you, the desire for it that rotted you from the inside out.

I knew turning them would change their lives forever, and maybe not for the better, but I also knew that I would do everything I could to help them navigate that new life. I would teach them how to control their hunger, how to harness their newfound abilities, and how to protect themselves from the dangers that lurked in the shadows.

The Council wouldn't like this; they would probably hunt me down and kill me for it, but I didn't care. It was my life or theirs, and I chose theirs.

The only one who had given me any information about the world I had stepped into was burned to ash. Constantine mentioned that the vampire Council had very strict rules regarding the turning of humans. They believed it was a violation of their sacred laws, an act of arrogance that threatened their very existence. They feared that a proliferation of vampires would lead to chaos and exposure, ultimately jeopardizing their carefully maintained secrecy. If any human knew of our existence, they would send a whole squad to kill both the human and their family.

To them, humans were nothing more than a food source, a means to an end. They were not to be respected, not to be trusted, and certainly not to be elevated to their level.

But I didn't care about their rules, their laws, or their twisted sense of morality. They could hunt me down; they could punish me, but I would not stand idly by while my family was slaughtered. I would do whatever it took to protect them, even if it meant defying the very beings that had given me this cursed existence.

The information that Constantine had given me flooded my mind. I was so confused by it all, and I didn't know what to do. I just hoped I could do something right.

For now, we had to focus on survival, on protecting ourselves from the immediate threat that loomed over us. We had to move deeper into the forest, find a safe haven, and prepare for the coming storm.

As I looked at my family, at the fear and uncertainty in their eyes, I knew that the journey ahead would be long and arduous.

"Turn us?" my mother gasped, her hand flying to her mouth, her beautiful eyes wide with disbelief and fear. "You mean... turn us into vampires?" The idea was ludicrous, a nightmare I hadn't even dared to imagine. Her world, already turned upside down by the revelation of my true nature and the existence of a hidden society of blood-drinkers, was now threatening to shatter completely.

"I don't want to do it," I quickly added, raising my hands in a placating gesture. The thought of turning my parents, forcing them into the same existence I led, filled me with a strange mix of guilt and terror. Turning them into vampires was risky, so I wouldn't do it now—at least not yet. And come to think of it, I didn't know how it all worked; Marcus turned me, so I would have to find him. After the fight, Marcus was gone. I thought he would stay after saving my life, but he left, leaving me with another puzzle to solve.

The process itself was a mystery, a dark art only Marcus seemed to truly understand. I remembered the burning pain, the agonizing transformation, the loss of innocence, and the surge of power that followed. To inflict that on my own parents, even to save them, felt like a betrayal. "Not unless I have no other choice. But if it comes down to it—if it's the only way to save you—I'll do it. I won't let you die." My eyes narrowed with determination.

My father stood abruptly, pacing the room in frustration. His tall frame was rigid, his hands clenched into fists. The idea of becoming a vampire was abhorrent to him, a violation of everything he believed in. He was a man of science, of reason, and the thought of embracing the supernatural, of becoming one of the creatures he'd only read about in books, filled him with dread. "We're not having this conversation," he said firmly, his voice rising, vibrating with an undercurrent of anger. "I will not let you turn us into monsters."

"It's not about becoming monsters," Micah interjected, stepping in front of our father, his voice calm and measured. He had always been the level-headed one, the mediator, the voice of reason. Now, he was using that ability to try and bridge the widening gap between my father's fear and the desperate reality we faced. "It's about survival. Look at me, Dad. Tristan's blood saved me. I was on the brink of death, and now I'm stronger than I've ever been. We need to be thinking ahead." He gestured to himself, flexing his bicep slightly. The effects of my blood were still evident in his improved health and energy levels—a tangible example of the power we were discussing.

"But you're not a vampire," my mother said, her eyes wide, fixated on Micah. "You're still... you're still human." She clung to that fact, the last vestige of normalcy in a world gone mad. I confirmed Micah was human by sniffing the air, catching his human scent and agreeing with Mom. "He still has my blood in him, but I'm not sure how long that will last. For now, he's alive," I said.

"For now," Micah admitted, his voice calm. "But Tristan's blood gave me a taste of what he's going through. I felt the power, the strength. And I'm telling you, we need to be prepared. We need options." He understood the danger better than anyone, having glimpsed the potential that lay within the blood of a vampire. He knew that if the Council found us, we would be defenseless.

My father stopped pacing, turning to Micah, his expression softening slightly. He saw the sincerity in Micah's eyes, the genuine concern for our safety. But the fear remained, a deep-seated dread of the unknown. "So what do you suggest we do? Just sit here and wait for these... these vampire

Council people to come for us?" His voice dripped with sarcasm, but beneath the surface, there was a genuine plea for guidance.

"No," Micah said, his voice steady. "We need a place where we can survive. I've been thinking about it. We need to disappear, fake our deaths or something, get off-grid deep in the forest, somewhere hard to find, and lay low until things cool off." He had been mulling over the options ever since he witnessed the fight, his mind searching for a solution that would keep us safe. He knew that staying here was not an option; we were sitting ducks waiting to be found.

"And what? ... farm?" my father said sarcastically. The idea of abandoning civilization and scratching out a living in the wilderness seemed absurd to him. He was a doctor, a man of science and technology, not a frontiersman.

"Yeah," Micah responded with enthusiasm. "We will need food, and Tristan can hunt meat for us. Easy." Micah saw it as an adventure, a challenge. A new beginning away from the city. He looked at Tristan, his eyes hopeful, knowing Tristan could handle himself.

"And what about me?" my mother asked, her voice small and uncertain. "I can't just... go live in the woods." She was a city woman, accustomed to comfort and convenience, and the thought of roughing it in the wilderness filled her with anxiety.

"We'll make it work," Micah said, stepping toward her and taking her hand. "We'll build a cabin, plant a garden, learn to hunt and fish. We'll do it together, as a family." His voice was filled with reassurance, but even he knew it wouldn't be easy.

I remained silent, listening to their exchange, my mind racing. The idea of running, of hiding in the forest, was appealing. It was a way to escape the Council and protect my family. But it was also a daunting prospect. I was a hunter, not a farmer. I knew how to survive in the wild as a vampire, but I had no idea how to build a home or grow food. The closest thing I had to a home was the little hideout I created when I first disappeared into the woods. Besides, the forest didn't feel safe anymore. Something was out there, something that made the hair on the back of my neck stand on end.

"We need to be careful," I said, my voice steady but laced with urgency. "We need to prepare. If we're going to venture into the forest, we must be ready for anything." The thought of the Council finding us again sent a chill down my spine, an unease that settled like a stone in my gut. Learning to navigate this new life as a vampire was already proving to be a monumental challenge; as if that weren't enough, the constant battle against my primal instincts weighed heavily on me.

Each day was an exercise in restraint, a relentless struggle to control the insatiable thirst that gnawed at my insides. I had managed to keep it at bay by feeding on animals, but the tantalizing pull of human blood was always there, lurking just beneath the surface—a dark temptation threatening to consume me whole.

"We need to gather supplies," Micah interjected, his voice cutting through the fog of my thoughts like a blade. "Food, water, weapons—anything we can use to defend ourselves against whatever might be lurking out there."

"I can hunt," I offered, a flicker of confidence igniting within me. "I can provide meat for us."

"We'll also need to learn how to build a shelter," my father chimed in, his mind already shifting into problem-solving mode, calculating the logistics of our survival. "And we need to find clean water. We can't risk drinking from just anywhere."

"We'll figure it out," Micah replied, his voice filled with unwavering determination. "We always do."

As I looked at my family, their faces weary but resolute, a wave of fierce protectiveness washed over me. They were scared, yes, but they were also willing to fight, to stand against the darkness of our reality. They were ready to do whatever it took to survive and protect each other, and in that moment, I knew I would do the same. Together, we would forge a path through the unknown, our bond the light guiding us through the shadows of the forest.

My father was silent for a long moment, his eyes shifting between me and Micah. The flickering candlelight danced across his weathered face, highlighting the deep lines etched by years of hard work and worry. He looked older than I remembered, the weight of our current predicament seemingly aging him overnight. Finally, he sighed heavily, the sound a weary expulsion of all the hopes and dreams he'd held for his family. He ran a hand through his graying hair, the gesture conveying a sense of utter defeat. "I never imagined my life would come to this," he muttered, his voice barely above a whisper. "Hiding in the woods from vampires... creatures I thought were mere legends. And now raising a farm... and probably a blood farm too... for my son... who's a vampire."

The words hung in the air, thick with disbelief and a profound sense of disappointment. It wasn't just the danger we faced, but the complete upheaval of everything he had believed in. He had always been a practical man, a man of the earth, grounded in reality. Vampires, blood farms, secret societies—these were the stuff of nightmares, not the reality he had built his life upon.

"I never imagined it either," I admitted, my voice low and laced with regret. I knew how difficult this was for him, for all of them. The path I had chosen—or rather, the path that had been thrust upon me—had dragged them all into a world of shadows and secrets. "But this is the reality we're living in now. We have to adapt if we want to survive."

My mother looked at me, her eyes filled with tears. They weren't tears of fear, I realized, but of heartbreak. Heartbreak for the life we had lost, for the innocence that had been stolen from us. "Tristan..." she said softly, her voice trembling. "Are you sure about this? Are you sure this is the only way?"

Her question was a plea, a desperate hope that I would offer an alternative, a way out of this nightmare. I wished I could give her that hope, but I couldn't lie. The truth was harsh, but it was the only thing I had to offer.

I nodded, feeling the weight of my decision settling in my chest like a leaden stone. "I don't know if it's the only way, but it's the best chance we have. And I'm not turning any of you unless there's no other choice." The thought of turning them, of forcing them to embrace this existence, was a constant source of torment. I would protect them, yes, but at what cost? To steal their humanity would be a betrayal beyond measure. I would only do it as a last resort, when all other options were exhausted.

Kat, ever the pragmatist, cut through the emotional undercurrent with a practical question. "And Marcus?" she asked quietly. "Do you think he'll help us?"

"I hope so," I replied, my voice thick with uncertainty. "But he's not easy to find. I don't even know where to start looking. But I have to try." He was our best hope for understanding the intricacies of the vampire world, for navigating the treacherous political landscape of the Council. We needed his guidance, his expertise. But first, we had to find him. The last time I saw him, flashes of his dark red eyes filled my memory. I could never forget those eyes because they were the eyes of a monster, and I just didn't know if he could be trusted.

Micah, ever the steady presence, stepped forward, placing a hand on my shoulder. His touch was grounding, a reminder that I wasn't alone in this. "We'll find him, Tristan. We'll figure this out. But in the meantime, let's focus on building this place. We need to make sure we're ready for whatever comes next."

He was right. We couldn't afford to be consumed by the uncertainty of the future. We had to focus on the present, on building a sanctuary—a fortress against the storm that was brewing. We needed to prepare for the inevitable confrontation with the Council, with the hunters, and with whatever else the vampire world decided to throw our way.

I watched as my family began to gather supplies, their movements purposeful despite the fear etched on their faces. The weight of our situation pressed down on me, but there was another sensation growing stronger by the minute—a gnawing emptiness that clawed at my insides.

The hunger was back, sharper and more demanding than before. I'd expended too much energy fighting Constantine, and now my body was demanding replenishment. My gums ached where my fangs wanted to descend, and I could feel my control slipping.

"I need to check the perimeter," I announced, my voice strained. "Make sure Constantine's men are really gone."

Dad looked up from where he was inventorying our supplies. "Is that safe? What if there are more of them out there?"

"I'll be careful," I promised. "And I... I need to feed. I used up a lot of energy in that fight."

The word "feed" hung in the air between us. My family froze, the reality of what I was hitting them anew.

"Oh," Mom said softly, her hand rising to her throat unconsciously.

"Not people," I clarified quickly. "Animals. Deer. It's how I've been surviving."

Kat gave me a tight nod. "Go. We'll be okay for a little while."

"Lock the doors behind me," I instructed, already moving toward the exit. "Don't open them for anyone but me."

The cool night air hit my face as I stepped outside, and I took a deep breath, filling my lungs with the scents of the forest. Under normal circumstances, I could pick up the trail of a deer from half a mile away, but now, weakened as I was, my senses felt dulled, muffled.

I moved through the trees, slower than my usual vampire speed. My limbs felt heavy, my reactions sluggish. The fight with Constantine had drained me more than I realized. I stumbled over a root that I would normally have sensed and avoided with ease.

I needed blood. Soon.

I pushed myself deeper into the forest, straining my senses. Finally, I caught it—the warm, earthy scent of a deer, its heartbeat a distant rhythm in my ears. I changed direction, moving toward it with single-minded focus.

The deer was grazing in a small clearing, its head bent to the ground, oblivious to the predator approaching. In my weakened state, I had to be more careful, more deliberate. I couldn't rely on sheer speed to catch my prey.

I crept closer, using the trees for cover. The deer's head snapped up, ears twitching, sensing danger. Before it could bolt, I launched myself forward, tackling it to the ground. We tumbled together, the deer struggling beneath me, but even in my weakened state, I was stronger.

I sank my fangs into its neck, and the warm blood flooded my mouth. The effect was immediate—a rush of energy flowing through me, filling the empty spaces, replenishing what I'd lost. But then something changed.

As I continued to drink, a new sensation washed over me. The air around me seemed to crackle with energy, like static electricity before a storm. Power surged through my veins, more intense than anything I'd experienced before. This wasn't just replenishment—this was something else entirely.

I pulled back, gasping, before I could drain the deer completely. The animal staggered to its feet and bounded away into the darkness.

I remained kneeling on the forest floor, trying to process what was happening to me. My skin buzzed with energy, my muscles felt coiled and ready to spring. I felt stronger than I ever had since my transformation—stronger, faster, more alive.

Testing my new strength, I leaped straight up, soaring higher than ever before, clearing the tops of the smaller trees. When I landed, the ground seemed to vibrate beneath my feet. I ran, and the forest blurred around me, my speed unprecedented.

What was happening to me? Was this normal for vampires after a significant fight? Or was there something special about this particular deer, this particular night?

I didn't have answers, only questions and this strange, buzzing energy coursing through my body. Whatever it was, I knew I needed to get back to my family.

I raced back toward the cabin, covering ground at an incredible pace, the trees nothing but smudges in my peripheral vision. The cabin came into view, and I slowed, not wanting to alarm my family with this strange new development.

I looked at my family, seeing the fear and uncertainty in their eyes, but also the glimmer of hope. They were scared—rightfully so—but they were willing to trust me. To follow me. It was a responsibility that weighed heavily on my shoulders, a burden I would carry until my last breath. Their faith in me was a precious gift, a source of strength in the face of overwhelming odds. I couldn't and I wouldn't let them down.

"All right," my father said at last, his voice heavy with resignation. The fight had gone out of him, replaced by a weary acceptance of our new reality. "We'll build this safe haven, or whatever. We'll make it work. But you need to promise me, Tristan—no matter what happens, you won't turn us unless there's no other way."

His words were a plea, a desperate attempt to hold onto the last vestiges of his humanity. He was willing to face danger, to endure hardship, but he didn't want to become one of them. He didn't want to lose himself, to become a creature of the night.

"I promise," I said, my voice firm. It was a sacred vow, a commitment I would uphold at all costs.

Micah gave me a nod, already moving toward the door. He was eager to get started, to channel his energy into something productive. "Let's get started then," he said. "We've got a lot of work to do."

As Micah led the way outside, I followed, my mind racing with everything that had just happened. My family was still in disbelief, still struggling to come to terms with the impossible. But they were with me. They trusted me. And that trust was the only thing that kept me going.

And now, more than ever, I knew I couldn't let them down. Their lives, their safety, their very existence depended on me. I would protect them, guide them, and lead them through this darkness.

We had to survive. We had to be ready. Because I knew—deep down—that this was only the beginning. The vampire world was vast and complex, filled with ancient secrets and hidden dangers. We had only scratched the surface, and I knew that the road ahead would be long and arduous. But we would face it together, as a family.

Chapter Twenty

NO WAY OUT

The trees closed in around us, gnarled branches twisting like skeletal fingers. The forest felt alive, its shadows whispering warnings. Each step grew heavier, laden with unspoken anxieties.

"You look... different," Mom said, her voice barely above a whisper. She glanced at me, then quickly away, her eyes darting nervously between me and the road ahead.

"Different how?" I asked, already knowing the answer. I could feel it in the way they looked at me—a mixture of fascination and fear.

"Sharper," Kat offered, her gaze lingering on my face. "Like a statue... carved from moonlight."

"It's the eyes, isn't it?" I ran a hand through my hair, the gesture feeling strange and unfamiliar.

Kat nodded slowly. "They're... brighter. And your skin..." She trailed off, reaching out a tentative hand as if to touch my cheek, then pulling it back. "It's... flawless."

"Flawless?" A bitter laugh escaped my lips. "It's the skin of a corpse, Kat. Beautiful on the outside, dead on the inside."

"Don't say that, Tris." Micah's voice was low, a rumble of warning. His hand rested on the small of her back, a protective gesture. "We'll figure this out. We'll get through this."

"Will we?" I stopped, turning to face them. The forest pressed in around us, a silent, watchful audience. "I've killed, Micah. I've tasted blood, and I liked it."

My mother gasped, her hand flying to her mouth. Kat's eyes widened, reflecting the moonlight filtering through the trees.

"It's not... you," she stammered. "It's... the monster."

"Is it?" I challenged, the question hanging heavy in the air. I looked at my hands, flexing my fingers, feeling the unnatural strength pulsing beneath my skin. "Or is the monster... me?"

Micah stepped forward, placing a hand on my shoulder. His grip was firm, grounding. "You're still Tristan. The man I know. The brother I respect. We'll fight this together."

"He's right," Kat added, her voice gaining newfound strength. "You're still our Tris. Just... a little... sharper." A faint smile touched her lips, a flicker of the Kat I knew and loved.

I wanted to believe them. I needed to believe them. But the darkness inside me stirred, a cold, hungry shadow lurking just beneath the surface.

I managed a weak smile. "I feel sharper too," I admitted, flexing my hand, marveling at the strength now residing within me. "Everything is... intensified."

Dad grunted, his eyes fixed on the road. "Intensified good or intensified bad?"

"Both," I replied honestly. "The world is... brighter. Louder. But the hunger..." I trailed off, not wanting to dwell on the gnawing emptiness that constantly pulsed within me.

"We need to keep a low profile for a bit." Micah said, his tone steady yet resolute.

"Lay low?" Mom's voice was sharp, laced with panic. "How? They'll find us. They'll..." She trailed off, unable to articulate the horrors her mind conjured.

"Not if we're smart," Micah reassured her, squeezing her hand. He looked at me, his gaze steady. "Tristan, what do you know about this... Council?"

I hesitated, feeling the weight of their fear pressing down on me like a thick fog. "I only know bits and pieces," I said, my voice shaky. "Constantine mentioned the Council. I think they're supposed to be the governing body of the vampire world."

My stomach twisted as I recalled Constantine's final words, his icy smirk haunting me.

"And I think Marcus turning me was illegal," I admitted, each word heavy with doubt. The faces around me mirrored my uncertainty—Mom's eyes wide with terror, Kat biting her lip as if she could will my thoughts to settle.

Micah furrowed his brow, his grip tightening on my shoulder. "What do you mean? Why would it be illegal?"

"I'm not sure," I continued, my pulse racing. "He didn't give me all the details. Just that... something was broken in the process." My mind churned, trying to piece together fragments of a conversation lost in the chaos. "Why does that matter?" Mom's voice trembled, her worry suffocating.

"It matters because if Marcus broke their rules..." My throat constricted at the thought. "They might come after us."

Kat shivered at my words, glancing toward the darkening woods surrounding us, as if unseen threats might spring to life.

"Illegal?" Kat asked, eyes wide.

"Yeah, and it means I'm a target," I explained, my voice flat. "And now... so are you."

"Because of you?" Dad's voice was rough, edged with accusation. He stopped, turning to face me, his eyes blazing. "You've put us all in danger."

"I know," I admitted, shame burning in my chest. "And I'll do everything I can to protect you. That's why we need to hide. Deep in the forest."

"The forest?" Mom's voice was barely a whisper. "But... there's nothing out there. No food. No shelter."

"We'll manage," Micah said, his voice unwavering. "We'll build a shelter. We'll hunt." He looked at me, a flicker of understanding passing between us. "We'll adapt."

"Adapt?" Kat echoed, her brow furrowed. "Adapt to what? Living like... animals?"

"Living like survivors," Micah corrected, his voice hardening. "We have to. It's our only chance."

A heavy silence fell over us, broken only by the rustling of leaves and the distant hoot of an owl. The forest seemed to hold its breath, waiting for our decision.

"What about... turning?" Kat asked, her voice barely audible. She glanced at me, her eyes filled with a strange mixture of fear and... hope?

"No," I said firmly, cutting her off before she could finish the thought. "I won't do that to you. Not unless... it's absolutely necessary."

Micah nodded, his expression grim. "We'll train. We'll learn to defend ourselves. We'll become... stronger." He looked at each of us in turn, his gaze unwavering.

We stood there for a moment longer, the forest closing in around us, a silent promise of both danger and sanctuary.

"And Constantine," Kat added, a shiver running through her. The name hung in the air like a noxious cloud, thick with memories of his brutal attack. I could still see the way he moved—swift, calculating, his eyes cold as ice. My stomach twisted at the thought of that moment when Micah fell, blood spilling across the floor.

I glanced at my sister, her face pale and drawn. "I know," I said softly, trying to keep my voice steady. The image of Micah's fading life haunted me. "We have to be ready for them."

The memory rushed back, uninvited but insistent—the power surge that erupted within me during that fight. I had felt it rising up like a tidal wave, an energy so intense it threatened to consume me. In that instant of desperation, I'd pushed Constantine back with a force I didn't fully understand, sending him crashing into a tree as if he were nothing more than a toy.

How had I done that? It felt so foreign yet exhilarating. What did it mean for me? For us?

Micah had been on the brink of death, and somehow, despite everything swirling around us in chaos and fear, I found strength within myself to protect him. That was when Marcus appeared with that glimmering silver blade—the very weapon that pierced Constantine's heart.

A shudder coursed through me as I remembered how Constantine had erupted into flames almost instantly after Marcus struck. The sight burned itself into my mind—a vivid reminder of how powerful the vampire world truly was and how precarious our situation remained.

"Tris?" Kat's voice pulled me back from my thoughts.

"Yeah?" I forced my attention back to her.

"You need to stay focused," she urged, her eyes searching mine for assurance—or perhaps something more desperate.

I nodded slowly but couldn't shake the fear tightening in my chest.

"I wish we could just forget all this," she said quietly.

"Me too." But the truth hung between us like an unwelcome guest. Forgetting wasn't an option; not anymore.

With a heavy heart and determination steeling within me, I met their gazes—Mom's wide with worry, Kat's fierce with resolve—and braced myself for what lay ahead.

"We'll be ready for them," I said, my voice laced with newfound steel. I had been prey for too long.

I nodded, my gaze drifting out the window. The city lights grew closer, a beacon in the encroaching darkness. It was a world I no longer fully belonged to, a world that both repelled and attracted me. It was a world I had to protect. For my family. For myself.

"Let's move," Micah urged, his voice firm as he slid into the driver's seat. I could see the tension in his shoulders, the way his hands gripped the wheel like it was a lifeline.

Kat climbed in next, her eyes darting around as if expecting shadows to leap from the trees at any moment. "We're really doing this?" she whispered, half to herself.

"Yeah," I said, forcing a calmness I didn't feel. "We are."

Mom settled into the backseat beside Kat, her fingers trembling as she fidgeted with her necklace. She cast a quick glance toward me before looking out the window again. The fear radiating from her tightened my chest, but there was also resolve simmering beneath it—a shared understanding that we were stepping into the unknown together.

Micah turned on the ignition, and the car roared to life with an eager growl. He glanced back at us through the rearview mirror, eyes steady but intense. "Keep your heads up. If anything feels off—"

"It will feel off," Kat interjected sharply, biting her lip.

I took a deep breath and squared my shoulders. "We'll be ready." The words felt heavier than I intended; they carried all our hopes and fears.

The city unfolded before us like an old friend turned stranger—familiar yet foreign under my new reality. Neon lights flickered in stark contrast against the darkening sky, illuminating faces that seemed blissfully unaware of what lurked just beneath their surface.

As we drove deeper into its heart, memories of laughter and late-night escapades clashed with the grim knowledge of what I had become. My fingers drummed nervously on my thigh, each beat echoing with uncertainty.

Mom's voice broke through my thoughts as she pointed ahead at an intersection lined with familiar cafes and shops.

"Tris," she said softly, "do you think we'll be safe?"

"I don't know," I replied honestly, feeling the weight of that admission settle heavily in the car's atmosphere.

The plan was simple—brutally so: gather the few remaining necessities, the meager remnants of our former lives, and then disappear deep into the woods, far beyond the reach of the Council and their grasping claws. Yet, the thought of such a drastic, permanent change filled me with a tumult of emotions, both exciting and terrifying.

The thrill of freedom, of finally escaping their suffocating control, warred furiously within me against the gut-wrenching fear of abandoning everything I had ever known. We were on the precipice of severing ties with the life we had grown accustomed to, stepping into the shadows to escape the looming threat that had cast a long, dark pall over our existence—a threat that had poisoned every moment and every breath we took, leaving an indelible mark on our souls. The stakes had never been higher, and with each step further from familiarity, I felt the weight of that choice pressing down on me like a relentless storm.

"Alright, here's the plan," Micah announced, his voice cutting through the quiet hum of the engine. He glanced at me in the rearview mirror, his eyes sharp and focused. "We split up."

"Split up?" Mom's voice was laced with alarm. "But... I thought we were staying together."

"We will," Micah reassured her, "but we can cover more ground this way. We'll meet back up at the fair near Pine Barrens. It's out of the way and should be deserted this time of year. From there, we head south to the Pine Barrens."

"The Pine Barrens?" Dad's voice was gruff. "That place is creepy as hell. Jersey Devil and all that."

I shifted in my seat, the mention of the creature stirring unsettling memories of childhood tales and shadowy figures lurking in the woods. I could almost smell the damp earth and pine needles, feel the chill of the forest air on my skin. "It's also the perfect place to disappear," I said, my voice low. "Miles of forest. No one will find us there."

"So, how do we split up?" Kat asked, her voice tight with apprehension.

"I'll go solo," Micah stated, his gaze fixed on the road ahead. "There's a military surplus store I know about, a few hours north. I need to stock up on... supplies."

"Supplies?" Mom's voice was barely a whisper. "What kind of supplies?"

Micah hesitated, his jaw tightening. "The kind that will keep us safe," he said finally, his voice clipped. "We're not dealing with... normal threats anymore."

A heavy silence settled in the car, the unspoken truth hanging in the air like a shroud. We were no longer just a family; we were fugitives, hunted by creatures we barely understood.

"You sure about this, Micah?" I asked, my voice laced with concern. "Going alone is risky."

He met my gaze in the rearview mirror, his eyes unwavering. "I'll be fine. I know what I'm doing. Mom and Dad, get the truck. Meet me at the Jersey Fair. Sunrise. Don't be late."

"What about... me?" Kat asked, her voice small.

"You're with me," I said, placing a reassuring hand on her arm. "We'll stick together."

She nodded, a flicker of gratitude in her eyes. But beneath it, I saw the fear—the same fear that gnawed at me, a constant reminder of the danger lurking just around the corner.

The fierce protectiveness I felt for my family surged, pushing back the tide of fear and uncertainty. We had to move fast. The Council wouldn't hesitate.

"Kat, we need to pack light. Essentials only," I said, turning to my sister. Her eyes, wide with a mixture of fear and resolve, met mine. She nodded, her lips pressed into a thin line.

"I'll get Mom and Dad started," she murmured, her voice barely above a whisper.

"Micah, what about weapons?" I asked, my gaze shifting to my brother-in-law. He was scanning the perimeter of the clearing, his military training kicking in.

The car rumbled to a stop in front of my parents' house, the familiar creak of the old wood sending a wave of nostalgia crashing over me. I caught a glimpse of my childhood—endless summers spent playing in the backyard, laughter ringing through the air—and now, here we were, standing on the precipice of an unknown future.

"Alright," Micah said, his voice low and steady as he climbed out. "We need to split up quickly. Mom and Dad, you'll take your truck."

Mom's eyes flickered with uncertainty. "Are you sure we should go out? What if they see us?"

Dad nodded resolutely. "We have to do this. We need cash and supplies to last us a while—food, tools... anything that can help us start over."

"Seeds too," Micah added. "Farming equipment will give us a fighting chance."

Kat glanced at me, her expression torn between fear and determination. I squeezed her hand for reassurance before we moved toward the back of the truck.

"Micah," I said, urgency creeping into my voice. "You know where to get weapons?"

"I've got a military surplus store in mind," he replied. "I'll grab guns, traps, anything high-tech for security." He paused, scanning our surroundings as if expecting shadows to leap from the trees. "Solar panels too—anything that can keep us off-grid."

I nodded, feeling the weight of responsibility settle on my shoulders again.

"Kat and I will handle the money and passports," I said, glancing at my sister. "We can swing by Benji's place and Jessica's on the way." The two of them would help without realizing how dire our situation truly was.

"Be careful," Mom said softly as she stepped toward us, her gaze filled with motherly worry.

"We will," Kat assured her. I felt her tension mirroring my own.

As their truck pulled away, I turned to Kat. "Let's move."

She nodded resolutely. We walked toward Mom's car parked in the garage—its familiar contours somehow both comforting and ominous now. I needed the keys, which were inside the house.

The front door creaks open as I step inside, Kat right behind me. Our childhood home greets us with the familiar scent of pine cleaner and cinnamon—Mom's signature combination that always meant home. Now it feels like we're trespassing in a museum of our former lives.

"Keys should be in the bowl by the door," I say, my voice unnaturally loud in the quiet house.

Kat runs her fingers along the wall, tracing the height markers where Mom and Dad had measured us every birthday. "Remember when you hit six feet and Dad acted like you'd just won the Olympics?"

I smile despite everything. "Yeah, and you were so mad because you stopped growing at five-four."

The living room sits frozen in time—Dad's recliner with the worn armrests, Mom's quilting project draped over the couch. Family photos line the mantel, capturing versions of us that no longer exist. I pause at one—Kat's high school graduation. My arm is slung around her shoulders, both of us grinning without a care in the world.

Mom steps into the living room, a worried expression on her face. "Have you found the keys yet?" she asks, her voice laced with anxiety.

"Not yet," I reply, turning to the kitchen.

Micah, standing close behind her, scans our surroundings with a soldier's vigilance. "Make it quick. We need to stay ahead of the Council."

Kat bites her lip, glancing at our mom and dad. "We're never coming back here, are we?" she whispers, her voice catching.

I can't bring myself to lie to her. "I don't know."

Dad's voice comes from the hallway, steady and firm. "We have to focus on what's important right now. Make sure to grab what you need for the journey."

Kat nods, swallowing hard. "I'll grab some photos. They should fit in my bag."

While she collects pieces of our past, I head to the kitchen. The bowl sits on the counter, a jumble of keys inside. I dig through them, finding Mom's car key with the worn rabbit's foot keychain she's had since college.

"Got it," I call out, then pause at the refrigerator. Magnets hold up crayon drawings from when we were kids, grocery lists in Mom's neat handwriting, a reminder for Dad's doctor appointment next week.

Kat appears in the doorway, her backpack bulging. "I took the important ones."

As she moves closer, I catch a flicker of tears she's trying to hide. I pretend not to see them, focusing instead on the task at hand. I jingle the keys. "Ready?"

She takes one last look around, her eyes lingering on the kitchen table where we'd eaten thousands of family dinners. "No. But we have to go anyway."

We step outside, locking the door behind us—a futile gesture of normalcy in a world that's anything but normal now.

"What's our story?" she asked as we climbed in.

"We'll say we're visiting friends out of town for a few weeks—something like that." My mind raced through possible scenarios as I gripped the steering wheel tightly.

"And what about Benji and Jessica?" Kat pressed.

"They can believe it's simply a pleasant drive to get some fresh air," I responded with a wave of my hand. We could rely on them; they would support us no matter what was hidden behind our shared grins.

We backed out of the driveway, the tires crunching on the gravel, and headed toward the city. The familiar streets blurred past, each landmark a reminder of a life that felt a million miles away. The world had shifted, tilted on its axis, and I struggled to find my footing in this new, unsettling reality. A tight knot formed in my stomach, twisting with anxiety as I remembered how quickly everything had spiraled out of control since Marcus bit me.

"Tris?" Kat's voice broke through my thoughts. She glanced at me, her brow furrowed with concern. "You okay?"

"Yeah," I replied, forcing a smile that didn't quite reach my eyes. "Just... thinking."

"About what?" she pressed.

I swallowed hard, unsure how to put it into words. "About everything."

As we drove deeper into the city, shadows loomed larger than ever in my mind. My childhood home receded behind us, and I couldn't shake the feeling that we were leaving more than just bricks and mortar; we were leaving behind a life that had been ours—a life before darkness seeped in.

The lights of downtown flickered like fireflies in the dusk as I navigated through the familiar streets tinged with fear. Each turn brought me closer to Benji's apartment and Jessica's place, but also deeper into danger.

"What if they don't believe us?" Kat said suddenly, her voice tight with worry.

"They will," I assured her. "They know us." But even as I said it, doubt gnawed at me like a hungry wolf. Would they understand? Would they grasp what we had become?

The weight of our circumstances pressed down on me—heavy and suffocating—as memories of laughter and carefree days danced mockingly in my head. I stole another glance at Kat; she was staring out the window, lost in thought.

I gripped the steering wheel, my knuckles white against the pressure, as we maneuvered through the bustling streets of downtown. The skyline loomed overhead, a jagged silhouette against the fading light. I felt Kat's anxious energy beside me, her gaze flitting from the window to my face.

"Let me call Benji," I said, pulling my phone from my pocket. My fingers trembled slightly as I scrolled to his contact.

"Now?" Kat asked, her voice laced with worry.

"Yeah, we need him," I replied, hitting the call button. The phone rang in my ear, each tone amplifying the tension coiling in my stomach.

"Come on, pick up," I muttered under my breath.

After what felt like an eternity, Benji's voice broke through. "Tris? Is that you?"

"Benji! It's me." I forced calm into my tone despite the chaos swirling in my mind.

"What the hell? It's been months! Where have you been?" His shock came through clearly, but it didn't matter right now.

"I need to meet you," I said quickly. "In person. It's not safe to talk over the phone."

"What do you mean not safe? What's going on?"

"Just trust me," I insisted, glancing at Kat. She leaned closer, her expression a mix of curiosity and concern. "Where can we meet?"

Benji paused for a moment; I could practically hear his mind racing. "You should come to my place. Downtown New York—should be safe enough."

"Alright." Relief washed over me at his suggestion; at least we had a plan. "We'll be there soon."

"You're really okay?" he asked again, his voice softening with genuine concern.

"I will be... Just hurry," I urged before hanging up.

Kat glanced at me, wide-eyed. "What did he say?"

"He wants us to meet at his place."

She nodded but didn't say anything more. As I navigated through traffic—each honk and shout of the city echoing around us—I couldn't shake the gnawing feeling that time was running out and that danger lurked just beyond our vision.

"Let's get there fast," I said tightly as I hit the gas, weaving through cars with urgency pulsing in my veins. We needed answers—and Benji was our first step in finding them.

"I'm starving, Tris," Kat complained, her discomfort evident as she fidgeted in her seat. The cityscape flew by in a neon blur, casting vibrant, colorful shadows over her features, illuminating the tension etched in her brow. "Can we stop for food?"

"Kat, we don't have time for detours," I countered, my grip on the steering wheel tightening further, the urgency of our situation weighing heavily on me. "We need to reach Benji's without delay."

She persisted, her voice tinged with hunger and frustration. "Come on, just a quick drive-through. It won't take long."

Exhaling a weary sigh, I conceded, knowing full well she wouldn't drop the matter. "Fine, but it's drive-through only. We won't stop any longer than necessary."

A faint smile of victory graced her lips. "Deal."

We diverted to the closest fast-food establishment, finding ourselves at the end of a long line of cars that coiled around the building like a snake, each vehicle inching forward at a frustratingly slow pace. With every passing second, my eyes darted about, vigilant of every shadow and rustle of sound that might hint at lurking danger in the night. The aroma of sizzling grease and salted fries permeated the air, turning my stomach despite its emptiness. It felt absurd to be craving food when our reality was so dire, the threat of the vampire world looming just beyond the horizon of our thoughts.

"What do you fancy?" Kat inquired, craning her neck toward the backlit menu, excitement tinged with impatience as she tried to distract herself from her gnawing hunger.

"Nothing," I responded tersely, feeling my appetite vanish as my thoughts spiraled back to our precarious situation. "I've lost my appetite."

Her gaze met mine, laced with concern as she tried to understand my mood, her worry a palpable thread in the air between us. "Are you certain? It might do you good to eat."

A forced smile crossed my lips, but I could tell it didn't reach my eyes. "Positive. Just get what you like."

She placed her order, her voice a mix of eagerness and urgency, and we crept forward in the line, each inch feeling like an eternity stretching out into the night. When it was our turn at the pick-up window, Kat exchanged a wad of cash for a tray laden with food, and we merged back into the flow of traffic, the smell of her burger wafting through the air, a tantalizing reminder of normalcy that felt so far out of reach.

"Finally," Kat exhaled in relief, peeling back the wrapper of her burger with eager hands. She savored the first bite, her eyes fluttering closed in bliss. "God, I was starving."

Her words had barely left her mouth when the startling flash of police lights caught my attention in the rearview mirror, slicing through the dim light of the evening like a knife through butter. My pulse skyrocketed, a surge of adrenaline flooding my system. "Damn it," I hissed under my breath, guiding the car to the roadside as dread crept in, my mind racing with thoughts of our situation.

The officer approached, his flashlight cutting through the darkness to illuminate us, casting sharp shadows across Kat's face, a stark contrast against the bright lights of the city. "License and registration, please," he requested, his voice imbued with authority that sent a shiver down my spine, making me acutely aware of how vulnerable we truly were.

I froze, the realization hitting hard that my license was lost near the cabin amidst the chaos of the fight. "Officer, I apologize, but my license isn't on me," I confessed, striving for composure as panic gnawed at the edges of my mind, threatening to unravel me like a fraying thread.

His brows arched, skepticism etching deeper lines into his forehead, and I could feel the weight of his gaze boring into me. "And why might that be?" he probed, his voice carrying an edge that made my stomach twist.

"It got misplaced," I explained, the words tumbling out as I fought against the pressure of his scrutiny, which felt like an iron weight on my chest, suffocating and relentless. My mind raced, wondering if he could sense the turmoil brewing beneath my surface. "I can provide my name, though. Tristan Blake. And this is my sister, Katherine Blake Adams. Her married name accounts for the difference." I hoped that sharing my name would somehow ease the tension, or at least redirect his focus.

Kat leaned in, her voice unwavering, a testament to her strength in our current predicament. "We're in our mom's car, on our way to catch up with our parents at the cinema. They went ahead." She kept her tone steady, but I could see the flicker of anxiety in her eyes, which only added to my unease.

The officer's eyes lingered on mine, a flicker of curiosity betraying his otherwise stoic demeanor as the flashlight's glow mingled with the unusual sheen of my eyes, a haunting reminder of the changes coursing through me.

The officer's eyes narrowed slightly as he assessed our situation, lingering on my face longer than I was comfortable with. "Hang tight while I check your names in the system," he said, stepping back from the car. His flashlight flickered away from us and toward the rear of the vehicle, illuminating the cabin's dull paint under the harsh glow.

Kat's breathing quickened beside me. I could feel her tension radiating through the air like static electricity. "What if he finds out?" she whispered, her voice barely audible over the engine's hum.

"Shh," I murmured, keeping my gaze locked on the officer as he returned to his patrol car. I fought against the primal urge to bolt into the night; instead, I sat rigidly, reminding myself to breathe.

The seconds felt like hours as I watched him type into his computer. A sickening knot twisted in my stomach—was it paranoia or instinct telling me we were exposed? I glanced at Kat, whose fingers fidgeted nervously with her burger wrapper, tearing it into smaller pieces like a stress ball.

"Just play it cool," I said quietly, trying to inject some calm into her frayed nerves. She nodded but kept her gaze glued to the officer's car.

I shifted in my seat, focusing on anything other than our predicament: the neon signs buzzing overhead, cars driving past us without a care in the world. How could life seem so normal when ours had spiraled into chaos?

Finally, after what felt like an eternity, the officer stepped out of his car and ambled back toward us. The look on his face shifted from skepticism to something more neutral—maybe even mildly curious.

"Alright," he announced as he approached our window again. "I checked your names against our system." He leaned against the door frame casually now, seeming less threatening than before.

I held my breath as he continued. "You two check out."

Kat let out a relieved sigh beside me; her shoulders relaxed a fraction. "Thank goodness."

"I pulled you over because your license plate light is out," he began, his tone serious but not unfriendly. "It's one of those little things that can turn into a big problem if left unchecked, you know? Just a warning this time, but I'd recommend getting it fixed."

"Absolutely, officer. I appreciate the heads-up," I replied, forcing a calmness I didn't entirely feel.

"I've seen a lot of people overlook those details," he continued, glancing at Kat before settling his gaze back on me. "You wouldn't believe how many lights can go out without anyone noticing. Safety first, that's what I always say."

"Definitely," I nodded, trying to sound engaged, but my mind raced, the need to protect my secrets swirling anxiously beneath the surface.

The officer shifted slightly, still observing me, and I felt the weight of his gaze—an inquisitiveness that lingered far longer than I anticipated. "But you know, you have a unique look about you. Those eyes of yours, they're—well, different," he remarked, a note of genuine curiosity edging into his voice.

Kat glanced at me, her expression caught between concern and intrigue. "Yeah, I guess they are a bit unusual," I added, trying to lighten the mood.

"Unusual is one way to put it," the officer said with a hint of a smile, leaning in closer. "What's going on with your eyes? I mean, they're striking—almost like they have a light of their own."

The urge to shield my secret surged within me. "Well," I managed, drawing out my response, "they're just contact lenses."

"Really?" he replied, tilting his head slightly, clearly intrigued. "I've seen a variety of styles, but nothing quite like that. Do they come in a lot of colors or designs?"

"Um, yeah, a whole range, actually," I said, my words tumbling out as I tried to maintain a lighthearted tone despite the truth of my situation. "I just thought it would be fun to mix things up a little."

"Good strategy," he remarked, stepping back but still looking at me intently. "Expressing yourself is important. Those contact lenses are pretty cool. This is why I love being a police officer; you never know who you're going to meet."

The conversation hung in the air, a thread of understanding weaving between us, and I sensed he was trying to show he meant well, wanting to connect on some level.

"Your brother has some intriguing contacts," he said, skepticism thinly veiled, the implications of his words hanging heavy like a storm cloud threatening to break. My thoughts spiraled, wondering how much he knew and if he could piece together the fragments of my reality.

Kat's laugh held a quiver of nerves, a small attempt to defuse the situation. "Yeah, he's an eccentric one. Has a thing for those exotic contacts." Her lighthearted response was a brave facade, but I could sense the underlying tension.

A chuckle escaped the officer as he shook his head in amusement, the tension momentarily lifted as if a fragile truce had been struck. "Alright, just make sure to replace that license. And fix the license plate light. Have a good evening." With that, he turned to walk back to his cruiser, leaving us in the oppressive silence of the night.

As he retreated, the tension that had gripped me dissipated, and I let out a breath that had been trapped in my chest. The officer's departure felt like a temporary reprieve, a fragile truce in the midst of our precarious situation.

"That was close," Kat whispered, her voice a breathy murmur that mirrored the relief flooding through me. Her wide eyes reflected the weight of our narrow escape, the gravity of our circumstances settling heavily upon us like a dark cloud. The secrets we carried felt like chains around our necks, a constant reminder of the dangers lurking just beyond our perception.

"Too close," I agreed, shifting back into the lane of traffic. The momentary respite felt fragile, as if it might shatter at any moment, and I was acutely aware of how tenuous our situation truly was. The road stretched ahead, shrouded in uncertainty, and I knew vigilance was our only ally.

Kat polished off her meal with quiet determination, the crinkling of paper wrappers filling the cramped car as she focused intently on her food. Gradually, the tension in her shoulders began to ease, but I could see a contemplative spark in her eyes as she cast a sideways glance my way, curiosity igniting a conversation.

"Tris, what's it actually like? You know, the whole blood-drinking thing?"

I paused, trying to figure out how to explain a reality that felt so far from normal now. "It's... different," I began slowly. "I mostly drink animal blood. I need just a bit to keep me going. And I always let them go afterward."

"Right," she nodded, brows knitting together in thought.

"When the hunger hits, it's this wild urge that makes everything feel sharper, like I'm alive in a way I've never experienced before."

Kat turned to me, eyes wide. "What do you mean?"

"It's hard to describe," I admitted, shifting a bit in my seat, "but when I drink, there's this amazing warmth that spreads through me. It feels like power flowing into my veins. Afterward, I feel strong—like I can take on anything. My senses sharpen, and my reflexes are quicker. It's like I'm seeing the world through a whole new lens."

"Wow," she breathed, leaning in. "So it's really that much of a change?"

"Totally," I replied, excitement creeping into my voice. "But trust me, after tasting that, regular food just seems... bland. Like it can't even compare. Besides, I'm pretty sure my body would reject it."

"So that's why you didn't want me to order food for you? You were saying it didn't smell good because you didn't want it, not just because we were in danger."

"Exactly," I said, grateful for her understanding. "After feeding, I feel incredible—clear-headed and full of energy. I can move faster and think sharper. It's like I've tapped into another level."

She nodded, the gears turning in her mind as she processed everything. "So if it's like that, it makes sense you wouldn't want anything else."

"Right," I confirmed, looking at her. "It's not like I have a choice, and it's not just about hunger anymore; it's about survival and mastering what I've become."

"Just promise me you won't go for human blood," Kat said, her voice turning serious again, concern threading through her words.

"I swear," I promised, relieved she understood. "I'll always stick to animals. I'd never hurt anyone, especially not you."

"Good," she said, giving me a small smile, the weight of our conversation lifting a little. "Just be careful, okay?"

"Always," I assured her, feeling a bit lighter in the cramped car. As we drove on, I couldn't shake the intensity of my new reality, but knowing Kat was right there with me helped a lot.

Kat absorbed my words in silence, her expression turning pensive before she probed further. "How much have you changed, Tris? Do you feel... different?"

Drawing a deep breath, I let the weight of everything settle in. It felt like my whole being had been turned upside down since the transformation. "You know, I feel... different. Like I've been reborn into this new version of myself. It's powerful, but honestly, a bit scary too. My senses are sharper; I can see, hear, and feel more than ever before."

I paused for a moment, the memory of that night flooding back—the moment when Constantine had come for me. "It's weird, Kat. Back when Constantine was about to kill me, there was this strange energy in the air, this feeling that built up inside me. Then, all of a sudden, I burst with power, knocking him back into a tree so hard it must have taken his breath away."

Kat's eyes widened as I spoke, clearly trying to digest what I was saying. "I passed out right then from the sheer force of it all. But when I woke up, I was in the woods, and I felt... different again. I felt this new overdrive in my being, like I was charged up. It was intense."

I glanced at her, searching for understanding as I tried to explain. "There's this vibration now, a kind of hum of energy that I can't quite shake. It's like I can almost feel everything around me vibrating. It's similar to that surge I felt when I fought Constantine. It's just... there, all the time. I don't know if that makes sense."

Her curiosity grounded me in what felt like swirling chaos. "What do you mean, vibration?"

"Honestly, I don't even know how to describe it," I said. "It's like I'm tuned into something I never noticed before, as if everything has its own rhythm, and I can feel it." I ran a hand through my hair, still trying to wrap my head around it. "I know it sounds crazy, but it's all pretty wild. After the power surge, I went hunting, and that's when it hit me how strong I really felt. Like I was in control of this new energy coursing through me."

She seemed to process my words, the weight of this new reality hanging between us. "So, you feel even more different now?"

"Yeah," I admitted, my voice low. "Way more than I did before. That first month of being turned, I felt extraordinary after I figured a few things out, but now? It's on a whole new level."

She fell quiet, returning her focus to the road as we navigated the bustling city, the lights dancing by us in a blur of motion. The tr-affic thickened as we neared downtown, and the resonance thrummed within me, a constant reminder of my transformation that echoed the uncertainty looming ahead.

As we drove on, Kat turned to me, her eyes alight with fascination. "Tris, you look incredible. I mean, your skin—it's so flawless and healthy.

I thought vampires were supposed to have pale, almost translucent skin, but you look... normal. Human, even."

I couldn't help but chuckle at her observation. "I know, right? It's one of the many surprises that came with this whole vampire thing." I glanced down at my hands, marveling at the subtle glow that seemed to emanate from my skin.

"And your eyes!" Kat exclaimed, leaning in closer. "They're so bright and vibrant, with these mesmerizing swirls of gold and silver. It's like they're alive or something." She shook her head in wonder. "I've never seen anything like it."

I felt a flush of self-consciousness creep up my neck. "Yeah, it's definitely one of the more noticeable changes. I'm still getting used to it myself."

Kat grinned, her earlier fear and tension seemingly forgotten. "Well, I think it's amazing. You look like some kind of otherworldly being, but in a good way. Like a model or something."

I rolled my eyes playfully. "Gee, thanks. I'm not sure if that's a compliment or not."

"Oh, come on," Kat laughed. "You know what I mean. You're practically glowing, Tris. It's kind of unfair, really."

I couldn't help but chuckle at her teasing. "Well, at least one of us is benefiting from this whole vampire thing."

The levity in the car slowly faded as the reality of our situation sank back in. "Speaking of which," I began, my voice growing serious, "the hunger is still something I'm trying to manage. It's a constant battle to suppress the urge to..." I trailed off, not wanting to voice the unspeakable.

Kat's expression sobered, and she reached over to give my hand a gentle squeeze. "I know, Tris. But I trust you. I know you'll never hurt anyone, especially not us."

I offered her a grateful smile and squeezed her hand back. "You're right. I'm determined to resist drinking human blood at all costs. It's the only way I can keep you and the rest of the family safe."

"How often do you need to... you know, feed?" Kat asked tentatively.

"About every nine days," I replied, my gaze fixed on the road ahead. "I can sustain myself on around three gallons of animal blood, but it's enough to keep the hunger at bay."

Kat nodded, her brow furrowed in thought. "Nine days, huh? That's a lot more manageable than I expected."

"Yeah, it's not too bad," I admitted. "But I still have to be vigilant. The cravings can be intense, and I have to be careful not to let them consume me."

As we drove on, the weight of our conversation hung in the air, a constant reminder of the challenges we faced. But with Kat by my side, I knew I had the strength to overcome them, no matter what the future held.

"But tell me one thing, Tris: are you okay?" Kat's voice cut through my reverie, laced with genuine concern, pulling me back into the present moment, away from the whirlpool of my thoughts.

I glanced at her, offering a semblance of reassurance, though I knew my inner turmoil was far from over. "I'm managing, Kat. Just... adapting."

Her hand found my arm, a comforting pressure that anchored me against the currents of fear and anxiety swirling around us, a reminder of our bond even amidst the turbulence. "You know you can confide in me, right? About anything."

I nodded, the warmth of her support lifting my spirits, even as uncertainty loomed like an ominous storm cloud on the horizon. "I'm aware. And when the time is right, I will."

She nodded, her eyes reflecting understanding and trust, a silent promise hanging between us like a fragile thread. "Okay. But promise me that when you need to talk, you'll reach out."

"I promise," I affirmed with conviction, feeling the weight of that promise settle between us—a steadfast anchor in the turbulent sea of our lives.

As we arrived at Benji's house, the gravity of our circumstances descended upon me like a heavy fog, the resonance a constant undercurrent to my newfound nature. But for the moment, we were armed with a plan and a sense of direction. And that was enough to propel me forward into the unknown, ready to face whatever lay ahead, united in our determination to survive.

CHAPTER TWENTY-ONE

BENJI'S HOUSE

I pulled up to Benji's house with Kat beside me, her eyes flickering nervously between me and the dimly lit street. I could feel her worry pressing down on my chest like a weight.

"Tris," she said, breaking into my thoughts, "we need to find you a pair of sunglasses. Mom should have some in here somewhere. You should really wear them."

Her words pulled me from my spiraling thoughts, and I quickly began rummaging through the glove compartment, my fingers fumbling over the various papers and odds and ends that cluttered it. "Where are they?" I muttered in frustration.

Kat leaned over, urgency matching the rising anxiety within me. "Here!" She reached in and pulled out a pair of sunglasses—slightly scratched but still functional. "You can wear these. Benji might freak if he sees your eyes."

I nodded and slid the sunglasses on, grateful for the shield they provided. The weight of the dark lenses felt comforting against the unsettling glow of my eyes, which had changed so much since the transformation.

"What should I tell him if he asks about it?" I asked, my voice strained by the gravity of our situation.

"Just say you've got a migraine or something," Kat suggested, her voice steady, though I could hear the tremor of anxiety beneath it. "He'll understand."

"Right, a migraine." I tried to muster a smile, but it felt forced, a mask for the storm inside me. The truth was much heavier than a simple headache.

I took a deep breath, turning off the engine and glancing at the familiar house before me—a place filled with laughter and memories that now felt lightyears away. Stepping out of the car, the cool night air pricked against my skin, and as we made our way toward the porch, I could feel my pulse quicken, fueled by the weight of secrets I couldn't share.

I glanced at Kat, who gave me an encouraging nod before we reached the door. "Let's just get this over with," I muttered, trying to convince myself as much as her. Even as I prepared to face Benji, I couldn't shake the gnawing doubts that haunted me—about my new reality, about keeping my family safe, and about the truth looming over us like a dark cloud.

Kat knocked on the door, her knuckles rapping against the wood with a firmness that belied her nerves. The seconds ticked by like hours, each one stretching the tension tighter. Finally, the door swung open, revealing Benji's familiar face, his eyes widening in surprise.

"Tris? Kat? Hurry, come in!" His gaze flicked between us, curiosity and concern etched on his features.

"Hey, Benji," I said, trying to keep my voice steady. "We need to talk."

Benji's brow furrowed, but he stepped aside, gesturing for us to come in. "Of course, come on in."

We trailed behind him into the living room, the warmth of the house a stark contrast to the chill outside. Benji motioned for us to sit on the couch, his eyes lingering on the sunglasses perched on my face.

"What's with the shades, man?" he asked, a hint of amusement in his voice. "You going for the rockstar look?"

I forced a chuckle, the sound hollow in my ears. "Nah, just a migraine. The light's been bothering me."

Benji nodded, his expression turning serious. "So, what's going on? You both look like you've seen a ghost."

Kat and I exchanged a glance, a silent understanding passing between us. She gave a slight nod, encouraging me to take the lead.

"Benji, we're in trouble," I began, my voice steady despite the turmoil inside me. "Serious trouble."

Benji leaned forward, his elbows resting on his knees. "What kind of trouble?"

I hesitated, the words sticking in my throat. How could I explain something so unbelievable, so terrifying? But I had to try. For Kat, for our family, I had to find a way.

"It's complicated," I said, choosing my words carefully. "But we need your help. We need to disappear."

Benji's eyes widened, shock written all over his face. "Disappear? What do you mean?"

Kat spoke up, her voice firm despite the fear I knew she felt. "We need new identities, Benji. We need to start over somewhere else."

Benji looked between us, disbelief warring with concern. "Why? What happened?"

I took a deep breath, steeling myself for the lies I had to tell. "There are people after us, Benji. Dangerous people. We can't stay here. It's not safe."

Benji's expression darkened, a protective instinct flaring in his eyes. "Who's after you? What did they do?"

I shook my head, avoiding his gaze. "I can't tell you that. The less you know, the safer you'll be."

Benji leaned back, running a hand through his hair. "This is crazy, Tris. You're talking about disappearing, about starting over. That's not something you do on a whim."

"We know," Kat interjected, her voice soft but insistent. "But we don't have a choice. We need to protect our family."

Benji looked at her, his expression softening. "And I want to help you, Kat. But I need to know what I'm getting into. I need to know why this is happening."

I could see the struggle in his eyes, the desire to help warring with the need for answers. But I couldn't give him the truth. Not yet. Not until I knew he was ready to accept it.

"Benji, I promise, I'll tell you everything when I can," I said, my voice earnest. "But right now, we need your help. We need to disappear, and we need to do it fast."

Benji sighed, his shoulders slumping in resignation. "Alright, Tris. I trust you. If you say you need to disappear, then I'll help you. But you have to promise me something."

"What's that?" I asked, a sense of relief washing over me.

"Promise me that when this is all over, you'll tell me the truth. The whole truth."

I nodded, a solemn vow in my eyes. "I promise, Benji. When this is all over, I'll tell you everything."

Benji stood up, a determined look on his face. "Alright, let's get to work. We've got a lot to do if we're going to make this happen."

As we followed Benji into his office, I couldn't shake the feeling of unease settling in the pit of my stomach. The lies weighed heavily on me, a constant reminder of the secrets I kept. But I pushed them aside, focusing on the task at hand. We had a plan, and we had to see it through—no matter what it took.

Benji sat down at his computer, his fingers flying over the keyboard as he pulled up various windows and programs. Kat and I stood behind him, watching as he navigated through a maze of code and data.

"First things first," Benji said, his eyes scanning the screen. "We need to get you some new identities. Names, social security numbers, the works."

Kat leaned in, her eyes wide with curiosity. "How are you going to do that?"

Benji grinned, a mischievous glint in his eyes. "Let's just say I have a few tricks up my sleeve and a few friends in low places."

I raised an eyebrow, a sense of amusement cutting through the tension. "Friends in low places, huh? Sounds like you've been busy since we last talked."

Benji chuckled, his fingers never slowing. "You have no idea, Tris. But don't worry; I've got this. I just need a little time to work my magic."

Kat nodded, her expression serious. "How long do you think it will take?"

Benji pursed his lips, considering. "A few hours, at least. Maybe more, depending on how deep I have to dig. But I'll get it done."

I placed a hand on his shoulder, gratitude welling up inside me. "Thank you, Benji. I don't know what we'd do without you."

Benji looked up at me, his expression softening. "You're my friend, Tris. I'd do anything for you. Besides, this is the most excitement I've had in months."

I laughed, the sound genuine and heartfelt. "Well, I'm glad we could provide some entertainment."

Benji turned back to the computer, his focus returning to the task at hand. "Alright, you two, make yourselves comfortable. This is going to take a while."

Kat and I exchanged a glance, a silent understanding passing between us. We had a long night ahead of us, but with Benji's help, we had a chance—a chance to disappear, to start over, to protect our family from the dangers that lurked in the shadows.

As we settled in, the weight of our situation pressing down on us, I couldn't help but feel a glimmer of hope. We had a plan, and we had each other. And for now, that was enough.

The hours ticked by, the silence broken only by the clicking of Benji's keyboard and the occasional murmur of conversation. Kat and I huddled together on the couch, our shoulders touching, a silent source of comfort and strength.

"How are you holding up?" I asked her, my voice low.

Kat sighed, her eyes reflecting the weariness we both felt. "I'm scared, Tris. Scared of what's happening, scared of what's to come. But I know we have to do this. For Mom, for Micah, for all of us."

I nodded, my hand finding hers, our fingers intertwining. "We'll get through this, Kat. Together."

She looked up at me, her eyes filled with determination. "Together."

As we sat there, the weight of our situation pressing down on us, I couldn't help but feel a sense of gratitude—gratitude for Kat, for her strength and courage; gratitude for Benji, for his unwavering support and willingness to help us, no matter the cost.

And as the night wore on, the tension in the air palpable, I knew that no matter what happened, no matter what challenges lay ahead, we would face them together—united in our determination to protect our family and survive the darkness that threatened to consume us.

Finally, after what felt like an eternity, Benji leaned back in his chair, a satisfied look on his face. "Alright, I think I've got something."

Kat and I stood up, her heart pounding with anticipation. "What did you find?" she asked, her voice barely above a whisper.

Benji turned to face us, his eyes gleaming with triumph. "I found you some new identities—names, social security numbers, the works. You're officially off the grid."

A wave of relief washed over me, quickly followed by a surge of questions. "Tell us everything," I urged, my voice laced with a mixture of excitement and apprehension.

Benji grinned, the glow of the computer screen reflecting in his eyes. "For you, Tristan, you'll be known as 'Ethan Miller,' a software developer from

Seattle—fitting, right? Kat, you're 'Sarah Johnson,' a freelance graphic designer from Portland. For your mom, I went with 'Evelyn Reed,' a retired teacher from Boise. Your dad is 'Richard Reed,' also retired, a former accountant. And Micah is now 'Mark Carter,' a construction worker from Denver."

He paused, clicking a few more keys. Images flashed on the screen—driver's licenses, passports, social security cards. They looked remarkably real, each with a different face and a different life attached. "I pulled your photos from various social media platforms and online databases," he explained, pointing to the slightly distorted but passable pictures on the IDs. "Had to do some tweaking, obviously, but they should pass a casual glance. The real magic is in the paperwork. These identities are squeaky clean, linked to real but dormant accounts. No red flags, no connections to your past lives."

Kat leaned closer, her eyes scanning the details of her new identity. "Sarah Johnson... I like it. It has a nice ring to it." A small, hesitant smile played on her lips, a brief flicker of light in the darkness that surrounded us.

"So, what's next?" I asked, my mind already racing ahead, planning our next moves.

"Next," Benji said, his voice turning serious, "we need to get these physical documents. I have a contact downtown—a specialist in acquiring certain items. We'll need to go tomorrow during the day. It's a risk, but it's necessary."

"What kind of risk?" Kat's voice tightened with worry.

"The usual," Benji said with a shrug. "Wrong place, wrong time. Unwanted attention. But I've worked with this guy before. He's reliable, discreet. We just need to be in and out, no fuss, no muss."

"And after that?" I pressed, my mind still reeling from the enormity of our plan.

"After that," Benji said, a determined glint in his eyes, "we fake your deaths. Stage a tragic accident, something untraceable. Make it look like you and your family... well, that you're no longer among the living. Then, while everyone's mourning, you disappear. Vanish into thin air. Start over with your new lives."

"And the money?" I reminded him, thinking of the massive amount we needed to transfer to make this work.

"That's already in motion," Benji assured me, his fingers dancing across the keyboard.

"I've initiated a series of transfers—small amounts, moving through various channels. Untraceable, undetectable. By the time we're ready to go, it'll all be waiting for you in a secure account, accessible only with your new identities." He paused, his brow furrowing slightly. "But for this to work, we'll need Jess's help. She knows the Palantir Technologies systems better than anyone."

Jess. Bringing her into this felt like adding another weight to the crushing burden I already carried. "Are you sure there's no other way?" I asked, my voice barely above a whisper.

"Not for a hack this complex," Benji replied, shaking his head. "We need access to Palantir's servers, and Jess is the only one who can get us in without raising alarms. With her and my combined skills... let's just say we can make magic happen." A flicker of his usual playful grin crossed his face, but it quickly faded. "Look, I know it's a risk. We could all lose our jobs if we get caught. But this isn't just about us anymore. This is about your family's safety. Think of it as a once-in-a-lifetime opportunity to play Robin Hood. We're taking from the corporate giants and giving to... well, ourselves. Besides," he added with a wink, "who needs a job when we're living off the grid with millions in the bank?"

"Benji's right," I chimed in, my voice firm despite the tremor of anxiety I felt. "We need Jess. We can't do this without her."

I looked from Kat to Benji, the weight of their words settling heavy in my chest. I knew they were right. We needed Jess. But the thought of exposing her to this danger, of dragging her into the mess I'd created... it made my stomach churn.

"Where is she, anyway?" Kat asked, glancing around the room.

"Jess?" Benji's fingers paused their dance across the keyboard. He swiveled in his chair, a sheepish look on his face. "Funny story about that. She's been helping me with this whole identity creation thing. She's the one who actually fabricated the documents. I just... uh... didn't tell her exactly what they were for."

My jaw dropped. "You're kidding me, right? You involved Jess without telling her the whole story?" I couldn't believe what I was hearing. This was getting more complicated by the minute.

Benji raised his hands in a placating gesture. "Hey, don't shoot the messenger! She's been itching for a challenge, and this was right up her alley. Besides," he added with a mischievous grin, "who's going to say no to a little anonymous hacking gig?"

"But what did you tell her?" Kat asked, her voice edged with concern.

"That I needed some... let's say 'creative samples' for a 'personal project,'" Benji replied, air-quoting liberally. "She knows I dabble in... alternative security solutions. She didn't ask too many questions."

I rubbed my temples, feeling a headache coming on. "And now she's going to find out the truth. Just great."

"Relax, Tris," Benji said, his voice reassuring. "She's a pro. She can handle it. Besides, she's already in this deep. Might as well see it through, right?"

"But to complete the transfer, we need access to Palantir's servers," Benji continued, his voice turning serious. "And that means a trip back to the office. Tonight."

I felt a knot tighten in my stomach. Going back to Palantir felt like walking into the lion's den. "Are you sure there's no other way?"

Benji shook his head. "Not if we want to do this quickly and cleanly. We need to be on-site, plugged into the network. It's the only way."

Kat looked at me, her eyes wide with apprehension. "Tonight? But what if someone sees us?"

"We'll be in and out before anyone even knows we're there," Benji assured her. "Besides, with Jess on the inside, we'll have eyes and ears everywhere. She'll disable the security cameras and clear our access paths. We'll be ghosts."

Benji turned back to his computer, his fingers flying across the keys once more. "In the meantime, we need to finalize the details—logistics, escape routes, contingencies. Every possible scenario needs to be accounted for."

Relief washed over me, a wave of gratitude threatening to overwhelm me. "Thank you, Benji. I don't know how we can ever repay you."

Benji waved a dismissive hand, a grin spreading across his face. "Don't worry about it, Tris. Just promise me you'll stay safe. And that you'll tell me the truth when this is all over."

I nodded, a solemn vow in my eyes.

Benji stood up, stretching his arms above his head. "Alright, now that we've got the hard part out of the way, let's talk logistics. You're going to need a place to stay and a way to get there..."

Kat stepped forward, her expression determined. "We've got a plan for that. We're going to fake our deaths and make it look like we died in a car accident. That way, no one will come looking for us."

Benji's eyes widened, shock and concern warring in his gaze. "Fake your deaths? That's... that's a big deal, Kat. Are you sure you want to go through with this?"

Kat nodded, her voice steady despite the fear I knew she felt. "We have to, Benji. It's the only way to keep our family safe."

Benji looked at me, his expression serious. "And you're on board with this, Tris? You're okay with faking your own death?"

I hesitated, the weight of the decision pressing down on me. But I knew there was no other way—not if we wanted to protect our family from the dangers that lurked in the shadows.

"I'm on board," I said, my voice firm. "It's the only way."

Benji sighed, resignation etched on his features. "Alright, then. Let's do this. Let's make you disappear."

As we delved into the details, the weight of our decision settling over us like a heavy cloak, I couldn't shake the feeling of unease that lingered in the pit of my stomach. The lies we told and the secrets we kept weighed heavily on me, a constant reminder of the truth lurking just beneath the surface.

But I pushed them aside, focusing on the task at hand. We had a plan, and we had to see it through—no matter what it took, no matter the cost.

And as the night wore on, the tension in the air palpable, I knew that no matter what happened, no matter what challenges lay ahead, we would face them together—united in our determination to protect our family and survive the darkness threatening to consume us.

"Alright," Benji said, his voice cutting through the silence. "I think we've got everything covered. You've got your new identities, a plan to fake your deaths, and a way to get out of town. But there's one more thing we need to discuss."

Kat and I exchanged a glance, a silent understanding passing between us. "What's that?" I asked, my voice steady despite the turmoil inside me.

Benji looked at us, his expression serious. "We need to talk about how you're going to stay hidden. How you're going to keep your family safe, even after you disappear."

I nodded, the weight of his words settling over me like a heavy cloak. "We've thought about that, Benji. We've got a plan."

Benji raised an eyebrow, a hint of skepticism in his gaze. "And what's that?"

Kat stepped forward, her voice firm despite the fear I knew she felt. "We're going off the grid completely. No phones, no internet, no contact with anyone from our old lives. We're going to disappear and stay hidden until it's safe to come out."

Benji nodded, a thoughtful expression on his face. "That's a good start. But you'll need more than that. You'll need a way to stay under the radar and avoid detection from anyone who might be looking for you."

I leaned forward, my eyes locked on Benji's. "And how do we do that?"

Benji grinned, a mischievous glint in his eyes. "That's where my friends in low places come in. I've got contacts, Tris. People who can help you stay hidden and provide the resources you need to stay off the grid."

Relief washed over me, a wave of gratitude threatening to overwhelm me. "Thank you, Benji. I don't know how we can ever repay you."

Benji waved a dismissive hand, a grin spreading across his face. "Don't worry about it, Tris. Just promise me you'll stay safe."

Benji's apartment felt like a haven, a stark contrast to the shadowy world I'd been navigating. But even here, shielded by his familiar, cluttered space, I couldn't fully relax. The sunglasses felt like a lead weight on my face, a constant reminder of the truth I was desperately trying to conceal.

"Dude, seriously, what's with the shades indoors?" Benji's voice cut through my internal turmoil. He was bouncing on the balls of his feet, his usual restless energy amplified by the sheer novelty of my bizarre accessory. "Are you trying to be some kind of mysterious celebrity? Because, let me tell you, it's not working. You look more like you're hiding from the sun... indoors."

I forced a chuckle, trying to inject light-heartedness into a situation I definitely wasn't feeling. "Just a bit sensitive to the light today, that's all. You know how it is." Smooth, Tristan, real smooth. I could practically feel the heat rising in my cheeks, betraying my discomfort.

"Sensitive to the light? Since when? You practically lived in the sun back in high school, trying to get that surfer tan you never quite achieved." Benji grinned, but I could see the curiosity simmering beneath the surface. He wasn't buying it, not even for a second, and I knew I needed to come up with a better excuse.

"Okay, okay, you got me," I said, feigning defeat. "I just thought they looked cool. Trying out a new look. What do you think? Rock star or international spy?" I struck a pose, hoping to distract him with sheer absurdity, but deep down I knew it was a futile attempt.

He rolled his eyes, but a smile tugged at the corner of his mouth. "More like a confused tourist who accidentally wandered into the wrong apartment. Take them off, man. It's weirding me out."

"Seriously, I'm good," I insisted, struggling to maintain my composure. "Just a bit of a headache. The light is really getting to me today."

My deflection only seemed to fuel his curiosity. He circled me slowly, like a predator sizing up its prey. "Come on, Tristan. You're acting like you have something to hide. You know you can tell me anything."

That was the problem, wasn't it? I *couldn't* tell him anything. Not without potentially dragging him into a world of shadows and ancient horrors that I was still trying to come to terms with myself. "Nothing to tell, Benji. Promise. Just a silly fashion choice gone wrong."

I kept the tone light, almost joking, but the undercurrent of tension was undeniable. I could feel Benji's eyes boring into me, his concern for my well-being evident, even as I struggled to maintain the facade of normalcy. The weight of my secret was becoming increasingly difficult to bear, and I knew that sooner or later, I would have to make a choice—to confide in my friend or to continue down this perilous path alone.

We eventually settled into Benji's living room, a chaotic yet comforting space filled with half-finished projects, stacks of books, and the lingering aroma of coffee. The familiar scent was different now—more intense, more complex. I could detect subtle notes of hazelnut and vanilla that I'd never noticed before, along with the faint metallic tang of computer components scattered across his desk.

He launched into a rapid-fire account of his latest coding triumph, a new security bypass he'd created that could supposedly crack any government database. I tried to focus, to match his enthusiasm, but my mind was still racing, my newfound senses overwhelmed by every minute detail around me

.

"... and then, BAM! I was in. It was like breaking into Fort Knox with a paperclip. Seriously, the security protocols were practically nonexistent! You wouldn't believe the kind of stuff they're hiding..." He trailed off, his eyes narrowing as he studied me. I could hear the subtle change in his heartbeat, the slight quickening that betrayed his growing concern.

The air suddenly shifted, the playful atmosphere replaced by a palpable sense of unease. He'd sensed something was off, something beyond my awkward attempts at humor and lame excuses. He knew me too well—we'd spent countless hours in this very room, planning coding projects and sharing dreams of digital conquests. Now those memories felt like they belonged to another lifetime.

"Okay, Tristan," he said slowly, his voice losing its usual levity. "What's really going on?" Each word felt like a weight dropping into the space between us, heavy with unspoken questions.

Before I could formulate another flimsy lie, he reached out, his hand moving with surprising speed. In one swift motion, the sunglasses were gone. My enhanced reflexes could have easily stopped him, but some part of me was tired of hiding, tired of pretending.

The world seemed to slow down, the moment stretching into an eternity. The fluorescent lights of Benji's living room felt blinding, and I instinctively flinched, my enhanced vision struggling to adjust. Exposed. I was exposed. I knew my eyes would betray me—the striking hazel irises with their telltale silver and gold swirls would be impossible to explain away with any normal excuse.

Benji's reaction was instantaneous and visceral. His jaw dropped, his eyes widening in disbelief as he stared at me, his expression a mixture of shock, confusion, and a dawning sense of horror. He looked like he'd seen a ghost, or worse, become one himself. The color drained from his face, leaving him a pasty white, a stark contrast to his usually vibrant complexion.

"Those... those aren't contacts, are they?" he stammered, his voice barely a whisper. He reached out, as if to touch my face, drawn to the unnatural glow of my eyes, but then hesitated, his hand hovering in the air between us. A flicker of fear sparked in his eyes, a primal instinct warning him away from the unknown danger that now radiated from me.

I could see the gears turning in his head, the pieces clicking slowly into place, the realization dawning that something profound and terrifying had happened to me. The playful banter, the light-hearted jokes we'd shared just moments before—they were all gone, vanished like smoke, replaced by a stark, unnerving silence that pressed down on us, heavy and suffocating. The air crackled with unspoken questions and a growing sense of dread that threatened to consume us both.

He backed away slightly, putting a small but significant distance between us, his eyes fixed on mine, transfixed by the swirling gold and silver flecks within the hazel. "What... what happened to you?" he finally managed to ask, his voice strained and laced with a tremor of fear, as if he already knew the answer but desperately hoped he was wrong.

Panic clawed at my throat, each ragged breath choking off my ability to articulate my thoughts. I reached out, grabbing Benji's arm, my grip tightening instinctively, as if anchoring myself to him would somehow shield him from the impending storm. "I can't tell you," I whispered, my voice raw with desperation, barely above a breath. "I can't tell you why they're like this. I don't want to put you in danger. You don't understand what you'd be getting into."

My words tumbled out in a rush, each syllable fueled by fear and an overwhelming need to protect him. The vampire world was a treacherous, brutal place; I couldn't bear the thought of dragging Benji into that abyss. He was too good, too innocent, too untainted by the darkness that loomed over my existence.

"If you know, you'll be in danger," I repeated, my voice trembling as the weight of my warning settled heavily between us. "They'll come after you. They'll come after everyone I care about." The thought sent a fresh wave of dread coursing through me, each heartbeat a reminder of the stakes at hand.

I loosened my grip on his arm, my hand falling limply to my side, feeling as if I had released a part of my very soul. The weight of my secret felt crushing, suffocating me in its grasp. I wanted to confide in him, to tell him everything—the truth that swirled within me like a tempest—but I knew I couldn't. Not if I wanted to keep him safe. The very act of sharing my burden could shatter the fragile safety we had left, and that was a risk I simply couldn't take.

The silence stretched on, thick with unspoken questions and mounting tension, wrapping around us like a suffocating fog. My mind raced as I braced myself for his reaction, expecting fear, revulsion, or even anger. But what I saw in Benji's eyes took me by surprise.

There was fear, yes, but also something else: a flicker of determination, a spark of unwavering loyalty that ignited a sense of hope within me. He was scared, but he wasn't backing down, and that steadied me somewhat amid the storm of my emotions.

"Whatever it is," he said, his voice firm despite the tremor in his hands, "just know that I'm here to help. You know that, right? We've been through everything together. If anyone can navigate this, it's me... it's us." His eyes locked onto mine, a quiet strength radiating from them, a lighthouse in the turbulent sea of uncertainty surrounding us.

He took a deep breath, visibly steeling himself for whatever was to come next. "Okay, so obviously something crazy is going on. We can freak out about it later. Right now, we need to figure out what to do." I could see the gears in his mind turning, his usual quick-thinking nature kicking in as he recalibrated our situation.

"First things first," he continued, pacing the room with an energy that was both comforting and infectious. "Why are those eyes a problem? Is it just a fashion faux pas, or is there something more to it?" His attempt at levity brought a small, grateful smile to my lips, even as my heart weighed heavy with the truth I had yet to reveal.

I hesitated, the words caught in my throat like a tangled web. I decided to give him a piece of the truth, carefully concealed within layers of vague explanation. "My... family. They need to disappear. Quickly. And these... eye changes... will make it difficult." The gravity of the situation settled over us both, a shared understanding igniting the air between us.

I paced the length of Benji's living room, the plush carpet beneath my feet doing little to quell the storm of anxiety within me. Kat perched on the edge of the couch, her fingers nervously tapping against her thigh, a fidget that mirrored my own unease. The weight of our situation was palpable, a silent specter looming over us.

"Alright, we're going to need a substantial amount of cash," she said, running a hand through her hair in frustration. "Around $300 million should be moved into private accounts—accounts that won't raise any flags."

I nodded, my brow furrowing as I considered the implications. "But how are we supposed to get that much without attracting attention? It's a massive sum. One wrong move, and we could have every agency from the FBI to Interpol breathing down our necks."

"Easy," Benji interjected, leaning back in his chair, a confident grin creeping onto his face. His casual demeanor was almost unnerving given the gravity of our situation. "I'll set up offshore accounts in all your new names. No one will ever know a thing. We'll be ghosts in the system. Before we do anything, we need to handle all the logistics tonight."

"Tonight?" Kat frowned, casting a worried glance at the clock on the wall. "What if we don't have enough time? We need to get in and out quickly. Every minute counts, and we can't afford any mistakes."

"No worries," Benji reassured her, his fingers tapping against the table with a rhythm that seemed to echo his unshakable confidence. "I've done this before. Depending on how smoothly this hack goes, we'll get it done. Now, let me call Jessica. She's the key to this whole operation."

Benji grabbed his phone, and I felt an electric anticipation crackle in the air, a mix of hope and fear surging through me. The thought of involving Jess brought both comfort and concern. "Jess needs to be in on this. Her skills will be invaluable, especially with accessing Palantir's servers. Until then, just keep your ears open for any hint that something's off. We can't afford to be caught off guard."

Moments later, Benji ended the call, a satisfied grin on his face as he leaned against the wall. "Jess is on her way," he announced, excitement brimming in his voice. "She said she'd be here in ten minutes."

Kat glanced at me, concern etched across her features. "Do you think we can trust Jess with everything? I mean, when this is over..."

"She's one of us, Kat," I replied, my confidence wavering slightly. "She's been with us through thick and thin. Besides, her tech skills are the best we've got. We need her if we're going to pull this off."

Just then, the door swung open, and Jessica stepped in, a whirlwind of energy. "What's the emergency?" she asked, scanning the room, her expression shifting from curiosity to concern as she noted the tension in the air.

"Glad you could make it, Jess," Benji said, gesturing for her to take a seat on the couch. "We've got a plan to move some funds around, and we need your expertise to pull it off."

"Funds?" she replied, raising an eyebrow. "What does that entail? Is it something legal? Because if it's not, I have a very strict policy about jail time."

"Relax, it's all legal," Benji assured her, waving his hands as if to brush away her worries. "We just need to hack into some accounts and funnel money into private offshore accounts under our names. Nothing that'll get us into trouble."

Benji leaned in, his eyes gleaming with a mix of excitement and determination. "Alright, here's the deal," he began, his voice low and conspiratorial. "Jess will be handling the technical side of things. She'll route the funds through a series of secure channels, making sure nothing gets traced back to us. For her efforts, she'll receive $8 million sent to an account of her choice."

Jessica nodded, a small smile playing at the corners of her mouth. "Sounds fair to me. I've got a few ideas on how to make this happen without raising any red flags."

Benji continued, "And for my part in this little adventure, I'll be getting the same—$8 million. Consider it payment for services rendered." He grinned, a mischievous glint in his eyes. "Plus, I've already got a plan in place for the passports and new IDs. You'll have everything you need to disappear without a trace."

Kat shifted uncomfortably on the couch, her eyes darting between Benji and Jessica. "And what about the rest of the money? How are we going to handle that?"

Benji leaned back, his expression turning serious. "The $300 million will be split up into five accounts, each connected to one of your new IDs. Offshore accounts, completely untraceable. Tristan, Kat, Micah, your mom, and your dad—each of you will have access to a substantial amount of money, enough to start a new life anywhere in the world."

I felt a wave of relief wash over me. The plan was coming together, the pieces falling into place. But there was still a lingering sense of unease, a gnawing worry that something could go wrong. I pushed the thought aside, focusing on the task at hand.

"So, what's the next step?" I asked, my voice steady despite the turmoil within me.

Benji's grin widened, his enthusiasm infectious. "Next step? We get to work. Jess and I will handle the technical side of things. You and Kat just need to focus on staying safe and keeping a low profile. Leave the rest to us."

Jessica chimed in, her voice filled with quiet confidence. "Don't worry, Tristan. We've got this. By the time we're done, it'll be like you and your family never existed. You'll be free to start over, to build a new life."

Her words were a balm, soothing the raw edges of my anxiety. I looked at Kat, saw the hope flickering in her eyes, and knew that we were on the right path. Whatever challenges lay ahead, we would face them together, united in our quest for freedom and safety.

Benji clapped his hands together, signaling that it was time to get started. "Alright, let's do this. The sooner we get the money moved, the sooner you can all disappear. And don't worry—we've got everything under control."

With that, we set to work, each of us playing our part in the intricate dance of deception and survival. The future was uncertain, but with Benji and Jessica by our side, I felt a glimmer of hope, a spark of determination that burned brighter with each passing moment. We were going to make it through this, no matter what it took.

I exchanged a quick glance with Benji. "We need to act fast. I have this new... situation, and we're in serious danger if we don't. It's not just about the money, Jess. It's about keeping us all safe."

Jessica nodded slowly, her expression softening as she grasped the gravity of our predicament. To lighten the mood, she tossed me a small box. "I brought these just in case." Inside were several pairs of high-quality contact lenses, perfect for hiding anything unusual about my eyes.

"Thought it'd be a good idea," Benji added, giving me a smile that masked his concern. "But you guys better explain everything once we're through this mess."

"Definitely," I said, slipping one pair into my pocket, already feeling slightly more secure. "Thanks, Jess. We couldn't do this without you."

As we gathered around the coffee table in the living room, tension settled over us, fueled by urgency. The weight of our mission hung heavy in the air, each of us acutely aware of the high stakes.

"Alright, let's get to work," Benji said, his fingers already flying across the keyboard of his laptop set up on the table. "The plan is to infiltrate our own company's servers. We can't afford to set off any alarms. We need to be ghosts."

An adrenaline rush coursed through me as I focused on the task ahead. The gravity of the situation wasn't lost on me; one wrong move could jeopardize everything. "What's the best way to get in?" I asked, leaning in for a better view of the screen.

Benji grinned, his confidence radiating and infectious. "I've already mapped out the security protocols. Timing is crucial. When the clock strikes three, we'll slip in while everyone is busy elsewhere. Kat's our getaway driver, and she'll stay in the car. We'll be in and out in minutes."

"Wait. Kat's not going to just sit there while we do all the heavy lifting!" Jessica protested, crossing her arms. "If she's driving, she deserves to know how everything works too."

"Trust me, she's safer in the car," Benji assured her, his voice steady and calm. "If anything goes wrong, she's our swift exit. I'll loop her in with the important details shortly before we head out."

I could sense Kat's agitation beneath the surface, her anxiety bubbling as she listened to the plan. Her eyes flicked between Benji and me, searching for reassurance. "Are you sure we can really blend in? What if someone sees us? This is my first time being involved in something like this."

I stepped in, trying to calm her fears. "You can trust Benji and Jess. They know what they're doing. Just keep your eyes peeled for anything out of the ordinary while you wait. If you see something, anything, don't hesitate to alert us."

"Now, onto the logistics," Benji said, pulling up a digital diagram of our company's security systems on the screen. "We need to disable the cameras first. Jess, I need you to bypass the security firewall. I'm counting on you. Once we're in, we'll need to move quickly and efficiently. Every second counts."

Jessica leaned forward, her fingers tapping lightly on the keyboard as she pulled up a series of windows, each filled with complex code and diagrams. The glow from the screen illuminated her face, revealing the determination etched across her features.

"Alright," she began, her voice steady. "To bypass the security firewall, we'll need a combination of tools. First up is Metasploit." She glanced at me, gauging my reaction. "It's a penetration testing framework that can help us find vulnerabilities in the system. I've been using it for years."

I nodded, trying to absorb every detail she shared while also feeling a surge of anxiety about what we were about to attempt.

"Next," she continued, her eyes flicking back to the screen, "I'll utilize Nmap to map out the network and identify any open ports that might give us access." She paused, biting her lip as if considering how much to divulge. "It's crucial for knowing what we're dealing with before diving in."

Kat shifted in her seat, clearly intrigued yet apprehensive. "So how does this all come together?"

Jessica smiled slightly, enjoying the explanation. "Once we've identified potential points of entry using Nmap, I'll craft some payloads in Metasploit. That's where I'll create specific commands that will exploit those vulnerabilities."

I leaned closer to the screen as she demonstrated a few lines of code. The intricacies fascinated me despite my underlying fear.

"After that," she continued, "I'll deploy an encryption tool called OpenVPN to secure our connection and mask our IP address. We can't have anyone tracing our activities back to us—especially now." Her gaze hardened momentarily at the thought.

"Will we need anything else?" I asked, feeling the weight of our plan settling on my shoulders.

"I've got a few other tricks up my sleeve," Jess said cryptically, shrugging off my question with a playful grin. "But trust me; it'll be fine as long as you all keep your heads down and stick to your roles."

Her confidence infused me with renewed determination as I glanced at Kat; I could see she was beginning to understand the gravity of what lay ahead too.

"Alright then," Benji said enthusiastically, cutting into our conversation as he pulled up another window on his laptop. "Let's make sure everything is ready for tonight."

Jessica cracked her knuckles, her eyes shining with determination. "Consider it done. I can get us in without anyone knowing—a little ghosting and we'll be smooth sailing. Just keep me updated on your end."

"Let's make this happen," I said firmly, adrenaline coursing through me.

CHAPTER TWENTY-TWO

PALANTIR TECHNOLOGIES

Jessica pulled me aside, her eyes sharp and probing. "Tris, something's off," she said, lowering her voice to a whisper. "I can feel it. What's going on?"

I shifted uncomfortably, my mind racing. Should I tell her? She was my best friend, the one person I could always count on, but the risks felt too high. The Council didn't just hunt vampires; they hunted anyone who even remotely stumbled into their world. I couldn't bear the thought of Jessica in danger because of me.

"It's nothing," I lied, forcing a smile that felt more like a grimace. "Just... work stuff."

"Don't give me that," she replied, crossing her arms defiantly. "You're not just acting weird because of work. You look different off somehow."

I looked away, unable to meet her gaze. The faint glow of silver and gold had been impossible to hide behind the sunglasses Kat found for me earlier. My eyes burned with secrets I wasn't ready to share.

"Jess, please..." I started but faltered. My voice barely broke above a whisper. "If I told you... if you found out what really happened to me—"

"Then what?" she pressed, urgency spilling from her tone. "You think I'd just walk away? You're like family to me."

That made it harder—so much harder—to keep the truth buried beneath layers of fear and shame. My mind raced as memories flooded back: the brutal attack from Constantine and Micah's lifeless body on the floor haunted my thoughts.

"You don't understand," I finally said, clenching my fists at my sides. "It's not just about me anymore; it's about you too! If you find out... if you dig too deep into this, they'll come after you and your family."

Her expression softened for a moment as she processed my words, but quickly hardened again with resolve. "You think I care about the risk? Tris, we've been through everything together! You don't have to go through this alone!"

"I'm protecting you!" My voice rose before I caught myself and lowered it again.

"I don't need protection from you," Jessica snapped back quietly but firmly.

Just then, Benji appeared at our side, sensing the tension in the air like a well-trained scout sniffing for danger. "Hey! What's going on over here?"

Jessica turned to him with an exasperated sigh while I racked my brain for something—anything—to distract us from the weight of the conversation.

"Nothing," Jess said quickly, though her eyes remained fixed on me.

Benji raised an eyebrow skeptically but decided not to push it further. "Okay then! Let's get back to work." He shot me a look that suggested he wouldn't let this go easily later.

As we began walking back toward our group, Jessica's gaze fell onto my sunglasses before flicking back to me with determination etched across her features.

"Tristan," she began softly, stopping mid-step and pulling my arm gently so that we faced each other again in private once more. "Those sunglasses... they're hiding something else."

I stiffened as dread washed over me like ice water. "What do you mean?"

"I saw the glow through them." Her voice dropped lower as if sharing a secret between sisters. "Your eyes—they're..."

I struggled for words while a million thoughts crashed in my mind—a tempest swirling with anxiety and regret.

Before I could formulate a response or deny it outright, Benji reappeared beside us like an unexpected guardian angel armed with pragmatism rather than magic.

"Tris! You ready? We should probably check on those contacts Jess brought for you."

"Contacts?" Jessica echoed curiously before glancing at me once more, as if piecing together some puzzle she didn't yet fully comprehend.

Benji nodded vigorously as he pulled out the small case from my pocket—a mundane object now loaded with significance in this absurd reality we were caught in.

"Yeah! The contacts should help conceal whatever's happening there." He pointed toward my face while ushering me along with gentle urgency that allowed no room for hesitation or protest.

Jessica narrowed her eyes playfully but shot me one last meaningful glance before Benji led me away toward the restroom down the hall—a temporary refuge from prying questions and restless minds swirling around us.

Inside the bathroom stall—thankfully deserted—I took a deep breath as Benji handed over the contact case filled with hope cloaked in plastic packaging.

"You got this." His encouragement felt sincere despite lingering doubts still clinging tightly to my chest as if daring hope to unravel entirely.

I unscrewed the lid and pulled out one of the contacts—its color vibrant yet foreign against my fingertips—and stared at myself in disbelief through the mirror's reflection shimmering under fluorescent lights above.

Benji walked out of the bathroom and shut the door behind him. "I'll give you a few minutes. Let me know when you're ready." His voice carried a hint of concern, a reminder that despite the chaos, I had people who cared.

I stared at myself in the mirror, the foreign contact resting on my fingertips. My eyes, once a dull hazel, now glowed with an otherworldly silver and gold swirl—a constant reminder of the darkness that had taken hold of me.

I held the first contact between trembling fingers, its artificial blue color a stark contrast to my transformed eyes. The mirror reflected back the ethereal swirls of silver and gold that had become my new reality.

Taking a deep breath, I stretched my eyelid and carefully placed the lens against my right eye. A slight burn followed as it settled into place.

The difference was immediate. Half of my supernatural gaze disappeared behind a veil of normalcy. The contact didn't completely hide the glow, but it dulled it enough that casual observers wouldn't notice anything unusual. Just a hint of luminescence remained, like sunshine filtering through autumn leaves.

I blinked several times, adjusting to the foreign sensation. My enhanced vision felt slightly muted through the artificial barrier, but it was a small price to pay for anonymity. With steady hands, I repeated the process with my left eye.

The face that stared back at me looked almost human again. Almost. There was still something otherworldly in my features—the too-perfect skin, the unnatural beauty that came with the change—but my eyes no longer betrayed my true nature.

Through the bathroom door, Benji and Jessica's hushed conversation drifted to my ears:

"What's really going on with him?" Jessica whispered.

"Jess, please... just trust that he has his reasons," Benji replied softly.

Their words were clear as crystal despite the barrier between us—another reminder of what I'd become. I adjusted my sunglasses back into place, an extra layer of protection against prying eyes.

"Jess, I'm not sure exactly, but Tris and his family are in danger. They need help to get out," Benji said, his tone laced with concern.

I tensed, waiting to hear Jessica's response. I knew I couldn't hide this from her forever, but the thought of dragging her into the vampiric world I now inhabited filled me with dread.

"Danger? Benji, what's going on?" Jessica's voice wavered slightly, the worry evident. "You randomly called me late at night. I'm not mad, just concerned. What's happening?"

Benji paused, and I could imagine him running a hand through his hair, a nervous habit of his. "I wish I could tell you more, Jess. But Tris is going through something..."

I sighed, knowing I could no longer avoid this. Steeling myself, I opened the bathroom door, meeting the concerned gazes of my two closest friends.

"Tris," Jessica breathed, her eyes searching mine, the contacts barely concealing the transformation that had taken place. "What's going on?"

I took a deep breath, trying to find the right words. "Jess, Benji... I'm in trouble. My family is in trouble. And I need your help."

Jessica's brow furrowed, and Benji placed a reassuring hand on her shoulder. "We're here for you, Tris. Whatever it is, we'll figure it out."

I nodded, grateful for their unwavering support, even as I grappled with the weight of the secrets I now carried.

"How's it look?" I asked Benji, blinking a few times to adjust to the foreign feel.

Benji leaned in, scrutinizing my face. "Perfect. You can barely tell a difference."

I let out a shaky breath, relieved that the contacts were doing their job of concealing the unnatural glow in my eyes. But the weight of the deception still hung heavy on my shoulders.

"Tris, you know you can't hide this forever, right?" Benji said, his tone laced with concern.

I nodded solemnly. "I know. But I have to try. I can't risk you, Jess, or anyone else getting dragged into this mess."

Jess placed a reassuring hand on my shoulder. "Hey, we've got your back. Whatever you need, Benji and I are here for you."

I managed a small smile, grateful for the unwavering support of my friends. "Thanks, guys. I just... I don't know what I'm going to do. Everything's changed, and I'm terrified of what might happen if the Council finds out about me."

"The Council?" Jessica's eyes narrowed at my slip. "What council?"

I shifted uncomfortably, my mind racing to find the right words without revealing too much. "They... think of them as this powerful organization that operates in the shadows. Old money, old power. They control more than you'd believe."

"Like some kind of secret society?" She leaned forward, her voice dropping to a whisper.

"Something like that. I'm sure they've got their fingers in everything—politics, business, technology. But they stay hidden, pulling strings from behind the scenes." I rubbed my temples, feeling the weight of each word. "And they don't take kindly to outsiders."

"And you somehow got mixed up with them?" Benji asked, his expression grave.

"Not by choice. I..." I paused, choosing my next words carefully. "I came across something I wasn't supposed to know about. And now I'm pretty sure they see me as a threat."

Jessica's face paled. "Are they the ones after your family?"

"Yes. They have strict rules about keeping their existence secret. Anyone who discovers them without permission..." I let the sentence hang, the implications clear.

"But why not just go to the authorities?" Jessica pressed.

I let out a bitter laugh. "The authorities? Jess, these people are the authorities. They've got judges, politicians, and CEOs in their pockets. They're practically untouchable."

"Jesus," Benji muttered. "No wonder you're trying to disappear."

"Now you understand why I need those new identities," I said, meeting Jessica's worried gaze.

"We'll figure it out," Benji said with determination. "You're not alone in this, okay?"

I took a deep breath, feeling a flicker of hope amidst the overwhelming uncertainty. "Okay. Let's get back out there before Kat starts wondering what's taking us so long."

Benji and Jess nodded, and we made our way back to Kat, the blue contacts concealing the truth that had become a heavy burden on my shoulders. As I rejoined the conversation, I couldn't help but feel a pang of guilt for keeping my friends in the dark. But the thought of them being in danger because of me was a risk I couldn't bear to take.

We gathered back in the living room, a motley crew of conspirators bound by necessity and friendship. Kat looked up from her perch on the couch, her eyes scanning over me with a mix of concern and amusement.

"Those contacts look way better than your freaky eyes, bro," she joked, a small smile playing at the corners of her mouth. The tension in the room eased slightly, the familiar banter a welcome reprieve from the heaviness of our situation.

Benji clapped his hands together, all business. "Alright, team. Let's gear up." He handed out dark hoodies, hats, and black medical masks from a bag he'd retrieved from his basement. "These should help conceal our identities from any security cameras. Can't be too careful, especially with what we're about to do."

I pulled the hoodie over my head, the fabric smelling faintly of mothballs and old storage. Kat wrinkled her nose but said nothing, slipping on her own disguise. Jess checked her reflection in the mirror, adjusting her hat to hide her distinctive blond hair. Every detail mattered; we couldn't afford any mistakes.

"We'll take my car," Jess said, keys jingling in her hand. "It's the least conspicuous and has tinted windows. Better safe than sorry."

Kat nodded, taking the keys from Jess. "I'll drive. I've got the most experience with... evasive maneuvers." She grinned, a flash of her old self shining through the worry. Her confidence was reassuring, a beacon in the storm of uncertainty we were about to face.

We piled into Jess's car, a sleek black sedan that blended seamlessly into the night. Kat started the engine, and we pulled out onto the quiet suburban street, leaving behind the safety of Benji's house. The drive was filled with nervous chatter, jumping from topic to topic like stones skimming across water.

Anything to avoid the heavy silence that threatened to settle over us. Benji recounted a story about a hacking job gone wrong, Jess shared an anecdote about her cat's latest antics, and Kat reminisced about a childhood camping trip.

I listened, half-heartedly contributing to the conversation, but my mind was elsewhere. The city lights blurred past the window, a smear of neon against the dark glass. I couldn't shake the feeling of unease, the constant prickle of danger at the back of my neck. The stakes were high, and the margin for error was slim.

"Tris, did you hear about the weird stuff going down at Palantir?" Benji asked, turning in his seat to face me.

I shook my head, pulling my attention back to the present. "No, what happened?"

Jess glanced at Benji, a silent exchange passing between them. "A few days ago, these men in suits showed up," she said, her voice dropping slightly. "They were demanding all of Kirkwood's files and information, claiming they were conducting an investigation."

I frowned, a sense of foreboding settling in my stomach. "What kind of investigation? And who were they?"

Benji shrugged. "They didn't say. But they had this... air about them. Like they were used to getting what they wanted, no questions asked. It was all very hush-hush."

"It's illegal to just hand over someone's personal information like that," I said, my brows furrowing. "Especially to some random group of people."

Jess nodded. "Exactly. But somehow, they got it. Ash was freaking out about it. She said they had some kind of warrant, but it all seemed shady as hell, like there was more going on than meets the eye."

"You think they were government?" I asked, looking between the two of them.

Jess bit her lip, considering. "Maybe. They had that vibe, you know? Like FBI or CIA. But something felt off. I can't quite put my finger on it. It's like they were operating outside the usual channels."

I leaned back in my seat, my mind racing. Kirkwood, the missing executive. The strange men in suits. The rising number of missing persons in the city. It all felt connected somehow, a web of intrigue and danger that we were caught in the middle of. The pieces were starting to fall into place, but the picture was still unclear.

"I'll check out the security footage when we get to Palantir," I said, determination settling in my voice. "Maybe we can catch a glimpse of these guys, figure out who they are and what they want. We need to know what we're dealing with."

Kat glanced at me in the rearview mirror, her eyes reflecting the city lights. "You think this has something to do with... everything?" she asked, her voice barely above a whisper.

I met her gaze, a silent understanding passing between us. "I don't know. But we can't ignore the possibility. We need to be prepared for anything."

The car fell silent, the weight of our mission settling over us like a shroud. We were no longer just a group of friends on a reckless adventure; we were conspirators, rebels fighting against an unseen enemy. The gravity of our situation was palpable, a heavy burden we all shared.

As we approached Palantir Technologies, the towering office building loomed before us like a monolith, its glass and steel facade reflecting the cold glow of the city. Kat pulled into the underground parking garage, the car's headlights slicing through the dimly lit space. The garage was quiet, the hum of the city above a distant murmur.

I looked around, my enhanced senses picking up the faint echoes of distant footsteps, the dull hum of electricity coursing through the building's veins. Every sound, every movement, felt amplified, a testament to the heightened state of my vampiric senses.

"Alright, let's do this," I said, my voice steady despite the turmoil within. We moved as one, a united front against the unknown, our footsteps echoing in the silent garage as we made our way toward the elevators. The plan was set, the players in motion. There was no turning back now. We were in this together, for better or for worse.

And as we stepped into the elevator, the doors sliding shut behind us, I couldn't shake the feeling that our lives would never be the same again. The reality of our situation was sinking in, and there was no going back to the way things were. We were on a path of no return, and the only way forward was through the danger that lay ahead.

The fluorescent lights buzzed overhead, casting an eerie glow on the sleek floors of Palantir Technologies. It was 3 AM, and I felt the weight of the darkness pressing in around me. The facility was quiet, save for the distant hum of machinery and the occasional shuffle of security guards. This was the perfect time for our covert operation, but the stillness added to my unease.

I adjusted my walkie-talkie, ensuring it was firmly in place. "Everyone ready?" I whispered as I flanked Benji and Jessica. Our plan was straightforward: infiltrate the server room, hack into the accounts of the wealthy, and disappear before anyone noticed we'd been there. But nothing felt straightforward in the swirling currents of danger around me.

"Just keep the walkie on," Benji replied, his eyes darting around for any signs of movement. "And remember to stick to the plan. We have a limited window."

Jessica pulled out a small device from her pocket and handed it to me. "You need to plug this into the security system. It'll loop the camera feeds for a while so we can move unseen." Her voice was steady, a stark contrast to the jittery energy in the air.

"Thanks, Jess," I said, pocketing the device. The glow of the screens highlighted the determination on her face; she seemed ready for anything.

As we approached the service door leading to the security room, I took a deep breath, reminding myself of the stakes. I needed to uncover more about Kirkwood and the strange men who had been desperately searching for him. With a few agile strides, I moved through the office space, my senses heightened amidst the buzzing atmosphere.

Jess and Benji flanked me, their expressions focused and determined. I paused before the door, listening intently for any signs of movement or voices on the other side. The silence was deafening, save for the faint hum of electronics.

"Alright, let's do this," I whispered, glancing at my friends. Jess nodded and quickly plugged a device into the security panel, her fingers flying across the keypad.

In hushed tones, Jess explained, "I can only disable one surveillance camera in the facility from this access panel. If we're lucky, that should draw the security guard away to investigate, giving Tris enough time to insert my USB drive and override the door locks before he comes back." She added under her breath that once I connected the drive, it would create a video loop, making us temporarily invisible on the security feeds.

I gripped the small flash drive, steeling myself for the critical next steps. "Alright, let's do this." I took a deep breath and moved to insert the drive, ready to seize the opportunity Jess had created.

"Ready?" Jess's voice was barely a whisper, yet it sliced through the thick silence surrounding us like a knife. I could feel the weight of the moment pressing down on me, and without hesitation, I nodded, preparing for what lay ahead.

"Three," she began the countdown, her fingers hovering over the controls. "Two... One."

The subtle click of a relay echoed in the small room, the only indication that something had changed. We held our breath, listening intently. Seconds ticked by, stretching into an eternity. The tension was thick enough to choke on. Then a faint creak reached my ears—the sound of a door opening.

A muffled voice, too low to decipher, drifted down the hallway. Jess gave me a curt nod, her eyes gleaming with a mixture of excitement and nerves. This was it—my chance. I slipped out of the shadows, adrenaline coursing through my veins. My enhanced speed made the short dash to the security room door a blur. I pressed my ear against the cool metal, listening for any sign that the guard was returning. Nothing.

With a swift, practiced movement, I inserted the USB drive Jess had given me. The small screen on the panel flickered, lines of code cascading down before settling on a looping image of the empty hallway. We were invisible, at least for a little while. I sent a silent prayer to whatever deity might be listening that it would be long enough.

"Jess, Benji, what's your status?" I whispered into the walkie-talkie while leaving the security room with the USB drive perfectly hidden.

"Just about to get in," Benji replied, his voice crisp.

I reached the server room door, a heavy steel barrier standing between us and our objective. Benji pulled out a small device, his fingers dancing over the keys with practiced ease. A soft whirring sound filled the air as the lock mechanism disengaged. The door swung open, revealing the blinking lights and humming servers within.

The air inside was cool, a stark contrast to the humid night outside. Rows upon rows of servers stretched into the darkness, their rhythmic hum a constant background noise. This was the heart of Palantir, the repository of secrets and data. And we were about to crack it wide open.

"Cover us while we work. This might take a few minutes," Benji whispered.

"Understood," I said, glancing through the glass panels of the server room. I could see Benji and Jess setting up their equipment, their focused expressions a mix of determination and urgency.

After they split off, I stealthily made my way to the archives, yearning to dig deeper into Kirkwood's files. It felt as if some unseen force compelled me to uncover the mysteries surrounding his disappearance, haunted by the enigmatic presence of the strange man who had visited me. Maybe Kirkwood was the key to understanding the shadows closing in around me.

The software systems were surprisingly easy to navigate. Using the skills I'd honed during my days at Palantir Technologies, I quickly located Kirkwood's file and accessed the CCTV footage from the day the strange men arrived. As I played the video, I carefully analyzed their body language and demeanor. They moved with an air of authority, their instincts honed and alert, as if they were scanning for anything unusual.

I swiftly connected a device to the server in the archives room, initiating a download of all files pertaining to Kirkwood. The progress bar on the screen flickered, indicating the process would be completed in roughly four minutes. This would provide me access to the entire Palantir database, including crucial security footage from the day the enigmatic individuals arrived.

My eyes darted between screens as files populated with Kirkwood's assets. Properties scattered across multiple states filled the display—vacation homes in the Hamptons, penthouses in Manhattan, private islands off the coast. The man had accumulated wealth beyond imagination, but something felt off about the paper trail.

I clicked through documents detailing his real estate holdings. A warehouse in Detroit caught my attention—purchased through a shell corporation with ties to offshore accounts. Similar patterns emerged: properties acquired through byzantine networks of dummy companies, all leading back to tax havens in the Cayman Islands.

Download Progress: 05%... 11%...

The download progress ticked up as I dug deeper. A sprawling compound in Montana stood out—500 acres of remote wilderness with state-of-the-art security systems. The blueprints showed underground facilities, but their purpose was unclear. What was Kirkwood preparing for?

More properties appeared: an abandoned missile silo in Kansas converted into a luxury bunker, a private airstrip in Nevada, research facilities masked as storage units. Each revelation painted a picture of a man systematically building something in the shadows. But what?

My enhanced vision caught every detail as I scanned through building permits and contractor invoices. Heavy security installations, reinforced walls, advanced filtration systems—these weren't normal vacation homes. They were fortresses designed to withstand disaster.

The loading bar crept forward as I absorbed the scope of Kirkwood's hidden empire. The official records showed a successful businessman, but these files revealed someone methodically preparing for something. Someone who knew secrets worth protecting at any cost.

Download Progress: 15%... 21%...

My fingers flew across the keyboard, downloading everything I could find about these properties. Whatever Kirkwood was involved in, these locations were clearly part of a larger plan. And understanding that plan might be key to unraveling the mystery of his disappearance.

Download Progress: 25%... 30%...

Suddenly, blaring alarms shattered the deceptive quiet, jolting me from my focus. A rush of adrenaline surged through me, knowing we had to move.

"Tristan!" I heard Benji's voice crackle through the static of my walkie-talkie. "We need to get out of here! Now!"

I turned the corner and saw Benji and Jess huddled in a nearby alcove, their faces tense. And standing with them was Ash.

My breath caught in my throat at the sight of Ash. Her presence threw me completely off balance—she wasn't part of the plan. Her dark eyes met mine, a mix of determination and something else I couldn't quite read.

"What are you doing here?" I asked, coming to a halt beside them.

"Trying not to get caught," Ash replied, her eyes wide with panic. "I heard the alarm while investigating Kirkwood's files."

"Great," I muttered, realizing the complications this would add. "That's just what we need right now."

"Tris, Ash is helping us," Benji explained quickly, glancing toward the approaching footsteps of the guards. "She ran into me when I was setting up. She agreed to help us with the money transfer."

"Seriously?" I looked at Ash, weighing her significance amidst the chaos.

"I'm in," she assured me, determination shining through her fear. "Whatever it takes to find out more about Kirkwood."

"We have to go!" Jess urged, her voice cutting through the tension as the sound of guards drawing nearer grew louder. "The guards are on high alert after that alarm."

I hesitated for a brief moment, knowing that my download still needed time. Download Progress: 50%... 55%... It was a critical window I couldn't afford to miss.

"Just hold on a second! I have to grab the device I connected—it's almost done!" I exclaimed, urgency driving my actions as I quickly slipped back into the archive computer room, my senses heightened. I could hear the footsteps of the guards approaching, bringing the pressure to a breaking point.

Racing against the clock, I felt the familiar thrill of my vampiric nature surging through me, propelling me forward. I rolled the USB drive into my hands and glanced at the download. Download Progress: 75%... 80%... I had to hurry—every second counted.

I perfected my movements, dodging shadows as the device finally chimed. Download Complete. A small victory surged within me as I pocketed the drive, taking a moment to steady my breath before racing back to join my friends just as the guards were closing in.

"Tris, now!" Benji shouted, urgency lacing his voice, and I turned sharply.

"Go! I got it!" I shouted as we swiftly pushed toward the nearest exit, adrenaline coursing through my veins.

My senses were finely attuned, honed to every detail of the chaotic surroundings.

"Where do we go?" Ash asked as we navigated through the dim lighting, tension palpable in the air.

"There's an emergency exit at the back of the building," I replied, trying to maintain my focus. "Let's stick together and stay low."

We moved as one, pushing through the corridor in a tight formation. As we approached the exit, I let out a breath of relief, the cool night air beckoning just outside the door.

"Almost there!" I urged, silently thanking fate that we were still a step ahead of the danger stalking us.

But just as we reached the door, security guards appeared around the corner. I barely had time to react before instinct took over. In a blur of motion, I weaved past them, moving with a speed that I hoped wouldn't betray my true nature.

"Go! I'll distract them!" I shouted over my shoulder. Without looking back, I sprinted down the hallway, firmly planting my feet as I redirected my attention to the guards.

"Tris, no!" Benji exclaimed behind me.

But I couldn't think about that right now—I had to keep everyone safe. With a quick turn, I disarmed one guard with a controlled motion, pushing him off balance and into the wall, relying on the strength I could muster without revealing my full capabilities.

I barely had time to think as the guards closed in. Their presence loomed—menacing, alert, and heavily armed. My instincts kicked in, sharp and clear, overriding any lingering hesitation.

I dashed forward, eyes locked on the first guard. He was tall and broad-shouldered, clearly a veteran. He raised his gun just as I lunged, sidestepping his aim with a speed that caught him off guard. My fist connected with his wrist in a quick jab, forcing him to drop the weapon with a clatter.

"What the hell?" he shouted, stumbling back as I used his momentum against him.

"Just a guy looking for answers," I shot back, already moving toward the next guard who appeared from around the corner.

Two more guards rushed me simultaneously. One of them shouted, "Hey! You're not supposed to be here! How many of you are there?" His voice was a mix of confusion and authority.

"Just me," I replied. The second guard swung at me with his baton; I ducked under it and struck back with an elbow to his stomach. He gasped and crumpled to the floor. The first guard regained his composure and tried to grapple with me from behind, but I twisted free just in time.

"Stop resisting!" he barked, struggling to keep up as I darted sideways into an open room lined with old office cubicles.

I needed space—a chance to regroup without being pinned down by too many at once. My heightened senses picked up another guard entering through the opposite door, gun raised.

"Freeze!" he yelled.

Instead of freezing, I surged forward and tackled him before he could pull the trigger. We hit the ground hard; I used my weight to pin him down while wrenching the weapon from his grip and tossing it aside. The chaos echoed through the room—a mixture of shouts and frantic movements blurred together in a cacophony of sound.

"You think this is funny?" Another guard barged in, flanked by yet another who came up from behind.

"Just trying to get out alive!" I shot back without slowing down.

They aimed their weapons at me; I threw myself low against a desk just as they fired shots that ricocheted off the walls. My body moved instinctively; using my speed again, I slid behind cover while catching sight of Benji peeking out from behind an office partition further down the hall.

"Go!" I yelled at him urgently, but he shook his head defiantly. "I'm not leaving you!"

I took a breath—this was going to take everything I had left in me if we were going to escape together.

I barely had a moment to catch my breath when I spotted a guard sneaking up behind Benji, eyes narrowed and intent on bringing him down. Panic surged through me, and without thinking, I tapped into that vampire speed that felt so alien yet exhilarating.

"Benji!" I shouted, propelling myself forward in a blur. I reached him just as the guard lunged, my body colliding with his and sending him crashing into a row of filing cabinets. The metal groaned under the impact.

Benji spun around, his face a mix of shock and confusion. "What the hell just happened?"

"Go! Get to the others!" I ordered, urgency coursing through my veins. The last thing I needed was for him to get caught up in this mess. "I'll handle the guards."

He hesitated, uncertainty flickering in his eyes, but then nodded slowly, backing away toward safety. "Tris... be careful."

"Just go!" I snapped, adrenaline fueling my every move as I darted away from him.

The remaining guards shifted their focus toward me as I dashed deeper into the office maze. My senses heightened; I could hear their shouts echoing behind me, their footsteps pounding against the floor. With each burst of speed, I pushed myself harder, knocking another guard off balance before he could react. He hit the ground with a thud.

"Hey! Over here!" I taunted as more guards rushed in my direction.

I darted between the desks, using the narrow space to my advantage. My body moved with a fluidity I had never known before—an instinctive grace that felt like second nature. I could hear the guards shouting behind me, their frustration palpable as they stumbled over each other in a desperate attempt to corner me.

"Stop right there!" one of them yelled, but his command fell flat as I leapt over a fallen chair, landing silently on the other side.

The agility coursing through me was exhilarating. I barely had time to think; it was all instinct now. I pushed off a desk with my foot, propelling myself into a somersault that landed me directly behind a guard who had just turned the corner. He barely registered my presence before I drove my shoulder into his back, sending him sprawling into the wall.

"Guess you should've been quicker," I muttered, adrenaline thrumming in my veins.

The remaining guards fanned out, clearly trying to encircle me. Their eyes widened as they struggled to keep up with my movements. I spotted another guard advancing from my right and pivoted sharply, throwing a fist that connected solidly with his jaw. He staggered back, shock evident on his face before he hit the ground.

"Damn it! It's like he's a ghost!" one guard shouted, exasperation creeping into his voice.

"Not a ghost—just faster than you," I shot back, scanning for an exit as more of them swarmed in from both sides.

I spotted a fire escape door at the end of the corridor—a possible way out if I could clear these guys first. The guards were closing in again; one reached for his weapon while another tried to grab me from behind. But this new body felt stronger—faster—I ducked under his grasp and spun around, catching him off guard with a swift kick to his knee. He went down with a grunt.

"Why can't you idiots work together?" I taunted as another guard lunged at me.

This time, instead of dodging backward, I sidestepped him and drove my fist into his ribs as he passed by—a calculated move that sent him crashing into a row of desks.

The adrenaline surged through me as I faced the guards, my instincts kicking into high gear. I felt alive—truly alive—in a way that I hadn't experienced before. Each of their movements felt exaggerated, slow in comparison to the blur of thoughts racing through my mind.

"Let's see what this body can really do," I muttered to myself, a smirk tugging at my lips.

Four guards surrounded me now, their faces tense and uncertain. They exchanged glances, trying to formulate a plan. But they had no idea how much had changed within me since my transformation. My senses heightened; I could hear their heartbeats thumping in rhythm, each one adding to the crescendo of chaos around us. The air was charged with tension, tinged with the metallic scent of sweat and fear.

I lunged forward, pivoting into a low sweep that knocked the first guard off his feet. He hit the ground hard with a grunt; a satisfied rush washed over me. This felt good—really good.

"Just like practice," I whispered as I shifted my weight, feeling every sinew in my body tighten and release in fluid motion.

Two more guards charged at me simultaneously. I ducked under one's flailing arms while launching upward onto a nearby desk. From there, I executed a perfect backflip, landing right behind them with grace that surprised even me.

"Nice try!" I laughed softly as they stumbled over each other in confusion.

The fourth guard tried to flank me from behind, but with a quick glance over my shoulder, I caught his movement just in time. I twisted on my heel and delivered a sharp elbow to his midsection that sent him wheezing into a wall.

"Keep it coming," I taunted lightly as they regrouped, determination evident on their faces despite their growing frustration.

With every strike and parry, my vampire senses fed into my reactions—my sight sharpened so that every flicker of movement stood out against the dull office backdrop; the sound of footsteps approached with an intensity that rang in my ears; even the texture of the air felt alive against my skin.

I advanced again, catching another guard off guard with an open palm strike to his chest followed by a swift knee to his stomach—a calculated effort not to inflict real harm but to incapacitate him long enough for him to reconsider his career choice.

"This is what it feels like," I thought excitedly as another guard lunged toward me. My foot shot out instinctively; it connected with his side and sent him sprawling across the floor.

"Control! Keep it together!" my internal voice reminded me as each blow fell perfectly into place—a testament not just to practice but to something deeper now.

With one last opponent left standing between me and freedom, everything slowed once again as he hesitated before advancing on me. The thrill surged anew within me; this was no longer just about survival—it was about reclaiming who I was becoming amidst this newfound chaos.

"Let's finish this."

Every punch and kick seemed to flow effortlessly from me; this was what it meant to embrace this new existence fully.

I slid past another guard and executed a swift strike to his chest—just enough to knock him out without causing serious harm.

Suddenly, my walkie-talkie buzzed against my hip, and Kat's voice crackled through with urgency. "Tristan! We're inside! Where are you?"

"Almost there!" I replied breathlessly.

The adrenaline propelled me toward an open window at the end of the hall. Without hesitating, I launched myself into the night air, landing softly on the ground just feet behind our getaway car parked under the cover of darkness.

Kat was there, her eyes widening in shock as she noticed me appear seemingly out of nowhere. Only she seemed aware of my entrance; her expression morphed from surprise to relief mixed with fear as she caught sight of me landing from a jump of thirty stories.

I slid inside the vehicle. "Drive!" I yelled as Kat revved the engine, her face etched with urgency.

"I thought you said it would be quick!" she exclaimed, glancing back at the chaos behind us.

"Keep it moving!" I said, trying to stay calm amidst the rising tension.

"I can't believe you fought off guards!" Ash marveled, disbelief mingling with admiration as we sped away from the building. "What are you, a ninja?"

"That was some impressive agility," Benji chimed in, a hint of laughter in his tone as he caught his breath.

I glanced at them, attempting to mask the internal turmoil. "Let's figure out what we got and how to move forward," I replied, casting a nervous glance back at where the facility faded into the distance. I knew we had escaped, but I could still feel the heaviness of our actions pressing down on me.

"What were you expecting to uncover?" I asked Ash, trying to keep my mind focused despite the chaos. "What made you come here?"

"I was digging into Kirkwood's disappearance," she replied, tension simmering in her voice. "Something about it felt off. He was involved in something shady before he vanished. I thought there'd be more answers here than at work."

"That's exactly it," I said, my mind racing. "I was looking for him too. He could be the thread that unravels this whole mess."

As Jess began discussing the transfers, her fingers danced over the keyboard, the glow of the screen illuminating her focused expression. I watched her, tension coiling in my stomach. Ash leaned closer, her brows furrowing deeper as she processed everything we had just done.

"Wait a minute," Ash said, her voice sharp with suspicion. "What exactly are you guys doing?" She leaned back in her chair, crossing her arms defensively. The shift in her demeanor was palpable; I could see her wheels turning.

Jess glanced up, momentarily caught off guard by Ash's tone. "We're just setting up some quick transfers to cover our tracks—"

"Cover your tracks? That's what you call it?" Ash interjected, skepticism intensifying. "I recognize that program running on your computer." She pointed an accusatory finger at the screen. "That's not just standard accounting software. Are you guys robbing the place?"

"Robbing?" I echoed, half-laughing at the absurdity while my mind raced to form a more convincing explanation.

Jess shifted uncomfortably in her seat but kept typing, as if ignoring Ash would make this all go away. "It's not like that," she insisted, trying to keep the conversation calm. "This is just a means to an end."

Ash wasn't buying it; I could see that much in her narrowed eyes. "Means to what end? You're stealing from your own company! Do you realize how dangerous this is?"

"It's not theft if we're taking back what they owe us," Jess replied quickly, now defensive as she faced Ash head-on. Her fingers hovered over the keyboard, awaiting my permission to proceed.

I ran a hand through my hair, frustration bubbling beneath the surface. "We're trying to secure our safety—our future," I explained, meeting Ash's gaze with a serious look that conveyed my urgency.

Her expression softened slightly but remained skeptical. "And how do you expect to get away with this? What if they find out?"

I could feel Jess's tension rise again as she continued typing—each keystroke echoing my mounting anxiety about how far we'd gone down this rabbit hole.

"Ash," I said slowly, trying to break through her doubt, "we need this."

She pointed at the screens where Jess and Benji were working. "You're stealing. This is illegal!"

"If we don't do this, we can't stay safe," Kat replied, her voice steady.

I could feel Ash's eyes burning into me, her skepticism palpable.

"Who's the driver?" she asked, glancing at Kat, her voice laced with suspicion. "I only recognize you three," she gestured between Benji, Jess, and me, "and you're all wearing disguises. Who is she?"

"Kat," I replied, keeping my tone steady as I sensed the tension in the air. "My sister."

Ash raised an eyebrow. "Your sister? Why didn't you say anything before?"

"It didn't seem important at the time," I said defensively. "We just needed to get out."

Benji cleared his throat awkwardly from the back seat. "We all have our reasons for keeping things under wraps." He turned toward Kat, trying to ease the atmosphere.

"Hi," Kat replied cautiously, but I could see her nerves simmering beneath the surface.

"Okay," Ash said slowly, clearly trying to process everything.

Jess took off her mask and hat first, shaking her head as if freeing herself from some invisible weight. Her blond hair tumbled down in soft waves; I could see Ash's surprise flicker across her face.

Benji followed suit, peeling off his cap and removing his mask. His bright smile remained intact as he looked between us.

"That was more exhausting than I thought it'd be," he joked lightly.

With each disguise removed, I felt layers of tension begin to lift from our group—like peeling away old skin to reveal something fresh underneath. But Ash still eyed me warily.

Slowly, I removed my own mask—the fabric sliding away felt both liberating and unnerving at once. When my face emerged into the light of the dim car interior, Ash stared at me with wide eyes that hinted at recognition mixed with apprehension.

Benji spoke up, glancing between us. "How about we transfer $8 million into your private account? It won't raise any flags, and we can keep this between us."

I was taken aback by Benji's boldness, but it made sense; aligning with Ash could bolster our safety as we navigated this unknown landscape.

After a tense moment, Ash finally nodded, resolve settling in her eyes. "Alright, but I need to be kept in the loop. No more secrets. If I'm part of this, I want to know everything."

I felt a rush of relief wash over me. "You'll be in the know. I promise."

She leaned forward, her expression turning serious. "I need to understand what's going on with Kirkwood. The whole situation feels off." Her voice softened as she continued, "The girl he hurt—she's my cousin."

I stared at her, surprise cutting through the tension in the air. "Your cousin?"

"Yeah," she said, rubbing her temples as if trying to ease the weight of it all. "She ended up in the hospital after Kirkwood lost it over that project failure. I had no idea it was that bad until I saw the reports about his outburst."

"So you've been investigating because of her?" I asked, trying to piece everything together.

Ash nodded vigorously. "Exactly! When those strange men in suits started showing up at Palantir Technologies, it raised all sorts of alarms for me." She crossed her arms tightly over her chest. "I had to find out what was happening—why they were there and why they seemed so interested in Kirkwood."

Benji exchanged a glance with Jess before shifting slightly in his seat, clearly intrigued by Ash's connection to this mess.

"I get that you want answers," Jess chimed in softly, glancing between Ash and me. "But we're already knee-deep in danger here. We can't afford any distractions."

"I'm not a distraction!" Ash shot back, fire igniting in her eyes again. "This is personal for me! If there's something bigger going on—if those guys are connected to Kirkwood's disappearance—I want to know what we're dealing with!"

I leaned back against my seat, considering Ash's words carefully. She wasn't just a friend caught up in this chaos; she had skin in the game now—her family was involved.

"Alright," I said finally, trying to quell any remaining doubts gnawing at my insides. "I downloaded all the files that Palantir Technologies had on Kirkwood through the main archives and server. I found some things, but we can look deeper at the files once we get clear."

Ash nodded firmly, determination radiating from her. It felt like we were solidifying an alliance amidst uncertainty—a pact born from shared purpose and desperation.

As we drove deeper into this tangled web of deceit and danger, I couldn't shake the feeling that things were about to get much worse before they got better.

As we sped away, ineffable shadows loomed over us, the looming threat of the future hanging heavy. Together, we would uncover the truths that lay hidden in the dark and navigate the dangerous waters ahead.

For now, we had escaped, and that was a victory worth celebrating.

CHAPTER TWENTY-THREE

KIRKWOOD

Morning arrived with a dull gray light filtering through the tinted windows of Jess's car. The cityscape blurred past us in a smear of steel and concrete; buildings that once towered proudly now seemed to hunch in the early dawn. The hum of the engine was a steady drone beneath our silence, the only consistent sound in an otherwise quiet ride.

Kat drove, her hands gripping the wheel tightly, knuckles white against the leather. Her eyes flicked to the navigation on Benji's phone clipped to the dash, brow furrowed in concentration. Each turn and lane change was executed with precision, a military precision that betrayed her anxiety.

Benji leaned forward from the backseat, pointing at the screen. "Take the next right, Kat. We're almost there." His voice was calm and reassuring, but I could hear the underlying tension, the tightly coiled spring of nerves just waiting to release.

I glanced at Jess beside me, her eyes scanning the streets warily, as if expecting danger to leap out from every alleyway. She caught my gaze and offered a small, tight smile, an unspoken promise that we would get through this together.

Ash sat in the far back, arms crossed, staring out the window. Her presence added another layer of tension, but there was comfort in numbers, a shared vigilance that bolstered my courage.

"You sure about this guy, Benji?" I asked, turning to look at him. His usual grin was replaced by a serious expression, eyebrows drawn together in thought. He nodded, meeting my gaze with determination in his eyes.

"Max is solid," he said confidently. "I've known him for years. He's helped me out of a few tight spots. If anyone can get us new IDs, it's him."

Kat took a sharp turn, the tires screeching slightly against the asphalt. "And he's okay with helping all of us?" Her voice was steady, but I could hear the undercurrent of anxiety, the fear that we were placing all our hopes on the shoulders of a stranger.

"He owes me one," Benji replied, leaning back in his seat. "Plus, he's not exactly a fan of the system. He likes to stick it to the man whenever he can."

Ash finally spoke up, her voice cutting through the tension like a knife. "And what makes you think he won't sell us out? If he's that connected, he must have a price."

Benji shook his head, a small smile playing at the corners of his mouth. "Max isn't like that. He's got his own code. Besides, I've got enough dirt on him to keep him in line."

Jess turned to look at Ash, her eyes flashing with a combination of defiance and understanding. "We don't have much choice here. We need those IDs if we're going to disappear."

Ash held her gaze for a moment before nodding slightly, conceding the point. The tension in the car seemed to lessen, if only slightly, as we all came to terms with the risks we were about to take.

The buildings grew older and more rundown as we ventured deeper into a part of the city I rarely visited. Graffiti sprawled across brick walls, the vibrant colors a stark contrast to the grime and dirt that coated everything.

The streets narrowed, cluttered with cars and debris, making it d-ifficult for Kat to navigate. She slowed the car, expertly maneuvering around potholes and stray cats darting across the road.

"This is it," Benji said, pointing to a nondescript building tucked between a boarded-up storefront and a grimy-looking bar. A faded sign hung above the door, reading "Max's Repairs" in chipped paint. The letters seemed to sag, as if the weight of the world was too much to bear.

Kat pulled over, the engine idling as we all stared at the building before us. It looked abandoned, forgotten by time and the city around it, as if it had been swallowed by the shadows of neglect. But Benji seemed confident, already opening his door and stepping out onto the cracked, uneven sidewalk that seemed to tell stories of its own.

"Come on," he called, a spark of enthusiasm in his voice as he beck-oned us forward. "Max is expecting us."

One by one, we exited the car, the cool morning air hitting me like a refreshing splash of reality, a stark contrast to the warmth that had enveloped us inside the vehicle.

I could smell the city here—exhaust fumes mingling with damp con-crete, the faint scent of garbage wafting up from the gutters. But beneath it all, there was something else, something uniquely human that stirred a primal instinct within me.

The smell of life, of blood pumping through veins, beating with a rhythm that echoed my own heartbeat—or rather, the absence of it. I pushed the thought away, forcing myself to focus on the task at hand, the mission that had drawn us to this forgotten corner of the city.

We followed Benji to the door, the glass so grimy it was impossible to see inside. He knocked, three sharp raps against the weathered wood, then paused before adding two more, as if to emphasize our urgency. A moment later, the door creaked open, revealing a dimly lit hallway that felt like the entrance to another world.

A gruff voice echoed from within, thick with familiarity. "About time you showed up, Benji."

Benji grinned in response, his enthusiasm unwavering as he stepped inside. "Good to see you too, Max." The tension in my shoulders eased slightly, though a part of me remained on high alert, aware of the complexities and dangers that lay ahead.

We filed in behind him, the door shutting firmly, sealing us off from the chaotic world outside. The hallway was narrow, the walls lined with peeling wallpaper that told stories of neglect and time, stained with age and perhaps a few secrets of their own.

A single bare bulb hung precariously from the ceiling, casting long shadows that danced and twisted with our movements, creating an eerie spectacle that was both captivating and unsettling. The air was thick with dust, carrying the scent of oil and something more elusive, hinting at the myriad secrets that lay hidden within these walls.

As we approached the end of the hallway, it opened into a cluttered room, a veritable treasure trove of old computers, tangled wires, and an assortment of tools scattered haphazardly across every available surface.

In the midst of this technological chaos sat Max, a burly man whose thick beard framed a face marked by experience. Tattoos snaked up his arms like vines, each one possibly a testament to his past.

His eyes were sharp and assessing as he looked up from the circuit board he had been examining, glinting with a mix of curiosity and caution. It felt as though he could take our measure in a single glance, evaluating not just the threat we might pose but also the potential profit we represented in this murky underworld we had stumbled into.

"Who are your friends, Benji?" he asked, his voice a low rumble that seemed to reverberate through the very foundations of the building, hinting at authority and experience.

Benji gestured to each of us in turn, his movements confident and sure, as if he were presenting prized possessions. "This is Tristan, Kat, Jess, and Ash. They're the ones I told you about," he said, pride evident in his tone.

Max nodded, but his gaze lingered on me for a moment longer than it did on the others. I met his stare unblinking, feeling the weight of his scrutiny, until he finally looked away, redirecting his attention back to Benji.

There was something unsettling about his gaze, a piercing intensity that suggested he could see through the carefully crafted facade I had built, exposing the truth of what I had become—the monstrous reality lurking beneath my human exterior.

"Alright," he said, leaning back in his chair, the ancient springs protesting with a groan that echoed the tension in the air. "Let's get down to business."

Benji stepped forward, his usual bravado tempered by the gravity of our situation. He looked more serious than I'd ever seen him, a stark contrast to his usual carefree demeanor. "Max, we need to talk business. You got the package?"

Max leaned back further, arms crossed over his broad chest, his posture exuding both confidence and a hint of reluctance. "You mean the IDs?" His expression remained inscrutable, but I sensed a flicker of curiosity beneath his tough exterior, as if he was weighing the potential consequences of our request.

"Yeah," Benji replied, urgency creeping into his tone, underscoring the weight of our predicament. "The ones I ordered."

With a grunt, Max pushed himself up from the chair, the wooden legs scraping against the concrete floor like nails on a chalkboard. He moved toward a battered filing cabinet tucked in the corner, rifling through its contents with practiced ease, a well-rehearsed dance that spoke volumes about the world we inhabited.

I glanced around the room, taking in the chaotic mix of technology and tools that surrounded us. It felt like stepping into a different world—one where survival hinged on information and quick thinking. My heart raced as I absorbed the reality of our situation; every gadget and piece of machinery seemed to pulse with the weight of our choices.

"You sure you want these?" Max asked over his shoulder, not bothering to look up as he continued his search, his voice gravelly and low. "Things could get messy if anyone finds out."

Benji shifted on his feet, anxiety etched across his face, the shadows of worry deepening his features. "We don't have much choice. We're not safe out there." He nodded toward the door, as if emphasizing the danger lurking just outside, a reminder that the world beyond these walls was filled with threats we couldn't afford to ignore.

Finally, after what felt like an eternity, Max produced a small manila envelope and tossed it onto a nearby table with a thud that resonated in the silence. "Here you go," he said gruffly, his tone leaving no room for further discussion. "IDs for each of you. They're clean—no strings attached."

I approached cautiously, my mind racing as I picked up the envelope and felt its weight in my hands. Inside lay our new identities—the lifelines that would allow us to disappear into obscurity.

My fingers brushed against the paper, and I hesitated for a moment, staring at Benji's determined face, which reflected both hope and the stark reality of our situation. This was more than just a piece of paper; it was a step into a new life, a desperate bid for safety in a world that threatened to engulf us.

"Did you get the payment?" Benji asked, his eyes fixed on Max, a tense edge to his voice.

Max's lips curved into a half-smile, a glint of satisfaction in his eyes. "Yeah, came through this morning. Clean transfer, just like you promised." He tapped a few keys on his keyboard, turning the monitor toward us. Numbers flashed across the screen—more zeros than I'd seen in a long time. A pang of unease hit me as I realized the magnitude of what we were doing.

"Thanks," Benji said, his voice steady. The IDs felt heavy in my hands, weighted with possibility and danger. Each piece of plastic represented a new life, a chance at survival, but also the death of who we used to be. The finality of it all sent a chill down my spine.

Max leaned against the wall, arms still crossed as he studied us closely, his gaze piercing. "Just remember," he cautioned in a low and serious voice, "you'll be starting fresh with these names. No pasts to carry forward. You'll be ghosts in the system."

I glanced down at the envelope, thoughts racing in my mind. Would this really help us? Would it shield us from what was coming? The thought churned in my stomach like acid, a mix of fear and determination swirling within me.

"Any chance you can help us set up some backup plans?" Kat asked quietly from behind me, her voice steady despite the uncertainty that hung thick in the air. Her eyes held a glimmer of hope, seeking any advantage we could get.

Max chuckled softly but shook his head slowly, a hint of finality in his gesture. "I'm not your babysitter. You're on your own from here." His words hung in the air, a stark reminder of the isolation we were stepping into.

Jess slid the flash drive into her laptop, the soft click echoing in the tense silence of Max's cluttered room. The screen flickered to life, casting a blue glow over her face as she began to sift through the files. Benji leaned over her shoulder, his eyes scanning the data with practiced intensity.

"Alright, let's see what we've got here," Jess murmured, her fingers dancing over the keyboard. The first few documents were straightforward—financial records, emails, nothing out of the ordinary. But as she delved deeper, her brows furrowed, and her typing slowed.

"What is it?" I asked, leaning in to get a better look at the screen. The air was thick with anticipation, the hum of the computer fan the only sound breaking the silence.

"These files... they're encrypted," Jess said, her voice tight. "And not just standard encryption. This is high-level stuff."

Benji let out a low whistle, his eyes widening as he took in the complex code. "Whoever did this didn't want anyone poking around."

Max, who had been watching from the sidelines with a mix of curiosity and skepticism, stepped forward. "Mind if I take a look?"

Jess glanced up at him, a question in her eyes. Benji nodded slightly, giving her the go-ahead. She slid the laptop toward Max, who began to scrutinize the screen with a critical eye.

"This isn't just about hiding information," Max muttered, more to himself than to us. "This is about protecting something... or someone."

Ash, who had been quietly observing from the corner, stepped forward. "You think this has something to do with Kirkwood's disappearance?"

Max looked up, his gaze sharp. "If he was involved in something this heavily guarded, then yeah, I'd say his disappearance is just the tip of the iceberg."

Jess took the laptop back, her determination renewed. "Alright, let's see what we can do about these encryptions."

Benji cracked his knuckles, a mischievous grin spreading across his face. "Time to put those old hacking skills to the test."

The room filled with the sound of rapid-fire typing, the occasional muttered curse, and the hum of concentration. I watched as Jess and Benji worked in tandem, their fingers flying over the keys with a synchronization that spoke of years of practice. Max chimed in occasionally, offering insights and suggestions that seemed to help them navigate the complex web of code.

"This is going to take a while," Jess muttered, her eyes never leaving the screen. "Whoever encrypted these files knew what they were doing."

Benji nodded, his brow furrowed in concentration. "We'll get through it. Just a matter of time."

I leaned against the wall, my arms crossed over my chest as I watched them work. The weight of our situation pressed down on me, the reality of what we were doing sinking in. We were delving into a world of secrets and deception, stepping into a game where the stakes were high and the consequences deadly.

Ash moved to stand beside me, her voice low. "You okay, Tristan?"

I glanced at her, meeting her concerned gaze. "Yeah, just... thinking."

She nodded, understanding in her eyes. "It's a lot to take in. But we're in this together. Remember that."

I offered her a small smile, appreciating her support. "Thanks, Ash. I know we are."

Hours passed, the room growing darker as the day waned. The only light came from the glow of the laptop screen, casting long shadows across the cluttered space. Jess and Benji continued to work, their focus unwavering, while Max observed, his expression thoughtful.

Finally, Jess let out a triumphant cry. "Got it!"

Benji whooped, clapping her on the back. "Knew you could do it, Jess."

Ash leaned in, her eyes scanning the newly unlocked files. "What do we have here?"

Jess began to open the documents one by one, her expression growing more serious with each reveal.

"These are records of transactions, meetings, communications... all tied to Kirkwood. But it's not just him. There are names here—powerful individuals—all connected in some way."

I leaned closer, peering over her shoulder at the screen. The rows of data blurred together, but as she scrolled through, certain names stood out—executives from companies I recognized, politicians with faces I'd seen on TV.

"Look at this," Jess said, pointing to a series of emails dated just before Kirkwood's outburst at Palantir. "They're discussing changes in financial allocations... and here." She highlighted another line that read: *Ensure our interests remain protected should any information surface.*

"What information?" I whispered, dread curling in my stomach.

Benji leaned in further, his brow furrowing as he absorbed the details. "They're worried about something coming to light. Kirkwood must have been caught up in something bigger than we realized."

Jess clicked on another file labeled "Meeting Minutes." The notes detailed a gathering among high-ranking officials and corporate leaders discussing a mysterious *Project Elysium*. "What the hell is that?" I asked.

"Sounds like something out of a sci-fi movie," Benji muttered under his breath.

"Or a cover for something sinister," Ash added, her tone grave.

As Jess continued to dig deeper, she found references to several shipments tied to overseas accounts—discrepancies that hinted at money laundering and possibly even human trafficking. My stomach turned as the implications sank in.

"They're not just hiding financial records; they're concealing lives," I said, anger flaring within me.

I leaned closer to the screen as Jess scrolled through the documents. The implications of what we were uncovering hit me like a punch to the gut. This was no ordinary corporate cover-up. Lives hung in the balance, and we were just scratching the surface.

"Jess," I said, my voice low but urgent. "We need to pivot back to those missing persons cases we heard about. This... this is bigger than we thought."

Her brow furrowed as she glanced up from the screen. "What do you mean?"

"Think about it. All those reports we dismissed as random disappearances? What if they're connected? Kirkwood was onto something—something serious."

Benji nodded, catching on quickly. "Those incidents were labeled as nothing significant in the news. Just another case of people vanishing in a city this size."

"But it's not just a coincidence," I pressed on, urgency coursing through me. "Kirkwood's outburst, the hidden transactions—this all leads somewhere dark."

Jess turned back to her laptop, fingers flying over the keyboard again as she searched for anything related to the missing persons cases. The tension in the room thickened, our breaths held as we waited for her findings.

"I remember some names from the news," Jess said, her eyes narrowing in concentration. "There were patterns—specific demographics targeted and disappearing under strange circumstances."

"Exactly," I replied, feeling a fire ignite within me. "Kirkwood must have stumbled upon a network that traffics these people or worse."

Ash stepped forward, crossing her arms tightly across her chest. "And what if he was silenced because of it? What if he got too close?"

The realization settled heavily in the air like an impending storm. The more I thought about it, the more convinced I became that Kirkwood had uncovered something vital—a tangled web of corruption that stretched far beyond our understanding.

"Let's dig deeper into those cases," I urged Jess. "If Kirkwood was involved in anything even remotely connected to human trafficking or exploitation..."

"I'm on it," she said resolutely, already pulling up additional files and searching through records from police reports and news articles.

The atmosphere shifted around us as we absorbed the gravity of our discovery—a dark truth waiting to be revealed. Each click of Jess's keys echoed my rising dread and determination to uncover whatever lurked beneath the surface.

Benji let out a low whistle as he read over her shoulder. "This is big, Jess. Really big."

As Jess and I sifted through the files, Benji leaned closer to the laptop screen, his brow furrowing in concentration. "Wait a minute," he muttered, his fingers flying across the keyboard. "I think I found something."

"What is it?" I asked, leaning in beside him. The tension in the air thickened, anticipation swirling around us.

"Look at this," Benji said, highlighting a name on one of the documents—a missing person's report. "This guy was reported missing about three weeks ago. But there's something strange here." He scrolled down, revealing a link to encrypted hospital records associated with the case.

Jess squinted at the screen. "Encrypted hospital records? That's not normal."

Benji nodded, clearly frustrated. "I can't crack this encryption. It's like they're hiding something specific about him." He sat back in his chair, running a hand through his hair. "But there's no record of him being admitted to any hospitals in the area."

"Then how did they get this file?" I wondered aloud.

Benji's eyes lit up with determination again. "Let me check the hospital records themselves for anything unusual."

He navigated away from the encrypted file and began searching through local hospital databases. Each click of the mouse felt like a step closer to uncovering a hidden truth.

After several tense moments, Benji leaned forward, eyes wide with disbelief. "There's nothing—no admissions under this name at any hospital. But look at this," he pointed to another entry that appeared almost hidden within layers of data.

"It's just basic medical info," he said slowly as Jess glanced over his shoulder. "Height, weight, blood type... but these results are dated recently."

"That's odd," Jess murmured as she took over again, pulling up more details on her screen.

This missing person had been logged somewhere—but it wasn't within standard channels or even hospitals that followed legal protocols. They were trapped in an encrypted void where information slipped away into shadows.

"What does this mean?" I asked quietly.

"It means someone is keeping track of them—monitoring them—without anyone knowing," Benji replied grimly.

"Let me try cracking into that encryption again," Jess said, her voice firm as she pulled up tools on her laptop while we all held our breath in anticipation of what we might find next.

Jess's fingers danced over the keyboard, her eyes scanning lines of code that seemed to stretch into infinity. The glow of the screen cast eerie shadows on her face, highlighting the furrow of her brow. "There's more," she murmured, her voice barely above a whisper. "Thousands of names. And the dates... they span decades. From the sixties all the way to this year."

I leaned in, my gaze flicking over the endless list. A chill ran down my spine. "What does this mean?"

Benji pulled up a chair, his expression grave. "Let's find out who's behind this. There must be a pattern, a common thread."

Jess nodded, her focus unwavering. She began to cross-reference the names with hospital records, her fingers flying over the keys with practiced ease. Minutes ticked by in tense silence, the only sound the hum of the computer and the distant murmur of the city outside.

"Nothing," Jess finally said, her voice laced with frustration. "It's like they just appear out of thin air. No admissions, no discharges, no doctors' notes. Just... nothing."

Benji leaned back, running a hand through his hair. "That's not possible. Everyone leaves a trail. We just need to find it."

I watched as Benji leaned closer to the screen, his brow furrowed in concentration. "Hold on," he muttered, scrolling through the encrypted files with a growing sense of urgency. The tension in the room thickened, each keystroke echoing my own mounting anxiety.

"What are you seeing?" I asked, my mind racing as I tried to piece together the puzzle we were uncovering.

"There are names here," Benji said slowly, his voice tightening. "A lot of names." He paused, running a hand through his hair. "These people... they all went missing."

"What do you mean?" I stepped closer, peering at the screen over his shoulder. The list seemed endless, rows and rows of names stretching into an abyss of forgotten lives.

He clicked on one name, pulling up a file that looked eerily familiar. "This one—Mark Johnson. He was reported missing last year." His voice grew more intense as he scrolled through more entries. "And here's another—Sarah Lopez—missing three months ago."

"Those cases were all over the news," I whispered.

"Exactly," Benji continued, eyes widening with disbelief. "They're connected to this encrypted database somehow." He highlighted a few more names, revealing a disturbing pattern that seemed to thread through them all.

Jess leaned closer too, her expression shifting from focus to concern as she began to recognize the implications. "You think these people are tied to Kirkwood's disappearance?"

Benji nodded vigorously. "It has to be! Look at the dates—most of these disappearances coincide with date entries of the encrypted files." He looked up at us, urgency flaring in his gaze. "What if Kirkwood found out something he shouldn't have? What if these disappearances are linked to whatever was going on?"

I felt a chill run down my spine as dread settled in my gut. The thought of innocent lives caught in this web sent a surge of anger through me. "We need to find out what happened to them."

"Right," Benji said resolutely as he continued scrolling through the files with newfound determination. "If we can trace these connections back to Kirkwood or whoever is behind this... we might uncover something that leads us straight to the truth."

As I watched him work, adrenaline coursed through me. The deeper we delved into this darkness, the clearer it became that we had stumbled upon something far bigger than ourselves—a sinister game where lives hung in the balance, and we were now entangled within its grasp.

Ash's eyes narrowed as she took in the information. "We need to follow this lead. If Kirkwood is involved in something this deep, we need to find out what it is."

I felt a pang of unease, a sense of foreboding that gnawed at the edges of my mind. But beneath it all, there was a spark of determination. Kirkwood had hurt Ash's cousin and left a trail of destruction in his wake. If there was a chance to bring him to justice, to uncover the truth behind his actions, I was willing to take the risk.

Ash leaned back in her chair, arms crossed, her gaze fixed on the screen. "We need to go back to those files—the ones with the locations. If Kirkwood is hiding, one of those places might give us a clue."

I nodded, the weight of our discovery pressing down on me. "You're right. We need to narrow it down."

Benji's fingers flew over the keyboard, pulling up the encrypted files again. The list of locations scrolled by, each one a potential hiding spot for a man who had everything to lose.

"Here," Jess pointed at the screen. "These are the most recent entries. If Kirkwood is on the run, he wouldn't have gone far."

I scanned the list, my eyes landing on a familiar address. "This one—it's an old warehouse downtown. Abandoned for years, but it's still standing."

Ash nodded, her expression thoughtful. "Makes sense. It's isolated, easy to defend. If he's hiding, that's where he'd go."

Benji looked up from the screen, his brow furrowed. "But what if he's not alone? What if someone got to him first?"

The room fell silent, the implication hanging heavy in the air. If Kirkwood had been taken, then we were walking into a trap. But if he was still out there, hiding, we had to find him.

"We have to check it out," I said, my voice firm. "We can't just sit here and do nothing."

Ash met my gaze, determination in her eyes. "Agreed. But we need to be careful. We don't know what we're walking into."

Jess nodded, already pulling up a map of the warehouse. "We'll scope it out first, make sure it's safe. Then we go in."

As we huddled around Jess's laptop, I felt the familiar weight of urgency settle in my gut. She scrolled through the live feeds from the warehouse, each flickering image a reminder of what was at stake. We needed to find Kirkwood—before it was too late.

Kat pulled me aside, her voice dropping to a low whisper. "Tris, we need to talk." Her eyes darted around the room, taking in the cluttered space filled with old computers and stacks of paper. She leaned in closer, her expression serious. "I'll call Mom, Dad, and Micah. It's starting to look like we need more time before we can meet up with them. I'll get the new IDs and head to Pine Barrens with them and wait for you there."

I nodded, feeling the weight of her words settle over me. The gravity of her statement hung in the air, revealing her desire to protect our family. "Okay, Kat. That sounds like a plan."

She hesitated for a moment, her eyes searching mine. "Tris, does this have anything to do with... the you-know-what stuff?"

I took a deep breath, choosing my words carefully. "With all the missing people, something must be going on. I'm not sure yet, but we need to be prepared for anything."

Kat's gaze held mine for a moment longer before she nodded resolutely. "Alright, I'll get everything ready. We'll be safe in Pine Barrens. Just make sure you join us as soon as you can."

As Kat turned to leave, Jess stepped forward, her voice steady. "Take my car, Kat. I can get another one."

Kat paused, looking back at Jess with gratitude. "Are you sure?"

Jess nodded firmly. "Yes, it's the least I can do."

Benji approached, a black backpack slung over his shoulder. He handed it to Kat, his expression serious. "Here, take this. It's got a few laptops and a gun. You might need them."

Kat took the backpack, her eyes widening slightly. "Thanks, Benji."

Benji reached into his pocket and pulled out a small flash drive. "All the money is on this drive. Just attach it to each of the computers, and the money will split and transfer automatically.

Use these black cards to take cash out of the ATM. They're untraceable, and you can use them like a credit or debit card. The funds are connected to the new offshore accounts I created for Micah, you, your mom, and dad. There are also burner phones in there, already programmed with our numbers."

Kat took the flash drive and the black cards, her expression a mix of determination and gratitude. "Thank you, Benji. This means a lot."

Benji nodded, a small smile playing on his lips. "No problem, Kat. Just be careful out there. Remember, Pine Barrens is vast and can be dangerous. Stick together and trust your instincts."

With a final nod, Kat turned and walked out of the room, leaving Jess, Benji, Ash, and me standing in silence. The weight of our mission hung heavily in the air, but there was also a sense of resolve. We were doing this to protect our family, and nothing would stand in our way.

As the door closed behind Kat, Jess turned to me, her expression thoughtful. "Tris, we need to focus on finding Kirkwood. If he's involved in something this deep, we need to uncover the truth. His disappearance might be the key to understanding what's happening in this city, and we can't afford to ignore the potential connection to the supernatural underworld."

I nodded, feeling a renewed sense of determination. "You're right. Let's get back to those files. There has to be something we missed."

Jess pulled up a grid of video feeds on her laptop, each square displaying a different angle of the abandoned warehouse. The images were grainy and flickering slightly, but they were live. "We've got eyes on the place," she said, her voice tense with focus. "But to see if Kirkwood ever walked in there, we'll need to access the main hub of the security system. It's not connected to the cloud, so we can't rewind from here."

I leaned in, scanning the screens. The warehouse looked deserted, but there were too many shadows, too many places to hide. "Where's the hub?" I asked, already knowing we'd have to go there.

"It's in the main office, on the second floor," Jess replied, her fingers dancing over the keyboard as she zoomed in on one of the feeds. "But Tris, it's been months since the incident at Palantir. The chances of finding anything…"

"Are better than doing nothing," I finished for her, determination gripping me. "We have to check it out. If there's even a slim chance that Kirkwood was there, we need to know."

Benji nodded, his expression serious. "I agree. We can't just sit here and hope for the best. We need to act."

Ash crossed her arms, her gaze fixed on the screens. "So, what's the plan? We just waltz in there and hope no one's home?"

Jess shook her head. "No, we do this smart. There are four entrances to the warehouse. We split up, scope out each entrance, and then regroup. If it's clear, we make our way to the main office and access the security footage."

I stood up, ready to move. "Let's do it. The sooner we get in, the sooner we find out what's going on."

Benji pushed his chair back, standing with me. "I'm with Tris. Let's get this show on the road."

Ash uncrossed her arms, a small smirk playing on her lips. "Fine, but if we get caught, I'm blaming you two."

"Let's keep looking," Jess said, determination threading through her voice. She pulled up another window filled with archived data from local reports, a treasure trove of information that could hold clues about Kirkwood's whereabouts.

I leaned closer as I watched her sift through records. "If we can connect any dots from previous cases…"

"Exactly," she replied, her fingers dancing over the keyboard again. A moment later, she leaned back and grinned triumphantly. "Here! I found three more potential locations where Kirkwood could be hiding or where we might find clues."

Benji and Ash gathered around her, anticipation evident in their expressions.

Jess pointed at the first location on the screen. "This one's an old industrial complex on the east side. It's been abandoned for years but is known to be a hotspot for illegal activities—drug deals and trafficking operations."

"Sounds promising," Benji said, his brow furrowing as he considered the implications.

She clicked on another file and continued. "The second place is a rundown motel off Main Street. It has a reputation for being a safe haven for people trying to stay off the grid."

"A perfect spot to lay low," I added, my mind racing with possibilities.

Jess nodded and pulled up one last location, this one slightly more surprising. "And finally, there's an old subway station that's been closed for renovations for ages. Rumor has it that people use it as a hideout."

I raised an eyebrow. "A subway station? That could be dangerous."

"Or it could be our best chance at finding him," Jess countered firmly as she began to jot down notes about each location on her notepad.

"We should hit all three," I suggested, excitement bubbling within me despite the gravity of our mission. "If Kirkwood is moving around, we need to cover ground quickly."

Ash nodded in agreement. "We can split up again after checking out the warehouse first."

"Then let's finalize our plan," Jess said decisively as she began to jot down notes about each location on her notepad.

With adrenaline surging through me, I felt ready to dive into whatever darkness awaited us next; there was no turning back now.

As we prepared to leave, I couldn't shake the feeling of unease that settled in my gut. We were stepping into the unknown, chasing shadows and secrets. But we had to find Kirkwood, no matter the cost. The truth was out there, waiting to be uncovered, and we were the ones who had to bring it to light.

Max watched us, his gaze thoughtful. "You're stepping into a world of trouble, you know that, right?"

I nodded, meeting his eyes with a steady gaze. "We know. But we can't just sit back and do nothing."

Max let out a sigh, running a hand through his beard. "Alright. I'll help you as much as I can. But you're on your own out there. I can't protect you from what's coming."

Ash stepped forward, her eyes gleaming with a mix of anger and determination. "We don't need protection. We need answers. And we're going to get them, one way or another."

The room seemed to pulse with a newfound energy, a sense of purpose that bound us together. Jess began to organize the files, her fingers moving swiftly over the keyboard, the click-clack of the keys echoing like a battle march.

"Alright, let's start by cross-referencing these names and locations. See if we can find any patterns or connections that might lead us to Kirkwood."

I leaned in, my eyes scanning the screens as Jess pulled up the data. The glow of the monitors cast eerie shadows on our faces, highlighting the mix of determination and anxiety that we all felt.

Benji and Ash flanked me, their expressions focused, ready to dive into the digital abyss to find the answers we needed. This was our chance to uncover the truth, to find out what happened to Kirkwood, and maybe, just maybe, shed some light on the larger mystery that had entangled us all.

"If Kirkwood is hiding, he's not going to make it easy for us to find him," Ash mused, her brow furrowed in concentration. Her sharp wit was already cutting through the layers of deceit, anticipating the challenges ahead.

"That's why we need to work together," Jess replied, her gaze unwavering. She was in her element, her past experiences with the FBI and CIA making her a formidable ally in this hunt. "We've got the resources and the skills to track him down. We just have to be smart about it."

Benji nodded, his fingers tapping against the desk, a nervous rhythm that betrayed his otherwise calm demeanor. "Okay, so we start with the warehouse. That's our best lead right now. What's the plan?"

I took a deep breath, feeling the weight of our mission settle on my shoulders. The responsibility was immense, but I was not alone. I had my friends, my family, and we were united in our quest for the truth. "We split up, like Jess said. Cover the different entrances, scope out the place, and then regroup. If it's clear, we make our way to the security hub and see what we can find."

Ash gave me a nod, her eyes gleaming with a hint of excitement. She was always ready for a challenge, and tonight was no different. "Sounds like a plan. Let's do this."

We quickly divided into teams: Jess and Benji took the north and east entrances, while Ash and I covered the south and west. As we stepped into the night, the city's shadows seemed to whisper secrets, daring us to uncover them.

The chill of the evening air contrasted sharply with the warmth of our determination, a silent promise that we would not return empty-handed. The hunt for Kirkwood had begun, plunging us deeper into the mysteries lurking in the heart of the city.

Max observed us critically as we gathered our gear. He stepped forward, holding out a set of keys. "You'll need more than just your wits out there. Take these." He handed each of us a compact, sleek gun, the metal cold and heavy in my hand.

Benji inspected each one with a practiced eye before passing them around. The weight of the gun served as a sobering reminder of the danger we were walking into.

"I hope you don't have to use these," Benji said, his voice low. "But better safe than sorry."

Max nodded, his expression serious. "Exactly. Now, follow me. I've got something else that might help."

We followed him through a maze of narrow corridors, the air thick with the scent of oil and metal. The fluorescent lights overhead flickered, casting eerie shadows on the walls.

He led us to a large garage, the door creaking open to reveal a beast of a truck. It was old but well-maintained, with a heavy-duty grille and reinforced tires. Max patted the hood affectionately, leaving a faint smudge on the otherwise gleaming paint.

"This is Bessie," he said, a hint of pride in his voice. "She's seen me through more scrapes than I can count. She's got a few modifications—armored plating, run-flat tires, and a few other surprises. She'll keep you safe."

Jess stepped forward, scanning the truck appreciatively. She ran her hand along the side, feeling the cool metal beneath her fingertips. "It's perfect, Max. Thank you."

Max tossed me the keys. "Tris, you're driving. I trust you to take care of her."

I caught the keys, feeling the weight of responsibility settle on my shoulders. They were cool and heavy in my palm, a tangible symbol of the trust Max was placing in me. "I will. Thanks, Max."

We climbed into the truck, the interior smelling of leather and old cigarettes, with a faint hint of Max's aftershave lingering in the air. Jess and Benji started setting up their laptops in the back, their fingers flying over the keyboards as they prepared for the mission ahead.

The glow of their screens cast long shadows across their faces, highlighting their intense concentration. Ash sat in the passenger seat, her eyes scanning the road ahead, already alert. Her fingers drummed nervously on the dashboard, missing nothing.

I slid the key into the ignition, and the engine roared to life with a deep, throaty growl. The truck vibrated beneath me, a beast ready to be unleashed. I gripped the steering wheel, a sense of determination settling over me.

We were ready. We had a plan. And we were going to find Kirkwood, no matter what it took. The city's secrets were out there, waiting to be uncovered, and we were the ones brave—or foolish—enough to dive in headfirst.

As I put the truck into gear, the garage door rumbled open, revealing the dark city streets beyond. The night air was cool, carrying the distant hum of traffic and the faint scent of rain.

I took a deep breath, steeling myself for whatever lay ahead. Then, with a final nod to Max, I pressed down on the accelerator, and we rolled into the night, the truck's headlights cutting through the darkness like a knife.

The city sprawled before us, a labyrinth of steel and shadows, hiding its secrets in the depths of the night. And we were ready to unravel them all.

CHAPTER TWENTY-FOUR
INTO THE ABYSS

The warehouse loomed before us, a monolithic structure of steel and concrete that seemed to swallow the dim light of the overcast sky. It was brand new, yet an ominous air surrounded it, as if the very walls whispered secrets of what lay hidden within. The air was thick with the scent of oil and metal; the distant hum of the city was a faint echo against the silence enveloping the building.

I stared at the warehouse, a mix of apprehension and excitement coursing through my veins. The adrenaline from our previous encounter still lingered, making the world feel sharper and the colors brighter. The weight of the gun in my hand was a comforting presence, a tangible reminder of the danger we were walking into.

"This place gives me the creeps," Ash murmured, her eyes scanning the building critically. "It's too quiet."

Benji nodded, his fingers tapping nervously against the laptop tucked under his arm. "Yeah, it's like a ghost town. Are you sure we should be doing this, Tris?"

Jess adjusted the strap of her bag, her expression serious. "We need to find out what's going on. Kirkwood's in there, and we need to know why."

I took a deep breath, the scent of the city filling my lungs. The nervous energy within me surged, a protective instinct flaring up. "We do this smart. There are four entrances to the warehouse. We split up, scope out each entrance, and then regroup. If it's clear, we make our way to the main office and access the security footage."

We quickly divided into teams, Jess and Benji taking the north and east entrances, while Ash and I covered the south and west. The sky above us was a canvas of dark clouds, hinting at an impending storm. The air was charged with tension, the silence broken only by the distant rumble of thunder.

As we approached the south entrance, I couldn't shake the feeling that something was off. The building was too new, too pristine. It was as if it had been constructed for a purpose, a facade hiding something sinister beneath.

Ash walked beside me, her steps measured and cautious. Her eyes were alert, missing nothing. "You feel it too, don't you?" she asked, her voice low.

I nodded, my fingers tightening around the gun. "Yeah. Something's not right here."

We reached the entrance, the metal door cold and unyielding. I pressed my ear against it, listening for any sounds from within. Silence greeted me—a heavy, oppressive silence that seemed to press against my eardrums.

"Clear," I whispered, stepping back. Ash nodded, her hand hovering over her own weapon.

As we made our way around the perimeter, I couldn't help but think back to the feeling I had experienced when I threw Constantine back. It had been an electric surge of power—exhilarating and frightening all at once. I could still feel the echo of it, a strange vibration that seemed to hum beneath my skin. It was unfamiliar yet somehow right, as if it had always been a part of me, waiting to be awakened.

We met up with Jess and Benji at the designated spot, their expressions grave. "Nothing on our end," Jess said, her voice barely above a whisper. "It's like the place is deserted."

Benji nodded, his eyes scanning the building nervously. "Same here. No signs of life."

I looked at each of them, seeing the concern etched on their faces. The weight of responsibility settled on my shoulders, a heavy burden I was determined to bear. "We go in. Stick to the plan. We find the security hub and see what we can uncover."

Jess nodded, her expression resolute. "Let's do this."

We slipped into the warehouse, the door creaking open to reveal a vast, empty space. The air was cool, the scent of metal and dust filling my nostrils. The silence was oppressive, the only sound the faint hum of the fluorescent lights overhead.

We moved cautiously, our steps echoing in the vast space. The warehouse was a labyrinth of steel and shadows, the rows of crates and machinery casting long, ominous shadows on the concrete floor.

While we navigated deeper into the building, I couldn't shake the feeling that we were being watched. The strange vibration beneath my skin seemed to intensify—a constant hum that set my nerves on edge. I gripped the gun tighter, my senses on high alert.

"Over there," Benji whispered, pointing to a door at the far end of the warehouse. "That must be the security hub."

We approached the door, our steps measured and cautious. The air was thick with tension, the silence broken only by the distant hum of the city outside.

As we reached the door, I paused, my hand hovering over the handle. The strange vibration beneath my skin seemed to pulse—a warning that sent a shiver down my spine. I looked at the others, seeing the concern etched on their faces.

"Ready?" I asked, my voice low.

They nodded, their expressions serious. I took a deep breath, steeling myself for whatever lay beyond the door. Then, with a final nod, I pushed it open.

The door creaked like an old man's joints, protesting our intrusion. The moment I stepped inside, a rush of stale air hit me, mixed with the metallic scent of machinery that clawed at my senses.

It felt like we had stumbled into a forgotten realm—one where time stood still, and the ghosts of long-dead machines whispered their secrets. The silence was almost deafening, broken only by the distant hum of the city outside, a world away from this abandoned place.

The interior was dimly lit, flickering overhead lights casting uneven shadows that danced across the walls. The beams struggled against the darkness, illuminating glimpses of rusted metal and dust-covered surfaces. A chill ran down my spine as echoes of forgotten machinery reverberated around us, heightening the eerie atmosphere. It was as if the very air was heavy with the weight of secrets hidden in the shadows.

"God, this place gives me the creeps," Ash muttered under her breath as she followed me inside, her sharp eyes scanning the room warily.

"Yeah," I replied quietly, scanning the room for any signs of life—or danger. "It's like we're walking into a horror movie."

We moved deeper into the room, where the real heart of the operation lay hidden behind a cluster of ancient-looking computers. The walls were lined with monitors displaying various camera feeds from different angles within the facility—some flickered to life with power while others remained dark and silent, their screens reflecting the dull glow of the struggling fluorescent lights. Cables snaked across the floor like dormant serpents, tangled in a chaotic web that seemed to have no beginning or end.

"This is it," I breathed out, feeling a surge of adrenaline as I realized we were on the brink of uncovering something significant. The strange vibration beneath my skin pulsed again, a warning that sent a shiver down my spine.

Jess stepped up to one of the terminals, her fingers hovering above the keyboard. "I just need a moment to bypass these security protocols," she said with confidence, though I could see her brow furrowed in concentration. Her eyes darted across the screen, her fingers moving with practiced ease as she navigated the digital labyrinth.

I turned my attention back to the monitors, scanning each feed for anything unusual. But then something else caught my attention—a familiar scent hung in the air. It clawed at my instincts like an unwelcome memory: blood mingled with sweat and something acrid.

A cold dread washed over me as I recalled that night when Constantine attacked my family. The smell lingered here; it was almost as if they had been present recently. But uncertainty held me back from saying anything to Ash or Jess; I wasn't sure if it was just remnants left behind or something more sinister.

Benji rummaged through some scattered files nearby while casting nervous glances at Jess. "You think they left anything useful lying around?" he asked, his voice barely above a whisper.

Ash knelt beside him, flipping through pages filled with technical jargon that made no sense to me. "This place is abandoned but looks like someone wanted it up and running," she murmured, her brow furrowed as she examined a broken piece of machinery on the floor.

"Focus on what matters," I urged them softly without taking my eyes off Jess as she worked quickly and efficiently on unlocking access to footage.

With a few rapid keystrokes, Jess cracked through layers of security protocols and began navigating through files displayed on-screen. Her eyes widened slightly as she brought up footage from one camera feed showing what looked like recent activity within this very room. The grainy images flickered, showing shadows moving in the dim light, hinting at a presence that sent a chill down my spine.

"Here we go!" she exclaimed excitedly while tapping on keys deftly, her voice echoing slightly in the silent room.

As different feeds blinked into view one after another—a hallway leading into darkness here, a storage area there—I couldn't shake off that nagging feeling that something, or someone, had come through here. The sense of unease grew stronger with each passing moment, a silent alarm bell ringing in the back of my mind.

"Rewind it, Jess," I said, my voice low. "Let's see if we can catch Kirkwood entering."

Jess's fingers danced across the keyboard, the footage rewinding at high speed. The grainy images flickered across the screen, a chaotic jumble of light and shadow. The tension in the room was palpable, thick enough to choke on.

"There!" Ash pointed at the screen, her voice sharp. "Those suits... aren't those the same guys who came to Palantir and took all of Kirkwood's files?"

Benji leaned closer, his eyes narrowed. "Holy crap, you're right. Same build, same... vibe. What the hell is going on, Tris?" He looked at me, worry etched across his face.

Jess paused the recording. The frozen image of the men in black suits stared back at us, their faces obscured by shadows. "This is way bigger than we thought," she murmured, her voice tight. "This isn't just about a missing executive anymore."

My gaze was fixed on the screen, my mind racing. They were just humans, albeit ones with an unsettling aura. Government agents? Private security? Something else entirely? Whatever they were, they were clearly

searching for something, and it seemed Kirkwood was at the center of it al
l.

"Keep going," I said, my voice steady. "Let's see what else is on here."

Jess hit play. The footage rolled, the grainy images flickering across the screen. For a few moments, nothing happened. Then, three figures appeared, seemingly out of nowhere. They moved with a speed that was almost impossible to follow, blurring across the frame like phantoms. My instincts screamed, a jolt of recognition coursing through my veins.

"What the...?" Benji's voice was barely a whisper.

"Did you see that?" Ash's eyes were wide with disbelief.

Jess's hand flew to her mouth, stifling a gasp. "That's... that's not possible."

I remained still, watching the figures as they moved through the warehouse. The way they moved, the unnatural speed and fluidity of their actions... it was something I had seen before, something I had felt within myself. Could they be...? The thought lingered, a dark shadow in the back of my mind. I couldn't voice it, not yet.

"What the hell was that?" Benji's voice trembled. "They moved like... like they weren't even human."

Ash nodded, her face pale. "I've never seen anything like it. It's like... sped-up footage or something."

Jess swallowed hard, her eyes still fixed on the screen. "There's no way... that was real."

I took a deep breath, forcing myself to remain calm. I couldn't let them see what I suspected, not yet. "It's just... a glitch," I said, my voice carefully neutral. "Some kind of interference. Maybe those guys had a jammer, something that messed with the recording."

Benji frowned. "A jammer? But... it looked so real."

"Yeah," Ash agreed. "But... what else could it be?"

Jess shook her head, still looking shaken. "I don't know... but it was freaky."

"It has to be some kind of technological explanation," I insisted, my voice firm. "There's got to be a logical reason for it."

They looked at me, their faces still etched with unease. But they wanted to believe me; they needed to believe me. And in their ignorance, they did.

"Maybe," Benji said slowly. "Maybe you're right."

Ash nodded, her gaze returning to the screen. "It has to be. Right?"

Jess took a deep breath, as if trying to compose herself. "Right. It has to be." She turned back to the keyboard, her fingers hovering over the keys. "Let's keep looking. Maybe there's something else on here."

The footage continued to play, but the image of those three figures, moving with unnatural speed, remained burned into my mind. I knew what I had seen. And I knew what it meant. But for now, I kept my suspicions to myself, a secret weighing heavily on my heart.

"We need to explore this place further," I said, my voice steady despite the turmoil inside. "There might be something here that can lead us to Kirkwood."

Jess nodded, her eyes sparkling with a mix of fear and excitement. Benji clapped his hands together, a nervous energy radiating from him. "Let's do this. Maybe we'll find something the suits missed."

Ash, however, looked less convinced. She cast a wary glance back at the video screens, her brow furrowed. "I don't know, Tris. That footage... it was weird. Really weird."

I stepped closer to her, lowering my voice. "I know it's unsettling, Ash. But we need to find out what's going on. For Kirkwood, for Laura."

She bit her lip, looking torn. Then, with a sigh, she nodded. "Alright. But we stick together. No splitting up this time."

I agreed, grateful for her trust. We moved out, our footsteps echoing in the vast, empty warehouse. The air was thick with dust and the faint smell of oil, the silence broken only by the distant hum of the city outside.

We started in the main office, rifling through desks and filing cabinets. Jess tackled the computers, her fingers flying over the keyboards as she delved into their digital depths. Benji and Ash sorted through paperwork, their eyes scanning each page with meticulous care.

I took a step back, letting my senses expand. The strange vibration beneath my skin pulsed gently, a silent alarm that kept me on edge. I scanned the room, my gaze landing on a small, seemingly insignificant detail—a faint scuff mark on the otherwise pristine floor.

Kneeling down, I ran my fingers over the mark. It was slight, barely noticeable, but it was there. And it led toward a heavy metal door at the far end of the room.

"Guys," I called out, my voice echoing in the silence. "I think I found something."

They gathered around me, their eyes following the faint trail on the floor. Benji whistled softly. "Good catch, Tris. Let's see where it leads."

The door was locked, but Jess made quick work of the electronic keypad, her hacking skills proving invaluable once again. The door clicked open, revealing a dimly lit staircase leading downwards.

Ash looked at me, her eyes wide. "You sure about this, Tris?"

I nodded, steeling myself for whatever lay ahead. "We've come this far. Let's see it through."

We descended into the darkness, our footsteps echoing ominously on the metal stairs. The air grew colder and damp, the scent of earth and decay filling my nostrils. We reached the bottom, the beam of our flashlights cutting through the gloom to reveal a vast underground chamber.

It was empty, save for a single, large crate in the center. The crate was unmarked, its wooden surface rough and splintered. A heavy padlock secured it, gleaming dully in the beam of our flashlights.

Benji looked at Jess, a grin spreading across his face. "Your turn, hacker girl."

Jess rolled her eyes but stepped forward, a small toolkit materializing from her pocket. She worked quickly, her brow furrowed in concentration. After a few tense moments, the padlock clicked open.

We gathered around the crate, our breaths misting in the cold air. I gripped the edge; the wood was rough against my fingers. With a nod to the others, I pulled. The crate groaned open, revealing its contents.

It was empty.

Disappointment surged through me, a bitter taste in my mouth. I looked at the others, seeing the same sentiment reflected in their eyes.

"Damn it," Jess muttered, kicking the crate in frustration. "All that for nothing."

Ash sighed, running a hand through her hair. "Maybe it's a sign, Tris. Maybe we should just... let this go."

I shook my head, determination burning within me. "No. We're not giving up. Not yet."

Benji looked at me, his expression serious. "So, what's the plan, Tris? Where do we go from here?"

I thought for a moment, my mind racing. Then it hit me. "The motel. The one off Main Street. Kirkwood owns that motel. Maybe he left something behind."

Jess nodded, her eyes gleaming with renewed determination. "It's worth a shot. Let's get out of here."

We made our way back up the stairs, leaving the empty crate and the cold, damp chamber behind. As we stepped out into the night, the city lights seemed to blur, the world shifting beneath my feet. I took a deep breath, steadying myself.

The motel off Main Street was a run-down, seedy place, the kind of establishment that rented rooms by the hour. The neon sign flickered intermittently, casting an eerie glow over the cracked pavement.

We parked in the shadows, our eyes scanning the area warily. The place seemed deserted, save for a lone figure behind the reception desk.

I turned to the others, my voice low. "Jess, Benji, see if you can access the motel's records. Find out which room Kirkwood was in. Ash and I will keep watch."

They nodded, slipping out of the car and melting into the shadows. Ash and I stayed behind, our eyes scanning the area for any signs of trouble.

The night was quiet, the only sound the distant hum of the city. I leaned against the car, my senses on high alert. The strange vibration beneath my skin had faded, leaving behind a sense of unease that gnawed at me.

Ash looked at me, her eyes reflecting the flickering neon light. "You okay, Tris? You've been... different lately."

I hesitated, unsure of how to respond. How could I explain the changes within me, the dark, primal urges that lurked beneath the surface? How could I tell her about the blood, the power, the risk?

Before I could formulate a response, Jess and Benji returned, their faces flushed with success.

"Room 207," Jess said, her voice breathless. "Kirkwood stayed there for a few weeks before he disappeared."

I nodded, pushing away from the car. "Let's go."

We made our way to the room, our footsteps echoing on the metal stairs. The motel was a labyrinth of faded doors and peeling paint, the air thick with the scent of decay and despair.

Room 207 was at the end of the corridor, the door slightly ajar. I paused, my hand hovering over the doorknob. The strange vibration beneath my skin pulsed again, a warning that sent a shiver down my spine.

I looked at the others, seeing the same tension reflected in their eyes. Then, with a deep breath, I pushed open the door.

The room was dark, with only a faint light filtering in through the grimy windows. I stepped inside, my senses on high alert. The air was thick with dust and a faint, unsettling scent.

I flicked on the light, the harsh glow revealing a sparse, rundown room. The bed was unmade, the sheets stained and rumpled. The desk was cluttered with papers, the drawers half-open as if someone had left in a hurry.

Jess moved to the desk, her fingers sifting through the papers. Benji checked the bathroom, his face twisting in disgust at its state. Ash stood by the door, her eyes scanning the room warily.

I approached the bed, my gaze landing on a small, seemingly insignificant detail—a faint stain on the pillow. Leaning in, I inhaled sharply. The scent hit me like a punch to the gut, a mix of sweat, fear, and something dark and metallic.

Blood.

I looked up, my eyes meeting Ash's. She saw the expression on my face and paled, her hand flying to her mouth.

"Tris... what is it?" she whispered, her voice barely audible.

Before I could respond, Jess called out sharply, "Guys, I found something."

We gathered around her, our eyes fixed on the piece of paper in her hand. It was a note, scrawled in hurried, barely legible handwriting.

"It's from Kirkwood," Jess said, her voice tight. "He says he found something... something big. And that he was in danger."

I took the note from her, my eyes scanning the words. The writing was erratic, the letters slanting wildly as if written in a state of extreme agitation. Each word stabbed at my veins like ice.

They're coming for me. They know what I found. I can't trust anyone. They're everywhere. I have to run. I have to hide. They'll kill me if they find me. I found the truth. I found the proof. They can't let it get out. They'll do anything to stop me. I have to keep moving. I can't stay here. They're coming. They're coming for me.

The note ended abruptly, the last words trailing off as if the writer had been interrupted. I looked up, meeting the others' eyes. The same horror reflected in their expressions, the same realization dawning on their faces.

Kirkwood wasn't just missing. He was running for his life. Whatever he had found had put him in the crosshairs of something far more sinister than we could have imagined.

"We have to find him," I said firmly. "Before they do."

The others nodded, their expressions grave. We knew the stakes and the risks, but we also knew we couldn't turn back—not now, not ever.

Watching Jess retreat down the hallway made me fidget. The air felt thick around me, and an instinctive desire to follow her bubbled up—she always knew how to take the initiative. It was unnerving to think about what she might find, but I had to trust her.

I had to believe that her skills, honed through years of navigating the complexities of Palantir Technologies and her past run-ins with the FBI, would guide her now.

The flickering fluorescent lights above cast strange shadows that transformed the corridor into a maze of uncertainty. Each echo of her footsteps felt magnified in the stillness, leaving me alone with my thoughts. The silence was almost deafening, a stark contrast to the usual hum of the office.

"You okay, Tris?" Ash asked, her voice cutting through the silence. Her sharp, perceptive eyes seemed to read right through me.

I glanced at her and forced a nod. "Yeah, just thinking," I replied, trying to keep my voice steady. I didn't want to worry her, but the truth was, my mind raced with possibilities, each darker than the last.

Benji chimed in, his voice filled with a confidence I wished I could share. "She'll find something. Jess always does." He adjusted his glasses, a small gesture hinting at his own nervous energy.

I appreciated their reassurance, but unease lingered. The motel's grimy walls seemed to close in on me, the smell of old cigarettes and despair heavy in the air. I could almost feel the desperation that had driven Kirkwood here, the same desperation that now drove us.

The stakes were high, and the risks were real. But we were too deep to turn back now. We had to find Kirkwood before whatever sinister force he had uncovered found him—and us.

My mind raced as Jess reached the office at the end of the corridor. I imagined her scanning the place for hidden cameras; this was her turf. She had an uncanny knack for digging into the digital depths of any situation.

"Think she'll find anything?" Ash whispered, her eyes fixed on the end of the hallway.

"If there's anything to find, she will," Benji replied, his confidence unwavering.

Ash nodded, though her eyes still held a hint of worry. "She's got a knack for this kind of thing. Remember the time she hacked into the FBI database just to prove a point?"

I chuckled, the memory lightening the mood slightly. "Yeah, she's always been a step ahead with tech. Let's hope that holds true now."

Benji leaned against the wall, his eyes scanning the corridor. "You know, I've been thinking. If Kirkwood was onto something big, something that got him into trouble, there must be more than just that note. There has to be evidence somewhere."

Ash frowned, her brow furrowing in thought. "But where? We've checked his office, his motel room... where else could he have hidden something?"

I glanced down the hallway, my mind racing. "Maybe it's not about where he hid it, but who he trusted. Kirkwood wasn't the kind of guy to do things alone. He always had someone else pulling the strings or covering his tracks."

Benji pushed his glasses up, a sign he was deep in thought. "You're right. We need to think like Kirkwood. If he was in trouble, if he knew he was being hunted, he would have made a backup plan. A contingency."

Ash looked at us, her eyes widening. "You think he left a trail? Something only he could follow?"

I nodded. "Exactly. If we can figure out what that trail is, we might be able to find him before it's too late."

Benji straightened, a determined look on his face. "Alright, let's start with what we know. Kirkwood was involved in shady business deals. He was funneling money, covering his tracks. There has to be a digital footprint somewhere."

Ash crossed her arms, her gaze fixed on the distant end of the hallway. "Jess is our best bet for that. She knows how to dig deep and find the hidden links. But we need to give her something to go on. A starting point."

I thought back to the note, the hurried scrawl, the desperate words. "The note mentioned 'they.' Who are 'they'? That's our starting point. We need to figure out who Kirkwood was afraid of, who he was running from."

Benji snapped his fingers, a spark of excitement in his eyes. "The missing persons cases. That's the link. Kirkwood's disappearance, the note, the fear—it all ties back to those cases. If we can find a connection there, we might unravel this whole thing."

Ash looked at us, her expression serious. "We need to be careful, though. If Kirkwood was taken out because of what he knew, we could be next."

I met her gaze, understanding the weight of her words. "You're right. We stick together, watch each other's backs."

The sound of footsteps echoed down the hallway, pulling our attention back to the present. Jess was returning, her face flushed with urgency.

"I found something," she said, breathless. "A hidden camera. And you won't believe what's on the footage."

I nodded, trying to quell the anxious thoughts swirling in my mind. The motel felt like a trap, a labyrinth of secrets and shadows closing in around us. The dull hum of the ancient fluorescent lights overhead heightened the sense of unease. I could almost feel the weight of the truth pressing down on us, waiting to be uncovered like some grim specter.

"What is it?" I asked, my voice barely above a whisper, as if the very walls had ears.

Jess held up a small USB drive, her eyes wide with a mix of excitement and trepidation. "I found the surveillance footage. Kirkwood was here, and he was desperate."

Benji whistled softly, his eyebrows raised in surprise. "Desperate how?"

Jess's expression darkened, her gaze flicking between each of us, underscoring the gravity of what she had discovered. "You need to see this."

The footage she described painted a grim picture of Kirkwood's state—the distress in his eyes as he stormed into the motel, the gun in his hand. My stomach twisted as I realized that this man we were searching for was now willing to threaten others.

"Play it," I said, my voice steady despite the turmoil inside me.

Jess plugged the USB into her laptop, and the screen flickered to life. The footage was grainy, but there was no mistaking Kirkwood's frantic movements as he entered the motel lobby. He looked disheveled, his eyes wild with fear and desperation. His suit, once pristine, was now wrinkled and stained, his hair tousled as if he'd been running his hands through it repeatedly.

"Look at him," Benji muttered, leaning in for a better view. "He's completely lost it."

Kirkwood paced the lobby, his eyes darting around as if expecting someone to jump out at him. He kept glancing over his shoulder, his hand gripping something tightly in his pocket. The camera angle shifted, capturing a close-up of his face—his jaw was set, his eyes bloodshot and filled with a mix of anger and terror.

"What's he holding?" Ash asked, her voice barely above a whisper.

Jess zoomed in on the footage, enhancing the image. Kirkwood's hand emerged from his pocket, revealing a small metallic object.

"Is that a gun?" I asked, my voice tight.

"Yeah," Jess confirmed, narrowing her eyes as she studied the screen. "He's armed and terrified."

On the screen, Kirkwood moved to the reception desk, slamming his hand down on the bell. The sound echoed through the lobby, a harsh, desperate call for attention. A moment later, a man appeared from the back, his eyes widening as he took in Kirkwood's state.

"I need a room," Kirkwood demanded, his voice shaking. "Now."

The receptionist hesitated, flicking his gaze between Kirkwood and the gun in his hand. "Sir, I—"

"Now!" Kirkwood barked, his voice resonating through the lobby.

The receptionist fumbled with the keys, his hands trembling as he handed one over to Kirkwood. "Room 207, sir. It's—"

Kirkwood snatched the key from his hand, cutting him off. "I don't need directions. Just give me the damn key."

With that, he turned and stormed up the stairs, his footsteps echoing through the motel. The camera followed him as he disappeared down the corridor, his figure shrinking into the distance.

Jess paused the footage, her eyes scanning the frozen image of Kirkwood's back. "He's running from something," she said firmly. "And whatever it is, it's got him terrified."

"We need to find out what," Benji added, his gaze fixed on the screen. "Before it finds us."

Ash looked at me, her eyes reflecting the same mix of determination and fear that I felt. "Tris, what's our next move?"

I took a deep breath, my mind racing with possibilities. We were in too deep to turn back now, and the stakes were higher than ever. Kirkwood was the key to unraveling this mystery, and we had to find him before it was too late.

"We keep digging," I said, my voice steady. "We find out what Kirkwood knew, what he was running from. And we do it fast."

The footage flickered, and suddenly Kirkwood was back in the frame, storming toward the motel manager's office. The camera angle was grainy but clear enough to capture the harsh lines etched into his face, a mix of fear and desperation aging him beyond his years.

"What's he doing?" Ash murmured, her eyes wide as she watched Kirkwood's erratic movements.

Jess leaned in, her brow furrowed in concentration. "Looks like he's about to lose it."

On the screen, Kirkwood slammed his fist against the manager's door, the sound echoing through the small office. The manager, a portly man with a receding hairline, looked up from his desk, his eyes widening in surprise.

"Can I help you?" the manager asked, his voice trembling slightly.

Kirkwood didn't waste time with pleasantries. "I need to see the security footage from last night," he demanded, urgency lacing his voice.

The manager hesitated, his gaze flicking to the gun in Kirkwood's hand. "Sir, I can't just—"

"Now!" Kirkwood barked, slamming his hand down on the desk. The sound was like a gunshot, making the manager flinch.

"Okay, okay," the manager stammered, his hands shaking as he turned to his computer. "But I have to warn you, the footage isn't great. The cameras are old and—"

"Just play it," Kirkwood snapped, his patience wearing thin.

The manager nodded, his fingers flying over the keyboard. A moment later, the security footage appeared on the screen, the images grainy and distorted. Kirkwood leaned in, his eyes scanning the footage intently.

"What is he looking for?" Benji asked, his voice barely above a whisper.

I shook my head, my gaze fixed on the screen. "I don't know. But whatever it is, it's got him spooked."

On the screen, Kirkwood's eyes widened as he watched the footage. He pointed at the screen, his voice shaking with fear and anger. "There! Who is that?"

The manager squinted at the screen, his brow furrowed in confusion. "I don't know, sir. Just looks like a guest to me."

Kirkwood's face darkened, his grip on the gun tightening. "No, it's not just a guest. It's them. They're here."

"Who's here?" the manager asked, his voice trembling.

Kirkwood looked up, his eyes meeting the manager's. "The people who are trying to kill me."

"He's losing it," Benji murmured, his voice barely audible.

Ash nodded, her eyes wide with shock. "We have to find him before he does something drastic."

I felt an internal tug-of-war—the growing sense of urgency battling the undercurrents of frustration and concern. Kirkwood was teetering on the edge, putting both him and us in grave danger.

Jess's voice cut through my thoughts, mixing urgency with fear. "We have to figure out where he went." I could sense the weight of her words pressing down on my chest; we needed to act and find Kirkwood before it was too late.

"Any clues in the footage?" I asked, my voice steady despite the turmoil inside me.

I watched as Jess's fingers danced across the keyboard, her focus unwavering. The soft glow of the screen cast shadows across her face, highlighting the determination in her eyes. She was a woman on a mission, and I could practically see the gears turning in her mind as she navigated through the digital labyrinth.

"The train station?" Benji leaned forward, his brows furrowed in confusion. "That old building on 5th?"

"Not exactly," Jess corrected, her eyes never leaving the screen. She pulled up a detailed map, zooming in on a location that seemed isolated and forgotten. "There's an abandoned station on the outskirts. Records show Kirkwood bought it through a shell company three years ago."

Ash crossed her arms, skepticism written all over her face. "Why would he buy an abandoned train station? It's not exactly prime real estate."

"Storage maybe?" I suggested, though even as the words left my mouth, something about it felt off. The pieces weren't fitting together quite right, and my gut told me there was more to this than met the eye.

"No," Jess shook her head, dismissing the idea. "Look at these power readings." She pointed to a graph on her screen, the lines spiking dramatically. "The place has been drawing massive amounts of electricity for the past year. Whatever he's doing there, it's not just storing old files."

"That doesn't make sense," Benji moved closer to the screen, his eyes scanning the data. "An abandoned station shouldn't need any power, let alone that much."

"Unless it's not abandoned," I said, the realization hitting me like a freight train. "What if he's been using it as some kind of base? A place to operate away from prying eyes?"

"Or a hideout," Ash added, her voice laced with concern. "Perfect place to disappear if you're running from something... or someone."

Jess's voice dropped lower, urgency creeping in. "The surveillance footage shows him making multiple trips there in the weeks before he vanished. He was planning something, and we need to find out what."

"Then that's where we need to go," I said, already calculating the risks and formulating a plan in my head. "How far is it?"

"About an hour outside the city," Jess replied, her eyes finally meeting mine. There was a silent understanding between us; we were stepping into uncharted territory, and the danger was palpable. "But Tris, we need to be careful. The footage shows he wasn't alone. We don't know what we're walking into."

The train station was an untamed wild, full of possibility and danger. My instincts prickled again, that strange energy rising within me as we made our plans. Whatever Kirkwood was hiding, we were going to find it. And I had a feeling that once we did, there would be no turning back.

Jess spoke with a hint of desperation. "We have to go to the train station! It's the last place he owned!" The gravity of her suggestion sank in, and I felt an electric surge of determination ripple through me.

The train station—an untamed wild, full of possibility and danger. It was a tangible lead, something we could grasp in the murky mystery of Kirkwood's disappearance.

"The train station?" Benji echoed, his voice tinged with disbelief. He looked at Jess, then me, his eyes reflecting the whirlwind of thoughts racing through his mind.

Jess nodded, her eyes bright with urgency. "It's our best lead. We have to check it out." She leaned forward, her hands gripping the table as if to emphasize her point.

Ash looked at me, her expression serious. "What do you think, Tris?" Her gaze pierced me, probing for the resolve she knew I had.

I took a deep breath, the weight of our decision pressing down on me. The train station was a nexus of the unknown, but it was also a beacon of hope. "We have to go. We can't let this slip away." The words felt heavy and significant, a declaration of intent.

I nodded, urgency pouring out of me as I said, "Let's gear up and move quickly. We can't waste time." My excitement surged at the thought of finally making significant progress toward finding Kirkwood. The sense of purpose was palpable, driving us forward.

Benji clapped his hands together, his expression determined. "Alright, let's do this. What do we need?" His enthusiasm was infectious, fueling our collective resolve.

Jess ticked off the list on her fingers. "Flashlights, maps, anything we can use to track him down." Her voice was steady, focused on the task ahead.

Ash nodded, her eyes serious. "And we need to be prepared for anything." Her tone held a warning, a reminder of the unpredictable nature of our quest.

I caught the resolve in my friends' eyes—they were with me, ready to dive into whatever awaited us. We swiftly gathered our gear, a sense of purpose weaving us together, uniting us in our mission.

The train station loomed in our minds—a challenge and an opportunity, a place where answers might be found or new dangers unveiled. But we were ready, determined to uncover the truth, no matter what it took.

The reality of our situation settled firmly in my mind; a mix of fear and determination filled me as I considered what we might encounter at the train station. Thoughts of Kirkwood's safety, my friends' unwavering support, and the urgent need to confront the shadows loomed ahead.

Kirkwood knew something—something dangerous enough to make him disappear without a trace. The weight of our mission pressed down on me, yet I found solace in the resolve etched on the faces of my friends.

Benji checked his backpack, his movements efficient and focused. "We're ready. Let's move." His steady voice grounded me in the moment.

Ash nodded, her expression serious, her eyes reflecting the gravity of our task. "Let's find Kirkwood and get some answers." Her words reminded us of the stakes, the secrets Kirkwood held, and the danger he might be in.

Jess looked at me, her eyes reflecting the same determination I felt. "Let's get back to the car. Benji, I sent you the location." Her tone was resolute, leaving no room for doubt or hesitation.

I took a deep breath, steeling myself for what lay ahead. "Let's go."

As we stepped outside into the night, the cool air pressed against my skin, and the scent of uncertainty hung in the atmosphere. I took a moment to breathe it in, feeling the sharpness of the moment. The city lights cast long, dancing shadows, a stark reminder of the world we were about to enter.

The silence of the night was broken only by the distant hum of traffic, a steady rhythm that echoed the pounding urgency within me. We moved swiftly, our footsteps resonating in the stillness, each step bringing us closer to the truth and the danger that awaited us.

CHAPTER TWENTY-FIVE

TICKETS PLEASE

The truck's engine hummed beneath us, a steady rhythm that should have been soothing. Instead, I felt a strange vibration, like a thousand tiny needles pricking at my senses. It wasn't just the truck; it was everything—the trees whispering secrets in the wind, the distant hum of the city, the heartbeats of my friends beside me. I could feel it all, but it was more than sound, more than touch. It was as if the world was pressing in on me, trying to tell me something I couldn't quite understand.

I shifted in my seat, trying to shake off the sensation. Benji glanced at me, his brow furrowing with concern. "You okay, Tris?"

"Yeah, just a bit on edge," I replied, forcing a smile. I couldn't tell him the truth—that I felt like I was standing on the precipice of something vast and unknown. That the world around me was alive in a way I'd never experienced before.

Jess looked back from the passenger seat, her eyes reflecting the passing streetlights. "We're almost there. You sure you're up for this?"

I nodded, more to convince myself than her. "I'm sure. We need to find Kirkwood."

Ash, sitting beside me, was quiet, her gaze fixed on the window. She was worried too; I could sense it. Her heartbeat was a steady, anxious rhythm, echoing my own unspoken fears.

I leaned back, trying to focus on the task ahead, but the sensation grew stronger. It was like a current running through me, a hum that resonated deep within. I clenched my fists, feeling a strange pressure building. It was different from hunger, different from heightened senses. This was something else, something new.

The truck turned a sharp corner, and the city lights faded behind us, giving way to the dark, looming silhouette of the abandoned train station. The hum inside me intensified, pulsing in time with the beat of the engine. I took a deep breath, trying to steady myself. Whatever this was, I had to keep it under control. I couldn't let my friends see the change; I couldn't let them know the truth.

"You sure you're okay, Tris?" Benji glanced at me from the driver's seat, his hands steady on the wheel. Max's truck was a beast, rumbling down the road like a tank.

I nodded, trying to push away the sensation. "Yeah, just...thinking about Kirkwood."

Ash leaned forward from the backseat, her eyes sharp. "It's all so strange, isn't it? The restricted hospital records, the data from Palantir Technologies, the missing people...it's like we're stuck in some weird conspiracy theory."

Jess chimed in, her voice thoughtful. "And Kirkwood's right at the center of it. What do you think he knows?"

I looked out the window, watching the city lights fade into the distance. "Something dangerous. Something worth disappearing for."

Benji's grip tightened on the wheel. "We'll find out soon enough. We're almost there."

The train station loomed ahead, a decaying relic of a bygone era. It was old and run-down, the kind of place you'd expect to find squatters or junkies—not a high-powered executive like Kirkwood. But as we pulled up, something felt off. The hairs on the back of my neck stood up, a primal response to an unseen threat.

"Look at this place," Ash muttered, her voice low. "It's creepy as hell."

Jess pointed toward the station. "And look at those cameras. They're everywhere."

She was right. The station was covered in surveillance cameras, all of them active, their little red lights blinking like malevolent eyes. It explained the power usage, but it was more than that. It was as if the station itself was watching us, waiting.

Benji killed the engine, and we sat in silence for a moment, taking it all in. Then Jess spoke up, her voice filled with determination. "Alright, let's do this. Benji, you ready to hack into those cameras?"

Benji grinned, pulling out his laptop. "Already on it."

We moved swiftly, our footsteps echoing in the stillness. The station was a maze of shadows and decay, the air thick with the scent of dust and rust. But beneath it all, there was something else—a faint, earthy smell that made my mouth water and my stomach churn. I pushed it away, focusing on the task at hand.

Benji and Jess worked quickly, their fingers flying over their keyboards as they tapped into the security system. I stood watch, my eyes scanning the darkness, my senses on high alert. Ash was beside me, her breath misting in the cool night air.

"You think he's here?" she asked, her voice barely a whisper.

I nodded. "Somewhere. We just have to find him."

Benji let out a triumphant whoop. "Got it! Cameras are looped. We're good to go."

Jess looked up, her eyes meeting mine. "Let's find Kirkwood."

We moved deeper into the station, our footsteps echoing in the silence. The vibration was stronger now, a steady hum that seemed to resonate in my very bones. I could feel the others too, their heartbeats like a symphony in the stillness. It was distracting, but I pushed through, focusing on the task at hand.

The station was a labyrinth of decaying corridors and abandoned platforms, each one more desolate than the last. But there was something else here too, something that hummed beneath the surface.

"This place is huge," Ash murmured, her eyes wide as she took it all in. "How are we supposed to find him?"

The station's decay was palpable, the air thick with dust and the faint scent of something unsettling beneath the grime. I could feel the others' heartbeats, a steady rhythm that grounded me amidst the eerie silence. Ash stood close, her breaths shallow, eyes scanning the shadows.

Jess looked up from her laptop, her face illuminated by the screen's glow. "Alright, we need to cover more ground. Let's split up." She pointed toward a corridor that branched off from the main platform. "Benji and I will take this side; you and Tris take the other. We'll meet back here in thirty minutes."

Benji nodded, closing his laptop. "Sounds good. Let's stay in touch with the walkies if we find something or Kirkwood."

Ash glanced at me, her eyes reflecting the dim light. "You good with that, Tris?"

I nodded, trying to ignore the humming sensation that seemed to grow stronger with each passing moment. "Yeah, let's do this."

Jess handed us each a walkie-talkie. "Keep these on. If you see anything, anything at all, let us know."

We split up, Ash and I taking the left corridor while Jess and Benji disappeared into the shadows on the right. The station was a labyrinth of decaying walls and rusted tracks, each step echoing ominously. The hum inside me pulsed in time with our footsteps, a steady beat that seemed to resonate with the station itself.

Ash walked beside me, her eyes sharp as she took in every detail. "This place is massive. How are we supposed to find him in all this?"

I shrugged, trying to keep my voice steady. "We just keep looking. He's here somewhere."

The corridor opened up into a larger room filled with old crates and forgotten machinery. The air was thick with dust, and the faint scent of something earthy lingered beneath it all. I could feel it—the hum growing stronger, pulling me forward.

Ash paused, her hand resting on a crate. "Tris, are you sure you're okay? You seem...distracted."

I forced a smile, pushing away the sensation. "I'm fine. Just focused on finding Kirkwood."

She nodded, but her eyes lingered on me for a moment longer before she turned away. We moved deeper into the room, our footsteps echoing in the silence. The hum was a constant now, a steady pulse that seemed to guide me, drawing me toward something unseen.

"You think he's still alive?" she asked, her voice barely a whisper.

I paused, considering her words. "I don't know. But we have to find out."

We moved deeper into the station, the darkness pressing in around us. The vibration was stronger now, a steady hum that seemed to resonate in my very bones. I could feel it all—the decay, the dust, the faint scent of something wild and dangerous. It was overwhelming, but I pushed through, focusing on the task at hand.

Ash's hand brushed against mine, her touch grounding me in the moment. "You look really good, by the way. It's been a while since I last saw your annoying face."

I chuckled, trying to hide my unease. "Thanks, Ash. It's good to see you too."

She paused, her eyes narrowing as she looked me over. "You've changed, Tris. You're different."

I shrugged, trying to play it off. "Just been working out, taking some classes. You know, self-improvement stuff."

Ash raised an eyebrow. "Classes? Like what, karate? Because the way you took down those guards at Palantir...that was impressive."

I forced a laugh. "Something like that. Just picked up a few tricks."

She wasn't convinced. I could see it in her eyes, the way she studied me. I had to be careful. I didn't want her to know the truth—that I was no longer the Tristan she knew.

"And the contacts," she said, leaning in closer. "They're cool. I can see something underneath, like a glow."

I stepped back, trying to put some distance between us. "Yeah, they're just for fun. Nothing special."

Ash's expression softened, and she looked away, her voice quieter. "Where have you been, Tris? We've all been worried about you. I've been worried about you."

Her words caught me off guard. I hadn't expected her to care, not like this. I hesitated, not sure what to say. "I...I needed some time away. To figure things out."

She turned back to me, her eyes searching mine. "Figure what out? What's going on, Tris? You can tell me."

I looked away, unable to meet her gaze. "It's complicated, Ash. I can't explain it right now."

She sighed but didn't press further. Instead, she changed the subject. "So, what do you think about this place? It's a dump, isn't it?"

I nodded, grateful for the shift in conversation. "Yeah, it's seen better days. But we should keep looking. Kirkwood might be hiding somewhere here."

We moved deeper into the station, our footsteps echoing in the silence. The hum was now a constant presence, a steady pulse that seemed to guide me, drawing me toward something unseen.

Ash paused, her hand resting on a rusted train car. "How long do you think this has been here?"

I shrugged, trying to keep my voice steady. "I'm not sure, but these train cars look old."

She nodded, but her eyes lingered on me for a moment longer before she turned away.

"You know, I never thought I'd say this," Ash began, her voice softening, "but I missed you, Tris. I missed your stupid jokes and your annoying laugh. I missed...you."

I stopped and turned to face her. Her words were unexpected, and I wasn't sure how to respond. "Ash, I—"

She cut me off, her voice barely a whisper. "I was worried about you, Tris. More than I thought I would be. I care about you, more than I should."

Her confession hung in the air between us, a fragile truth I wasn't sure how to handle. I opened my mouth to respond, but she shook her head, stopping me.

"You don't have to say anything. I just needed you to know. And I need you to be careful, Tris. Whatever you're involved in, whatever you're hiding...it's dangerous. I can feel it."

I nodded, unable to find the words to respond. She was right—it was dangerous. More dangerous than she could ever imagine. But I couldn't tell her that. I couldn't tell her the truth.

We continued our search, the silence between us filled with unspoken words and lingering confessions. The station was a maze of decaying corridors and abandoned platforms, each one more desolate than the last. But there was something else here too, something that hummed beneath the surface.

"Look at this," Ash said, pointing to a pile of old crates. "These haven't been moved in years. This place is a dead end."

I shook my head, the hum growing stronger. "No, there's something here. I can feel it."

She looked at me, her eyes filled with concern. "Tris, are you sure you're okay? You've been acting strange since we got here."

I forced a smile, trying to reassure her. "I'm fine, Ash. Just...trust me. We need to keep looking."

She hesitated for a moment before nodding. "Alright, Tris. I trust you."

Her words sent a pang through me, a mix of guilt and gratitude. She trusted me, and I was lying to her. But I had to. I had to protect her, protect all of them, from the truth.

We ventured further into the station., the hum growing stronger with each step. I could feel it, the pulse of something hidden, something waiting to be found. And I knew, with a certainty that shook me to my core, that we were close. Close to finding Kirkwood, close to uncovering the truth.

But with that truth came danger—a danger that I wasn't sure we were ready to face. A danger I wasn't sure I could protect them from. But I had to try. I had to keep them safe, no matter what it cost me.

Because that's what family did. That's what friends did. And Ash, Benji, Jess—they were my family, my friends. And I would do whatever it took to keep them safe.

Even if it meant lying to them. Even if it meant hiding the truth. Even if it meant facing the danger alone.

The hum intensified, pulsing through me like a second heartbeat. I tried to focus on Ash, her words washing over me, but the sensation was overwhelming. It was as if the station itself was alive, its energy coursing through my veins, resonating with every fiber of my being.

"Tris, are you even listening to me?" Ash's voice cut through the haze, her eyes narrowing as she studied me.

I forced a nod, trying to ground myself in her gaze. "Yeah, I'm here. Just...there's something about this place, Ash. It's like it's alive."

She raised an eyebrow, her lips quirking into a half-smile. "Alive? Tris, it's just an old train station. Creepy, yes. Alive, no."

I opened my mouth to respond, but the hum surged, drowning out my words. It was too strong, too intense. I could feel it building inside me, a pressure that threatened to explode. I had to get away, had to find a safe spot before it was too late.

"Ash, I...I need a moment," I managed to choke out, stepping back. "I'll be right back."

Her eyes widened, concern etched on her face. "Tris, what's wrong? You look like you've seen a ghost."

I shook my head, unable to explain. "I just need a moment. Stay here; I'll be right back."

I turned and walked away, my steps echoing in the silence. I could feel Ash's gaze on my back, her concern following me like a shadow. But I couldn't stop, couldn't turn back. The pressure was building, the hum growing louder, more insistent.

I found a secluded spot, hidden behind a pile of old crates. The hum was deafening now, a roar that filled my ears and my mind. I could feel it pulsing through me, a wave of energy that threatened to consume me. I remembered the last time this happened, the explosion of power that had sent Constantine crashing into a tree. I couldn't let that happen again, not with Ash so close.

I tried to control it, to push it down. But it was too strong, too wild. The hum intensified, building like a crescendo, a symphony of chaos echoing in my bones. The air around me crackled, alive with an unseen force. I gritted my teeth, my hands clenched into fists, trying to rein in the surging power.

But it was too much. The wave crested, and I couldn't hold it back any longer. It burst from me, a surge of telekinetic energy that sent crates flying, metal groaning as it twisted and bent. The station seemed to shudder, dust and debris exploding outward in a violent storm. The walls shook, the ground trembled, and the air filled with the deafening roar of unleashed power.

I could feel it all—the force pulsing through my veins, the chaos unraveling around me. Crates splintered into fragments, raining down like shrapnel. Metal beams groaned and twisted, contorting into impossible shapes. The air was thick with dust, the scent of rust and decay mingling with the earthy, electric smell of raw power.

The ground beneath me trembled, sending shockwaves that rippled outward, disrupting the decaying equilibrium of the station. The vibrations intensified, resonating through the soles of my feet, up my legs, and into my core. It was as if the very essence of the station was responding to the surge within me, amplifying it, feeding it.

A rusted sign, once proudly displaying the station's name, tore from its mount and hurtled through the air, narrowly missing me as it crashed into a distant wall. The impact sent a cascade of debris tumbling down, adding to the cacophony of destruction. Shards of glass from long-abandoned windows exploded outward, glinting like deadly confetti in the dim light filtering through the crumbling roof.

I struggled to control the maelstrom, my hands clenched into fists, nails digging into my palms. The power was wild, unruly, a beast unleashed from the depths of my being. It clawed at my insides, demanding release, yearning to break free from the constraints of my flesh. I gritted my teeth, fighting to rein it in, to shape it, to make it m ine.

But it was too strong, too primal. The energy surged, a tidal wave of force that crashed against the walls of my consciousness. I could feel every splinter of wood, every fragment of metal, every grain of dust as it danced in the air, caught in the vortex of my power. The station groaned around me, its bones creaking under the strain, threatening to collapse under the weight of my unleashed fury.

A massive iron girder, once part of the station's skeleton, wrenched free from its moorings and soared through the air. It spun end over end, a lethal projectile that could have leveled a building. I reached out with my mind, my hand stretching toward the girder as if I could physically grasp it. The power within me responded, latching onto the spinning metal, halting its deadly trajectory mere inches from a crumbling wall.

My breath came in ragged gasps as I fought to maintain control. The girder hung suspended in mid-air, a testament to the raw, untamed force coursing through my veins. I could feel the weight of it, the cold, unyielding metal pressing against my will. It was a battle, a struggle between the wild, primal power and the fragile remnants of my humanity.

The air crackled with energy, the scent of ozone sharp and pungent. Sparks danced along the girder, arcing and snapping like miniature lightning bolts. It was exhilarating, terrifying—a rush of sensation that threatened to consume me, to sweep me away in its relentless tide.

But I held on, my will a fragile barrier against the storm. I could feel the power bending to my command, the wild, unruly force slowly, painstakingly submitting to my control. The girder trembled, its spin slowing, its trajectory shifting as I guided it gently, carefully, to the ground.

The station seemed to sigh in relief as the girder touched down, the groaning of metal and the crackling of energy fading into silence. The air was still thick with dust, the scent of rust and decay lingering like a ghostly reminder of the chaos that had been unleashed. But the storm had passed, the power tamed, the beast subdued.

Yet, amidst the chaos, there was a sense of control—a thread of consciousness that allowed me to guide the explosion. I could feel the energy responding to my will, the crates and metal bending to my command. It wasn't a massive, uncontrolled blast like before; this time, it was focused and contained, a concentrated burst of force that left the rest of the station untouched.

In the aftermath, I stood there panting, my body shaking from the force of the explosion. I looked around, taking in the destruction. And then I saw her: Ash, standing at the edge of the chaos, her eyes wide with shock and fear.

"Ash," I breathed, stepping toward her. But she didn't move or speak. She just stood there, staring at me as if I were a stranger.

Then I noticed it—the metal rod protruding from her stomach. Blood seeped from the wound, staining her shirt and dripping onto the dusty floor. She looked down, her eyes widening as she took in the sight. Then she screamed.

I was by her side in an instant, my arms wrapping around her as she crumpled to the ground. "Ash, oh God, Ash," I murmured, my hands shaking as I assessed the wound. It was bad—too bad. She was losing too much blood, too fast.

Ash's breath hitched, her eyes widening as she looked down at her stomach, at the rod that impaled her. Her hands trembled as she reached for the metal, but I stopped her, my voice steady despite the panic clawing at my insides.

"Don't, Ash. Let me."

I pulled the rod from her stomach, her scream echoing through the station. Blood pulsed from the wound, the scent filling the air—a stark contrast to the dust and decay. I pressed my wrist against her stomach, my blood dripping onto the wound.

Ash's eyes were on me, wide with pain and fear, but also with something else—maybe awe or disbelief. She watched as my blood seeped into her wound, as the flesh began to knit together.

She gasped, her body convulsing as the healing began. Her hands clutched at the dusty floor, her nails digging into the dirt. I could see the pain in her eyes, the agony of her body repairing itself.

"Tris," she gasped, her voice barely a whisper. "What...what's happening?"

I couldn't answer or explain. I just held her, my wrist pressed against her stomach, my blood flowing into her.

Her clothes, all black, were damp with sweat and blood, clinging to her body as it contorted and healed. The fabric of her shirt was torn where the rod had impaled her, the edges stained a dark, almost black, red. Her pants were smeared with dust and dirt, her shoes scuffed and worn.

She screamed again, her body arching off the ground as the wound closed, the skin pulling together and sealing shut. The flow of blood slowed, then stopped, leaving the stain on her shirt as the only evidence of the injury.

Her breath came in ragged gasps, her chest heaving as the pain subsided. She looked up at me, her eyes filled with a mix of fear, awe, and confusion.

"Tris," she whispered, her voice hoarse from screaming. "What did you do?"

I sighed, running a hand through my hair. "Ash, listen to me. What just happened...it's complicated. I need you to promise me something."

Her eyes were wide, still filled with a mix of fear and awe. She nodded slowly, her hands clutching her now-healed stomach. "Okay, Tris. What is it?"

I leaned in, my voice low and steady. "You can't tell anyone about this. Not Jess, not Benji. No one can know what happened here. It's important, Ash. It's for your safety and theirs."

She stared at me, her brow furrowing as she processed my words. "Tris, what are you talking about? What do you mean, 'what happened here'? You saved me; that's what happened."

I shook my head, my gaze holding hers. "It's more than that, Ash. The blood...it's not just mine. It's different. It heals, but it also changes things. It ties you to a world that's dangerous—a world you don't want to be a part of."

She looked down at her stomach, then back up at me, her eyes filled with questions. "Tris, what are you saying? What world? What's going on?"

I hesitated, the words stuck in my throat. I didn't want to lie to her, but I couldn't tell her the truth—not all of it. "Ash, I can't explain everything right now. Just please, promise me you won't tell anyone. It's important."

She studied me for a moment, her gaze searching mine. Then she nodded, her voice soft but determined. "Okay, Tris. I promise. I won't tell anyone."

Relief washed over me, but it was short-lived. There was still so much she didn't know, so much I couldn't tell her. But for now, her promise would have to be enough.

I stood up, offering her my hand. "Come on, we should get out of here. The others are probably wondering where we are."

She took my hand, her grip firm as I pulled her to her feet. She looked around at the destruction, her eyes lingering on the crates and twisted metal. "Tris, what about all this?"

I scanned the area, my thoughts swirling. "I don't really know what all this is, but for now, we need to concentrate on Kirkwood."

I took off my hoodie and handed it to Ash, who gratefully slipped it on. The fabric enveloped her, hiding the torn and bloodied shirt underneath.

"Here, this should cover up the...blood," I said, my voice low.

Ash nodded, pulling the hoodie over herself. "Thanks, Tris. I don't know what's going on, but I trust you. Just tell me one thing: are we in danger?"

I hesitated, weighing my words carefully. "The truth is, I'm not entirely sure. But I need to keep you and the others safe. That's why I need you to keep this between us for now, okay?"

Suddenly, Ash's walkie crackled to life. Benji's voice came through, filled with static. "We found something. It's...it's not good. You guys need to see this."

Ash and I exchanged a glance, the urgency in Benji's voice sending a chill down my spine. We turned back, retracing our steps through the labyrinth of the station. The hum was no longer there, but I could feel every object around me as if they were extensions of my body, waiting for my command.

"Tris, what was that back there?" Ash asked, her voice barely above a whisper as we navigated through the dimly lit station.

I shook my head, not ready to explain. "Later, Ash. Right now, we need to focus on finding the others."

She nodded, though I could see the questions lingering in her eyes. We moved swiftly, our footsteps echoing in the silence. The station was a maze of shadows and dust—a graveyard of forgotten memories. But we pressed on, guided by the urgency in Benji's voice.

We found them huddled in a small room, the air thick with tension. Benji looked up as we entered, relief washing over his face. "Tris, Ash, you gotta see this."

Jess stood in front of an unremarkable door, her fingers gliding along the edge as if looking for a concealed seam. After a swift look at us, she pressed down firmly, and the door clicked ajar, exposing a narrow strip of darkness.

"How did you—?" Benji started, but Jess just smirked, cutting him off.

"I've got my ways," she said, pushing the door wide.

The room yawned before us—large and shadowed. Jess stepped in first, her hand finding a switch. Light flickered on, row by row, illuminating a space that was both eerie and impressive. The walls were lined with monitors, some displaying static, others showing grainy feeds of what looked like the city streets. Computers hummed softly, their lights blinking like mechanical eyes.

As we stepped further inside, the first thing that hit me was the unsettling stillness of the room. There was no sign of Kirkwood, but the signs of his presence were undeniable. Leftover boxes of food were haphazardly piled on a nearby table, remnants of hastily consumed meals. My stomach twisted slightly at the sight.

"Wow, looks like he was living here," Jess said, glancing around. "But where did he go?"

"We don't have time to wonder about that," Benji replied, nudging a pile of dirty clothes scattered across the floor. "This stuff looks like it's been left in a hurry. We need to focus on finding out what he was doing."

"Right," Ash added, her voice tight. "This is bad. Whatever he was mixed up in, it must've been serious for him to leave like this."

The atmosphere felt thick with tension, and I couldn't shake the feeling that we were on the brink of discovering something monumental. I scanned the room, taking in the chaos. "Kirkwood's not just missing; it looks like he was in panic mode," I said, trying to sound calm.

"Do you think he was hiding something?" Jess asked, stepping closer to the table, her brow furrowed. "If he was, we could be walking into a trap."

"No one hurries away from an apartment loaded with food and dirty laundry unless they're scared," Benji replied, his tone serious. "We should check the monitors over there."

"What if he's watching us right now?" I shot back, the thought sending a shiver down my spine.

Ash shook her head. "We can't think that way, Tris. We need answers, or we'll be in the dark about whatever happened to him."

"Okay, what's the plan then?" Benji asked, glancing from Ash to Jess. "We split up and search?"

"I don't think that's a good idea," Jess interjected. "We should stick together as much as possible. There's strength in numbers, right?"

"Yeah, but if the place starts to feel too small, we might not have a way out," I warned, unease creeping into my voice. "Let's not forget what happened at Palantir."

"Tris has a point," Ash said reluctantly. "But we can't give in to fear, either. We must keep moving forward. If Kirkwood was keeping track of something important, it'll be in this room somewhere."

I felt a surge of determination at Ash's words. "Then let's check those monitors," I suggested, moving toward a cluster of screens lined along the wall. "Maybe there's something that indicates where he could be."

Benji shot me a quick nod, and the three of them stepped closer, hearts racing in anticipation of what we might uncover. I took a deep breath, trying to quell the whirlwind of thoughts and emotions churning inside m e.

"Whatever he was monitoring, it has to be connected to his disappearance," Jess said, peering at the screens.

"Or the people he was involved with," Ash added. "We need to watch our backs. If anyone else is watching this place, we can't expose ourselves."

"Right," I said, feeling the weight of her words. "Let's be smart about this. We can't afford to let our guard down. Kirkwood might be the key to understanding everything—his disappearance and us becoming potential targets. We can't leave until we know what he was working on."

As we began to sift through the remnants of Kirkwood's life, I couldn't shake the feeling that we were peeling back layers of a conspiracy that threatened to consume us. We were in deep, but I reminded myself—together, we were stronger. And as long as we stayed focused, there was hope in uncovering the truth.

"Whoa," Ash breathed, stepping beside me. "This is... this is something else."

Benji whistled low, his eyes scanning the tech. "Kirkwood wasn't messing around," he murmured, moving to a nearby keyboard. His fingers flew over the keys, and the screens responded with a cascade of code.

The air was cool, filled with the hum of electronics and the faint scent of ozone. The hairs on the back of my neck stood up—a primal response to the unseen eyes of the cameras and the silent whisper of data streaming through cables.

"Tris," Ash called from another station. "You need to see this."

I tore my gaze away from the screen and joined Ash at her terminal. She pointed to a data stream, her finger tracing the lines of code. "These are records," she said. "Financial transactions, communications, surveillance logs. It's all here. Kirkwood was watching everything, tracking everything."

I peered over Ash's shoulder, my eyes scanning the data streams she had uncovered. The sheer volume of information was staggering—financial records, communications logs, even surveillance footage. It was clear that Kirkwood had been meticulously tracking everything, leaving no stone unturned.

"This is crazy," I murmured, my mind racing to connect the dots. "He was monitoring everyone and everything, but for what purpose?"

Ash shook her head, her brow furrowed in concentration. "I'm not sure, but it looks like it goes deeper than we thought. These files are linked to the missing persons cases we've been investigating, as well as some high-profile individuals in government and business."

As Ash showed me the data streams, my mind raced to piece together the implications. Kirkwood had been monitoring an intricate web of high-profile individuals and organizations—it was mind-boggling.

"Look at this," Ash said, pointing to a series of names and companies. "There's Jonah Brewer, the city's mayor, and Abigail Blackwood, the CEO of Xenon Pharmaceuticals. And over here, it looks like he was tracking financial transactions between Palantir Technologies and a company called Lumin Enterprises."

I leaned in, studying the information displayed on the screen. The connections were staggering—it was clear that Kirkwood had been privy to sensitive information involving some of the most powerful people and corporations in the city.

"Do you think Kirkwood was trying to expose something?" I asked, my voice low. "Was he blackmailing these people?"

Ash shook her head, her expression grave. "I'm not sure, but it seems like he was in over his head. These are powerful people he was messing with. No wonder he disappeared."

I felt a chill run down my spine. If Kirkwood had truly uncovered something damning about these individuals, then we could be in grave danger as well. I glanced around the room, half-expecting to see shadowy figures lurking in the corners.

"We need to be careful," I said, my voice barely above a whisper. "If Kirkwood was tracking this kind of information, then whoever he was involved with might be after us too."

Ash nodded, her eyes narrowed with determination. "We have to find out what Kirkwood knew and why he was monitoring all of this. There has to be a reason he disappeared so suddenly."

I opened my mouth to respond, but a sudden commotion from the other side of the room caught my attention. Benji and Jess were huddled over another set of screens, their faces etched with concern.

"Guys, you need to see this," Benji called out, his voice laced with urgency.

Ash and I exchanged a glance before hurrying over to join them. As we approached, the images on the screens became clearer, and my breath caught in my throat.

The footage showed a series of missing persons reports, each one connected to a different high-profile individual or company. The faces of the victims were hauntingly familiar—I recognized several of them from the data Ash had uncovered.

"This is bad," Jess said, her voice tight with worry. "Kirkwood wasn't just monitoring these people—he was tracking their disappearances."

I felt a knot of dread form in the pit of my stomach. "You're saying Kirkwood was investigating the missing persons cases?"

Benji nodded, his expression grim. "And it looks like he was getting close to something. These disappearances... they're all connected to the people Kirkwood was monitoring."

Ash's eyes widened with realization. "Then that means whoever is behind these disappearances... they're the ones who made Kirkwood vanish."

The weight of her words hung in the air, the implications sending a chill through the room. I clenched my fists, my mind racing with a thousand questions. What had Kirkwood stumbled upon? And who was powerful enough to make him, and all these other people, simply disappear?

Just then, Benji called out. "Guys, you're not going to believe this. The hospital records we accessed match up with a lot of the data Kirkwood was tracking. There's a clear pattern emerging here."

Jess joined him, her expression grave. "This isn't just about Kirkwood's disappearance anymore. It's about a much larger conspiracy, one that's been in the shadows for who knows how long."

A shiver coursed through me. as the implications sank in. Kirkwood had stumbled upon something massive, something that had put his life in jeopardy. And now, by following his trail, we were putting ourselves in the crosshairs as well.

"What do we do?" I asked, my voice barely above a whisper. "If Kirkwood was right to be scared, then we're in over our heads."

Benji looked up from his station, his eyes meeting mine. "Tris, this is big," he said, his voice barely above a whisper. "This is bigger than Kirkwood, bigger than Palantir. This is... something else entirely."

The room hummed with the low thrum of computers, the air thick with the scent of ozone and the tang of old coffee. Benji and Jess huddled together, their faces bathed in the cold glow of the monitors, fingers dancing over keyboards in a rhythm that was almost hypnotic. I stood behind them, Ash by my side, our eyes scanning the streams of code that cascaded down the screens like digital waterfalls.

"Alright, I've got the primary firewall down," Benji muttered, his brow furrowed in concentration. "But there's a secondary layer here, something custom. Jess, can you handle the decryption?"

Jess nodded, her ponytail bobbing with the motion. "On it." Her fingers flew over the keys, her gaze locked onto the screen. The room filled with the soft click-clack of the keyboard, a symphony of hacking that was both tense and strangely soothing.

I leaned in, watching as lines of code began to unravel, revealing the hidden heart of Kirkwood's digital fortress. The air was electric, charged with the thrill of discovery and the undercurrent of danger. We were trespassing in the mind of a man who had vanished without a trace, a man who had been tangled in a web of secrets and lies.

"Got it," Jess breathed, a note of triumph in her voice. The screen flickered, and suddenly, we were in. Files began to populate the monitor, a sprawling landscape of data that stretched back years, maybe even decades.

Benji whistled low, his eyes scanning the list. "This is... really big, guys."

Ash stepped closer, her gaze flicking over the files. "What are we looking at here?"

Benji pointed to a series of folders, each one labeled with a string of numbers and letters that seemed to follow no discernible pattern. "These are encrypted, but the metadata suggests they're medical records. Except... they're not from any hospital I recognize."

Jess opened one of the files, her brow furrowing as she scanned the contents. "These are restricted hospital files, but there's no hospital name. Just a list of people, dates, treatments..." Her voice trailed off, her eyes widening as she scrolled through the data.

"What is it, Jess?" I asked, a sense of unease prickling at the back of my neck.

She looked up at me, her face pale. "These files... they go back to the 1960s. And they're not just missing people, Tris. They're people who were pronounced dead, people on death row, cancer patients... all listed as alive and well, with up-to-date records."

A chill ran down my spine, the implications of her words sending a shiver through the room. Ash leaned in, her eyes scanning the list. "This doesn't make sense. How could these people still be alive?"

Benji shook his head, his expression grave. "I don't know, but it's clear that Kirkwood was involved in something huge—something that goes far beyond Palantir."

The room fell silent, the weight of our discovery settling over us like a shroud. I could feel the tension in the air, the unspoken questions hanging between us. What had Kirkwood uncovered? And what did it mean for us, now that we were following in his footsteps?

Suddenly, the screens flickered, and a new set of images began to load. They were grainy and poorly lit, but there was no mistaking the horror they depicted. People hooked up to machines, tubes and wires snaking across their bodies, their faces contorted in pain. The machines were unlike anything I had ever seen—a grotesque parody of medical equipment designed to inflict suffering rather than heal.

"What is this place?" Ash whispered, her voice barely audible.

Benji's face was a mask of horror, his eyes fixed on the screen. "I... I don't know. But it looks like some kind of... experiment."

Jess scrolled through the images, her face pale. "These are cell phone pictures—short video clips. Kirkwood must have taken them himself."

I felt a chill run down my spine as the images on the screen came into focus. Rows upon rows of unconscious people, hooked up to strange, twisted machines that seemed designed to inflict pain rather than heal.

"What is this place?" I breathed, my voice barely above a whisper.

Benji shook his head, his expression one of pure horror. "I don't know, but it looks like some kind of... experiment."

Jess scrolled through the images, her face still pale. My mind raced as she pulled up the first video. The image was grainy and poorly lit, but I could make out a figure standing in the center of the room, surrounded by the unconscious victims.

"This is... unbelievable," the figure, whom I assumed was Kirkwood, murmured. "Look, this part looks like it's sending nutrients... ah, water... food. And this line of cables—it looks like a monitoring system, like the ones hospitals use."

He moved closer to one of the machines, his face etched with a mix of fascination and horror. "The people in these pods are unresponsive. I'm not sure if anyone is home. It's like nothing I've ever encountered. I need to understand what's happening here, but I can't risk being caught."

The video cut out, and Jess moved on to the next one. This time, Kirkwood was standing in a dimly lit hallway, his eyes darting around nervously.

"I've been trying to piece together what's happening here, but the more I dig, the more I realize just how deep this goes," he said, his voice barely above a whisper. "These people... they're not just missing. They're being held here against their will, subjected to these... experiments."

He paused, his expression darkening. "And the worst part is, I think I know who's behind it all. But if I'm right, then I'm in way over my head. I need to get out of here before they realize I'm onto them."

The video ended, and Jess moved on to the next one. This time, Kirkwood was in a small, cramped room, his face lit by the glow of a computer screen.

"I've managed to access some of their records, but it's heavily encrypted," he murmured, his fingers flying across the keyboard. "Whatever they're doing here, they're going to great lengths to keep it hidden. I need to find a way to expose this, to bring it all to light, but I don't know how much time I have."

He paused, his expression suddenly fearful. "I think they're on to me. I need to get out of here, fast. If they find me, I don't know what they'll do."

The video cut out, and the room fell silent, the weight of what we had just witnessed hanging in the air.

I had seen enough horror in my own transformation to recognize the signs of something unnatural and twisted. This was not the work of humans, but something else entirely.

The room spun around me, the walls closing in as the weight of our discovery crashed down. This was not just about Kirkwood or Palantir. This was something far bigger and darker—a conspiracy that stretched back decades, a web of lies and deceit that had ensnared countless lives.

Jess leaned back in her chair, her eyes never leaving the screen. "There's one more file here. It's... different."

I moved closer, the glow of the monitor casting eerie shadows on our faces. "Different how?"

"It's an unsent email," she said, her voice barely above a whisper. "With a video attachment. And there's a code—a sequence of numbers and letters. It looks like a personal message, meant for someone specific."

Benji glanced over, his brow furrowed. "Can you decrypt it?"

Jess nodded, her fingers already dancing over the keys. "I think so. It's complex, but it's not like anything we've seen before. It's almost like it was meant to be deciphered by someone who knows the pattern."

Ash stepped closer, her eyes scanning the code. "It's a substitution cipher. But the sequence... it's not random. It's a date. A birthday, maybe?"

I felt a chill run down my spine. "Kirkwood has a daughter. She's a reporter, a blogger. If anyone could decipher this, it would be her."

Jess looked up at me, her expression grave. "Then we need to send this to her. If Kirkwood left this message, it's important. It could be the key to exposing whatever he found."

Benji nodded, his voice steady. "We can't just send it blindly. We need to make sure it's safe, that it won't be intercepted."

Ash leaned in, her eyes locked onto the screen. "We can use a secure server, bounce the signal around. Make it look like it's coming from somewhere else."

I felt a knot of tension in my stomach. This was it—the moment of truth. We were about to step into the unknown, to send a message that could change everything. I nodded, my voice firm. "Do it. Send the email."

Jess took a deep breath, her fingers poised over the keys. "Alright. Here goes nothing."

The room fell silent as she hit send, the weight of our decision hanging in the air. I could feel the tension, the uncertainty, and the hope that we had made the right choice.

Suddenly, the screen flickered, and the video began to play. Kirkwood's face filled the frame, his eyes haunted, his voice filled with regret.

"Emily," he said, his voice barely above a whisper. "If you're watching this, then I'm gone. I'm sorry, sweetheart. I'm so sorry for everything."

He paused, his eyes flicking away from the camera, as if checking for something—or someone.

"I never meant for any of this to happen. I thought I could control it, that I could keep you safe. But I was wrong. I was so wrong."

He looked back at the camera, his expression grave. "I found something, Emily. Something big, something dangerous. I tried to expose it, to bring it to light, but they found me first. They're coming for me, and I don't know how much time I have left."

He leaned closer, his voice dropping to a whisper. "But I managed to gather evidence. It's all here, in these files. You can download them, expose them. You're the only one I trust, Emily. The only one who can bring the truth to light."

He paused, his eyes filling with tears. "I love you, Emily. I always have. And I'm sorry for everything—for not being there, for not being the father you deserved. But you can make this right. You can expose the truth and bring them to justice."

The video cut out, and the room fell silent, the weight of Kirkwood's words settling over us like a shroud. I felt a lump form in my throat, the reality of our situation crashing down on me. We had just sent a message that could change everything, that could expose a conspiracy far beyond anything we had ever imagined.

Jess looked up at me, her eyes filled with uncertainty. "Did we do the right thing, Tris? Did we just put Kirkwood's daughter in danger?"

I shook my head, my voice steady. "We did what we had to do. Kirkwood left that message for a reason. He wanted his daughter to expose the truth and bring the people responsible to justice. We just gave her the chance to do that."

Benji nodded, his expression grave. "We can't turn back now. We're in this, for better or for worse. We have to see it through."

Ash stepped closer, her voice filled with determination. "Then let's make sure we do this right. Let's ensure that Kirkwood's daughter gets the message and can expose the truth. We owe it to him—and to all the people who have disappeared—to bring this to light."

I felt a surge of resolve, a fire burning within me. This was our fight now, our battle. We had stepped into the unknown, into a world of shadows and secrets, and there was no turning back. We had to see this through, no matter the cost.

Jess turned back to the screen, her fingers flying over the keys. "Alright. Let's make this message untraceable. Let's ensure it gets to Kirkwood's daughter, no matter what."

I watched as she worked, the lines of code cascading down the screen like a waterfall. This was our moment, our chance to make a difference. We had stepped into the unknown, into a world of danger and deception, and there was no turning back.

I looked at Ash, Benji, and Jess, their faces mirroring my own horror and disbelief. We had set out to find the truth about Kirkwood's disappearance, to uncover the secrets he had been hiding. But now, as we stood on the precipice of a revelation that threatened to shatter our world, I couldn't help but wonder if we had bitten off more than we could chew.

CHAPTER TWENTY-SIX

RUN & HIDE

Jess, Benji, and Ash huddled over their laptops, fingers dancing across keyboards as they downloaded Kirkwood's files with focused intensity. The air was thick with the scent of dust and the faint electric hum of computers, the silence broken only by the occasional tap of a key or the soft murmur of a discovered file.

I stood watch, my senses on high alert. The atmosphere shifted subtly, like a change in air pressure before a storm. My eyes scanned the dimly lit station, where rows of old, rusted tracks stretched out like skeletal fingers into the darkness. A shiver ran down my spine, an instinctual warning that something was off.

"Got another batch," Jess whispered, her eyes fixed on the screen. Beside her, Benji nodded, his fingers flying over the keys, oblivious to the change in the air.

Suddenly, the first camera flickered and went out. A small black square on Jess's screen turned to static. She frowned, her fingers pausing mid-stroke. "What the—"

Another camera blinked out. Then another. The darkness seemed to creep closer, shadows deepening around us. I inhaled sharply, and the scent hit me like a punch to the gut: blood and rotting flesh, a putrid mix that sent a wave of nausea crashing over me. My fangs threatened to descend, a primal response to the smell of death.

"Guys," I said, my voice low and urgent. "We need to go. Now."

Ash looked up, her eyes meeting mine. She saw something in my expression that made her pause, her brow furrowing with concern. "Tris, what's wrong?"

I couldn't tell them the truth. Not here, not now. Not ever, if I wanted to keep them safe. I gestured to the screens, the growing black squares of dead cameras. "Something's interfering with the feed. We're not safe here."

Benji finally looked up, his eyes wide behind his glasses. "You think someone's coming?"

I nodded, my senses screaming at me to run. "We can't stay here. Grab what you can; we're leaving."

Jess started to protest, her fingers hovering over the keyboard. "But we're not done. We need more time—"

"There is no more time," I snapped, my voice harsher than intended. I softened my tone, trying to keep the urgency in check. "Please, Jess. We have to

go."She searched my face, her own pale with worry. Then she nodded, her fingers moving swiftly to eject the USB drives from the laptops. Benji and Ash followed suit, their movements hurried and tense.

I moved to the edge of the platform, scanning the darkness. The scent was stronger now, a thick, cloying stench that clung to the back of my throat. I could feel them, the vampires, lurking in the shadows, their presence pressing down on my chest. I had to get my friends out of here, away from the danger they didn't even know existed.

"Stay close," I murmured, my voice barely audible. "And be quiet. We don't want to draw any attention."

Ash nodded, her eyes wide with fear. She clutched her laptop to her chest, her breath coming in quick, shallow gasps. Benji slipped the USB drives into his pocket, his eyes darting nervously around the station. Jess closed her laptop with a soft click, her face set in a determined expression.

I led them along the platform, my footsteps silent on the dusty concrete. The others followed, their steps echoing softly in the vast, empty space. The scent of blood and decay grew stronger, a sickening miasma that clung to the air like a shroud. I could feel the vampires moving, their presence like a dark tide washing over us.

We reached the stairs, the metal steps creaking softly under our weight. I paused, straining to pinpoint the locations of the vampires. They were close—too close. We needed to move faster.

"Quickly," I whispered, barely more than a breath. "Up the stairs, then straight to the car. Don't stop, don't look back."

They nodded, their faces pale and tense. I took the lead, the metal railing cold and damp under my hand. The scent of blood was overpowering now, a thick, choking fog that filled my lungs and set my nerves on edge.

We reached the top of the stairs, the dim light of the street filtering in through the grimy windows. The car was parked just outside, a dark silhouette against the night sky. I could see the shadows moving, the vampires closing in. We were running out of time.

"Go," I hissed, my voice barely more than a whisper. "Now."

They ran, their footsteps echoing in the empty station, the sound of their hearts pounding in my ears. I followed, my senses heightened, scanning the darkness for any sign of movement. The vampires were near, their presence looming like a dark cloud in my consciousness.

The chill of the station clung to my skin, the air thick with the scent of decay and something far more sinister. We huddled together—Jess, Benji, and Ash hearts beating in a rhythm of fear that resonated in my ears. I could taste their anxiety, a bitter tang on my tongue. We were not alone.

A figure materialized from the shadows, his silhouette cutting through the dim light like a blade. He was pale, his skin almost luminescent against the darkness, and his eyes burned a deep, unsettling red. A British accent sliced through the air, sharp and cold. "Not so fast, you lot. Our sensors went off, and here you are." He sniffed, his nostrils flaring. "Do you know where Kirkwood is?"

Jess stepped back, her breath hitching. The vampire's gaze flicked to her, a predatory gleam in his eyes. Behind us, another figure emerged from the shadows, blocking our escape. The darkness seemed to stretch, reaching out with dark tendrils, as if the very air conspired against us.

Benji, ever the diplomat, stepped forward. "Hey, man. We're just exploring this old station. It's supposed to be haunted, you know? We don't know anything about a Kirkwood."

The first vampire, the one with the British accent, took a step closer. His eyes narrowed, scrutinizing Benji like a specimen under a microscope. "Is that so? You expect me to believe you just happened to stumble upon this place? That you know nothing about Kirkwood?"

The second vampire, silent until now, moved closer. His eyes were the same dark red, but there was something different about him—a quiet menace that made the hairs on the back of my neck stand up.

Ash spoke up, her voice steady despite the fear coursing through her. "We're telling the truth. We don't know who Kirkwood is. We were just curious about the station."

The British vampire chuckled, a sound like ice cracking. "Curious, hmm? Well, curiosity killed the cat, didn't it?" He leaned in, his voice dropping to a low growl. "And we don't like trespassers."

I could see it in their eyes: the intent to kill. They weren't here to ask questions; they were here to eliminate a threat. I couldn't let that happen. Not to my friends.

The vampire's eyes narrowed as he focused on Jess, a predatory gleam shining in his crimson gaze. I could see his muscles coil, ready to pounce, and a surge of protectiveness flooded my veins.

In a blur of motion, I darted forward, slamming into the vampire's side and knocking him off course. He hissed in surprise, his clawed hand swiping at me, but I was faster. I shoved him back with a telekinetic push, sending him crashing into the old ticket booth. The wood splintered, and he slumped to the ground, unmoving.

Jess stared at me, her eyes wide with a mix of fear and awe. "Tris, what...?"

I didn't have time to explain. "We need to go, now," I said. "That won't keep him down for long."

I turned to my friends, my voice urgent. "Run. Now."

Jess, Benji, and Ash stared at me, frozen in place. Then Ash's eyes widened, and a gasp escaped her lips. "Tris, your... your face."

I felt it then, the familiar prick of my fangs descending. I clenched my jaw, trying to rein in the beast within, but it was too late. They had seen the truth.

Jess took a step back, her laptop slipping from her fingers and clattering to the ground. Benji's eyes darted between the fallen vampire and me, his brow furrowed in disbelief and curiosity. "Dude, what the hell is going on?"

They hesitated for a moment, shock etched on their faces. Jess's eyes widened, her laptop forgotten on the ground. Benji's mouth hung open, his glasses askew. Ash's gaze flicked between the fallen vampire and me, her breath hitching in her throat. The air was thick with the scent of decay and the electric hum of tension.

Then they moved, their footsteps echoing sharply against the cold concrete. Jess snatched her laptop from the ground, clutching it to her chest like a shield. Benji pushed his glasses up his nose, his eyes darting around nervously. Ash grabbed Jess's arm, her fingers digging into the fabric of her jacket, urging her forward.

I turned to face the second vampire, my knife drawn. The blade glinted in the dim light, a cold, deadly promise. His eyes narrowed, a low growl rumbling in his chest. He was taller than I was, with broad shoulders and muscles taut beneath his dark clothing. His skin was pale, almost luminescent, and his eyes burned like hot coals.

I could feel the power radiating off him, a dark, pulsating energy that clawed at the air. But I didn't back down. I couldn't—not with my friends' lives at stake. I planted my feet firmly on the ground. The silver swirls in my eyes intensified, a silent warning of the storm brewing within me.

The vampire circled me like a predator, his movements fluid and precise. I mirrored his steps, my eyes never leaving his. The air crackled with tension, the silence broken only by the soft scrape of our feet against the concrete. I could hear my friends' heartbeats, a faint, distant drumming echoing in my ears.

He sniffed the air, his eyes narrowing as he took in my scent. "What are you, boy?"

I didn't answer; my focus was honed on his every movement. He lunged, his speed matching mine. I deflected his strike with my knife, the blade glinting in the dim light. He was strong, but so was I.

We danced around each other, a deadly ballet of kicks and flips. I could feel the power coursing through me, my telekinesis amplifying every move. He lunged, his fist aimed at my jaw, but I ducked just in time, the air whistling past my ear. I retaliated with a swift kick, my foot connecting with his chest. He staggered back, but only for a moment; his recovery was swift and fluid.

His fighting style was unlike anything I'd encountered. He utilized his surroundings, the shadows seeming to bend to his will. He grabbed a rusted metal pipe from the ground, swinging it with a force that should have shattered bones. I threw up a telekinetic shield, the pipe clanging against an invisible barrier, sparks flying.

Seizing the moment, I used my power to wrench the pipe from his grasp. It flew across the station, clattering against the far wall. His eyes narrowed, a sinister smile playing on his lips. "Impressive," he murmured, circling me like a predator.

I didn't respond; my focus was honed on his every movement. He lunged again, this time aiming low. I jumped, twisting in the air to avoid his strike. I landed gracefully, my hand reaching out, fingers splayed. A nearby pile of debris lifted, chunks of concrete and metal hurtling toward hi m.

He dodged most of the projectiles, but a jagged piece of metal grazed his cheek, drawing blood. The scent hit me like a punch, a primal urge surging within me. I fought it back, my control slipping but still intact. He touched his cheek, his fingers coming away red. His smile widened—a chilling sight. "You're making this fun," he said, his voice a low growl.

He charged, his speed matching mine. I met him head-on, our fists clashing, the force of the impact reverberating through my bones. We traded blows in a whirlwind of punches and kicks, each landing with brutal force. I could feel the power pulsing through me, my telekinesis amplifying my strength and speed. But he was relentless, his attacks fueled by a dark energy that seemed to grow with every exchange.

I needed an edge, something to tip the scales in my favor. I reached out with my mind, my telekinesis latching onto a crumbling section of the ceiling. With a mental shove, I sent it crashing down, a hail of stone and dust raining on him. He dodged, but not fast enough. A large chunk of concrete struck him, sending him sprawling.

I moved in, my knife glinting in the dim light. But he wasn't down—not yet. He rolled, his foot lashing out and catching me off guard. I stumbled, my balance thrown. He rose, his eyes burning with dark intensity.

"You're good," he said, his voice barely more than a whisper. "But not good enough."

He lunged, his fist aimed at my face. I blocked, my arm shaking from the force of the impact. He pressed his advantage, his attacks coming fast and furious. I was on the defensive, my focus split between blocking his strikes and trying to land a counterattack. It was a losing battle; his relentless assault pushed me back, my strength waning.

He leaped back, his hands moving in a fluid motion. Dark tendrils snaked out from the shadows, writhing and twisting like serpents. They lashed out, striking me with a force that sent me reeling. I hit the ground hard, pain exploding through my body.

Struggling to my feet, I gasped for breath. What was this? I had never seen anything like it.

The vampire advanced, his eyes glowing with malice. "You're stronger than you look, boy. But you're no match for me."

I gritted my teeth, my hand clenching around the knife. I couldn't let him win. I couldn't let him hurt my friends. I had to try something—anything.

I needed to end this, and fast. I reached deep within, tapping into the reservoir of power inside me. My telekinesis surged, a wave of energy that sent him crashing into a nearby wall. He slumped to the ground, gasping for breath. I stood over him, my knife poised.

I focused, my mind reaching out, searching for that connection, that vibrational energy linking me to the world around me. I could feel it—the hum of power, the potential waiting to be unleashed.

The vampire lunged, the shadows lashing out like whips. I raised another telekinetic barrier, the air shimmering as the shadows collided with it. He snarled, his eyes widening in surprise.

I pushed back, my mind straining with the effort. The shadows recoiled, writhing as if in pain. The vampire stumbled, his face contorted with shock and rage.

I pressed my advantage, my mind lashing out, searching for something—anything—I could use. There it was: an old train cart, rusted and forgotten. I focused, bending the metal to my command. It groaned, the sound of protesting metal echoing through the station as it tore free from its moorings.

It flew through the air, wrapping around the vampire and pinning him to the ground. He struggled, his eyes burning with fury, but the cart held firm, the metal bending and twisting to conform to my will.

I stood there, breath coming in ragged gasps, my body trembling with the effort. I could feel the power coursing through me, a wild, untamed force threatening to consume me. But I held on, my will unyielding.

The vampire snarled, fangs bared, eyes promising retribution. But he was trapped, his body pinned, his limbs ensnared. He wasn't going anywhere.

Before I could deliver the final blow, a sound echoed through the station—a soft, barely audible whisper. "Tristan..."

I turned to see my friends huddled behind me, their faces pale with shock. Jess's eyes were wide, her hand pressed to her mouth. Benji stared, his glasses askew, breath coming in quick, shallow gasps. Ash's eyes reflected a mix of fear and awe, her hand clutching her side as blood seeped through her fingers.

I moved toward them, my steps faltering. I was covered in blood, clothes torn, body aching. But I was alive. And so were they.

Ash looked up at me, her eyes locking onto mine. "Tris, your eyes..."

I froze, the realization hitting me like a punch to the gut. My contacts were gone, lost in the fight. My friends were seeing me, the real me, for the first time.

The station fell silent, save for the ragged breaths of my friends. Ash's eyes widened, her hand clenched in fear. Jess stood frozen, her face a mask of shock. Benji's glasses hung askew, his mouth agape. I could see the reflection of my glowing eyes in their stares, the truth of what I was laid bare.

I looked down at my body, a mess of blood and torn clothes. But even as I watched, the deep gash on my arm began to knit itself back together. The jagged bone of my broken rib shifted, realigning with an audible crack. My friends gasped, their eyes tracking the impossible healing of my wounds.

The claw marks on my chest smoothed over, skin regenerating as if time itself were reversing. My broken arm straightened, the bone mending with a series of soft pops. The pain ebbed away, replaced by a warm, tingling sensation that spread throughout my body.

Jess stepped forward, her hand reaching out tentatively. She touched my shoulder, fingers brushing against the spot where the bone had protruded just moments before. Her eyes met mine, filled with disbelief and awe. "How... how is this possible?" she murmured.

Benji pushed up his glasses, his eyes scanning me from head to toe. He let out a low whistle, a sound that broke the tense silence. "Dude," he said, a nervous laugh bubbling in his throat. "You're like Wolverine or something. But with... you know... the glowy eyes thing."

Ash looked at him, her eyebrows raised. "Glowy eyes thing?" she echoed, a hint of her usual wit returning.

Benji shrugged, a grin spreading across his face. "Well, you have to admit, it's not something you see every day. I mean, Tris here just went full-on superhero on us."

Ash stepped forward, her hand reaching out to brush against my cheek. "They're beautiful," she whispered, her voice filled with wonder.

This was it—the moment of truth. They knew, they saw, they understood. And yet, they didn't run, scream, or turn away in fear or disgust. They stood by me.

Ash's nose wrinkled, her eyes narrowing as she scanned the darkness. "Wait," she said, lowering her voice to a whisper. "I think there's something out there."

I heard her voice cut through the aftermath of the fight, tightening every muscle in my body.

"Wait," she whispered again, eyes narrowing as she surveyed the shadows beyond the station entrance.

I closed my eyes, focusing my heightened senses outward. The sounds of the night filtered in—distant traffic, the rustle of leaves, the scurrying of small animals. Then I caught it: the faintest disruption in the natural rhythm, a controlled breathing pattern that didn't belong to any animal.

"You're right," I murmured, opening my eyes to meet Ash's worried gaze. "Someone's out there."

Benji shifted nervously beside me. "What is it? What are they?"

I couldn't be sure, but my instincts screamed danger. "I'll go out first. Just wait for my signal before you make a run for the car."

Jess grabbed my arm. "Tris, you can't—"

"The car's hidden. You'll be safe if you move fast enough." I gently removed her hand. "Trust me."

I moved toward the entrance, every sense on high alert. The night air hit my face as I stepped outside, scanning the surroundings. The parking lot stretched before me, bathed in moonlight and shadows.

Before I could fully register the danger, something slammed into my side with brutal force. The impact sent me flying, my body crashing against the station's brick wall. Pain exploded through my ribs as I crumpled to the ground, my vision swimming.

Through the haze of pain, I saw Ash at the top of the stairs, moving toward me. I thrust my hand up in a desperate signal for her to stop, relief washing over me when she froze.

My attacker had vanished into the shadows, but I knew they were still there, watching and waiting. I pushed myself to my feet, feeling my broken ribs shift and knit back together. The pain receded to a dull throb as my vampiric healing kicked in.

A figure stepped into the moonlight, and my breath caught. She was tall—impossibly tall, at least 6 feet 10 inches—with platinum blonde hair that seemed to absorb the moonlight. Her movements were fluid and elegant, like a dancer performing for an audience of one. But it was her eyes that held me captive—cold, calculating, ancient.

Another vampire.

She tilted her head, studying me with clinical detachment. "You're not what I expected," she said, her voice musical yet sharp, like glass wind chimes in a storm.

I tensed, ready to spring. "What were you expecting?"

Her lips curved into a smile that never reached her eyes. "Something more... impressive."

She flicked her wrist, and the shadows around her writhed and twisted, condensing into solid forms—spears and daggers, weapons born from darkness itself. One moment they were shadows; the next, they were solid enough to kill.

I'd never seen anything like it. Was this another vampire ability I didn't know about?

There was no time to wonder. She launched a shadow dagger at my head with blinding speed. I ducked, feeling it slice through the air where my throat had been just a split second before.

I called on my old parkour training, relying on the muscle memory of countless hours spent vaulting, jumping, and rolling through urban landscapes. Combined with the basic Kung Fu I'd learned years ago, it wasn't much against a vampire of her caliber, but it was all I had.

I charged, closing the distance between us in a burst of speed. I threw a combination of strikes—jab, cross, hook—movements that would have been blurs to human eyes.

She blocked my first punch with her forearm, the impact sending shockwaves up my arm. She dodged my second strike with a slight tilt of her head, her expression almost bored. My kick connected with her side, but it felt like hitting concrete.

Her counterattack came faster than I could track—a palm strike to my sternum sent me skidding backward. I barely maintained my footing, gasping as my newly healed ribs protested.

"Is that all?" she taunted, shadows coiling around her fingers like living serpents.

I needed to buy time for my friends. I feinted left, then dove right, rolling across the pavement as shadow spikes impaled the ground where I'd been. Coming up in a crouch, I focused my telekinesis on a nearby dumpster and hurled it toward her with all my mental strength.

The dumpster flew at her with tremendous force. She raised her hands, shadows forming a barrier before her, but the impact still knocked her back several steps. Her eyes widened slightly—the first hint of surprise I had seen.

I seized the moment, launching myself at her with every ounce of vampiric speed I possessed. My fist connected with her jaw, the satisfying crack confirming I had landed a solid hit. I followed with a knee to her midsection and then an elbow strike aimed at her temple.

She caught my arm mid-strike, her grip like iron. "Interesting," she murmured, then twisted, flipping me over her shoulder and slamming me into the ground with enough force to crack the pavement.

Stars exploded across my vision. I rolled away just as her foot stomped down where my head had been, the concrete shattering under the impact.

From the corner of my eye, I saw movement—Ash, Benji, and Jess making a break for it, darting between shadows toward where we had parked the car. Good. I just needed to keep this vampire occupied long enough for them to escape.

I pushed myself up, blood trickling from a cut on my forehead, already healing. "Who are you?" I demanded, circling her warily.

"Names have power," she replied, shadows dancing between her fingers. "You're not ready for mine."

She lunged, a blur of motion. I sidestepped but not fast enough to avoid the shadow blade that materialized in her hand, slicing across my chest. Pain flared, hot and sharp, as blood soaked my shirt.

I staggered back, pressing my hand against the deep wound, which was already beginning to close. I needed to end this—and fast.

Focusing my telekinesis, I reached out to everything around me—loose gravel, broken glass, discarded trash. The debris rose into the air, swirling around me in a cyclone of potential projectiles. With a mental push, I sent it all flying toward her in a deadly barrage.

She waved her hand, and shadows formed a shield that deflected most of the improvised missiles. But not all. A jagged piece of metal caught her across the cheek, drawing a line of dark blood, while a chunk of concrete struck her shoulder, making her stumble.

I pressed my advantage, charging in with renewed determination. I launched a flurry of strikes—some connecting, most blocked or dodged. She was too fast, too skilled, but I was desperate and unpredictable.

I feinted a punch, then dropped low, sweeping her legs out from under her. She fell, surprise flashing across her face as she hit the ground. I pounced, straddling her and raining down punches with all my strength.

She conjured a shadow shield between us, absorbing most of the impact, but I could feel it weakening under my assault. Behind me, I heard the roar of an engine coming to life—my friends had made it to the car.

Relief flooded through me, momentarily distracting me from the fight. It was all the opening she needed.

A shadow spike erupted from the ground beside us, piercing through my shoulder and lifting me off her. I cried out, the pain white-hot and blinding. She rose to her feet, dusting herself off with casual disdain.

The shadow spike pinning my shoulder sent waves of agony through my body as I hung suspended above the ground. Blood ran down my arm in rivulets, dripping onto the pavement below. I gritted my teeth, refusing to give her the satisfaction of hearing me scream again.

She approached with predatory grace, her platinum hair gleaming in the moonlight. Her cold, calculating eyes studied me with a mixture of curiosity and contempt.

"You fight well," she said, circling beneath me like a shark. She paused, her nostrils flaring slightly as she inhaled. A flicker of confusion crossed her face. "But you're still just a child playing at being a monster."

Her head tilted, those ancient eyes narrowing as she examined me more closely. "You're... unusual," she continued, reaching up to touch my blood-soaked shirt. "You move like one of us, yet..." She brought her fingertips to her nose, sniffing my blood with evident puzzlement.

"You smell... different. Forest floor and animal blood." She stepped back, reassessing. "And that power?"

I focused through the pain, gathering my strength. The shadow spike began to tremble as I pushed against it with my mind.

"What exactly are you?" she demanded, her composure slipping for the first time.

I didn't answer. Instead, I channeled everything I had into breaking her hold. The shadow spike shattered like glass, and I dropped to the ground, landing in a crouch despite the searing pain in my shoulder.

"I'm a nobody!" I snarled, getting back on my feet as my injury started to heal. "You don't need to be concerned about me."

Her eyes widened fractionally. "Impossible," she whispered, watching my healing flesh with undisguised fascination. "You're not pure vampire, yet you heal like one. You don't smell right. You shouldn't exist."

I straightened, feeling my strength returning with each passing second. The pain in my shoulder faded to a dull ache, the flesh knitting back together with astonishing speed. As the vampire circled me, her eyes filled with a mixture of curiosity and contempt, I reached out with my mind, focusing on the discarded pipes littering the ground nearby. They trembled, then rose into the air, hovering behind her, ready to strike at my command.

"You're an anomaly," she murmured, her gaze flicking over me as if trying to peel back the layers of my existence. "You shouldn't be able to heal like that. You shouldn't be able to do... this." She gestured to the debris still swirling around us, remnants of my earlier telekinetic outburst.

I kept my expression neutral, my focus split between her and the pipes floating behind her. "Maybe you don't know as much as you think you do." My voice was steady, betraying none of the tension coiling within me.

She stepped closer, her eyes narrowing as she inhaled deeply, trying to catch my scent. "You smell of earth and wild things, but there's something else. Something... unusual."

"You're not like the others," she whispered, her brow furrowing in confusion. "You're not pure. Yet, you're not quite human either. What are you?"

I could see the gears turning in her mind as she struggled to categorize me, to fit me into her understanding of the world. Behind her, the pipes shifted, aligning themselves with her back, poised to strike at my mental command.

"I'm just someone trying to protect what's important to me," I said, my voice low, my eyes locked onto hers. I needed to keep her distracted, to buy just a few more seconds.

Her lips curved into a smirk as she withdrew her hand from my face. "Protect? You think you can shield anything from us? You're a fool. You're just a—"

Now.

The pipes shot forward, aimed at her back. But suddenly, something slammed into my back with tremendous force, yanking me backward off the spike. Fresh pain exploded through me as I hit the ground, rolling several times before coming to a stop.

...TO BE CONTINUED...

AFTERWORD

Thank You & What's Next

If you loved *Requiem: The Quiet Bloom*, the journey doesn't stop here.

Get updates, behind-the-scenes content, and access to the next book before anyone else:

Join the mailing list at Xkaii.com

Don't miss the next chapter: *Requiem: Beneath the Veil* – coming soon.

Tristan's story deepens as new powers awaken, old secrets surface, and the line between humanity and darkness begins to blur.

A Personal Note from Harrison C. Songolo

Thank you for walking through the shadows with me. *Requiem* is more than a vampire story — it's about identity, transformation, and the parts of ourselves we try to hide. Through Tristan's struggle, I wanted to explore the quiet power of choosing who you become, even when the world wants to define you.

This series is deeply personal, and I hope it offered you moments of reflection, adrenaline, and connection. The darkness may be vast, but so is the light we carry.

About the Author

Harrison C. Songolo, also known musically as *Xkaii*, is a storyteller, performer, and worldbuilder with a passion for supernatural fiction and emotional depth. With over half a million fans across TikTok and Instagram, his voice blends music, myth, and memory into unforgettable experiences.

When he's not writing novels or performing live, he's exploring foggy forests, composing under the stars, or dreaming up the next twist in a world not quite like ours.

Acknowledgements

To my readers — thank you for being here.

To my friends, family, and early supporters — your encouragement gave this story wings.□

To the mentors, editors, and quiet believers behind the curtain — this wouldn't exist without you.

Want More?

Check out more stories, exclusive scenes, music and character backstories at:□

Xkaii.com

Or follow me on TikTok & Instagram:

@xkaii

Book Club Questions

1. How does Tristan's transformation challenge his identity?

2. Which friendships in *Requiem* felt the most real or meaningful to you?

3. What role does fear play in shaping the characters' choices?

4. How did the urban setting elevate the tension in the story?

5. Which moment stayed with you the most — and why?